MW01026748

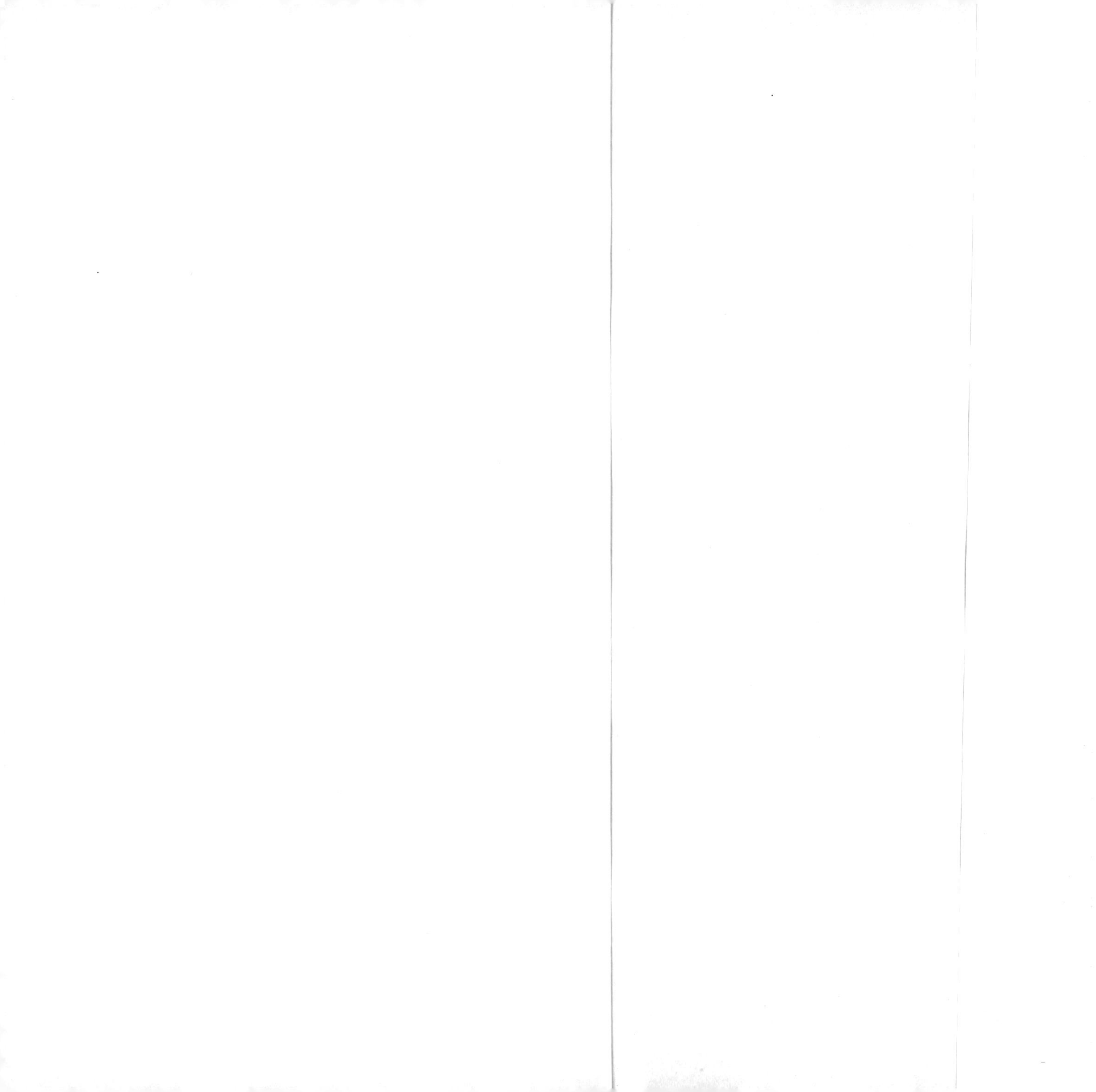

BOOTH TARKINGTON

BOOTH TARKINGTON

NOVELS & STORIES

The Magnificent Ambersons
Alice Adams
In the Arena: Stories of Political Life

Thomas Mallon, *editor*

THE LIBRARY OF AMERICA

BOOTH TARKINGTON: NOVELS & STORIES

Published in the United States by Library of America.
Visit our website at www.loa.org.

This paper exceeds the requirements of
ANSI/NISO Z39.48–1992 (Permanence of Paper).

Distributed to the trade in the United States
by Penguin Random House Inc.
and in Canada by Penguin Random House Canada Ltd.

Library of Congress Control Number: 2018962315
ISBN 978–1–59853–620–1

First Printing
The Library of America—319

Manufactured in the United States of America

Contents

THE MAGNIFICENT AMBERSONS

To Susanah

Chapter I

MAJOR AMBERSON had "made a fortune" in 1873, when other people were losing fortunes, and the magnificence of the Ambersons began then. Magnificence, like the size of a fortune, is always comparative, as even Magnificent Lorenzo may now perceive, if he has happened to haunt New York in 1916; and the Ambersons were magnificent in their day and place. Their splendour lasted throughout all the years that saw their Midland town spread and darken into a city, but reached its topmost during the period when every prosperous family with children kept a Newfoundland dog.

In that town, in those days, all the women who wore silk or velvet knew all the other women who wore silk or velvet, and when there was a new purchase of sealskin, sick people were got to windows to see it go by. Trotters were out, in the winter afternoons, racing light sleighs on National Avenue and Tennessee Street; everybody recognized both the trotters and the drivers; and again knew them as well on summer evenings, when slim buggies whizzed by in renewals of the snow-time rivalry. For that matter, everybody knew everybody else's family horse-and-carriage, could identify such a silhouette half a mile down the street, and thereby was sure who was going to market, or to a reception, or coming home from office or store to noon dinner or evening supper.

During the earlier years of this period, elegance of personal appearance was believed to rest more upon the texture of garments than upon their shaping. A silk dress needed no remodelling when it was a year or so old; it remained distinguished by merely remaining silk. Old men and governors wore broadcloth; "full dress" was broadcloth with "doeskin" trousers; and there were seen men of all ages to whom a hat meant only that rigid, tall silk thing known to impudence as a "stove-pipe." In town and country these men would wear no other hat, and, without self-consciousness, they went rowing in such hats.

Shifting fashions of shape replaced aristocracy of texture: dressmakers, shoemakers, hatmakers, and tailors, increasing in cunning and in power, found means to make new clothes old.

The long contagion of the "Derby" hat arrived: one season the crown of this hat would be a bucket; the next it would be a spoon. Every house still kept its bootjack, but high-topped boots gave way to shoes and "congress gaiters"; and these were played through fashions that shaped them now with toes like box-ends and now with toes like the prows of racing shells.

Trousers with a crease were considered plebeian; the crease proved that the garment had lain upon a shelf, and hence was "ready-made"; these betraying trousers were called "hand-me-downs," in allusion to the shelf. In the early 'eighties, while bangs and bustles were having their way with women, that variation of dandy known as the "dude" was invented: he wore trousers as tight as stockings, dagger-pointed shoes, a spoon "Derby," a single-breasted coat called a "Chesterfield," with short flaring skirts, a torturing cylindrical collar, laundered to a polish and three inches high, while his other neckgear might be a heavy, puffed cravat or a tiny bow fit for a doll's braids. With evening dress he wore a tan overcoat so short that his black coat-tails hung visible, five inches below the overcoat; but after a season or two he lengthened his overcoat till it touched his heels, and he passed out of his tight trousers into trousers like great bags. Then, presently, he was seen no more, though the word that had been coined for him remained in the vocabularies of the impertinent.

It was a hairier day than this. Beards were to the wearers' fancy, and things as strange as the Kaiserliche boar-tusk moustache were commonplace. "Side-burns" found nourishment upon childlike profiles; great Dundreary whiskers blew like tippets over young shoulders; moustaches were trained as lambrequins over forgotten mouths; and it was possible for a Senator of the United States to wear a mist of white whisker upon his throat only, not a newspaper in the land finding the ornament distinguished enough to warrant a lampoon. Surely no more is needed to prove that so short a time ago we were living in another age!

. . . At the beginning of the Ambersons' great period most of the houses of the Midland town were of a pleasant architecture. They lacked style, but also lacked pretentiousness, and whatever does not pretend at all has style enough. They stood in commodious yards, well shaded by leftover forest trees, elm and walnut and beech, with here and there a line of tall sycamores where the land had been made by filling bayous from the creek. The house of a "prominent resident," facing Military Square, or National Avenue, or Tennessee Street, was built of brick upon a stone foundation, or of wood upon a brick foundation. Usually it had a "front porch" and a "back porch"; often a "side porch," too. There was a "front hall"; there was a "side hall"; and sometimes a "back hall." From the "front hall" opened three rooms, the "parlour," the "sitting room," and the "library"; and the library could show warrant to its title—for some reason these people bought books. Commonly, the family sat more in the library than in the "sitting room," while callers, when they came formally, were kept to the "parlour," a place of formidable polish and discomfort. The upholstery of the library furniture was a little shabby; but the hostile chairs and sofa of the "parlour" always looked new. For all the wear and tear they got they should have lasted a thousand years.

Upstairs were the bedrooms; "mother-and-father's room" the largest; a smaller room for one or two sons, another for one or two daughters; each of these rooms containing a double bed, a "washstand," a "bureau," a wardrobe, a little table, a rocking-chair, and often a chair or two that had been slightly damaged downstairs, but not enough to justify either the expense of repair or decisive abandonment in the attic. And there was always a "spare-room," for visitors (where the sewing-machine usually was kept), and during the 'seventies there developed an appreciation of the necessity for a bathroom. Therefore the architects placed bathrooms in the new houses, and the older houses tore out a cupboard or two, set up a boiler beside the kitchen stove, and sought a new godliness, each with its own bathroom. The great American plumber joke, that many-branched evergreen, was planted at this time.

At the rear of the house, upstairs, was a bleak little chamber, called "the girl's room," and in the stable there was another bedroom, adjoining the hayloft, and called "the hired man's room." House and stable cost seven or eight thousand dollars to build, and people with that much money to invest in such comforts were classified as the Rich. They paid the inhabitant of "the girl's room" two dollars a week, and, in the latter part of this period, two dollars and a half, and finally three dollars a week. She was Irish, ordinarily, or German, or it might be Scandinavian, but never native to the land unless she happened to be a person of colour. The man or youth who lived in the stable had like wages, and sometimes he, too, was lately a steerage voyager, but much oftener he was coloured.

After sunrise, on pleasant mornings, the alleys behind the stables were gay; laughter and shouting went up and down their dusty lengths, with a lively accompaniment of currycombs knocking against back fences and stable walls, for the darkies loved to curry their horses in the alley. Darkies always prefer to gossip in shouts instead of whispers; and they feel that profanity, unless it be vociferous, is almost worthless. Horrible phrases were caught by early rising children and carried to older people for definition, sometimes at inopportune moments; while less investigative children would often merely repeat the phrases in some subsequent flurry of agitation, and yet bring about consequences so emphatic as to be recalled with ease in middle life.

. . . They have passed, those darky hired-men of the Midland town; and the introspective horses they curried and brushed and whacked and amiably cursed—those good old horses switch their tails at flies no more. For all their seeming permanence they might as well have been buffaloes—or the buffalo laprobes that grew bald in patches and used to slide from the careless drivers' knees and hang unconcerned, half way to the ground. The stables have been transformed into other likenesses, or swept away, like the woodsheds where were kept the stove-wood and kindling that the "girl" and the "hired-man" always quarrelled over: who should fetch it. Horse and stable and woodshed, and the whole tribe of the "hired-man," all are gone. They went quickly, yet so silently that we whom they served have not yet really noticed that they are vanished.

So with other vanishings. There were the little bunty streetcars on the long, single track that went its troubled way among the cobblestones. At the rear door of the car there was no platform, but a step where passengers clung in wet clumps when the weather was bad and the car crowded. The patrons —if not too absent-minded—put their fares into a slot; and no conductor paced the heaving floor, but the driver would rap remindingly with his elbow upon the glass of the door to his little open platform if the nickels and the passengers did not appear to coincide in number. A lone mule drew the car, and sometimes drew it off the track, when the passengers would get out and push it on again. They really owed it courtesies like this, for the car was genially accommodating: a lady could whistle to it from an upstairs window, and the car would halt at once and wait for her while she shut the window, put on her hat and cloak, went downstairs, found an umbrella, told the "girl" what to have for dinner, and came forth from the house.

The previous passengers made little objection to such gallantry on the part of the car: they were wont to expect as much for themselves on like occasion. In good weather the mule pulled the car a mile in a little less than twenty minutes, unless the stops were too long; but when the trolley-car came, doing its mile in five minutes and better, it would wait for nobody. Nor could its passengers have endured such a thing, because the faster they were carried the less time they had to spare! In the days before deathly contrivances hustled them through their lives, and when they had no telephones—another ancient vacancy profoundly responsible for leisure—they had time for everything: time to think, to talk, time to read, time to wait for a lady!

They even had time to dance "square dances," quadrilles, and "lancers"; they also danced the "racquette," and schottisches and polkas, and such whims as the "Portland Fancy." They pushed back the sliding doors between the "parlour" and the "sitting room," tacked down crash over the carpets, hired a few palms in green tubs, stationed three or four Italian musicians under the stairway in the "front hall"—and had great nights!

But these people were gayest on New Year's Day; they made it a true festival—something no longer known. The women gathered to "assist" the hostesses who kept "Open House"; and the carefree men, dandified and perfumed, went about in sleighs, or in carriages and ponderous "hacks," going from Open House to Open House, leaving fantastic cards in fancy baskets as they entered each doorway, and emerging a little later, more carefree than ever, if the punch had been to their liking. It always was, and, as the afternoon wore on, pedestrians saw great gesturing and waving of skin-tight lemon gloves, while ruinous fragments of song were dropped behind as the carriages rolled up and down the streets.

"Keeping Open House" was a merry custom; it has gone, like the all-day picnic in the woods, and like that prettiest of all vanished customs, the serenade. When a lively girl visited the town she did not long go unserenaded, though a visitor was not indeed needed to excuse a serenade. Of a summer night, young men would bring an orchestra under a pretty girl's window—or, it might be, her father's, or that of an ailing maiden aunt—and flute, harp, fiddle, 'cello, cornet, and bass viol would presently release to the dulcet stars such melodies as sing through "You'll Remember Me," "I Dreamt That I Dwelt in Marble Halls," "Silver Threads Among the Gold," "Kathleen Mavourneen," or "The Soldier's Farewell."

They had other music to offer, too, for these were the happy days of "Olivette" and "The Mascotte" and "The Chimes of Normandy" and "Giroflé-Girofla" and "Fra Diavolo." Better than that, these were the days of "Pinafore" and "The Pirates of Penzance" and of "Patience." This last was needed in the Midland town, as elsewhere, for the "æsthetic movement" had reached thus far from London, and terrible things were being done to honest old furniture. Maidens sawed what-nots in two, and gilded the remains. They took the rockers from rocking-chairs and gilded the inadequate legs; they gilded the easels that supported the crayon portraits of their deceased uncles. In the new spirit of art they sold old clocks for new, and threw wax flowers and wax fruit, and the protecting glass domes, out upon the trash-heap. They filled vases with peacock feathers, or cat-tails, or sumach, or sunflowers, and set the vases upon mantelpieces and marble-topped tables. They embroidered daisies (which they called "marguerites") and sunflowers and sumach and cat-tails and owls and peacock feathers upon plush screens and upon heavy cushions, then strewed these cushions upon floors where fathers fell over them in the dark. In the teeth of sinful oratory, the daughters went on embroidering: they embroidered daisies and sunflowers and sumach and cat-tails and owls and peacock feathers upon "throws" which they had the courage to drape upon horsehair sofas; they painted owls and daisies and sunflowers and sumach and cat-tails and peacock feathers upon tambourines. They hung Chinese umbrellas of paper to the chandeliers; they nailed paper fans to the walls. They "studied" painting on china, these girls; they sang Tosti's new songs; they sometimes still practised the old, genteel habit of lady-fainting, and were most charming of all when they drove forth, three or four in a basket phaeton, on a spring morning.

Croquet and the mildest archery ever known were the sports of people still young and active enough for so much exertion; middle-age played euchre. There was a theatre, next door to the Amberson Hotel, and when Edwin Booth came for a night, everybody who could afford to buy a ticket was there, and all the "hacks" in town were hired. "The Black Crook" also filled the theatre, but the audience then was almost entirely of men who looked uneasy as they left for home when the final curtain fell upon the shocking girls dressed as fairies. But the theatre did not often do so well; the people of the town were still too thrifty.

They were thrifty because they were the sons or grandsons of the "early settlers," who had opened the wilderness and had reached it from the East and the South with wagons and axes and guns, but with no money at all. The pioneers were thrifty or they would have perished: they had to store away food for the winter, or goods to trade for food, and they often feared they had not stored enough—they left traces of that fear in their sons and grandsons. In the minds of most of these, indeed, their thrift was next to their religion: to save, even for the sake of saving, was their earliest lesson and discipline. No matter how prosperous they were, they could not spend money either upon "art," or upon mere luxury and entertainment, without a sense of sin.

Against so homespun a background the magnificence of the Ambersons was as conspicuous as a brass band at a funeral. Major Amberson bought two hundred acres of land at the end of National Avenue; and through this tract he built broad streets and cross-streets; paved them with cedar block, and curbed them with stone. He set up fountains, here and there, where the streets intersected, and at symmetrical intervals placed cast-iron statues, painted white, with their titles clear upon the pedestals: Minerva, Mercury, Hercules, Venus, Gladiator,

Emperor Augustus, Fisher Boy, Stag-hound, Mastiff, Greyhound, Fawn, Antelope, Wounded Doe, and Wounded Lion. Most of the forest trees had been left to flourish still, and, at some distance, or by moonlight, the place was in truth beautiful; but the ardent citizen, loving to see his city grow, wanted neither distance nor moonlight. He had not seen Versailles, but, standing before the Fountain of Neptune in Amberson Addition, at bright noon, and quoting the favourite comparison of the local newspapers, he declared Versailles outdone. All this Art showed a profit from the start, for the lots sold well and there was something like a rush to build in the new Addition. Its main thoroughfare, an oblique continuation of National Avenue, was called Amberson Boulevard, and here, at the juncture of the new Boulevard and the Avenue, Major Amberson reserved four acres for himself, and built his new house—the Amberson Mansion, of course.

This house was the pride of the town. Faced with stone as far back as the dining-room windows, it was a house of arches and turrets and girdling stone porches: it had the first porte-cochère seen in that town. There was a central "front hall" with a great black walnut stairway, and open to a green glass skylight called the "dome," three stories above the ground floor. A ballroom occupied most of the third story; and at one end of it was a carved walnut gallery for the musicians. Citizens told strangers that the cost of all this black walnut and wood-carving was sixty thousand dollars. "Sixty thousand dollars for the woodwork *alone*! Yes, sir, and hardwood floors all over the house! Turkish rugs and no carpets at all, except a Brussels carpet in the front parlour—I hear they call it the 'reception-room.' Hot and cold water upstairs and down, and stationary washstands in every last bedroom in the place! Their sideboard's built right into the house and goes all the way across one end of the dining room. It isn't walnut, it's solid mahogany! Not veneering—solid mahogany! Well, sir, I presume the President of the United States would be tickled to swap the White House for the new Amberson Mansion, if the Major'd give him the chance—but by the Almighty Dollar, you bet your sweet life the Major wouldn't!"

The visitor to the town was certain to receive further enlightenment, for there was one form of entertainment never omitted: he was always patriotically taken for "a little drive around our city," even if his host had to hire a hack, and the climax of the display was the Amberson Mansion. "Look at that greenhouse they've put up there in the side yard," the escort would continue. "And look at that brick stable! Most folks would think that stable plenty big enough and good enough to live in; it's got running water and four rooms up-stairs for two hired men and one of 'em's family to live in. They keep one hired man loafin' in the house, and they got a married hired man out in the stable, and his wife does the washing. They got box-stalls for four horses, and they keep a coupay, and some new kinds of fancy rigs you never saw the beat of! 'Carts' they call two of 'em—'way up in the air they are—too high for me! I guess they got every new kind of fancy rig in there that's been invented. And harness—well, everybody in town can tell when Ambersons are out driving after dark, by the jingle. This town never did see so much style as Ambersons are putting on, these days; and I guess it's going to be expensive, because a lot of other folks'll try to keep up with 'em. The Major's wife and the daughter's been to Europe, and my wife tells me since they got back they make tea there every afternoon about five o'clock, and drink it. Seems to me it would go against a person's stomach, just before supper like that, and anyway tea isn't fit for much—not unless you're sick or something. My wife says Ambersons don't make lettuce salad the way other people do; they don't chop it up with sugar and vinegar at all. They pour olive oil on it with their vinegar, and they have it separate—not along with the rest of the meal. And they *eat* these olives, too: green things they are, something like a hard plum, but a friend of mine told me they tasted a good deal like a bad hickory-nut. My wife says she's going to buy some; you got to eat nine and then you get to like 'em, she says. Well, I wouldn't eat nine bad hickory-nuts to get to like *them*, and I'm going to let these olives alone. Kind of a woman's dish, anyway, I suspect, but most everybody'll be makin' a stagger to worm through nine of 'em, now Ambersons brought 'em to town. Yes, sir, the rest'll eat 'em, whether they get sick or not! Looks to me like some people in this city'd be willing to go crazy if they thought that would help 'em to be as high-toned as

Ambersons. Old Aleck Minafer—he's about the closest old codger we got—he come in my office the other day, and he pretty near had a stroke tellin' me about his daughter Fanny. Seems Miss Isabel Amberson's got some kind of a dog—they call it a Saint Bernard—and Fanny was bound to have one, too. Well, old Aleck told her he didn't like dogs except rat-terriers, because a rat-terrier cleans up the mice, but she kept on at him, and finally he said all right she could have one. Then, by George! she says Ambersons *bought* their dog, and you can't get one without paying for it: they cost from fifty to a hundred dollars up! Old Aleck wanted to know if I ever heard of anybody buyin' a dog before, because, of course, even a Newfoundland or a setter you can usually get somebody to give you one. He says he saw some sense in payin' a nigger a dime, or even a quarter, to *drown* a dog for you, but to pay out fifty dollars and maybe more—well, sir, he like to choked himself to death, right there in my office! Of course everybody realizes that Major Amberson is a fine business man, but what with throwin' money around for dogs, and every which and what, some think all this style's bound to break him up, if his family don't quit!"

One citizen, having thus discoursed to a visitor, came to a thoughtful pause, and then added, "Does seem pretty much like squandering, yet when you see that dog out walking with this Miss Isabel, he seems worth the money."

"What's she look like?"

"Well, sir," said the citizen, "she's not more than just about eighteen or maybe nineteen years old, and I don't know as I know just how to put it—but she's kind of a *delightful* lookin' young lady!"

Chapter II

ANOTHER CITIZEN said an eloquent thing about Miss Isabel Amberson's looks. This was Mrs. Henry Franklin Foster, the foremost literary authority and intellectual leader of the community—for both the daily newspapers thus described Mrs. Foster when she founded the Women's Tennyson Club; and her word upon art, letters, and the drama was accepted more as law than as opinion. Naturally, when "Hazel Kirke" finally reached the town, after its long triumph in larger places, many people waited to hear what Mrs. Henry Franklin Foster thought of it before they felt warranted in expressing any estimate of the play. In fact, some of them waited in the lobby of the theatre, as they came out, and formed an inquiring group about her.

"I didn't see the play," she informed them.

"What! Why, we saw you, right in the middle of the fourth row!"

"Yes," she said, smiling, "but I was sitting just behind Isabel Amberson. I couldn't look at anything except her wavy brown hair and the wonderful back of her neck."

The ineligible young men of the town (they were all ineligible) were unable to content themselves with the view that had so charmed Mrs. Henry Franklin Foster: they spent their time struggling to keep Miss Amberson's face turned toward them. She turned it most often, observers said, toward two: one excelling in the general struggle by his sparkle, and the other by that winning if not winsome old trait, persistence. The sparkling gentleman "led germans" with her, and sent sonnets to her with his bouquets—sonnets lacking neither music nor wit. He was generous, poor, well-dressed, and his amazing persuasiveness was one reason why he was always in debt. No one doubted that he would be able to persuade Isabel, but he unfortunately joined too merry a party one night, and, during a moonlight serenade upon the lawn before the Amberson Mansion, was easily identified from the windows as the person who stepped through the bass viol and had to be assisted to a waiting carriage. One of Miss Amberson's brothers was among the serenaders, and, when the party had dispersed, remained propped against the front door in a state of helpless liveliness; the Major going down in a dressing-gown and slippers to bring him in, and scolding mildly, while imperfectly concealing strong impulses to laughter. Miss Amberson also laughed at this brother, the next day, but for the suitor it was a different matter: she refused to see him when he called to apologize. "You seem to care a great deal about bass viols!" he wrote her. "I promise never to break another." She made no response to the note, unless it was an answer, two weeks later, when her engagement was announced. She took the persistent one, Wilbur Minafer, no breaker of bass viols or of hearts, no serenader at all.

A few people, who always foresaw everything, claimed that they were not surprised, because though Wilbur Minafer "might not be an Apollo, as it were," he was "a steady young business man, and a good church-goer," and Isabel Amberson was "pretty sensible—for such a showy girl." But the engagement astounded the young people, and most of their fathers and mothers, too; and as a topic it supplanted literature at the next meeting of the "Women's Tennyson Club."

"Wilbur *Minafer*!" a member cried, her inflection seeming to imply that Wilbur's crime was explained by his surname. "Wilbur *Minafer*! It's the queerest thing I ever heard! To think of her taking Wilbur Minafer, just because a man *any* woman would like a thousand times better was a little wild one night at a serenade!"

"No," said Mrs. Henry Franklin Foster. "It isn't that. It isn't even because she's afraid he'd be a dissipated husband and she wants to be safe. It isn't because she's religious or hates wildness; it isn't even because she hates wildness in *him*."

"Well, but look how she's thrown him over for it."

"No, that wasn't her reason," said the wise Mrs. Henry Franklin Foster. "If men only knew it—and it's a good thing they don't—a woman doesn't really care much about whether a man's wild or not, if it doesn't affect herself, and Isabel Amberson doesn't care a thing!"

"Mrs. *Foster*!"

"No, she doesn't. What she minds is his making a clown of himself in her front yard! It made her think he didn't care much about *her*. She's probably mistaken, but that's what she thinks, and it's too late for her to think anything else now, because she's going to be married right away—the invitations will be out next week. It'll be a big Amberson-style thing, raw oysters floating in scooped-out blocks of ice and a band from out-of-town—champagne, showy presents; a colossal present from the Major. Then Wilbur will take Isabel on the carefulest little wedding trip he can manage, and she'll be a good wife to him, but they'll have the worst spoiled lot of children this town will ever see."

"How on earth do you make *that* out, Mrs. Foster?"

"She couldn't love Wilbur, could she?" Mrs. Foster demanded, with no challengers. "Well, it will all go to her children, and she'll ruin 'em!"

The prophetess proved to be mistaken in a single detail merely: except for that, her foresight was accurate. The wedding was of Ambersonian magnificence, even to the floating oysters; and the Major's colossal present was a set of architect's designs for a house almost as elaborate and impressive as the Mansion, the house to be built in Amberson Addition by the Major. The orchestra was certainly not that local one which had suffered the loss of a bass viol; the musicians came, according to the prophecy and next morning's paper, from afar; and at midnight the bride was still being toasted in champagne, though she had departed upon her wedding journey at ten. Four days later the pair had returned to town, which promptness seemed fairly to demonstrate that Wilbur had indeed taken Isabel upon the carefulest little trip he could manage. According to every report, she was from the start "a good wife to him," but here in a final detail the prophecy proved inaccurate. Wilbur and Isabel did not have children; they had only one.

"Only one," Mrs. Henry Franklin Foster admitted. "But I'd like to know if he isn't spoiled enough for a whole carload!"

Again she found none to challenge her.

At the age of nine, George Amberson Minafer, the Major's one grandchild, was a princely terror, dreaded not only in Amberson Addition but in many other quarters through which he galloped on his white pony. "By golly, I guess you think you own this town!" an embittered labourer complained, one day, as Georgie rode the pony straight through a pile of sand the man was sieving. "I will when I grow up," the undisturbed child replied. "I guess my grandpa owns it now, you bet!" And the baffled workman, having no means to controvert what seemed a mere exaggeration of the facts, could only mutter "Oh, pull down your vest!"

"Don't haf to! Doctor says it ain't healthy!" the boy returned promptly. "But I tell you what I'll do: I'll pull down my vest if you'll wipe off your chin!"

This was stock and stencil: the accustomed argot of street badinage of the period; and in such matters Georgie was an expert. He had no vest to pull down; the incongruous fact was that a fringed sash girdled the juncture of his velvet blouse and breeches, for the Fauntleroy period had set in, and Georgie's mother had so poor an eye for appropriate things, where Georgie was concerned, that she dressed him according to the doctrine of that school in boy decoration. Not only did he wear a silk sash, and silk stockings, and a broad lace collar, with his little black velvet suit: he had long brown curls, and often came home with burrs in them.

Except upon the surface (which was not his own work, but his mother's) Georgie bore no vivid resemblance to the fabulous little Cedric. The storied boy's famous "Lean on *me*, grandfather," would have been difficult to imagine upon the lips of Georgie. A month after his ninth birthday anniversary, when the Major gave him his pony, he had already become acquainted with the toughest boys in various distant parts of the town, and had convinced them that the toughness of a rich little boy with long curls might be considered in many respects superior to their own. He fought them, learning how to go baresark at a certain point in a fight, bursting into tears of anger, reaching for rocks, uttering wailed threats of murder and attempting to fulfil them. Fights often led to intimacies, and he acquired the art of saying things more exciting than "Don't haf to!" and "Doctor says it ain't healthy!" Thus, on a summer afternoon, a strange boy, sitting bored upon the gatepost of the Reverend Malloch Smith, beheld George Amberson Minafer rapidly approaching on his white pony, and was impelled by bitterness to shout: "Shoot the ole jackass! Look at the girly curls! Say, bub, where'd you steal your mother's ole sash!"

"Your sister stole it for me!" Georgie instantly replied, checking the pony. "She stole it off our clo'es-line an' gave it to me."

"You go get your hair cut!" said the stranger hotly. "Yah! I haven't got any sister!"

"I know you haven't at home," Georgie responded. "I mean the one that's in jail."

"I dare you to get down off that pony!"

Georgie jumped to the ground, and the other boy descended from the Reverend Mr. Smith's gate-post—but he descended inside the gate. "I dare you outside that gate," said Georgie.

"Yah! I dare you half way here. I dare you——"

But these were luckless challenges, for Georgie immediately vaulted the fence—and four minutes later Mrs. Malloch Smith, hearing strange noises, looked forth from a window; then screamed, and dashed for the pastor's study. Mr. Malloch Smith, that grim-bearded Methodist, came to the front yard and found his visiting nephew being rapidly prepared by Master Minafer to serve as a principal figure in a pageant of massacre. It was with great physical difficulty that Mr. Smith managed to give his nephew a chance to escape into the house, for Georgie was hard and quick, and, in such matters, remarkably intense; but the minister, after a grotesque tussle, got him separated from his opponent, and shook him.

"You stop that, you!" Georgie cried fiercely; and wrenched himself away. "I guess you don't know who I am!"

"Yes, I do know!" the angered Mr. Smith retorted. "I know who you are, and you're a disgrace to your mother! Your mother ought to be ashamed of herself to allow——"

"Shut up about my mother bein' ashamed of herself!"

Mr. Smith, exasperated, was unable to close the dialogue with dignity. "She ought to be ashamed," he repeated. "A woman that lets a bad boy like you——"

But Georgie had reached his pony and mounted. Before setting off at his accustomed gallop, he paused to interrupt the Reverend Malloch Smith again. "You pull down your vest, you ole Billygoat, you!" he shouted, distinctly. "Pull down your vest, wipe off your chin—an' go to hell!"

Such precocity is less unusual, even in children of the Rich, than most grown people imagine. However, it was a new experience for the Reverend Malloch Smith, and left him in a state of excitement. He at once wrote a note to Georgie's mother, describing the crime according to his nephew's testimony; and the note reached Mrs. Minafer before Georgie did. When he got home she read it to him sorrowfully.

DEAR MADAM:

Your son has caused a painful distress in my household. He made an unprovoked attack upon a little nephew of mine who is visiting in my household, insulted him by calling him vicious names and falsehoods, stating that ladies of his family were in jail. He then tried to make his pony kick him, and when the child, who is only eleven years old, while your son is much older and stronger, endeavoured to avoid his indignities and withdraw quietly, he pursued him into the enclosure of my property and brutally assaulted him. When I appeared upon this scene he deliberately called insulting words to me, concluding with profanity, such as "go to hell," which was heard not only by myself but by my wife and the lady who lives next door. I trust such a state of undisciplined behaviour may be remedied for the sake of the reputation for propriety, if nothing higher, of the family to which this unruly child belongs.

Georgie had muttered various interruptions, and as she concluded the reading he said:

"He's an ole liar!"

"Georgie, you mustn't say 'liar.' Isn't this letter the truth?"

"Well," said Georgie, "how old am I?"

"Ten."

"Well, look how he says I'm older than a boy eleven years old."

"That's true," said Isabel. "He does. But isn't some of it true, Georgie?"

Georgie felt himself to be in a difficulty here, and he was silent.

"Georgie, did you say what he says you did?"

"Which one?"

"Did you tell him to—to—— Did you say, 'Go to hell?'"

Georgie looked worried for a moment longer; then he brightened. "Listen here, mamma; grandpa wouldn't wipe his shoe on that ole story-teller, would he?"

"Georgie, you mustn't——"

"I mean: none of the Ambersons wouldn't have anything to do with him, would they? He doesn't even know *you*, does he, mamma?"

"That hasn't anything to do with it."

"Yes, it has! I mean: none of the Amberson family go to see him, and they never have him come in their house; they wouldn't ask him to, and they prob'ly wouldn't even let him."

"That isn't what we're talking about."

"I bet," said Georgie emphatically, "I bet if he wanted to see any of 'em, he'd haf to go around to the side door!"

"No, dear, they——"

"Yes, they would, mamma! So what does it matter if I did say somep'm' to him he didn't like? That kind o' people, I don't see why you can't say anything you want to, to 'em!"

"No, Georgie. And you haven't answered me whether you said that dreadful thing he says you did."

"Well——" said Georgie. "Anyway, he said somep'm' to me that made me mad." And upon this point he offered no further details; he would not explain to his mother that what had made him "mad" was Mr. Smith's hasty condemnation of herself: "Your mother ought to be ashamed," and, "A woman that lets a bad boy like you——" Georgie did not even consider excusing himself by quoting these insolences.

Isabel stroked his head. "They were terrible words for you to use, dear. From his letter he doesn't seem a very tactful person, but——"

"He's just riffraff," said Georgie.

"You mustn't say so," his mother gently agreed. "Where did you learn those bad words he speaks of? Where did you hear any one use them?"

"Well, I've heard 'em serreval places. I guess Uncle George Amberson was the *first* I ever heard say 'em. Uncle George Amberson said 'em to papa once. Papa didn't like it, but Uncle George was just laughin' at papa, an' then he said 'em while he was laughin'."

"That was wrong of him," she said, but almost instinctively he detected the lack of conviction in her tone. It was Isabel's great failing that whatever an Amberson did seemed right to her, especially if the Amberson was either her brother George, or her son George. She knew that she should be more severe with the latter now, but severity with him was beyond her power; and the Reverend Malloch Smith had succeeded only in rousing her resentment against himself. Georgie's symmetrical face—altogether an Amberson face—had looked never more beautiful to her. It always looked unusually beautiful when she tried to be severe with him. "You must promise me," she said feebly, "never to use those bad words again."

"I promise not to," he said promptly—and he whispered an immediate codicil under his breath: "Unless I get mad at somebody!" This satisfied a code according to which, in his own sincere belief, he never told lies.

"That's a good boy," she said, and he ran out to the yard, his punishment over. Some admiring friends were gathered there; they had heard of his adventure, knew of the note, and were waiting to see what was going to "happen" to him. They hoped for an account of things, and also that he would allow them to "take turns" riding his pony to the end of the alley and back.

They were really his henchmen: Georgie was a lord among boys. In fact, he was a personage among certain sorts of grown people, and was often fawned upon; the alley negroes delighted in him, chuckled over him, flattered him slavishly. For that matter, he often heard well-dressed people speaking of him admiringly: a group of ladies once gathered about him on the pavement where he was spinning a top. "I *know* this is Georgie!" one exclaimed, and turned to the others with the impressiveness of a showman. "Major Amberson's only grandchild!" The others said, "It *is*?" and made clicking sounds with their mouths; two of them loudly whispering, "*So* handsome!"

Georgie, annoyed because they kept standing upon the circle he had chalked for his top, looked at them coldly and offered a suggestion:

"Oh, go hire a hall!"

As an Amberson, he was already a public character, and the story of his adventure in the Reverend Malloch Smith's front yard became a town topic. Many people glanced at him with great distaste, thereafter, when they chanced to encounter him, which meant nothing to Georgie, because he innocently believed most grown people to be necessarily cross-looking as a normal phenomenon resulting from the adult state; and he failed to comprehend that the distasteful glances had any personal bearing upon himself. If he had perceived such a bearing, he would have been affected only so far, probably, as to mutter, "Riffraff!" Possibly he would have shouted it; and, certainly, most people believed a story that went round the town just after Mrs. Amberson's funeral, when Georgie was eleven. Georgie was reported to have differed with the undertaker about the seating of the family; his indignant voice had become audible: "Well, who *is* the most important person at my own grandmother's funeral?" And later he had projected his head from the window of the foremost mourners' carriage, as the undertaker happened to pass.

"Riffraff!"

There were people—grown people they were—who expressed themselves longingly: they *did* hope to live to see the day, they said, when that boy would get his come-upance! (They used that honest word, so much better than "deserts," and not until many years later to be more clumsily rendered as "what is coming to him.") *Something* was bound to take him down, some day, and they only wanted to *be* there! But Georgie heard nothing of this, and the yearners for his taking down went unsatisfied, while their yearning grew the greater as the happy day of fulfilment was longer and longer postponed. His grandeur was not diminished by the Malloch Smith story; the rather it was increased, and among other children (especially among little girls) there was added to the prestige of his gilded position that diabolical glamour which must inevitably attend a boy who has told a minister to go to hell.

Chapter III

UNTIL HE reached the age of twelve, Georgie's education was a domestic process; tutors came to the house; and those citizens who yearned for his taking down often said: "Just wait till he has to go to public school; *then* he'll get it!" But at twelve Georgie was sent to a private school in the town, and there came from this small and dependent institution no report, or even rumour, of Georgie's getting anything that he was thought to deserve; therefore the yearning still persisted, though growing gaunt with feeding upon itself. For, although Georgie's pomposities and impudence in the little school were often almost unbearable, the teachers were fascinated by him. They did not like him—he was too arrogant for that—but he kept them in such a state of emotion that they thought more about him than they did about all of the other ten pupils. The emotion he kept them in was usually one resulting from injured self-respect, but sometimes it was dazzled admiration. So far as their conscientious observation went, he "studied" his lessons sparingly; but sometimes, in class, he flashed an admirable answer, with a comprehension not often shown by the pupils they taught; and he passed his examinations easily. In all, without discernible effort, he acquired at this school some rudiments of a liberal education and learned nothing whatever about himself.

The yearners were still yearning when Georgie, at sixteen, was sent away to a great "Prep School." "Now," they said brightly, "he'll get it! He'll find himself among boys just as important in their home towns as he is, and they'll knock the stuffing out of him when he puts on his airs with them! Oh, but that *would* be worth something to see!" They were mistaken, it appeared, for when Georgie returned, a few months later, he still seemed to have the same stuffing. He had been deported by the authorities, the offense being stated as "insolence and profanity"; in fact, he had given the principal of the school instructions almost identical with those formerly objected to by the Reverend Malloch Smith.

But he had not got his come-upance, and those who counted upon it were embittered by his appearance upon the down-town streets driving a dog-cart at a criminal speed, making pedestrians retreat from the crossings, and behaving generally as if he "owned the earth." A disgusted hardware dealer of middle age, one of those who hungered for Georgie's downfall, was thus driven back upon the sidewalk to avoid being run over, and so far forgot himself as to make use of the pet street insult of the year: "Got 'ny *sense*! See here, bub, does your mother know you're out?"

Georgie, without even seeming to look at him, flicked the long lash of his whip dexterously, and a little spurt of dust came from the hardware man's trousers, not far below the waist. He was not made of hardware: he raved, looking for a missile; then, finding none, commanded himself sufficiently to shout after the rapid dog-cart: "Turn down your pants, you would-be dude! Raining in dear ole Lunnon! Git off the earth!"

Georgie gave him no encouragement to think that he was heard. The dog-cart turned the next corner, causing indignation there, likewise, and, having proceeded some distance farther, halted in front of the "Amberson Block"—an old-fashioned four-story brick warren of lawyers' offices, insurance and real-estate offices, with a "drygoods store" occupying the ground floor. Georgie tied his lathered trotter to a telegraph pole, and stood for a moment looking at the building critically: it seemed shabby, and he thought his grandfather ought to replace it with a fourteen-story skyscraper, or even a higher one, such as he had lately seen in New York—when he stopped there for a few days of recreation and rest on his way home from the bereaved school. About the entryway to the stairs were various tin signs, announcing the occupation and location of upper-floor tenants, and Georgie decided to take some of these with him if he should ever go to college. However, he did not stop to collect them at this time, but climbed the worn stairs—there was no elevator—to the fourth floor, went down a dark corridor, and rapped three times upon a door. It was a mysterious door, its upper half, of opaque glass, bearing no sign to state the business or profession of the occupants within; but overhead, upon the lintel, four letters had been smearingly inscribed, partly with purple ink and partly with a soft lead pencil, "F. O. T. A." and upon the plaster wall, above the lintel, there was a drawing dear to male adolescence: a skull and crossbones.

Three raps, similar to Georgie's, sounded from within the room. Georgie then rapped four times; the rapper within the room rapped twice, and Georgie rapped seven times. This ended precautionary measures; and a well-dressed boy of sixteen opened the door; whereupon Georgie entered quickly, and the door was closed behind him. Seven boys of congenial age were seated in a semicircular row of damaged office chairs, facing a platform whereon stood a solemn, red-haired young personage with a table before him. At one end of the room there was a battered sideboard, and upon it were some empty beer bottles, a tobacco can about two-thirds full, with a web of mold over the surface of the tobacco, a dusty cabinet photograph (not inscribed) of Miss Lillian Russell, several withered old pickles, a caseknife, and a half-petrified section of icing-cake on a sooty plate. At the other end of the room were two rickety card-tables and a stand of bookshelves where were displayed under dust four or five small volumes of M. Guy de Maupassant's stories, "Robinson Crusoe," "Sappho," "Mr. Barnes of New York," a work by Giovanni Boccaccio, a Bible, "The Arabian Nights' Entertainment," "Studies of the Human Form Divine," "The Little Minister," and a clutter of monthly magazines and illustrated weeklies of about that crispness one finds in such articles upon a doctor's ante-room table. Upon the wall, above the sideboard, was an old framed lithograph of Miss Della Fox in "Wang"; over the bookshelves there was another lithograph purporting to represent Mr. John L. Sullivan in a boxing costume, and beside it a halftone reproduction of "A Reading From Homer." The final decoration consisted of damaged papier-mâché—a round shield with two battle-axes and two cross-hilted swords, upon the wall over the little platform where stood the red-haired presiding officer. He addressed Georgie in a serious voice:

"Welcome, Friend of the Ace."

"Welcome, Friend of the Ace," Georgie responded, and all of the other boys repeated the words, "Welcome, Friend of the Ace."

"Take your seat in the secret semicircle," said the presiding officer. "We will now proceed to——"

But Georgie was disposed to be informal. He interrupted, turning to the boy who had admitted him: "Look here, Charlie Johnson, what's Fred Kinney doing in the president's chair? That's my place, isn't it? What you men been up to here, anyhow? Didn't you all agree I was to be president just the same, even if I was away at school?"

"Well——" said Charlie Johnson uneasily. "Listen! I didn't have much to do with it. Some of the other members thought that long as you weren't in town or anything, and Fred gave the sideboard, why——"

Mr. Kinney, presiding, held in his hand, in lieu of a gavel, and considered much more impressive, a Civil War relic known as a "horse-pistol." He rapped loudly for order. "All Friends of the Ace will take their seats!" he said sharply. "I'm president of the F. O. T. A. now, George Minafer, and don't you forget it! You and Charlie Johnson sit down, because I was elected perfectly fair, and we're goin' to hold a meeting here."

"Oh, you are, are you?" said George skeptically.

Charlie Johnson thought to mollify him. "Well, didn't we call this meeting just especially because you told us to? You said yourself we ought to have a kind of celebration because you've got back to town, George, and that's what we're here for now, and everything. What do you care about being president? All it amounts to is just calling the roll and——"

The president *de facto* hammered the table. "This meeting will now proceed to——"

"No, it won't," said George, and he advanced to the desk, laughing contemptuously. "Get off that platform."

"This meeting will come to order!" Mr. Kinney commanded fiercely.

"You put down that gavel," said George. "Whose is it, I'd like to know? It belongs to my grandfather, and you quit hammering it that way or you'll break it, and I'll have to knock your head off."

"This meeting will come to order! I was legally elected here, and I'm not going to be bulldozed!"

"All right," said Georgie. "You're president. Now we'll hold another election."

"We will not!" Fred Kinney shouted. "We'll have our reg'lar meeting, and then we'll play euchre a nickel a corner, what we're here for. This meeting will now come to ord——"

Georgie addressed the members. "I'd like to know who got up this thing in the first place," he said. "Who's the founder of the F.O.T.A., if you please? Who got this room rent free? Who got the janitor to let us have most of this furniture? You suppose you could keep this clubroom a minute if I told my grandfather I didn't want it for a literary club any more? I'd like to say a word on how you members been acting, too! When I went away I said I didn't care if you had a *vice*-president or something while I was gone, but here I hardly turned my back and you had to go and elect Fred Kinney president! Well, if that's what you want, you can have it. I was going to have a little celebration down here some night pretty soon, and bring some port wine, like we drink at school in our crowd there, and I *was* going to get my grandfather to give the club an extra room across the hall, and prob'ly I could get my Uncle George to give us his old billiard table, because he's got a new one, and the club could put it in the other room. Well, you got a new president now!" Here Georgie moved toward the door and his tone became plaintive, though undeniably there was disdain beneath his sorrow. "I guess all I better do is—resign!"

And he opened the door, apparently intending to withdraw.

"All in favour of having a new election," Charlie Johnson shouted hastily, "say, 'Aye'!"

"Aye" was said by everyone present except Mr. Kinney, who began a hot protest, but it was immediately smothered.

"All in favour of me being president instead of Fred Kinney," shouted Georgie, "say 'Aye.' The 'Ayes' have it!"

"I resign," said the red-headed boy, gulping as he descended from the platform. "I resign from the club!"

Hot-eyed, he found his hat and departed, jeers echoing after him as he plunged down the corridor. Georgie stepped upon the platform, and took up the emblem of office.

"Ole red-head Fred'll be around next week," said the new chairman. "He'll be around boot-lickin' to get us to take him back in again, but I guess we don't want him: that fellow always was a trouble-maker. We will now proceed with our meeting. Well, fellows, I suppose you want to hear from your president.

I don't know that I have much to say, as I have already seen most of you a few times since I got back. I had a good time at the old school, back East, but had a little trouble with the faculty and came on home. My family stood by me as well as I could ask, and I expect to stay right here in the old town until whenever I decide to enter college. Now, I don't suppose there's any more business before the meeting. I guess we might as well play cards. Anybody that's game for a little quarter-limit poker or any limit they say, why I'd like to have 'em sit at the president's card-table."

When the diversions of the Friends of the Ace were concluded for that afternoon, Georgie invited his chief supporter, Mr. Charlie Johnson, to drive home with him to dinner, and as they jingled up National Avenue in the dog-cart, Charlie asked:

"What sort of men did you run up against at that school, George?"

"Best crowd there: finest set of men I ever met."

"How'd you get in with 'em?"

Georgie laughed. "I let them get in with *me*, Charlie," he said in a tone of gentle explanation. "It's vulgar to do any other way. Did I tell you the nickname they gave me—'King'? That was what they called me at that school, 'King Minafer.'"

"How'd they happen to do that?" his friend asked innocently.

"Oh, different things," George answered lightly. "Of course, any of 'em that came from anywhere out in this part the country knew about the family and all that, and so I suppose it was a good deal on account of—oh, on account of the family and the way I do things, most likely."

Chapter IV

WHEN MR. George Amberson Minafer came home for the holidays at Christmastide, in his sophomore year, probably no great change had taken place inside him, but his exterior was visibly altered. Nothing about him encouraged any hope that he had received his come-upance; on the contrary, the yearners for that stroke of justice must yearn even more itchingly: the gilded youth's manner had become polite, but his politeness was of a kind which democratic people found hard to bear. In a word, M. le Duc had returned from the gay life of the capital to show himself for a week among the loyal peasants belonging to the old château, and their quaint habits and costumes afforded him a mild amusement.

Cards were out for a ball in his honour, and this pageant of the tenantry was held in the ballroom of the Amberson Mansion the night after his arrival. It was, as Mrs. Henry Franklin Foster said of Isabel's wedding, "a big Amberson-style thing," though that wise Mrs. Henry Franklin Foster had long ago gone the way of all wisdom, having stepped out of the Midland town, unquestionably into heaven—a long step, but not beyond her powers. She had successors, but no successor; the town having grown too large to confess that it was intellectually led and literarily authoritated by one person; and some of these successors were not invited to the ball, for dimensions were now so metropolitan that intellectual leaders and literary authorities loomed in outlying regions unfamiliar to the Ambersons. However, all "old citizens" recognizable as gentry received cards, and of course so did their dancing descendants.

The orchestra and the caterer were brought from away, in the Amberson manner, though this was really a gesture—perhaps one more of habit than of ostentation—for servitors of gaiety as proficient as these importations were nowadays to be found in the town. Even flowers and plants and roped vines were brought from afar—not, however, until the stock of the local florists proved insufficient to obliterate the interior structure of the big house, in the Amberson way. It was the last of the great, long-remembered dances that "everybody talked about"—there were getting to be so many people in town that no later than the next year there were too many for "everybody" to hear of even such a ball as the Ambersons'.

George, white-gloved, with a gardenia in his buttonhole, stood with his mother and the Major, embowered in the big red and gold drawing room downstairs, to "receive" the guests; and, standing thus together, the trio offered a picturesque example of good looks persistent through three generations. The Major, his daughter, and his grandson were of a type all Amberson: tall, straight, and regular, with dark eyes, short noses, good chins; and the grandfather's expression, no less than the grandson's, was one of faintly amused condescension. There was a difference, however. The grandson's unlined young face had nothing to offer except this condescension; the grandfather's had other things to say. It was a handsome, worldly old face, conscious of its importance, but persuasive rather than arrogant, and not without tokens of sufferings withstood. The Major's short white hair was parted in the middle, like his grandson's, and in all he stood as briskly equipped to the fashion as exquisite young George.

Isabel, standing between her father and her son, caused a vague amazement in the mind of the latter. Her age, just under forty, was for George a thought of something as remote as the moons of Jupiter: he could not possibly have conceived such an age ever coming to be his own: five years was the limit of his thinking in time. Five years ago he had been a child not yet fourteen; and those five years were an abyss. Five years hence he would be almost twenty-four; what the girls he knew called "one of the older men." He could imagine himself at twenty-four, but beyond that, his powers staggered and refused the task. He saw little essential difference between thirty-eight and eighty-eight, and his mother was to him not a woman but wholly a mother. He had no perception of her other than as an adjunct to himself, his mother; nor could he imagine her thinking or doing anything—falling in love, walking with a friend, or reading a book—as a woman, and not as his mother. The woman, Isabel, was a stranger to her son; as completely a stranger as if he had never in his life seen her or heard her voice.

And it was to-night, while he stood with her, "receiving," that he caught a disquieting glimpse of this stranger whom he thus fleetingly encountered for the first time.

Youth cannot imagine romance apart from youth. That is why the rôles of the heroes and heroines of plays are given by the managers to the most youthful actors they can find among the competent. Both middle-aged people and young people enjoy a play about young lovers; but only middle-aged people will tolerate a play about middle-aged lovers; young people will not come to see such a play, because, for them, middle-aged lovers are a joke—not a very funny one. Therefore, to bring both the middle-aged people and the young people into his house, the manager makes his romance as young as he can. Youth will indeed be served, and its profound instinct is to be not only scornfully amused but vaguely angered by middle-age romance. So, standing beside his mother, George was disturbed by a sudden impression, coming upon him out of nowhere, so far as he could detect, that her eyes were brilliant, that she was graceful and youthful—in a word, that she was romantically lovely.

He had one of those curious moments that seem to have neither a cause nor any connection with actual things. While it lasted, he was disquieted not by thoughts—for he had no definite thoughts—but by a slight emotion like that caused in a dream by the presence of something invisible, soundless, and yet fantastic. There was nothing different or new about his mother, except her new black and silver dress: she was standing there beside him, bending her head a little in her greetings, smiling the same smile she had worn for the half-hour that people had been passing the "receiving" group. Her face was flushed, but the room was warm; and shaking hands with so many people easily accounted for the pretty glow that was upon her. At any time she could have "passed" for twenty-five or twenty-six—a man of fifty would have honestly guessed her to be about thirty but possibly two or three years younger—and though extraordinary in this, she had been extraordinary in it for years. There was nothing in either her looks or her manner to explain George's uncomfortable feeling; and yet it increased, becoming suddenly a vague resentment, as if she had done something unmotherly to him.

The fantastic moment passed; and even while it lasted, he was doing his duty, greeting two pretty girls with whom he had grown up, as people say, and warmly assuring them that he remembered them very well—an assurance which might have surprised them "in anybody but Georgie Minafer!" It seemed unnecessary, since he had spent many hours with them no longer ago than the preceding August. They had with them their parents and an uncle from out of town; and George negligently gave the parents the same assurance he had given the daughters, but murmured another form of greeting to the out-of-town uncle, whom he had never seen before. This person George absently took note of as a "queer-looking duck." Undergraduates had not yet adopted "bird." It was a period previous to that in which a sophomore would have thought of the Sharon girls' uncle as a "queer-looking bird," or, perhaps a "funny-face bird." In George's time, every human male was to be defined, at pleasure, as a "duck"; but "duck" was not spoken with admiring affection, as in its former feminine use to signify a "dear"—on the contrary, "duck" implied the speaker's personal detachment and humorous superiority. An indifferent amusement was what George felt when his mother, with a gentle emphasis, interrupted his interchange of courtesies with the nieces to present him to the queer-looking duck, their uncle. This emphasis of Isabel's, though slight, enabled George to perceive that she considered the queer-looking duck a person of some importance; but it was far from enabling him to understand why. The duck parted his thick and longish black hair on the side; his tie was a forgetful looking thing, and his coat, though it fitted a good enough middle-aged figure, no product of this year, or of last year either. One of his eyebrows was noticeably higher than the other; and there were whimsical lines between them, which gave him an apprehensive expression; but his apprehensions were evidently more humorous than profound, for his prevailing look was that of a genial man of affairs, not much afraid of anything whatever. Nevertheless, observing only his unfashionable hair, his eyebrows, his preoccupied tie and his old coat, the olympic George set him down as a queer-looking duck, and having thus completed his portrait, took no interest in him.

The Sharon girls passed on, taking the queer-looking duck with them, and George became pink with mortification as his mother called his attention to a white-bearded guest waiting to shake his hand. This was George's great-uncle, old John Minafer: it was old John's boast that in spite of his connection by marriage with the Ambersons, he never had worn and never would wear a swaller-tail coat. Members of his family had exerted their influence uselessly—at eighty-nine conservative people seldom form radical new habits, and old John wore his "Sunday suit" of black broadcloth to the Amberson ball. The coat was square, with skirts to the knees; old John called it a "Prince Albert" and was well enough pleased with it, but his great-nephew considered it the next thing to an insult. George's purpose had been to ignore the man, but he had to take his hand for a moment; whereupon old John began to tell George that he was looking well, though there had been a time, during his fourth month, when he was so puny that nobody thought he would live. The great-nephew, in a fury of blushes, dropped old John's hand with some vigour, and seized that of the next person in the line. "'Member you v'ry well 'ndeed!" he said fiercely.

The large room had filled, and so had the broad hall and the rooms on the other side of the hall, where there were tables for whist. The imported orchestra waited in the ballroom on the third floor, but a local harp, 'cello, violin, and flute were playing airs from "The Fencing Master" in the hall, and people were shouting over the music. Old John Minafer's voice was louder and more penetrating than any other, because he had been troubled with deafness for twenty-five years, heard his own voice but faintly, and liked to hear it. "Smell o' flowers like this always puts me in mind o' funerals," he kept telling his niece, Fanny Minafer, who was with him; and he seemed to get a great deal of satisfaction out of this reminder. His tremulous yet strident voice cut through the voluminous sound that filled the room, and he was heard everywhere: "Always got to think o' funerals when I smell so many flowers!" And, as the pressure of people forced Fanny and himself against the white marble mantelpiece, he pursued this train of cheery thought, shouting, "Right here's where the Major's wife was laid out at *her* funeral. They had her in a good light from that big bow window." He paused to chuckle mournfully. "I s'pose that's where they'll put the Major when *his* time comes."

Presently George's mortification was increased to hear this sawmill droning harshly from the midst of the thickening crowd: "Ain't the dancin' broke out yet, Fanny? Hoopla! Le's push through and go see the young women-folks crack their heels! Start the circus! Hoopse-daisy!" Miss Fanny Minafer, in charge of the lively veteran, was almost as distressed as her nephew George, but she did her duty and managed to get old John through the press and out to the broad stairway, which numbers of young people were now ascending to the ballroom. And here the sawmill voice still rose over all others: "Solid black walnut every inch of it, balustrades and all. Sixty thousand dollars' worth o' carved woodwork in the house! Like water! Spent money like water! Always did! Still do! Like water! God knows where it all comes from!"

He continued the ascent, barking and coughing among the gleaming young heads, white shoulders, jewels, and chiffon, like an old dog slowly swimming up the rapids of a sparkling river; while down below, in the drawing room, George began to recover from the degradation into which this relic of early settler days had dragged him. What restored him completely was a dark-eyed little beauty of nineteen, very knowing in lustrous blue and jet; at sight of this dashing advent in the line of guests before him, George was fully an Amberson again.

"Remember you very well *indeed*!" he said, his graciousness more earnest than any he had heretofore displayed. Isabel heard him and laughed.

"But you don't, George!" she said. "You don't remember her yet, though of course you *will*! Miss Morgan is from out of town, and I'm afraid this is the first time you've ever seen her. You might take her up to the dancing; I think you've pretty well done your duty here."

"Be d'lighted," George responded formally, and offered his arm, not with a flourish, certainly, but with an impressiveness inspired partly by the appearance of the person to whom he offered it, partly by his being the hero of this fête, and partly by his youthfulness—for when manners are new they are apt to be elaborate. The little beauty entrusted her gloved fingers to his coat-sleeve, and they moved away together.

Their progress was necessarily slow, and to George's mind it did not lack stateliness. How could it? Musicians, hired especially for him, were sitting in a grove of palms in the hall and now tenderly playing "Oh, Promise Me" for his pleasuring; dozens and scores of flowers had been brought to life and tended to this hour that they might sweeten the air for him while they died; and the evanescent power that music and floral scents hold over youth stirred his appreciation of strange, beautiful qualities within his own bosom: he seemed to himself to be mysteriously angelic, and about to do something dramatic which would overwhelm the beautiful young stranger upon his arm.

Elderly people and middle-aged people moved away to let him pass with his honoured fair beside him. Worthy middle-class creatures, they seemed, leading dull lives but appreciative of better things when they saw them—and George's bosom was fleetingly touched with a pitying kindness. And since the primordial day when caste or heritage first set one person, in his own esteem, above his fellow-beings, it is to be doubted if anybody ever felt more illustrious, or more negligently grand, than George Amberson Minafer felt at this party.

As he conducted Miss Morgan through the hall, toward the stairway, they passed the open double doors of a card room, where some squadrons of older people were preparing for action, and, leaning gracefully upon the mantelpiece of this room, a tall man, handsome, high-mannered, and sparklingly point-device, held laughing converse with that queer-looking duck, the Sharon girls' uncle. The tall gentleman waved a gracious salutation to George, and Miss Morgan's curiosity was stirred. "Who is that?"

"I didn't catch his name when my mother presented him to me," said George. "You mean the queer-looking duck."

"I mean the aristocratic duck."

"That's my Uncle George. Honourable George Amberson. I thought everybody knew him."

"He looks as though everybody ought to know him," she said. "It seems to run in your family."

If she had any sly intention, it skipped over George harmlessly. "Well, of course, I suppose most everybody does," he admitted—"out in this part of the country especially. Besides,

Uncle George is in Congress; the family like to have someone there."

"Why?"

"Well, it's sort of a good thing in one way. For instance, my Uncle Sydney Amberson and his wife, Aunt Amelia, they haven't got much of anything to do with themselves—get bored to death around here, of course. Well, probably Uncle George'll have Uncle Sydney appointed minister or ambassador, or something like that, to Russia or Italy or somewhere, and that'll make it pleasant when any of the rest of the family go travelling, or things like that. I expect to do a good deal of travelling myself when I get out of college."

On the stairway he pointed out this prospective ambassadorial couple, Sydney and Amelia. They were coming down, fronting the ascending tide, and as conspicuous over it as a king and queen in a play. Moreover, as the clear-eyed Miss Morgan remarked, the very least they looked was ambassadorial. Sydney was an Amberson exaggerated, more pompous than gracious; too portly, flushed, starched to a shine, his stately jowl furnished with an Edward the Seventh beard. Amelia, likewise full-bodied, showed glittering blond hair exuberantly dressed; a pink, fat face cold under a white-hot tiara; a solid, cold bosom under a white-hot necklace; great, cold, gloved arms, and the rest of her beautifully upholstered. Amelia was an Amberson born, herself, Sydney's second-cousin: they had no children, and Sydney was without a business or a profession; thus both found a great deal of time to think about the appropriateness of their becoming Excellencies. And as George ascended the broad stairway, they were precisely the aunt and uncle he was most pleased to point out, to a girl from out of town, as his appurtenances in the way of relatives. At sight of them the grandeur of the Amberson family was instantly conspicuous as a permanent thing: it was impossible to doubt that the Ambersons were entrenched, in their nobility and riches, behind polished and glittering barriers which were as solid as they were brilliant, and would last.

Chapter V

THE HERO of the fête, with the dark-eyed little beauty upon his arm, reached the top of the second flight of stairs; and here, beyond a spacious landing, where two proud-like darkies tended a crystalline punch bowl, four wide archways in a rose-vine lattice framed gliding silhouettes of waltzers, already smoothly at it to the castanets of "*La Paloma*." Old John Minafer, evidently surfeited, was in the act of leaving these delights. "D'want 'ny more o' that!" he barked. "Just slidin' around! Call that dancin'? Rather see a jig any day in the world! They ain't very modest, some of 'em. I don't mind *that*, though. Not me!"

Miss Fanny Minafer was no longer in charge of him: he emerged from the ballroom escorted by a middle-aged man of commonplace appearance. The escort had a dry, lined face upon which, not ornamentally but as a matter of course, there grew a business man's short moustache; and his thin neck showed an Adam's apple, but not conspicuously, for there was nothing conspicuous about him. Baldish, dim, quiet, he was an unnoticeable part of this festival, and although there were a dozen or more middle-aged men present, not casually to be distinguished from him in general aspect, he was probably the last person in the big house at whom a stranger would have glanced twice. It did not enter George's mind to mention to Miss Morgan that this was his father, or to say anything whatever about him.

Mr. Minafer shook his son's hand unobtrusively in passing.

"I'll take Uncle John home," he said, in a low voice. "Then I guess I'll go on home myself—I'm not a great hand at parties, you know. Good-night, George."

George murmured a friendly enough good-night without pausing. Ordinarily he was not ashamed of the Minafers; he seldom thought about them at all, for he belonged, as most American children do, to the mother's family—but he was anxious not to linger with Miss Morgan in the vicinity of old John, whom he felt to be a disgrace.

He pushed brusquely through the fringe of calculating youths who were gathered in the arches, watching for chances to dance only with girls who would soon be taken off their hands, and led his stranger lady out upon the floor. They caught the time instantly, and were away in the waltz.

George danced well, and Miss Morgan seemed to float as part of the music, the very dove itself of "*La Paloma*." They said nothing as they danced; her eyes were cast down all the while—the prettiest gesture for a dancer—and there was left in the universe, for each of them, only their companionship in this waltz; while the faces of the other dancers, swimming by, denoted not people but merely blurs of colour. George became conscious of strange feelings within him: an exaltation of soul, tender, but indefinite, and seemingly located in the upper part of his diaphragm.

The stopping of the music came upon him like the waking to an alarm clock; for instantly six or seven of the calculating persons about the entryways bore down upon Miss Morgan to secure dances. George had to do with one already established as a belle, it seemed.

"Give me the next and the one after that," he said hurriedly, recovering some presence of mind, just as the nearest applicant reached them. "And give me every third one the rest of the evening."

She laughed. "Are you asking?"

"What do you mean, 'asking'?"

"It sounded as though you were just telling me to give you all those dances."

"Well, I want 'em!" George insisted.

"What about all the other girls it's your duty to dance with?"

"They'll have to go without," he said heartlessly; and then, with surprising vehemence: "Here! I want to know: Are you going to give me those——"

"Good gracious!" she laughed. "Yes!"

The applicants flocked round her, urging contracts for what remained, but they did not dislodge George from her side, though he made it evident that they succeeded in annoying him; and presently he extricated her from an accumulating siege—she must have connived in the extrication—and bore her off to sit beside him upon the stairway that led to the musicians' gallery, where they were sufficiently retired, yet had a view of the room.

"How'd all those ducks get to know you so quick?" George inquired, with little enthusiasm.

"Oh, I've been here a week."

"Looks as if you'd been pretty busy!" he said. "Most of those ducks, I don't know what my mother wanted to invite 'em here for."

"Don't you like them?"

"Oh, I used to see something of a few of 'em. I was president of a club we had here, and some of 'em belonged to it, but I don't care much for that sort of thing any more. I really don't see why my mother invited 'em."

"Perhaps it was on account of their parents," Miss Morgan suggested mildly. "Maybe she didn't want to offend their fathers and mothers."

"Oh, hardly! I don't think my mother need worry much about offending anybody in this old town."

"It must be wonderful," said Miss Morgan. "It must be wonderful, Mr. Amberson—Mr. Minafer, I mean."

"What must be wonderful?"

"To be so important as that!"

"*That* isn't 'important,'" George assured her. "Anybody that really is anybody ought to be able to do about as they like in their own town, I should think!"

She looked at him critically from under her shading lashes —but her eyes grew gentler almost at once. In truth, they became more appreciative than critical. George's imperious good looks were altogether manly, yet approached actual beauty as closely as a boy's good looks should dare; and dance-music and flowers have some effect upon nineteen-year-old girls as well as upon eighteen-year-old boys. Miss Morgan turned her eyes slowly from George, and pressed her face among the lilies-of-the-valley and violets of the pretty bouquet she carried, while, from the gallery above, the music of the next dance carolled out merrily in a new two-step. The musicians made the melody gay for the Christmastime with chimes of sleighbells, and the entrance to the shadowed stairway framed the passing flushed and lively dancers, but neither George nor Miss Morgan suggested moving to join the dance.

The stairway was draughty: the steps were narrow and uncomfortable; no older person would have remained in such a place. Moreover, these two young people were strangers to each other; neither had said anything in which the other had discovered the slightest intrinsic interest; there had not arisen between them the beginnings of congeniality, or even of friendliness—but stairways near ballrooms have more to answer for than have moonlit lakes and mountain sunsets. Some day the laws of glamour must be discovered, because they are so important that the world would be wiser now if Sir Isaac Newton had been hit on the head, not by an apple, but by a young lady.

Age, confused by its own long accumulation of follies, is everlastingly inquiring, "What does *she* see in *him*?" as if young love came about through thinking—or through conduct. Age wants to know: "What on earth can they *talk* about?" as if talking had anything to do with April rains! At seventy, one gets up in the morning, finds the air sweet under a bright sun, feels lively; thinks, "I am hearty, to-day," and plans to go for a drive. At eighteen, one goes to a dance, sits with a stranger on a stairway, feels peculiar, thinks nothing, and becomes incapable of any plan whatever. Miss Morgan and George stayed where they were.

They had agreed to this in silence and without knowing it; certainly without exchanging glances of intelligence—they had exchanged no glances at all. Both sat staring vaguely out into the ballroom, and, for a time, they did not speak. Over their heads the music reached a climax of vivacity: drums, cymbals, triangle, and sleighbells, beating, clashing, tinkling. Here and there were to be seen couples so carried away that, ceasing to move at the decorous, even glide, considered most knowing, they pranced and whirled through the throng, from wall to wall, galloping bounteously in abandon. George suffered a shock of vague surprise when he perceived that his aunt, Fanny Minafer, was the lady-half of one of these wild couples.

Fanny Minafer, who rouged a little, was like fruit which in some climates dries with the bloom on. Her features had remained prettily childlike; so had her figure, and there were times when strangers, seeing her across the street, took her to be about twenty; there were other times when at the same distance they took her to be about sixty, instead of forty, as she was. She had old days and young days; old hours and young hours; old minutes and young minutes; for the change might be that quick. An alteration in her expression, or a difference in the attitude of her head, would cause astonishing indentations to appear—and behold, Fanny was an old lady! But she had been never more childlike than she was to-night as she flew over the floor in the capable arms of the queer-looking duck; for this person was her partner.

The queer-looking duck had been a real dancer in his day, it appeared; and evidently his day was not yet over. In spite of the headlong, gay rapidity with which he bore Miss Fanny about the big room, he danced authoritatively, avoiding without effort the lightest collision with other couples, maintaining sufficient grace throughout his wildest moments, and all the while laughing and talking with his partner. What was most remarkable to George, and a little irritating, this stranger in the Amberson Mansion had no vestige of the air of deference proper to a stranger in such a place: he seemed thoroughly at home. He seemed offensively so, indeed, when, passing the entrance to the gallery stairway, he disengaged his hand from Miss Fanny's for an instant, and not pausing in the dance, waved a laughing salutation more than cordial, then capered lightly out of sight.

George gazed stonily at this manifestation, responding neither by word nor sign. "How's that for a bit of freshness?" he murmured.

"What was?" Miss Morgan asked.

"That queer-looking duck waving his hand at me like that. Except he's the Sharon girls' uncle I don't know him from Adam."

"You don't need to," she said. "He wasn't waving his hand to you: he meant me."

"Oh, he did?" George was not mollified by the explanation. "Everybody seems to mean you! You certainly do seem to've been pretty busy this week you've been here!"

She pressed her bouquet to her face again, and laughed into

it, not displeased. She made no other comment, and for another period neither spoke. Meanwhile the music stopped; loud applause insisted upon its renewal; an encore was danced; there was an interlude of voices; and the changing of partners began.

"Well," said George finally, "I must say you don't seem to be much of a prattler. They say it's a great way to get a reputation for being wise, never saying much. Don't you ever talk *any*?"

"When people can understand," she answered.

He had been looking moodily out at the ballroom but he turned to her quickly, at this, saw that her eyes were sunny and content, over the top of her bouquet; and he consented to smile.

"Girls are usually pretty fresh!" he said. "They ought to go to a man's college about a year: they'd get taught a few things about freshness! What you got to do after two o'clock to-morrow afternoon?"

"A whole lot of things. Every minute filled up."

"All right," said George. "The snow's fine for sleighing: I'll come for you in a cutter at ten minutes after two."

"I can't possibly go."

"If you don't," he said, "I'm going to sit in the cutter in front of the gate, wherever you're visiting, all afternoon, and if you try to go out with anybody else he's got to whip me before he gets you." And as she laughed—though she blushed a little, too—he continued, seriously: "If you think I'm not in earnest you're at liberty to make quite a big experiment!"

She laughed again. "I don't think I've often had so large a compliment as that," she said, "especially on such short notice—and yet, I don't think I'll go with you."

"You be ready at ten minutes after two."

"No, I won't."

"Yes, you will!"

"Yes," she said, "I will!" And her partner for the next dance arrived, breathless with searching.

"Don't forget I've got the third from now," George called after her.

"I won't."

"And every third one after that."

"I know!" she called, over her partner's shoulder, and her voice was amused—but meek.

When "the third from now" came, George presented himself before her without any greeting, like a brother, or a mannerless old friend. Neither did she greet him, but moved away with him, concluding, as she went, an exchange of badinage with the preceding partner: she had been talkative enough with him, it appeared. In fact, both George and Miss Morgan talked much more to every one else that evening, than to each other; and they said nothing at all at this time. Both looked preoccupied, as they began to dance, and preserved a gravity of expression to the end of the number. And when "the third one after that" came, they did not dance, but went back to the gallery stairway, seeming to have reached an understanding without any verbal consultation, that this suburb was again the place for them.

"Well," said George, coolly, when they were seated, "what did you say your name was?"

"Morgan."

"Funny name!"

"Everybody else's name always is."

"I didn't mean it was really funny," George explained. "That's just one of my crowd's bits of horsing at college. We always say 'funny name' no matter what it is. I guess we're pretty fresh sometimes; but I knew your name was Morgan because my mother said so downstairs. I meant: what's the rest of it?"

"Lucy."

He was silent.

"Is 'Lucy' a funny name, too?" she inquired.

"No. Lucy's very much all right!" he said, and he went so far as to smile. Even his Aunt Fanny admitted that when George smiled "in a certain way" he was charming.

"Thanks about letting my name be Lucy," she said.

"How old are you?" George asked.

"I don't really know, myself."

"What do you mean: you don't really know yourself?"

"I mean I only know what they tell me. I believe them, of course, but believing isn't really knowing. You believe some certain day is your birthday—at least, I suppose you do—but you don't really know it is because you can't remember."

"Look here!" said George. "Do you always talk like this?"

Miss Lucy Morgan laughed forgivingly, put her young head

on one side, like a bird, and responded cheerfully: "I'm willing to learn wisdom. What are you studying in school?"

"College!"

"At the university! Yes. What are you studying there?"

George laughed. "Lot o' useless guff!"

"Then why don't you study some useful guff?"

"What do you mean: 'useful'?"

"Something you'd use later, in your business or profession?"

George waved his hand impatiently. "I don't expect to go into any 'business or profession.'"

"No?"

"Certainly not!" George was emphatic, being sincerely annoyed by a suggestion which showed how utterly she failed to comprehend the kind of person he was.

"Why not?" she asked mildly.

"Just look at 'em!" he said, almost with bitterness, and he made a gesture presumably intended to indicate the business and professional men now dancing within range of vision. "That's a fine career for a man, isn't it! Lawyers, bankers, politicians! What do they get out of life, I'd like to know! What do they ever know about *real* things? Where do they ever *get*?"

He was so earnest that she was surprised and impressed. Evidently he had deep-seated ambitions, for he seemed to speak with actual emotion of these despised things which were so far beneath his planning for the future. She had a vague, momentary vision of Pitt, at twenty-one, prime minister of England; and she spoke, involuntarily in a lowered voice, with deference:

"What do you want to be?" she asked.

George answered promptly.

"A yachtsman," he said.

Chapter VI

HAVING THUS, in a word, revealed his ambition for a career above courts, marts, and polling booths, George breathed more deeply than usual, and, turning his face from the lovely companion whom he had just made his confidant, gazed out at the dancers with an expression in which there was both sternness and a contempt for the squalid lives of the unyachted Midlanders before him. However, among them, he marked his mother; and his sombre grandeur relaxed momentarily; a more genial light came into his eyes.

Isabel was dancing with the queer-looking duck; and it was to be noted that the lively gentleman's gait was more sedate than it had been with Miss Fanny Minafer, but not less dexterous and authoritative. He was talking to Isabel as gaily as he had talked to Miss Fanny, though with less laughter, and Isabel listened and answered eagerly: her colour was high and her eyes had a look of delight. She saw George and the beautiful Lucy on the stairway, and nodded to them. George waved his hand vaguely: he had a momentary return of that inexplicable uneasiness and resentment which had troubled him downstairs.

"How lovely your mother is!" Lucy said.

"I think she is," he agreed gently.

"She's the gracefulest woman in that ballroom. She dances like a girl of sixteen."

"Most girls of sixteen," said George, "are bum dancers. Anyhow, I wouldn't dance with one unless I had to."

"Well, you'd better dance with your mother! I never saw anybody lovelier. How wonderfully they dance together!"

"Who?"

"Your mother and—and the queer-looking duck," said Lucy. "I'm going to dance with him pretty soon."

"I don't care—so long as you don't give him one of the numbers that belong to me."

"I'll try to remember," she said, and thoughtfully lifted to her face the bouquet of violets and lilies, a gesture which George noted without approval.

"Look here! Who sent you those flowers you keep makin' such a fuss over?"

"He did."

"Who's 'he'?"

"The queer-looking duck."

George feared no such rival; he laughed loudly. "I s'pose he's some old widower!" he said, the object thus described seeming ignominious enough to a person of eighteen, without additional characterization. "Some old widower!"

Lucy became serious at once. "Yes, he is a widower," she said. "I ought to have told you before; he's my father."

George stopped laughing abruptly. "Well, that's a horse on me. If I'd known he was your father, of course I wouldn't have made fun of him. I'm sorry."

"Nobody could make fun of him," she said quietly.

"Why couldn't they?"

"It wouldn't make him funny: it would only make themselves silly."

Upon this, George had a gleam of intelligence. "Well, I'm not going to make myself silly any more, then; I don't want to take chances like that with *you*. But I thought he was the Sharon girls' uncle. He came with them——"

"Yes," she said, "I'm always late to everything: I wouldn't let them wait for me. We're visiting the Sharons."

"About time I knew that! You forget my being so fresh about your father, will you? Of course he's a distinguished looking man, in a way."

Lucy was still serious. "'In a way?'" she repeated. "You mean, not in your way, don't you?"

George was perplexed. "How do you mean: not in my way?"

"People pretty often say 'in a way' and 'rather distinguished looking,' or 'rather' so-and-so, or 'rather' anything, to show that *they're* superior, don't they? In New York last month I overheard a climber sort of woman speaking of me as 'little Miss Morgan,' but she didn't mean my height; she meant that she was important. Her husband spoke of a friend of mine as 'little Mr. Pembroke' and 'little Mr. Pembroke' is six-feet-three. This husband and wife were really so terribly unimportant that the only way they knew to pretend to be important was calling people 'little' Miss or Mister so-and-so. It's a kind of snob slang, I think. Of course people don't always say 'rather' or 'in a way' to be superior."

"I should say not! I use both of 'em a great deal myself," said George. "One thing I don't see though: What's the use of a man being six-feet-three? Men that size can't handle themselves as well as a man about five-feet-eleven and a half can. Those long, gangling men, they're nearly always too kind of wormy to be any good in athletics, and they're so awkward they keep falling over chairs or——"

"Mr. Pembroke is in the army," said Lucy primly. "He's extraordinarily graceful."

"In the army? Oh, I suppose he's some old friend of your father's."

"They got on very well," she said, "after I introduced them."

George was a straightforward soul, at least. "See here!" he said. "Are you engaged to anybody?"

"No."

Not wholly mollified, he shrugged his shoulders. "You seem to know a good many people! Do you live in New York?"

"No. We don't live anywhere."

"What you mean: you don't live anywhere?"

"We've lived all over," she answered. "Papa used to live here in this town, but that was before I was born."

"What do you keep moving around so for? Is he a promoter?"

"No. He's an inventor."

"What's he invented?"

"Just lately," said Lucy, "he's been working on a new kind of horseless carriage."

"Well, I'm sorry for him," George said, in no unkindly spirit. "Those things are never going to amount to anything. People aren't going to spend their lives lying on their backs in the road and letting grease drip in their faces. Horseless carriages are pretty much a failure, and your father better not waste his time on 'em."

"Papa'd be so grateful," she returned, "if he could have your advice."

Instantly George's face became flushed. "I don't know that I've done anything to be insulted for!" he said. "I don't see that what I said was particularly fresh."

"No, indeed!"

"Then what do you——"

She laughed gaily. "I don't! And I don't mind your being such a lofty person at all. I think it's ever so interesting—but papa's a great man!"

"Is he?" George decided to be good-natured. "Well, let us hope so. I hope so, I'm sure."

Looking at him keenly, she saw that the magnificent youth was incredibly sincere in this bit of graciousness. He spoke as a tolerant, elderly statesman might speak of a promising young politician; and with her eyes still upon him, Lucy shook her head in gentle wonder. "I'm just beginning to understand," she said.

"Understand what?"

"What it means to be a real Amberson in this town. Papa told me something about it before we came, but I see he didn't say half enough!"

George superbly took this all for tribute. "Did your father say he knew the family before he left here?"

"Yes. I believe he was particularly a friend of your Uncle George; and he didn't say so, but I imagine he must have known your mother very well, too. He wasn't an inventor then; he was a young lawyer. The town was smaller in those days, and I believe he was quite well known."

"I dare say. I've no doubt the family are all very glad to see him back, especially if they used to have him at the house a good deal, as he told you."

"I don't think he meant to boast of it," she said. "He spoke of it quite calmly."

George stared at her for a moment in perplexity, then perceiving that her intention was satirical, "Girls really ought to go to a man's college," he said—"just a month or two, anyhow. It'd take *some* of the freshness out of 'em!"

"I can't believe it," she retorted, as her partner for the next dance arrived. "It would only make them a little politer on the surface—they'd be really just as awful as ever, after you got to know them a few minutes."

"What do you mean: 'after you got to know them a——'"

She was departing to the dance. "Janie and Mary Sharon told me all about what sort of a *little* boy you were," she said, over her shoulder. "You must think it out!"

She took wing away on the breeze of the waltz, and George, having stared gloomily after her for a few moments, postponed filling an engagement, and strolled round the fluctuating outskirts of the dance to where his uncle, George Amberson, stood smilingly watching, under one of the rose-vine arches at the entrance to the room.

"Hello, young namesake," said the uncle. "Why lingers the laggard heel of the dancer? Haven't you got a partner?"

"She's sitting around waiting for me somewhere," said George. "See here: Who is this fellow Morgan that Aunt Fanny Minafer was dancing with a while ago?"

Amberson laughed. "He's a man with a pretty daughter, Georgie. Meseemed you've been spending the evening noticing something of that sort—or do I err?"

"Never mind! What sort is he?"

"I think we'll have to give him a character, Georgie. He's an old friend; used to practise law here—perhaps he had more debts than cases, but he paid 'em all up before he left town. Your question is purely mercenary, I take it: you want to know his true worth before proceeding further with the daughter. I cannot inform you, though I notice signs of considerable prosperity in that becoming dress of hers. However, you never can tell. It is an age when every sacrifice is made for the young, and how your own poor mother managed to provide those genuine pearl studs for you out of her allowance from father, I can't——"

"Oh, dry up!" said the nephew. "I understand this Morgan——"

"Mr. Eugene Morgan," his uncle suggested. "Politeness requires that the young should——"

"I guess the 'young' didn't know much about politeness in your day," George interrupted. "I understand that Mr. Eugene Morgan used to be a great friend of the family."

"Oh, the Minafers?" the uncle inquired, with apparent innocence. "No, I seem to recall that he and your father were not——"

"I mean the Ambersons," George said impatiently. "I understand he was a good deal around the house here."

"What is your objection to that, George?"

"What do you mean: my objection?"

"You seemed to speak with a certain crossness."

"Well," said George, "I meant he seems to feel awfully at home here. The way he was dancing with Aunt Fanny——"

Amberson laughed. "I'm afraid your Aunt Fanny's heart was stirred by ancient recollections, Georgie."

"You mean she used to be silly about him?"

"She wasn't considered singular," said the uncle. "He was —he was popular. Could you bear a question?"

"What do you mean: could I bear——"

"I only wanted to ask: Do you take this same passionate interest in the parents of every girl you dance with? Perhaps it's a new fashion we old bachelors ought to take up. Is it the thing this year to——"

"Oh, go on!" said George, moving away. "I only wanted to know——" He left the sentence unfinished, and crossed the room to where a girl sat waiting for his nobility to find time to fulfil his contract with her for this dance.

"Pardon f' keep' wait," he muttered, as she rose brightly to meet him; and she seemed pleased that he came at all—but George was used to girls looking radiant when he danced with them, and she had little effect upon him. He danced with her perfunctorily, thinking the while of Mr. Eugene Morgan and his daughter. Strangely enough, his thoughts dwelt more upon the father than the daughter, though George could not possibly have given a reason—even to himself—for this disturbing preponderance.

By a coincidence, though not an odd one, the thoughts and conversation of Mr. Eugene Morgan at this very time were concerned with George Amberson Minafer, rather casually, it is true. Mr. Morgan had retired to a room set apart for smoking, on the second floor, and had found a grizzled gentleman lounging in solitary possession.

"'Gene Morgan!" this person exclaimed, rising with great heartiness. "I'd heard you were in town—I don't believe you know me!"

"Yes, I do, Fred Kinney!" Mr. Morgan returned with equal friendliness. "Your real face—the one I used to know—it's just underneath the one you're masquerading in to-night. You ought to have changed it more if you wanted a disguise."

"Twenty years!" said Mr. Kinney. "It makes some difference in faces, but more in behaviour!"

"It does *so*!" his friend agreed with explosive emphasis. "My own behaviour began to be different about that long ago—quite suddenly."

"I remember," said Mr. Kinney sympathetically. "Well, life's odd enough as we look back."

"Probably it's going to be odder still—if we could look forward."

"Probably."

They sat and smoked.

"However," Mr. Morgan remarked presently, "I still dance like an Indian. Don't you?"

"No. I leave that to my boy Fred. He does the dancing for the family."

"I suppose he's upstairs hard at it?"

"No, he's not here." Mr. Kinney glanced toward the open door and lowered his voice. "He wouldn't come. It seems that a couple of years or so ago he had a row with young Georgie Minafer. Fred was president of a literary club they had, and he said this young Georgie got himself elected instead, in an overbearing sort of way. Fred's red-headed, you know—I suppose you remember his mother? You were at the wedding——"

"I remember the wedding," said Mr. Morgan. "And I remember your bachelor dinner—most of it, that is."

"Well, my boy Fred's as red-headed now," Mr. Kinney went on, "as his mother was then, and he's very bitter about his row with Georgie Minafer. He says he'd rather burn his foot off than set it inside any Amberson house or any place else where young Georgie is. Fact is, the boy seemed to have so much feeling over it I had my doubts about coming myself, but my wife said it was all nonsense; we mustn't humour Fred in a grudge over such a little thing, and while she despised that Georgie Minafer, herself, as much as any one else did, she wasn't going to miss a big Amberson show just on account of a boys' rumpus, and so on and so on; and so we came."

"Do people dislike young Minafer generally?"

"I don't know about 'generally.' I guess he gets plenty of toadying; but there's certainly a lot of people that are glad to express their opinions about him."

"What's the matter with him?"

"Too much Amberson, I suppose, for one thing. And for another, his mother just fell down and worshipped him from the day he was born. That's what beats me! I don't have to tell you what Isabel Amberson is, Eugene Morgan. She's got a touch of the Amberson high stuff about her, but you can't get anybody that ever knew her to deny that she's just about the finest woman in the world."

"No," said Eugene Morgan. "You can't get anybody to deny that."

"Then I can't see how she doesn't see the truth about that boy. He thinks he's a little tin god on wheels—and honestly, it makes some people weak and sick just to think about him! Yet that high-spirited, intelligent woman, Isabel Amberson, actually sits and worships him! You can hear it in her voice when she speaks to him or speaks of him. You can see it in her eyes when she looks at him. My Lord! What *does* she see when she looks at him?"

Morgan's odd expression of genial apprehension deepened whimsically, though it denoted no actual apprehension whatever, and cleared away from his face altogether when he smiled; he became surprisingly winning and persuasive when he smiled. He smiled now, after a moment, at this question of his old friend. "She sees something that we don't see," he said.

"What does she see?"

"An angel."

Kinney laughed aloud. "Well, if she sees an angel when she looks at Georgie Minafer, she's a funnier woman than I thought she was!"

"Perhaps she is," said Morgan. "But that's what she sees."

"My Lord! It's easy to see you've only known him an hour or so. In that time have you looked at Georgie and seen an angel?"

"No. All I saw was a remarkably good-looking fool-boy with the pride of Satan and a set of nice new drawing-room manners that he probably couldn't use more than half an hour at a time without busting."

"Then what——"

"Mothers are right," said Morgan. "Do you think this young George is the same sort of creature when he's with his mother that he is when he's bulldozing your boy Fred? Mothers see the angel in us because the angel is there. If it's shown to the mother, the son has got an angel to show, hasn't he? When a son cuts somebody's throat the mother only sees it's possible for a misguided angel to act like a devil—and she's entirely right about that!"

Kinney laughed, and put his hand on his friend's shoulder. "I remember what a fellow you always were to argue," he said. "You mean Georgie Minafer is as much of an angel as any murderer is, and that Georgie's mother is always right."

"I'm afraid she always has been," Morgan said lightly.

The friendly hand remained upon his shoulder. "She was wrong once, old fellow. At least, so it seemed to me."

"No," said Morgan, a little awkwardly. "No——"

Kinney relieved the slight embarrassment that had come upon both of them: he laughed again. "Wait till you know young Georgie a little better," he said. "Something tells me you're going to change your mind about his having an angel to show, if you see anything of him!"

"You mean beauty's in the eye of the beholder, and the angel is all in the eye of the mother. If you were a painter, Fred, you'd paint mothers with angels' eyes holding imps in their laps. Me, I'll stick to the Old Masters and the cherubs."

Mr. Kinney looked at him musingly. "Somebody's eyes must have been pretty angelic," he said, "if they've been persuading you that Georgie Minafer is a cherub!"

"They are," said Morgan heartily. "They're more angelic than ever." And as a new flourish of music sounded overhead he threw away his cigarette, and jumped up briskly. "Goodbye, I've got this dance with her."

"With whom?"

"With Isabel!"

The grizzled Mr. Kinney affected to rub his eyes. "It startles me, your jumping up like that to go and dance with Isabel Amberson! Twenty years seem to have passed—but have they? Tell me, have you danced with poor old Fanny, too, this evening?"

"Twice!"

"My Lord!" Kinney groaned, half in earnest. "Old times starting all over again! My Lord!"

"Old times?" Morgan laughed gaily from the doorway. "Not a bit! There aren't any old times. When times are gone they're not old, they're dead! There aren't any times but new times!"

And he vanished in such a manner that he seemed already to have begun dancing.

Chapter VII

THE APPEARANCE of Miss Lucy Morgan the next day, as she sat in George's fast cutter, proved so charming that her escort was stricken to soft words instantly, and failed to control a poetic impulse. Her rich little hat was trimmed with black fur; her hair was almost as dark as the fur; a great boa of black fur was about her shoulders; her hands were vanished into a black muff; and George's laprobe was black. "You look like—" he said. "Your face looks like—it looks like a snowflake on a lump of coal. I mean a—a snowflake that would be a rose-leaf, too!"

"Perhaps you'd better look at the reins," she returned. "We almost upset just then."

George declined to heed this advice. "Because there's too much pink in your cheeks for a snowflake," he continued. "What's that fairy story about snow-white and rose-red——"

"We're going pretty fast, Mr. Minafer!"

"Well, you see, I'm only here for two weeks."

"I mean the sleigh!" she explained. "We're not the only people on the street, you know."

"Oh, *they'll* keep out of the way."

"That's very patrician charioteering, but it seems to me a horse like this needs guidance. I'm sure he's going almost twenty miles an hour."

"That's nothing," said George; but he consented to look forward again. "He can trot under three minutes, all right." He laughed. "I suppose your father thinks he can build a horseless carriage to go that fast!"

"They go that fast already, sometimes."

"Yes," said George; "they do—for about a hundred feet! Then they give a yell and burn up."

Evidently she decided not to defend her father's faith in horseless carriages, for she laughed, and said nothing. The cold air was polka-dotted with snowflakes, and trembled to the loud, continuous jingling of sleighbells. Boys and girls, all aglow and panting jets of vapour, darted at the passing sleighs to ride on the runners, or sought to rope their sleds to any vehicle whatever, but the fleetest no more than just touched the flying cutter, though a hundred soggy mittens grasped for it, then reeled and whirled till sometimes the wearers of those daring mittens plunged flat in the snow and lay a-sprawl, reflecting. For this was the holiday time, and all the boys and girls in town were out, most of them on National Avenue.

But there came panting and chugging up that flat thoroughfare a thing which some day was to spoil all their sleigh-time merriment—save for the rashest and most disobedient. It was vaguely like a topless surry, but cumbrous with unwholesome excrescences fore and aft, while underneath were spinning leather belts and something that whirred and howled and seemed to stagger. The ride-stealers made no attempt to fasten their sleds to a contrivance so nonsensical and yet so fearsome. Instead, they gave over their sport and concentrated all their energies in their lungs, so that up and down the street the one cry shrilled increasingly: "Git a hoss! Git a hoss! Git a hoss! Mister, why don't you git a hoss?" But the mahout in charge, sitting solitary on the front seat, was unconcerned—he laughed, and now and then ducked a snowball without losing any of his good-nature. It was Mr. Eugene Morgan who exhibited so cheerful a countenance between the forward visor of a deer-stalker cap and the collar of a fuzzy gray ulster. "Git a hoss!" the children shrieked, and gruffer voices joined them. "Git a hoss! Git a hoss! Git a *hoss*!"

George Minafer was correct thus far: the twelve miles an hour of such a machine would never overtake George's trotter. The cutter was already scurrying between the stone pillars at the entrance to Amberson Addition.

"That's my grandfather's," said George, nodding toward the Amberson Mansion.

"I ought to know that!" Lucy exclaimed. "We stayed there late enough last night: papa and I were almost the last to go. He and your mother and Miss Fanny Minafer got the musicians to play another waltz when everybody else had gone downstairs and the fiddles were being put away in their cases. Papa danced part of it with Miss Minafer and the rest with your mother. Miss Minafer's your aunt, isn't she?"

"Yes; she lives with us. I tease her a good deal."

"What about?"

"Oh, anything handy—whatever's easy to tease an old maid about."

"Doesn't she mind?"

"She usually has sort of a grouch on me," laughed George. "Nothing much. That's our house just beyond grandfather's." He waved a sealskin gauntlet to indicate the house Major Amberson had built for Isabel as a wedding gift. "It's almost the same as grandfather's, only not as large and hasn't got a regular ballroom. We gave the dance, last night, at grandfather's on account of the ballroom, and because I'm the only grandchild, you know. Of course, some day that'll be my house, though I expect my mother will most likely go on living where she does now, with father and Aunt Fanny. I suppose I'll probably build a country house, too—somewhere East, I guess." He stopped speaking, and frowned as they passed a closed carriage and pair. The body of this comfortable vehicle sagged slightly to one side; the paint was old and seamed with hundreds of minute cracks like little rivers on a black map; the coachman, a fat and elderly darky, seemed to drowse upon the box; but the open window afforded the occupants of the cutter a glimpse of a tired, fine old face, a silk hat, a pearl tie, and an astrachan collar, evidently out to take the air.

"There's your grandfather now," said Lucy. "Isn't it?"

George's frown was not relaxed. "Yes, it is; and he ought to give that rat-trap away and sell those old horses. They're a disgrace, all shaggy—not even clipped. I suppose he doesn't notice it—people get awful funny when they get old; they seem to lose their self-respect, sort of."

"He seemed a real Brummell to me," she said.

"Oh, he keeps up about what he *wears*, well enough, but—well, look at that!" He pointed to a statue of Minerva, one of the cast-iron sculptures Major Amberson had set up in opening the Addition years before. Minerva was intact, but a blackish streak descended unpleasantly from her forehead to the point of her straight nose, and a few other streaks were sketched in a repellent dinge upon the folds of her drapery.

"That must be from soot," said Lucy. "There are so many houses around here."

"Anyhow, somebody ought to see that these statues are kept clean. My grandfather owns a good many of these houses, I guess, for renting. Of course, he sold most of the lots—there aren't any vacant ones, and there used to be heaps of 'em when I was a boy. Another thing I don't think he ought to allow: a good many of these people bought big lots and they built houses on 'em; then the price of the land kept getting higher, and they'd sell part of their yards and let the people that bought it build houses on it to live in, till they haven't hardly any of 'em got big, open yards any more, and it's getting all too much built up. The way it used to be, it was like a gentleman's country estate, and that's the way my grandfather ought to keep it. He lets these people take too many liberties: they do anything they want to."

"But how could he stop them?" Lucy asked, surely with reason. "If he sold them the land, it's theirs, isn't it?"

George remained serene in the face of this apparently difficult question. "He ought to have all the trades-people boycott the families that sell part of their yards that way. All he'd have to do would be to tell the trades-people they wouldn't get any more orders from the family if they didn't do it."

"From 'the family'? What family?"

"Our family," said George, unperturbed. "The Ambersons."

"I see!" she murmured, and evidently she did see something that he did not, for, as she lifted her muff to her face, he asked:

"What are you laughing at now?"

"Why?"

"You always seem to have some little secret of your own to get happy over!"

"'Always!'" she exclaimed. "What a big word, when we only met last night!"

"That's another case of it," he said, with obvious sincerity. "One of the reasons I don't like you—much!—is you've got that way of seeming quietly superior to everybody else."

"I!" she cried. "I have?"

"Oh, you think you keep it sort of confidential to yourself, but it's plain enough! I don't believe in that kind of thing."

"You don't?"

"No," said George emphatically. "Not with *me*! I think the world's like this: there's a few people that their birth and position, and so on, puts them at the top, and they ought to treat each other entirely as equals." His voice betrayed a little emotion as he added, "I wouldn't speak like this to everybody."

"You mean you're confiding your deepest creed—or code, whatever it is—to me?"

"Go on, make fun of it, then!" George said bitterly. "You do think you're terribly clever! It makes me tired!"

"Well, as you don't like my seeming 'quietly superior,' after this I'll be noisily superior," she returned cheerfully. "We aim to please!"

"I had a notion before I came for you to-day that we were going to quarrel," he said.

"No, we won't; it takes two!" She laughed and waved her muff toward a new house, not quite completed, standing in a field upon their right. They had passed beyond Amberson Addition, and were leaving the northern fringes of the town for the open country. "Isn't that a beautiful house!" she exclaimed. "Papa and I call it our Beautiful House."

George was not pleased. "Does it belong to you?"

"Of course not! Papa brought me out here the other day, driving in his machine, and we both loved it. It's so spacious and dignified and plain."

"Yes, it's plain enough!" George grunted.

"Yet it's lovely; the gray-green roof and shutters give just enough colour, with the trees, for the long white walls. It seems to me the finest house I've seen in this part of the country."

George was outraged by an enthusiasm so ignorant—not ten minutes ago they had passed the Amberson Mansion. "Is that a sample of your taste in architecture?" he asked.

"Yes. Why?"

"Because it strikes me you better go somewhere and study the subject a little!"

Lucy looked puzzled. "What makes you have so much feeling about it? Have I offended you?"

"'Offended' nothing!" George returned brusquely. "Girls usually think they know it all as soon as they've learned to dance and dress and flirt a little. They never know anything about things like architecture, for instance. That house is about as bum a house as any house I ever saw!"

"Why?"

"'Why?'" George repeated. "Did you ask me 'why?'"

"Yes."

"Well, for one thing—" he paused—"for one thing—well, just look at it! I shouldn't think you'd have to do any more than look at it if you'd ever given any attention to architecture."

"What is the matter with its architecture, Mr. Minafer?"

"Well, it's this way," said George. "It's like this. Well, for instance, that house—well, it was built like a town house." He spoke of it in the past tense, because they had now left it far behind them—a human habit of curious significance. "It was like a house meant for a street in the city. What kind of a house was that for people of any taste to build out here in the country?"

"But papa says it's built that way on purpose. There are a lot of other houses being built in this direction, and papa says the city's coming out this way; and in a year or two that house will be right in town."

"It was a bum house, anyhow," said George crossly. "I don't even know the people that are building it. They say a lot of riffraff come to town every year nowadays and there's other riffraff that have always lived here, and have made a little money, and act as if they owned the place. Uncle Sydney was talking about it yesterday: he says he and some of his friends are organizing a country club, and already some of these riffraff are worming into it—people he never heard of at all! Anyhow, I guess it's pretty clear you don't know a great deal about architecture."

She demonstrated the completeness of her amiability by laughing. "I'll know something about the North Pole before long," she said, "if we keep going much farther in this direction!"

At this he was remorseful. "All right, we'll turn and drive south awhile till you get warmed up again. I expect we have been going against the wind about long enough. Indeed, I'm sorry!"

He said, "Indeed, I'm sorry," in a nice way, and looked very strikingly handsome when he said it, she thought. No doubt it is true that there is more rejoicing in heaven over one sinner repented than over all the saints who consistently remain holy, and the rare, sudden gentlenesses of arrogant people have infinitely more effect than the continual gentleness of gentle people. Arrogance turned gentle melts the heart; and Lucy gave her companion a little sidelong, sunny nod of acknowledgment. George was dazzled by the quick glow of her eyes, and found himself at a loss for something to say.

Having turned about, he kept his horse to a walk, and at this gait the sleighbells tinkled but intermittently. Gleaming wanly through the whitish vapour that kept rising from the trotter's body and flanks, they were like tiny fog-bells, and made the only sounds in a great winter silence. The white road ran between lonesome rail fences; and frozen barnyards beyond the fences showed sometimes a harrow left to rust, with its iron seat half filled with stiffened snow, and sometimes an old dead buggy, its wheels forever set, it seemed, in the solid ice of deep ruts. Chickens scratched the metallic earth with an air of protest, and a masterless ragged colt looked up in sudden horror at the mild tinkle of the passing bells, then blew fierce clouds of steam at the sleigh. The snow no longer fell, and far ahead, in a grayish cloud that lay upon the land, was the town.

Lucy looked at this distant thickening reflection. "When we get this far out we can see there must be quite a little smoke hanging over the town," she said. "I suppose that's because it's growing. As it grows bigger it seems to get ashamed of itself, so it makes this cloud and hides in it. Papa says it used to be a bit nicer when he lived here: he always speaks of it differently—he always has a gentle look, a particular tone of voice, I've noticed. He must have been very fond of it. It must have been a lovely place: everybody must have been so jolly. From the way he talks, you'd think life here then was just one long midsummer serenade. He declares it was always sunshiny, that the air wasn't like the air anywhere else—that, as he remembers it, there always seemed to be gold-dust in the air. I doubt it! I think it doesn't seem to be duller air to him now just on account of having a little soot in it sometimes, but probably because he was twenty years younger then. It seems to me the gold-dust he thinks was here is just his being young that he remembers. I think it was just youth. It *is* pretty pleasant to be young, isn't it?" She laughed absently, then appeared to become wistful. "I wonder if we really do enjoy it as much as we'll look back and think we did! I don't suppose so. Anyhow, for my part I feel as if I must be missing something about it, somehow, because I don't ever seem to be thinking about what's happening at the present moment; I'm always looking forward to something—thinking about things that will happen when I'm older."

"You're a funny girl," George said gently. "But your voice sounds pretty nice when you think and talk along together like that!"

The horse shook himself all over, and the impatient sleigh-bells made his wish audible. Accordingly, George tightened the reins, and the cutter was off again at a three-minute trot, no despicable rate of speed. It was not long before they were again passing Lucy's Beautiful House, and here George thought fit to put an appendix to his remark. "You're a funny girl, and you know a lot—but I don't believe you know much about architecture!"

Coming toward them, black against the snowy road, was a strange silhouette. It approached moderately and without visible means of progression, so the matter seemed from a distance; but as the cutter shortened the distance, the silhouette was revealed to be Mr. Morgan's horseless carriage, conveying four people atop: Mr. Morgan with George's mother beside him, and, in the rear seat, Miss Fanny Minafer and the Honorable George Amberson. All four seemed to be in the liveliest humour, like high-spirited people upon a new adventure; and Isabel waved her handkerchief dashingly as the cutter flashed by them.

"For the Lord's sake!" George gasped.

"Your mother's a dear," said Lucy. "And she does wear the most bewitching *things*! She looked like a Russian princess, though I doubt if they're that handsome."

George said nothing; he drove on till they had crossed Amberson Addition and reached the stone pillars at the head of National Avenue. There he turned.

"Let's go back and take another look at that old sewing-machine," he said. "It certainly is the weirdest, craziest——"

He left the sentence unfinished, and presently they were again in sight of the old sewing-machine. George shouted mockingly.

Alas! three figures stood in the road, and a pair of legs, with the toes turned up, indicated that a fourth figure lay upon its back in the snow, beneath a horseless carriage that had decided to need a horse.

George became vociferous with laughter, and coming up at his trotter's best gait, snow spraying from runners and every hoof, swerved to the side of the road and shot by, shouting, "Git a hoss! Git a hoss! Git a hoss!"

Three hundred yards away he turned and came back, racing; leaning out as he passed, to wave jeeringly at the group about the disabled machine: "Git a hoss! Git a hoss! Git a——"

The trotter had broken into a gallop, and Lucy cried a warning: "Be careful!" she said. "Look where you're driving! There's a ditch on that side. *Look*——"

George turned too late; the cutter's right runner went into the ditch and snapped off; the little sleigh upset, and, after dragging its occupants some fifteen yards, left them lying together in a bank of snow. Then the vigorous young horse kicked himself free of all annoyances, and disappeared down the road, galloping cheerfully.

Chapter VIII

WHEN GEORGE regained some measure of his presence of mind, Miss Lucy Morgan's cheek, snowy and cold, was pressing his nose slightly to one side; his right arm was firmly about her neck; and a monstrous amount of her fur boa seemed to mingle with an equally unplausible quantity of snow in his mouth. He was confused, but conscious of no objection to any of these juxtapositions. She was apparently uninjured, for she sat up, hatless, her hair down, and said mildly:

"Good heavens!"

Though her father had been under his machine when they passed, he was the first to reach them. He threw himself on his knees beside his daughter, but found her already laughing, and was reassured. "They're all right," he called to Isabel, who was running toward them, ahead of her brother and Fanny Minafer. "This snowbank's a feather bed—nothing the matter with them at all. Don't look so pale!"

"Georgie!" she gasped. "*Georgie!*"

Georgie was on his feet, snow all over him.

"Don't make a fuss, mother! Nothing's the matter. That darned silly horse——"

Sudden tears stood in Isabel's eyes. "To see you down underneath—dragging—oh!——" Then with shaking hands she began to brush the snow from him.

"Let me alone," he protested. "You'll ruin your gloves. You're getting snow all over you, and——"

"No, no!" she cried. "You'll catch cold; you mustn't catch cold!" And she continued to brush him.

Amberson had brought Lucy's hat; Miss Fanny acted as lady's-maid; and both victims of the accident were presently restored to about their usual appearance and condition of apparel. In fact, encouraged by the two older gentlemen, the entire party, with one exception, decided that the episode was after all a merry one, and began to laugh about it. But George was glummer than the December twilight now swiftly closing in.

"That darned horse!" he said.

"I wouldn't bother about Pendennis, Georgie," said his uncle. "You can send a man out for what's left of the cutter tomorrow, and Pendennis will gallop straight home to his stable: he'll be there a *long* while before we will, because all we've got to depend on to get us home is Gene Morgan's broken-down chafing-dish yonder."

They were approaching the machine as he spoke, and his friend, again underneath it, heard him. He emerged, smiling. "She'll go," he said.

"What!"

"All aboard!"

He offered his hand to Isabel. She was smiling but still pale, and her eyes, in spite of the smile, kept upon George in a shocked anxiety. Miss Fanny had already mounted to the rear seat, and George, after helping Lucy Morgan to climb up beside his aunt, was following. Isabel saw that his shoes were light things of patent leather, and that snow was clinging to them. She made a little rush toward him, and, as one of his feet rested on the iron step of the machine, in mounting, she began to clean the snow from his shoe with her almost aërial lace handkerchief. "You mustn't catch cold!" she cried.

"Stop that!" George shouted, and furiously withdrew his foot.

"Then stamp the snow off," she begged. "You mustn't ride with wet feet."

"They're not!" George roared, thoroughly outraged. "For heaven's sake get in! You're standing in the snow yourself. Get in!"

Isabel consented, turning to Morgan, whose habitual expression of apprehensiveness was somewhat accentuated. He climbed up after her, George Amberson having gone to the other side. "You're the same Isabel I used to know!" he said in a low voice. "You're a divinely ridiculous woman."

"Am I, Eugene?" she said, not displeased. "'Divinely' and 'ridiculous' just counterbalance each other, don't they? Plus one and minus one equal nothing; so you mean I'm nothing in particular?"

"No," he answered, tugging at a lever. "That doesn't seem

to be precisely what I meant. There!" This exclamation referred to the subterranean machinery, for dismaying sounds came from beneath the floor, and the vehicle plunged, then rolled noisily forward.

"Behold!" George Amberson exclaimed. "She does move! It must be another accident."

"'Accident?'" Morgan shouted over the din. "No! She breathes, she stirs; she seems to feel a thrill of life along her keel!" And he began to sing "The Star Spangled Banner."

Amberson joined him lustily, and sang on when Morgan stopped. The twilight sky cleared, discovering a round moon already risen; and the musical congressman hailed this bright presence with the complete text and melody of "The Danube River."

His nephew, behind, was gloomy. He had overheard his mother's conversation with the inventor: it seemed curious to him that this Morgan, of whom he had never heard until last night, should be using the name "Isabel" so easily; and George felt that it was not just the thing for his mother to call Morgan "Eugene"; the resentment of the previous night came upon George again. Meanwhile, his mother and Morgan continued their talk; but he could no longer hear what they said; the noise of the car and his uncle's songful mood prevented. He marked how animated Isabel seemed; it was not strange to see his mother so gay, but it was strange that a man not of the family should be the cause of her gaiety. And George sat frowning.

Fanny Minafer had begun to talk to Lucy. "Your father wanted to prove that his horseless carriage would run, even in the snow," she said. "It really does, too."

"Of course!"

"It's so interesting! He's been telling us how he's going to change it. He says he's going to have wheels all made of rubber and blown up with air. I don't understand what he means at all; I should think they'd explode—but Eugene seems to be very confident. He always was confident, though. It seems so like old times to hear him talk!"

She became thoughtful, and Lucy turned to George. "You tried to swing underneath me and break the fall for me when we went over," she said. "I knew you were doing that, and—it was nice of you."

"Wasn't any fall to speak of," he returned brusquely. "Couldn't have hurt either of us."

"Still it was friendly of you—and awfully quick, too. I'll not —I'll not forget it!"

Her voice had a sound of genuineness, very pleasant; and George began to forget his annoyance with her father. This annoyance of his had not been alleviated by the circumstance that neither of the seats of the old sewing-machine was designed for three people, but when his neighbour spoke thus gratefully, he no longer minded the crowding—in fact, it pleased him so much that he began to wish the old sewing-machine would go even slower. And she had spoken no word of blame for his letting that darned horse get the cutter into the ditch. George presently addressed her hurriedly, almost tremulously, speaking close to her ear:

"I forgot to tell you something: you're pretty nice! I thought so the first second I saw you last night. I'll come for you to-night and take you to the Assembly at the Amberson Hotel. You're going, aren't you?"

"Yes, but I'm going with papa and the Sharons. I'll see you there."

"Looks to me as if you were awfully conventional," George grumbled; and his disappointment was deeper than he was willing to let her see—though she probably did see. "Well, we'll dance the cotillion together, anyhow."

"I'm afraid not. I promised Mr. Kinney."

"What!" George's tone was shocked, as at incredible news. "Well, you could break *that* engagement, I guess, if you wanted to! Girls always can get out of things when they want to. Won't you?"

"I don't think so."

"Why not?"

"Because I promised him. Several days ago."

George gulped, and lowered his pride, "I don't—oh, look here! I only want to go to that thing to-night to get to see something of you; and if you don't dance the cotillion with me, how can I? I'll only be here two weeks, and the others have got all the rest of your visit to see you. *Won't* you do it, please?"

"I couldn't."

"See here!" said the stricken George. "If you're going to

decline to dance that cotillion with me simply because you've promised a—a—a miserable red-headed outsider like Fred Kinney, why we might as well quit!"

"Quit what?"

"You know perfectly well what I mean," he said huskily.

"I don't."

"Well, you ought to!"

"But I don't at all!"

George, thoroughly hurt, and not a little embittered, expressed himself in a short outburst of laughter: "Well, I ought to have seen it!"

"Seen what?"

"That you might turn out to be a girl who'd like a fellow of the red-headed Kinney sort. I ought to have seen it from the first!"

Lucy bore her disgrace lightly. "Oh, dancing a cotillion with a person doesn't mean that you like him—but I don't see anything in particular the matter with Mr. Kinney. What is?"

"If you don't see anything the matter with him for yourself," George responded, icily, "I don't think pointing it out would help you. You probably wouldn't understand."

"You might try," she suggested. "Of course I'm a stranger here, and if people have done anything wrong or have something unpleasant about them, I wouldn't have any way of knowing it, just at first. If poor Mr. Kinney——"

"I prefer not to discuss it," said George curtly. "He's an enemy of mine."

"Why?"

"I prefer not to discuss it."

"Well, but——"

"I prefer not to discuss it!"

"Very well." She began to hum the air of the song which Mr. George Amberson was now discoursing, "O moon of my delight that knows no wane"—and there was no further conversation on the back seat.

They had entered Amberson Addition, and the moon of Mr. Amberson's delight was overlaid by a slender Gothic filagree; the branches that sprang from the shade trees lining the street. Through the windows of many of the houses rosy lights were flickering; and silver tinsel and evergreen wreaths and brilliant little glass globes of silver and wine colour could be seen, and glimpses were caught of Christmas trees, with people decking them by firelight—reminders that this was Christmas Eve. The ride-stealers had disappeared from the highway, though now and then, over the gasping and howling of the horseless carriage, there came a shrill jeer from some young passer-by upon the sidewalk:

"Mister, fer heaven's sake go an' git a hoss! Git a hoss! *Git* a hoss!"

The contrivance stopped with a heart-shaking jerk before Isabel's house. The gentlemen jumped down, helping Isabel and Fanny to descend; there were friendly leavetakings—and one that was not precisely friendly.

"It's 'au revoir,' till to-night, isn't it?" Lucy asked, laughing.

"Good afternoon!" said George, and he did not wait, as his relatives did, to see the old sewing-machine start briskly down the street, toward the Sharons'; its lighter load consisting now of only Mr. Morgan and his daughter. George went into the house at once.

He found his father reading the evening paper in the library. "Where are your mother and your Aunt Fanny?" Mr. Minafer inquired, not looking up.

"They're coming," said his son; and, casting himself heavily into a chair, stared at the fire.

His prediction was verified a few moments later; the two ladies came in cheerfully, unfastening their fur cloaks. "It's all right, Georgie," said Isabel. "Your Uncle George called to us that Pendennis got home safely. Put your shoes close to the fire, dear, or else go and change them." She went to her husband and patted him lightly on the shoulder, an action which George watched with sombre moodiness. "You might dress before long," she suggested. "We're all going to the Assembly, after dinner, aren't we? Brother George said he'd go with us."

"Look here," said George abruptly. "How about this man Morgan and his old sewing-machine? Doesn't he want to get grandfather to put money into it? Isn't he trying to work Uncle George for that? Isn't that what he's up to?"

It was Miss Fanny who responded. "You little silly!" she cried, with surprising sharpness. "What on earth are you talking about? Eugene Morgan's perfectly able to finance his own inventions these days."

"I'll bet he borrows money of Uncle George," the nephew insisted.

Isabel looked at him in grave perplexity. "Why do you say such a thing, George?" she asked.

"He strikes me as that sort of man," he answered doggedly. "Isn't he, father?"

Minafer set down his paper for the moment. "He was a fairly wild young fellow twenty years ago," he said, glancing at his wife absently. "He was like you in one thing, Georgie; he spent too much money—only he didn't have any mother to get money out of a grandfather for him, so he was usually in debt. But I believe I've heard he's done fairly well of late years. No, I can't say I think he's a swindler, and I doubt if he needs anybody else's money to back his horseless carriage."

"Well, what's he brought the old thing here for, then? People that own elephants don't take their elephants around with 'em when they go visiting. What's he got it here for?"

"I'm sure I don't know," said Mr. Minafer, resuming his paper. "You might ask him."

Isabel laughed and patted her husband's shoulder again. "Aren't you going to dress? Aren't we all going to the dance?"

He groaned faintly. "Aren't your brother and Georgie escorts enough for you and Fanny?"

"Wouldn't you enjoy it at all?"

"You know I don't."

Isabel let her hand remain upon his shoulder a moment longer; she stood behind him, looking into the fire, and George, watching her broodingly, thought there was more colour in her face than the reflection of the flames accounted for. "Well, then," she said indulgently, "stay at home and be happy. We won't urge you if you'd really rather not."

"I really wouldn't," he said contentedly.

Half an hour later, George was passing through the upper hall, in a bath-robe stage of preparation for the evening's gaieties, when he encountered his Aunt Fanny. He stopped her. "Look here!" he said.

"What in the world is the matter with you?" she demanded, regarding him with little amiability. "You look as if you were rehearsing for a villain in a play. Do change your expression!"

His expression gave no sign of yielding to the request; on

the contrary, its sombreness deepened. "I suppose you don't know why father doesn't want to go to-night," he said solemnly. "You're his only sister, and yet you don't know!"

"He never wants to go anywhere that I ever heard of," said Fanny. "What *is* the matter with you?"

"He doesn't want to go because he doesn't like this man Morgan."

"Good gracious!" Fanny cried impatiently. "Eugene Morgan isn't in your father's thoughts at all, one way or the other. Why should he be?"

George hesitated. "Well—it strikes me—— Look here, what makes you and—and everybody—so excited over him?"

"'Excited!'" she jeered. "Can't people be glad to see an old friend without silly children like you having to make a to-do about it? I've just been in your mother's room suggesting that she might give a little dinner for them——"

"For who?"

"For *whom*, Georgie! For Mr. Morgan and his daughter."

"Look here!" George said quickly. "Don't do that! Mother mustn't do that. It wouldn't look well."

"'Wouldn't look well!'" Fanny mocked him; and her suppressed vehemence betrayed a surprising acerbity. "See here, Georgie Minafer, I suggest that you just march straight on into your room and finish your dressing! Sometimes you say things that show you have a pretty mean little mind!"

George was so astounded by this outburst that his indignation was delayed by his curiosity. "Why, what upsets *you* this way?" he inquired.

"I know what you mean," she said, her voice still lowered, but not decreasing in sharpness. "You're trying to insinuate that I'd get your mother to invite Eugene Morgan here on my account because he's a widower!"

"I *am*?" George gasped, nonplussed. "I'm trying to insinuate that you're setting your cap at him and getting mother to help you? Is that what you mean?"

Beyond a doubt that was what Miss Fanny meant. She gave him a white-hot look. "You attend to your own affairs!" she whispered fiercely, and swept away.

George, dumfounded, returned to his room for meditation.

He had lived for years in the same house with his Aunt

Fanny, and it now appeared that during all those years he had been thus intimately associating with a total stranger. Never before had he met the passionate lady with whom he had just held a conversation in the hall. So she wanted to get married! And wanted George's mother to help her with this horseless-carriage widower!

"Well, I *will* be shot!" he muttered aloud. "I will—I certainly will be shot!" And he began to laugh. "Lord 'lmighty!"

But presently, at the thought of the horseless-carriage widower's daughter, his grimness returned, and he resolved upon a line of conduct for the evening. He would nod to her carelessly when he first saw her; and, after that, he would notice her no more: he would not dance with her; he would not favour her in the cotillion—he would not go near her!

. . . He descended to dinner upon the third urgent summons of a coloured butler, having spent two hours dressing—and rehearsing.

Chapter IX

THE HONOURABLE George Amberson was a congressman who led cotillions—the sort of congressman an Amberson would be. He did it negligently, to-night, yet with infallible dexterity, now and then glancing humorously at the spectators, people of his own age. They were seated in a tropical grove at one end of the room whither they had retired at the beginning of the cotillion, which they surrendered entirely to the twenties and the late 'teens. And here, grouped with that stately pair, Sydney and Amelia Amberson, sat Isabel with Fanny, while Eugene Morgan appeared to bestow an amiable devotion impartially upon the three sisters-in-law. Fanny watched his face eagerly, laughing at everything he said; Amelia smiled blandly, but rather because of graciousness than because of interest; while Isabel, looking out at the dancers, rhythmically moved a great fan of blue ostrich feathers, listened to Eugene thoughtfully, yet all the while kept her shining eyes on Georgie.

Georgie had carried out his rehearsed projects with precision. He had given Miss Morgan a nod studied into perfection during his lengthy toilet before dinner. "Oh, yes, I do seem to remember that curious little outsider!" this nod seemed to say. Thereafter, all cognizance of her evaporated: the curious little outsider was permitted no further existence worth the struggle. Nevertheless, she flashed in the corner of his eye too often. He was aware of her dancing demurely, and of her viciously flirtatious habit of never looking up at her partner, but keeping her eyes concealed beneath downcast lashes; and he had over-sufficient consciousness of her between the dances, though it was not possible to see her at these times, even if he had cared to look frankly in her direction—she was invisible in a thicket of young dresscoats. The black thicket moved as she moved, and her location was hatefully apparent, even if he had not heard her voice laughing from the thicket. It was annoying how her voice, though never loud, pursued him. No matter how vociferous were other voices, all about, he seemed unable to prevent himself from constantly recognizing hers. It had a quaver in it, not pathetic—rather humorous than pathetic—a quality which annoyed him to the point of rage, because it was so difficult to get away from. She seemed to be having a "wonderful time!"

An unbearable soreness accumulated in his chest: his dislike of the girl and her conduct increased until he thought of leaving this sickening Assembly and going home to bed. *That* would show her! But just then he heard her laughing, and decided that it wouldn't show her. So he remained.

When the young couples seated themselves in chairs against the walls, round three sides of the room, for the cotillion, George joined a brazen-faced group clustering about the doorway—youths with no partners, yet eligible to be "called out" and favoured. He marked that his uncle placed the infernal Kinney and Miss Morgan, as the leading couple, in the first chairs at the head of the line upon the leader's right; and this disloyalty on the part of Uncle George was inexcusable, for in the family circle the nephew had often expressed his opinion of Fred Kinney. In his bitterness, George uttered a significant monosyllable.

The music flourished; whereupon Mr. Kinney, Miss Morgan, and six of their neighbours rose and waltzed knowingly. Mr. Amberson's whistle blew; then the eight young people went to the favour-table and were given toys and trinkets wherewith to delight the new partners it was now their privilege to select. Around the walls, the seated non-participants in this ceremony looked rather conscious; some chattered, endeavouring not to appear expectant; some tried not to look wistful; and others were frankly solemn. It was a trying moment; and whoever secured a favour, this very first shot, might consider the portents happy for a successful evening.

Holding their twinkling gewgaws in their hands, those about to bestow honour came toward the seated lines, where expressions became feverish. Two of the approaching girls seemed to wander, not finding a predetermined object in sight; and these two were Janie Sharon, and her cousin, Lucy. At this, George Amberson Minafer, conceiving that he had little to anticipate from either, turned a proud back upon the room and affected to converse with his friend, Mr. Charlie Johnson.

The next moment a quick little figure intervened between the two. It was Lucy, gayly offering a silver sleighbell decked with white ribbon.

"I almost couldn't find you!" she cried.

George stared, took her hand, led her forth in silence, danced with her. She seemed content not to talk; but as the whistle blew, signalling that this episode was concluded, and he conducted her to her seat, she lifted the little bell toward him. "You haven't taken your favour. You're supposed to pin it on your coat," she said. "Don't you want it?"

"If you insist!" said George stiffly. And he bowed her into her chair; then turned and walked away, dropping the sleighbell haughtily into his trousers' pocket.

The figure proceeded to its conclusion, and George was given other sleighbells, which he easily consented to wear upon his lapel; but, as the next figure began, he strolled with a bored air to the tropical grove, where sat his elders, and seated himself beside his Uncle Sydney. His mother leaned across Miss Fanny, raising her voice over the music to speak to him.

"Georgie, nobody will be able to see you here. You'll not be favoured. You ought to be where you can dance."

"Don't care to," he returned. "Bore!"

"But you ought——" She stopped and laughed, waving her fan to direct his attention behind him. "Look! Over your shoulder!"

He turned, and discovered Miss Lucy Morgan in the act of offering him a purple toy balloon.

"I found you!" she laughed.

George was startled. "Well——" he said.

"Would you rather 'sit it out?'" Lucy asked quickly, as he did not move. "I don't care to dance if you——"

"No," he said, rising. "It would be better to dance." His tone was solemn, and solemnly he departed with her from the grove. Solemnly he danced with her.

Four times, with not the slightest encouragement, she brought him a favour: four times in succession. When the fourth came, "Look here!" said George huskily. "You going to keep this up all night? What do you mean by it?"

For an instant she seemed confused. "That's what cotillions are for, aren't they?" she murmured.

"What do you mean: what they're for?"

"So that a girl can dance with a person she wants to?"

George's huskiness increased. "Well, do you mean you—you want to dance with me all the time—all evening?"

"Well, this much of it—evidently!" she laughed.

"Is it because you thought I tried to keep you from getting hurt this afternoon when we upset?"

She shook her head.

"Was it because you want to even things up for making me angry—I mean, for hurting my feelings on the way home?"

With her eyes averted—for girls of nineteen can be as shy as boys, sometimes—she said, "Well—you only got angry because I couldn't dance the cotillion with you. I—I didn't feel terribly hurt with you for getting angry about *that*!"

"Was there any other reason? Did my telling you I liked you have anything to do with it?"

She looked up gently, and, as George met her eyes, something exquisitely touching, yet queerly delightful, gave him a catch in the throat. She looked instantly away, and, turning, ran out from the palm grove, where they stood, to the dancing-floor.

"Come on!" she cried. "Let's dance!"

He followed her.

"See here—I—I——" he stammered. "You mean—— Do you——"

"No, no!" she laughed. "Let's dance!"

He put his arm about her almost tremulously, and they began to waltz. It was a happy dance for both of them.

Christmas day is the children's, but the holidays are youth's dancing-time. The holidays belong to the early twenties and the 'teens, home from school and college. These years possess the holidays for a little while, then possess them only in smiling, wistful memories of holly and twinkling lights and dance-music, and charming faces all aglow. It is the liveliest time in life, the happiest of the irresponsible times in life. Mothers echo its happiness—nothing is like a mother who has a son home from college, except another mother with a son home from college. Bloom does actually come upon these mothers; it is a visible thing; and they run like girls, walk like athletes, laugh like sycophants. Yet they give up their sons to the daughters of other mothers, and find it proud rapture enough to be allowed to sit and watch.

Thus Isabel watched George and Lucy dancing, as together they danced away the holidays of that year into the past.

"They seem to get along better than they did at first, those two children," Fanny Minafer said, sitting beside her at the Sharons' dance, a week after the Assembly. "They seemed to be always having little quarrels of some sort, at first. At least George did: he seemed to be continually pecking at that lovely, dainty, little Lucy, and being cross with her over nothing."

"'*Pecking?*'" Isabel laughed. "What a word to use about Georgie! I think I never knew a more angelically amiable disposition in my life!"

Miss Fanny echoed her sister-in-law's laugh, but it was a rueful echo, and not sweet. "He's amiable to you!" she said. "That's all the side of him you ever happen to see. And why wouldn't he be amiable to anybody that simply fell down and worshipped him every minute of her life? Most of us would!"

"Isn't he worth worshipping? Just look at him! Isn't he *charming* with Lucy! See how hard he ran to get it when she dropped her handkerchief back there."

"Oh, I'm not going to argue with you about George!" said Miss Fanny. "I'm fond enough of him, for that matter. He *can* be charming, and he's certainly stunning *looking*, if only——"

"Let the 'if only' go, dear," Isabel suggested good-naturedly. "Let's talk about that dinner you thought I should——"

"I?" Miss Fanny interrupted quickly. "Didn't you want to give it yourself?"

"Indeed, I did, my dear!" said Isabel heartily. "I only meant that unless you had proposed it, perhaps I wouldn't——"

But here Eugene came for her to dance, and she left the sentence uncompleted. Holiday dances can be happy for youth renewed as well as for youth in bud—and yet it was not with the air of a rival that Miss Fanny watched her brother's wife dancing with the widower. Miss Fanny's eyes narrowed a little, but only as if her mind engaged in a hopeful calculation. She looked pleased.

Chapter X

A FEW days after George's return to the university it became evident that not quite everybody had gazed with complete benevolence upon the various young collegians at their holiday sports. The Sunday edition of the principal morning paper even expressed some bitterness under the heading, "Gilded Youths of the Fin-de-Siècle"—this was considered the knowing phrase of the time, especially for Sunday supplements—and there is no doubt that from certain references in this bit of writing some people drew the conclusion that Mr. George Amberson Minafer had not yet got his comeupance, a postponement still irritating. Undeniably, Fanny Minafer was one of the people who drew this conclusion, for she cut the article out and enclosed it in a letter to her nephew, having written on the border of the clipping, "I wonder whom it can mean!"

George read part of it:

We debate sometimes what is to be the future of this nation when we think that in a few years public affairs may be in the hands of the *fin-de-siècle* gilded youths we see about us during the Christmas holidays. Such foppery, such luxury, such insolence, was surely never practised by the scented, overbearing patricians of the Palatine, even in Rome's most decadent epoch. In all the wild orgy of wastefulness and luxury with which the nineteenth century reaches its close, the gilded youth has been surely the worst symptom. With his airs of young milord, his fast horses, his gold and silver cigarette-cases, his clothes from a New York tailor, his recklessness of money showered upon him by indulgent mothers or doting grandfathers, he respects nothing and nobody. He is blasé, if you please. Watch him at a social function, how condescendingly he deigns to select a partner for the popular waltz or two-step; how carelessly he shoulders older people out of his way, with what a blank stare he returns the salutation of some old acquaintance whom he may choose in his royal whim to forget! The unpleasant part of all this is that the young women he so condescendingly selects as partners for the dance greet him with seeming rapture, though in their hearts they must feel humiliated by his languid hauteur, and many older people beam upon him almost fawningly if he unbends so far as to throw them a careless, disdainful word!

One wonders what has come over the new generation. Of such as these the Republic was not made. Let us pray that the future of our country is not in the hands of these *fin-de-siècle* gilded youths, but rather in the calloused palms of young men yet unknown, labouring upon the farms of the land. When we compare the young manhood of Abraham Lincoln with the specimens we are now producing, we see too well that it bodes ill for the twentieth century——

George yawned, and tossed the clipping into his waste-basket, wondering why his aunt thought such dull nonsense worth the sending. As for her insinuation, pencilled upon the border, he supposed she meant to joke—a supposition which neither surprised him nor altered his lifelong opinion of her wit.

He read her letter with more interest:

. . . The dinner your mother gave for the Morgans was a lovely affair. It was last Monday evening, just ten days after you left. It was peculiarly appropriate that your mother should give this dinner, because her brother George, your uncle, was Mr. Morgan's most intimate friend before he left here a number of years ago, and it was a pleasant occasion for the formal announcement of some news which you heard from Lucy Morgan before you returned to college. At least she told me she had told you the night before you left that her father had decided to return here to live. It was appropriate that your mother, herself an old friend, should assemble a representative selection of Mr. Morgan's old friends around him at such a time. He was in great spirits and most entertaining. As your time was so charmingly taken up during your visit home with a *younger member* of his family, you probably overlooked opportunities of hearing him talk, and do not know what an interesting man he can be.

He will soon begin to build his factory here for the manufacture of *automobiles*, which he says is a term he prefers to "horseless carriages." Your Uncle George told me he would like to invest in this factory, as George thinks there is a future for automobiles; perhaps not for general use, but as an interesting novelty, which people with sufficient means would like to own for their amusement and the sake of variety. However, he said Mr. Morgan laughingly declined his offer, as Mr. M. was fully able to finance this venture, though not starting in a very large way. Your uncle said other people are manufacturing automobiles in different parts of the country with success. Your father is not very well, though he is not actually ill, and the doctor tells him he ought not to be so much at his office, as the long years of application indoors with no exercise are beginning to affect him unfavourably, but I believe your father would die if he had to give up his work, which is all that has ever interested him outside of his family. I never could understand it. Mr. Morgan took your mother and me with Lucy to see Modjeska in "Twelfth Night" yesterday evening, and Lucy said she thought the Duke looked rather like you, only much more democratic in his manner. I suppose you will think I have written a great deal about the Morgans in this letter, but thought you would be interested because of your interest in a *younger member* of his family. Hoping that you are finding college still as attractive as ever,

Affectionately,
AUNT FANNY.

George read one sentence in this letter several times. Then he dropped the missive in his waste-basket to join the clipping, and strolled down the corridor of his dormitory to borrow a copy of "Twelfth Night." Having secured one, he returned to his study and refreshed his memory of the play—but received no enlightenment that enabled him to comprehend Lucy's strange remark. However, he found himself impelled in the direction of correspondence, and presently wrote a letter—not a reply to his Aunt Fanny.

DEAR LUCY:

No doubt you will be surprised at hearing from me so soon again, especially as this makes two in answer to the one received from you since getting back to the old place. I hear you have been making comments about me at the theatre, that some actor was more democratic in his manners than I am, which I do not understand. You know my theory of life because I explained it to you on our first drive together, when I told you I would not talk to everybody about things I feel like the way I spoke to you of my theory of life. I believe those who are able should have a true theory of life, and I developed my theory of life long, long ago.

Well, here I sit smoking my faithful briar pipe, indulging in the fragrance of my *tabac* as I look out on the campus from my many-paned window, and things are different with me from the way they were way back in Freshman year. I can see now how boyish in many ways I was then. I believe what has changed me as much as anything was my visit home at the time I met you. So I sit here with my faithful briar and dream the old dreams over as it were, dreaming of the waltzes we waltzed together and of that last night before we parted, and you told me the good news you were going to live there, and I would *find my friend waiting for me*, when I get home next summer.

I will be glad my friend *will* be waiting for me. I am not capable of friendship except for the very few, and, looking back over my life, I remember there were times when I doubted if I could feel a great friendship for anybody—especially girls. I do not take a great interest in many people, as you know, for I find most of them shallow. Here in the old place I do not believe in being hail-fellow-well-met with every Tom, Dick, and Harry just because he happens to be a classmate, any more than I do at home, where I have always been careful who I was seen with, largely on account of the family, but also because my disposition ever since my boyhood has been to encourage real intimacy from but the few.

What are you reading now? I have finished both "Henry Esmond" and "The Virginians." I like Thackeray because he is not trashy, and because he writes principally of nice people. My theory of literature is an author who does not indulge in trashiness—writes about people you could introduce into your own home. I agree with my Uncle Sydney, as I once heard him say he did not care to read a book or go to a play about people he would not care to meet at his own dinner table. I believe we should live by certain standards and ideals, as you know from my telling you my theory of life.

Well, a letter is no place for deep discussions, so I will not go into the subject. From several letters from my mother, and one from Aunt Fanny, I hear you are seeing a good deal of the family since I left. I hope sometimes you think of the member who is absent. I got a silver frame for your photograph in New York, and I keep it on my desk. It is the only girl's photograph I ever took the trouble to have framed, though, as I told you frankly, I have had any number of other girls' photographs, yet all were only passing fancies, and oftentimes I have questioned in years past if I was capable of much friendship toward the feminine sex, which I usually found shallow until our own friendship began. When I look at your photograph, I say to myself, "At last, at last here is one that will not prove shallow."

My faithful briar has gone out. I will have to rise and fill it, then once more in the fragrance of My Lady Nicotine, I will sit and dream the old dreams over, and think, too, of the true friend at home awaiting my return in June for the summer vacation.

Friend, this is from your friend,

G. A. M.

George's anticipations were not disappointed. When he came home in June his friend was awaiting him; at least, she was so pleased to see him again that for a few minutes after their first encounter she was a little breathless, and a great deal glowing, and quiet withal. Their sentimental friendship continued, though sometimes he was irritated by her making it less sentimental than he did, and sometimes by what he called her "air of superiority." Her air was usually, in truth, that of a fond but amused older sister; and George did not believe such an attitude was warranted by her eight months of seniority.

Lucy and her father were living at the Amberson Hotel, while Morgan got his small machine-shops built in a western outskirt of the town; and George grumbled about the shabbiness and the old-fashioned look of the hotel, though it was "still the best in the place, of course." He remonstrated with his grandfather, declaring that the whole Amberson Estate would be getting "run-down and out-at-heel, if things weren't taken in hand pretty soon." He urged the general need of rebuilding, renovating, varnishing, and lawsuits. But the Major, declining to hear him out, interrupted querulously, saying that he had enough to bother him without any advice from George; and retired to his library, going so far as to lock the door audibly.

"Second childhood!" George muttered, shaking his head; and he thought sadly that the Major had not long to live. However, this surmise depressed him for only a moment or so. Of course, people couldn't be expected to live forever, and it would be a good thing to have someone in charge of the Estate who wouldn't let it get to looking so rusty that riffraff dared to make fun of it. For George had lately undergone the annoyance of calling upon the Morgans, in the rather stuffy red velours and gilt parlour of their apartment at the hotel, one evening when Mr. Frederick Kinney also was a caller, and Mr. Kinney had not been tactful. In fact, though he adopted a humorous tone of voice, in expressing his sympathy for people who, through the city's poverty in hotels, were obliged to stay at the Amberson, Mr. Kinney's intention was interpreted by the other visitor as not at all humorous, but, on the contrary, personal and offensive.

George rose abruptly, his face the colour of wrath. "Good-night, Miss Morgan. Good-night, Mr. Morgan," he said. "I shall take pleasure in calling at some other time when a more courteous sort of people may be present."

"Look here!" the hot-headed Fred burst out. "Don't you try to make me out a boor, George Minafer! I wasn't hinting anything at you; I simply forgot all about your grandfather owning this old building. Don't you try to put *me* in the light of a boor! I won't——"

But George walked out in the very course of this vehement protest, and it was necessarily left unfinished.

Mr. Kinney remained only a few moments after George's departure; and as the door closed upon him, the distressed Lucy turned to her father. She was plaintively surprised to find him in a condition of immoderate laughter.

"I didn't—I didn't think I could hold out!" he gasped, and, after choking until tears came to his eyes, felt blindly for the chair from which he had risen to wish Mr. Kinney an indistinct good-night. His hand found the arm of the chair; he collapsed feebly, and sat uttering incoherent sounds.

"Papa!"

"It brings things back so!" he managed to explain. "This very Fred Kinney's father and young George's father, Wilbur Minafer, used to do just such things when they were at that age—and, for that matter, so did George Amberson and I, and all the rest of us!" And, in spite of his exhaustion, he began to imitate: "'Don't you try to put *me* in the light of a boor!' 'I shall take pleasure in calling at some time when a more courteous sort of people——'" He was unable to go on.

There is a mirth for every age, and Lucy failed to comprehend her father's, but tolerated it a little ruefully.

"Papa, I think they were shocking. Weren't they *awful*!"

"Just—just boys!" he moaned, wiping his eyes.

But Lucy could not smile at all; she was beginning to look indignant. "I can forgive that poor Fred Kinney," she said. "He's just blundering—but George—oh, George behaved outrageously!"

"It's a difficult age," her father observed, his calmness somewhat restored. "Girls don't seem to have to pass through it quite as boys do, or their *savoir faire* is instinctive—or something!" And he gave away to a return of his convulsion.

She came and sat upon the arm of his chair. "Papa, *why* should George behave like that?"

"He's sensitive."

"Rather! But why is he? He does anything he likes to, without any regard for what people think. Then why should he mind so furiously when the least little thing reflects upon him, or on anything or anybody connected with him?"

Eugene patted her hand. "That's one of the greatest puzzles of human vanity, dear; and I don't pretend to know the answer. In all my life, the most arrogant people that I've known have been the most sensitive. The people who have done the most in contempt of other people's opinion, and who consider themselves the highest above it, have been the most furious if it went against them. Arrogant and domineering people can't stand the least, lightest, faintest breath of criticism. It just kills them."

"Papa, do you think George is *terribly* arrogant and domineering?"

"Oh, he's still only a boy," said Eugene consolingly. "There's plenty of fine stuff in him—can't help but be, because he's Isabel Amberson's son."

Lucy stroked his hair, which was still almost as dark as her own. "You liked her pretty well once, I guess, papa."

"I do still," he said quietly.

"She's lovely—lovely! Papa—" she paused, then continued —"I wonder sometimes——"

"What?"

"I wonder just how she happened to marry Mr. Minafer."

"Oh, Minafer's all right," said Eugene. "He's a quiet sort of man, but he's a good man and a kind man. He always was, and those things count."

"But in a way—well, I've heard people say there wasn't anything to him at all except business and saving money. Miss Fanny Minafer herself told me that everything George and his mother have of their own—that is, just to spend as they like—she says it has always come from Major Amberson."

"Thrift, Horatio!" said Eugene lightly. "Thrift's an inheritance, and a common enough one here. The people who settled the country *had* to save, so making and saving were taught as virtues, and the people, to the third generation, haven't found out that making and saving are only means to an end. Minafer doesn't believe in money being spent. He believes God made it to be invested and saved."

"But George isn't saving. He's reckless, and even if he is arrogant and conceited and bad-tempered, he's awfully generous."

"Oh, he's an Amberson," said her father. "The Ambersons aren't saving. They're too much the other way, most of them."

"I don't think I should have called George bad-tempered," Lucy said thoughtfully. "No. I don't think he is."

"Only when he's cross about something?" Morgan suggested, with a semblance of sympathetic gravity.

"Yes," she said brightly, not perceiving that his intention was humorous. "All the rest of the time he's really very amiable. Of course, he's much more a perfect *child*, the whole time, than he realizes! He certainly behaved awfully to-night." She jumped up, her indignation returning. "He did, indeed, and it won't do to encourage him in it. I think he'll find me pretty cool—for a week or so!"

Whereupon her father suffered a renewal of his attack of uproarious laughter.

Chapter XI

IN THE matter of coolness, George met Lucy upon her own predetermined ground; in fact, he was there first, and, at their next encounter, proved loftier and more formal than she did. Their estrangement lasted three weeks, and then disappeared without any preliminary treaty: it had worn itself out, and they forgot it.

At times, however, George found other disturbances to the friendship. Lucy was "too much the village belle," he complained; and took a satiric attitude toward his competitors, referring to them as her "local swains and bumpkins," sulking for an afternoon when she reminded him that he, too, was at least "local." She was a belle with older people as well; Isabel and Fanny were continually taking her driving, bringing her home with them to lunch or dinner, and making a hundred little engagements with her, and the Major had taken a great fancy to her, insisting upon her presence and her father's at the Amberson family dinner at the Mansion every Sunday evening. She knew how to flirt with old people, he said, as she sat next him at the table on one of these Sunday occasions; and he had always liked her father, even when Eugene was a "terror" long ago. "Oh, yes, he was!" the Major laughed, when she remonstrated. "He came up here with my son George and some others for a serenade one night, and Eugene stepped into a bass fiddle, and the poor musicians just gave up! I had a pretty half-hour getting my son George upstairs. I remember! It was the last time Eugene ever touched a drop—but he'd touched plenty before that, young lady, and he daren't deny it! Well, well; there's another thing that's changed: hardly anybody drinks nowadays. Perhaps it's just as well, but things used to be livelier. That serenade was just before Isabel was married—and don't you fret, Miss Lucy: your father remembers it well enough!" The old gentleman burst into laughter, and shook his finger at Eugene across the table. "The fact is," the Major went on hilariously, "I believe if Eugene hadn't broken that bass fiddle and given himself away, Isabel would never have taken Wilbur! I shouldn't be surprised if that was about all the reason that Wilbur got her! What do you think, Wilbur?"

"I shouldn't be surprised," said Wilbur placidly. "If your notion is right, I'm glad 'Gene broke the fiddle. He was giving me a hard run!"

The Major always drank three glasses of champagne at his Sunday dinner, and he was finishing the third. "What do *you* say about it, Isabel? By Jove!" he cried, pounding the table. "She's blushing!"

Isabel did blush, but she laughed. "Who wouldn't blush!" she cried, and her sister-in-law came to her assistance.

"The important thing," said Fanny jovially, "is that Wilbur did get her, and not only got her, but kept her!"

Eugene was as pink as Isabel, but he laughed without any sign of embarrassment other than his heightened colour. "There's another important thing—that is, for me," he said. "It's the only thing that makes me forgive that bass viol for getting in my way."

"What is it?" the Major asked.

"Lucy," said Morgan gently.

Isabel gave him a quick glance, all warm approval, and there was a murmur of friendliness round the table.

George was not one of those who joined in this applause. He considered his grandfather's nonsense indelicate, even for second childhood, and he thought that the sooner the subject was dropped the better. However, he had only a slight recurrence of the resentment which had assailed him during the winter at every sign of his mother's interest in Morgan; though he was still ashamed of his aunt sometimes, when it seemed to him that Fanny was almost publicly throwing herself at the widower's head. Fanny and he had one or two arguments in which her fierceness again astonished and amused him.

"You drop your criticisms of your relatives," she bade him, hotly, one day, "and begin thinking a little about your own behaviour! You say people will 'talk' about my—about my merely being pleasant to an old friend! What do I care how they talk? I guess if people are talking about anybody in this family they're talking about the impertinent little snippet that hasn't any respect for anything, and doesn't even know enough to attend to his own affairs!"

"'Snippet,' Aunt Fanny!" George laughed. "How elegant! And '*little* snippet'—when I'm over five-feet-eleven?"

"I said it!" she snapped, departing. "I don't see how Lucy can stand you!"

"You'd make an amiable stepmother-in-law!" he called after her. "I'll be careful about proposing to Lucy!"

These were but roughish spots in a summer that glided by evenly and quickly enough, for the most part, and, at the end, seemed to fly. On the last night before George went back to be a Junior, his mother asked him confidently if it had not been a happy summer.

He hadn't thought about it, he answered. "Oh, I suppose so. Why?"

"I just thought it would be nice to hear you say so," she said, smiling. "I mean, it's pleasant for people of my age to know that people of your age realize that they're happy."

"People of your age!" he repeated. "You know you don't look precisely like an old woman, mother. Not precisely!"

"No," she said. "And I suppose I feel about as young as you do, inside, but it won't be many years before I must begin to *look* old. It does come!" She sighed, still smiling. "It's seemed to me that it must have been a happy summer for you—a real 'summer of roses and wine'—without the wine, perhaps. 'Gather ye roses while ye may'—or was it primroses? Time does really fly, or perhaps it's more like the sky—and smoke——"

George was puzzled. "What do you mean: time being like the sky and smoke?"

"I mean the things that we have and that we think are so solid—they're like smoke, and time is like the sky that the smoke disappears into. You know how a wreath of smoke goes up from a chimney, and seems all thick and black and busy against the sky, as if it were going to do such important things and last forever, and you see it getting thinner and thinner—and then, in such a little while, it isn't there at all; nothing is left but the sky, and the sky keeps on being just the same forever."

"It strikes me you're getting mixed up," said George cheerfully. "I don't see much resemblance between time and the sky, or between things and smoke-wreaths; but I do see one reason you like Lucy Morgan so much. She talks that same kind of wistful, moony way sometimes—I don't mean to say I mind it in either of you, because I rather like to listen to it, and you've got a very good voice, mother. It's nice to listen to, no matter how much smoke and sky, and so on, you talk. So's Lucy's, for that matter; and I see why you're congenial. She talks that way to her father, too; and he's right there with the same kind of guff. Well, it's all right with *me*!" He laughed, teasingly, and allowed her to retain his hand, which she had fondly seized. "I've got plenty to think about when people drool along!"

She pressed his hand to her cheek, and a tear made a tiny warm streak across one of his knuckles.

"For heaven's sake!" he said. "What's the matter? Isn't everything all right?"

"You're going away!"

"Well, I'm coming back, don't you suppose? Is *that* all that worries you?"

She cheered up, and smiled again, but shook her head. "I never can bear to see you go—that's the most of it. I'm a little bothered about your father, too."

"Why?"

"It seems to me he looks so badly. Everybody thinks so."

"What nonsense!" George laughed. "He's been looking that way all summer. He isn't much different from the way he's looked all his life, that I can see. What's the matter with him?"

"He never talks much about his business to me but I think he's been worrying about some investments he made last year. I think his worry has affected his health."

"What investments?" George demanded. "He hasn't gone into Mr. Morgan's automobile concern, has he?"

"No," Isabel smiled. "The 'automobile concern' is all Eugene's, and it's so small I understand it's taken hardly anything. No; your father has always prided himself on making only the most absolutely safe investments, but two or three years ago he and your Uncle George both put a great deal—pretty much everything they could get together, I think—into the stock of rolling-mills some friends of theirs owned, and I'm afraid the mills haven't been doing well."

"What of that? Father needn't worry. You and I could take care of him the rest of his life on what grandfather——"

"Of course," she agreed. "But your father's always lived so for his business and taken such pride in his sound investments; it's a passion with him. I——"

"Pshaw! *He* needn't worry! You tell him we'll look after him: we'll build him a little stone bank in the backyard, if he busts up, and he can go and put his pennies in it every morning. That'll keep him just as happy as he ever was!" He kissed her. "Good-night, I'm going to tell Lucy good-bye. Don't sit up for me."

She walked to the front gate with him, still holding his hand, and he told her again not to "sit up" for him.

"Yes, I will," she laughed. "You won't be very late."

"Well—it's my last night."

"But I know Lucy, and she knows I want to see you, too, your last night. You'll see: she'll send you home promptly at eleven!"

But she was mistaken: Lucy sent him home promptly at ten.

Chapter XII

ISABEL'S UNEASINESS about her husband's health—sometimes reflected in her letters to George during the winter that followed—had not been alleviated when the accredited Senior returned for his next summer vacation, and she confided to him in his room, soon after his arrival, that "something" the doctor had said to her lately had made her more uneasy than ever.

"Still worrying over his rolling-mills investments?" George asked, not seriously impressed.

"I'm afraid it's past that stage from what Dr. Rainey says. His worries only aggravate his condition now. Dr. Rainey says we ought to get him away."

"Well, let's do it, then."

"He won't go."

"He's a man awfully set in his ways; that's true," said George. "I don't think there's anything much the matter with him, though, and he looks just the same to me. Have you seen Lucy lately? How is she?"

"Hasn't she written you?"

"Oh, about once a month," he answered carelessly. "Never says much about herself. How's she look?"

"She looks—pretty!" said Isabel. "I suppose she wrote you they've moved?"

"Yes; I've got her address. She said they were building."

"They did. It's all finished, and they've been in it a month. Lucy is so capable; she keeps house exquisitely. It's small, but oh, such a pretty little house!"

"Well, that's fortunate," George said. "One thing I've always felt they didn't know a great deal about is architecture."

"Don't they?" asked Isabel, surprised. "Anyhow, their house is charming. It's way out beyond the end of Amberson Boulevard; it's quite near that big white house with a gray-green roof somebody built out there a year or so ago. There are any number of houses going up, out that way; and the trolley-line runs within a block of them now, on the next street, and the traction people are laying tracks more than three miles beyond. I suppose you'll be driving out to see Lucy to-morrow."

"I thought——" George hesitated. "I thought perhaps I'd go after dinner this evening."

At this, his mother laughed, not astonished. "It was only my feeble joke about 'to-morrow,' Georgie! I was pretty sure you couldn't wait that long. Did Lucy write you about the factory?"

"No. What factory?"

"The automobile shops. They had rather a dubious time at first, I'm afraid, and some of Eugene's experiments turned out badly, but this spring they've finished eight automobiles and sold them all, and they've got twelve more almost finished, and they're sold already! Eugene's so gay over it!"

"What do his old sewing-machines look like? Like that first one he had when they came here?"

"No, indeed! These have rubber tires blown up with air—pneumatic! And they aren't so high; they're very easy to get into, and the engine's in front—Eugene thinks that's a great improvement. They're very interesting to look at; behind the driver's seat there's a sort of box where four people can sit, with a step and a little door in the rear, and——"

"I know all about it," said George. "I've seen any number like that, East. You can see all you want of 'em, if you stand on Fifth Avenue half an hour, any afternoon. I've seen half-a-dozen go by almost at the same time—within a few minutes, anyhow; and of course electric hansoms are a common sight there any day. I hired one, myself, the last time I was there. How fast do Mr. Morgan's machines go?"

"Much *too* fast! It's very exhilarating—but rather frightening; and they do make a fearful uproar. He says, though, he thinks he sees a way to get around the noisiness in time."

"I don't mind the noise," said George. "Give me a horse, for mine, though, any day. I must get up a race with one of these things: Pendennis'll leave it one mile behind in a two-mile run. How's grandfather?"

"He looks well, but he complains sometimes of his heart: I suppose that's natural at his age—and it's an Amberson trouble." Having mentioned this, she looked anxious instantly. "Did *you* ever feel any weakness there, Georgie?"

"No!" he laughed.

"Are you *sure*, dear?"

"No!" And he laughed again. "Did you?"

"Oh, I think not—at least, the doctor told me he thought my heart was about all right. He said I needn't be alarmed."

"I should think not! Women do seem to be always talking about health: I suppose they haven't got enough else to think of!"

"That must be it," she said gayly. "We're an idle lot!"

George had taken off his coat. "I don't like to hint to a lady," he said, "but I do want to dress before dinner."

"Don't be long; I've got to do a lot of looking at you, dear!" She kissed him and ran away, singing.

But his Aunt Fanny was not so fond; and at the dinner-table there came a spark of liveliness into her eye when George patronizingly asked her what was the news in her own "particular line of sport."

"What do you mean, Georgie?" she asked quietly.

"Oh I mean: What's the news in the fast set generally? You been causing any divorces lately?"

"No," said Fanny, the spark in her eye getting brighter. "I haven't been causing anything."

"Well, what's the gossip? You usually hear pretty much everything that goes on around the nooks and crannies in this town, I hear. What's the last from the gossips' corner, auntie?"

Fanny dropped her eyes, and the spark was concealed, but a movement of her lower lip betokened a tendency to laugh, as she replied, "There hasn't been much gossip lately, except the report that Lucy Morgan and Fred Kinney are engaged—and that's quite old, by this time."

Undeniably, this bit of mischief was entirely successful, for there was a clatter upon George's plate. "What—what do you think you're talking about?" he gasped.

Miss Fanny looked up innocently. "About the report of Lucy Morgan's engagement to Fred Kinney."

George turned dumbly to his mother, and Isabel shook her head reassuringly. "People are always starting rumours," she said. "I haven't paid any attention to this one."

"But you—you've heard it?" he stammered.

"Oh, one hears all sorts of nonsense, dear. I haven't the slightest idea that it's true."

"Then you *have* heard it!"

"I wouldn't let it take my appetite," his father suggested drily. "There are plenty of girls in the world!"

George turned pale.

"Eat your dinner, Georgie," his aunt said sweetly. "Food will do you good. I didn't say I knew this rumour was true. I only said I'd heard it."

"When? When did you hear it!"

"Oh, months ago!" And Fanny found any further postponement of laughter impossible.

"Fanny, you're a hard-hearted creature," Isabel said gently. "You *really* are. Don't pay any attention to her, George. Fred Kinney's only a clerk in his uncle's hardware place: he couldn't marry for ages—even if anybody would accept him!"

George breathed tumultuously. "I don't care anything about 'ages'! What's that got to do with it?" he said, his thoughts appearing to be somewhat disconnected. "'Ages,' don't mean anything! I only want to know—I want to know—— I want——" He stopped.

"What do you want?" his father asked crossly. "Why don't you say it? Don't make such a fuss."

"I'm not—not at all," George declared, pushing his chair back from the table.

"You must finish your dinner, dear," his mother urged. "Don't——"

"I have finished. I've eaten all I want. I don't want any more than I wanted. I don't want—I——" He rose, still incoherent. "I prefer—I want—— Please excuse me!"

He left the room, and a moment later the screens outside the open front door were heard to slam.

"Fanny! You shouldn't——"

"Isabel, don't reproach me. He did have plenty of dinner, and I only told the truth: everybody has been saying——"

"But there isn't any truth in it."

"We don't actually know there isn't," Miss Fanny insisted, giggling. "We've never *asked* Lucy."

"I wouldn't ask her anything so absurd!"

"George would," George's father remarked. "That's what he's gone to do."

Mr. Minafer was not mistaken: that was what his son had

gone to do. Lucy and her father were just rising from their dinner table when the stirred youth arrived at the front door of the new house. It was a cottage, however, rather than a house; and Lucy had taken a free hand with the architect, achieving results in white and green, outside, and white and blue, inside, to such effect of youth and daintiness that her father complained of "too much springtime!" The whole place, including his own bedroom, was a young damsel's boudoir, he said, so that nowhere could he smoke a cigar without feeling like a ruffian. However, he was smoking when George arrived, and he encouraged George to join him in the pastime, but the caller, whose air was both tense and preoccupied, declined with something like agitation.

"I never smoke—that is, I'm seldom—I mean, no thanks," he said. "I mean not at all. I'd rather not."

"Aren't you well, George?" Eugene asked, looking at him in perplexity. "Have you been overworking at college? You do look rather pa——"

"I don't work," said George. "I mean I don't work. I think, but I don't work. I only work at the end of the term. There isn't much to do."

Eugene's perplexity was little decreased, and a tinkle of the door-bell afforded him obvious relief. "It's my foreman," he said, looking at his watch. "I'll take him out in the yard to talk. This is no place for a foreman." And he departed, leaving the "living room" to Lucy and George. It was a pretty room, white panelled and blue curtained—and no place for a foreman, as Eugene said. There was a grand piano, and Lucy stood leaning back against it, looking intently at George, while her fingers, behind her, absently struck a chord or two. And her dress was the dress for that room, being of blue and white, too; and the high colour in her cheeks was far from interfering with the general harmony of things—George saw with dismay that she was prettier than ever, and naturally he missed the reassurance he might have felt had he been able to guess that Lucy, on her part, was finding him better looking than ever. For, however unusual the scope of George's pride, vanity of beauty was not included; he did not think about his looks.

"What's wrong, George?" she asked softly.

"What do you mean: 'What's wrong?'"

"You're awfully upset about something. Didn't you get through your examination all right?"

"Certainly I did. What makes you think anything's 'wrong' with me?"

"You do look pale, as papa said, and it seemed to me that the way you talked sounded—well, a little confused."

"'Confused'! I said I didn't care to smoke. What in the world is confused about that?"

"Nothing. But——"

"See here!" George stepped close to her. "Are you glad to see me?"

"You needn't be so fierce about it!" Lucy protested, laughing at his dramatic intensity. "Of course I am! How long have I been looking forward to it?"

"I don't know," he said sharply, abating nothing of his fierceness. "How long have you?"

"Why—ever since you went away!"

"Is that true? Lucy, is that true?"

"You *are* funny!" she said. "Of course it's true. Do tell me what's the matter with you, George!"

"I will!" he exclaimed. "I was a boy when I saw you last. I see that now, though I didn't then. Well, I'm not a boy any longer. I'm a man, and a man has a right to demand a totally different treatment."

"Why has he?"

"What?"

"I don't seem to be able to understand you at all, George. Why shouldn't a boy be treated just as well as a man?"

George seemed to find himself at a loss. "Why shouldn't—— Well, he shouldn't, because a man has a right to certain explanations."

"What explanations?"

"Whether he's been made a toy of!" George almost shouted. "*That's* what I want to know!"

Lucy shook her head despairingly. "You *are* the queerest person! You say you're a man now, but you talk more like a boy than ever. What *does* make you so excited?"

"'Excited'!" he stormed. "Do you dare to stand there and call me 'excited'? I tell you, I never have been more calm or calmer in my life! I don't know that a person needs to be called 'excited' because he demands explanations that are his simple due!"

"What in the world do you want me to explain?"

"Your conduct with Fred *Kinney*!" George shouted.

Lucy uttered a sudden cry of laughter; she was delighted. "It's been awful!" she said. "I don't know that I ever heard of worse misbehaviour! Papa and I have been twice to dinner with his family, and I've been three times to church with Fred —and once to the circus! I don't know when they'll be here to arrest me!"

"Stop that!" George commanded fiercely. "I want to know just one thing, and I mean to know it, too!"

"Whether I enjoyed the circus?"

"I want to know if you're engaged to him!"

"No!" she cried, and lifting her face close to his for the shortest instant possible, she gave him a look half merry, half defiant, but all fond. It was an adorable look.

"*Lucy!*" he said huskily.

But she turned quickly from him, and ran to the other end of the room. He followed awkwardly, stammering:

"Lucy, I want—I want to ask you. Will you—will you—will you be engaged to *me*?"

She stood at a window, seeming to look out into the summer darkness, her back to him.

"Will you, Lucy?"

"No," she murmured, just audibly.

"Why not?"

"I'm older than you."

"Eight months!"

"You're too young."

"Is that—" he said, gulping —"is that the only reason you won't?"

She did not answer.

As she stood, persistently staring out of the window, with her back to him, she did not see how humble his attitude had become; but his voice was low, and it shook so that she could have no doubt of his emotion. "Lucy, please forgive me for making such a row," he said, thus gently. "I've been—I've been terribly upset—terribly! You know how I feel about you, and always have felt about you. I've shown it in every single thing

I've done since the first time I met you, and I know you know it. Don't you?"

Still she did not move or speak.

"Is the only reason you won't be engaged to me you think I'm too young, Lucy?"

"It's—it's reason enough," she said faintly.

At that he caught one of her hands, and she turned to him: there were tears in her eyes, tears which he did not understand at all.

"Lucy, you little dear!" he cried. "I *knew* you——"

"No, no!" she said, and she pushed him away, withdrawing her hand. "George, let's not talk of solemn things."

"'Solemn things!' Like what?"

"Like—being engaged."

But George had become altogether jubilant, and he laughed triumphantly. "Good gracious, *that* isn't solemn!"

"It is, too!" she said, wiping her eyes. "It's too solemn for us."

"No, it isn't! I——"

"Let's sit down and be sensible, dear," she said. "You sit over there——"

"I will if you'll call me 'dear' again."

"No," she said. "I'll only call you that once again this summer—the night before you go away."

"That will have to do, then," he laughed, "so long as I know we're engaged."

"But we're not!" she protested. "And we never will be, if you don't promise not to speak of it again until—until I tell you to!"

"I won't promise that," said the happy George. "I'll only promise not to speak of it till the next time you call me 'dear'; and you've promised to call me that the night before I leave for my senior year."

"Oh, but I didn't!" she said earnestly, then hesitated. "Did I?"

"Didn't you?"

"I don't think I meant it," she murmured, her wet lashes flickering above troubled eyes.

"I know *one* thing about you," he said gayly, his triumph

increasing. "You never went back on anything you said, yet, and I'm not afraid of this being the first time!"

"But we mustn't let——" she faltered; then went on tremulously, "George, we've got on so well together, we won't let this make a difference between us, will we?" And she joined in his laughter.

"It will all depend on what you tell me the night before I go away. You agree we're going to settle things then, don't you, Lucy?"

"I don't promise."

"Yes, you do! Don't you?"

"Well——"

Chapter XIII

THAT NIGHT George began a jubilant warfare upon his Aunt Fanny, opening the campaign upon his return home at about eleven o'clock. Fanny had retired, and was presumably asleep, but George, on the way to his own room, paused before her door, and serenaded her in a full baritone;

> "As I walk along the Boy de Balong
> With my independent air,
> The people all declare,
> 'He must be a millionaire!'
> *Oh*, you hear them sigh, and wish to die,
> And see them wink the other eye
> At the man that broke the bank at Monte Carlo!"

Isabel came from George's room, where she had been reading, waiting for him. "I'm afraid you'll disturb your father, dear. I wish you'd sing more, though—in the daytime! You have a splendid voice."

"Good-night, old lady!"

"I thought perhaps I—— Didn't you want me to come in with you and talk a little?"

"Not to-night. You go to bed. Good-night, old lady!"

He kissed her hilariously, entered his room with a skip, closed his door noisily; and then he could be heard tossing things about, loudly humming "The Man that Broke the Bank at Monte Carlo."

Smiling, his mother knelt outside his door to pray; then, with her "Amen," pressed her lips to the bronze door-knob; and went silently to her own apartment.

. . . After breakfasting in bed, George spent the next morning at his grandfather's and did not encounter his Aunt Fanny until lunch, when she seemed to be ready for him.

"Thank you so much for the serenade, George!" she said. "Your poor father tells me he'd just got to sleep for the first time in two nights, but after your kind attentions he lay awake the rest of last night."

"Perfectly true," Mr. Minafer said grimly.

"Of course, I didn't know, sir," George hastened to assure him. "I'm awfully sorry. But Aunt Fanny was so gloomy and excited before I went out, last evening, I thought she needed cheering up."

"*I!*" Fanny jeered. "*I* was gloomy? *I* was excited? You mean about that engagement?"

"Yes. Weren't you? I thought I heard you worrying over somebody's being engaged. Didn't I hear you say you'd heard Mr. Eugene Morgan was engaged to marry some pretty little seventeen-year-old girl?"

Fanny was stung, but she made a brave effort. "Did you ask Lucy?" she said, her voice almost refusing the teasing laugh she tried to make it utter. "Did you ask her when Fred Kinney and she——"

"Yes. *That* story wasn't true. But the other one——" Here he stared at Fanny, and then affected dismay. "Why, what's the matter with your face, Aunt Fanny? It seems agitated!"

"'Agitated!'" Fanny said disdainfully, but her voice undeniably lacked steadiness. "'Agitated!'"

"Oh, come!" Mr. Minafer interposed. "Let's have a little peace!"

"I'm willing," said George. "*I* don't want to see poor Aunt Fanny all stirred up over a rumour I just this minute invented myself. She's so excitable—about certain subjects—it's hard to control her." He turned to his mother. "What's the matter with grandfather?"

"Didn't you see him this morning?" Isabel asked.

"Yes. He was glad to see me, and all that, but he seemed pretty fidgety. Has he been having trouble with his heart again?"

"Not lately. No."

"Well, he's not himself. I tried to talk to him about the estate; it's disgraceful—it really is—the way things are looking. He wouldn't listen, and he seemed upset. What's he upset over?"

Isabel looked serious; however, it was her husband who suggested gloomily, "I suppose the Major's bothered about this Sydney and Amelia business, most likely."

"What Sydney and Amelia business?" George asked.

"Your mother can tell you, if she wants to," Minafer said. "It's not my side of the family, so I keep off."

"It's rather disagreeable for all of us, Georgie," Isabel began. "You see, your Uncle Sydney wanted a diplomatic position, and he thought brother George, being in Congress, could arrange it. George did get him the offer of a South American ministry, but Sydney wanted a European ambassadorship, and he got quite indignant with poor George for thinking he'd take anything smaller—and he believes George didn't work hard enough for him. George had done his best, of course, and now he's out of Congress, and won't run again—so there's Sydney's idea of a big diplomatic position gone for good. Well, Sydney and your Aunt Amelia are terribly disappointed, and they say they've been thinking for years that this town isn't really fit to live in—'for a gentleman,' Sydney says—and it *is* getting rather big and dirty. So they've sold their house and decided to go abroad to live permanently; there's a villa near Florence they've often talked of buying. And they want father to let them have their share of the estate now, instead of waiting for him to leave it to them in his will."

"Well, I suppose that's fair enough," George said. "That is, in case he intended to leave them a certain amount in his will."

"Of course that's understood, Georgie. Father explained his will to us long ago; a third to them, and a third to brother George, and a third to us."

Her son made a simple calculation in his mind. Uncle George was a bachelor, and probably would never marry; Sydney and Amelia were childless. The Major's only grandchild appeared to remain the eventual heir of the entire property, no matter if the Major did turn over to Sydney a third of it now. And George had a fragmentary vision of himself, in mourning, arriving to take possession of a historic Florentine villa —he saw himself walking up a cypress-bordered path, with ancient carven stone balustrades in the distance, and servants in mourning livery greeting the new signore. "Well, I suppose it's grandfather's own affair. He can do it or not, just as he likes. I don't see why he'd mind much."

"He seemed rather confused and pained about it," Isabel said. "I think they oughtn't to urge it. George says that the estate won't stand taking out the third that Sydney wants, and that Sydney and Amelia are behaving like a couple of pigs." She laughed, continuing, "Of course *I* don't know whether they are or not: I never have understood any more about business myself than a little pig would! But I'm on George's side, whether he's right or wrong; I always was from the time we were children: and Sydney and Amelia are hurt with me about it, I'm afraid. They've stopped speaking to George entirely. Poor father! Family rows at his time of life."

George became thoughtful. If Sydney and Amelia were behaving like pigs, things might not be so simple as at first they seemed to be. Uncle Sydney and Aunt Amelia might live an *awful* long while, he thought; and besides, people didn't always leave their fortunes to relatives. Sydney might die first, leaving everything to his widow, and some curly-haired Italian adventurer might get round her, over there in Florence; she might be fool enough to marry again—or even adopt somebody!

He became more and more thoughtful, forgetting entirely a plan he had formed for the continued teasing of his Aunt Fanny; and, an hour after lunch, he strolled over to his grandfather's, intending to apply for further information, as a party rightfully interested.

He did not carry out this intention, however. Going into the big house by a side entrance, he was informed that the Major was upstairs in his bedroom, that his sons Sydney and George were both with him, and that a serious argument was in progress. "You kin stan' right in de middle dat big sta'y-way," said Old Sam, the ancient negro, who was his informant, "an' you kin heah all you a-mind to wivout goin' on up no fudda. Mist' Sydney an' Mist' Jawge talkin' louduh'n I evuh heah nobody ca'y on in nish heah house! Quollin', honey, big quollin'!"

"All right," said George shortly. "You go on back to your own part of the house, and don't make any talk. Hear me?"

"Yessuh, yessuh," Sam chuckled, as he shuffled away. "Plenty talkin' wivout Sam! Yessuh!"

George went to the foot of the great stairway. He could hear angry voices overhead—those of his two uncles—and a plaintive murmur, as if the Major tried to keep the peace.

Such sounds were far from encouraging to callers, and George decided not to go upstairs until this interview was over. His decision was the result of no timidity, nor of a too sensitive delicacy. What he felt was, that if he interrupted the scene in his grandfather's room, just at this time, one of the three gentlemen engaging in it might speak to him in a peremptory manner (in the heat of the moment) and George saw no reason for exposing his dignity to such mischances. Therefore he turned from the stairway, and going quietly into the library, picked up a magazine—but he did not open it, for his attention was instantly arrested by his Aunt Amelia's voice, speaking in the next room. The door was open and George heard her distinctly.

"Isabel does? *Isabel!*" she exclaimed, her tone high and shrewish. "You needn't tell me anything about Isabel Minafer, I guess, my dear old Frank Bronson! I know her a little better than you do, don't you think?"

George heard the voice of Mr. Bronson replying—a voice familiar to him as that of his grandfather's attorney-in-chief and chief intimate as well. He was a contemporary of the Major's, being over seventy, and they had been through three years of the War in the same regiment. Amelia addressed him now, with an effect of angry mockery, as "my dear old Frank Bronson"; but that (without the mockery) was how the Amberson family almost always spoke of him: "dear old Frank Bronson." He was a hale, thin old man, six feet three inches tall, and without a stoop.

"I doubt your knowing Isabel," he said stiffly. "You speak of her as you do because she sides with her brother George, instead of with you and Sydney."

"*Poot!*" Aunt Amelia was evidently in a passion. "You know what's been going on over there, well enough, Frank Bronson!"

"I don't even know what you're talking about."

"Oh, you don't? You don't know that Isabel takes George's side simply because he's Eugene Morgan's best friend?"

"It seems to me you're talking pure nonsense," said Bronson sharply. "Not impure nonsense, I hope!"

Amelia became shrill. "I thought you were a man of the world: don't tell me you're blind! For nearly two years Isabel's been pretending to chaperone Fanny Minafer with Eugene, and all the time she's been dragging that poor fool Fanny around to chaperone *her* and Eugene! Under the circumstances, she knows people will get to thinking Fanny's a pretty slim kind of chaperone, and Isabel wants to please George because she thinks there'll be less talk if she can keep her own brother around, seeming to approve. 'Talk!' She'd better look out! The whole town will be talking, the first thing she knows! She——"

Amelia stopped, and stared at the doorway in a panic, for her nephew stood there.

She kept her eyes upon his white face for a few strained moments, then, regaining her nerve, looked away and shrugged her shoulders.

"You weren't intended to hear what I've been saying, George," she said quietly. "But since you seem to——"

"Yes, I did."

"So!" She shrugged her shoulders again. "After all, I don't know but it's just as well, in the long run."

He walked up to where she sat. "You—you——" he said thickly. "It seems—it seems to me you're—you're pretty common!"

Amelia tried to give the impression of an unconcerned person laughing with complete indifference, but the sounds she produced were disjointed and uneasy. She fanned herself, looking out of the open window near her. "Of course, if you want to make more trouble in the family than we've already got, George, with your eavesdropping, you can go and repeat——"

Old Bronson had risen from his chair in great distress. "Your aunt was talking nonsense because she's piqued over a business matter, George," he said. "She doesn't mean what she said, and neither she nor any one else gives the slightest credit to such foolishness—no one in the world!"

George gulped, and wet lines shone suddenly along his lower eyelids. "They—they'd better not!" he said, then stalked out of the room, and out of the house. He stamped fiercely across the stone slabs of the front porch, descended the steps, and halted abruptly, blinking in the strong sunshine.

In front of his own gate, beyond the Major's broad lawn, his mother was just getting into her victoria, where sat already his Aunt Fanny and Lucy Morgan. It was a summer fashion-picture: the three ladies charmingly dressed, delicate parasols aloft; the lines of the victoria graceful as those of a violin; the trim pair of bays in glistening harness picked out with silver, and the serious black driver whom Isabel, being an Amberson, dared even in that town to put into a black livery coat, boots, white breeches, and cockaded hat. They jingled smartly away, and, seeing George standing on the Major's lawn, Lucy waved, and Isabel threw him a kiss.

But George shuddered, pretending not to see them, and stooped as if searching for something lost in the grass, protracting that posture until the victoria was out of hearing. And ten minutes later, George Amberson, somewhat in the semblance of an angry person plunging out of the Mansion, found a pale nephew waiting to accost him.

"I haven't time to talk, Georgie."

"Yes, you have. You'd better!"

"What's the matter, then?"

His namesake drew him away from the vicinity of the house. "I want to tell you something I just heard Aunt Amelia say, in there."

"I don't want to hear it," said Amberson. "I've been hearing entirely too much of what 'Aunt Amelia, says,' lately."

"She says my mother's on your side about this division of the property because you're Eugene Morgan's best friend."

"What in the name of heaven has that got to do with your mother's being on my side?"

"She said——" George paused to swallow. "She said——" He faltered.

"You look sick," said his uncle, and laughed shortly. "If it's because of anything Amelia's been saying, I don't blame you! What else did she say?"

George swallowed again, as with nausea, but under his uncle's encouragement he was able to be explicit. "She said my mother wanted you to be friendly to her about Eugene Morgan. She said my mother had been using Aunt Fanny as a chaperone."

Amberson emitted a laugh of disgust. "It's wonderful what tommy-rot a woman in a state of spite can think of! I suppose you don't doubt that Amelia Amberson created this specimen of tommy-rot herself?"

"I know she did."

"Then what's the matter?"

"She said——" George faltered again. "She said—she implied people were—were talking about it."

"Of all the damn nonsense!" his uncle exclaimed.

George looked at him haggardly. "You're sure they're not?"

"Rubbish! Your mother's on my side about this division because she knows Sydney's a pig and always has been a pig, and so has his spiteful wife. I'm trying to keep them from getting the better of your mother as well as from getting the better of me, don't you suppose? Well, they're in a rage because Sydney always could do what he liked with father unless your mother interfered, and they know I got Isabel to ask him not to do what they wanted. They're keeping up the fight and they're sore—and Amelia's a woman who always says any damn thing that comes into her head! That's all there is to it."

"But she said," George persisted wretchedly; "she said there was *talk*. She said——"

"Look here, young fellow!" Amberson laughed good-naturedly. "There probably *is* some harmless talk about the way your Aunt Fanny goes after poor Eugene, and I've no doubt I've abetted it myself. People can't help being amused by a thing like that. Fanny was always languishing at him, twenty-odd years ago, before he left here. Well, we can't blame the poor thing if she's got her hopes up again, and I don't know that I blame her, myself, for using your mother the way she does."

"How do you mean?"

Amberson put his hand on George's shoulder. "You like to tease Fanny," he said, "but I wouldn't tease her about this, if I were you. Fanny hasn't got much in her life. You know, Georgie, just being an aunt isn't really the great career it may sometimes appear to you! In fact, I don't know of anything much that Fanny *has* got, except her feeling about Eugene. She's always had it—and what's funny to us is pretty much life-and-death to her, I suspect. Now, I'll not deny that Eugene Morgan is attracted to your mother. He is; and that's another case of 'always was'; but I know him, and he's a knight, George—a crazy one, perhaps, if you've read 'Don Quixote.' And I think your mother likes him better than she likes any man outside her own family, and that he interests her more than anybody else—and 'always has.' And that's all there is to it, except——"

"Except what?" George asked quickly, as he paused.

"Except that I suspect——" Amberson chuckled, and began over: "I'll tell you in confidence. I think Fanny's a fairly tricky customer, for such an innocent old girl! There isn't any real harm in her, but she's a great diplomatist—lots of cards up her lace sleeves, Georgie! By the way, did you ever notice how proud she is of her arms? Always flashing 'em at poor Eugene!" And he stopped to laugh again.

"I don't see anything confidential about that," George complained. "I thought——"

"Wait a minute! My idea is—don't forget it's a confidential one, but I'm devilish right about it, young Georgie!—it's this: Fanny uses your mother for a decoy duck. She does everything in the world she can to keep your mother's friendship with Eugene going, because she thinks that's what keeps Eugene about the place, so to speak. Fanny's always with your mother, you see; and whenever he sees Isabel he sees Fanny. Fanny thinks he'll get used to the idea of her being around, and some day her chance may come! You see, she's probably afraid—perhaps she even knows, poor thing!—that she wouldn't get to see much of Eugene if it weren't for Isabel's being such a friend of his. There! D'you see?"

"Well—I suppose so." George's brow was still dark, however. "If you're sure whatever talk there is, is about Aunt Fanny. If that's so——"

"Don't be an ass," his uncle advised him lightly, moving away. "I'm off for a week's fishing to forget that woman in there, and her pig of a husband." (His gesture toward the Mansion indicated Mr. and Mrs. Sydney Amberson.) "I recommend a like course to you, if you're silly enough to pay any attention to such rubbishings! Good-bye!"

. . . George was partially reassured, but still troubled: a word haunted him like the recollection of a nightmare. "*Talk!*"

He stood looking at the houses across the street from the Mansion; and though the sunshine was bright upon them, they seemed mysteriously threatening. He had always despised them, except the largest of them, which was the home of his henchman, Charlie Johnson. The Johnsons had originally owned a lot three hundred feet wide, but they had sold all of it except the meagre frontage before the house itself, and five houses were now crowded into the space where one used to squire it so spaciously. Up and down the street, the same transformation had taken place: every big, comfortable old brick house now had two or three smaller frame neighbours crowding up to it on each side, cheap-looking neighbours, most of them needing paint and not clean—and yet, though they were cheap looking, they had cost as much to build as the big brick houses, whose former ample yards they occupied. Only where George stood was there left a sward as of yore; the great, level, green lawn that served for both the Major's house and his daughter's. This serene domain —unbroken, except for the two gravelled carriage-drives— alone remained as it had been during the early glories of the Amberson Addition.

George stared at the ugly houses opposite, and hated them more than ever; but he shivered. Perhaps the riffraff living in those houses sat at the windows to watch their betters; perhaps they dared to gossip——

He uttered an exclamation, and walked rapidly toward his own front gate. The victoria had returned with Miss Fanny alone; she jumped out briskly and the victoria waited.

"Where's mother?" George asked sharply, as he met her.

"At Lucy's. I only came back to get some embroidery, because we found the sun too hot for driving. I'm in a hurry."

But, going into the house with her, he detained her when she would have hastened upstairs.

"I haven't time to talk now, Georgie; I'm going right back. I promised your mother——"

"You listen!" said George.

"What on earth——"

He repeated what Amelia had said. This time, however, he spoke coldly, and without the emotion he had exhibited during the recital to his uncle: Fanny was the one who showed agitation during this interview, for she grew fiery red, and her eyes dilated. "What on earth do you want to bring such trash to *me* for?" she demanded, breathing fast.

"I merely wished to know two things: whether it is your duty or mine to speak to father of what Aunt Amelia——"

Fanny stamped her foot. "You little fool!" she cried. "You *awful* little fool!"

"I decline——"

"Decline, my hat! Your father's a sick man, and you——"

"He doesn't seem so to me."

"Well, he does to me! And you want to go troubling him with an Amberson family row! It's just what that cat would *love* you to do!"

"Well, I——"

"Tell your father if you like! It will only make him a little sicker to think he's got a son silly enough to listen to such craziness!"

"Then you're *sure* there isn't any talk?"

Fanny disdained a reply in words. She made a hissing sound of utter contempt and snapped her fingers. Then she asked scornfully: "What's the other thing you wanted to know?"

George's pallor increased. "Whether it mightn't be better, under the circumstances," he said, "if this family were not so intimate with the Morgan family—at least for a time. It might be better——"

Fanny stared at him incredulously. "You mean you'd quit seeing Lucy?"

"I hadn't thought of that side of it, but if such a thing were necessary on account of talk about my mother, I—I——" He hesitated unhappily. "I suggested that if all of us—for a time—perhaps only for a time—it might be better if——"

"See here," she interrupted. "We'll settle this nonsense right now. If Eugene Morgan comes to this house, for instance, to see *me*, your mother can't get up and leave the place the minute he gets here, can she? What do you want her to do: insult him? Or perhaps you'd prefer she'd insult Lucy? That would do just as well. What is it you're up to, anyhow? Do you really love your Aunt Amelia so much that you want to please her? Or do you really hate your Aunt *Fanny* so much that you want to—that you want to——"

She choked and sought for her handkerchief; suddenly she began to cry.

"Oh, see here," George said. "I don't hate you, Aunt Fanny. That's silly. I don't——"

"You do! You *do*! You want to—you want to destroy the only thing—that I—that I ever——" And, unable to continue, she became inaudible in her handkerchief.

George felt remorseful, and his own troubles were lightened: all at once it became clear to him that he had been worrying about nothing. He perceived that his Aunt Amelia was indeed an old cat, and that to give her scandalous meanderings another thought would be the height of folly. By no means insusceptible to such pathos as that now exposed before him, he did not lack pity for Fanny, whose almost spoken confession was lamentable; and he was granted the vision to understand that his mother also pitied Fanny infinitely more than he did. This seemed to explain everything.

He patted the unhappy lady awkwardly upon her shoulder. "There, there!" he said. "I didn't mean anything. Of course the only thing to do about Aunt Amelia is to pay no attention to her. It's all right, Aunt Fanny. Don't cry. I feel a lot better now, myself. Come on; I'll drive back there with you. It's all over, and nothing's the matter. Can't you cheer up?"

Fanny cheered up; and presently the customarily hostile aunt and nephew were driving out Amberson Boulevard amiably together in the hot sunshine.

Chapter XIV

"ALMOST" WAS Lucy's last word on the last night of George's vacation—that vital evening which she had half consented to agree upon for "settling things" between them. "Almost engaged," she meant. And George, discontented with the "almost," but contented that she seemed glad to wear a sapphire locket with a tiny photograph of George Amberson Minafer inside it, found himself wonderful in a new world at the final instant of their parting. For, after declining to let him kiss her "good-bye," as if his desire for such a ceremony were the most preposterous absurdity in the world, she had leaned suddenly close to him and left upon his cheek the veriest feather from a fairy's wing.

She wrote him a month later:

No. It must keep on being almost.

Isn't almost pretty pleasant? You know well enough that I care for you. I did from the first minute I saw you, and I'm pretty sure you knew it—I'm afraid you did. I'm afraid you always knew it. I'm not conventional and cautious about being engaged, as you say I am, dear. (I always read over the "dears" in *your* letters a time or two, as you say you do in mine—only I read all of your letters a time or two!) But it's such a solemn thing it scares me. It means a good deal to a lot of people besides you and me, and that scares me, too. You write that I take your feeling for me "too lightly" and that I "take the whole affair too lightly." Isn't that odd! Because to myself I seem to take it as something so much more solemn than you do. I shouldn't be a bit surprised to find myself an old lady, some day, still thinking of you—while you'd be away and away with somebody else perhaps, and me forgotten ages ago! "Lucy Morgan," you'd say, when you saw my obituary. "Lucy Morgan? Let me see: I seem to remember the name. Didn't I know some Lucy Morgan or other, once upon a time?" Then you'd shake your big white head and stroke your long white beard—you'd have such a distinguished long white beard! and you'd say, 'No. I don't seem to remember any Lucy Morgan; I wonder what made me think I did?' And poor me! I'd be deep in the ground, wondering if you'd heard about it and what you were saying! Good-bye for to-day. Don't work too hard—dear!

George immediately seized pen and paper, plaintively but vigorously requesting Lucy not to imagine him with a beard, distinguished or otherwise, even in the extremities of age. Then, after inscribing his protest in the matter of this visioned beard, he concluded his missive in a tone mollified to tenderness, and proceeded to read a letter from his mother which had reached him simultaneously with Lucy's. Isabel wrote from Asheville, where she had just arrived with her husband.

I think your father looks better already, darling, though we've been here only a few hours. It may be we've found just the place to build him up. The doctors said they hoped it would prove to be, and if it is, it would be worth the long struggle we had with him to get him to give up and come. Poor dear man, he was so blue, not about his health but about giving up the worries down at his office and forgetting them for a time—if he only will forget them! It took the pressure of the family and all his best friends, to get him to come—but father and brother George and Fanny and Eugene Morgan all kept at him so constantly that he just had to give in. I'm afraid that in my anxiety to get him to do what the doctors wanted him to, I wasn't able to back up brother George as I should in his difficulty with Sydney and Amelia. I'm so sorry! George is more upset than I've ever seen him—they've got what they wanted, and they're sailing before long, I hear, to live in Florence. Father said he couldn't stand the constant persuading—I'm afraid the word he used was "nagging." I can't understand people behaving like that. George says they may be Ambersons, but they're vulgar! I'm afraid I almost agree with him. At least, I think they were inconsiderate. But I don't see why I'm unburdening myself of all this to you, poor darling! We'll have forgotten all about it long before you come home for the holidays, and it should mean little or nothing to you, anyway. Forget that I've been so foolish!

Your father is waiting for me to take a walk with him—that's a splendid sign, because he hasn't felt he could walk much, at home, lately. I mustn't keep him waiting. Be careful to wear your mackintosh and rubbers in rainy weather, and, as soon as it begins to get colder, your ulster. Wish you could see your father now. Looks *so* much better! We plan to stay six weeks if the place agrees with him. It does really seem to already! He's just called in the door to say he's waiting. Don't smoke too much, darling boy.

Devotedly, your mother

ISABEL.

But she did not keep her husband there for the six weeks she anticipated. She did not keep him anywhere that long. Three weeks after writing this letter, she telegraphed suddenly to George that they were leaving for home at once; and four days later, when he and a friend came whistling into his study, from lunch at the club, he found another telegram upon his desk.

He read it twice before he comprehended its import.

Papa left us at ten this morning, dearest.

MOTHER.

The friend saw the change in his face. "Not bad news?"

George lifted utterly dumfounded eyes from the yellow paper.

"My father," he said weakly. "She says—she says he's *dead*. I've got to go home."

. . . His Uncle George and the Major met him at the station when he arrived—the first time the Major had ever come to meet his grandson. The old gentleman sat in his closed carriage (which still needed paint) at the entrance to the station, but he got out and advanced to grasp George's hand tremulously, when the latter appeared. "Poor fellow!" he said, and patted him repeatedly upon the shoulder. "Poor fellow! Poor Georgie!"

George had not yet come to a full realization of his loss: so far, his condition was merely dazed; and as the Major continued to pat him, murmuring "Poor fellow!" over and over, George was seized by an almost irresistible impulse to tell his grandfather that he was not a poodle. But he said "Thanks," in a low voice, and got into the carriage, his two relatives following with deferential sympathy. He noticed that the Major's tremulousness did not disappear, as they drove up the street, and that he seemed much feebler than during the summer. Principally, however, George was concerned with his own emotion, or rather, with his lack of emotion; and the anxious sympathy of his grandfather and his uncle made him feel hypocritical. He was not grief-stricken; but he felt that he ought to be, and, with a secret shame, concealed his callousness beneath an affectation of solemnity.

But when he was taken into the room where lay what was left of Wilbur Minafer, George had no longer to pretend; his grief was sufficient. It needed only the sight of that forever inert semblance of the quiet man who had been always so quiet a part of his son's life—so quiet a part that George had seldom been consciously aware that his father was indeed a part of his life. As the figure lay there, its very quietness was what was most lifelike; and suddenly it struck George hard. And in that unexpected, racking grief of his son, Wilbur Minafer became more vividly George's father than he had ever been in life.

When George left the room, his arm was about his black-robed mother, his shoulders were still shaken with sobs. He leaned upon his mother; she gently comforted him; and presently he recovered his composure and became self-conscious enough to wonder if he had not been making an unmanly display of himself. "I'm all right again, mother," he said awkwardly. "Don't worry about me: you'd better go lie down, or something; you look pretty pale."

Isabel did look pretty pale, but not ghastly pale, as Fanny did. Fanny's grief was overwhelming; she stayed in her room, and George did not see her until the next day, a few minutes before the funeral, when her haggard face appalled him. But by this time he was quite himself again, and during the short service in the cemetery his thoughts even wandered so far as to permit him a feeling of regret not directly connected with his father. Beyond the open flower-walled grave was a mound where new grass grew; and here lay his great-uncle, old John Minafer, who had died the previous autumn; and beyond this were the graves of George's grandfather and grandmother Minafer, and of his grandfather Minafer's second wife, and her three sons, George's half-uncles, who had been drowned together in a canoe accident when George was a child—Fanny was the last of the family. Next beyond was the Amberson family lot, where lay the Major's wife and their sons Henry and Milton, uncles whom George dimly remembered; and beside them lay Isabel's older sister, his Aunt Estelle, who had died in her girlhood, long before George was born. The Minafer monument was a granite block, with the name chiselled upon its one polished side, and the Amberson monument was a white marble shaft, taller than any other in that neighbourhood. But farther on there was a newer section of the cemetery, an addition which had been thrown open to occupancy only a few years before, after dexterous modern treatment by a landscape specialist. There were some large new mausoleums here, and shafts taller than the Ambersons', as well as a number of monuments of some sculptural pretentiousness; and altogether the new section appeared to be a more fashionable and important quarter than that older one which contained the Amberson and Minafer lots. This was what caused George's regret, during the moment or two when his mind strayed from his father and the reading of the service.

. . . On the train, going back to college, ten days later, this regret (though it was as much an annoyance as a regret) recurred to his mind, and a feeling developed within him that the new quarter of the cemetery was in bad taste—not architecturally or sculpturally perhaps, but in presumption: it seemed to flaunt a kind of parvenu ignorance, as if it were actually pleased to be unaware that all the aristocratic and really important families were buried in the old section.

The annoyance gave way before a recollection of the sweet mournfulness of his mother's face, as she had said good-bye to him at the station, and of how lovely she looked in her mourning. He thought of Lucy, whom he had seen only twice, and he could not help feeling that in these quiet interviews he had appeared to her as tinged with heroism—she had shown, rather than said, how brave she thought him in his sorrow. But what came most vividly to George's mind, during these retrospections, was the despairing face of his Aunt Fanny. Again and again he thought of it; he could not avoid its haunting. And for days, after he got back to college, the stricken likeness of Fanny would appear before him unexpectedly, and without a cause that he could trace in his immediately previous thoughts. Her grief had been so silent, yet it had so amazed him.

George felt more and more compassion for this ancient antagonist of his, and he wrote to his mother about her:

I'm afraid poor Aunt Fanny might think now father's gone we won't want her to live with us any longer and because I always teased her so much she might think I'd be for turning her out. I don't know where on earth she'd go or what she could live on if we did do something like this, and of course we never would do such a thing, but I'm pretty sure she had something of the kind on her mind. She didn't say anything, but the way she looked is what makes me think so. Honestly, to me she looked just scared sick. You tell her there isn't any danger in the world of my treating her like that. Tell her everything is to go on just as it always has. Tell her to cheer up!

Chapter XV

ISABEL DID more for Fanny than telling her to cheer up. Everything that Fanny inherited from her father, old Aleck Minafer, had been invested in Wilbur's business; and Wilbur's business, after a period of illness corresponding in dates to the illness of Wilbur's body, had died just before Wilbur did. George Amberson and Fanny were both "wiped out to a miracle of precision," as Amberson said. They "owned not a penny and owed not a penny," he continued, explaining his phrase. "It's like the moment just before drowning: you're not under water and you're not out of it. All you know is that you're not dead yet."

He spoke philosophically, having his "prospects" from his father to fall back upon; but Fanny had neither "prospects" nor philosophy. However, a legal survey of Wilbur's estate revealed the fact that his life insurance was left clear of the wreck; and Isabel, with the cheerful consent of her son, promptly turned this salvage over to her sister-in-law. Invested, it would yield something better than nine hundred dollars a year, and thus she was assured of becoming neither a pauper nor a dependent, but proved to be, as Amberson said, adding his efforts to the cheering up of Fanny, "an heiress, after all, in spite of rolling mills and the devil." She was unable to smile, and he continued his humane gayeties. "See what a wonderfully desirable income nine hundred dollars is, Fanny: a bachelor, to be in your class, must have exactly forty-nine thousand one hundred a year. Then, you see, all you need to do, in order to have fifty thousand a year, is to be a little encouraging when some bachelor in your class begins to show by his haberdashery what he wants you to think about him!"

She looked at him wanly, murmured a desolate response —she had "sewing to do"—and left the room; while Amberson shook his head ruefully at his sister. "I've often thought that humour was not my forte," he sighed. "Lord! She doesn't 'cheer up' much!"

*

The collegian did not return to his home for the holidays. Instead, Isabel joined him, and they went South for the two weeks. She was proud of her stalwart, good-looking son at the hotel where they stayed, and it was meat and drink to her when she saw how people stared at him in the lobby and on the big verandas—indeed, her vanity in him was so dominant that she was unaware of their staring at her with more interest and an admiration friendlier than George evoked. Happy to have him to herself for this fortnight, she loved to walk with him, leaning upon his arm, to read with him, to watch the sea with him—perhaps most of all she liked to enter the big dining room with him.

Yet both of them felt constantly the difference between this Christmastime and other Christmastimes of theirs—in all, it was a sorrowful holiday. But when Isabel came East for George's commencement, in June, she brought Lucy with her—and things began to seem different, especially when George Amberson arrived with Lucy's father on Class Day. Eugene had been in New York, on business; Amberson easily persuaded him to this outing; and they made a cheerful party of it, with the new graduate of course the hero and centre of it all.

His uncle was a fellow alumnus. "Yonder was where I roomed when I was here," he said, pointing out one of the university buildings to Eugene. "I don't know whether George would let my admirers place a tablet to mark the spot, or not. He owns all these buildings now, you know."

"Didn't you, when you were here? Like uncle, like nephew."

"Don't tell George you think he's like me. Just at this time we should be careful of the young gentleman's feelings."

"Yes," said Eugene. "If we weren't he mightn't let us exist at all."

"I'm sure I didn't have it so badly at his age," Amberson said reflectively, as they strolled on through the commencement crowd. "For one thing, I had brothers and sisters, and my mother didn't just sit at my feet as George's does; and I wasn't an only grandchild, either. Father's always spoiled Georgie a lot more than he did any of his own children."

Eugene laughed. "You need only three things to explain all that's good and bad about Georgie."

"Three?"

"He's Isabel's only child. He's an Amberson. He's a boy."

"Well, Mister Bones, of these three things which are the good ones and which are the bad ones?"

"All of them," said Eugene.

It happened that just then they came in sight of the subject of their discourse. George was walking under the elms with Lucy, swinging a stick and pointing out to her various objects and localities which had attained historical value during the last four years. The two older men marked his gestures, careless and graceful; they observed his attitude, unconsciously noble, his easy proprietorship of the ground beneath his feet and round about, of the branches overhead, of the old buildings beyond, and of Lucy.

"I don't know," Eugene said, smiling whimsically. "I don't know. When I spoke of his being a human being—I don't know. Perhaps it's more like deity."

"I wonder if I *was* like that!" Amberson groaned. "You don't suppose every Amberson has had to go through it, do you?"

"Don't worry! At least half of it is a combination of youth, good looks, and college; and even the noblest Ambersons get over their nobility and come to be people in time. It takes more than time, though."

"I should say it *did* take more than time!" his friend agreed, shaking a rueful head.

Then they walked over to join the loveliest Amberson, whom neither time nor trouble seemed to have touched. She stood alone, thoughtful under the great trees, chaperoning George and Lucy at a distance; but, seeing the two friends approaching, she came to meet them.

"It's charming, isn't it!" she said, moving her black-gloved hand to indicate the summery dressed crowd strolling about them, or clustering in groups, each with its own hero. "They seem so eager and so confident, all these boys—it's touching. But of course youth doesn't know it's touching."

Amberson coughed. "No, it doesn't seem to take itself as pathetic, precisely! Eugene and I were just speaking of something like that. Do you know what I think whenever I see these smooth, triumphal young faces? I always think: '*Oh*, how you're going to catch it'!"

"George!"

"Oh, yes," he said. "Life's most ingenious: it's got a special walloping for every mother's son of 'em!"

"Maybe," said Isabel, troubled—"maybe some of the mothers can take the walloping for them."

"Not one!" her brother assured her, with emphasis. "Not any more than she can take on her own face the lines that are bound to come on her son's. I suppose you know that all these young faces have got to get lines on 'em?"

"Maybe they won't," she said, smiling wistfully. "Maybe times will change, and nobody will have to wear lines."

"Times have changed like that for only one person that I know," Eugene said. And as Isabel looked inquiring, he laughed, and she saw that she was the "only one person." His implication was justified, moreover, and she knew it. She blushed charmingly.

"Which is it puts the lines on the faces?" Amberson asked. "Is it age or trouble? Of course we can't decide that wisdom does it—we must be polite to Isabel."

"I'll tell you what puts the lines there," Eugene said. "Age puts some, and trouble puts some, and work puts some, but the deepest are carved by lack of faith. The serenest brow is the one that believes the most."

"In what?" Isabel asked gently.

"In everything!"

She looked at him inquiringly, and he laughed as he had a moment before, when she looked at him that way. "Oh, yes, you do!" he said.

She continued to look at him inquiringly a moment or two longer, and there was an unconscious earnestness in her glance, something trustful as well as inquiring, as if she knew that whatever he meant it was all right. Then her eyes drooped thoughtfully, and she seemed to address some inquiries to herself. She looked up suddenly. "Why, I believe," she said, in a tone of surprise, "I believe I do!"

And at that both men laughed. "Isabel!" her brother exclaimed. "You're a foolish person! There are times when you look exactly fourteen years old!"

But this reminded her of her real affair in that part of the world. "Good gracious!" she said. "Where have the children got to? We must take Lucy pretty soon, so that George can go and sit with the class. We must catch up with them."

She took her brother's arm, and the three moved on, looking about them in the crowd.

"Curious," Amberson remarked, as they did not immediately discover the young people they sought. "Even in such a concourse one would think we couldn't fail to see the proprietor."

"Several hundred proprietors to-day," Eugene suggested.

"No; they're only proprietors of the university," said George's uncle. "We're looking for the proprietor of the universe."

"There he is!" cried Isabel fondly, not minding this satire at all. "And doesn't he look it!"

Her escorts were still laughing at her when they joined the proprietor of the universe and his pretty friend, and though both Amberson and Eugene declined to explain the cause of their mirth, even upon Lucy's urgent request, the portents of the day were amiable, and the five made a happy party—that is to say, four of them made a happy audience for the fifth, and the mood of this fifth was gracious and cheerful.

George took no conspicuous part in either the academic or the social celebrations of his class; he seemed to regard both sets of exercises with a tolerant amusement, his own "crowd" "not going in much for either of those sorts of things," as he explained to Lucy. What his crowd had gone in for remained ambiguous; some negligent testimony indicating that, except for an astonishing reliability which they all seemed to have attained in matters relating to musical comedy, they had not gone in for anything. Certainly the question one of them put to Lucy, in response to investigations of hers, seemed to point that way: "Don't you think," he said, "really, don't you think that being things is rather better than doing things?"

He said "rahthuh bettuh" for "rather better," and seemed to do it deliberately, with perfect knowledge of what he was doing. Later, Lucy mocked him to George, and George refused to smile: he somewhat inclined to such pronunciations, himself. This inclination was one of the things that he had acquired in the four years.

What else he had acquired, it might have puzzled him to state, had anybody asked him and required a direct reply within a reasonable space of time. He had learned how to pass examinations by "cramming"; that is, in three or four days and nights he could get into his head enough of a selected fragment of some scientific or philosophical or literary or linguistic subject to reply plausibly to six questions out of ten. He could retain the information necessary for such a feat just long enough to give a successful performance; then it would evaporate utterly from his brain, and leave him undisturbed. George, like his "crowd," not only preferred "being things" to "doing things," but had contented himself with four years of "being things" as a preparation for going on "being things." And when Lucy rather shyly pressed him for his friend's probable definition of the "things" it seemed so superior and beautiful to be, George raised his eyebrows slightly, meaning that she should have understood without explanation; but he did explain: "Oh, family and all that—being a gentleman, I suppose."

Lucy gave the horizon a long look, but offered no comment.

Chapter XVI

"AUNT FANNY doesn't look much better," George said to his mother, a few minutes after their arrival, on the night they got home. He stood with a towel in her doorway, concluding some sketchy ablutions before going downstairs to a supper which Fanny was hastily preparing for them. Isabel had not telegraphed; Fanny was taken by surprise when they drove up in a station cab at eleven o'clock; and George instantly demanded "a little decent food." (Some criticisms of his had publicly disturbed the composure of the dining-car steward four hours previously.) "I never saw anybody take things so hard as she seems to," he observed, his voice muffled by the towel. "Doesn't she get over it at all? I thought she'd feel better when we turned over the insurance to her—gave it to her absolutely, without any strings to it. She looks about a thousand years old!"

"She looks quite girlish, sometimes, though," his mother said.

"Has she looked that way much since father——"

"Not so much," Isabel said thoughtfully. "But she will, as times goes on."

"Time'll have to hurry, then, it seems to me," George observed, returning to his own room.

When they went down to the dining room, he pronounced acceptable the salmon salad, cold beef, cheese, and cake which Fanny made ready for them without disturbing the servants. The journey had fatigued Isabel, she ate nothing, but sat to observe with tired pleasure the manifestations of her son's appetite, meanwhile giving her sister-in-law a brief summary of the events of commencement. But presently she kissed them both good-night—taking care to kiss George lightly upon the side of his head, so as not to disturb his eating—and left aunt and nephew alone together.

"It never was becoming to her to look pale," Fanny said absently, a few moments after Isabel's departure.

"Wha'd you say, Aunt Fanny?"

"Nothing. I suppose your mother's been being pretty gay? Going a lot?"

"How could she?" George asked cheerfully. "In mourning, of course all she could do was just sit around and look on. That's all Lucy could do either, for the matter of that."

"I suppose so," his aunt assented. "How did Lucy get home?"

George regarded her with astonishment. "Why, on the train with the rest of us, of course."

"I didn't mean that," Fanny explained. "I meant from the station. Did you drive out to their house with her before you came here?"

"No. She drove home with her father, of course."

"Oh, I see. So Eugene came to the station to meet you."

"'To meet us?'" George echoed, renewing his attack upon the salmon salad. "How could he?"

"I don't know what you mean," Fanny said drearily, in the desolate voice that had become her habit. "I haven't seen him while your mother's been away."

"Naturally," said George. "He's been East himself."

At this Fanny's drooping eyelids opened wide.

"Did you *see* him?"

"Well, naturally, since he made the trip home with us!"

"He did?" she said sharply. "He's been with you all the time?"

"No; only on the train and the last three days before we left. Uncle George got him to come."

Fanny's eyelids drooped again, and she sat silent until George pushed back his chair and lit a cigarette, declaring his satisfaction with what she had provided. "You're a fine housekeeper," he said benevolently. "You know how to make things look dainty as well as taste the right way. I don't believe you'd stay single very long if some of the bachelors and widowers around town could just once see——"

She did not hear him. "It's a little odd," she said.

"What's odd?"

"Your mother's not mentioning that Mr. Morgan had been with you."

"Didn't think of it, I suppose," said George carelessly; and, his benevolent mood increasing, he conceived the idea that a little harmless rallying might serve to elevate his aunt's drooping spirits. "I'll tell you something, in confidence," he said solemnly.

She looked up, startled. "What?"

"Well, it struck me that Mr. Morgan was looking pretty absent-minded, most of the time; and he certainly is dressing better than he used to. Uncle George told me he heard that the automobile factory had been doing quite well—won a race, too! I shouldn't be a bit surprised if all the young fellow had been waiting for was to know he had an assured income before he proposed."

"What 'young fellow'?"

"This young fellow Morgan," laughed George. "Honestly, Aunt Fanny, I shouldn't be a bit surprised to have him request an interview with me any day, and declare that his intentions are honourable, and ask my permission to pay his addresses to you. What had I better tell him?"

Fanny burst into tears.

"Good heavens!" George cried. "I was only teasing. I didn't mean——"

"Let me alone," she said lifelessly; and, continuing to weep, rose and began to clear away the dishes.

"Please, Aunt Fanny——"

"Just let me alone."

George was distressed. "I didn't mean anything, Aunt Fanny! I didn't know you'd got so sensitive as all that."

"You'd better go up to bed," she said desolately, going on with her work and her weeping.

"Anyhow," he insisted, "do let these things wait. Let the servants 'tend to the table in the morning."

"No."

"But, why not?"

"Just let me alone."

"Oh, Lord!" George groaned, going to the door. There he turned. "See here, Aunt Fanny, there's not a bit of use your bothering about those dishes to-night. What's the use of a butler and three maids if——"

"Just let me alone."

He obeyed, and could still hear a pathetic sniffing from the dining room as he went up the stairs.

"By George!" he grunted, as he reached his own room; and his thought was that living with a person so sensitive to kindly raillery might prove lugubrious. He whistled, long and low, then went to the window and looked through the darkness to the great silhouette of his grandfather's house. Lights were burning over there, upstairs; probably his newly arrived uncle was engaged in talk with the Major.

George's glance lowered, resting casually upon the indistinct ground, and he beheld some vague shapes, unfamiliar to him. Formless heaps, they seemed; but, without much curiosity, he supposed that sewer connections or water pipes might be out of order, making necessary some excavations. He hoped the work would not take long; he hated to see that sweep of lawn made unsightly by trenches and lines of dirt, even temporarily. Not greatly disturbed, however, he pulled down the shade, yawned, and began to undress, leaving further investigation for the morning.

But in the morning he had forgotten all about it, and raised his shade, to let in the light, without even glancing toward the ground. Not until he had finished dressing did he look forth from his window, and then his glance was casual. The next instant his attitude became electric, and he gave utterance to a bellow of dismay. He ran from his room, plunged down the stairs, out of the front door, and, upon a nearer view of the destroyed lawn, began to release profanity upon the breezeless summer air, which remained unaffected. Between his mother's house and his grandfather's, excavations for the cellars of five new houses were in process, each within a few feet of its neighbour. Foundations of brick were being laid; everywhere were piles of brick and stacked lumber, and sand heaps and mortar beds.

It was Sunday, and so the workmen implicated in these defacings were denied what unquestionably they would have considered a treat; but as the fanatic orator continued the monologue, a gentleman in flannels emerged upward from one of the excavations, and regarded him contemplatively.

"Obtaining any relief, nephew?" he inquired with some

interest. "You must have learned quite a number of those expressions in childhood—it's so long since I'd heard them I fancied they were obsolete."

"Who wouldn't swear?" George demanded hotly. "In the name of God, what does grandfather mean, doing such things?"

"My private opinion is," said Amberson gravely, "he desires to increase his income by building these houses to rent."

"Well, in the name of God, can't he increase his income any other way but this?"

"In the name of God, it would appear he couldn't."

"It's beastly! It's a damn degradation! It's a crime!"

"I don't know about its being a crime," said his uncle, stepping over some planks to join him. "It might be a mistake, though. Your mother said not to tell you until we got home, so as not to spoil commencement for you. She rather feared you'd be upset."

"Upset! Oh, my Lord, I should think I *would* be upset! He's in his second childhood. What did you let him *do* it for, in the name of——"

"Make it in the name of heaven this time, George; it's Sunday. Well, I thought, myself, it was a mistake."

"I should say so!"

"Yes," said Amberson. "I wanted him to put up an apartment building instead of these houses."

"An apartment building! *Here?*"

"Yes; that was my idea."

George struck his hands together despairingly. "An apartment house! Oh, my Lord!"

"Don't worry! Your grandfather wouldn't listen to me, but he'll wish he had, some day. He says that people aren't going to live in miserable little flats when they can get a whole house with some grass in front and plenty of backyard behind. He sticks it out that apartment houses will never do in a town of this type, and when I pointed out to him that a dozen or so of 'em already *are* doing, he claimed it was just the novelty, and that they'd all be empty as soon as people got used to 'em. So he's putting up these houses."

"Is he getting miserly in his old age?"

"Hardly! Look what he gave Sydney and Amelia!"

"I don't mean he's a miser, of course," said George. "Heaven knows he's liberal enough with mother and me; but why on earth didn't he *sell* something or other rather than do a thing like this?"

"As a matter of fact," Amberson returned coolly, "I believe he *has* sold something or other, from time to time."

"Well, in heaven's name," George cried, "what did he do it for?"

"To get money," his uncle mildly replied. "That's my deduction."

"I suppose you're joking—or trying to!"

"That's the best way to look at it," Amberson said amiably. "Take the whole thing as a joke—and in the meantime, if you haven't had your breakfast——"

"I haven't!"

"Then if I were you I'd go in and get some. And"—he paused, becoming serious—"and if I were you I wouldn't say anything to your grandfather about this."

"I don't think I could trust myself to speak to him about it," said George. "I want to treat him respectfully, because he *is* my grandfather, but I don't believe I could if I talked to him about such a thing as this!"

And with a gesture of despair, plainly signifying that all too soon after leaving bright college years behind him he had entered into the full tragedy of life, George turned bitterly upon his heel and went into the house for his breakfast.

His uncle, with his head whimsically upon one side, gazed after him not altogether unsympathetically, then descended again into the excavation whence he had lately emerged. Being a philosopher he was not surprised, that afternoon, in the course of a drive he took in the old carriage with the Major, when George was encountered upon the highway, flashing along in his runabout with Lucy beside him and Pendennis doing better than three minutes.

"He seems to have recovered," Amberson remarked: "Looks in the highest good spirits."

"I beg your pardon."

"Your grandson," Amberson explained. "He was inclined to melancholy this morning, but seemed jolly enough just now when they passed us."

"What was he melancholy about? Not getting remorseful

about all the money he's spent at college, was he?" The Major chuckled feebly, but with sufficient grimness. "I wonder what he thinks I'm made of," he concluded querulously.

"Gold," his son suggested, adding gently, "And he's right about part of you, father."

"What part?"

"Your heart."

The Major laughed ruefully. "I suppose that may account for how heavy it feels, sometimes, nowadays. This town seems to be rolling right over that old heart you mentioned, George —rolling over it and burying it under! When I think of those devilish workmen digging up my lawn, yelling around my house——"

"Never mind, father. Don't think of it. When things are a nuisance it's a good idea not to keep remembering 'em."

"I *try* not to," the old gentleman murmured. "I try to keep remembering that I won't be remembering anything very long." And, somehow convinced that this thought was a mirthful one, he laughed loudly, and slapped his knee. "Not so very long now, my boy!" he chuckled, continuing to echo his own amusement. "Not so very long. Not so very long!"

Chapter XVII

YOUNG GEORGE paid his respects to his grandfather the following morning, having been occupied with various affairs and engagements on Sunday until after the Major's bedtime; and topics concerned with building or excavations were not introduced into the conversation, which was a cheerful one until George lightly mentioned some new plans of his. He was a skillful driver, as the Major knew, and he spoke of his desire to extend his proficiency in this art: in fact, he entertained the ambition to drive a four-in-hand. However, as the Major said nothing, and merely sat still, looking surprised, George went on to say that he did not propose to "go in for coaching just at the start"; he thought it would be better to begin with a tandem. He was sure Pendennis could be trained to work as a leader; and all that one needed to buy at present, he said, would be "comparatively inexpensive—a new trap, and the harness, of course, and a good bay to match Pendennis." He did not care for a special groom; one of the stablemen would do.

At this point the Major decided to speak. "You say one of the stablemen would do?" he inquired, his widened eyes remaining fixed upon his grandson. "That's lucky, because one's all there is, just at present, George. Old fat Tom does it all. Didn't you notice, when you took Pendennis out, yesterday?"

"Oh, that will be all right, sir. My mother can lend me her man."

"Can she?" The old gentleman smiled faintly. "I wonder——" He paused.

"What, sir?"

"Whether you mightn't care to go to law-school somewhere perhaps. I'd be glad to set aside a sum that would see you through."

This senile divergence from the topic in hand surprised George painfully. "I have no interest whatever in the law," he said. "I don't care for it, and the idea of being a professional man has never appealed to me. None of the family has ever gone in for that sort of thing, to my knowledge, and I don't care to be the first. I was speaking of driving a tandem——"

"I know you were," the Major said quietly.

George looked hurt. "I beg your pardon. Of course if the idea doesn't appeal to you——" And he rose to go.

The Major ran a tremulous hand through his hair, sighing deeply. "I—I don't like to refuse you anything, Georgie," he said. "I don't know that I often have refused you whatever you wanted—in reason——"

"You've always been more than generous, sir," George interrupted quickly. "And if the idea of a tandem doesn't appeal to you, why—of course——" And he waved his hand, heroically dismissing the tandem.

The Major's distress became obvious. "Georgie, I'd like to, but—but I've an idea tandems are dangerous to drive, and your mother might be anxious. She——"

"No, sir; I think not. She felt it would be rather a good thing—help to keep me out in the open air. But if perhaps your finances——"

"Oh, it isn't that so much," the old gentleman said hurriedly. "I wasn't thinking of that altogether." He laughed uncomfortably. "I guess we could still afford a new horse or two, if need be——"

"I thought you said——"

The Major waved his hand airily. "Oh, a few retrenchments where things were useless: nothing gained by a raft of idle darkies in the stable—nor by a lot of extra land that might as well be put to work for us in rentals. And if you want this thing so very much——"

"It's not important enough to bother about, really, of course."

"Well, let's wait till autumn then," said the Major in a tone of relief. "We'll see about it in the autumn, if you're still in the mind for it then. That will be a great deal better. You remind me of it, along in September—or October. We'll see what can be done." He rubbed his hands cheerfully. "We'll see what can be done about it then, Georgie. We'll see."

And George, in reporting this conversation to his mother, was ruefully humorous. "In fact, the old boy cheered up so much," he told her, "you'd have thought he'd got a real load off his mind. He seemed to think he'd fixed *me* up perfectly, and that I was just as good as driving a tandem around his library right that minute! Of course I know he's anything but miserly; still I can't help thinking he must be salting a lot of money away. I know prices are higher than they used to be, but he doesn't spend within thousands of what he used to, and *we* certainly can't be spending more than we always have spent. Where does it all go to? Uncle George told me grandfather had sold some pieces of property, and it looks a little queer. If he's really 'property poor,' of course we ought to be more saving than we are, and help him out. *I* don't mind giving up a tandem if it seems a little too expensive just now. I'm perfectly willing to live quietly till he gets his bank balance where he wants it. But I have a faint suspicion, not that he's getting miserly—not that at all—but that old age has begun to make him timid about money. There's no doubt about it, he's getting a little queer: he can't keep his mind on a subject long. Right in the middle of talking about one thing he'll wander off to something else; and I shouldn't be surprised if he turned out to be a lot better off than any of us guess. It's entirely possible that whatever he's sold just went into government bonds, or even his safety deposit box. There was a friend of mine in college had an old uncle like that: made the whole family think he was poor as dirt—and then left seven millions. People get terribly queer as they get old, sometimes, and grandfather certainly doesn't act the way he used to. He seems to be a totally different man. For instance, he said he thought tandem driving might be dangerous——"

"Did he?" Isabel asked quickly. "Then I'm glad he doesn't want you to have one. I didn't dream——"

"But it's not. There isn't the slightest——"

Isabel had a bright idea. "Georgie! Instead of a tandem wouldn't it interest you to get one of Eugene's automobiles?"

"I don't think so. They're fast enough, of course. In fact, running one of those things is getting to be quite on the cards for sport, and people go all over the country in 'em. But they're dirty things, and they keep getting out of order, so that you're always lying down on your back in the mud, and——"

"Oh, no," she interrupted eagerly. "Haven't you noticed? You don't see nearly so many people doing that nowadays as you did two or three years ago, and, when you do, Eugene says it's apt to be one of the older patterns. The way they make them now, you can get at most of the machinery from the top. I do think you'd be interested, dear."

George remained indifferent. "Possibly—but I hardly think so. I know a lot of good people are really taking them up, but still——"

"'But still' what?" she said as he paused.

"But still—well, I suppose I'm a little old-fashioned and fastidious, but I'm afraid being a sort of engine driver never will appeal to me, mother. It's exciting, and I'd like that part of it, but still it doesn't seem to me precisely the thing a gentleman ought to do. Too much overalls and monkey-wrenches and grease!"

"But Eugene says people are hiring mechanics to do all that sort of thing for them. They're beginning to have them just the way they have coachmen; and he says it's developing into quite a profession."

"I know that, mother, of course; but I've seen some of these mechanics, and they're not very satisfactory. For one thing, most of them only pretend to understand the machinery and they let people break down a hundred miles from nowhere, so that about all these fellows are good for is to hunt up a farmer and hire a horse to pull the automobile. And friends of mine at college that've had a good deal of experience tell me the mechanics who do understand the engines have no training at all as servants. They're awful! They say anything they like, and usually speak to members of the family as 'Say!' No, I believe I'd rather wait for September and a tandem, mother."

Nevertheless, George sometimes consented to sit in an automobile, while waiting for September, and he frequently went driving in one of Eugene's cars with Lucy and her father. He even allowed himself to be escorted with his mother and Fanny through the growing factory, which was now, as the foreman of the paint shop informed the visitors, "turning out a car and a quarter a day." George had seldom been more excessively bored, but his mother showed a lively interest in everything, wishing to have all the machinery explained to her. It was Lucy who did most of the explaining, while her father looked on and laughed at the mistakes she made, and Fanny remained in the background with George, exhibiting a bleakness that overmatched his boredom.

From the factory Eugene took them to lunch at a new restaurant, just opened in the town, a place which surprised Isabel with its metropolitan air, and, though George made fun of it to her, in a whisper, she offered everything the tribute of pleased exclamations; and her gayety helped Eugene's to make the little occasion almost a festive one.

George's ennui disappeared in spite of himself, and he laughed to see his mother in such spirits. "I didn't know mineral waters could go to a person's head," he said. "Or perhaps it's this place. It might pay to have a new restaurant opened somewhere in town every time you get the blues."

Fanny turned to him with a wan smile. "Oh, *she* doesn't 'get the blues,' George!" Then she added, as if fearing her remark might be thought unpleasantly significant, "I never knew a person of a more even disposition. I wish I could be like that!" And though the tone of this afterthought was not so enthusiastic as she tried to make it, she succeeded in producing a fairly amiable effect.

"No," Isabel said, reverting to George's remark, and overlooking Fanny's. "What makes me laugh so much at nothing is Eugene's factory. Wouldn't anybody be delighted to see an old friend take an idea out of the air like that—an idea that most people laughed at him for—wouldn't any old friend of his be happy to see how he'd made his idea into such a splendid, humming thing as that factory—all shiny steel, clicking and buzzing away, and with all those workmen, such *muscled* looking men and yet so intelligent looking?"

"Hear! Hear!" George applauded. "We seem to have a lady orator among us. I hope the waiters won't mind."

Isabel laughed, not discouraged. "It's beautiful to see such a thing," she said. "It makes us all happy, dear old Eugene!"

And with a brave gesture she stretched out her hand to him across the small table. He took it quickly, giving her a look in which his laughter tried to remain, but vanished before a gratitude threatening to become emotional in spite of him. Isabel, however, turned instantly to Fanny. "Give him your hand, Fanny," she said gayly; and, as Fanny mechanically obeyed, "There!" Isabel cried. "If brother George were here, Eugene would have his three oldest and best friends congratulating him all at once. We know what brother George thinks about it, though. It's just beautiful, Eugene!"

Probably if her brother George had been with them at the little table, he would have made known what he thought about herself, for it must inevitably have struck him that she was in the midst of one of those "times" when she looked "exactly fourteen years old." Lucy served as a proxy for Amberson, perhaps, when she leaned toward George and whispered: "Did you *ever* see anything so lovely?"

"As what?" George inquired, not because he misunderstood, but because he wished to prolong the pleasant neighbourliness of whispering.

"As your mother! Think of her doing that! She's a darling! And papa"—here she imperfectly repressed a tendency to laugh—"papa looks as if he were either going to explode or utter loud sobs!"

Eugene commanded his features, however, and they resumed their customary apprehensiveness. "I used to write verse," he said—"if you remember——"

"Yes," Isabel interrupted gently. "I remember."

"I don't recall that I've written any for twenty years or so," he continued. "But I'm almost thinking I could do it again, to thank you for making a factory visit into such a kind celebration."

"Gracious!" Lucy whispered, giggling. "Aren't they sentimental!"

"People that age always are," George returned. "They get sentimental over anything at all. Factories or restaurants, it doesn't matter what!"

And both of them were seized with fits of laughter which they managed to cover under the general movement of departure, as Isabel had risen to go.

Outside, upon the crowded street, George helped Lucy into his runabout, and drove off, waving triumphantly, and laughing at Eugene who was struggling with the engine of his car, in the tonneau of which Isabel and Fanny had established themselves. "Looks like a hand-organ man grinding away for pennies," said George, as the runabout turned the corner and into National Avenue. "I'll still take a horse, any day."

He was not so cocksure, half an hour later, on an open road, when a siren whistle wailed behind him, and before the sound had died away, Eugene's car, coming from behind with what seemed fairly like one long leap, went by the runabout and dwindled almost instantaneously in perspective, with a lace handkerchief in a black-gloved hand fluttering sweet derision as it was swept onward into minuteness—a mere white speck—and then out of sight.

George was undoubtedly impressed. "Your father does know how to drive some," the dashing exhibition forced him to admit. "Of course Pendennis isn't as young as he was, and I don't care to push him too hard. I wouldn't mind handling one of those machines on the road like that, myself, if that was all there was to it—no cranking to do, or fooling with the engine. Well, I enjoyed part of that lunch quite a lot, Lucy."

"The salad?"

"No. Your whispering to me."

"Blarney!"

George made no response, but checked Pendennis to a walk. Whereupon Lucy protested quickly: "Oh, don't!"

"Why? Do you want him to trot his legs off?"

"No, but——"

"'No, but'—what?"

She spoke with apparent gravity: "I know when you make him walk it's so you can give all your attention to—to proposing to me again!"

And as she turned a face of exaggerated colour to him, "By the Lord, but you're a little witch!" George cried.

"George, *do* let Pendennis trot again!"

"I won't!"

She clucked to the horse. "Get up, Pendennis! Trot! Go on! Commence!"

Pendennis paid no attention; she meant nothing to him, and George laughed at her fondly. "You *are* the prettiest thing in this world, Lucy!" he exclaimed. "When I see you in winter, in furs, with your cheeks red, I think you're prettiest then, but when I see you in summer, in a straw hat and a shirtwaist and a duck skirt and white gloves and those little silver buckled slippers, and your rose-coloured parasol, and your cheeks not red but with a kind of pinky glow about them, then I see I must have been wrong about the winter! When are you going to drop the 'almost' and say we're really engaged?"

"Oh, not for *years*! So there's the answer, and let's trot again."

But George was persistent; moreover, he had become serious during the last minute or two. "I want to know," he said. "I really mean it."

"Let's don't be serious, George," she begged him hopefully. "Let's talk of something pleasant."

He was a little offended. "Then it isn't pleasant for you to know that I want to marry you?"

At this she became as serious as he could have asked; she looked down, and her lip quivered like that of a child about to cry. Suddenly she put her hand upon one of his for just an instant, and then withdrew it.

"Lucy!" he said huskily. "Dear, what's the matter? You look as if you were going to cry. You always do that," he went on plaintively, "whenever I can get you to talk about marrying me."

"I know it," she murmured.

"Well, why do you?"

Her eyelids flickered, and then she looked up at him with a sad gravity, tears seeming just at the poise. "One reason's because I have a feeling that it's never going to be."

"Why?"

"It's just a feeling."

"You haven't any reason or——"

"It's just a feeling."

"Well, if that's all," George said, reassured, and laughing confidently, "I guess I won't be very much troubled!" But at once he became serious again, adopting the tone of argument. "Lucy, how is anything ever going to get a *chance* to come of it, so long as you keep sticking to 'almost'? Doesn't it strike you as unreasonable to have a 'feeling' that we'll never be married, when what principally stands between us is the fact that you won't be really engaged to me? That does seem pretty absurd! Don't you *care* enough about me to marry me?"

She looked down again, pathetically troubled. "Yes."

"Won't you always care that much about me?"

"I'm—yes—I'm afraid so, George. I never do change much about anything."

"Well, then, why in the world won't you drop the 'almost'?"

Her distress increased. "Everything is—everything——"

"What about 'everything'?"

"Everything is so—so unsettled."

And at that he uttered an exclamation of impatience. "If you aren't the queerest girl! *What* is 'unsettled'?"

"Well, for one thing," she said, able to smile at his vehemence, "you haven't settled on anything to do. At least, if you have you've never spoken of it."

As she spoke, she gave him the quickest possible side glance of hopeful scrutiny; then looked away, not happily. Surprise and displeasure were intentionally visible upon the countenance of her companion; and he permitted a significant period of silence to elapse before making any response. "Lucy," he said, finally, with cold dignity, "I should like to ask you a few questions."

"Yes?"

"The first is: Haven't you perfectly well understood that I don't mean to go into business or adopt a profession?"

"I wasn't quite sure," she said gently. "I really didn't know—quite."

"Then of course it's time I did tell you. I never have been able to see any occasion for a man's going into trade, or being a lawyer, or any of those things if his position and family were such that he didn't need to. You know, yourself, there are a lot of people in the East—in the South, too, for that matter—that don't think we've got any particular family or position or culture in this part of the country. I've met plenty of that kind of provincial snobs myself, and they're pretty galling. There were one or two men in my crowd at college, their families had lived on their income for three generations, and they never dreamed there was anybody in their class out here. I had to show them a thing or two, right at the start, and I guess they won't forget it! Well, I think it's time all their sort found out that three generations *can* mean just as much out here as anywhere else. That's the way I feel about it, and let me tell you I feel it pretty deeply!"

"But what *are* you going to do, George?" she cried.

George's earnestness surpassed hers; he had become flushed and his breathing was emotional. As he confessed, with simple genuineness, he did feel what he was saying "pretty deeply"; and in truth his state approached the tremulous. "I expect to live an honourable life," he said. "I expect to contribute my share to charities, and to take part in—in movements."

"What kind?"

"Whatever appeals to me," he said.

Lucy looked at him with grieved wonder. "But you really don't mean to have any regular business or profession at *all*?"

"I certainly do not!" George returned promptly and emphatically.

"I was afraid so," she said in a low voice.

George continued to breathe deeply throughout another protracted interval of silence. Then he said, "I should like to revert to the questions I was asking you, if you don't mind."

"No, George. I think we'd better——"

"Your father is a business man——"

"He's a mechanical genius," Lucy interrupted quickly. "Of course he's both. And he was a lawyer once—he's done all sorts of things."

"Very well. I merely wished to ask if it's his influence that makes you think I ought to 'do' something?"

Lucy frowned slightly. "Why, I suppose almost everything I think or say must be owing to his influence in one way or another. We haven't had anybody but each other for so many years, and we always think about alike, so of course——"

"I see!" And George's brow darkened with resentment. "So that's it, is it? It's your father's idea that I ought to go into business and that you oughtn't to be engaged to me until I do."

Lucy gave a start, her denial was so quick. "No! I've never once spoken to him about it. Never!"

George looked at her keenly, and he jumped to a conclusion not far from the truth. "But you know without talking to him that it's the way he does feel about it? I see."

She nodded gravely. "Yes."

George's brow grew darker still. "Do you think I'd be much of a man," he said, slowly, "if I let any other man dictate to me my own way of life?"

"George! Who's 'dictating' your——"

"It seems to me it amounts to that!" he returned.

"Oh, *no*! I only know how papa thinks about things. He's never, never spoken unkindly, or 'dictatingly' of you." She lifted her hand in protest, and her face was so touching in its distress that for the moment George forgot his anger. He seized that small, troubled hand.

"Lucy," he said huskily. "Don't you know that I love you?"

"Yes—I do."

"Don't you love me?"

"Yes—I do."

"Then what does it matter what your father thinks about my doing something or not doing anything? He has his way, and I have mine. I don't believe in the whole world scrubbing dishes and selling potatoes and trying law cases. Why, look at your father's best friend, my Uncle George Amberson—he's never done anything in his life, and——"

"Oh, yes, he has," she interrupted. "He was in politics."

"Well, I'm glad he's out," George said. "Politics is a dirty business for a gentleman, and Uncle George would tell you that himself. Lucy, let's not talk any more about it. Let me tell mother when I get home that we're engaged. Won't you, dear?"

She shook her head.

"Is it because——"

For a fleeting instant she touched to her cheek the hand that held hers. "No," she said, and gave him a sudden little look of renewed gayety. "Let's let it stay 'almost'."

"Because your father——"

"Oh, because it's better!"

George's voice shook. "Isn't it your father?"

"It's his ideals I'm thinking of—yes."

George dropped her hand abruptly and anger narrowed his eyes. "I know what you mean," he said. "I dare say I don't care for your father's ideals any more than he does for mine!"

He tightened the reins, Pendennis quickening eagerly to the trot; and when George jumped out of the runabout before Lucy's gate, and assisted her to descend, the silence in which they parted was the same that had begun when Pendennis began to trot.

Chapter XVIII

THAT EVENING, after dinner, George sat with his mother and his Aunt Fanny upon the veranda. In former summers, when they sat outdoors in the evening, they had customarily used an open terrace at the side of the house, looking toward the Major's, but that more private retreat now afforded too blank and abrupt a view of the nearest of the new houses; so, without consultation, they had abandoned it for the Romanesque stone structure in front, an oppressive place.

Its oppression seemed congenial to George; he sat upon the copestone of the stone parapet, his back against a stone pilaster; his attitude not comfortable, but rigid, and his silence not comfortable, either, but heavy. However, to the eyes of his mother and his aunt, who occupied wicker chairs at a little distance, he was almost indistinguishable except for the stiff white shield of his evening frontage.

"It's so nice of you always to dress in the evening, Georgie," his mother said, her glance resting upon this surface. "Your Uncle George always used to, and so did father, for years; but they both stopped quite a long time ago. Unless there's some special occasion, it seems to me we don't see it done any more, except on the stage and in the magazines."

He made no response, and Isabel, after waiting a little while, as if she expected one, appeared to acquiesce in his mood for silence, and turned her head to gaze thoughtfully out at the street.

There, in the highway, the evening life of the Midland city had begun. A rising moon was bright upon the tops of the shade trees, where their branches met overhead, arching across the street, but only filtered splashings of moonlight reached the block pavement below; and through this darkness flashed the firefly lights of silent bicycles gliding by in pairs and trios—or sometimes a dozen at a time might come, and not so silent, striking their little bells; the riders' voices calling and laughing; while now and then a pair of invisible experts would pass, playing mandolin and guitar as if handle-bars were of no account in the world—their music would come swiftly, and then too swiftly die away. Surreys rumbled lightly by, with the plod-plod of honest old horses, and frequently there was the glitter of whizzing spokes from a runabout or a sporting buggy, and the sharp, decisive hoof-beats of a trotter. Then, like a cowboy shooting up a peaceful camp, a frantic devil would hurtle out of the distance, bellowing, exhaust racketing like a machine gun gone amuck—and at these horrid sounds the surreys and buggies would hug the curbstone, and the bicycles scatter to cover, cursing; while children rushed from the sidewalks to drag pet dogs from the street. The thing would roar by, leaving a long wake of turbulence; then the indignant street would quiet down for a few minutes—till another came.

"There are a great many more than there used to be," Miss Fanny observed, in her lifeless voice, as the lull fell after one of these visitations. "Eugene is right about that; there seem to be at least three or four times as many as there were last summer, and you never hear the ragamuffins shouting 'Get a horse!' nowadays; but I think he may be mistaken about their going on increasing after this. I don't believe we'll see so many next summer as we do now."

"Why?" asked Isabel.

"Because I've begun to agree with George about their being more a fad than anything else, and I think it must be the height of the fad just now. You know how roller-skating came in—everybody in the world seemed to be crowding to the rinks—and now only a few children use rollers for getting to school. Besides, people won't permit the automobiles to be used. Really, I think they'll make laws against them. You see how they spoil the bicycling and the driving; people just seem to hate them! They'll never stand it—never in the world! Of course I'd be sorry to see such a thing happen to Eugene, but I shouldn't be really surprised to see a law passed forbidding the sale of automobiles, just the way there is with concealed weapons."

"Fanny!" exclaimed her sister-in-law. "You're not in earnest?"

"I am, though!"

Isabel's sweet-toned laugh came out of the dusk where she sat. "Then you didn't mean it when you told Eugene you'd enjoyed the drive this afternoon?"

"I didn't say it so very enthusiastically, did I?"

"Perhaps not, but he certainly thought he'd pleased you."

"I don't think I gave him any right to think he'd pleased me," Fanny said slowly.

"Why not? Why shouldn't you, Fanny?"

Fanny did not reply at once, and when she did, her voice was almost inaudible, but much more reproachful than plaintive. "I hardly think I'd want any one to get the notion he'd pleased me just now. It hardly seems time, yet—to me."

Isabel made no response, and for a time the only sound upon the dark veranda was the creaking of the wicker rocking-chair in which Fanny sat—a creaking which seemed to denote content and placidity on the part of the chair's occupant, though at this juncture a series of human shrieks could have been little more eloquent of emotional disturbance. However, the creaking gave its hearer one great advantage: it could be ignored.

"Have you given up smoking, George?" Isabel asked presently.

"No."

"I hoped perhaps you had, because you've not smoked since dinner. We shan't mind if you care to."

"No, thanks."

There was silence again, except for the creaking of the rocking-chair; then a low, clear whistle, singularly musical, was heard softly rendering an old air from "Fra Diavolo." The creaking stopped.

"Is that you, George?" Fanny asked abruptly.

"Is that me what?"

"Whistling 'On Yonder Rock Reclining'?"

"It's I," said Isabel.

"Oh," Fanny said dryly.

"Does it disturb you?"

"Not at all. I had an idea George was depressed about something, and merely wondered if he could be making such a cheerful sound." And Fanny resumed her creaking.

"Is she right, George?" his mother asked quickly, leaning forward in her chair to peer at him through the dusk. "You didn't eat a very hearty dinner, but I thought it was probably because of the warm weather. Are you troubled about anything?"

"*No!*" he said angrily.

"That's good. I thought we had such a nice day, didn't you?"

"I suppose so," he muttered, and, satisfied, she leaned back in her chair; but "Fra Diavolo" was not revived. After a time she rose, went to the steps, and stood for several minutes looking across the street. Then her laughter was faintly heard.

"Are you laughing about something?" Fanny inquired.

"Pardon?" Isabel did not turn, but continued her observation of what had interested her upon the opposite side of the street.

"I asked: Were you laughing at something?"

"Yes, I was!" And she laughed again. "It's that funny, fat old Mrs. Johnson. She has a habit of sitting at her bedroom window with a pair of opera-glasses."

"Really!"

"Really. You can see the window through the place that was left when we had the dead walnut tree cut down. She looks up and down the street, but mostly at father's and over here. Sometimes she forgets to put out the light in her room, and there she is, spying away for all the world to see!"

However, Fanny made no effort to observe this spectacle, but continued her creaking. "I've always thought her a very good woman," she said primly.

"So she is," Isabel agreed. "She's a good, friendly old thing, a little too intimate in her manner, sometimes, and if her poor old opera-glasses afford her the quiet happiness of knowing what sort of young man our new cook is walking out with, I'm the last to begrudge it to her! Don't you want to come and look at her, George?"

"What? I beg your pardon. I hadn't noticed what you were talking about."

"It's nothing," she laughed. "Only a funny old lady—and she's gone now. I'm going, too—at least, I'm going indoors to read. It's cooler in the house, but the heat's really not bad anywhere, since nightfall. Summer's dying. How quickly it goes, once it begins to die."

When she had gone into the house, Fanny stopped rocking, and, leaning forward, drew her black gauze wrap about her shoulders and shivered. "Isn't it queer," she said drearily, "how your mother can use such words?"

"What words are you talking about?" George asked.

"Words like 'die' and 'dying.' I don't see how she can bear to use them so soon after your poor father——" She shivered again.

"It's almost a year," George said absently, and he added: "It seems to me you're using them yourself."

"I? Never!"

"Yes, you did."

"When?"

"Just this minute."

"Oh!" said Fanny. "You mean when I repeated what *she* said? That's hardly the same thing, George."

He was not enough interested to argue the point. "I don't think you'll convince anybody that mother's unfeeling," he said indifferently.

"I'm not trying to convince anybody. I mean merely that in my opinion—well, perhaps it may be just as wise for me to keep my opinions to myself."

She paused expectantly, but her possible anticipation that George would urge her to discard wisdom and reveal her opinion was not fulfilled. His back was toward her, and he occupied himself with opinions of his own about other matters. Fanny may have felt some disappointment as she rose to withdraw.

However, at the last moment she halted with her hand upon the latch of the screen door.

"There's *one* thing I hope," she said. "I hope at least she won't leave off her full mourning on the *very* anniversary of Wilbur's death!"

The light door clanged behind her, and the sound annoyed her nephew. He had no idea why she thus used inoffensive wood and wire to dramatize her departure from the veranda, the impression remaining with him being that she was critical of his mother upon some point of funeral millinery. Throughout the desultory conversation he had been profoundly concerned with his own disturbing affairs, and now was preoccupied with a dialogue taking place (in his mind) between himself and Miss Lucy Morgan. As he beheld the vision, Lucy had just thrown herself at his feet. "George, you *must* forgive me!" she cried. "Papa was utterly wrong! I have told him so, and the truth is that I have come to rather dislike him as you do, and as you always have, in your heart of hearts. George, I understand you:

thy people shall be my people and thy gods my gods. George, won't you take me back?"

"Lucy, are you *sure* you understand me?" And in the darkness George's bodily lips moved in unison with those which uttered the words in his imaginary rendering of this scene. An eavesdropper, concealed behind the column, could have heard the whispered word "sure," the emphasis put upon it in the vision was so poignant. "You say you understand me, but are you *sure*?"

Weeping, her head bowed almost to her waist, the ethereal Lucy made reply: "*Oh*, so sure! I will never listen to father's opinions again. I do not even care if I never see him again!"

"Then I pardon you," he said gently.

This softened mood lasted for several moments—until he realized that it had been brought about by processes strikingly lacking in substance. Abruptly he swung his feet down from the copestone to the floor of the veranda. "Pardon nothing!" No meek Lucy had thrown herself in remorse at his feet; and now he pictured her as she probably really was at this moment: sitting on the white steps of her own front porch in the moonlight, with red-headed Fred Kinney and silly Charlie Johnson and four or five others—all of them laughing, most likely, and some idiot playing the guitar!

George spoke aloud: "Riffraff!"

And because of an impish but all too natural reaction of the mind, he could see Lucy with much greater distinctness in this vision than in his former pleasing one. For a moment she was miraculously real before him, every line and colour of her. He saw the moonlight shimmering in the chiffon of her skirt, brightest on her crossed knee and the tip of her slipper; saw the blue curve of the characteristic shadow behind her, as she leaned back against the white step; saw the watery twinkling of sequins in the gauze wrap over her white shoulders as she moved, and the faint, symmetrical lights in her black hair—and not one alluring, exasperating twentieth-of-an-inch of her laughing profile was spared him as she seemed to turn to the infernal Kinney——

"Riffraff!" And George began furiously to pace the stone floor. "Riffraff!" By this hard term—a favourite with him since childhood's scornful hour—he meant to indicate, not Lucy, but the young gentlemen who, in his vision, surrounded her. "Riffraff!" he said again, aloud, and again:

"Riffraff!"

At that moment, as it happened, Lucy was playing chess with her father; and her heart, though not remorseful, was as heavy as George could have wished. But she did not let Eugene see that she was troubled, and he was pleased when he won three games of her. Usually she beat him.

Chapter XIX

GEORGE WENT driving the next afternoon alone, and, encountering Lucy and her father on the road, in one of Morgan's cars, lifted his hat, but nowise relaxed his formal countenance as they passed. Eugene waved a cordial hand quickly returned to the steering-wheel; but Lucy only nodded gravely and smiled no more than George did. Nor did she accompany Eugene to the Major's for dinner, the following Sunday evening, though both were bidden to attend that feast, which was already reduced in numbers and gayety by the absence of George Amberson. Eugene explained to his host that Lucy had gone away to visit a school-friend.

The information, delivered in the library, just before old Sam's appearance to announce dinner, set Miss Minafer in quite a flutter. "Why, George!" she said, turning to her nephew. "How does it happen you didn't tell us?" And with both hands opening, as if to express her innocence of some conspiracy, she exclaimed to the others, "He's never said one word to us about Lucy's planning to go away!"

"Probably afraid to," the Major suggested. "Didn't know but he might break down and cry if he tried to speak of it!" He clapped his grandson on the shoulder, inquiring jocularly, "That it, Georgie?"

Georgie made no reply, but he was red enough to justify the Major's developing a chuckle into laughter; though Miss Fanny, observing her nephew keenly, got an impression that this fiery blush was in truth more fiery than tender. She caught a glint in his eye less like confusion than resentment, and saw a dilation of his nostrils which might have indicated not so much a sweet agitation as an inaudible snort. Fanny had never been lacking in curiosity, and, since her brother's death, this quality was more than ever alert. The fact that George had spent all the evenings of the past week at home had not been lost upon her, nor had she failed to ascertain, by diplomatic inquiries, that since the day of the visit to Eugene's shops George had gone driving alone.

At the dinner-table she continued to observe him, sidelong;

and toward the conclusion of the meal she was not startled by an episode which brought discomfort to the others. After the arrival of coffee the Major was rallying Eugene upon some rival automobile shops lately built in a suburb, and already promising to flourish.

"I suppose they'll either drive you out of the business," said the old gentleman, "or else the two of you'll drive all the rest of us off the streets."

"If we do, we'll even things up by making the streets five or ten times as long as they are now," Eugene returned.

"How do you propose to do that?"

"It isn't the distance from the centre of a town that counts," said Eugene; "it's the time it takes to get there. This town's already spreading; bicycles and trolleys have been doing their share, but the automobile is going to carry city streets clear out to the county line."

The Major was skeptical. "Dream on, fair son!" he said. "It's lucky for us that you're only dreaming; because if people go to moving that far, real estate values in the old residence part of town are going to be stretched pretty thin."

"I'm afraid so," Eugene assented. "Unless you keep things so bright and clean that the old section will stay more attractive than the new ones."

"Not very likely! How are things going to be kept 'bright and clean' with soft coal and our kind of city government?"

"They aren't," Eugene replied quickly. "There's no hope of it, and already the boarding-house is marching up National Avenue. There are two in the next block below here, and there are a dozen in the half-mile below that. My relatives, the Sharons, have sold their house and are building in the country—at least, they call it 'the country.' It will be city in two or three years."

"Good gracious!" the Major exclaimed, affecting dismay. "So your little shops are going to ruin all your old friends, Eugene!"

"Unless my old friends take warning in time, or abolish smoke and get a new kind of city government. I should say the best chance is to take warning."

"Well, well!" the Major laughed. "You have enough faith in miracles, Eugene—granting that trolleys and bicycles and automobiles are miracles. So you think they're to change the face of the land, do you?"

"They're already doing it, Major; and it can't be stopped. Automobiles——"

At this point he was interrupted. George was the interrupter. He had said nothing since entering the dining room, but now he spoke in a loud and peremptory voice, using the tone of one in authority who checks idle prattle and settles a matter forever.

"Automobiles are a useless nuisance," he said.

There fell a moment's silence.

Isabel gazed incredulously at George, colour slowly heightening upon her cheeks and temples, while Fanny watched him with a quick eagerness, her eyes alert and bright. But Eugene seemed merely quizzical, as if not taking this brusquerie to himself. The Major was seriously disturbed.

"What did you say, George?" he asked, though George had spoken but too distinctly.

"I said all automobiles were a nuisance," George answered, repeating not only the words but the tone in which he had uttered them. And he added, "They'll never amount to anything but a nuisance. They had no business to be invented."

The Major frowned. "Of course you forget that Mr. Morgan makes them, and also did his share in inventing them. If you weren't so thoughtless he might think you rather offensive."

"That would be too bad," said George coolly. "I don't think I could survive it."

Again there was a silence, while the Major stared at his grandson, aghast. But Eugene began to laugh cheerfully.

"I'm not sure he's wrong about automobiles," he said. "With all their speed forward they may be a step backward in civilization—that is, in spiritual civilization. It may be that they will not add to the beauty of the world, nor to the life of men's souls. I am not sure. But automobiles have come, and they bring a greater change in our life than most of us suspect. They are here, and almost all outward things are going to be different because of what they bring. They are going to alter war, and they are going to alter peace. I think men's minds are going to be changed in subtle ways because of automobiles; just how, though, I could hardly guess. But you can't have the immense outward changes that they will cause without some inward ones, and it may be that George is right, and that the spiritual alteration will be bad for us. Perhaps, ten or twenty years from now, if we can see the inward change in men by that time, I shouldn't be able to defend the gasoline engine, but would have to agree with him that automobiles 'had no business to be invented.'" He laughed good-naturedly, and looking at his watch, apologized for having an engagement which made his departure necessary when he would so much prefer to linger. Then he shook hands with the Major, and bade Isabel, George, and Fanny a cheerful good-night—a collective farewell cordially addressed to all three of them together—and left them at the table.

Isabel turned wondering, hurt eyes upon her son. "George, dear!" she said. "What *did* you mean?"

"Just what I said," he returned, lighting one of the Major's cigars, and his manner was imperturbable enough to warrant the definition (sometimes merited by imperturbability) of stubbornness.

Isabel's hand, pale and slender, upon the tablecloth, touched one of the fine silver candlesticks aimlessly: the fingers were seen to tremble. "Oh, he was hurt!" she murmured.

"I don't see why he should be," George said. "I didn't say anything about *him*. He didn't seem to me to be hurt—seemed perfectly cheerful. What made you think he was hurt?"

"I know him!" was all of her reply, half whispered.

The Major stared hard at George from under his white eyebrows. "You didn't mean '*him*,' you say, George? I suppose if we had a clergyman as a guest here you'd expect him not to be offended, and to understand that your remarks were neither personal nor untactful, if you said the church was a nuisance and ought never to have been invented. By Jove, but you're a puzzle!"

"In what way, may I ask, sir?"

"We seem to have a new kind of young people these days," the old gentleman returned, shaking his head. "It's a new style of courting a pretty girl, certainly, for a young fellow to go deliberately out of his way to try and make an enemy of her father by attacking his business! By Jove! That's a new way to win a woman!"

George flushed angrily and seemed about to offer a retort, but held his breath for a moment; and then held his peace. It was Isabel who responded to the Major. "Oh, no!" she said. "Eugene would never be anybody's enemy—he couldn't!—and last of all Georgie's. I'm afraid he was hurt, but I don't fear his not having understood that George spoke without thinking of what he was saying—I mean, without realizing its bearing on Eugene."

Again George seemed upon the point of speech, and again controlled the impulse. He thrust his hands in his pockets, leaned back in his chair, and smoked, staring inflexibly at the ceiling.

"Well, well," said his grandfather, rising. "It wasn't a very successful little dinner!"

Thereupon he offered his arm to his daughter, who took it fondly, and they left the room, Isabel assuring him that all his little dinners were pleasant, and that this one was no exception.

George did not move, and Fanny, following the other two, came round the table, and paused close beside his chair; but George remained posed in his great imperturbability, cigar between teeth, eyes upon ceiling, and paid no attention to her. Fanny waited until the sound of Isabel's and the Major's voices became inaudible in the hall. Then she said quickly, and in a low voice so eager that it was unsteady:

"George, you've struck *just* the treatment to adopt: you're doing the right thing!"

She hurried out, scurrying after the others with a faint rustling of her black skirts, leaving George mystified but incurious. He did not understand why she should bestow her approbation upon him in the matter, and cared so little whether she did or not that he spared himself even the trouble of being puzzled about it.

In truth, however, he was neither so comfortable nor so imperturbable as he appeared. He felt some gratification: he had done a little to put the man in his place—that man whose influence upon his daughter was precisely the same thing as a contemptuous criticism of George Amberson Minafer, and of George Amberson Minafer's "ideals of life." Lucy's going away without a word was intended, he supposed, as a bit of punishment. Well, he wasn't the sort of man that people were allowed to punish: he could demonstrate that to them—since they started it!

It appeared to him as almost a kind of insolence, this abrupt departure—not even telephoning! Probably she wondered how he would take it; she even might have supposed he would show some betraying chagrin when he heard of it.

He had no idea that this was just what he had shown; and he was satisfied with his evening's performance. Nevertheless, he was not comfortable in his mind; though he could not have explained his inward perturbations, for he was convinced, without any confirmation from his Aunt Fanny, that he had done "just the right thing."

Chapter XX

Isabel came to George's door that night, and when she had kissed him good-night she remained in the open doorway with her hand upon his shoulder and her eyes thoughtfully lowered, so that her wish to say something more than good-night was evident. Not less obvious was her perplexity about the manner of saying it; and George, divining her thought, amiably made an opening for her.

"Well, old lady," he said indulgently, "you needn't look so worried. I won't be tactless with Morgan again. After this I'll just keep out of his way."

Isabel looked up, searching his face with the fond puzzlement which her eyes sometimes showed when they rested upon him; then she glanced down the hall toward Fanny's room, and, after another moment of hesitation, came quickly in, and closed the door.

"Dear," she said, "I wish you'd tell me something: Why don't you like Eugene?"

"Oh, I like him well enough," George returned, with a short laugh, as he sat down and began to unlace his shoes. "I like him well enough—in his place."

"No, dear," she said hurriedly. "I've had a feeling from the very first that you didn't really like him—that you really never liked him. Sometimes you've seemed to be friendly with him, and you'd laugh with him over something in a jolly, companionable way, and I'd think I was wrong, and that you really did like him, after all; but to-night I'm sure my other feeling was the right one: you don't like him. I can't understand it, dear; I don't see what can be the matter."

"Nothing's the matter."

This easy declaration naturally failed to carry great weight, and Isabel went on, in her troubled voice, "It seems so queer, especially when you feel as you do about his daughter."

At this, George stopped unlacing his shoes abruptly, and sat up. "How do I feel about his daughter?" he demanded.

"Well, it's seemed—as if—as if——" Isabel began timidly. "It did seem—— At least, you haven't looked at any other girl, ever since they came here, and—and certainly you've seemed very much interested in her. Certainly you've been very great *friends*?"

"Well, what of that?"

"It's only that I'm like your grandfather: I can't see how you could be so much interested in a girl and—and not feel very pleasantly toward her father."

"Well, I'll tell you something," George said slowly; and a frown of concentration could be seen upon his brow, as from a profound effort at self-examination. "I haven't ever thought much on that particular point, but I admit there may be a little something in what you say. The truth is, I don't believe I've ever thought of the two together, exactly—at least, not until lately. I've always thought of Lucy just as Lucy, and of Morgan just as Morgan. I've always thought of her as a person herself, not as anybody's daughter. I don't see what's very extraordinary about that. You've probably got plenty of friends, for instance, that don't care much about your son——"

"No, indeed!" she protested quickly. "And if I knew anybody who felt like that, I wouldn't——"

"Never mind," he interrupted. "I'll try to explain a little more. If I have a friend, I don't see that it's incumbent upon me to like that friend's relatives. If I didn't like them, and pretended to, I'd be a hypocrite. If that friend likes me and wants to stay my friend he'll have to stand my not liking his relatives, or else he can quit. I decline to be a hypocrite about it; that's all. Now, suppose I have certain ideas or ideals which I have chosen for the regulation of my own conduct in life. Suppose some friend of mine has a relative with ideals directly the opposite of mine, and my friend believes more in the relative's ideals than in mine: Do you think I ought to give up my own just to please a person who's taken up ideals that I really despise?"

"No, dear; of course people can't give up their ideals; but I don't see what this has to do with dear little Lucy and——"

"I didn't say it had anything to do with them," he interrupted. "I was merely putting a case to show how a person would be justified in being a friend of one member of a family, and feeling anything but friendly toward another. I don't say, though, that I feel unfriendly to Mr. Morgan. I don't say that I feel friendly to him, and I don't say that I feel unfriendly; but if you really think that I was rude to him to-night——"

"Just thoughtless, dear. You didn't see that what you said to-night——"

"Well, I'll not say anything of that sort again where he can hear it. There, isn't that enough?"

This question, delivered with large indulgence, met with no response; for Isabel, still searching his face with her troubled and perplexed gaze, seemed not to have heard it. On that account, George repeated it, and rising, went to her and patted her reassuringly upon the shoulder. "There, old lady, you needn't fear my tactlessness will worry you again. I can't quite promise to like people I don't care about one way or another, but you can be sure I'll be careful, after this, not to let them see it. It's all right, and you'd better toddle along to bed, because I want to undress."

"But, George," she said earnestly, "you *would* like him, if you'd just let yourself. You say you don't dislike him. Why don't you like him? I can't understand at all. *What* is it that you don't——"

"There, there!" he said. "It's all right, and you toddle along."

"But, George——"

"Now, now! I really do want to get into bed. Good-night, old lady."

"Good-night, dear. But——"

"Let's not talk of it any more," he said. "It's all right, and nothing in the world to worry about. So good-night, old lady. I'll be polite enough to him, never fear—if we happen to be thrown together. So *good*-night!"

"But, George, dear——"

"I'm going to bed, old lady; so good-night."

Thus the interview closed perforce. She kissed him again before going slowly to her own room, her perplexity evidently not dispersed; but the subject was not renewed between them the next day or subsequently. Nor did Fanny make any allusion to the cryptic approbation she had bestowed upon her nephew after the Major's "not very successful little dinner"; though she annoyed George by looking at him oftener and longer than he cared to be looked at by an aunt. He could not glance her way, it seemed, without finding her red-rimmed eyes fixed upon him eagerly, with an alert and hopeful calculation in them which he declared would send a nervous man into fits. For thus, one day, he broke out, in protest:

"It would!" he repeated vehemently. "Given time it would —straight into fits! What do you find the matter with me? Is my tie *always* slipping up behind? Can't you look at something else? My Lord! We'd better buy a cat for you to stare at, Aunt Fanny! A cat could stand it, maybe. What in the name of goodness do you expect to *see*?"

But Fanny laughed good-naturedly, and was not offended. "It's more as if I expected *you* to see something, isn't it?" she said quietly, still laughing.

"Now, what do you mean by that?"

"Never mind!"

"All right, I don't. But for heaven's sake stare at somebody else awhile. Try it on the housemaid!"

"Well, well," Fanny said indulgently, and then chose to be more obscure in her meaning than ever, for she adopted a tone of deep sympathy for her final remark, as she left him: "I don't wonder you're nervous these days, poor boy!"

And George indignantly supposed that she referred to the ordeal of Lucy's continued absence. During this period he successfully avoided contact with Lucy's father, though Eugene came frequently to the house, and spent several evenings with Isabel and Fanny; and sometimes persuaded them and the Major to go for an afternoon's motoring. He did not, however, come again to the Major's Sunday evening dinner, even when George Amberson returned. Sunday evening was the time, he explained, for going over the week's work with his factory managers.

. . . When Lucy came home the autumn was far enough advanced to smell of burning leaves, and for the annual editorials, in the papers, on the purple haze, the golden branches, the ruddy fruit, and the pleasure of long tramps in the brown forest. George had not heard of her arrival, and he met her, on the afternoon following that event, at the Sharons', where he had gone in the secret hope that he might hear something about her. Janie Sharon had just begun to tell him that she heard

Lucy was expected home soon, after having "a perfectly gorgeous time"—information which George received with no responsive enthusiasm—when Lucy came demurely in, a proper little autumn figure in green and brown.

Her cheeks were flushed, and her dark eyes were bright indeed; evidences, as George supposed, of the excitement incidental to the perfectly gorgeous time just concluded; though Janie and Mary Sharon both thought they were the effect of Lucy's having seen George's runabout in front of the house as she came in. George took on colour, himself, as he rose and nodded indifferently; and the hot suffusion to which he became subject extended its area to include his neck and ears. Nothing could have made him much more indignant than his consciousness of these symptoms of the icy indifference which it was his purpose not only to show but to feel.

She kissed her cousins, gave George her hand, said "How d'you do," and took a chair beside Janie with a composure which augmented George's indignation.

"How d'you do," he said. "I trust that ah—I trust—I do trust——"

He stopped, for it seemed to him that the word "trust" sounded idiotic. Then, to cover his awkwardness, he coughed, and even to his own rosy ears his cough was ostentatiously a false one. Whereupon, seeking to be plausible, he coughed again, and instantly hated himself: the sound he made was an atrocity. Meanwhile, Lucy sat silent, and the two Sharon girls leaned forward, staring at him with strained eyes, their lips tightly compressed; and both were but too easily diagnosed as subject to an agitation which threatened their self-control. He began again.

"I tr—I hope you have had a—a pleasant time. I tr—I hope you are well. I hope you are extremely—I hope extremely—extremely——" And again he stopped in the midst of his floundering, not knowing how to progress beyond "extremely," and unable to understand why the infernal word kept getting into his mouth.

"I beg your pardon?" Lucy said.

George was never more furious; he felt that he was "making a spectacle of himself"; and no young gentleman in the world was more loath than George Amberson Minafer to look a figure of fun. And while he stood there, undeniably such a figure, with Janie and Mary Sharon threatening to burst at any moment, if laughter were longer denied them, Lucy sat looking at him with her eyebrows delicately lifted in casual, polite inquiry. Her own complete composure was what most galled him.

"Nothing of the slightest importance!" he managed to say. "I was just leaving. *Good* afternoon!" And with long strides he reached the door, and hastened through the hall; but before he closed the front door he heard from Janie and Mary Sharon the outburst of wild, irrepressible emotion which his performance had inspired.

He drove home in a tumultuous mood, and almost ran down two ladies who were engaged in absorbing conversation at a crossing. They were his Aunt Fanny and the stout Mrs. Johnson; a jerk of the reins at the last instant saved them by a few inches; but their conversation was so interesting that they were unaware of their danger, and did not notice the runabout, nor how close it came to them. George was so furious with himself and with the girl whose unexpected coming into a room could make him look such a fool, that it might have soothed him a little if he had actually run over the two absorbed ladies without injuring them beyond repair. At least, he said to himself that he wished he had; it might have taken his mind off of himself for a few minutes. For, in truth, to be ridiculous (and know it) was one of several things that George was unable to endure. He was savage.

He drove into the Major's stable too fast, the sagacious Pendennis saving himself from going through a partition by a swerve which splintered a shaft of the runabout and almost threw the driver to the floor. George swore, and then swore again at the fat old darkey, Tom, for giggling at his swearing.

"Hoopee!" said old Tom. "Mus' been some white lady use Mist' Jawge mighty bad! White lady say, 'No, suh, I ain' go'n out ridin' 'ith Mist' Jawge no mo'!' Mist' Jawge drive in. 'Dam de dam worl'! Dam de dam hoss! Dam de dam nigga'! Dam de dam dam!' Hoopee!"

"That'll do!" George said sternly.

"Yessuh!"

George strode from the stable, crossed the Major's back yard, then passed behind the new houses, on his way home. These structures were now approaching completion, but still in a state of rawness hideous to George—though, for that matter, they were never to be anything except hideous to him. Behind them, stray planks, bricks, refuse of plaster and lath, shingles, straw, empty barrels, strips of twisted tin and broken tiles were strewn everywhere over the dried and pitted gray mud where once the suave lawn had lain like a green lake around those stately islands, the two Amberson houses. And George's state of mind was not improved by his present view of this repulsive area, nor by his sensations when he kicked an uptilted shingle only to discover that what uptilted it was a brickbat on the other side of it. After that, the whole world seemed to be one solid conspiracy of malevolence.

In this temper he emerged from behind the house nearest to his own, and, glancing toward the street, saw his mother standing with Eugene Morgan upon the cement path that led to the front gate. She was bareheaded, and Eugene held his hat and stick in his hand; evidently he had been calling upon her, and she had come from the house with him, continuing their conversation and delaying their parting.

They had paused in their slow walk from the front door to the gate, yet still stood side by side, their shoulders almost touching, as though neither Isabel nor Eugene quite realized that their feet had ceased to bear them forward; and they were not looking at each other, but at some indefinite point before them, as people do who consider together thoughtfully and in harmony. The conversation was evidently serious; his head was bent, and Isabel's lifted left hand rested against her cheek; but all the significances of their thoughtful attitude denoted companionableness and a shared understanding. Yet, a stranger, passing, would not have thought them married: somewhere about Eugene, not quite to be located, there was a romantic gravity; and Isabel, tall and graceful, with high colour and absorbed eyes, was visibly no wife walking down to the gate with her husband.

George stared at them. A hot dislike struck him at the sight of Eugene; and a vague revulsion, like a strange, unpleasant taste in his mouth, came over him as he looked at his mother: her manner was eloquent of so much thought about her companion and of such reliance upon him. And the picture the two thus made was a vivid one indeed, to George, whose angry eyes, for some reason, fixed themselves most intently upon Isabel's lifted hand, upon the white ruffle at her wrist, bordering the graceful black sleeve, and upon the little indentations in her cheek where the tips of her fingers rested. She should not have worn white at her wrist, or at the throat either, George felt; and then, strangely, his resentment concentrated upon those tiny indentations at the tips of her fingers—actual changes, however slight and fleeting, in his mother's face, made because of Mr. Eugene Morgan. For the moment, it seemed to George that Morgan might have claimed the ownership of a face that changed for him. It was as if he owned Isabel.

The two began to walk on toward the gate, where they stopped again, turning to face each other, and Isabel's glance, passing Eugene, fell upon George. Instantly she smiled and waved her hand to him; while Eugene turned and nodded; but George, standing as in some rigid trance, and staring straight at them, gave these signals of greeting no sign of recognition whatever. Upon this, Isabel called to him, waving her hand again.

"Georgie!" she called, laughing. "Wake up, dear! Georgie, hello!"

George turned away as if he had neither seen nor heard, and stalked into the house by the side door.

Chapter XXI

HE WENT to his room, threw off his coat, waistcoat, collar, and tie, letting them lie where they chanced to fall, and then, having violently enveloped himself in a black velvet dressing-gown, continued this action by lying down with a vehemence that brought a wheeze of protest from his bed. His repose was only a momentary semblance, however, for it lasted no longer than the time it took him to groan "Riffraff!" between his teeth. Then he sat up, swung his feet to the floor, rose, and began to pace up and down the large room.

He had just been consciously rude to his mother for the first time in his life; for, with all his riding down of populace and riffraff, he had never before been either deliberately or impulsively disregardful of her. When he had hurt her it had been accidental; and his remorse for such an accident was always adequate compensation—and more—to Isabel. But now he had done a rough thing to her; and he did not repent; the rather he was the more irritated with her. And when he heard her presently go by his door with a light step, singing cheerfully to herself as she went to her room, he perceived that she had mistaken his intention altogether, or, indeed, had failed to perceive that he had any intention at all. Evidently she had concluded that he refused to speak to her and Morgan out of sheer absent-mindedness, supposing him so immersed in some preoccupation that he had not seen them or heard her calling to him. Therefore there was nothing of which to repent, even if he had been so minded; and probably Eugene himself was unaware that any disapproval had recently been expressed. George snorted. What sort of a dreamy loon did they take him to be?

There came a delicate, eager tapping at his door, not done with a knuckle but with the tip of a fingernail, which was instantly clarified to George's mind's eye as plainly as if he saw it: the long and polished white-mooned pink shield on the end of his Aunt Fanny's right forefinger. But George was in no mood for human communications, and even when things went well he had little pleasure in Fanny's society. Therefore it is not surprising that at the sound of her tapping, instead of bidding her enter, he immediately crossed the room with the intention of locking the door to keep her out.

Fanny was too eager, and, opening the door before he reached it, came quickly in, and closed it behind her. She was in a street dress and a black hat, with a black umbrella in her black-gloved hand—for Fanny's heavy mourning, at least, was nowhere tempered with a glimpse of white, though the anniversary of Wilbur's death had passed. An infinitesimal perspiration gleamed upon her pale skin; she breathed fast, as if she had run up the stairs; and excitement was sharp in her widened eyes. Her look was that of a person who had just seen something extraordinary or heard thrilling news.

"Now, what on earth do *you* want?" her chilling nephew demanded.

"George," she said hurriedly, "I saw what you did when you wouldn't speak to them. I was sitting with Mrs. Johnson at her front window, across the street, and I saw it all."

"Well, what of it?"

"You did right!" Fanny said with a vehemence not the less spirited because she suppressed her voice almost to a whisper. "You did exactly right! You're behaving splendidly about the whole thing, and I want to tell you I know your father would thank you if he could see what you're doing."

"My Lord!" George broke out at her. "You make me dizzy! For heaven's sake quit the mysterious detective business—at least do quit it around me! Go and try it on somebody else, if you like; but *I* don't want to hear it!"

She began to tremble, regarding him with a fixed gaze. "You don't care to hear then," she said huskily, "that I approve of what you're doing?"

"Certainly not! Since I haven't the faintest idea what you think I'm 'doing,' naturally I don't care whether you approve of it or not. All I'd like, if you please, is to be alone. I'm not giving a tea here, this afternoon, if you'll permit me to mention it!"

Fanny's gaze wavered; she began to blink; then suddenly she sank into a chair and wept silently, but with a terrible desolation.

"Oh, for the Lord's sake!" he moaned. "What in the world is wrong with you?"

"You're always picking on me," she quavered wretchedly, her voice indistinct with the wetness that bubbled into it from her tears. "You do—you always pick on me! You've always done it—always—ever since you were a little boy! Whenever anything goes wrong with you, you take it out on me! You do! You always——"

George flung to heaven a gesture of despair; it seemed to him the last straw that Fanny should have chosen this particular time to come and sob in his room over his mistreatment of her!

"Oh, my Lord!" he whispered; then, with a great effort, addressed her in a reasonable tone: "Look here, Aunt Fanny; I don't see what you're making all this fuss about. Of course I know I've teased you sometimes, but——"

"'*Teased*' me?" she wailed. "'*Teased*' me! Oh, it does seem too hard, sometimes—this mean old life of mine does seem too hard! I don't think I *can* stand it! Honestly, I don't think I can! I came in here just to show you I sympathized with you—just to say something *pleasant* to you, and you treat me as if I were—oh, no, you *wouldn't* treat a servant the way you treat me! You wouldn't treat anybody in the world like this except old Fanny! 'Old Fanny' you say. 'It's nobody but old Fanny, so I'll kick her—nobody will resent it. I'll kick her all I want to!' You do! That's how you think of me—I know it! And you're right: I haven't got anything in the world, since my brother died—nobody—nothing—nothing!"

"Oh my *Lord*!" George groaned.

Fanny spread out her small, soaked handkerchief, and shook it in the air to dry it a little, crying as damply and as wretchedly during this operation as before—a sight which gave George a curious shock to add to his other agitations, it seemed so strange. "I ought not to have come," she went on, "because I might have known it would only give you an excuse to pick on me again! I'm sorry enough I came, I can tell you! I didn't mean to speak of it again to you, at all; and I wouldn't have, but I saw how you treated them, and I guess I got excited about it, and couldn't help following the impulse—but I'll know better next time, I can tell you! I'll keep my mouth shut as I meant to, and as I would have, if I hadn't got excited and if I hadn't felt sorry for you. But what does it matter to anybody if I'm sorry for them? I'm only old Fanny!"

"Oh, good gracious! How *can* it matter to me who's sorry for me when I don't know what they're sorry about!"

"You're so proud," she quavered, "and so hard! I *tell* you I didn't mean to speak of it to you, and I never, never in the world would have *told* you about it, nor have made the faintest reference to it, if I hadn't seen that somebody else had told you, or you'd found out for yourself some way. I——"

In despair of her intelligence, and in some doubt of his own, George struck the palms of his hands together. "Somebody else had told me what? I'd found *what* out for myself?"

"How people are talking about your mother."

Except for the incidental teariness of her voice, her tone was casual, as though she mentioned a subject previously discussed and understood; for Fanny had no doubt that George had only pretended to be mystified because, in his pride, he would not in words admit that he knew what he knew.

"What did you say?" he asked incredulously.

"Of course *I* understood what you were doing," Fanny went on, drying her handkerchief again. "It puzzled other people when you began to be rude to Eugene, because they couldn't see how you could treat him as you did when you were so interested in Lucy. But I remembered how you came to me, that other time when there was so much talk about Isabel; and I knew you'd give Lucy up in a minute, if it came to a question of your mother's reputation, because you said then that——"

"Look here," George interrupted in a shaking voice. "Look here, I'd like——" He stopped, unable to go on, his agitation was so great. His chest heaved as from hard running, and his complexion, pallid at first, had become mottled; fiery splotches appearing at his temples and cheeks. "What do you mean by telling me—telling me there's talk about—about——" He gulped, and began again: "What do you mean by using such words as 'reputation'? What do you mean, speaking of a 'question' of my—my mother's reputation?"

Fanny looked up at him woefully over the handkerchief which she now applied to her reddened nose. "God knows I'm sorry for you, George," she murmured. "I wanted to say so, but it's only old Fanny, so whatever she says—even when it's sympathy—pick on her for it! Hammer her!" She sobbed. "Hammer her! It's only poor old lonely Fanny!"

"You look here!" George said harshly. "When I spoke to my Uncle George after that rotten thing I heard Aunt Amelia say about my mother, he said if there was any gossip it was about *you*! He said people might be laughing about the way you ran after Morgan, but that was all."

Fanny lifted her hands, clenched them, and struck them upon her knees. "Yes; it's always Fanny!" she sobbed. "Ridiculous old Fanny—always, always!"

"You listen!" George said. "After I'd talked to Uncle George I saw *you*; and you said I had a mean little mind for thinking there might be truth in what Aunt Amelia said about people talking. You denied it. And that wasn't the only time; you'd attacked me before then, because I intimated that Morgan might be coming here too often. You made me believe that mother let him come entirely on your account, and *now* you say——"

"I think he did," Fanny interrupted desolately. "I think he did come as much to see me as anything—for a *while* it looked like it. Anyhow, he liked to dance with me. He danced with me as much as he danced with her, and he acted as if he came on my account at least as much as he did on hers. He *did* act a good deal that way—and if Wilbur hadn't died——"

"You told me there *wasn't* any talk."

"I didn't think there was much, then," Fanny protested. "*I* didn't know how much there was."

"What!"

"People don't come and tell such things to a person's family, you know. You don't suppose anybody was going to say to George Amberson that his sister was getting herself talked about, do you? Or that they were going to say much to *me*?"

"You told me," said George, fiercely, "that mother never saw him except when she was chaperoning you."

"They weren't much alone together, then," Fanny returned. "Hardly ever, before Wilbur died. But you don't suppose *that* stops people from talking, do you? Your father never went anywhere, and people saw Eugene with her everywhere she went—and though I was with them people just thought"—she choked—"they just thought I didn't count! 'Only old Fanny

Minafer,' I suppose they'd say! Besides, everybody knew that he'd been engaged to her——"

"What's that?" George cried.

"Everybody knows it. Don't you remember your grandfather speaking of it at the Sunday dinner one night?"

"He didn't say they were engaged or——"

"Well, they were! Everybody knows it; and she broke it off on account of that serenade when Eugene didn't know what he was doing. He drank when he was a young man, and she wouldn't stand it, but everybody in this town knows that Isabel has never really cared for any other man in her life! Poor Wilbur! He was the only soul alive that didn't know it!"

Nightmare had descended upon the unfortunate George; he leaned back against the foot-board of his bed, gazing wildly at his aunt. "I believe I'm going crazy," he said. "You mean when you told me there wasn't any talk, you told me a falsehood?"

"No!" Fanny gasped.

"You did!"

"I tell you I didn't know how much talk there *was*, and it wouldn't have amounted to much if Wilbur had lived." And Fanny completed this with a fatal admission: "I didn't want you to interfere."

George overlooked the admission; his mind was not now occupied with analysis. "What do you mean," he asked, "when you say that if father had lived, the talk wouldn't have amounted to anything?"

"Things might have been—they might have been different."

"You mean Morgan might have married *you*?"

Fanny gulped. "No. Because I don't know that I'd have accepted him." She had ceased to weep, and now she sat up stiffly. "I certainly didn't care enough about him to marry him; I wouldn't have let myself care that much until he showed that he wished to marry me. I'm not that sort of person!" The poor lady paid her vanity this piteous little tribute. "What I mean is, if Wilbur hadn't died, people wouldn't have had it proved before their very *eyes* that what they'd been talking about was true!"

"You say—you say that people believe——" George shuddered, then forced himself to continue, in a sick voice: "They believe my mother is—is in love with that man?"

"Of course!"

"And because he comes here—and they see her with him driving—and all that—they think they were right when they said she was in—in love with him before—before my father died?"

She looked at him gravely with her eyes now dry between their reddened lids. "Why, George," she said, gently, "don't *you* know that's what they say? You *must* know that everybody in town thinks they're going to be married very soon."

George uttered an incoherent cry; and sections of him appeared to writhe. He was upon the verge of actual nausea.

"You know it!" Fanny cried, getting up. "You don't think I'd have spoken of it to you unless I was sure you knew it?" Her voice was wholly genuine, as it had been throughout the wretched interview: Fanny's sincerity was unquestionable. "George, *I* wouldn't have told you, if you didn't know. What other reason could you have for treating Eugene as you did, or for refusing to speak to them like that, a while ago in the yard? Somebody *must* have told you?"

"Who told *you*?" he said.

"What?"

"Who told you there was talk? Where *is* this talk? Where does it come from? Who does it?"

"Why, I suppose pretty much everybody," she said. "I know it must be pretty general."

"Who said so?"

"What?"

George stepped close to her. "You say people don't speak to a person of gossip about that person's family. Well, how did you hear it, then? How did you get hold of it? Answer me!"

Fanny looked thoughtful. "Well, of course nobody not one's most intimate friends would speak to them about such things, and then only in the kindest, most considerate way."

"Who's spoken of it to you in any way at all?" George demanded.

"Why——" Fanny hesitated.

"You answer me!"

"I hardly think it would be fair to give names."

"Look here," said George. "One of your most intimate friends is that mother of Charlie Johnson's, for instance. Has *she* ever mentioned this to you? You say everybody is talking. Is she one?"

"Oh, she may have intimated——"

"I'm asking you: Has she ever spoken of it to you?"

"She's a very kind, discreet woman, George; but she may have intimated——"

George had a sudden intuition, as there flickered into his mind the picture of a street-crossing and two absorbed ladies almost run down by a fast horse. "You and she have been talking about it to-day!" he cried. "You were talking about it with her not two hours ago. Do you deny it?"

"I——"

"Do you deny it?"

"No!"

"All right," said George. "That's enough!"

She caught at his arm as he turned away. "What are you going to do, George?"

"I'll not talk about it, now," he said heavily. "I think you've done a good deal for one day, Aunt Fanny!"

And Fanny, seeing the passion in his face, began to be alarmed. She tried to retain possession of the black velvet sleeve which her fingers had clutched, and he suffered her to do so, but used this leverage to urge her to the door. "George, you know I'm sorry for you, whether you care or not," she whimpered. "I never in the world would have spoken of it, if I hadn't thought you knew all about it. I wouldn't have——"

But he had opened the door with his free hand. "Never mind!" he said, and she was obliged to pass out into the hall, the door closing quickly behind her.

Chapter XXII

GEORGE took off his dressing-gown and put on a collar and a tie, his fingers shaking so that the tie was not his usual success; then he picked up his coat and waistcoat, and left the room while still in process of donning them, fastening the buttons as he ran down the front stairs to the door. It was not until he reached the middle of the street that he realized that he had forgotten his hat; and he paused for an irresolute moment, during which his eye wandered, for no reason, to the Fountain of Neptune. This castiron replica of too elaborate sculpture stood at the next corner, where the Major had placed it when the Addition was laid out so long ago. The street corners had been shaped to conform with the great octagonal basin, which was no great inconvenience for horse-drawn vehicles, but a nuisance to speeding automobiles; and, even as George looked, one of the latter, coming too fast, saved itself only by a dangerous skid as it rounded the fountain. This skid was to George's liking, though he would have been more pleased to see the car go over, for he was wishing grief and destruction, just then, upon all the automobiles in the world.

His eyes rested a second or two longer upon the Fountain of Neptune, not an enlivening sight even in the shielding haze of autumn twilight. For more than a year no water had run in the fountain: the connections had been broken, and the Major was evasive about restorations, even when reminded by his grandson that a dry fountain is as gay as a dry fish. Soot streaks and a thousand pits gave Neptune the distinction, at least, of leprosy, which the mermaids associated with him had been consistent in catching; and his trident had been so deeply affected as to drop its prongs. Altogether, this heavy work of heavy art, smoked dry, hugely scabbed, cracked, and crumbling, was a dismal sight to the distracted eye of George Amberson Minafer, and its present condition of craziness may have added a mite to his own. His own was sufficient, with no additions, however, as he stood looking at the Johnsons' house and those houses on both sides of it—that row of riffraff dwellings he had thought so damnable, the day when he stood in his grandfather's yard, staring at them, after hearing what his Aunt Amelia said of the "talk" about his mother.

He decided that he needed no hat for the sort of call he intended to make, and went forward hurriedly. Mrs. Johnson was at home, the Irish girl who came to the door informed him, and he was left to await the lady, in a room like an elegant well—the Johnsons' "reception room": floor space, nothing to mention; walls, blue calcimined; ceiling, twelve feet from the floor; inside shutters and gray lace curtains; five gilt chairs, a brocaded sofa, soiled, and an inlaid walnut table, supporting two tall alabaster vases; a palm, with two leaves, dying in a corner.

Mrs. Johnson came in, breathing noticeably; and her round head, smoothly but economically decorated with the hair of an honest woman, seemed to be lingering far in the background of the Alpine bosom which took precedence of the rest of her everywhere; but when she was all in the room, it was to be seen that her breathing was the result of hospitable haste to greet the visitor, and her hand, not so dry as Neptune's Fountain, suggested that she had paused for only the briefest ablutions. George accepted this cold, damp lump mechanically.

"Mr. Amberson—I mean Mr. Minafer!" she exclaimed. "I'm really delighted: I understood you asked for me. Mr. Johnson's out of the city, but Charlie's downtown and I'm looking for him at any minute, now, and he'll be so pleased that you——"

"I didn't want to see Charlie," George said. "I want——"

"Do sit down," the hospitable lady urged him, seating herself upon the sofa. "Do sit down."

"No, I thank you. I wish——"

"Surely you're not going to run away again, when you've just come. Do sit down, Mr. Minafer. I hope you're all well at your house and at the dear old Major's, too. He's looking——"

"Mrs. Johnson" George said, in a strained loud voice which arrested her attention immediately, so that she was abruptly silent, leaving her surprised mouth open. She had already been concealing some astonishment at this unexampled visit, however, and the condition of George's ordinarily smooth hair (for he had overlooked more than his hat) had not alleviated her perplexity. "Mrs. Johnson," he said, "I have come to ask you a few questions which I would like you to answer, if you please."

She became grave at once. "Certainly, Mr. Minafer. Anything I can——"

He interrupted sternly, yet his voice shook in spite of its sternness. "You were talking with my Aunt Fanny about my mother this afternoon."

At this Mrs. Johnson uttered an involuntary gasp, but she recovered herself. "Then I'm sure our conversation was a very pleasant one, if we were talking of your mother, because——"

Again he interrupted. "My aunt has told me what the conversation virtually was, and I don't mean to waste any time, Mrs. Johnson. You were talking about a——" George's shoulders suddenly heaved uncontrollably; but he went fiercely on: "You were discussing a scandal that involved my mother's name."

"Mr. Minafer!"

"Isn't that the truth?"

"I don't feel called upon to answer, Mr. Minafer," she said with visible agitation. "I do not consider that you have any right——"

"My aunt told me you repeated this scandal to her."

"I don't think your aunt can have said that," Mrs. Johnson returned sharply. "I did not repeat a scandal of any kind to your aunt and I think you are mistaken in saying she told you I did. We may have discussed some matters that have been a topic of comment about town——"

"Yes!" George cried. "I think you may have! That's what I'm here about, and what I intend to——"

"Don't tell *me* what you intend, please," Mrs. Johnson interrupted crisply. "And I should prefer that you would not make your voice quite so loud in this house, which I happen to own. Your aunt may have told you—though I think it would have been very unwise in her if she did, and not very considerate of *me*—she may have told you that we discussed some such topic as I have mentioned, and possibly that would have been true. If I talked it over with her, you may be sure I spoke in the most charitable spirit, and without sharing in other people's disposition to put an evil interpretation on what *may* be nothing more than unfortunate appearances and——"

"My God!" said George. "I can't stand this!"

"You have the option of dropping the subject," Mrs. Johnson suggested tartly, and she added: "Or of leaving the house."

"I'll do that soon enough, but first I mean to know——"

"I am perfectly willing to tell you anything you wish if you will remember to ask it quietly. I'll also take the liberty of reminding you that I had a perfect right to discuss the subject with your aunt. Other people may be less considerate in not confining their discussion of it, as I have, to charitable views expressed only to a member of the family. Other people——"

"Other people!" the unhappy George repeated viciously. "That's what I want to know about—these other people!"

"I beg your pardon."

"I want to ask you about them. You say you know of other people who talk about this."

"I presume they do."

"How many?"

"What?"

"I want to know how many other people talk about it?"

"Dear, dear!" she protested. "How should I know that?"

"Haven't you heard anybody mention it?"

"I presume so."

"Well, how *many* have you heard?"

Mrs. Johnson was becoming more annoyed than apprehensive, and she showed it. "Really, this isn't a court-room," she said. "And I'm not a defendant in a libel-suit, either!"

The unfortunate young man lost what remained of his balance. "You may be!" he cried. "I intend to know just who's dared to say these things, if I have to force my way into every house in town, and I'm going to make them take every word of it back! I mean to know the name of every slanderer that's spoken of this matter to you and of every tattler you've passed it on to yourself. I mean to know——"

"You'll know *something* pretty quick!" she said, rising with difficulty; and her voice was thick with the sense of insult. "You'll know that you're out in the street. Please to leave my house!"

George stiffened sharply. Then he bowed, and strode out of the door.

Three minutes later, dishevelled and perspiring, but cold all over, he burst into his Uncle George's room at the Major's without knocking. Amberson was dressing.

"Good gracious, Georgie!" he exclaimed. "What's up?"

"I've just come from Mrs. Johnson's—across the street," George panted.

"You have your own tastes!" was Amberson's comment.

"But curious as they are, you ought to do something better with your hair, and button your waistcoat to the right buttons —even for Mrs. Johnson! What were you doing over there?"

"She told me to leave the house," George said desperately. "I went there because Aunt Fanny told me the whole town was talking about my mother and that man Morgan—that they say my mother is going to marry him and that proves she was too fond of him before my father died—she said this Mrs. Johnson was one that talked about it, and I went to her to ask who were the others."

Amberson's jaw fell in dismay. "Don't tell me you did that!" he said, in a low voice; and then, seeing that it was true, "Oh, now you *have* done it!"

Chapter XXIII

"I'VE 'DONE it'?" George cried. "What do you mean: I've done it? And what have I done?"

Amberson had collapsed into an easy chair beside his dressing-table, the white evening tie he had been about to put on dangling from his hand, which had fallen limply on the arm of the chair. The tie dropped to the floor before he replied; and the hand that had held it was lifted to stroke his graying hair reflectively. "By Jove!" he muttered. "That *is* too bad!"

George folded his arms bitterly. "Will you kindly answer my question? What have I done that wasn't honourable and right? Do you think these riffraff can go about bandying my mother's name——"

"They can now," said Amberson. "I don't know if they could before, but they certainly can now!"

"What do you mean by that?"

His uncle sighed profoundly, picked up his tie, and, preoccupied with despondency, twisted the strip of white lawn till it became unwearable. Meanwhile, he tried to enlighten his nephew. "Gossip is never fatal, Georgie," he said, "until it is denied. Gossip goes on about every human being alive and about all the dead that are alive enough to be remembered, and yet almost never does any harm until some defender makes a controversy. Gossip's a nasty thing, but it's sickly, and if people of good intentions will let it entirely alone, it will die, ninety-nine times out of a hundred."

"See here," George said: "I didn't come to listen to any generalizing dose of philosophy! I ask you——"

"You asked me what you've done, and I'm telling you." Amberson gave him a melancholy smile, continuing: "Suffer me to do it in my own way. Fanny says there's been talk about your mother, and that Mrs. Johnson does some of it. I don't know, because naturally nobody would come to me with such stuff or mention it before me; but it's presumably true—I suppose it is. I've seen Fanny with Mrs. Johnson quite a lot; and that old lady is a notorious gossip, and that's why she ordered you out of her house when you pinned her down that she'd been gossiping. I have a suspicion Mrs. Johnson has been quite a comfort to Fanny in their long talks; but she'll probably quit speaking to her over this, because Fanny told you. I suppose it's true that the 'whole town,' a lot of others, that is, do share in the gossip. In this town, naturally, anything about any Amberson has always been a stone dropped into the centre of a pond, and a lie would send the ripples as far as a truth would. I've been on a steamer when the story went all over the boat, the second day out, that the prettiest girl on board didn't have any ears; and you can take it as a rule that when a woman's past thirty-five the prettier her hair is, the more certain you are to meet somebody with reliable information that it's a wig. You can be sure that for many years there's been more gossip in this place about the Ambersons than about any other family. I dare say it isn't so much so now as it used to be, because the town got too big long ago, but it's the truth that the more prominent you are the more gossip there is about you, and the more people would like to pull you down. Well, they can't do it as long as you refuse to know what gossip there is about you. But the minute you notice it, it's got you! I'm not speaking of certain kinds of slander that sometimes people have got to take to the courts; I'm talking of the wretched buzzing the Mrs. Johnsons do—the thing you seem to have such a horror of—people 'talking'—the kind of thing that has assailed your mother. People who have repeated slander either get ashamed or forget it, if they're let alone. Challenge them, and in self-defense they believe everything they've said: they'd rather believe you a sinner than believe themselves liars, naturally. Submit to gossip and you kill it; fight it and you make it strong. People will forget almost any slander except one that's been fought."

"Is that all?" George asked.

"I suppose so," his uncle murmured sadly.

"Well, then, may I ask what you'd have done, in my place?"

"I'm not sure, Georgie. When I was your age I was like you in many ways, especially in not being very cool-headed, so I can't say. Youth can't be trusted for much, except asserting itself and fighting and making love."

"Indeed!" George snorted. "May I ask what you think I *ought* to have done?"

"Nothing."

"'Nothing?'" George echoed, mocking bitterly. "I suppose you think I mean to let my mother's good name——"

"Your mother's good name!" Amberson cut him off impatiently. "Nobody has a good name in a bad mouth. Nobody has a good name in a silly mouth, either. Well, your mother's name was in some silly mouths, and all you've done was to go and have a scene with the worst old woman gossip in the town —a scene that's going to make her into a partisan against your mother, whereas she was a mere prattler before. Don't you suppose she'll be all over town with this to-morrow? To-morrow? Why, she'll have her telephone going to-night as long as any of her friends are up! People that never heard anything about this are going to hear it all now, with embellishments. And she'll see to it that everybody who's hinted anything about poor Isabel will know that you're on the warpath; and that will put them on the defensive and make them vicious. The story will grow as it spreads and——"

George unfolded his arms to strike his right fist into his left palm. "But do you suppose I'm going to tolerate such things?" he shouted. "What do you suppose *I'll* be doing?"

"Nothing helpful."

"Oh, you think so, do you?"

"You can do absolutely nothing," said Amberson. "Nothing of any use. The more you do the more harm you'll do."

"You'll see! I'm going to stop this thing if I have to force my way into every house on National Avenue and Amberson Boulevard!"

His uncle laughed rather sourly, but made no other comment.

"Well, what do *you* propose to do?" George demanded. "Do you propose to sit there——"

"Yes."

"—and let this riffraff bandy my mother's good name back and forth among them? Is that what *you* propose to do?"

"It's all I *can* do," Amberson returned. "It's all any of us can do now: just sit still and hope that the thing may die down in time, in spite of your stirring up that awful old woman."

George drew a long breath, then advanced and stood close before his uncle. "Didn't you understand me when I told you that people are saying my mother means to marry this man?"

"Yes, I understood you."

"You say that my going over there has made matters worse,"

George went on. "How about it if such a—such an unspeakable marriage did take place? Do you think *that* would make people believe they'd been wrong in saying—you know what they say."

"No," said Amberson deliberately; "I don't believe it would. There'd be more badness in the bad mouths and more silliness in the silly mouths, I dare say. But it wouldn't hurt Isabel and Eugene, if they never heard of it; and if they did hear of it, then they could take their choice between placating gossip or living for their own happiness. If they have decided to marry——"

George almost staggered. "Good God!" he gasped. "You speak of it calmly!"

Amberson looked up at him inquiringly. "Why shouldn't they marry if they want to?" he asked. "It's their own affair."

"Why shouldn't they?" George echoed. "Why shouldn't they?"

"Yes. Why shouldn't they? I don't see anything precisely monstrous about two people getting married when they're both free and care about each other. What's the matter with their marrying?"

"It *would* be monstrous!" George shouted. "Monstrous even if *this* horrible thing hadn't happened, but *now* in the face of *this*—oh, that you can sit there and even speak of it! Your own sister! O God! Oh——" He became incoherent, swinging away from Amberson and making for the door, wildly gesturing.

"For heaven's sake, don't be so theatrical!" said his uncle, and then, seeing that George was leaving the room: "Come back here. You mustn't speak to your mother of this!"

"Don't 'tend to," George said indistinctly; and he plunged out into the big dimly lit hall. He passed his grandfather's room on the way to the stairs; and the Major was visible within, his white head brightly illumined by a lamp, as he bent low over a ledger upon his roll-top desk. He did not look up, and his grandson strode by the door, not really conscious of the old figure stooping at its tremulous work with long additions and subtractions that refused to balance as they used to. George went home and got a hat and overcoat without seeing either his mother or Fanny. Then he left word that he would be out for dinner, and hurried away from the house.

He walked the dark streets of Amberson Addition for an

hour, then went downtown and got coffee at a restaurant. After that he walked through the lighted parts of the town until ten o'clock, when he turned north and came back to the purlieus of the Addition. He strode through the length and breadth of it again, his hat pulled down over his forehead, his overcoat collar turned up behind. He walked fiercely, though his feet ached, but by and by he turned homeward, and, when he reached the Major's, went in and sat upon the steps of the huge stone veranda in front—an obscure figure in that lonely and repellent place. All lights were out at the Major's, and finally, after twelve, he saw his mother's window darken at home.

He waited half an hour longer, then crossed the front yards of the new houses and let himself noiselessly in the front door. The light in the hall had been left burning, and another in his own room, as he discovered when he got there. He locked the door quickly and without noise, but his fingers were still upon the key when there was a quick footfall in the hall outside.

"Georgie, dear?"

He went to the other end of the room before replying.

"Yes?"

"I'd been wondering where you were, dear."

"Had you?"

There was a pause; then she said timidly: "Wherever it was, I hope you had a pleasant evening."

After a silence, "Thank you," he said, without expression.

Another silence followed before she spoke again.

"You wouldn't care to be kissed good-night, I suppose?" And with a little flurry of placative laughter, she added: "At your age, of course!"

"I'm going to bed, now," he said. "Good-night."

Another silence seemed blanker than those which had preceded it, and finally her voice came—it was blank, too.

"Good-night."

. . . After he was in bed his thoughts became more tumultuous than ever; while among all the inchoate and fragmentary sketches of this dreadful day, now rising before him, the clearest was of his uncle collapsed in a big chair with a white tie dangling from his hand; and one conviction, following upon that picture, became definite in George's mind: that his Uncle

George Amberson was a hopeless dreamer from whom no help need be expected, an amiable imbecile lacking in normal impulses, and wholly useless in a struggle which required honour to be defended by a man of action.

Then would return a vision of Mrs. Johnson's furious round head, set behind her great bosom like the sun far sunk on the horizon of a mountain plateau—and her crackling, asthmatic voice . . . "Without sharing in other people's disposition to put an evil interpretation on what *may* be nothing more than unfortunate appearances." . . . "Other people may be less considerate in not confining their discussion of it, as I have, to charitable views." . . . "You'll know *something* pretty quick! You'll know you're out in the street." . . . And then George would get up again—and again—and pace the floor in his bare feet.

That was what the tormented young man was doing when daylight came gauntly in at his window—pacing the floor, rubbing his head in his hands, and muttering:

"It can't be true: this can't be happening to *me*!"

Chapter XXIV

BREAKFAST WAS brought to him in his room, as usual; but he did not make his normal healthy raid upon the dainty tray: the food remained untouched, and he sustained himself upon coffee—four cups of it, which left nothing of value inside the glistening little percolator. During this process he heard his mother being summoned to the telephone in the hall, not far from his door, and then her voice responding: "Yes? Oh, it's you! . . . Indeed I should! . . . Of course. . . . Then I'll expect you about three. . . . Yes. . . . Good-bye till then." A few minutes later he heard her speaking to someone beneath his window and, looking out, saw her directing the removal of plants from a small garden bed to the Major's conservatory for the winter. There was an air of briskness about her; as she turned away to go into the house, she laughed gaily with the Major's gardener over something he said, and this unconcerned cheerfulness of her was terrible to her son.

He went to his desk, and, searching the jumbled contents of a drawer, brought forth a large, unframed photograph of his father, upon which he gazed long and piteously, till at last hot tears stood in his eyes. It was strange how the inconsequent face of Wilbur seemed to increase in high significance during this belated interview between father and son; and how it seemed to take on a reproachful nobility—and yet, under the circumstances, nothing could have been more natural than that George, having paid but the slightest attention to his father in life, should begin to deify him, now that he was dead. "Poor, poor father!" the son whispered brokenly. "Poor man, I'm glad you didn't know!"

He wrapped the picture in a sheet of newspaper, put it under his arm, and, leaving the house hurriedly and stealthily, went downtown to the shop of a silversmith, where he spent sixty dollars on a resplendently festooned silver frame for the picture. Having lunched upon more coffee, he returned to the house at two o'clock, carrying the framed photograph with him, and placed it upon the centre-table in the library, the room most used by Isabel and Fanny and himself. Then he went to a front window of the long "reception room," and sat looking out through the lace curtains.

The house was quiet, though once or twice he heard his mother and Fanny moving about upstairs, and a ripple of song in the voice of Isabel—a fragment from the romantic ballad of Lord Bateman.

"Lord Bateman was a noble lord,
A noble lord of high degree;
And he sailed West and he sailed East,
Far countries for to see. . . ."

The words became indistinct; the air was hummed absently; the humming shifted to a whistle, then drifted out of hearing, and the place was still again.

George looked often at his watch, but his vigil did not last an hour. At ten minutes of three, peering through the curtain, he saw an automobile stop in front of the house and Eugene Morgan jump lightly down from it. The car was of a new pattern, low and long, with an ample seat in the tonneau, facing forward; and a professional driver sat at the wheel, a strange figure in leather, goggled out of all personality and seemingly part of the mechanism.

Eugene himself, as he came up the cement path to the house, was a figure of the new era which was in time to be so disastrous to stiff hats and skirted coats; and his appearance afforded a debonair contrast to that of the queer-looking duck capering at the Amberson Ball in an old dress coat, and next day chugging up National Avenue through the snow in his nightmare of a sewing-machine. Eugene, this afternoon, was richly in the new outdoor mode: his motoring coat was soft gray fur; his cap and gloves were of gray suede; and though Lucy's hand may have shown itself in the selection of these high garnitures, he wore them easily, even with a becoming hint of jauntiness. Some change might be seen in his face, too, for a successful man is seldom to be mistaken, especially if his temper be genial. Eugene had begun to look like a millionaire.

But above everything else, what was most evident about him, as he came up the path, was his confidence in the happiness promised by his present errand; the anticipation in his eyes could have been read by a stranger. His look at the door of

Isabel's house was the look of a man who is quite certain that the next moment will reveal something ineffably charming, inexpressibly dear.

. . . When the bell rang, George waited at the entrance of the "reception room" until a housemaid came through the hall on her way to answer the summons.

"You needn't mind, Mary," he told her. "I'll see who it is and what they want. Probably it's only a pedlar."

"Thank you, sir, Mister George," said Mary; and returned to the rear of the house.

George went slowly to the front door, and halted, regarding the misty silhouette of the caller upon the ornamental frosted glass. After a minute of waiting, this silhouette changed outline so that an arm could be distinguished—an arm outstretched toward the bell, as if the gentleman outside doubted whether or not it had sounded, and were minded to try again. But before the gesture was completed George abruptly threw open the door, and stepped squarely upon the middle of the threshold.

A slight change shadowed the face of Eugene; his look of happy anticipation gave way to something formal and polite. "How do you do, George," he said. "Mrs. Minafer expects to go driving with me, I believe—if you'll be so kind as to send her word that I'm here."

George made not the slightest movement.

"No," he said.

Eugene was incredulous, even when his second glance revealed how hot of eye was the haggard young man before him. "I beg your pardon. I said——"

"I heard you," said George. "You said you had an engagement with my mother, and I told you, No!"

Eugene gave him a steady look, and then he asked quietly: "What is the—the difficulty?"

George kept his own voice quiet enough, but that did not mitigate the vibrant fury of it. "My mother will have no interest in knowing that you came for her to-day," he said. "Or any other day!"

Eugene continued to look at him with a scrutiny in which began to gleam a profound anger, none the less powerful because it was so quiet. "I am afraid I do not understand you."

"I doubt if I could make it much plainer," George said, raising his voice slightly, "but I'll try. You're not wanted in this house, Mr. Morgan, now or at any other time. Perhaps you'll understand—this!"

And with the last word he closed the door in Eugene's face.

Then, not moving away, he stood just inside the door, and noted that the misty silhouette remained upon the frosted glass for several moments, as if the forbidden gentleman debated in his mind what course to pursue. "Let him ring again!" George thought grimly. "Or try the side door—or the kitchen!"

But Eugene made no further attempt; the silhouette disappeared; footsteps could be heard withdrawing across the floor of the veranda; and George, returning to the window in the "reception room," was rewarded by the sight of an automobile manufacturer in baffled retreat, with all his wooing furs and fineries mocking him. Eugene got into his car slowly, not looking back at the house which had just taught him such a lesson; and it was easily visible—even from a window seventy feet distant—that he was not the same light suitor who had jumped so gallantly from the car only a few minutes earlier. Observing the heaviness of his movements as he climbed into the tonneau, George indulged in a sickish throat rumble which bore a distant cousinship to mirth.

The car was quicker than its owner; it shot away as soon as he had sunk into his seat; and George, having watched its impetuous disappearance from his field of vision, ceased to haunt the window. He went to the library, and, seating himself beside the table whereon he had placed the photograph of his father, picked up a book, and pretended to be engaged in reading it.

Presently Isabel's buoyant step was heard descending the stairs, and her low, sweet whistling, renewing the air of "Lord Bateman." She came into the library, still whistling thoughtfully, a fur coat over her arm, ready to put on, and two veils round her small black hat, her right hand engaged in buttoning the glove upon her left; and, as the large room contained too many pieces of heavy furniture, and the inside shutters excluded most of the light of day, she did not at once perceive George's presence. Instead, she went to the bay window at the end of the room, which afforded a view of the street, and glanced out expectantly; then bent her attention upon her glove; after that, looked out toward the street again, ceased to whistle, and turned toward the interior of the room.

"Why, Georgie!"

She came, leaned over from behind him, and there was a faint, exquisite odour as from distant apple-blossoms as she kissed his cheek. "Dear, I waited lunch almost an hour for you, but you didn't come! Did you lunch out somewhere?"

"Yes." He did not look up from the book.

"Did you have plenty to eat?"

"Yes."

"Are you sure? Wouldn't you like to have Maggie get you something now in the dining room? Or they could bring it to you here, if you think it would be cosier. Shan't I——"

"No."

A tinkling bell was audible, and she moved to the doorway into the hall. "I'm going out driving, dear. I'm——" She interrupted herself to address the house-maid, who was passing through the hall: "I think it's Mr. Morgan, Mary. Tell him I'll be there at once."

"Yes, ma'am."

Mary returned. "'Twas a pedlar, ma'am."

"Another one?" Isabel said, surprised. "I thought you said it was a pedlar when the bell rang a little while ago."

"Mister George said it was, ma'am; he went to the door," Mary informed her, disappearing.

"There seem to be a great many of them," Isabel mused. "What did yours want to sell, George?"

"He didn't say."

"You must have cut him off short!" she laughed; and then, still standing in the doorway, she noticed the big silver frame upon the table beside him. "Gracious, Georgie!" she exclaimed. "You *have* been investing!" and as she came across the room for a closer view, "Is it—is it Lucy?" she asked half timidly, half archly. But the next instant she saw whose likeness was thus set forth in elegiac splendour—and she was silent, except for a long, just-audible "*Oh!*"

He neither looked up nor moved.

"That was nice of you, Georgie," she said, in a low voice

presently. "I ought to have had it framed, myself, when I gave it to you."

He said nothing, and, standing beside him, she put her hand gently upon his shoulder, then as gently withdrew it, and went out of the room. But she did not go upstairs; he heard the faint rustle of her dress in the hall, and then the sound of her footsteps in the "reception room." After a time, silence succeeded even these slight tokens of her presence; whereupon George rose and went warily into the hall, taking care to make no noise, and he obtained an oblique view of her through the open double doors of the "reception room." She was sitting in the chair which he had occupied so long; and she was looking out of the window expectantly—a little troubled.

He went back to the library, waited an interminable half hour, then returned noiselessly to the same position in the hall, where he could see her. She was still sitting patiently by the window.

Waiting for that man, was she? Well, it might be quite a long wait! And the grim George silently ascended the stairs to his own room, and began to pace his suffering floor.

Chapter XXV

HE LEFT his door open, however, and when he heard the front door-bell ring, by and by, he went half way down the stairs and stood to listen. He was not much afraid that Morgan would return, but he wished to make sure.

Mary appeared in the hall below him, but, after a glance toward the front of the house, turned back, and withdrew. Evidently Isabel had gone to the door. Then a murmur was heard, and George Amberson's voice, quick and serious: "I want to talk to you, Isabel" . . . and another murmur; then Isabel and her brother passed the foot of the broad, dark stairway, but did not look up, and remained unconscious of the watchful presence above them. Isabel still carried her cloak upon her arm, but Amberson had taken her hand, and retained it; and as he led her silently into the library there was something about her attitude, and the pose of her slightly bent head, that was both startled and meek. Thus they quickly disappeared from George's sight, hand in hand; and Amberson at once closed the massive double doors of the library.

For a time all that George could hear was the indistinct sound of his uncle's voice: what he was saying could not be surmised, though the troubled brotherliness of his tone was evident. He seemed to be explaining something at considerable length, and there were moments when he paused, and George guessed that his mother was speaking, but her voice must have been very low, for it was entirely inaudible to him.

Suddenly he did hear her. Through the heavy doors her outcry came, clear and loud:

"Oh, *no!*"

It was a cry of protest, as if something her brother told her must be untrue, or, if it were true, the fact he stated must be undone; and it was a sound of sheer pain.

Another sound of pain, close to George, followed it; this was a vehement sniffling which broke out just above him, and, looking up, he saw Fanny Minafer on the landing, leaning over the banisters and applying her handkerchief to her eyes and nose.

"I can guess what *that* was about," she whispered huskily. "He's just told her what you did to Eugene!"

George gave her a dark look over his shoulder. "You go on back to your room!" he said; and he began to descend the stairs; but Fanny, guessing his purpose, rushed down and caught his arm, detaining him.

"You're not going in *there*?" she whispered huskily. "You don't——"

"Let go of me!"

But she clung to him savagely. "No, you don't, Georgie Minafer! You'll keep away from there! You will!"

"You let go of——"

"I won't! You come back here! You'll come upstairs and let them alone; that's what you'll do!" And with such passionate determination did she clutch and tug, never losing a grip of him somewhere, though George tried as much as he could, without hurting her, to wrench away—with such utter forgetfulness of her maiden dignity did she assault him, that she forced him, stumbling upward, to the landing.

"Of all the ridiculous——" he began furiously; but she spared one hand from its grasp of his sleeve and clapped it over his mouth.

"Hush up!" Never for an instant in this grotesque struggle did Fanny raise her voice above a husky whisper. "Hush up! It's indecent—like squabbling outside the door of an operating-room! Go on to the top of the stairs—go on!"

And when George had most unwillingly obeyed, she planted herself in his way, on the top step. "There!" she said. "The idea of your going in there now! I never heard of such a thing!" And with the sudden departure of the nervous vigour she had shown so amazingly, she began to cry again. "I was an *awful* fool! I thought you knew what was going on or I never, never would have done it. Do you suppose I *dreamed* you'd go making everything into such a tragedy? Do you?"

"I don't care what you dreamed," George muttered.

But Fanny went on, always taking care to keep her voice from getting too loud, in spite of her most grievous agitation. "Do you dream I thought you'd go making such a fool of yourself at Mrs. Johnson's? Oh, I saw her this morning! She wouldn't talk to me, but I met George Amberson on my way back, and he told me what you'd done over there! And do you dream I thought you'd do what you've done here this afternoon to Eugene? Oh, I knew that, too! I was looking out of the front bedroom window, and I saw him drive up, and then go away again, and I knew you'd been to the door. Of course he went to George Amberson about it, and that's why George is here. He's got to tell Isabel the whole thing now, and you wanted to go in there interfering—God knows what! You stay here and let her brother tell her; he's got some consideration for her!"

"I suppose you think I haven't!" George said, challenging her, and at that Fanny laughed witheringly.

"You! Considerate of anybody!"

"I'm considerate of her good name!" he said hotly. "It seems to me that's about the first thing to be considerate of, in being considerate of a person! And look here: it strikes me you're taking a pretty different tack from what you did yesterday afternoon!"

Fanny wrung her hands. "I did a terrible thing!" she lamented. "Now that it's done and too late, I know what it *was*! I didn't have sense enough just to let things go on. I didn't have any business to interfere, and I didn't *mean* to interfere —I only wanted to talk, and let out a little! I did think you already knew everything I told you. I did! And I'd rather have cut my hand off than stir you up to doing what you *have* done! I was just suffering so that I wanted to let out a little—I didn't mean any real harm. But now I *see* what's happened—oh, I was a fool! I hadn't any business interfering. Eugene never would have looked at me, anyhow, and, oh, why couldn't I have seen that before! He never came here a single time in his life except on her account, never! and I might have let them alone, because he wouldn't have looked at me even if he'd never seen Isabel. And they haven't done any harm: she made Wilbur happy, and she was a true wife to him as long as he lived. It wasn't a crime for her to care for Eugene all the time; she certainly never *told* him she did—and she gave me every chance in the world! She left us alone together every time she could—even since Wilbur died—but what was the use? And here I go, not doing myself a bit of good by it, and just"—Fanny wrung her hands again—"just ruining them!"

"I suppose you mean I'm doing that," George said bitterly.

"Yes, I do!" she sobbed, and drooped upon the stairway railing, exhausted.

"On the contrary, I mean to save my mother from a calamity."

Fanny looked at him wanly, in a tired despair; then she stepped by him and went slowly to her own door, where she paused and beckoned to him.

"What do you want?"

"Just come here a minute."

"What for?" he asked impatiently.

"I just wanted to say something to you."

"Well, for heaven's sake, say it! There's nobody to hear." Nevertheless, after a moment, as she beckoned him again, he went to her, profoundly annoyed. "Well, what is it?"

"George," she said in a low voice, "I think you ought to be told something. If I were you, I'd let my mother alone."

"Oh, my Lord!" he groaned. "I'm doing these things *for* her, not against her!"

A mildness had come upon Fanny, and she had controlled her weeping. She shook her head gently. "No, I'd let her alone if I were you. I don't think she's very well, George."

"She! I never saw a healthier person in my life."

"No. She doesn't let anybody know, but she goes to the doctor regularly."

"Women are always going to doctors regularly."

"No. He told her to."

George was not impressed. "It's nothing at all; she spoke of it to me years ago—some kind of family failing. She said grandfather had it, too; and look at him! Hasn't proved very serious with him! You act as if I'd done something wrong in sending that man about his business, and as if I were going to persecute my mother, instead of protecting her. By Jove, it's sickening! *You* told me how all the riffraff in town were busy with her name, and then the minute I lift my hand to protect her, you begin to attack me and——"

"*Sh!*" Fanny checked him, laying her hand on his arm. "Your uncle is going."

The library doors were heard opening, and a moment later there came the sound of the front door closing.

George moved toward the head of the stairs, then stood listening; but the house was silent.

Fanny made a slight noise with her lips to attract his attention, and, when he glanced toward her, shook her head at him urgently. "Let her alone," she whispered. "She's down there by herself. Don't go down. Let her alone."

She moved a few steps toward him and halted, her face pallid and awestruck, and then both stood listening for anything that might break the silence downstairs. No sound came to them; that poignant silence was continued throughout long, long minutes, while the two listeners stood there under its mysterious spell; and in its plaintive eloquence—speaking, as it did, of the figure alone in the big, dark library, where dead Wilbur's new silver frame gleamed in the dimness—there was something that checked even George.

Above the aunt and nephew, as they kept this strange vigil, there was a triple window of stained glass, to illumine the landing and upper reaches of the stairway. Figures in blue and amber garments posed gracefully in panels, conceived by some craftsman of the Eighties to represent Love and Purity and Beauty, and these figures, leaded to unalterable attitudes, were little more motionless than the two human beings upon whom fell the mottled faint light of the window. The colours were growing dull; evening was coming on.

Fanny Minafer broke the long silence with a sound from her throat, a stifled gasp; and with that great companion of hers, her handkerchief, retired softly to the loneliness of her own chamber. After she had gone George looked about him bleakly, then on tiptoe crossed the hall and went into his own room, which was filled with twilight. Still tiptoeing, though he could not have said why, he went across the room and sat down heavily in a chair facing the window. Outside there was nothing but the darkening air and the wall of the nearest of the new houses. He had not slept at all, the night before, and he had eaten nothing since the preceding day at lunch, but he felt neither drowsiness nor hunger. His set determination filled him, kept him but too wide awake, and his gaze at the grayness beyond the window was wide-eyed and bitter.

Darkness had closed in when there was a step in the room

behind him. Then someone knelt beside the chair, two arms went round him with infinite compassion, a gentle head rested against his shoulder, and there came the faint scent as of apple-blossoms far away.

"You mustn't be troubled, darling," his mother whispered.

Chapter XXVI

George choked. For an instant he was on the point of breaking down, but he commanded himself, bravely dismissing the self-pity roused by her compassion. "How can I help but be?" he said.

"No, no." She soothed him. "You mustn't. You mustn't be troubled, no matter what happens."

"That's easy enough to say!" he protested; and he moved as if to rise.

"Just let's stay like this a little while, dear. Just a minute or two. I want to tell you: brother George has been here, and he told me everything about—about how unhappy you'd been—and how you went so gallantly to that old woman with the opera-glasses." Isabel gave a sad little laugh. "What a terrible old woman she is! What a really terrible thing a vulgar old woman can be!"

"Mother, I——" And again he moved to rise.

"Must you? It seemed to me such a comfortable way to talk. Well——" She yielded; he rose, helped her to her feet, and pressed the light into being.

As the room took life from the sudden lines of fire within the bulbs Isabel made a deprecatory gesture, and, with a faint laugh of apologetic protest, turned quickly away from George. What she meant was: "You mustn't see my face until I've made it nicer for you." Then she turned again to him, her eyes downcast, but no sign of tears in them, and she contrived to show him that there was the semblance of a smile upon her lips. She still wore her hat, and in her unsteady fingers she held a white envelope, somewhat crumpled.

"Now, mother——"

"Wait, dearest," she said; and though he stood stone cold, she lifted her arms, put them round him again, and pressed her cheek lightly to his. "Oh, you do look so troubled, poor dear! One thing you couldn't doubt, beloved boy: you know I could never care for anything in the world as I care for you—never, never!"

"Now, mother——"

She released him, and stepped back. "Just a moment more, dearest. I want you to read this first. We can get at things better." She pressed into his hand the envelope she had brought with her, and as he opened it, and began to read the long enclosure, she walked slowly to the other end of the room; then stood there, with her back to him, and her head drooping a little, until he had finished.

The sheets of paper were covered with Eugene's handwriting.

George Amberson will bring you this, dear Isabel. He is waiting while I write. He and I have talked things over, and before he gives this to you he will tell you what has happened. Of course I'm rather confused, and haven't had time to think matters out very definitely, and yet I believe I should have been better prepared for what took place to-day—I ought to have known it was coming, because I have understood for quite a long time that young George was getting to dislike me more and more. Somehow, I've never been able to get his friendship; he's always had a latent distrust of me—or something like distrust—and perhaps that's made me sometimes a little awkward and diffident with him. I think it may be he felt from the first that I cared a great deal about you, and he naturally resented it. I think perhaps he felt this even during all the time when I was so careful—at least I thought I was—not to show, even to you, how immensely I did care. And he may have feared that you were thinking too much about me—even when you weren't and only liked me as an old friend. It's perfectly comprehensible to me, also, that at his age one gets excited about gossip. Dear Isabel, what I'm trying to get at, in my confused way, is that you and I don't care about this nonsensical gossip, ourselves, at all. Yesterday I thought the time had come when I could ask you to marry me, and you were dear enough to tell me "some time it might come to that." Well, you and I, left to ourselves, and knowing what we have been and what we are, we'd pay as much attention to "talk" as we would to any other kind of old cats' mewing! We'd not be very apt to let such things keep us from the plenty of life we have left to us for making up to ourselves for old unhappinesses and mistakes. But now we're faced with—not the slander and not our own fear of it, because we haven't any, but someone else's fear of it—your son's. And, oh, dearest woman in the world, I know what your son is to you, and it frightens me! Let me explain a little: I don't think he'll change—at twenty-one or twenty-two so many things appear solid and permanent and terrible which forty sees are nothing but disappearing miasma.

Forty can't *tell* twenty about this; that's the pity of it! Twenty can find out only by getting to be forty. And so we come to this, dear: Will you live your own life your way, or George's way? I'm going a little further, because it would be fatal not to be wholly frank now. George will act toward you only as your long worship of him, your sacrifices—all the unseen little ones every day since he was born—will make him act. Dear, it breaks my heart for you, but what you have to oppose now is the history of your own selfless and perfect motherhood. I remember saying once that what you worshipped in your son was the angel you saw in him—and I still believe that is true of every mother. But in a mother's worship she may not see that the Will in her son should not always be offered incense along with the angel. I grow sick with fear for you—for both you and me—when I think how the Will against us two has grown strong through the love you have given the angel—and how long your own sweet Will has served that other. Are you strong enough, Isabel? Can you make the fight? I promise you that if you will take heart for it, you will find so quickly that it has all amounted to nothing. You shall have happiness, and, in a little while, *only* happiness. You need only to write me a line—I can't come to your house—and tell me where you will meet me. We will come back in a month, and the angel in your son will bring him to you; I promise it. What is good in him will grow so fine, once you have beaten the turbulent Will—but it must be beaten!

Your brother, that good friend, is waiting with such patience; I should not keep him longer—and I am saying too much for wisdom, I fear. But, oh, my dear, won't you be strong—such a little short strength it would need! Don't strike my life down twice, dear—this time I've not deserved it.

EUGENE.

Concluding this missive, George tossed it abruptly from him so that one sheet fell upon his bed and the others upon the floor; and at the faint noise of their falling Isabel came, and, kneeling, began to gather them up.

"Did you read it, dear?"

George's face was pale no longer, but pink with fury. "Yes, I did."

"All of it?" she asked gently, as she rose.

"Certainly!"

She did not look at him, but kept her eyes downcast upon the letter in her hands, tremulously rearranging the sheets in order as she spoke—and though she smiled, her smile was as tremulous as her hands. Nervousness and an irresistible timidity possessed her. "I—I wanted to say, George," she faltered. "I felt that if—if some day it *should* happen—I mean, if you came to feel differently about it, and Eugene and I—that is if we found that it seemed the most sensible thing to do—I was afraid you might think it would be a little queer about—Lucy. I mean if—if she were your step-sister. Of course, she'd not be even legally related to you, and if you—if you cared for her——"

Thus far she got stumblingly with what she wanted to say, while George watched her with a gaze that grew harder and hotter; but here he cut her off. "I have already given up all idea of Lucy," he said. "Naturally, I couldn't have treated her father as I deliberately did treat him—I could hardly have done that and expected his daughter ever to speak to me again."

Isabel gave a quick cry of compassion, but he allowed her no opportunity to speak. "You needn't think I'm making any particular sacrifice," he said sharply, "though I would, quickly enough, if I thought it necessary in a matter of honour like this. I *was* interested in her, and I could even say I did care for her; but she proved pretty satisfactorily that she cared little enough about me! She went away right in the midst of a—of a difference of opinion we were having; she didn't even let me know she was going, and never wrote a line to me, and then came back telling everybody she'd had 'a perfectly gorgeous time!' That's quite enough for me. I'm not precisely the sort to arrange for that kind of thing to be done to me more than once! The truth is, we're not congenial and we'd found that much out, at least, before she left. We should never have been happy; she was 'superior' all the time, and critical of me—not very pleasant, that! I was disappointed in her, and I might as well say it. I don't think she has the very deepest nature in the world, and——"

But Isabel put her hand timidly on his arm. "Georgie, dear, this is only a quarrel: all young people have them before they get adjusted, and you mustn't let——"

"If you please!" he said emphatically, moving back from her. "This isn't that kind. It's all over, and I don't care to speak of it again. It's settled. Don't you understand?"

"But, dear——"

"No. I want to talk to you about this letter of her father's."

"Yes, dear, that's why——"

"It's simply the most offensive piece of writing that I've ever held in my hands!"

She stepped back from him, startled. "But, dear, I thought ——"

"I can't understand your even showing me such a thing!" he cried. "How *did* you happen to bring it to me?"

"Your uncle thought I'd better. He thought it was the simplest thing to do, and he said that he'd suggested it to Eugene, and Eugene had agreed. They thought——"

"Yes!" George said bitterly. "I should like to hear what they thought!"

"They thought it would be the most straightforward thing."

George drew a long breath. "Well, what do *you* think, mother?"

"I thought it would be the simplest and most straightforward thing; I thought they were right."

"Very well! We'll agree it was simple and straightforward. Now, what do you think of that letter itself?"

She hesitated, looking away. "I—of course I don't agree with him in the way he speaks of you, dear—except about the angel! I don't agree with some of the things he implies. You've always been unselfish—nobody knows that better than your mother. When Fanny was left with nothing, you were so quick and generous to give up what really should have come to you, and——"

"And yet," George broke in, "you see what he implies about me. Don't you think, really, that this was a pretty insulting letter for that man to be asking you to hand your son?"

"Oh, no!" she cried. "You can see how fair he means to be, and he didn't ask for me to give it to you. It was brother George who——"

"Never mind that, now! You say he tries to be fair, and yet do you suppose it ever occurs to him that I'm doing my simple duty? That I'm doing what my *father* would do if he were alive? That I'm doing what my father would ask me to do if he could speak from his grave out yonder? Do you suppose it ever occurs to that man for one minute that I'm *protecting* my mother?" George raised his voice, advancing upon the helpless lady fiercely; and she could only bend her head before him. "He talks about my 'Will'—how it must be beaten down; yes, and he asks my *mother* to do that little thing to please him! What for? *Why* does he want me 'beaten' by my mother? Because I'm trying to protect her name! He's got my mother's name bandied up and down the streets of this town till I can't *step* in those streets without wondering what every soul I meet is thinking of me and of my family, and now he wants you to marry him so that every gossip in town will say 'There! What did I tell you? I guess *that* proves it's true!' You can't get away from it; that's exactly what they'd say, and this man pretends he cares for you, and yet asks you to marry him and give them the *right* to say it. He says he and you don't care what they say, but I know better! He may not care—probably he's that kind—but you do. There never was an Amberson yet that would let the Amberson name go trailing in the dust like that! It's the proudest name in this town and it's going to stay the proudest; and I tell you that's the deepest thing in my nature—not that I'd expect Eugene Morgan to understand—the very deepest thing in my nature is to protect that name, and to fight for it to the last breath when danger threatens it, as it does now—through my mother!" He turned from her, striding up and down and tossing his arms about, in a tumult of gesture. "I can't believe it of you, that you'd *think* of such a sacrilege! That's what it would be—sacrilege! When he talks about your unselfishness toward me, he's right—you have been unselfish and you have been a perfect mother. But what about him? Is it unselfish of him to want you to throw away your good name just to please him? That's all he asks of you—and to quit being my mother! Do you think I can believe you *really* care for him? I don't! You are my mother and you're an Amberson—and I believe you're too proud! You're too proud to care for a man who could write such a letter as that!" He stopped, faced her, and spoke with more self-control: "Well, what are you going to do about it, mother?"

George was right about his mother's being proud. And even when she laughed with a negro gardener, or even those few times in her life when people saw her weep, Isabel had a proud look—something that was independent and graceful and strong. But she did not have it now: she leaned against the wall, beside his dressing-table, and seemed beset with humility and with weakness. Her head drooped.

"What answer are you going to make to such a letter?" George demanded, like a judge on the bench.

"I—I don't quite know, dear," she murmured.

"You don't?" he cried. "You——"

"Wait," she begged him. "I'm so—confused."

"I want to know what you're going to write him. Do you think if you did what he wants you to I could bear to stay another day in this town, mother? Do you think I could ever bear even to see you again if you married him? I'd want to, but you surely know I just—couldn't!"

She made a futile gesture, and seemed to breathe with difficulty. "I—I wasn't—quite sure," she faltered, "about—about it's being wise for us to be married—even before knowing how you feel about it. I wasn't even sure it was quite fair to—to Eugene. I have—I seem to have that family trouble—like father's—that I spoke to you about once." She managed a deprecatory little dry laugh. "Not that it amounts to much, but I wasn't at all sure that it would be fair to him. Marrying doesn't mean so much, after all—not at my age. It's enough to know that—that people think of you—and to see them. I thought we were all—oh, pretty happy the way things were, and I don't think it would mean giving up a great deal for him or me, either, if we just went on as we have been. I—I see him almost every day, and——"

"Mother!" George's voice was loud and stern. "Do you think you could go on seeing him after *this*!"

She had been talking helplessly enough before; her tone was little more broken now. "Not—not even—see him?"

"How could you?" George cried. "Mother, it seems to me that if he ever set foot in this house again—oh! I can't speak of it! *Could* you see him, knowing what talk it makes every time he turns into this street, and knowing what that means to me! Oh, I *don't* understand all this—I don't! If you'd told me, a year ago, that such things were going to happen, I'd have thought you were insane—and now I believe *I* am!"

Then, after a preliminary gesture of despair, as though he meant harm to the ceiling, he flung himself heavily, face downward, upon the bed. His anguish was none the less real for its vehemence; and the stricken lady came to him instantly and bent over him, once more enfolding him in her arms. She said nothing, but suddenly her tears fell upon his head; she saw them, and seemed to be startled.

"Oh, this won't do!" she said. "I've never let you see me cry before, except when your father died. I mustn't!"

And she ran from the room.

. . . A little while after she had gone, George rose and began solemnly to dress for dinner. At one stage of these conscientious proceedings he put on, temporarily, his long black velvet dressing-gown, and, happening to catch sight in his pier glass of the picturesque and mediæval figure thus presented, he paused to regard it; and something profoundly theatrical in his nature came to the surface.

His lips moved; he whispered, half-aloud, some famous fragments:

> "'Tis not alone my inky cloak, good mother,
> Nor customary suits of solemn black . . ."

For, in truth, the mirrored princely image, with hair dishevelled on the white brow, and the long tragic fall of black velvet from the shoulders, had brought about (in his thought, at least) some comparisons of his own times, so out of joint, with those of that other gentle prince and heir whose widowed mother was minded to marry again.

> "But I have that within which passeth show;
> These but the trappings and the suits of Woe."

Not less like Hamlet did he feel and look as he sat gauntly at the dinner table with Fanny to partake of a meal throughout which neither spoke. Isabel had sent word "not to wait" for her, an injunction it was as well they obeyed, for she did not come at all. But with the renewal of sustenance furnished to his system, some relaxation must have occurred within the high-strung George. Dinner was not quite finished when, without warning, sleep hit him hard. His burning eyes could no longer restrain the lids above them; his head sagged beyond control; and he got to his feet, and went lurching upstairs, yawning with exhaustion. From the door of his room, which he closed mechanically, with his eyes shut, he went blindly to his bed, fell upon it soddenly, and slept—with his face full upturned to the light.

. . . It was after midnight when he woke, and the room was dark. He had not dreamed, but he woke with the sense that somebody or something had been with him while he slept —somebody or something infinitely compassionate; somebody or something infinitely protective, that would let him come to no harm and to no grief.

He got up, and pressed the light on. Pinned to the cover of his dressing-table was a square envelope, with the words, "For you, dear," written in pencil upon it. But the message inside was in ink, a little smudged here and there.

I have been out to the mail-box, darling, with a letter I've written to Eugene, and he'll have it in the morning. It would be unfair not to let him know at once, and my decision could not change if I waited. It would always be the same. I think it is a little better for me to write to you, like this, instead of waiting till you wake up and then telling you, because I'm foolish and might cry again, and I took a vow once, long ago, that you should never see me cry. Not that I'll feel like crying when we talk things over to-morrow. I'll be "all right and fine" (as you say so often) by that time—don't fear. I think what makes me most ready to cry now is the thought of the terrible suffering in your poor face, and the unhappy knowledge that it is I, your mother, who put it there. It shall never come again! I love you better than anything and everything else on earth. God gave you to me—and oh! how thankful I have been every day of my life for that sacred gift—and nothing can ever come between me and God's gift. I cannot hurt you, and I cannot let you stay hurt as you have been—not another instant after you wake up, my darling boy! It is beyond my power. And Eugene was right—I know you couldn't change about this. Your suffering shows how deep-seated the feeling is within you. So I've written him just about what I think you would like me to—though I told him I would always be fond of him and always his best friend, and I hoped his dearest friend. He'll understand about not seeing him. He'll understand that, though I didn't say it in so many words. You mustn't trouble about that—he'll understand. Good-night, my darling, my beloved, my beloved! You mustn't be troubled. I think I shouldn't mind anything very much so long as I have you "all to myself"—as people say—to make up for your long years away from me at college. We'll talk of what's best to do in the morning, shan't we? And for all this pain you'll forgive your loving and devoted mother.

ISABEL.

Chapter XXVII

Having finished some errands downtown, the next afternoon, George Amberson Minafer was walking up National Avenue on his homeward way when he saw in the distance, coming toward him, upon the same side of the street, the figure of a young lady—a figure just under the middle height, comely indeed, and to be mistaken for none other in the world—even at two hundred yards. To his sharp discomfiture his heart immediately forced upon him the consciousness of its acceleration; a sudden warmth about his neck made him aware that he had turned red, and then, departing, left him pale. For a panicky moment he thought of facing about in actual flight; he had little doubt that Lucy would meet him with no token of recognition, and all at once this probability struck him as unendurable. And if she did not speak, was it the proper part of chivalry to lift his hat and take the cut bareheaded? Or should the finer gentleman acquiesce in the lady's desire for no further acquaintance, and pass her with stony mien and eyes constrained forward? George was a young man badly flustered.

But the girl approaching him was unaware of his trepidation, being perhaps somewhat preoccupied with her own. She saw only that he was pale, and that his eyes were darkly circled. But here he was advantaged with her, for the finest touch to his good looks was given by this toning down; neither pallor nor dark circles detracting from them, but rather adding to them a melancholy favour of distinction. George had retained his mourning, a tribute completed down to the final details of black gloves and a polished ebony cane (which he would have been pained to name otherwise than as a "walking-stick") and in the aura of this sombre elegance his straight figure and drawn face were not without a tristful and appealing dignity.

In everything outward he was cause enough for a girl's cheek to flush, her heart to beat faster, and her eyes to warm with the soft light that came into Lucy's now, whether she would or no. If his spirit had been what his looks proclaimed it, she would have rejoiced to let the light glow forth which now shone in spite of her. For a long time, thinking of that spirit of his, and what she felt it should be, she had a persistent sense: "It must be there!" but she had determined to believe this folly no longer. Nevertheless, when she met him at the Sharons', she had been far less calm than she seemed.

People speaking casually of Lucy were apt to define her as "a little beauty," a definition short of the mark. She was "a little beauty," but an independent, masterful, self-reliant little American, of whom her father's earlier gipsyings and her own sturdiness had made a woman ever since she was fifteen. But though she was the mistress of her own ways and no slave to any lamp save that of her own conscience, she had a weakness: she had fallen in love with George Amberson Minafer at first sight, and no matter how she disciplined herself, she had never been able to climb out. The thing had happened to her; that was all. George had looked just the way she had always wanted someone to look—the riskiest of all the moonshine ambushes wherein tricky romance snares credulous young love. But what was fatal to Lucy was that this thing having happened to her, she could not change it. No matter what she discovered in George's nature she was unable to take away what she had given him; and though she could think differently about him, she could not feel differently about him, for she was one of those too faithful victims of glamour. When she managed to keep the picture of George away from her mind's eye, she did well enough; but when she let him become visible, she could not choose but love what she disdained. She was a little angel who had fallen in love with high-handed Lucifer; quite an experience, and not apt to be soon succeeded by any falling in love with a tamer party—and the unhappy truth was that George did make better men seem tame. But though she was a victim, she was a heroic one, anything but helpless.

As they drew nearer, George tried to prepare himself to meet her with some remnants of aplomb. He decided that he would keep on looking straight ahead, and lift his hand toward his hat at the very last moment when it would be possible for her to see him out of the corner of her eye: then when she thought it over later, she would not be sure whether he had saluted her or merely rubbed his forehead. And there was the added benefit that any third person who might chance to look from a window, or from a passing carriage, would not think that he was receiving a snub, because he did not intend to lift his hat, but, timing the gesture properly, would in fact actually rub his forehead. These were the hasty plans which occupied his thoughts until he was within about fifty feet of her—when he ceased to have either plans or thoughts. He had kept his eyes from looking full at her until then, and as he saw her, thus close at hand, and coming nearer, a regret that was dumfounding took possession of him. For the first time he had the sense of having lost something of overwhelming importance.

Lucy did not keep to the right, but came straight to meet him, smiling, and with her hand offered to him.

"Why—you——" he stammered, as he took it. "Haven't you——" What he meant to say was, "Haven't you heard?"

"Haven't I what?" she asked; and he saw that Eugene had not yet told her.

"Nothing!" he gasped. "May I—may I turn and walk with you a little way?"

"Yes, indeed!" she said cordially.

He would not have altered what had been done: he was satisfied with all that—satisfied that it was right, and that his own course was right. But he began to perceive a striking inaccuracy in some remarks he had made to his mother. Now when he had put matters in such shape that even by the relinquishment of his "ideals of life" he could not have Lucy, knew that he could never have her, and knew that when Eugene told her the history of yesterday he could not have a glance or word even friendly from her—now when he must in good truth "give up all idea of Lucy," he was amazed that he could have used such words as "no particular sacrifice," and believed them when he said them! She had looked never in his life so bewitchingly pretty as she did to-day; and as he walked beside her he was sure that she was the most exquisite thing in the world.

"Lucy," he said huskily, "I want to tell you something. Something that matters."

"I hope it's a lively something then," she said; and laughed. "Papa's been so glum to-day he's scarcely spoken to me. Your Uncle George Amberson came to see him an hour ago and they shut themselves up in the library, and your uncle looked as glum as papa. I'd be glad if you'll tell me a funny story, George."

"Well, it may seem one to you," he said bitterly. "Just to begin with: when you went away you didn't let me know; not even a word—not a line——"

Her manner persisted in being inconsequent. "Why, no," she said. "I just trotted off for some visits."

"Well, at least you might have——"

"Why, no," she said again briskly. "Don't you remember, George? We'd had a grand quarrel, and didn't speak to each other all the way home from a long, long drive! So, as we couldn't play together like good children, of course it was plain that we oughtn't to play at all."

"'Play!'" he cried.

"Yes. What I mean is that we'd come to the point where it was time to quit playing—well, what we were playing."

"At being lovers, you mean, don't you?"

"Something like that," she said lightly. "For us two, playing at being lovers was just the same as playing at cross-purposes. I had all the purposes, and that gave you all the crossness: things weren't getting along at all. It was absurd!"

"Well, have it your own way," he said. "It needn't have been absurd."

"No, it couldn't help but be!" she informed him cheerfully. "The way I am and the way you are, it couldn't ever be anything else. So what was the use?"

"I don't know," he sighed, and his sigh was abysmal. "But what I wanted to tell you is this: when you went away, you didn't let me know and didn't care how or when I heard it, but I'm not like that with you. This time, *I*'m going away. That's what I wanted to tell you. I'm going away to-morrow night—indefinitely."

She nodded sunnily. "That's nice for you. I hope you'll have ever so jolly a time, George."

"I don't expect to have a particularly 'jolly time'."

"Well, then," she laughed, "if I were you I don't think I'd go."

It seemed impossible to impress this distracting creature, to make her serious. "Lucy," he said desperately, "this is our last walk together."

"Evidently!" she said. "If you're going away to-morrow night."

"Lucy—this may be the last time I'll see you—ever—ever in my life."

At that she looked at him quickly, across her shoulder, but she smiled as brightly as before, and with the same cordial inconsequence: "Oh, I can hardly think that!" she said. "And of course I'd be awfully sorry to think it. You're not moving away, are you, to live?"

"No."

"And even if you were, of course you'd be coming back to visit your relatives every now and then."

"I don't know when I'm coming back. Mother and I are starting to-morrow night for a trip around the world."

At this she did look thoughtful. "Your mother is going with you?"

"Good heavens!" he groaned. "Lucy, doesn't it make any difference to you that *I* am going?"

At this her cordial smile instantly appeared again. "Yes, of course," she said. "I'm sure I'll miss you ever so much. Are you to be gone long?"

He stared at her wanly. "I told you indefinitely," he said. "We've made no plans—at all—for coming back."

"That does sound like a long trip!" she exclaimed admiringly. "Do you plan to be travelling all the time, or will you stay in some one place the greater part of it? I think it would be lovely to——"

"Lucy!"

He halted; and she stopped with him. They had come to a corner at the edge of the "business section" of the city, and people were everywhere about them, brushing against them, sometimes, in passing.

"I can't stand this," George said, in a low voice. "I'm just about ready to go in this drug-store here, and ask the clerk for something to keep me from dying in my tracks! It's quite a shock, you see, Lucy!"

"What is?"

"To find out certainly, at last, how deeply you've cared for me! To see how much difference this makes to you! By Jove, I *have* mattered to you!"

Her cordial smile was tempered now with good-nature. "George!" She laughed indulgently. "Surely you don't want me to do pathos on a downtown corner!"

"*You* wouldn't 'do pathos' anywhere!"

"Well—don't you think pathos is generally rather foozling?"

"I can't stand this any longer," he said. "I can't! Good-bye, Lucy!" He took her hand. "It's good-bye—I think it's good-bye for good, Lucy!"

"Good-bye! I do hope you'll have the most splendid trip." She gave his hand a cordial little grip, then released it lightly. "Give my love to your mother. Good-bye!"

He turned heavily away, and a moment later glanced back over his shoulder. She had not gone on, but stood watching him, that same casual, cordial smile on her face to the very last; and now, as he looked back, she emphasized her friendly unconcern by waving her small hand to him cheerily, though perhaps with the slightest hint of preoccupation, as if she had begun to think of the errand that brought her downtown.

In his mind, George had already explained her to his own poignant dissatisfaction—some blond pup, probably, whom she had met during that "perfectly gorgeous time!" And he strode savagely onward, not looking back again.

But Lucy remained where she was until he was out of sight. Then she went slowly into the drug-store which had struck George as a possible source of stimulant for himself.

"Please let me have a few drops of aromatic spirits of ammonia in a glass of water," she said, with the utmost composure.

"Yes, *ma'am*!" said the impressionable clerk, who had been looking at her through the display window as she stood on the corner.

But a moment later, as he turned from the shelves of glass jars against the wall, with the potion she had asked for in his hand, he uttered an exclamation: "For goshes' sake, Miss!" And, describing this adventure to his fellow-boarders, that evening, "Sagged pretty near to the counter, she was," he said. "'F I hadn't been a bright, quick, ready-for-anything young fella she'd 'a' flummixed plum! I was watchin' her out the window —talkin' to some young s'iety fella, and she was all right then. She was all right when she come in the store, too. Yes, sir; the prettiest girl that ever walked in our place and took one good look at me. I reckon it must be the truth what some you town wags say about my face!"

Chapter XXVIII

At that hour the heroine of the susceptible clerk's romance was engaged in brightening the rosy little coal fire under the white mantelpiece in her pretty white-and-blue boudoir. Four photographs all framed in decorous plain silver went to the anthracite's fierce destruction—frames and all—and three packets of letters and notes in a charming Florentine treasure-box of painted wood; nor was the box, any more than the silver frames, spared this rousing finish. Thrown heartily upon live coal, the fine wood sparkled forth in stars, then burst into an alarming blaze which scorched the white mantelpiece, but Lucy stood and looked on without moving.

It was not Eugene who told her what had happened at Isabel's door. When she got home, she found Fanny Minafer waiting for her—a secret excursion of Fanny's for the purpose, presumably, of "letting out" again; because that was what she did. She told Lucy everything (except her own lamentable part in the production of the recent miseries) and concluded with a tribute to George: "The worst of it is, he thinks he's been such a hero, and Isabel does, too, and that makes him more than twice as awful. It's been the same all his life: everything he did was noble and perfect. He had a domineering nature to begin with, and she let it go on, and fostered it till it absolutely ruled her. I never saw a plainer case of a person's fault making them pay for having it! She goes about, overseeing the packing and praising George and pretending to be perfectly cheerful about what he's making her do and about the dreadful things he's done. She pretends he did such a fine thing—so manly and protective—going to Mrs. Johnson. And so heroic—doing what his 'principles' made him—even though he knew what it would cost him with you! And all the while it's almost killing her—what he said to your father! She's always been lofty enough, so to speak, and had the greatest idea of the Ambersons being superior to the rest of the world, and all that, but rudeness, or anything like a 'scene,' or any bad manners—they always just made her sick! But she could never see what George's manners were—oh, it's been a terrible adulation! . . . It's going to be a task for me, living in that big house, all alone: you must come and see me—I mean after they've gone, of course. I'll go crazy if I don't see something of people. I'm sure you'll come as often as you can. I know you too well to think you'll be sensitive about coming there, or being reminded of George. Thank heaven you're too well-balanced," Miss Fanny concluded, with a profound fervour, "you're too well-balanced to let anything affect you deeply about that—that monkey!"

The four photographs and the painted Florentine box went to their cremation within the same hour that Miss Fanny spoke; and a little later Lucy called her father in, as he passed her door, and pointed to the blackened area on the underside of the mantelpiece, and to the burnt heap upon the coal, where some metallic shapes still retained outline. She flung her arms about his neck in passionate sympathy, telling him that she knew what had happened to him; and presently he began to comfort her and managed an embarrassed laugh.

"Well, well——" he said. "I was too old for such foolishness to be getting into my head, anyhow."

"No, no!" she sobbed. "And if you knew how I despise myself for—for ever having thought one instant about—oh, Miss Fanny called him the right name: that *monkey*! He is!"

"There, I think I agree with you," Eugene said grimly, and in his eyes there was a steady light of anger that was to last. "Yes, I think I agree with you about *that*!"

"There's only one thing to do with such a person," she said vehemently. "That's to put him out of our thoughts forever —*forever*!"

And yet, the next day, at six o'clock, which was the hour, Fanny had told her, when George and his mother were to leave upon their long journey, Lucy touched that scorched place on her mantel with her hand just as the little clock above it struck. Then, after this odd, unconscious gesture, she went to a window and stood between the curtains, looking out into the cold November dusk; and in spite of every reasoning and reasonable power within her, a pain of loneliness struck through her heart. The dim street below her window, the dark houses across the way, the vague air itself—all looked empty, and cold and (most of all) uninteresting. Something more sombre than November dusk took the colour from them and gave them that air of desertion.

The light of her fire, flickering up behind her, showed suddenly a flying group of tiny snowflakes nearing the window-pane; and for an instant she felt the sensation of being dragged through a snow-drift under a broken cutter, with a boy's arms about her—an arrogant, handsome, too-conquering boy, who nevertheless did his best to get hurt himself, keeping her from any possible harm.

She shook the picture out of her eyes indignantly, then came and sat before her fire, and looked long and long at the blackened mantelpiece. She did not have the mantelpiece repainted —and, since she did not, might as well have kept his photographs. One forgets what made the scar upon his hand but not what made the scar upon his wall.

She played no *marche funèbre* upon her piano, even though Chopin's romantic lamentation was then at the top of nine-tenths of the music-racks in the country, American youth having recently discovered the distinguished congeniality between itself and this deathless bit of deathly gloom. She did not even play "Robin Adair"; she played "Bedelia" and all the new cake-walks, for she was her father's housekeeper, and rightly looked upon the office as being the same as that of his heart-keeper. Therefore it was her affair to keep both house and heart in what state of cheerfulness might be contrived. She made him "go out" more than ever; made him take her to all the gayeties of that winter, declining to go herself unless he took her, and, though Eugene danced no more, and quoted Shakespeare to prove all light-foot caperings beneath the dignity of his age, she broke his resolution for him at the New Year's Eve "Assembly" and half coaxed, half dragged him forth upon the floor, and made him dance the New Year in with her.

. . . New faces appeared at the dances of the winter; new faces had been appearing everywhere, for that matter, and familiar ones were disappearing, merged in the increasing crowd, or gone forever and missed a little and not long; for the town was growing and changing as it never had grown and changed before.

It was heaving up in the middle incredibly; it was spreading incredibly; and as it heaved and spread, it befouled itself and darkened its sky. Its boundary was mere shapelessness on the run; a raw, new house would appear on a country road; four or five others would presently be built at intervals between it and the outskirts of the town; the country road would turn into an asphalt street with a brick-faced drug-store and a frame grocery at a corner; then bungalows and six-room cottages would swiftly speckle the open green spaces—and a farm had become a suburb, which would immediately shoot out other suburbs into the country, on one side, and, on the other, join itself solidly to the city. You drove between pleasant fields and woodland groves one spring day; and in the autumn, passing over the same ground, you were warned off the tracks by an interurban trolley-car's gonging, and beheld, beyond cement sidewalks just dry, new house-owners busy "moving in." Gasoline and electricity were performing the miracles Eugene had predicted.

But the great change was in the citizenry itself. What was left of the patriotic old-stock generation that had fought the Civil War, and subsequently controlled politics, had become venerable and was little heeded. The descendants of the pioneers and early settlers were merging into the new crowd, becoming part of it, little to be distinguished from it. What happened to Boston and to Broadway happened in degree to the Midland city; the old stock became less and less typical, and of the grown people who called the place home, less than a third had been born in it. There was a German quarter; there was a Jewish quarter; there was a negro quarter—square miles of it—called "Bucktown"; there were many Irish neighbourhoods; and there were large settlements of Italians, and of Hungarians, and of Rumanians, and of Servians and other Balkan peoples. But not the emigrants, themselves, were the almost dominant type on the streets downtown. That type was the emigrant's prosperous offspring: descendant of the emigrations of the Seventies and Eighties and Nineties, those great folk-journeyings in search not so directly of freedom and democracy as of more money for the same labour. A new Midlander—in fact, a new American—was beginning dimly to emerge.

A new spirit of citizenship had already sharply defined itself. It was idealistic, and its ideals were expressed in the new kind of young men in business downtown. They were optimists

—optimists to the point of belligerence—their motto being "Boost! Don't Knock!" And they were hustlers, believing in hustling and in honesty because both paid. They loved their city and worked for it with a plutonic energy which was always ardently vocal. They were viciously governed, but they sometimes went so far as to struggle for better government on account of the helpful effect of good government on the price of real estate and "betterment" generally; the politicians could not go too far with them, and knew it. The idealists planned and strove and shouted that their city should become a better, better, and better city—and what they meant, when they used the word "better," was "more prosperous," and the core of their idealism was this: "The more prosperous my beloved city, the more prosperous beloved I!" They had one supreme theory: that the perfect beauty and happiness of cities and of human life was to be brought about by more factories; they had a mania for factories; there was nothing they would not do to cajole a factory away from another city; and they were never more piteously embittered than when another city cajoled one away from them.

What they meant by Prosperity was credit at the bank; but in exchange for this credit they got nothing that was not dirty, and, therefore, to a sane mind, valueless; since whatever was cleaned was dirty again before the cleaning was half done. For, as the town grew, it grew dirty with an incredible completeness. The idealists put up magnificent business buildings and boasted of them, but the buildings were begrimed before they were finished. They boasted of their libraries, of their monuments and statues; and poured soot on them. They boasted of their schools, but the schools were dirty, like the children within them. This was not the fault of the children or their mothers. It was the fault of the idealists, who said: "The more dirt, the more prosperity." They drew patriotic, optimistic breaths of the flying powdered filth of the streets, and took the foul and heavy smoke with gusto into the profundities of their lungs. "Boost! Don't knock!" they said. And every year or so they boomed a great Clean-Up Week, when everybody was supposed to get rid of the tin cans in his back-yard.

They were happiest when the tearing down and building up were most riotous, and when new factory districts were thundering into life. In truth, the city came to be like the body of a great dirty man, skinned, to show his busy works, yet wearing a few barbaric ornaments; and such a figure carved, coloured, and discoloured, and set up in the market-place, would have done well enough as the god of the new people. Such a god they had indeed made in their own image, as all peoples make the god they truly serve; though of course certain of the idealists went to church on Sunday, and there knelt to Another, considered to be impractical in business. But while the Growing went on, this god of their market-place was their true god, their familiar and spirit-control. They did not know that they were his helplessly obedient slaves, nor could they ever hope to realize their serfdom (as the first step toward becoming free men) until they should make the strange and hard discovery that matter should serve man's spirit.

"Prosperity" meant good credit at the bank, black lungs, and housewives' Purgatory. The women fought the dirt all they could; but if they let the air into their houses they let in the dirt. It shortened their lives, and kept them from the happiness of ever seeing anything white. And thus, as the city grew, the time came when Lucy, after a hard struggle, had to give up her blue-and-white curtains and her white walls. Indoors, she put everything into dull gray and brown, and outside had the little house painted the dark green nearest to black. Then she knew, of course, that everything was as dirty as ever, but was a little less distressed because it no longer looked so dirty as it was.

These were bad times for Amberson Addition. This quarter, already old, lay within a mile of the centre of the town, but business moved in other directions; and the Addition's share of Prosperity was only the smoke and dirt, with the bank credit left out. The owners of the original big houses sold them, or rented them to boarding-house keepers, and the tenants of the multitude of small houses moved "farther out" (where the smoke was thinner) or into apartment houses, which were built by dozens now. Cheaper tenants took their places, and the rents were lower and lower, and the houses shabbier and shabbier—for all these shabby houses, burning soft coal, did their best to help in the destruction of their own value. They helped to make the quarter so dingy and the air so foul to breathe that no one would live there who had money enough to get "farther out" where there were glimpses of ungrayed sky and breaths of cleaner winds. And with the coming of the new speed, "farther out" was now as close to business as the Addition had been in the days of its prosperity. Distances had ceased to matter.

The five new houses, built so closely where had been the fine lawn of the Amberson Mansion, did not look new. When they were a year old they looked as old as they would ever look; and two of them were vacant, having never been rented, for the Major's mistake about apartment houses had been a disastrous one. "He guessed wrong," George Amberson said. "He guessed wrong at just the wrong time! Housekeeping in a house is harder than in an apartment; and where the smoke and dirt are as thick as they are in the Addition, women can't stand it. People were crazy for apartments—too bad he couldn't have seen it in time. Poor man! he digs away at his ledgers by his old gas drop-light lamp almost every night—he still refuses to let the Mansion be torn up for wiring, you know. But he had one painful satisfaction this spring: he got his taxes lowered!"

Amberson laughed ruefully, and Fanny Minafer asked how the Major could have managed such an economy. They were sitting upon the veranda at Isabel's one evening during the third summer of the absence of their nephew and his mother; and the conversation had turned toward Amberson finances.

"I said it was a '*painful* satisfaction,' Fanny," he explained. "The property has gone down in value, and they assessed it lower than they did fifteen years ago."

"But farther out——"

"Oh, yes, 'farther out!' Prices are magnificent 'farther out,' and farther in, too! We just happen to be the wrong spot, that's all. Not that I don't think something could be done if father would let me have a hand; but he won't. He can't, I suppose I ought to say. He's 'always done his own figuring,' he says; and it's his lifelong habit to keep his affairs, and even his books, to himself, and just hand us out the money. Heaven knows he's done enough of that!"

He sighed; and both were silent, looking out at the long flares of the constantly passing automobile headlights, shifting in vast geometric demonstrations against the darkness. Now and then a bicycle wound its nervous way among these portents, or, at long intervals, a surrey or buggy plodded forlornly by.

"There seem to be so many ways of making money nowadays," Fanny said thoughtfully. "Every day I hear of a new fortune some person has got hold of, one way or another—nearly always it's somebody you never heard of. It doesn't seem all to be in just making motor cars; I hear there's a great deal in manufacturing these things that motor cars use—new inventions particularly. I met dear old Frank Bronson the other day, and he told me——"

"Oh, yes, even dear old Frank's got the fever," Amberson laughed. "He's as wild as any of them. He told me about this invention he's gone into, too. 'Millions in it!' Some new electric headlight better than anything yet—'every car in America can't *help* but have 'em,' and all that. He's putting half he's laid by into it, and the fact is, he almost talked me into getting father to 'finance me' enough for me to go into it. Poor father! he's financed me before! I suppose he would again if I had the heart to ask him; and this seems to be a good thing, though probably old Frank is a *little* too sanguine. At any rate, I've been thinking it over."

"So have I," Fanny admitted. "He seemed to be certain it would pay twenty-five per cent. the first year, and enormously more after that; and I'm only getting four on my little principal. People *are* making such enormous fortunes out of everything to do with motor cars, it does seem as if——" She paused. "Well, I told him I'd think it over seriously."

"We may turn out to be partners and millionaires then," Amberson laughed. "I thought I'd ask Eugene's advice."

"I wish you would," said Fanny. "He probably knows exactly how much profit there would be in this."

Eugene's advice was to "go slow": he thought electric lights for automobiles were "coming—*some* day," but probably not until certain difficulties could be overcome. Altogether, he was discouraging, but by this time his two friends "had the fever" as thoroughly as old Frank Bronson himself had it; for they had been with Bronson to see the light working beautifully in a machine shop. They were already enthusiastic, and after asking Eugene's opinion they argued with him, telling him how they had seen with their own eyes that the difficulties he mentioned *had* been overcome. "Perfectly!" Fanny cried. "And if it worked in the shop it's bound to work any place else, isn't it?"

He would not agree that it was "bound to"—yet, being pressed, was driven to admit that "it *might*," and, retiring from what was developing into an oratorical contest, repeated a warning about not "putting too much into it."

George Amberson also laid stress on this caution later, though the Major had "financed him" again, and he was "going in." "You must be careful to leave yourself a 'margin of safety,' Fanny," he said. "I'm confident that is a pretty conservative investment of its kind, and all the chances are with us, but you must be careful to leave yourself enough to fall back on, in case anything *should* go wrong."

Fanny deceived him. In the impossible event of "anything going wrong" she would have enough left to "live on," she declared, and laughed excitedly, for she was having the best time that had come to her since Wilbur's death. Like so many women for whom money has always been provided without their understanding how, she was prepared to be a thorough and irresponsible plunger.

Amberson, in his wearier way, shared her excitement, and in the winter, when the exploiting company had been formed, and he brought Fanny her importantly engraved shares of stock, he reverted to his prediction of possibilities, made when they first spoke of the new light.

"We seem to be partners, all right," he laughed. "Now let's go ahead and be millionaires before Isabel and young George come home."

"When they come home!" she echoed sorrowfully—and it was a phrase which found an evasive echo in Isabel's letters. In these letters Isabel was always planning pleasant things that she and Fanny and the Major and George and "brother George" would do—when she and her son came home. "They'll find things pretty changed, I'm afraid," Fanny said. "If they ever do come home!"

Amberson went over, the next summer, and joined his sister and nephew in Paris, where they were living. "Isabel does want to come home," he told Fanny gravely, on the day of his return, in October. "She's wanted to for a long while—and she ought to come while she can stand the journey——" And he amplified this statement, leaving Fanny looking startled and solemn when Lucy came by to drive him out to dinner at the new house Eugene had just completed.

This was no white-and-blue cottage, but a great Georgian picture in brick, five miles north of Amberson Addition, with four acres of its own hedged land between it and its next neighbour; and Amberson laughed wistfully as they turned in between the stone and brick gate pillars, and rolled up the crushed stone driveway. "I wonder, Lucy, if history's going on forever repeating itself," he said. "I wonder if this town's going on building up things and rolling over them, as poor father once said it was rolling over his poor old heart. It looks like it: here's the Amberson Mansion again, only it's Georgian instead of nondescript Romanesque; but it's just the same Amberson Mansion that my father built long before you were born. The only difference is that it's your father who's built this one now. It's all the same, in the long run."

Lucy did not quite understand, but she laughed as a friend should, and, taking his arm, showed him through vasty rooms where ivory-panelled walls and trim window hangings were reflected dimly in dark, rugless floors, and the sparse furniture showed that Lucy had been "collecting" with a long purse. "By Jove!" he said. "You *have* been going it! Fanny tells me you had a great 'house-warming' dance, and you keep right on being the belle of the ball, not any softer-hearted than you used to be. Fred Kinney's father says you've refused Fred so often that he got engaged to Janie Sharon just to prove that someone would have him in spite of his hair. Well, the material world do move, and you've got the new kind of house it moves into nowadays—if it has the new price! And even the grand old expanses of plate glass we used to be so proud of at the other Amberson Mansion—they've gone, too, with the crowded heavy gold and red stuff. Curious! *We've* still got the plate glass windows, though all we can see out of 'em is the smoke and the old Johnson house, which is a counter-jumper's boarding-house now, while you've got a view, and you cut it all up into little panes. Well, you're pretty refreshingly out of the smoke up here."

"Yes, for a while," Lucy laughed. "Until it comes and we have to move out farther."

"No, you'll stay here," he assured her. "It will be somebody else who'll move out farther."

He continued to talk of the house after Eugene arrived, and gave them no account of his journey until they had retired from the dinner table to Eugene's library, a gray and shadowy room, where their coffee was brought. Then, equipped with a cigar, which seemed to occupy his attention, Amberson spoke in a casual tone of his sister and her son.

"I found Isabel as well as usual," he said, "only I'm afraid 'as usual' isn't particularly well. Sydney and Amelia had been up to Paris in the spring, but she hadn't seen them. Somebody told her they were there, it seems. They'd left Florence and were living in Rome; Amelia's become a Catholic and is said to give great sums to charity and to go about with the gentry in consequence, but Sydney's ailing and lives in a wheel-chair most of the time. It struck me Isabel ought to be doing the same thing."

He paused, bestowing minute care upon the removal of the little band from his cigar; and as he seemed to have concluded his narrative, Eugene spoke out of the shadow beyond a heavily shaded lamp: "What do you mean by that?" he asked quietly.

"Oh, she's cheerful enough," said Amberson, still not looking at either his young hostess or her father. "At least," he added, "she manages to seem so. I'm afraid she hasn't been really well for several years. She isn't stout you know—she hasn't changed in looks much—and she seems rather alarmingly short of breath for a slender person. Father's been that way for years, of course; but never nearly so much as Isabel is now. Of course she makes nothing of it, but it seemed rather serious to me when I noticed she had to stop and rest twice to get up the one short flight of stairs in their two-floor apartment. I told her I thought she ought to make George let her come home."

"'Let her?'" Eugene repeated, in a low voice. "Does she want to?"

"She doesn't urge it. George seems to like the life there—in his grand, gloomy, and peculiar way; and of course she'll never change about being proud of him and all that—he's quite a swell. But in spite of anything she said, rather than because,

I know she does indeed want to come. She'd like to be with father, of course; and I think she's—well, she intimated one day that she feared it might even happen that she wouldn't get to see him again. At the time I thought she referred to his age and feebleness, but on the boat, coming home, I remembered the little look of wistfulness, yet of resignation, with which she said it, and it struck me all at once that I'd been mistaken: I saw she was really thinking of her own state of health."

"I see," Eugene said, his voice even lower than it had been before. "And you say he won't 'let' her come home?"

Amberson laughed, but still continued to be interested in his cigar. "Oh, I don't think he uses force! He's very gentle with her. I doubt if the subject is mentioned between them, and yet—and yet, knowing my interesting nephew as you do, wouldn't you think that was about the way to put it?"

"Knowing him as I do—yes," said Eugene slowly. "Yes, I should think that was about the way to put it."

A murmur out of the shadows beyond him—a faint sound, musical and feminine, yet expressive of a notable intensity—seemed to indicate that Lucy was of the same opinion.

Chapter XXIX

"LET HER" was correct; but the time came—and it came in the spring of the next year—when it was no longer a question of George's letting his mother come home. He had to bring her, and to bring her quickly if she was to see her father again; and Amberson had been right: her danger of never seeing him again lay not in the Major's feebleness of heart but in her own. As it was, George telegraphed his uncle to have a wheeled chair at the station, for the journey had been disastrous, and to this hybrid vehicle, placed close to the car platform, her son carried her in his arms when she arrived. She was unable to speak, but patted her brother's and Fanny's hands and looked "very sweet," Fanny found the desperate courage to tell her. She was lifted from the chair into a carriage, and seemed a little stronger as they drove home; for once she took her hand from George's, and waved it feebly toward the carriage window.

"Changed," she whispered. "So changed."

"You mean the town," Amberson said. "You mean the old place is changed, don't you, dear?"

She smiled and moved her lips: "Yes."

"It'll change to a happier place, old dear," he said, "now that you're back in it, and going to get well again."

But she only looked at him wistfully, her eyes a little frightened.

When the carriage stopped, her son carried her into the house, and up the stairs to her own room, where a nurse was waiting; and he came out a moment later, as the doctor went in. At the end of the hall a stricken group was clustered: Amberson, and Fanny, and the Major. George, deathly pale and speechless, took his grandfather's hand, but the old gentleman did not seem to notice his action.

"When are they going to let me see my daughter?" he asked querulously. "They told me to keep out of the way while they carried her in, because it might upset her. I wish they'd let me go in and speak to my daughter. I think she wants to see me."

He was right—presently the doctor came out and beckoned

to him; and the Major shuffled forward, leaning on a shaking cane; his figure, after all its years of proud soldierliness, had grown stooping at last, and his untrimmed white hair straggled over the back of his collar. He looked old—old and divested of the world—as he crept toward his daughter's room. Her voice was stronger, for the waiting group heard a low cry of tenderness and welcome as the old man reached the open doorway. Then the door was closed.

Fanny touched her nephew's arm. "George, you must need something to eat—I know she'd want you to. I've had things ready: I knew she'd want me to. You'd better go down to the dining room: there's plenty on the table, waiting for you. She'd want you to eat something."

He turned a ghastly face to her, it was so panic-stricken. "I don't want anything to *eat*!" he said savagely. And he began to pace the floor, taking care not to go near Isabel's door, and that his footsteps were muffled by the long, thick hall rug. After a while he went to where Amberson, with folded arms and bowed head, had seated himself near the front window. "Uncle George," he said hoarsely. "I didn't——"

"Well?"

"Oh, my God, I didn't think this thing the matter with her could ever be serious! I——" He gasped. "When that doctor I had meet us at the boat——" He could not go on.

Amberson only nodded his head, and did not otherwise change his attitude.

. . . Isabel lived through the night. At eleven o'clock Fanny came timidly to George in his room. "Eugene is here," she whispered. "He's downstairs. He wants——" She gulped. "He wants to know if he can't *see* her. I didn't know what to say. I said I'd see. I didn't know—the doctor said——"

"The doctor said we 'must keep her peaceful,'" George said sharply. "Do you think that man's coming would be very soothing? My God! if it hadn't been for him this mightn't have happened: we could have gone on living here quietly, and—why, it would be like taking a stranger into her room! She hasn't even spoken of him more than twice in all the time we've been away. Doesn't he know how *sick* she is? You tell him the doctor said she had to be quiet and peaceful. That's what he did say, isn't it?"

Fanny acquiesced tearfully. "I'll tell him. I'll tell him the doctor said she was to be kept very quiet. I—I didn't know——" And she pottered out.

An hour later the nurse appeared in George's doorway; she came noiselessly, and his back was toward her; but he jumped as if he had been shot, and his jaw fell, he so feared what she was going to say.

"She wants to see you."

The terrified mouth shut with a click; and he nodded and followed her; but she remained outside his mother's room while he went in.

Isabel's eyes were closed, and she did not open them or move her head, but she smiled and edged her hand toward him as he sat on a stool beside the bed. He took that slender, cold hand, and put it to his cheek.

"Darling, did you—get something to eat?" She could only whisper, slowly and with difficulty. It was as if Isabel herself were far away, and only able to signal what she wanted to say.

"Yes, mother."

"All you—needed?"

"Yes, mother."

She did not speak again for a time; then, "Are you sure you didn't—didn't catch cold—coming home?"

"I'm all right, mother."

"That's good. It's sweet—it's sweet——"

"What is, mother darling?"

"To feel—my hand on your cheek. I—I *can* feel it."

But this frightened him horribly—that she seemed so glad she could feel it, like a child proud of some miraculous seeming thing accomplished. It frightened him so that he could not speak, and he feared that she would know how he trembled; but she was unaware, and again was silent. Finally she spoke again:

"I wonder if—if Eugene and Lucy know that we've come —home."

"I'm sure they do."

"Has he—asked about me?"

"Yes, he was here."

"Has he—gone?"

"Yes, mother."

She sighed faintly. "I'd like——"

"What, mother?"

"I'd like to have—seen him." It was just audible, this little regretful murmur. Several minutes passed before there was another. "Just—just once," she whispered, and then was still.

She seemed to have fallen asleep, and George moved to go, but a faint pressure upon his fingers detained him, and he remained, with her hand still pressed against his cheek. After a while he made sure she was asleep, and moved again, to let the nurse come in, and this time there was no pressure of the fingers to keep him. She was not asleep, but, thinking that if he went he might get some rest, and be better prepared for what she knew was coming, she commanded those longing fingers of hers—and let him go.

He found the doctor standing with the nurse in the hall; and, telling them that his mother was drowsing now, George went back to his own room, where he was startled to find his grandfather lying on the bed, and his uncle leaning against the wall. They had gone home two hours before, and he did not know they had returned.

"The doctor thought we'd better come over," Amberson said, then was silent, and George, shaking violently, sat down on the edge of the bed. His shaking continued, and from time to time he wiped heavy sweat from his forehead.

The hours passed, and sometimes the old man upon the bed would snore a little, stop suddenly, and move as if to rise, but George Amberson would set a hand upon his shoulder, and murmur a reassuring word or two. Now and then, either uncle or nephew would tiptoe into the hall and look toward Isabel's room, then come tiptoeing back, the other watching him haggardly.

Once George gasped defiantly: "That doctor in New York said she *might* get better! Don't you know he did? Don't you know he said she might?"

Amberson made no answer.

Dawn had been murking through the smoky windows, growing stronger for half an hour, when both men started violently at a sound in the hall; and the Major sat up on the bed, unchecked. It was the voice of the nurse speaking to Fanny Minafer, and the next moment, Fanny appeared in the doorway, making contorted efforts to speak.

Amberson said weakly: "Does she want us—to come in?"

But Fanny found her voice, and uttered a long, loud cry. She threw her arms about George, and sobbed in an agony of loss and compassion:

"She loved you!" she wailed. "She loved you! She loved you! Oh, how she did love you!"

Isabel had just left them.

Chapter XXX

MAJOR AMBERSON remained dry-eyed through the time that followed: he knew that this separation from his daughter would be short; that the separation which had preceded it was the long one. He worked at his ledgers no more under his old gas drop-light, but would sit all evening staring into the fire, in his bedroom, and not speaking unless someone asked him a question. He seemed almost unaware of what went on around him, and those who were with him thought him dazed by Isabel's death, guessing that he was lost in reminiscences and vague dreams. "Probably his mind is full of pictures of his youth, or the Civil War, and the days when he and mother were young married people and all of us children were jolly little things—and the city was a small town with one cobbled street and the others just dirt roads with board sidewalks." This was George Amberson's conjecture, and the others agreed; but they were mistaken. The Major was engaged in the profoundest thinking of his life. No business plans which had ever absorbed him could compare in momentousness with the plans that absorbed him now, for he had to plan how to enter the unknown country where he was not even sure of being recognized as an Amberson—not sure of anything, except that Isabel would help him if she could. His absorption produced the outward effect of reverie, but of course it was not. The Major was occupied with the first really important matter that had taken his attention since he came home invalided, after the Gettysburg campaign, and went into business; and he realized that everything which had worried him or delighted him during this lifetime between then and to-day—all his buying and building and trading and banking—that it all was trifling and waste beside what concerned him now.

He seldom went out of his room, and often left untouched the meals they brought to him there; and this neglect caused them to shake their heads mournfully, again mistaking for dazedness the profound concentration of his mind. Meanwhile, the life of the little bereft group still forlornly centring upon him began to pick up again, as life will, and to emerge from its own period of dazedness. It was not Isabel's father but her son who was really dazed.

A month after her death he walked abruptly into Fanny's room, one night, and found her at her desk, eagerly adding columns of figures with which she had covered several sheets of paper. This mathematical computation was concerned with her future income to be produced by the electric headlight, now just placed on the general market; but Fanny was ashamed to be discovered doing anything except mourning, and hastily pushed the sheets aside, even as she looked over her shoulder to greet her hollow-eyed visitor.

"George! You startled me."

"I beg your pardon for not knocking," he said huskily. "I didn't think."

She turned in her chair and looked at him solicitously. "Sit down, George, won't you?"

"No. I just wanted——"

"I could hear you walking up and down in your room," said Fanny. "You were doing it ever since dinner, and it seems to me you're at it almost every evening. I don't believe it's good for you—and I know it would worry your mother terribly if she——" Fanny hesitated.

"See here," George said, breathing fast, "I want to tell you once more that what I did was right. How could I have done anything else but what I did do?"

"About what, George?"

"About everything!" he exclaimed; and he became vehement. "I did the right thing, I tell you! In heaven's name, I'd like to know what else there was for anybody in my position to do! It would have been a dreadful thing for me to just let matters go on and not interfere—it would have been terrible! What else on earth was there *for* me to do? I *had* to stop that talk, didn't I? Could a son do less than I did? Didn't it *cost* me something to do it? Lucy and I'd had a quarrel, but that would have come round in time—and it meant the end forever when I turned her father back from our door. I knew what it meant, yet I went ahead and did it because I knew it had to be done if the talk was to be stopped. I took mother away for the same reason. I knew that would help to stop it. And she was happy over there—she was perfectly happy. I tell you, I think she had a happy life, and that's my only consolation. She didn't live to be old; she was still beautiful and young looking, and I feel she'd rather have gone before she got old. She'd had a good husband, and all the comfort and luxury that anybody could have—and how could it be called anything but a happy life? She was always cheerful, and when I think of her I can always see her laughing—I can always hear that pretty laugh of hers. When I can keep my mind off of the trip home, and that last night, I *always* think of her gay and laughing. So how on earth *could* she have had anything but a happy life? People that aren't happy don't look cheerful all the time, do they? They look unhappy if they *are* unhappy; that's how they look! See here"— he faced her challengingly—"do *you* deny that I did the right thing?"

"Oh, I don't pretend to judge," Fanny said soothingly, for his voice and gesture both partook of wildness. "I know you think you did, George."

"'Think I did!'" he echoed violently. "My God in heaven!" And he began to walk up and down the floor. "What else *was* there to do? What *choice* did I have? Was there any other way of stopping the talk?" He stopped, close in front of her, gesticulating, his voice harsh and loud: "Don't you hear me? I'm asking you: Was there any other way on earth of protecting her from the talk?"

Miss Fanny looked away. "It died down before long, I think," she said nervously.

"*That* shows I was right, doesn't it?" he cried. "If I hadn't acted as I did, that slanderous old Johnson woman would have kept on with her slanders—she'd *still* be——"

"No," Fanny interrupted. "She's dead. She dropped dead with apoplexy one day about six weeks after you left. I didn't mention it in my letters because I didn't want—I thought——"

"Well, the *other* people would have kept on, then. *They'd* have——"

"I don't know," said Fanny, still averting her troubled eyes. "Things are so changed here, George. The other people you speak of—one hardly knows what's become of them. Of course not a great many were doing the talking, and they—well, some of them are dead, and some might as well be—you never see them any more—and the rest, whoever they were, are probably so mixed in with the crowds of new people that seem never even to have heard of *us*—and I'm sure we certainly never heard of *them*—and people seem to forget things so soon—they seem to forget anything. You can't imagine how things have changed here!"

George gulped painfully before he could speak. "You—you mean to sit there and tell me that if I'd just let things go on—— Oh!" He swung away, walking the floor again. "I tell you I did the only right thing! If you don't think so, why in the name of heaven can't you say what *else* I should have done? It's easy enough to criticize, but the person who criticizes a man ought at least to tell him what *else* he should have done! You think I was wrong!"

"I'm not saying so," she said.

"You did at the time!" he cried. "You said enough then, I think! Well, what have you to say now, if you're so sure I was wrong?"

"Nothing, George."

"It's only because you're afraid to!" he said, and he went on with a sudden bitter divination: "You're reproaching yourself with what *you* had to do with all that; and you're trying to make up for it by doing and saying what you think mother would want you to, and you think I couldn't stand it if I got to thinking I might have done differently. Oh, I know! That's exactly what's in your mind: you *do* think I was wrong! So does Uncle George. I challenged him about it the other day, and he answered just as you're answering—evaded, and tried to be gentle! I don't care to be handled with gloves! I tell you I was right, and I don't need any coddling by people that think I wasn't! And I suppose you believe I was wrong not to let Morgan see her that last night when he came here, and she—she was dying. If you do, why in the name of God did you come and ask *me*? *You* could have taken him in! She *did* want to see him. She——"

Miss Fanny looked startled. "You think——"

"She told me so!" And the tortured young man choked. "She said—'just once.' She said 'I'd like to have seen him—just once!' She meant—to tell him good-bye! *That's* what she meant! And you put this on me, too; you put this responsibility on me! But I tell you, and I told Uncle George, that the responsibility isn't *all* mine! If you were so sure I was wrong all the time—when I took her away, and when I turned Morgan out—if you were so sure, what did you let me do it for? You and Uncle George were grown people, both of you, weren't you? You were older than I, and if you were so sure you were *wiser* than I, why did you just stand around with your hands hanging down, and let me go ahead? You could have stopped it if it was wrong, couldn't you?"

Fanny shook her head. "No, George," she said slowly. "Nobody could have stopped you. You were too strong, and——"

"And what?" he demanded loudly.

"And she loved you—too well."

George stared at her hard, then his lower lip began to move convulsively, and he set his teeth upon it but could not check its frantic twitching.

He ran out of the room.

She sat still, listening. He had plunged into his mother's room, but no sound came to Fanny's ears after the sharp closing of the door; and presently she rose and stepped out into the hall—but could hear nothing. The heavy black walnut door of Isabel's room, as Fanny's troubled eyes remained fixed upon it, seemed to become darker and vaguer; the polished wood took the distant ceiling light, at the end of the hall, in dim reflections which became mysterious; and to Fanny's disturbed mind the single sharp point of light on the bronze door-knob was like a continuous sharp cry in the stillness of night. What interview was sealed away from human eye and ear within the lonely darkness on the other side of that door—in that darkness where Isabel's own special chairs were, and her own special books, and the two great walnut wardrobes filled with her dresses and wraps? What tragic argument might be there vainly striving to confute the gentle dead? "In God's name, what else could I have done?" For his mother's immutable silence was surely answering him as Isabel in life would never have answered him, and he was beginning to understand how eloquent the dead can be. They cannot stop their eloquence, no matter how they have loved the living: they cannot choose. And so, no matter in what agony George should cry out, "What else could

I have done?" and to the end of his life no matter how often he made that wild appeal, Isabel was doomed to answer him with the wistful, faint murmur:

"I'd like to have—seen him. Just—just once."

A cheerful darkey went by the house, loudly and tunelessly whistling some broken thoughts upon women, fried food and gin; then a group of high-school boys, returning homeward after important initiations, were heard skylarking along the sidewalk, rattling sticks on the fences, squawking hoarsely, and even attempting to sing in the shocking new voices of uncompleted adolescence. For no reason, and just as a poultry yard falls into causeless agitation, they stopped in front of the house, and for half an hour produced the effect of a noisy multitude in full riot.

To the woman standing upstairs in the hall, this was almost unbearable; and she felt that she would have to go down and call to them to stop; but she was too timid, and after a time went back to her room, and sat at her desk again. She left the door open, and frequently glanced out into the hall, but gradually became once more absorbed in the figures which represented her prospective income from her great plunge in electric lights for automobiles. She did not hear George return to his own room.

. . . A superstitious person might have thought it unfortunate that her partner in this speculative industry (as in Wilbur's disastrous rolling-mills) was that charming but too haphazardous man of the world, George Amberson. He was one of those optimists who believe that if you put money into a great many enterprises one of them is sure to turn out a fortune, and therefore, in order to find the lucky one, it is only necessary to go into a large enough number of them. Altogether gallant in spirit, and beautifully game under catastrophe, he had gone into a great many, and the unanimity of their "bad luck," as he called it, gave him one claim to be a distinguished person, if he had no other. In business he was ill fated with a consistency which made him, in that alone, a remarkable man; and he declared, with some earnestness, that there was no accounting for it except by the fact that there had been so much good luck in his family before he was born that something had to balance it.

"You ought to have thought of my record and stayed out," he told Fanny, one day the next spring, when the affairs of the headlight company had begun to look discouraging. "I feel the old familiar sinking that's attended all my previous efforts to prove myself a business genius. I think it must be something like the feeling an aeronaut has when his balloon bursts, and, looking down, he sees below him the old home farm where he used to live—I mean the feeling he'd have just before he flattened out in that same old clay barnyard. Things do look bleak, and I'm only glad you didn't go into this confounded thing to the extent I did."

Miss Fanny grew pink. "But it *must* go right!" she protested. "We saw with our own eyes how perfectly it worked in the shop. The light was so bright no one could face it, and so there *can't* be any reason for it not to work. It simply——"

"Oh, you're right about that," Amberson said. "It certainly was a perfect thing—in the shop! The only thing *we* didn't know was how fast an automobile had to go to keep the light going. It appears that this was a matter of some importance."

"Well, how fast *does* one have to——"

"To keep the light from going entirely out," he informed her with elaborate deliberation, "it is computed by those enthusiasts who have bought our product—and subsequently returned it to us and got their money back—they compute that a motor car must maintain a speed of twenty-five miles an hour, or else there won't be any light at all. To make the illumination bright enough to be noticed by an approaching automobile, they state the speed must be more than thirty miles an hour. At thirty-five, objects in the path of the light begin to become visible; at forty they are revealed distinctly; and at fifty and above we have a real headlight. Unfortunately many people don't care to drive that fast at all times after dusk, especially in the traffic, or where policemen are likely to become objectionable."

"But think of that test on the road when we——"

"That test was lovely," he admitted. "The inventor made us happy with his oratory, and you and Frank Bronson and I went whirling through the night at a speed that thrilled us. It was an intoxicating sensation: we were intoxicated by the lights, the lights and the music. We must never forget that drive, with the cool wind kissing our cheeks and the road lit up for miles ahead. We must never forget it—and we never shall. It cost——"

"But something's got to be done."

"It has, indeed! *My* something would seem to be leaving my watch at my uncle's. Luckily, you——"

The pink of Fanny's cheeks became deeper. "But isn't that man going to *do* anything to remedy it? Can't he try to——"

"He can try," said Amberson. "He *is* trying, in fact. I've sat in the shop watching him try for several beautiful afternoons, while outside the windows all Nature was fragrant with spring and smoke. He hums ragtime to himself as he tries, and I think his mind is wandering to something else less tedious—to some new invention in which he'd take more interest."

"But you mustn't let him," she cried. "You must *make* him keep on trying!"

"Oh, yes. He understands that's what I sit there for. I'll keep sitting!"

However, in spite of the time he spent sitting in the shop, worrying the inventor of the fractious light, Amberson found opportunity to worry himself about another matter of business. This was the settlement of Isabel's estate.

"It's curious about the deed to her house," he said to his nephew. "You're absolutely sure it wasn't among her papers?"

"Mother didn't have any papers," George told him. "None at all. All she ever had to do with business was to deposit the cheques grandfather gave her and then write her own cheques against them."

"The deed to the house was never recorded," Amberson said thoughtfully. "I've been over to the courthouse to see. I asked father if he never gave her one, and he didn't seem able to understand me at first. Then he finally said he thought he must have given her a deed long ago; but he wasn't sure. I rather think he never did. I think it would be just as well to get him to execute one now in your favour. I'll speak to him about it."

George sighed. "I don't think I'd bother him about it: the house is mine, and you and I understand that it is. That's enough for me, and there isn't likely to be much trouble between you and me when we come to settling poor grandfather's estate. I've just been with him, and I think it would only confuse him for you to speak to him about it again. I notice he seems distressed if anybody tries to get his attention —he's a long way off, somewhere, and he likes to stay that way. I think—I think mother wouldn't want us to bother him about it; I'm sure she'd tell us to let him alone. He looks so white and queer."

Amberson shook his head. "Not much whiter and queerer than you do, young fellow! You'd better begin to get some air and exercise and quit hanging about in the house all day. I won't bother him any more than I can help; but I'll have the deed made out ready for his signature."

"I wouldn't bother him at all. I don't see——"

"You might see," said his uncle uneasily. "The estate is just about as involved and mixed-up as an estate can well get, to the best of my knowledge; and I haven't helped it any by what he let me have for this infernal headlight scheme which has finally gone trolloping forever to where the woodbine twineth. Leaves me flat, and poor old Frank Bronson just half flat, and Fanny—well, thank heaven! I kept her from going in so deep that it would leave *her* flat. It's rough on her as it is, I suspect. You ought to have that deed."

"No. Don't bother him."

"I'll bother him as little as possible. I'll wait till some day when he seems to brighten up a little."

But Amberson waited too long. The Major had already taken eleven months since his daughter's death to think important things out. He had got as far with them as he could, and there was nothing to detain him longer in the world. One evening his grandson sat with him—the Major seemed to like best to have young George with him, so far as they were able to guess his preferences—and the old gentleman made a queer gesture: he slapped his knee as if he had made a sudden discovery, or else remembered that he had forgotten something.

George looked at him with an air of inquiry, but said nothing. He had grown to be almost as silent as his grandfather. However, the Major spoke without being questioned.

"It must be in the sun," he said. "There wasn't anything here but the sun in the first place, and the earth came out of the sun, and we came out of the earth. So, whatever we are, we must have been in the sun. We go back to the earth we came out of, so the earth will go back to the sun that it came out of. And time means nothing—nothing at all—so in a little while we'll all be back in the sun together. I wish——"

He moved his hand uncertainly as if reaching for something, and George jumped up. "Did you want anything, grandfather?"

"What?"

"Would you like a glass of water?"

"No—no. No; I don't want anything." The reaching hand dropped back upon the arm of his chair, and he relapsed into silence; but a few minutes later he finished the sentence he had begun:

"I wish—somebody could tell me!"

The next day he had a slight cold, but he seemed annoyed when his son suggested calling the doctor, and Amberson let him have his own way so far, in fact, that after he had got up and dressed, the following morning, he was all alone when he went away to find out what he hadn't been able to think out —all those things he had wished "somebody" would tell him.

Old Sam, shuffling in with the breakfast tray, found the Major in his accustomed easy-chair by the fireplace—and yet even the old darkey could see instantly that the Major was not there.

Chapter XXXI

WHEN THE great Amberson Estate went into court for settlement, "there wasn't any," George Amberson said—that is, when the settlement was concluded there was no estate. "I guessed it," Amberson went on. "As an expert on prosperity, my career is disreputable, but as a prophet of calamity I deserve a testimonial banquet." He reproached himself bitterly for not having long ago discovered that his father had never given Isabel a deed to her house. "And those pigs, Sydney and Amelia!" he added, for this was another thing he was bitter about. "They won't do anything. I'm sorry I gave them the opportunity of making a polished refusal. Amelia's letter was about half in Italian; she couldn't remember enough ways of saying no in English. One has to live quite a long while to realize there *are* people like that! The estate was badly crippled, even before they took out their 'third,' and the 'third' they took was the only good part of the rotten apple. Well, I didn't ask them for restitution on my own account, and at least it will save *you* some trouble, young George. Never waste any time writing to them; you mustn't count on them."

"I don't," George said quietly. "I don't count on anything."

"Oh, we'll not feel that things are quite desperate," Amberson laughed, but not with great cheerfulness. "We'll survive, Georgie—*you* will, especially. For my part I'm a little too old and too accustomed to fall back on somebody else for supplies to start a big fight with life: I'll be content with just surviving, and I can do it on an eighteen-hundred-dollar-a-year consulship. An ex-congressman can always be pretty sure of getting some such job, and I hear from Washington the matter's about settled. I'll live pleasantly enough with a pitcher of ice under a palm tree, and black folks to wait on me—that part of it will be like home—and I'll manage to send you fifty dollars every now and then, after I once get settled. So much for me! But you—of course you've had a poor training for making your own way, but you're only a boy after all, and the stuff of the old stock is in you. It'll come out and do something. I'll never forgive myself about that deed: it would have given you something substantial to start with. Still, you have a little tiny bit, and you'll have a little tiny salary, too; and of course your Aunt Fanny's here, and she's got something you can fall back on if you get *too* pinched, until I can begin to send you a dribble now and then."

George's "little tiny bit" was six hundred dollars which had come to him from the sale of his mother's furniture; and the "little tiny salary" was eight dollars a week which old Frank Bronson was to pay him for services as a clerk and student-at-law. Old Frank would have offered more to the Major's grandson, but since the death of that best of clients and his own experience with automobile headlights, he was not certain of being able to pay more and at the same time settle his own small bills for board and lodging. George had accepted haughtily, and thereby removed a burden from his uncle's mind.

Amberson himself, however, had not even a "tiny bit"; though he got his consular appointment; and to take him to his post he found it necessary to borrow two hundred of his nephew's six hundred dollars. "It makes me sick, George," he said. "But I'd better get there and get that salary started. Of course Eugene would do anything in the world, and the fact is he wanted to, but I felt that—ah—under the circumstances——"

"Never!" George exclaimed, growing red. "I can't imagine one of the family——" He paused, not finding it necessary to explain that "the family" shouldn't turn a man from the door and then accept favours from him. "I wish you'd take more."

Amberson declined. "One thing I'll say for you, young George; you haven't a stingy bone in your body. That's the Amberson stock in you—and I like it!"

He added something to this praise of his nephew on the day he left for Washington. He was not to return, but to set forth from the capital on the long journey to his post. George went with him to the station, and their farewell was lengthened by the train's being several minutes late.

"I may not see you again, Georgie," Amberson said; and his voice was a little husky as he set a kind hand on the young man's shoulder. "It's quite probable that from this time on we'll only know each other by letter—until you're notified as my next of kin that there's an old valise to be forwarded to you, and perhaps some dusty curios from the consulate mantelpiece. Well, it's an odd way for us to be saying good-bye: one wouldn't have thought it, even a few years ago, but here we are, two gentlemen of elegant appearance in a state of bustitude. We can't ever tell what will happen at all, can we? Once I stood where we're standing now, to say good-bye to a pretty girl—only it was in the old station before this was built, and we called it the 'dépôt.' She'd been visiting your mother, before Isabel was married, and I was wild about her, and she admitted she didn't mind that. In fact, we decided we couldn't live without each other, and we were to be married. But she had to go abroad first with her father, and when we came to say good-bye we knew we wouldn't see each other again for almost a year. I thought I couldn't live through it—and she stood here crying. Well, I don't even know where she lives now, or if she *is* living—and I only happen to think of her sometimes when I'm here at the station waiting for a train. If she ever thinks of me she probably imagines I'm still dancing in the ballroom at the Amberson Mansion, and she probably thinks of the Mansion as still beautiful—still the finest house in town. Life and money both behave like loose quicksilver in a nest of cracks. And when they're gone we can't tell where—or what the devil we did with 'em! But I believe I'll say now—while there isn't much time left for either of us to get embarrassed about it—I believe I'll say that I've always been fond of you, Georgie, but I can't say that I always liked you. Sometimes I've felt you were distinctly *not* an acquired taste. Until lately, one had to be fond of you just *naturally*—this isn't very 'tactful,' of course—for if he didn't, well, he wouldn't! We all spoiled you terribly when you were a little boy and let you grow up *en prince*—and I must say you took to it! But you've received a pretty heavy jolt, and I had enough of your disposition, myself, at your age, to understand a little of what cocksure youth has to go through inside when it finds that it *can* make terrible mistakes. Poor old fellow! You get both kinds of jolts together, spiritual and material—and you've taken them pretty quietly and—well, with my train coming into the shed, you'll forgive me for saying that there have been times when I thought you ought to be hanged—but I've always been fond of you, and now I *like* you! And just for a last word: there may be somebody else in this town who's always felt about you like that—fond of you, I mean, no matter how much it seemed you ought to be hanged. You might try—— Hello, I must run. I'll send back the money as fast as they pay me—so, good-bye and God bless you, Georgie!"

He passed through the gates, waved his hat cheerily from the other side of the iron screen, and was lost from sight in the hurrying crowd. And as he disappeared, an unexpected poignant loneliness fell upon his nephew so heavily and so suddenly that he had no energy to recoil from the shock. It seemed to him that the last fragment of his familiar world had disappeared, leaving him all alone forever.

He walked homeward slowly through what appeared to be the strange streets of a strange city; and, as a matter of fact, the city was strange to him. He had seen little of it during his years in college, and then had followed the long absence and his tragic return. Since then he had been "scarcely outdoors at all," as Fanny complained, warning him that his health would suffer, and he had been downtown only in a closed carriage. He had not realized the great change.

The streets were thunderous; a vast energy heaved under the universal coating of dinginess. George walked through the begrimed crowds of hurrying strangers and saw no face that he remembered. Great numbers of the faces were even of a kind he did not remember ever to have seen; they were partly like the old type that his boyhood knew, and partly like types he knew abroad. He saw German eyes with American wrinkles at their corners; he saw Irish eyes and Neapolitan eyes, Roman eyes, Tuscan eyes, eyes of Lombardy, of Savoy, Hungarian eyes, Balkan eyes, Scandinavian eyes—all with a queer American look in them. He saw Jews who had been German Jews, Jews who had been Russian Jews, Jews who had been Polish Jews but were no longer German or Russian or Polish Jews. All the people were soiled by the smoke-mist through which they hurried, under the heavy sky that hung close upon the new skyscrapers; and nearly all seemed harried by something impending, though here and there a woman with bundles would be laughing to a companion about some adventure of the department stores, or perhaps an escape from the charging traffic of the streets—and not infrequently a girl, or a free-and-easy young matron, found time to throw an encouraging look to George.

He took no note of these, and, leaving the crowded sidewalks, turned north into National Avenue, and presently reached the quieter but no less begrimed region of smaller shops and old-fashioned houses. Those latter had been the homes of his boyhood playmates; old friends of his grandfather had lived here;—in this alley he had fought with two boys at the same time, and whipped them; in that front yard he had been successfully teased into temporary insanity by a Sunday-school class of pinky little girls. On that sagging porch a laughing woman had fed him and other boys with doughnuts and gingerbread; yonder he saw the staggered relics of the iron picket fence he had made his white pony jump, on a dare, and in the shabby, stone-faced house behind the fence he had gone to children's parties, and, when he was a little older he had danced there often, and fallen in love with Mary Sharon, and kissed her, apparently by force, under the stairs in the hall. The double front doors, of meaninglessly carved walnut, once so glossily varnished, had been painted smoke gray, but the smoke grime showed repulsively, even on the smoke gray; and over the doors a smoked sign proclaimed the place to be a "Stag Hotel."

Other houses had become boarding-houses too genteel for signs, but many were franker, some offering "board by the day, week or meal," and some, more laconic, contenting themselves with the label: "Rooms." One, having torn out part of an old stone-trimmed bay window for purposes of commercial display, showed forth two suspended petticoats and a pair of oyster-coloured flannel trousers to prove the claims of its black-and-gilt sign: "French Cleaning and Dye House." Its next neighbour also sported a remodelled front and permitted no doubt that its mission in life was to attend cosily upon death: "J. M. Rolsener. Caskets. The Funeral Home." And beyond that, a plain old honest four-square gray-painted brick house was flamboyantly decorated with a great gilt scroll on the railing of the old-fashioned veranda: "Mutual Benev't Order Cavaliers and Dames of Purity." This was the old Minafer house.

George passed it without perceptibly wincing; in fact, he

held his head up, and except for his gravity of countenance and the prison pallor he had acquired by too constantly remaining indoors, there was little to warn an acquaintance that he was not precisely the same George Amberson Minafer known aforetime. He was still so magnificent, indeed, that there came to his ears a waft of comment from a passing automobile. This was a fearsome red car, glittering in brass, with half-a-dozen young people in it whose motorism had reached an extreme manifestation in dress. The ladies of this party were favourably affected at sight of the pedestrian upon the sidewalk, and, as the machine was moving slowly, and close to the curb, they had time to observe him in detail, which they did with a frankness not pleasing to the object of their attentions. "One sees so many nice-looking people one doesn't know nowadays," said the youngest of the young ladies. "This old town of ours is really getting enormous. I shouldn't mind knowing who he is."

"*I* don't know," the youth beside her said, loudly enough to be heard at a considerable distance. "I don't know who he is, but from his looks I know who he thinks he is: he thinks he's the Grand Duke Cuthbert!" There was a burst of tittering as the car gathered speed and rolled away, with the girl continuing to look back until her scandalized companions forced her to turn by pulling her hood over her face. She made an impression upon George, so deep a one, in fact, that he unconsciously put his emotion into a muttered word:

"Riffraff!"

This was the last "walk home" he was ever to take by the route he was now following: up National Avenue to Amberson Addition and the two big old houses at the foot of Amberson Boulevard; for to-night would be the last night that he and Fanny were to spend in the house which the Major had forgotten to deed to Isabel. To-morrow they were to "move out," and George was to begin his work in Bronson's office. He had not come to this collapse without a fierce struggle—but the struggle was inward, and the rolling world was not agitated by it, and rolled calmly on. For of all the "ideals of life" which the world, in its rolling, inconsiderately flattens out to nothingness, the least likely to retain a profile is that ideal which depends upon inheriting money. George Amberson, in spite of his record of failures in business, had spoken shrewdly when he realized at last that money, like life, was "like quicksilver in a nest of cracks." And his nephew had the awakening experience of seeing the great Amberson Estate vanishing into such a nest—in a twinkling, it seemed, now that it was indeed so utterly vanished.

His uncle had suggested that he might write to college friends; perhaps they could help him to something better than the prospect offered by Bronson's office; but George flushed and shook his head, without explaining. In that small and quietly superior "crowd" of his he had too emphatically supported the ideal of being rather than doing. He could not appeal to one of its members now to help him to a job. Besides, they were not precisely the warmest-hearted crew in the world, and he had long ago dropped the last affectation of a correspondence with any of them. He was as aloof from any survival of intimacy with his boyhood friends in the city, and, in truth, had lost track of most of them. "The Friends of the Ace," once bound by oath to succour one another in peril or poverty, were long ago dispersed; one or two had died; one or two had gone to live elsewhere; the others were disappeared into the smoky bigness of the heavy city. Of the brethren, there remained within his present cognizance only his old enemy, the red-haired Kinney, now married to Janie Sharon, and Charlie Johnson, who, out of deference to his mother's memory, had passed the Amberson Mansion one day, when George stood upon the front steps, and, looking in fiercely, had looked away with continued fierceness—his only token of recognition.

. . . On this last homeward walk of his, when George reached the entrance to Amberson Addition—that is, when he came to where the entrance had formerly been—he gave a little start, and halted for a moment to stare. This was the first time he had noticed that the stone pillars, marking the entrance, had been removed. Then he realized that for a long time he had been conscious of a queerness about this corner without being aware of what made the difference. National Avenue met Amberson Boulevard here at an obtuse angle, and the removal of the pillars made the Boulevard seem a cross-street of no overpowering importance—certainly it did not seem to be a boulevard!

At the next corner Neptune's Fountain remained, and one could still determine with accuracy what its designer's intentions had been. It stood in sore need of just one last kindness; and if the thing had possessed any friends they would have done that doleful shovelling after dark.

George did not let his eyes linger upon the relic; nor did he look steadfastly at the Amberson Mansion. Massive as the old house was, it managed to look gaunt: its windows stared with the skull emptiness of all windows in empty houses that are to be lived in no more. Of course the rowdy boys of the neighbourhood had been at work: many of these haggard windows were broken; the front door stood ajar, forced open; and idiot salacity, in white chalk, was smeared everywhere upon the pillars and stone-work of the verandas.

George walked by the Mansion hurriedly, and came home to his mother's house for the last time.

Emptiness was there, too, and the closing of the door resounded through bare rooms; for downstairs there was no furniture in the house except a kitchen table in the dining room, which Fanny had kept "for dinner," she said, though as she was to cook and serve that meal herself George had his doubts about her name for it. Upstairs, she had retained her own furniture, and George had been living in his mother's room, having sent everything from his own to the auction. Isabel's room was still as it had been, but the furniture would be moved with Fanny's to new quarters in the morning. Fanny had made plans for her nephew as well as herself; she had found a "three-room kitchenette apartment" in an apartment house where several old friends of hers had established themselves—elderly widows of citizens once "prominent" and other retired gentry. People used their own "kitchenettes" for breakfast and lunch, but there was a table-d'hôte arrangement for dinner on the ground floor; and after dinner bridge was played all evening, an attraction powerful with Fanny. She had "made all the arrangements," she reported, and nervously appealed for approval, asking if she hadn't shown herself "pretty practical" in such matters. George acquiesced absent-mindedly, not thinking of what she said and not realizing to what it committed him.

He began to realize it now, as he wandered about the dismantled house; he was far from sure that he was willing to go and live in a "three-room apartment" with Fanny and eat breakfast and lunch with her (prepared by herself in the "kitchenette") and dinner at the table d'hôte in "such a pretty Colonial dining room" (so Fanny described it) at a little round table they would have all to themselves in the midst of a dozen little round tables which other relics of disrupted families would have all to themselves. For the first time, now that the change was imminent, George began to develop before his mind's eye pictures of what he was in for; and they appalled him. He decided that such a life verged upon the sheerly unbearable, and that after all there were some things left that he just couldn't stand. So he made up his mind to speak to his aunt about it at "dinner," and tell her that he preferred to ask Bronson to let him put a sofa-bed, a trunk, and a folding rubber bathtub behind a screen in the dark rear room of the office. George felt that this would be infinitely more tolerable; and he could eat at restaurants, especially as about all he ever wanted nowadays was coffee.

But at "dinner" he decided to put off telling Fanny of his plan until later: she was so nervous, and so distressed about the failure of her efforts with sweetbreads and macaroni; and she was so eager in her talk of how comfortable they would be "by this time to-morrow night." She fluttered on, her nervousness increasing, saying how "nice" it would be for him, when he came from work in the evenings, to be among "nice people—people who know who we *are*," and to have a pleasant game of bridge with "people who are really old friends of the family."

When they stopped probing among the scorched fragments she had set forth, George lingered downstairs, waiting for a better opportunity to introduce his own subject, but when he heard dismaying sounds from the kitchen he gave up. There was a crash, then a shower of crashes; falling tin clamoured to be heard above the shattering of porcelain; and over all rose Fanny's wail of lamentation for the treasures saved from the sale, but now lost forever to the "kitchenette." Fanny was nervous indeed; so nervous that she could not trust her hands.

For a moment George thought she might have been injured, but, before he reached the kitchen, he heard her sweeping at the fragments, and turned back. He put off speaking to Fanny until morning.

Things more insistent than his vague plans for a sofa-bed in Bronson's office had possession of his mind as he went upstairs, moving his hand slowly along the smooth walnut railing of the balustrade. Half way to the landing he stopped, turned, and stood looking down at the heavy doors masking the black emptiness that had been the library. Here he had stood on what he now knew was the worst day of his life; here he had stood when his mother passed through that doorway, hand-in-hand with her brother, to learn what her son had done.

He went on more heavily, more slowly; and, more heavily and slowly still, entered Isabel's room and shut the door. He did not come forth again, and bade Fanny good-night through the closed door when she stopped outside it later.

"I've put all the lights out, George," she said. "Everything's all right."

"Very well," he called. "Good-night."

She did not go. "I'm sure we're going to enjoy the new little home, George," she said timidly. "I'll try hard to make things nice for you, and the people really are lovely. You mustn't feel as if things are altogether gloomy, George. I know everything's going to turn out all right. You're young and strong and you have a good mind and I'm sure—" she hesitated—"I'm sure your mother's watching over you, Georgie. Good-night, dear."

"Good-night, Aunt Fanny."

His voice had a strangled sound in spite of him; but she seemed not to notice it, and he heard her go to her own room and lock herself in with bolt and key against burglars. She had said the one thing she should not have said just then: "I'm sure your mother's watching over you, Georgie." She had meant to be kind, but it destroyed his last chance for sleep that night. He would have slept little if she had not said it, but since she had said it, he did not sleep at all. For he knew that it was true—if it *could* be true—and that his mother, if she still lived in spirit, would be weeping on the other side of the wall of silence, weeping and seeking for some gate to let her through so that she could come and "watch over him."

He felt that if there were such gates they were surely barred: they were like those awful library doors downstairs, which had shut her in to begin the suffering to which he had consigned her.

The room was still Isabel's. Nothing had been changed: even the photographs of George, of the Major, and of "brother George" still stood on her dressing-table, and in a drawer of her desk was an old picture of Eugene and Lucy, taken together, which George had found, but had slowly closed away again from sight, not touching it. To-morrow everything would be gone; and he had heard there was not long to wait before the house itself would be demolished. The very space which to-night was still Isabel's room would be cut into new shapes by new walls and floors and ceilings; yet the room would always live, for it could not die out of George's memory. It would live as long as he did, and it would always be murmurous with a tragic, wistful whispering.

And if space itself can be haunted, as memory is haunted, then some time, when the space that was Isabel's room came to be made into the small bedrooms and "kitchenettes" already designed as its destiny, that space might well be haunted and the new occupants come to feel that some seemingly causeless depression hung about it—a wraith of the passion that filled it throughout the last night that George Minafer spent there.

Whatever remnants of the old high-handed arrogance were still within him, he did penance for his deepest sin that night—and it may be that to this day some impressionable, overworked woman in a "kitchenette," after turning out the light, will seem to see a young man kneeling in the darkness, shaking convulsively, and, with arms outstretched through the wall, clutching at the covers of a shadowy bed. It may seem to her that she hears the faint cry, over and over:

"Mother, forgive me! *God*, forgive me!"

Chapter XXXII

At least, it may be claimed for George that his last night in the house where he had been born was not occupied with his own disheartening future, but with sorrow for what sacrifices his pride and youth had demanded of others. And early in the morning he came downstairs and tried to help Fanny make coffee on the kitchen range.

"There was something I wanted to say to you last night, Aunt Fanny," he said, as she finally discovered that an amber fluid, more like tea than coffee, was as near ready to be taken into the human system as it would ever be. "I think I'd better do it now."

She set the coffee-pot back upon the stove with a little crash, and, looking at him in a desperate anxiety, began to twist her dainty apron between her fingers without any consciousness of what she was doing.

"Why—why——" she stammered; but she knew what he was going to say, and that was why she had been more and more nervous. "Hadn't—perhaps—perhaps we'd better get the—the things moved to the little new home first, George. Let's——"

He interrupted quietly, though at her phrase, "the little new home," his pungent impulse was to utter one loud shout and run. "It was about this new place that I wanted to speak. I've been thinking it over, and I've decided. I want you to take all the things from mother's room and use them and keep them for me, and I'm sure the little apartment will be just what you like; and with the extra bedroom probably you could find some woman friend to come and live there, and share the expense with you. But I've decided on another arrangement for myself, and so I'm not going with you. I don't suppose you'll mind much, and I don't see why you *should* mind—particularly, that is. I'm not very lively company these days, or any days, for that matter. I can't imagine you, or any one else, being much attached to me, so——"

He stopped in amazement: no chair had been left in the

kitchen, but Fanny gave a despairing glance around her, in search of one, then sank abruptly, and sat flat upon the floor.

"You're going to leave me in the lurch!" she gasped.

"What on earth——" George sprang to her. "Get up, Aunt Fanny!"

"I can't. I'm too weak. Let me alone, George!" And as he released the wrist he had seized to help her, she repeated the dismal prophecy which for days she had been matching against her hopes: "You're going to leave me—in the lurch!"

"Why no, Aunt Fanny!" he protested. "At first I'd have been something of a burden on you. I'm to get eight dollars a week; about thirty-two a month. The rent's thirty-six dollars a month, and the table-d'hôte dinner runs up to over twenty-two dollars apiece, so with my half of the rent—eighteen dollars—I'd have less than nothing left out of my salary to pay my share of the groceries for all the breakfasts and luncheons. You see you'd not only be doing all the housework and cooking, but you'd be paying more of the expenses than I would."

She stared at him with such a forlorn blankness as he had never seen. "I'd be paying——" she said feebly. "I'd be paying——"

"Certainly you would. You'd be using more of your money than——"

"My money!" Fanny's chin drooped upon her thin chest, and she laughed miserably. "I've got twenty-eight dollars. That's all."

"You mean until the interest is due again?"

"I mean that's all," Fanny said. "I mean that's all there is. There won't be any more interest because there isn't any principal."

"Why, you told——"

She shook her head. "No. I haven't told you anything."

"Then it was Uncle George. *He* told me you had enough to fall back on. That's just what he said: 'to fall back on.' He said you'd lost more than you should, in the headlight company, but he'd insisted that you should hold out enough to live on, and you'd very wisely followed his advice."

"I know," she said weakly. "I told him so. He didn't know, or else he'd forgotten, how much Wilbur's insurance amounted to, and I—oh, it seemed such a sure way to make a real fortune out of a little—and I thought I could do something for *you*, George, if you ever came to need it—and it all looked so bright I just thought I'd put it all in. I did—every cent except my last interest payment—and it's gone."

"Good Lord!" George began to pace up and down the worn planks of the bare floor. "Why on earth did you wait till now to tell such a thing as this?"

"I *couldn't* tell till I had to," she said piteously. "I couldn't till George Amberson went away. He couldn't do anything to help, anyhow, and I just didn't want him to talk to me about it—he's been at me so much about not putting more in than I could afford to lose, and said he considered he had my—my word I *wasn't* putting more than that in it. So I thought: What was the use? What was the use of going over it all with him and having him reproach me, and probably reproach himself? It wouldn't do any good—not any good on earth." She got out her lace handkerchief and began to cry. "Nothing does any good, I guess, in this old world! Oh, how tired of this old world I am! I didn't know *what* to do. I just tried to go ahead and be as practical as I could, and arrange *some* way for us to live. Oh, I knew you didn't want me, George! You always teased me and berated me whenever you had a chance from the time you were a little boy—you did *so*! Later, you've tried to be kinder to me, but you don't want me around—oh, I can see *that* much! You don't suppose I want to thrust myself on you, do you? It isn't very pleasant to be thrusting yourself on a person you know doesn't want you—but I knew you oughtn't to be left all alone in the world; it isn't good. I knew your mother'd want me to watch over you and try to have *something* like a home for you—I know she'd want me to do what I tried to do!" Fanny's tears were bitter now, and her voice, hoarse and wet, was tragically sincere. "I tried—I tried to be practical —to look after your interests—to make things as nice for you as I could—I walked my heels down looking for a place for us to live—I walked and walked over this town—I didn't ride one block on a street-car—I wouldn't use five cents no matter how tired I—— Oh!" She sobbed uncontrollably. "Oh! and now—you don't want—you want—you want to leave me in the lurch! You——"

George stopped walking. "In God's name, Aunt Fanny," he said, "quit spreading out your handkerchief and drying it and then getting it all wet again! I mean stop crying! Do! And for heaven's sake, get up. Don't sit there with your back against the boiler and——"

"It's not hot," Fanny sniffled. "It's cold; the plumbers disconnected it. I wouldn't mind if they hadn't. *I* wouldn't mind if it burned me, George."

"Oh, my *Lord*!" He went to her, and lifted her. "For God's sake, get up! Come, let's take the coffee into the other room, and see what's to be done."

He got her to her feet; she leaned upon him, already somewhat comforted, and, with his arm about her, he conducted her to the dining room and seated her in one of the two kitchen chairs which had been placed at the rough table. "There!" he said, "get over it!" Then he brought the coffee-pot, some lumps of sugar in a tin pan, and, finding that all the coffee-cups were broken, set water glasses upon the table, and poured some of the pale coffee into them. By this time Fanny's spirits had revived appreciably: she looked up with a plaintive eagerness. "I *had* bought all my fall clothes, George," she said; "and I paid every bill I owed. I don't owe a cent for clothes, George."

"That's good," he said wanly, and he had a moment of physical dizziness that decided him to sit down quickly. For an instant it seemed to him that he was not Fanny's nephew, but married to her. He passed his pale hand over his paler forehead. "Well, let's see where we stand," he said feebly. "Let's see if we can afford this place you've selected."

Fanny continued to brighten. "I'm sure it's the most practical plan we could possibly have worked out, George—and it *is* a comfort to be among nice people. I think we'll both enjoy it, because the truth is we've been keeping too much to ourselves for a long while. It isn't good for people."

"I was thinking about the money, Aunt Fanny. You see——"

"I'm sure we can manage it," she interrupted quickly. "There really isn't a cheaper place in town that we could actually live in and be——" Here she interrupted herself. "Oh! There's one *great* economy I forgot to tell you, and it's especially an economy for you, because you're always too generous about such things: they don't allow any tipping. They have signs that prohibit it."

"That's good," he said grimly. "But the rent is thirty-six dollars a month; the dinner is twenty-two and a half for each of us, and we've got to have some provision for other food. We won't need any clothes for a year, perhaps——"

"Oh, longer!" she exclaimed. "So you see——"

"I see that forty-five and thirty-six make eighty-one," he said. "At the lowest, we need a hundred dollars a month—and I'm going to make thirty-two."

"I thought of that, George," she said confidently, "and I'm sure it will be all right. You'll be earning a great deal more than that very soon."

"I don't see any prospect of it—not till I'm admitted to the bar, and that will be two years at the earliest."

Fanny's confidence was not shaken. "I know *you'll* be getting on faster than——"

"'Faster?'" George echoed gravely. "We've got to have more than that to start with."

"Well, there's the six hundred dollars from the sale. Six hundred and twelve dollars it was."

"It isn't six hundred and twelve now," said George. "It's about one hundred and sixty."

Fanny showed a momentary dismay. "Why, how——"

"I lent Uncle George two hundred; I gave fifty apiece to old Sam and those two other old darkies that worked for grandfather so long, and ten to each of the servants here——"

"And you gave me thirty-six," she said thoughtfully, "for the first month's rent, in advance."

"Did I? I'd forgotten. Well, with about a hundred and sixty in bank and our expenses a hundred a month, it doesn't seem as if this new place——"

"Still," she interrupted, "we *have* paid the first month's rent in advance, and it does seem to be the most practical——"

George rose. "See here, Aunt Fanny," he said decisively. "You stay here and look after the moving. Old Frank doesn't expect me until afternoon, this first day, but I'll go and see him now."

. . . It was early, and old Frank, just established at his big, flat-topped desk, was surprised when his prospective assistant and pupil walked in. He was pleased, as well as surprised, however, and rose, offering a cordial old hand. "The real flare!" he said. "The real flare for the law. That's right! Couldn't wait till afternoon to begin! I'm delighted that you——"

"I wanted to say——" George began, but his patron cut him off.

"Wait just a minute, my boy. I've prepared a little speech of welcome, and even though you're five hours ahead of time, I mean to deliver it. First of all, your grandfather was my old war-comrade and my best client; for years I prospered through my connection with his business, and his grandson is welcome in my office and to my best efforts in his behalf. But I want to confess, Georgie, that during your earlier youth I may have had some slight feeling of—well, prejudice, not altogether in your favour; but whatever slight feeling it was, it began to vanish on that afternoon, a good while ago, when you stood up to your Aunt Amelia Amberson as you did in the Major's library, and talked to her as a man and a gentleman should. I saw then what good stuff was in you—and I always wanted to mention it. If my prejudice hadn't altogether vanished after that, the last vestiges disappeared during these trying times that have come upon you this past year, when I have been a witness to the depth of feeling you've shown and your quiet consideration for your grandfather and for everyone else around you. I just want to add that I think you'll find an honest pleasure now in industry and frugality that wouldn't have come to you in a more frivolous career. The law is a jealous mistress and a stern mistress, but a——"

George had stood before him in great and increasing embarrassment; and he was unable to allow the address to proceed to its conclusion.

"I can't do it!" he burst out. "I can't take her for my mistress."

"What?"

"I've come to tell you, I've got to find something that's quicker. I can't——"

Old Frank got a little red. "Let's sit down," he said. "What's the trouble?"

George told him.

The old gentleman listened sympathetically, only murmuring: "Well, well!" from time to time, and nodding acquiescence.

"You see she's set her mind on this apartment," George explained. "She's got some old cronies there, and I guess she's been looking forward to the games of bridge and the kind of harmless gossip that goes on in such places. Really, it's a life she'd like better than anything else—better than that she's lived at home, I really believe. It struck me she's just about got to have it, and after all she could hardly have anything less."

"This comes pretty heavily upon me, you know," said old Frank. "I got her into that headlight company, and she fooled me about her resources as much as she did your Uncle George. I was never your father's adviser, if you remember, and when the insurance was turned over to her some other lawyer arranged it—probably your father's. But it comes pretty heavily on me, and I feel a certain responsibility."

"Not at all. I'm taking the responsibility." And George smiled with one corner of his mouth. "She's not *your* aunt, you know, sir."

"Well, I'm unable to see, even if she's yours, that a young man is morally called upon to give up a career at the law to provide his aunt with a favourable opportunity to play bridge whist!"

"No," George agreed. "But I haven't begun my 'career at the law' so it can't be said I'm making any considerable sacrifice. I'll tell you how it is, sir." He flushed, and, looking out of the streaked and smoky window beside which he was sitting, spoke with difficulty. "I feel as if—as if perhaps I had one or two pretty important things in my life to make up for. Well, I can't. I can't make them up to—to whom I would. It's struck me that, as I couldn't, I might be a little decent to somebody else, perhaps—if I could manage it! I never have been particularly decent to poor old Aunt Fanny."

"Oh, I don't know: I shouldn't say that. A little youthful teasing—I doubt if she's minded so much. She felt your father's death terrifically, of course, but it seems to me she's had a fairly comfortable life—up to now—if she was disposed to take it that way."

"But 'up to now' is the important thing," George said. "Now is now—and you see I can't wait two years to be admitted to the bar and begin to practice. I've got to start in at something else that pays from the start, and that's what I've come to you about. I have an idea, you see."

"Well, I'm glad of that!" said old Frank, smiling. "I can't think of anything just at this minute that pays from the start."

"I only know of one thing, myself."

"What is it?"

George flushed again, but managed to laugh at his own embarrassment. "I suppose I'm about as ignorant of business as anybody in the world," he said. "But I've heard they pay very high wages to people in dangerous trades; I've always heard they did, and I'm sure it must be true. I mean people that handle touchy chemicals or high explosives—men in dynamite factories, or who take things of that sort about the country in wagons, and shoot oil wells, I thought I'd see if you couldn't tell me something more about it, or else introduce me to someone who could, and then I thought I'd see if I couldn't get something of the kind to do as soon as possible. My nerves are good; I'm muscular, and I've got a steady hand; it seemed to me that this was about the only line of work in the world that I'm fitted for. I wanted to get started to-day if I could."

Old Frank gave him a long stare. At first this scrutiny was sharply incredulous; then it was grave; finally it developed into a threat of overwhelming laughter; a forked vein in his forehead became more visible and his eyes seemed about to protrude.

But he controlled his impulse; and, rising, took up his hat and overcoat. "All right," he said. "If you'll promise not to get blown up, I'll go with you to see if we can find the job." Then, meaning what he said, but amazed that he did mean it, he added: "You certainly are the most practical young man I ever met!"

Chapter XXXIII

THEY FOUND the job. It needed an apprenticeship of only six weeks, during which period George was to receive fifteen dollars a week; after that he would get twenty-eight. This settled the apartment question, and Fanny was presently established in a greater contentment than she had known for a long time. Early every morning she made something she called (and believed to be) coffee for George, and he was gallant enough not to undeceive her. She lunched alone in her "kitchenette," for George's place of employment was ten miles out of town on an interurban trolley-line, and he seldom returned before seven. Fanny found partners for bridge by two o'clock almost every afternoon, and she played until about six. Then she got George's "dinner clothes" out for him—he maintained this habit—and she changed her own dress. When he arrived he usually denied that he was tired, though he sometimes looked tired, particularly during the first few months; and he explained to her frequently—looking bored enough with her insistence—that his work was "fairly light, and fairly congenial, too." Fanny had the foggiest idea of what it was, though she noticed that it roughened his hands and stained them. "Something in those new chemical works," she explained to casual inquirers. It was not more definite in her own mind.

Respect for George undoubtedly increased within her, however, and she told him she'd always had a feeling he might "turn out to be a mechanical genius, or something." George assented with a nod, as the easiest course open to him. He did not take a hand at bridge after dinner: his provisions for Fanny's happiness refused to extend that far, and at the table d'hôte he was a rather discouraging boarder. He was considered "affected" and absurdly "up-stage" by the one or two young men, and the three or four young women, who enlivened the elderly retreat; and was possibly less popular there than he had been elsewhere during his life, though he was now nothing worse than a coldly polite young man who kept to himself. After dinner he would escort his aunt from the table in some state (not wholly unaccompanied by a leerish wink or two from the wags of the place) and he would leave her at the door of the communal parlours and card rooms, with a formality in his bow of farewell which afforded an amusing contrast to Fanny's always voluble protests. (She never failed to urge loudly that he really *must* come and play, just this once, and not go hiding from everybody in his room *every* evening like this!) At least some of the other inhabitants found the contrast amusing, for sometimes, as he departed stiffly toward the elevator, leaving her still entreating in the doorway (though with one eye already on her table, to see that it was not seized) a titter would follow him which he was no doubt meant to hear. He did not care whether they laughed or not.

And once, as he passed the one or two young men of the place entertaining the three or four young women, who were elbowing and jerking on a settee in the lobby, he heard a voice inquiring quickly, as he passed:

"What makes people tired?"

"Work?"

"No."

"Well, what's the answer?"

Then, with an intentional outbreak of mirth, the answer was given by two loudly whispering voices together:

"A stuck-up boarder!"

George didn't care.

On Sunday mornings Fanny went to church and George took long walks. He explored the new city, and found it hideous, especially in the early spring, before the leaves of the shade trees were out. Then the town was fagged with the long winter and blacked with the heavier smoke that had been held close to the earth by the smoke-fog it bred. Everything was damply streaked with the soot: the walls of the houses, inside and out, the gray curtains at the windows, the windows themselves, the dirty cement and unswept asphalt underfoot, the very sky overhead. Throughout this murky season he continued his explorations, never seeing a face he knew—for, on Sunday, those whom he remembered, or who might remember him, were not apt to be found within the limits of the town, but were congenially occupied with the new outdoor life which had come to be the mode since his boyhood. He and Fanny were pretty thoroughly buried away within the bigness of the city.

One of his Sunday walks, that spring, he made into a sour pilgrimage. It was a misty morning of belated snow slush, and suited him to a perfection of miserableness, as he stood before the great dripping department store which now occupied the big plot of ground where once had stood both the Amberson Hotel and the Amberson Opera House. From there he drifted to the old "Amberson Block," but this was fallen into a backwater; business had stagnated here. The old structure had not been replaced, but a cavernous entryway for trucks had been torn in its front, and upon the cornice, where the old separate metal letters had spelt "Amberson Block," there was a long billboard sign: "Doogan Storage."

To spare himself nothing, he went out National Avenue and saw the piles of slush-covered wreckage where the Mansion and his mother's house had been, and where the Major's ill-fated five "new" houses had stood; for these were down, too, to make room for the great tenement already shaped in unending lines of foundation. But the Fountain of Neptune was gone at last—and George was glad that it was!

He turned away from the devastated site, thinking bitterly that the only Amberson mark still left upon the town was the name of the boulevard—Amberson Boulevard. But he had reckoned without the city council of the new order, and by an unpleasant coincidence, while the thought was still in his mind, his eye fell upon a metal oblong sign upon the lamp-post at the corner. There were two of these little signs upon the lamp-post, at an obtuse angle to each other, one to give passers-by the name of National Avenue, the other to acquaint them with Amberson Boulevard. But the one upon which should have been stencilled "Amberson Boulevard" exhibited the words "Tenth Street."

George stared at it hard. Then he walked quickly along the boulevard to the next corner and looked at the little sign there. "Tenth Street."

It had begun to rain, but George stood unheeding, staring at the little sign. "Damn them!" he said finally, and, turning up his coat-collar, plodded back through the soggy streets toward "home."

The utilitarian impudence of the city authorities put a thought into his mind. A week earlier he had happened to stroll into the large parlour of the apartment house, finding it empty, and on the centre-table he noticed a large, red-bound, gilt-edged book, newly printed, bearing the title: "A Civic History," and beneath the title, the rubric, "Biographies of the 500 Most Prominent Citizens and Families in the History of the City." He had glanced at it absently, merely noticing the title and sub-title, and wandered out of the room, thinking of other things and feeling no curiosity about the book. But he had thought of it several times since with a faint, vague uneasiness; and now when he entered the lobby he walked directly into the parlour where he had seen the book. The room was empty, as it always was on Sunday mornings, and the flamboyant volume was still upon the table—evidently a fixture as a sort of local Almanach de Gotha, or Burke, for the enlightenment of tenants and boarders.

He opened it, finding a few painful steel engravings of placid, chin-bearded faces, some of which he remembered dimly; but much more numerous, and also more unfamiliar to him, were the pictures of neat, aggressive men, with clipped short hair and clipped short moustaches—almost all of them strangers to him. He delayed not long with these, but turned to the index where the names of the five hundred Most Prominent Citizens and Families in the History of the City were arranged in alphabetical order, and ran his finger down the column of *A*'s:

Abbett
Abbott
Abrams
Adams
Adams
Adler
Akers
Albertsmeyer
Alexander
Allen
Ambrose
Ambuhl
Anderson
Andrews
Appenbasch
Archer
Arszman
Ashcraft
Austin
Avey

George's eyes remained for some time fixed on the thin space between the names "Allen" and "Ambrose." Then he closed the book quietly, and went up to his own room, agreeing with the elevator boy, on the way, that it was getting to be a mighty nasty wet and windy day outside.

The elevator boy noticed nothing unusual about him and neither did Fanny, when she came in from church with her hat ruined, an hour later. And yet something had happened —a thing which, years ago, had been the eagerest hope of many, many good citizens of the town. They had thought of it, longed for it, hoping acutely that they might live to see the day when it would come to pass. And now it had happened at last: Georgie Minafer had got his come-upance.

He had got it three times filled and running over. The city had rolled over his heart, burying it under, as it rolled over the Major's and buried it under. The city had rolled over the Ambersons and buried them under to the last vestige; and it mattered little that George guessed easily enough that most of the five hundred Most Prominent had paid something substantial "to defray the cost of steel engraving, etc."—the Five Hundred had heaved the final shovelful of soot upon that heap of obscurity wherein the Ambersons were lost forever from sight and history. "Quicksilver in a nest of cracks!"

Georgie Minafer had got his come-upance, but the people who had so longed for it were not there to see it, and they never knew it. Those who were still living had forgotten all about it and all about him.

Chapter XXXIV

THERE WAS one border section of the city which George never explored in his Sunday morning excursions. This was far out to the north where lay the new Elysian Fields of the millionaires, though he once went as far in that direction as the white house which Lucy had so admired long ago—her "Beautiful House." George looked at it briefly and turned back, rumbling with an interior laugh of some grimness. The house was white no longer; nothing could be white which the town had reached, and the town reached far beyond the beautiful white house now. The owners had given up and painted it a despairing chocolate, suitable to the freight-yard life it was called upon to endure.

George did not again risk going even so far as that, in the direction of the millionaires, although their settlement began at least two miles farther out. His thought of Lucy and her father was more a sensation than a thought, and may be compared to that of a convicted cashier beset by recollections of the bank he had pillaged—there are some thoughts to which one closes the mind. George had seen Eugene only once since their calamitous encounter. They had passed on opposite sides of the street, downtown; each had been aware of the other, and each had been aware that the other was aware of him, and yet each kept his eyes straight forward, and neither had shown a perceptible alteration of countenance. It seemed to George that he felt emanating from the outwardly imperturbable person of his mother's old friend a hate that was like a hot wind.

At his mother's funeral and at the Major's he had been conscious that Eugene was there: though he had afterward no recollection of seeing him, and, while certain of his presence, was uncertain how he knew of it. Fanny had not told him, for she understood George well enough not to speak to him of Eugene or Lucy. Nowadays Fanny almost never saw either of them and seldom thought of them—so sly is the way of time with life. She was passing middle age, when old intensities and longings grow thin and flatten out as Fanny herself was thinning and flattening out; and she was settling down contentedly to her apartment house intimacies. She was precisely suited by the table-d'hôte life, with its bridge, its variable alliances and shifting feuds, and the long whisperings of elderly ladies at corridor corners—those eager but suppressed conversations, all sibilance, of which the elevator boy declared he heard the words "*she said*" a million times and the word "*she*," five million. The apartment house suited Fanny and swallowed her.

The city was so big, now, that people disappeared into it unnoticed, and the disappearance of Fanny and her nephew was not exceptional. People no longer knew their neighbours as a matter of course; one lived for years next door to strangers—that sharpest of all the changes since the old days—and a friend would lose sight of a friend for a year, and not know it.

One May day George thought he had a glimpse of Lucy. He was not certain, but he was sufficiently disturbed, in spite of his uncertainty. A promotion in his work now frequently took him out of town for a week, or longer, and it was upon his return from one of these absences that he had the strange experience. He had walked home from the station, and as he turned the corner which brought him in sight of the apartment house entrance, though two blocks distant from it, he saw a charming little figure come out, get into a shiny landaulet automobile, and drive away. Even at that distance no one could have any doubt that the little figure was charming; and the height, the quickness and decision of motion, even the swift gesture of a white glove toward the chauffeur—all were characteristic of Lucy. George was instantly subjected to a shock of indefinable nature, yet definitely a shock: he did not know what he felt—but he knew that he felt. Heat surged over him: probably he would not have come face to face with her if the restoration of all the ancient Amberson magnificence could have been his reward. He went on slowly, his knees shaky.

But he found Fanny not at home; she had been out all afternoon; and there was no record of any caller—and he began to wonder, then to doubt if the small lady he had seen in the distance was Lucy. It might as well have been, he said to himself—since any one who looked like her could give him "a jolt like that!"

Lucy had not left a card. She never left one when she called on Fanny; though she did not give her reasons a quite definite form in her own mind. She came seldom; this was but the third time that year, and, when she did come, George was not mentioned, either by her hostess or by herself—an oddity contrived between the two ladies without either of them realizing how odd it was. For, naturally, while Fanny was with Lucy, Fanny thought of George, and what time Lucy had George's aunt before her eyes she could not well avoid the thought of him. Consequently, both looked absent-minded as they talked, and each often gave a wrong answer which the other consistently failed to notice.

At other times Lucy's thoughts of George were anything but continuous, and weeks went by when he was not consciously in her mind at all. Her life was a busy one: she had the big house "to keep up"; she had a garden to keep up, too, a large and beautiful garden; she represented her father as a director for half a dozen public charity organizations, and did private charity work of her own, being a proxy mother of several large families; and she had "danced down," as she said, groups from eight or nine classes of new graduates returned from the universities, without marrying any of them, but she still danced—and still did not marry.

Her father, observing this circumstance happily, yet with some hypocritical concern, spoke of it to her one day as they stood in her garden. "I suppose I'd want to shoot him," he said, with attempted lightness. "But I mustn't be an old pig. I'd build you a beautiful house close by—just over yonder."

"No, no! That would be like——" she began impulsively; then checked herself. George Amberson's comparison of the Georgian house to the Amberson Mansion had come into her mind, and she thought that another new house, built close by for her, would be like the house the Major built for Isabel.

"Like what?"

"Nothing." She looked serious, and when he reverted to his idea of "some day" grudgingly surrendering her up to a suitor, she invented a legend. "Did you ever hear the Indian name for that little grove of beech trees on the other side of the house?" she asked him.

"No—and you never did either!" he laughed.

"Don't be so sure! I read a great deal more than I used to—getting ready for my bookish days when I'll have to do something solid in the evenings and won't be asked to dance any more, even by the very youngest boys who think it's a sporting event to dance with the oldest of the 'older girls.' The name of the grove was 'Loma-Nashah' and it means 'They-Couldn't-Help-It'."

"Doesn't sound like it."

"Indian names don't. There was a bad Indian chief lived in the grove before the white settlers came. He was the worst Indian that ever lived, and his name was—it was 'Vendonah.' That means 'Rides-Down-Everything'."

"What?"

"His name was Vendonah, the same thing as Rides-Down-Everything."

"I see," said Eugene thoughtfully. He gave her a quick look and then fixed his eyes upon the end of the garden path. "Go on."

"Vendonah was an unspeakable case," Lucy continued. "He was so proud that he wore iron shoes, and he walked over people's faces with them. He was always killing people that way, and so at last the tribe decided that it wasn't a good enough excuse for him that he was young and inexperienced—he'd have to go. They took him down to the river, and put him in a canoe, and pushed him out from shore; and then they ran along the bank and wouldn't let him land, until at last the current carried the canoe out into the middle, and then on down to the ocean, and he never got back. They didn't want him back, of course, and if he'd been able to manage it, they'd have put him in another canoe and shoved him out into the river again. But still, they didn't elect another chief in his place. Other tribes thought that was curious, and wondered about it a lot, but finally they came to the conclusion that the beech grove people were afraid a new chief might turn out to be a bad Indian, too, and wear iron shoes like Vendonah. But they were wrong, because the real reason was that the tribe had led such an exciting life under Vendonah that they couldn't settle down to anything tamer. He was awful, but he always kept things happening—terrible things, of course. They hated him, but they weren't able to discover any other warrior that they wanted to make chief in his place. I suppose it was a little like drinking a glass of too strong wine and then trying to take the taste out of your mouth with barley water. They couldn't help feeling that way."

"I see," said Eugene. "So that's why they named the place 'They-Couldn't-Help-It'!"

"It must have been."

"And so you're going to stay here in your garden," he said musingly. "You think it's better to keep on walking these sunshiny gravel paths between your flower-beds, and growing to look like a pensive garden lady in a Victorian engraving."

"I suppose I'm like the tribe that lived here, papa. I had too much unpleasant excitement. It was unpleasant—but it was excitement. I don't want any more; in fact, I don't want anything but you."

"You don't?" He looked at her keenly, and she laughed and shook her head; but he seemed perplexed, rather doubtful. "What was the name of the grove?" he asked. "The Indian name, I mean."

"Mola-Haha."

"No, it wasn't; that wasn't the name you said."

"I've forgotten."

"I see you have," he said, his look of perplexity remaining. "Perhaps you remember the chief's name better."

She shook her head again. "I don't!"

At this he laughed, but not very heartily, and walked slowly to the house, leaving her bending over a rose-bush, and a shade more pensive than the most pensive garden lady in any Victorian engraving.

. . . Next day, it happened that this same "Vendonah" or "Rides-Down-Everything" became the subject of a chance conversation between Eugene and his old friend Kinney, father of the fire-topped Fred. The two gentlemen found themselves smoking in neighbouring leather chairs beside a broad window at the club, after lunch.

Mr. Kinney had remarked that he expected to get his family established at the seashore by the Fourth of July, and, following a train of thought, he paused and chuckled. "Fourth of July reminds me," he said. "Have you heard what that Georgie Minafer is doing?"

"No, I haven't," said Eugene, and his friend failed to notice the crispness of the utterance.

"Well, sir," Kinney chuckled again, "it beats the devil! My boy Fred told me about it yesterday. He's a friend of this young Henry Akers, son of F. P. Akers of the Akers Chemical Company. It seems this young Akers asked Fred if he knew a fellow named Minafer, because he knew Fred had always lived here, and young Akers had heard some way that Minafer used to be an old family name here, and was sort of curious about it. Well, sir, you remember this young Georgie sort of disappeared, after his grandfather's death, and nobody seemed to know much what had become of him—though I did hear, once or twice, that he was still around somewhere. Well, sir, he's working for the Akers Chemical Company, out at their plant on the Thomasville Road."

He paused, seeming to reserve something to be delivered only upon inquiry, and Eugene offered him the expected question, but only after a cold glance through the nose-glasses he had lately found it necessary to adopt. "What does he do?"

Kinney laughed and slapped the arm of his chair. "He's a nitro-glycerin expert!"

He was gratified to see that Eugene was surprised, if not, indeed, a little startled.

"He's what?"

"He's an expert on nitro-glycerin. Doesn't that beat the devil! Yes, sir! Young Akers told Fred that this George Minafer had worked like a houn'-dog ever since he got started out at the works. They have a special plant for nitro-glycerin, way off from the main plant, o' course—in the woods somewhere—and George Minafer's been working there, and lately they put him in charge of it. He oversees shooting oil-wells, too, and shoots 'em himself, sometimes. They aren't allowed to carry it on the railroads, you know—have to team it. Young Akers says George rides around over the bumpy roads, sitting on as much as three hundred quarts of nitro-glycerin! My Lord! Talk about romantic tumbles! If he gets blown sky-high some day he won't have a bigger drop, when he comes down, than he's already had! Don't it beat the devil! Young Akers said he's got all the nerve there is in the world. Well, he always did have plenty of *that*—from the time he used to ride around here on his white pony and fight all the Irish boys in Can-Town, with his long curls all handy to be pulled out. Akers says he gets a fair salary, and I should think he ought to! Seems to me I've heard the average life in that sort of work is somewhere around four years, and agents don't write any insurance at all for nitro-glycerin experts. Hardly!"

"No," said Eugene. "I suppose not."

Kinney rose to go. "Well, it's a pretty funny thing—pretty odd, I mean—and I suppose it would be pass-around-the-hat for old Fanny Minafer if he blew up. Fred told me that they're living in some apartment house, and said Georgie supports her. He was going to study law, but couldn't earn enough that way to take care of Fanny, so he gave it up. Fred's wife told him all this. Says Fanny doesn't do anything but play bridge these days. Got to playing too high for awhile and lost more than she wanted to tell Georgie about, and borrowed a little from old Frank Bronson. Paid him back, though. Don't know how Fred's wife heard it. Women do hear the darndest things!"

"They do," Eugene agreed.

"I thought you'd probably heard about it—thought most likely Fred's wife might have said something to your daughter, especially as they're cousins."

"I think not."

"Well, I'm off to the store," said Mr. Kinney briskly; yet he lingered. "I suppose we'll all have to club in and keep old Fanny out of the poorhouse if he does blow up. From all I hear it's usually only a question of time. They say she hasn't got anything else to depend on."

"I suppose not."

"Well—I wondered——" Kinney hesitated. "I was wondering why you hadn't thought of finding something around your works for him. They say he's an all-fired worker and he certainly does seem to have hid some decent stuff in him under all his damfoolishness. And you used to be such a tremendous friend of the family—I thought perhaps you—of course I know he's a queer lot—I know he's——"

"Yes, I think he is," said Eugene. "No. I haven't anything to offer him."

"I suppose not," Kinney returned thoughtfully, as he went out. "I don't know that I would myself. Well, we'll probably see his name in the papers some day if he stays with that job!"

. . . However, the nitro-glycerin expert of whom they spoke did not get into the papers as a consequence of being blown up, although his daily life was certainly a continuous exposure to that risk. Destiny has a constant passion for the incongruous, and it was George's lot to manipulate wholesale quantities of terrific and volatile explosives in safety, and to be laid low by an accident so commonplace and inconsequent that it was a comedy. Fate had reserved for him the final insult of riding him down under the wheels of one of those juggernauts at which he had once shouted "Git a hoss!" Nevertheless, Fate's ironic choice for Georgie's undoing was not a big and swift and momentous car, such as Eugene manufactured; it was a specimen of the hustling little type that was flooding the country, the cheapest, commonest, hardiest little car ever made.

The accident took place upon a Sunday morning, on a downtown crossing, with the streets almost empty, and no reason in the world for such a thing to happen. He had gone out for his Sunday morning walk, and he was thinking of an automobile at the very moment when the little car struck him; he was thinking of a shiny landaulet and a charming figure stepping into it, and of the quick gesture of a white glove toward the chauffeur, motioning him to go on. George heard a shout but did not look up, for he could not imagine anybody's shouting at him, and he was too engrossed in the question "Was it Lucy?" He could not decide, and his lack of decision in this matter probably superinduced a lack of decision in another, more pressingly vital. At the second and louder shout he did look up; and the car was almost on him; but he could not make up his mind if the charming little figure he had seen was Lucy's and he could not make up his mind whether to go backward or forward: these questions became entangled in his mind. Then, still not being able to decide which of two ways to go, he tried to go both—and the little car ran him down. It was not moving very rapidly, but it went all the way over George.

He was conscious of gigantic violence; of roaring and jolting and concussion; of choking clouds of dust, shot with lightning, about his head; he heard snapping sounds as loud as shots from a small pistol, and was stabbed by excruciating pains in his legs.

Then he became aware that the machine was being lifted off of him. People were gathering in a circle round him, gabbling.

His forehead was bedewed with the sweat of anguish, and he tried to wipe off this dampness, but failed. He could not get his arm that far.

"Nev' mind," a policeman said; and George could see above his eyes the skirts of the blue coat, covered with dust and sunshine. "Amb'lance be here in a minute. Nev' mind tryin' to move any. You want 'em to send for some special doctor?"

"No." George's lips formed the word.

"Or to take you to some private hospital?"

"Tell them to take me," he said faintly, "to the City Hospital."

"A' right."

A smallish young man in a duster fidgeted among the crowd, explaining and protesting, and a strident voiced girl, his companion, supported his argument, declaring to everyone her willingness to offer testimony in any court of law that every blessed word he said was the God's truth.

"It's the fella that hit you," the policeman said, looking down on George. "I guess he's right; you must of b'en thinkin' about somep'm' or other. It's wunnerful the damage them little machines can do—you'd never think it—but I guess they ain't much case ag'in this fella that was drivin' it."

"You bet your life they ain't no case on me!" the young man in the duster agreed, with great bitterness. He came and stood at George's feet, addressing him heatedly: "I'm sorry fer *you* all right, and I don't say I ain't. I hold nothin' against you, but it wasn't any more my fault than the state-house! You run into me, much as I run into you, and if you get well you ain't goin' to get not one single cent out o' me! This lady here was settin' with me and we both yelled at you. Wasn't goin' a *step* over eight mile an hour! I'm perfectly willing to say I'm sorry for you though, and so's the lady with me. We're both willing to say that much, but that's all, understand!"

George's drawn eyelids twitched; his misted glance rested fleetingly upon the two protesting motorists, and the old imperious spirit within him flickered up in a single word. Lying on his back in the middle of the street, where he was regarded by an increasing public as an unpleasant curiosity, he spoke this word clearly from a mouth filled with dust, and from lips smeared with blood.

. . . It was a word which interested the policeman. When the ambulance clanged away, he turned to a fellow patrolman who had joined him. "Funny what he says to the little cuss that done the damage. That's all he *did* call him—nothin' else at all—and the cuss had broke both his legs fer him and God-knows-what-all!"

"I wasn't here then. What was it?"

"'Riffraff!'"

Chapter XXXV

EUGENE'S FEELING about George had not been altered by his talk with Kinney in the club window, though he was somewhat disturbed. He was not disturbed by Kinney's hint that Fanny Minafer might be left on the hands of her friends through her nephew's present dealings with nitro-glycerin, but he was surprised that Kinney had "led up" with intentional tact to the suggestion that a position might be made for George in the Morgan factory. Eugene did not care to have any suggestions about Georgie Minafer made to him. Kinney had represented Georgie as a new Georgie—at least in spots —a Georgie who was proving that decent stuff had been hid in him; in fact, a Georgie who was doing rather a handsome thing in taking a risky job for the sake of his aunt, poor old silly Fanny Minafer! Eugene didn't care what risks Georgie took, or how much decent stuff he had in him: nothing that Georgie would ever do in this world or the next could change Eugene Morgan's feeling toward him.

If Eugene could possibly have brought himself to offer Georgie a position in the automobile business, he knew full well the proud devil wouldn't have taken it from him; though Georgie's proud reason would not have been the one attributed to him by Eugene. George would never reach the point where he could accept anything material from Eugene and preserve the self-respect he had begun to regain.

But if Eugene had wished, he could easily have taken George out of the nitro-glycerin branch of the chemical works. Always interested in apparent impossibilities of invention, Eugene had encouraged many experiments in such gropings as those for the discovery of substitutes for gasoline and rubber; and, though his mood had withheld the information from Kinney, he had recently bought from the elder Akers a substantial quantity of stock on the condition that the chemical company should establish an experimental laboratory. He intended to buy more; Akers was anxious to please him; and a word from Eugene would have placed George almost anywhere in the chemical works. George need never have known it, for

Eugene's purchases of stock were always quiet ones: the transaction remained, so far, between him and Akers, and could be kept between them.

The possibility just edged itself into Eugene's mind; that is, he let it become part of his perceptions long enough for it to prove to him that it was actually a possibility. Then he half started with disgust that he should be even idly considering such a thing over his last cigar for the night, in his library. "No!" And he threw the cigar into the empty fireplace and went to bed.

His bitterness for himself might have worn away, but never his bitterness for Isabel. He took that thought to bed with him —and it was true that nothing George could do would ever change this bitterness of Eugene. Only George's mother could have changed it.

And as Eugene fell asleep that night, thinking thus bitterly of Georgie, Georgie in the hospital was thinking of Eugene. He had come "out of ether" with no great nausea, and had fallen into a reverie, though now and then a white sailboat staggered foolishly into the small ward where he lay. After a time he discovered that this happened only when he tried to open his eyes and look about him; so he kept his eyes shut, and his thoughts were clearer. He thought of Eugene Morgan and of the Major; they seemed to be the same person for awhile, but he managed to disentangle them and even to understand why he had confused them. Long ago his grandfather had been the most striking figure of success in the town: "As rich as Major Amberson!" they used to say. Now it was Eugene. "If I had Eugene Morgan's money," he would hear the workmen day-dreaming at the chemical works; or, "If Eugene Morgan had hold of this place you'd see things hum!" And the boarders at the table d'hôte spoke of "the Morgan Place" as an eighteenth-century Frenchman spoke of Versailles. Like his uncle, George had perceived that the "Morgan Place" was the new Amberson Mansion. His reverie went back to the palatial days of the Mansion, in his boyhood, when he would gallop his pony up the driveway and order the darkey stablemen about, while they whooped and obeyed, and his grandfather, observing from a window, would laugh and call out to him, "That's right, Georgie. Make those lazy rascals jump!" He remembered his gay young uncles, and how the town was eager concerning everything about them, and about himself. What a clean, pretty town it had been! And in his reverie he saw like a pageant before him the magnificence of the Ambersons—its passing, and the passing of the Ambersons themselves. They had been slowly engulfed without knowing how to prevent it, and almost without knowing what was happening to them. The family lot, in the shabby older quarter, out at the cemetery, held most of them now; and the name was swept altogether from the new city. But the new great people who had taken their places—the Morgans and Akerses and Sheridans—they would go, too. George saw that. They would pass, as the Ambersons had passed, and though some of them might do better than the Major and leave the letters that spelled a name on a hospital or a street, it would be only a word and it would not stay forever. Nothing stays or holds or keeps where there is growth, he somehow perceived vaguely but truly. Great Cæsar dead and turned to clay stopped no hole to keep the wind away; dead Cæsar was nothing but a tiresome bit of print in a book that schoolboys study for awhile and then forget. The Ambersons had passed, and the new people would pass, and the new people that came after them, and then the next new ones, and the next—and the next——

He had begun to murmur, and the man on duty as night nurse for the ward came and bent over him.

"Did you want something?"

"There's nothing in this family business," George told him confidentially. "Even George Washington is only something in a book."

. . . Eugene read a report of the accident in the next morning's paper. He was on the train, having just left for New York, on business, and with less leisure would probably have overlooked the obscure item:

LEGS BROKEN

G. A. Minafer, an employe of the Akers Chemical Co., was run down by an automobile yesterday at the corner of Tennessee and Main and had both legs broken. Minafer was to blame for the accident according to patrolman F. A. Kax, who witnessed the affair. The automobile was a small one driven by Herbert Cottleman of 2173 Noble Avenue who stated that he was making less than 4 miles an hour. Minafer is said to belong to a family formerly of considerable prominence in the city. He was taken to the City Hospital where physicians stated later that he was suffering from internal injuries besides the fracture of his legs but might recover.

Eugene read the item twice, then tossed the paper upon the opposite seat of his compartment, and sat looking out of the window. His feeling toward Georgie was changed not a jot by his human pity for Georgie's human pain and injury. He thought of Georgie's tall and graceful figure, and he shivered, but his bitterness was untouched. He had never blamed Isabel for the weakness which had cost them the few years of happiness they might have had together; he had put the blame all on the son, and it stayed there.

He began to think poignantly of Isabel: he had seldom been able to "see" her more clearly than as he sat looking out of his compartment window, after reading the account of this accident. She might have been just on the other side of the glass, looking in at him—and then he thought of her as the pale figure of a woman, seen yet unseen, flying through the air, beside the train, over the fields of springtime green and through the woods that were just sprouting out their little leaves. He closed his eyes and saw her as she had been long ago. He saw the brown-eyed, brown-haired, proud, gentle, laughing girl he had known when first he came to town, a boy just out of the State College. He remembered—as he had remembered ten thousand times before—the look she gave him when her brother George introduced him to her at a picnic; it was "like hazel starlight" he had written her, in a poem, afterward. He remembered his first call at the Amberson Mansion, and what a great personage she seemed, at home in that magnificence; and yet so gay and friendly. He remembered the first time he had danced with her—and the old waltz song began to beat in his ears and in his heart. They laughed and sang it together as they danced to it:

> "Oh, love for a year, a week, a day,
> But alas for the love that lasts alway——"

Most plainly of all he could see her dancing; and he became articulate in the mourning whisper: "So graceful—oh, so graceful——"

All the way to New York it seemed to him that Isabel was near him, and he wrote of her to Lucy from his hotel the next night:

> I saw an account of the accident to George Minafer. I'm sorry, though the paper states that it was plainly his own fault. I suppose it may have been as a result of my attention falling upon the item that I thought of his mother a great deal on the way here. It seemed to me that I had never seen her more distinctly or so constantly, but, as you know, thinking of his mother is not very apt to make me admire *him*! Of course, however, he has my best wishes for his reeovery.

He posted the letter, and by the morning's mail received one from Lucy written a few hours after his departure from home. She enclosed the item he had read on the train.

> I thought you might not see it,
>
> I have seen Miss Fanny and she has got him put into a room by himself. Oh, *poor* Rides-Down-Everything! I have been thinking so constantly of his mother and it seemed to me that I have never seen her more distinctly. How lovely she was—and how she loved him!

If Lucy had not written this letter Eugene might not have done the odd thing he did that day. Nothing could have been more natural than that both he and Lucy should have thought intently of Isabel after reading the account of George's accident, but the fact that Lucy's letter had crossed his own made Eugene begin to wonder if a phenomenon of telepathy might not be in question, rather than a chance coincidence. The reference to Isabel in the two letters was almost identical: he and Lucy, it appeared, had been thinking of Isabel at the same time —both said "constantly" thinking of her—and neither had ever "seen her more distinctly." He remembered these phrases in his own letter accurately.

Reflection upon the circumstance stirred a queer spot in Eugene's brain—he had one. He was an adventurer; if he had lived in the sixteeth century he would have sailed the unknown new seas, but having been born in the latter part of the nineteenth, when geography was a fairly well-settled matter, he had become an explorer in mechanics. But the fact that he was a "hard-headed business man" as well as an adventurer did not keep him from having a queer spot in his brain, because hard-headed business men are as susceptible to such spots as adventurers are. Some of them are secretly troubled when they do not see the new moon over the lucky shoulder; some of them have strange, secret incredulities—they do not believe in geology, for instance; and some of them think they have had supernatural experiences. "Of course there was nothing in it—still it *was* queer!" they say.

Two weeks after Isabel's death, Eugene had come to New York on urgent business and found that the delayed arrival of a steamer gave him a day with nothing to do. His room at the hotel had become intolerable; outdoors was intolerable; everything was intolerable. It seemed to him that he must see Isabel once more, hear her voice once more; that he *must* find some way to her, or lose his mind. Under this pressure he had gone, with complete scepticism, to a "trance-medium" of whom he had heard wild accounts from the wife of a business acquaintance. He thought despairingly that at least such an excursion would be "trying to do *some*thing!" He remembered the woman's name; found it in the telephone book, and made an appointment.

The experience had been grotesque, and he came away with an encouraging message from his father, who had failed to identify himself satisfactorily, but declared that everything was "on a higher plane" in his present state of being, and that all life was "continuous and progressive." Mrs. Horner spoke of herself as a "psychic"; but otherwise she seemed oddly unpretentious and matter-of-fact; and Eugene had no doubt at all of her sincerity. He was sure that she was not an intentional fraud, and though he departed in a state of annoyance with himself, he came to the conclusion that if any credulity were played upon by Mrs. Horner's exhibitions, it was her own.

Nevertheless, his queer spot having been stimulated to action by the coincidence of the letters, he went to Mrs. Horner's after his directors' meeting to-day. He used the telephone booth in the directors' room to make the appointment; and he laughed feebly at himself, and wondered what the group of men in that mahogany apartment would think if they knew what he was doing. Mrs. Horner had changed her address, but he found the new one, and somebody purporting to be a niece of hers talked to him and made an appointment for a "sitting" at five o'clock.

He was prompt, and the niece, a dull-faced fat girl with a magazine under her arm, admitted him to Mrs. Horner's apartment, which smelt of camphor; and showed him into a room with gray painted walls, no rug on the floor and no furniture except a table (with nothing on it) and two chairs: one a leather easy-chair and the other a stiff little brute with a wooden seat. There was one window with the shade pulled down to the sill, but the sun was bright outside, and the room had light enough.

Mrs. Horner appeared in the doorway, a wan and unenterprising looking woman in brown, with thin hair artificially waved—but not recently—and parted in the middle over a bluish forehead. Her eyes were small and seemed weak, but she recognized the visitor.

"Oh, you been here before," she said, in a thin voice, not unmusical. "I recollect you. Quite a time ago, wa'n't it?"

"Yes, quite a long time."

"I recollect because I recollect you was disappointed. Anyway, you was kind of cross." She laughed faintly.

"I'm sorry if I seemed so," Eugene said. "Do you happen to have found out my name?"

She looked surprised and a little reproachful. "Why, no. I never try to find out people's names. Why should I? I don't claim anything for the power; I only know I have it—and some ways it ain't always such a blessing, neither, I can tell you!"

Eugene did not press an investigation of her meaning, but said vaguely, "I suppose not. Shall we——"

"All right," she assented, dropping into the leather chair, with her back to the shaded window. "You better set down, too, I reckon. I hope you'll get something this time so you won't feel cross, but I dunno. *I* can't never tell what they'll do. Well——"

She sighed, closed her eyes, and was silent, while Eugene, seated in the stiff chair across the table from her, watched her profile, thought himself an idiot, and called himself that and other names. And as the silence continued, and the impassive woman in the easy-chair remained impassive, he began to wonder what had led him to be such a fool. It became clear to him that the similarity of his letter and Lucy's needed no explanation involving telepathy, and was not even an extraordinary coincidence. What, then, had brought him back to this absurd place and caused him to be watching this absurd woman taking a nap in a chair? In brief: What the devil did he mean by it? He had not the slightest interest in Mrs. Horner's naps—or in her teeth, which were being slightly revealed by the unconscious parting of her lips, as her breathing became heavier. If the vagaries of his own mind had brought him into such a grotesquerie as this, into what did the vagaries of other men's minds take them? Confident that he was ordinarily saner than most people, he perceived that since he was capable of doing a thing like this, other men did even more idiotic things, in secret. And he had a fleeting vision of sober-looking bankers and manufacturers and lawyers, well-dressed church-going men, sound citizens—and all as queer as the deuce inside!

How long was he going to sit here presiding over this unknown woman's slumbers? It struck him that to make the picture complete he ought to be shooing flies away from her with a palm-leaf fan.

Mrs. Horner's parted lips closed again abruptly, and became compressed; her shoulders moved a little, then jerked repeatedly; her small chest heaved; she gasped, and the compressed lips relaxed to a slight contortion, then began to move, whispering and bringing forth indistinguishable mutterings.

Suddenly she spoke in a loud, husky voice:

"Lopa is here!"

"Yes," Eugene said dryly. "That's what you said last time. I remember 'Lopa.' She's your 'control' I think you said."

"*I*'m Lopa," said the husky voice. "*I*'m Lopa herself."

"You mean I'm to suppose you're not Mrs. Horner now?"

"Never was Mrs. Horner!" the voice declared, speaking undeniably from Mrs. Horner's lips—but with such conviction that Eugene, in spite of everything, began to feel himself in the presence of a third party, who was none the less an individual, even though she might be another edition of the apparently somnambulistic Mrs. Horner. "Never was Mrs. Horner or anybody but just Lopa. Guide."

"You mean you're Mrs. Horner's guide?" he asked.

"*Your* guide now," said the voice with emphasis, to which was incongruously added a low laugh. "You came here once before. Lopa remembers."

"Yes—so did Mrs. Horner."

Lopa overlooked his implication, and continued quickly: "You build. Build things that go. You came here once and old gentleman on this side, he spoke to you. Same old gentleman here now. He tell Lopa he's your grandfather—no, he says 'father.' He's your father."

"What's his appearance?"

"How?"

"What does he look like?"

"Very fine! White beard, but not long beard. He says someone else wants to speak to you. See here. Lady. Not his wife, though. No. Very fine lady! Fine lady, fine lady!"

"Is it my sister?" Eugene asked.

"Sister? No. She is shaking her head. She has pretty brown hair. She is fond of you. She is someone who knows you very well but she is not your sister. She is very anxious to say something to you—very anxious. Very fond of you; very anxious to talk to you. Very glad you came here—oh, *very* glad!"

"What is her name?"

"Name," the voice repeated, and seemed to ruminate. "Name hard to get—always very hard for Lopa. Name. She wants to tell me her name to tell you. She wants you to understand names are hard to make. She says you must think of something that makes a sound." Here the voice seemed to put a question to an invisible presence and to receive an answer. "A little sound or a big sound? She says it might be a little sound or a big sound. She says a ring—oh, Lopa knows! She means a bell! That's it, a bell."

Eugene looked grave. "Does she mean her name is Belle?"

"Not quite. Her name is longer."

"Perhaps," he suggested, "she means that she was a belle."

"No. She says she thinks you know what she means. She says you must think of a colour. What colour?" Again Lopa addressed the unknown, but this time seemed to wait for an answer.

"Perhaps she means the colour of her eyes," said Eugene.

"No. She says her colour is light—it's a light colour and you can see through it."

"Amber?" he said, and was startled, for Mrs. Horner, with her eyes still closed, clapped her hands, and the voice cried out in delight:

"Yes! She says you know who she is from amber. Amber! Amber! That's it! She says you understand what her name is from a bell and from amber. She is laughing and waving a lace handkerchief at me because she is pleased. She says I have made you know who it is."

This was the strangest moment of Eugene's life, because, while it lasted, he believed that Isabel Amberson, who was dead, had found means to speak to him. Though within ten minutes he doubted it, he believed it then.

His elbows pressed hard upon the table, and, his head between his hands, he leaned forward, staring at the commonplace figure in the easy-chair. "What does she wish to say to me?"

"She is happy because you know her. No—she is troubled. Oh—a great trouble! Something she wants to tell you. She wants so *much* to tell you. She wants Lopa to tell you. This is a great trouble. She says—oh, yes, she wants you to be—to be kind! That's what she says. That's it. To be kind."

"Does she——"

"She wants you to be kind," said the voice. "She nods when I tell you this. Yes; it must be right. She is a very fine lady. Very pretty. She is so anxious for you to understand. She hopes and hopes you will. Someone else wants to speak to you. This is a man. He says——"

"I don't want to speak to any one else," said Eugene quickly. "I want——"

"This man who has come says that he is a friend of yours. He says——"

Eugene struck the table with his fist. "I don't want to speak to any one else, I tell you!" he cried passionately. "If she is there I——" He caught his breath sharply, checked himself, and sat in amazement. Could his mind so easily accept so stupendous a thing as true? Evidently it could!

Mrs. Horner spoke languidly in her own voice: "Did you get anything satisfactory?" she asked. "I certainly hope it wasn't like that other time when you was cross because they couldn't get anything for you."

"No, no," he said hastily. "This was different. It was very interesting."

He paid her, went to his hotel, and thence to his train

for home. Never did he so seem to move through a world of dream-stuff: for he knew that he was not more credulous than other men, and if he could believe what he had believed, though he had believed it for no longer than a moment or two, what hold had he or any other human being on reality?

His credulity vanished (or so he thought) with his recollection that it was he, and not the alleged "Lopa," who had suggested the word "amber." Going over the mortifying, plain facts of his experience, he found that Mrs. Horner, or the subdivision of Mrs. Horner known as "Lopa," had told him to think of a bell and of a colour, and that being furnished with these scientific data, he had leaped to the conclusion that he spoke with Isabel Amberson!

For a moment he had believed that Isabel was *there*, believed that she was close to him, entreating him—entreating him "to be kind." But with this recollection a strange agitation came upon him. After all, *had* she not spoken to him? If his own unknown consciousness had told the "psychic's" unknown consciousness how to make the picture of the pretty brown-haired, brown-eyed lady, hadn't the picture been a true one? And hadn't the true Isabel—oh, indeed her very soul!—called to him out of his own true memory of her?

And as the train roared through the darkened evening he looked out beyond his window, and saw her as he had seen her on his journey, a few days ago—an ethereal figure flying beside the train, but now it seemed to him that she kept her face toward his window with an infinite wistfulness.

. . . "To be kind!" If it had been Isabel, was that what she would have said? If she were anywhere, and could come to him through the invisible wall, what would be the first thing she would say to him?

Ah, well enough, and perhaps bitterly enough, he knew the answer to that question! "To be kind"—to Georgie!

. . . A red-cap at the station, when he arrived, leaped for his bag, abandoning another which the Pullman porter had handed him. "Yessuh, Mist' Morgan. Yessuh. You' car waitin' front the station fer you, Mist' Morgan, suh!"

And people in the crowd about the gates turned to stare, as he passed through, whispering, "*That's Morgan.*"

Outside, the neat chauffeur stood at the door of the touring-car like a soldier in whip-cord.

"I'll not go home now, Harry," said Eugene, when he had got in. "Drive to the City Hospital."

"Yes, sir," the man returned. "Miss Lucy's there. She said she expected you'd come there before you went home."

"She did?"

"Yes, sir."

Eugene stared. "I suppose Mr. Minafer must be pretty bad," he said.

"Yes, sir. I understand he's liable to get well, though, sir." He moved his lever into high speed, and the car went through the heavy traffic like some fast, faithful beast that knew its way about, and knew its master's need of haste. Eugene did not speak again until they reached the hospital.

Fanny met him in the upper corridor, and took him to an open door.

He stopped on the threshold, startled; for, from the waxen face on the pillow, almost it seemed the eyes of Isabel herself were looking at him: never before had the resemblance between mother and son been so strong—and Eugene knew that now he had once seen it thus startlingly, he need divest himself of no bitterness "to be kind" to Georgie.

George was startled, too. He lifted a white hand in a queer gesture, half forbidding, half imploring, and then let his arm fall back upon the coverlet. "You must have thought my mother wanted you to come," he said, "so that I could ask you to—to forgive me."

But Lucy, who sat beside him, lifted ineffable eyes from him to her father, and shook her head. "No, just to take his hand—gently!"

She was radiant.

But for Eugene another radiance filled the room. He knew that he had been true at last to his true love, and that through him she had brought her boy under shelter again. Her eyes would look wistful no more.

ALICE ADAMS

To S. S. McClure

Chapter I

THE PATIENT, an old-fashioned man, thought the nurse made a mistake in keeping both of the windows open, and her sprightly disregard of his protests added something to his hatred of her. Every evening he told her that anybody with ordinary gumption ought to realize that night air was bad for the human frame. "The human frame won't stand everything, Miss Perry," he warned her, resentfully. "Even a child, if it had just ordinary gumption, ought to know enough not to let the night air blow on sick people—yes, nor well people, either! 'Keep out of the night air, no matter how well you feel.' That's what my mother used to tell me when I was a boy. 'Keep out of the night air, Virgil,' she'd say. 'Keep out of the night air.'"

"I expect probably her mother told her the same thing," the nurse suggested.

"Of course she did. My grandmother——"

"Oh, I guess your *grand*mother thought so, Mr. Adams! That was when all this flat central country was swampish and hadn't been drained off yet. I guess the truth must been the swamp mosquitoes bit people and gave 'em malaria, especially before they began to put screens in their windows. Well, we got screens in these windows, and no mosquitoes are goin' to bite us; so just you be a good boy and rest your mind and go to sleep like you need to."

"Sleep?" he said. "Likely!"

He thought the night air worst of all in April; he hadn't a doubt it would kill him, he declared. "It's miraculous what the human frame *will* survive," he admitted on the last evening of that month. "But you and the doctor ought to both be taught it won't stand too dang much! You poison a man and poison and poison him with this April night air——"

"Can't poison you with much more of it," Miss Perry interrupted him, indulgently. "To-morrow it'll be May night air, and I expect that'll be a lot better for you, don't you? Now let's just sober down and be a good boy and get some nice sound sleep."

She gave him his medicine, and, having set the glass upon the center table, returned to her cot, where, after a still interval, she snored faintly. Upon this, his expression became that of a man goaded out of overpowering weariness into irony.

"Sleep? Oh, *certainly*, thank you!"

However, he did sleep intermittently, drowsed between times, and even dreamed; but, forgetting his dreams before he opened his eyes, and having some part of him all the while aware of his discomfort, he believed, as usual, that he lay awake the whole night long. He was conscious of the city as of some single great creature resting fitfully in the dark outside his windows. It lay all round about, in the damp cover of its night cloud of smoke, and tried to keep quiet for a few hours after midnight, but was too powerful a growing thing ever to lie altogether still. Even while it strove to sleep it muttered with digestions of the day before, and these already merged with rumblings of the morrow. "Owl" cars, bringing in last passengers over distant trolley-lines, now and then howled on a curve; far-away metallic stirrings could be heard from factories in the sooty suburbs on the plain outside the city; east, west, and south, switch-engines chugged and snorted on sidings; and everywhere in the air there seemed to be a faint, voluminous hum as of innumerable wires trembling overhead to vibration of machinery underground.

In his youth Adams might have been less resentful of sounds such as these when they interfered with his night's sleep: even during an illness he might have taken some pride in them as proof of his citizenship in a "live town"; but at fifty-five he merely hated them because they kept him awake. They "pressed on his nerves," as he put it; and so did almost everything else, for that matter.

He heard the milk-wagon drive into the cross-street beneath his windows and stop at each house. The milkman carried his jars round to the "back porch," while the horse moved slowly ahead to the gate of the next customer and waited there. "He's gone into Pollocks'," Adams thought, following this progress. "I hope it'll sour on 'em before breakfast. Delivered the Andersons'. Now he's getting out ours. Listen to the darn brute! What's *he* care who wants to sleep!" His complaint was of the horse, who casually shifted weight with a clink of steel shoes on the worn brick pavement of the street, and then heartily shook himself in his harness, perhaps to dislodge a fly far ahead of its season. Light had just filmed the windows; and with that the first sparrow woke, chirped instantly, and roused neighbours in the trees of the small yard, including a loud-voiced robin. Vociferations began irregularly, but were soon unanimous.

"Sleep? Dang likely now, ain't it!"

Night sounds were becoming day sounds; the far-away hooting of freight-engines seemed brisker than an hour ago in the dark. A cheerful whistler passed the house, even more careless of sleepers than the milkman's horse had been; then a group of coloured workmen came by, and although it was impossible to be sure whether they were homeward bound from night-work or on their way to day-work, at least it was certain that they were jocose. Loose, aboriginal laughter preceded them afar, and beat on the air long after they had gone by.

The sick-room night-light, shielded from his eyes by a newspaper propped against a water-pitcher, still showed a thin glimmering that had grown offensive to Adams. In his wandering and enfeebled thoughts, which were much more often imaginings than reasonings, the attempt of the night-light to resist the dawn reminded him of something unpleasant, though he could not discover just what the unpleasant thing was. Here was a puzzle that irritated him the more because he could not solve it, yet always seemed just on the point of a solution. However, he may have lost nothing cheerful by remaining in the dark upon the matter; for if he had been a little sharper in this introspection he might have concluded that the squalor of the night-light, in its seeming effort to show against the forerunning of the sun itself, had stimulated some half-buried perception within him to sketch the painful little synopsis of an autobiography.

In spite of noises without, he drowsed again, not knowing that he did; and when he opened his eyes the nurse was just rising from her cot. He took no pleasure in the sight, it may be said. She exhibited to him a face mismodelled by sleep, and set like a clay face left on its cheek in a hot and dry studio. She was still only in part awake, however, and by the time she had extinguished the night-light and given her patient his tonic, she had recovered enough plasticity. "Well, isn't that grand!

We've had another good night," she said as she departed to dress in the bathroom.

"Yes, you had another!" he retorted, though not until after she had closed the door.

Presently he heard his daughter moving about in her room across the narrow hall, and so knew that she had risen. He hoped she would come in to see him soon, for she was the one thing that didn't press on his nerves, he felt; though the thought of her hurt him, as, indeed, every thought hurt him. But it was his wife who came first.

She wore a lank cotton wrapper, and a crescent of gray hair escaped to one temple from beneath the handkerchief she had worn upon her head for the night and still retained; but she did everything possible to make her expression cheering.

"Oh, you're better again! I can see that, as soon as I look at you," she said. "Miss Perry tells me you've had another splendid night."

He made a sound of irony, which seemed to dispose unfavourably of Miss Perry, and then, in order to be more certainly intelligible, he added, "She slept well, as usual!"

But his wife's smile persisted. "It's a good sign to be cross; it means you're practically convalescent right now."

"Oh, I am, am I?"

"No doubt in the world!" she exclaimed. "Why, you're practically a well man, Virgil—all except getting your strength back, of course, and that isn't going to take long. You'll be right on your feet in a couple of weeks from now."

"Oh, I will?"

"Of course you will!" She laughed briskly, and, going to the table in the center of the room, moved his glass of medicine an inch or two, turned a book over so that it lay upon its other side, and for a few moments occupied herself with similar futilities, having taken on the air of a person who makes things neat, though she produced no such actual effect upon them. "Of course you will," she repeated, absently. "You'll be as strong as you ever were; maybe stronger." She paused for a moment, not looking at him, then added, cheerfully, "So that you can fly around and find something really good to get into."

Something important between them came near the surface here, for though she spoke with what seemed but a casual cheerfulness, there was a little betraying break in her voice, a trembling just perceptible in the utterance of the final word. And she still kept up the affectation of being helpfully preoccupied with the table, and did not look at her husband—perhaps because they had been married so many years that without looking she knew just what his expression would be, and preferred to avoid the actual sight of it as long as possible. Meanwhile, he stared hard at her, his lips beginning to move with little distortions not lacking in the pathos of a sick man's agitation.

"So that's it," he said. "That's what you're hinting at."

"'Hinting?'" Mrs. Adams looked surprised and indulgent. "Why, I'm not doing any hinting, Virgil."

"What did you say about my finding 'something good to get into?'" he asked, sharply. "Don't you call that hinting?"

Mrs. Adams turned toward him now; she came to the bedside and would have taken his hand, but he quickly moved it away from her.

"You mustn't let yourself get nervous," she said. "But of course when you get well there's only one thing to do. You mustn't go back to that old hole again."

"'Old hole?' That's what you call it, is it?" In spite of his weakness, anger made his voice strident, and upon this stimulation she spoke more urgently.

"You just mustn't go back to it, Virgil. It's not fair to any of us, and you know it isn't."

"Don't tell me what I know, please!"

She clasped her hands, suddenly carrying her urgency to plaintive entreaty. "Virgil, you *won't* go back to that hole?"

"That's a nice word to use to me!" he said. "Call a man's business a hole!"

"Virgil, if you don't owe it to me to look for something different, don't you owe it to your children? Don't tell me you won't do what we all want you to, and what you know in your heart you ought to! And if you *have* got into one of your stubborn fits and are bound to go back there for no other reason except to have your own way, don't tell me so, for I can't bear it!"

He looked up at her fiercely. "You've got a fine way to cure a sick man!" he said; but she had concluded her appeal—for that time—and instead of making any more words in the matter, let him see that there were tears in her eyes, shook her head, and left the room.

Alone, he lay breathing rapidly, his emaciated chest proving itself equal to the demands his emotion put upon it. "Fine!" he repeated, with husky indignation. "Fine way to cure a sick man! Fine!" Then, after a silence, he gave forth whispering sounds as of laughter, his expression the while remaining sore and far from humour.

"And give us our daily bread!" he added, meaning that his wife's little performance was no novelty.

Chapter II

IN FACT, the agitation of Mrs. Adams was genuine, but so well under her control that its traces vanished during the three short steps she took to cross the narrow hall between her husband's door and the one opposite. Her expression was matter-of-course, rather than pathetic, as she entered the pretty room where her daughter, half dressed, sat before a dressing-table and played with the reflections of a three-leafed mirror framed in blue enamel. That is, just before the moment of her mother's entrance, Alice had been playing with the mirror's reflections—posturing her arms and her expressions, clasping her hands behind her neck, and tilting back her head to foreshorten the face in a tableau conceived to represent sauciness, then one of smiling weariness, then one of scornful toleration, and all very piquant; but as the door opened she hurriedly resumed the practical, and occupied her hands in the arrangement of her plentiful brownish hair.

They were pretty hands, of a shapeliness delicate and fine. "The best things she's got!" a cold-blooded girl friend said of them, and meant to include Alice's mind and character in the implied list of possessions surpassed by the notable hands. However that may have been, the rest of her was well enough. She was often called "a right pretty girl"—temperate praise meaning a girl rather pretty than otherwise, and this she deserved, to say the least. Even in repose she deserved it, though repose was anything but her habit, being seldom seen upon her except at home. On exhibition she led a life of gestures, the unkind said to make her lovely hands more memorable; but all of her usually accompanied the gestures of the hands, the shoulders ever giving them their impulses first, and even her feet being called upon, at the same time, for eloquence.

So much liveliness took proper place as only accessory to that of the face, where her vivacity reached its climax; and it was unfortunate that an ungifted young man, new in the town, should have attempted to define the effect upon him of all this generosity of emphasis. He said that "the way she used her cute hazel eyes and the wonderful glow of her facial expression gave her a mighty spiritual quality." His actual rendition of the word was "spirichul"; but it was not his pronunciation that embalmed this outburst in the perennial laughter of Alice's girl friends; they made the misfortune far less his than hers.

Her mother comforted her too heartily, insisting that Alice had "plenty enough spiritual qualities," certainly more than possessed by the other girls who flung the phrase at her, wooden things, jealous of everything they were incapable of themselves; and then Alice, getting more championship than she sought, grew uneasy lest Mrs. Adams should repeat such defenses "outside the family"; and Mrs. Adams ended by weeping because the daughter so distrusted her intelligence. Alice frequently thought it necessary to instruct her mother.

Her morning greeting was an instruction to-day; or, rather, it was an admonition in the style of an entreaty, the more petulant as Alice thought that Mrs. Adams might have had a glimpse of the posturings to the mirror. This was a needless worry; the mother had caught a thousand such glimpses, with Alice unaware, and she thought nothing of the one just flitted.

"For heaven's sake, mama, come clear inside the room and shut the door! *Please* don't leave it open for everybody to look at me!"

"There isn't anybody to see you," Mrs. Adams explained, obeying. "Miss Perry's gone downstairs, and——"

"Mama, I heard you in papa's room," Alice said, not dropping the note of complaint. "I could hear both of you, and I don't think you ought to get poor old papa so upset—not in his present condition, anyhow."

Mrs. Adams seated herself on the edge of the bed. "He's better all the time," she said, not disturbed. "He's almost well. The doctor says so and Miss Perry says so; and if we don't get him into the right frame of mind now we never will. The first day he's outdoors he'll go back to that old hole—you'll see! And if he once does that, he'll settle down there and it'll be too late and we'll never get him out."

"Well, anyhow, I think you could use a little more tact with him."

"I do try to," the mother sighed. "It never was much use with him. I don't think you understand him as well as I do, Alice."

"There's one thing I don't understand about either of you," Alice returned, crisply. "Before people get married they can do anything they want to with each other. Why can't they do the same thing after they're married? When you and papa were young people and engaged, he'd have done anything you wanted him to. That must have been because you knew how to manage him then. Why can't you go at him the same way now?"

Mrs. Adams sighed again, and laughed a little, making no other response; but Alice persisted. "Well, *why* can't you? Why can't you ask him to do things the way you used to ask him when you were just in love with each other? Why don't you anyhow try it, mama, instead of ding-donging at him?"

"'Ding-donging at him,' Alice?" Mrs. Adams said, with a pathos somewhat emphasized. "Is that how my trying to do what I can for you strikes you?"

"Never mind that; it's nothing to hurt your feelings." Alice disposed of the pathos briskly. "Why don't you answer my question? What's the matter with using a little more tact on papa? Why can't you treat him the way you probably did when you were young people, before you were married? I never have understood why people can't do that."

"Perhaps you *will* understand some day," her mother said, gently. "Maybe you will when you've been married twenty-five years."

"You keep evading. Why don't you answer my question right straight out?"

"There are questions you can't answer to young people, Alice."

"You mean because we're too young to understand the answer? I don't see that at all. At twenty-two a girl's supposed to have some intelligence, isn't she? And intelligence is the ability to understand, isn't it? Why do I have to wait till I've lived with a man twenty-five years to understand why you can't be tactful with papa?"

"You may understand some things before that," Mrs. Adams said, tremulously. "You may understand how you hurt me sometimes. Youth can't know everything by being intelligent, and by the time you could understand the answer you're asking for you'd know it, and wouldn't need to ask. You don't understand your father, Alice; you don't know what it takes to change him when he's made up his mind to be stubborn."

Alice rose and began to get herself into a skirt. "Well, I don't think making scenes ever changes anybody," she grumbled. "I think a little jolly persuasion goes twice as far, myself."

"'A little jolly persuasion!'" Her mother turned the echo of this phrase into an ironic lament. "Yes, there was a time when I thought that, too! It didn't work; that's all."

"Perhaps you left the 'jolly' part of it out, mama."

For the second time that morning—it was now a little after seven o'clock—tears seemed about to offer their solace to Mrs. Adams. "I might have expected you to say that, Alice; you never do miss a chance," she said, gently. "It seems queer you don't some time miss just *one* chance!"

But Alice, progressing with her toilet, appeared to be little concerned. "Oh, well, I think there are better ways of managing a man than just hammering at him."

Mrs. Adams uttered a little cry of pain. "'Hammering,' Alice?"

"If you'd left it entirely to me," her daughter went on, briskly, "I believe papa'd already be willing to do anything we want him to."

"That's it; tell me I spoil everything. Well, I won't interfere from now on, you can be sure of it."

"Please don't talk like that," Alice said, quickly. "I'm old enough to realize that papa may need pressure of all sorts; I only think it makes him more obstinate to get him cross. You probably do understand him better, but that's one thing I've found out and you haven't. There!" She gave her mother a friendly tap on the shoulder and went to the door. "I'll hop in and say hello to him now."

As she went, she continued the fastening of her blouse, and appeared in her father's room with one hand still thus engaged, but she patted his forehead with the other.

"Poor old papa-daddy!" she said, gaily. "Every time he's better somebody talks him into getting so mad he has a relapse. It's a shame!"

Her father's eyes, beneath their melancholy brows, looked up at her wistfully. "I suppose you heard your mother going for me," he said.

"I heard you going for her, too!" Alice laughed. "What was it all about?"

"Oh, the same danged old story!"

"You mean she wants you to try something new when you get well?" Alice asked, with cheerful innocence. "So we could all have a lot more money?"

At this his sorrowful forehead was more sorrowful than ever. The deep horizontal lines moved upward to a pattern of suffering so familiar to his daughter that it meant nothing to her; but he spoke quietly. "Yes; so we wouldn't have any money at all, most likely."

"Oh, no!" she laughed, and, finishing with her blouse, patted his cheeks with both hands. "Just think how many grand openings there must be for a man that knows as much as you do! I always did believe you could get rich if you only cared to, papa."

But upon his forehead the painful pattern still deepened. "Don't you think we've always had enough, the way things are, Alice?"

"Not the way things *are*!" She patted his cheeks again; laughed again. "It used to be enough, maybe—anyway we did skimp along on it—but the way things are now I expect mama's really pretty practical in her ideas, though, I think it's a shame for her to bother you about it while you're so weak. Don't you worry about it, though; just think about other things till you get strong."

"You know," he said; "you know it isn't exactly the easiest thing in the world for a man of my age to find these grand openings you speak of. And when you've passed half-way from fifty to sixty you're apt to see some risk in giving up what you know how to do and trying something new."

"My, what a frown!" she cried, blithely. "Didn't I tell you to stop thinking about it till you get *all* well?" She bent over him, giving him a gay little kiss on the bridge of his nose. "There! I must run to breakfast. Cheer up now! *Au 'voir!*" And with her pretty hand she waved further encouragement from the closing door as she departed.

Lightsomely descending the narrow stairway, she whistled as she went, her fingers drumming time on the rail; and, still whistling, she came into the dining-room, where her mother and her brother were already at the table. The brother, a thin and sallow boy of twenty, greeted her without much approval as she took her place.

"Nothing seems to trouble you!" he said.

"No; nothing much," she made airy response. "What's troubling yourself, Walter?"

"Don't let that worry you!" he returned, seeming to consider this to be repartee of an effective sort; for he furnished a short laugh to go with it, and turned to his coffee with the manner of one who has satisfactorily closed an episode.

"Walter always seems to have so many secrets!" Alice said, studying him shrewdly, but with a friendly enough amusement in her scrutiny. "Everything he does or says seems to be acted for the benefit of some mysterious audience inside himself, and he always gets its applause. Take what he said just now: he seems to think it means something, but if it does, why, that's just another secret between him and the secret audience inside of him! We don't really know anything about Walter at all, do we, mama?"

Walter laughed again, in a manner that sustained her theory well enough; then after finishing his coffee, he took from his pocket a flattened packet in glazed blue paper; extracted with stained fingers a bent and wrinkled little cigarette, lighted it, hitched up his belted trousers with the air of a person who turns from trifles to things better worth his attention, and left the room.

Alice laughed as the door closed. "He's *all* secrets," she said. "Don't you think you really ought to know more about him, mama?"

"I'm sure he's a good boy," Mrs. Adams returned, thoughtfully. "He's been very brave about not being able to have the advantages that are enjoyed by the boys he's grown up with. I've never heard a word of complaint from him."

"About his not being sent to college?" Alice cried. "I should think you wouldn't! He didn't even have enough ambition to finish high school!"

Mrs. Adams sighed. "It seemed to me Walter lost his ambition when nearly all the boys he'd grown up with went to Eastern schools to prepare for college, and we couldn't afford to send him. If only your father would have listened——"

Alice interrupted: "What nonsense! Walter hated books and studying, and athletics, too, for that matter. He doesn't care for anything nice that I ever heard of. What do you suppose he does like, mama? He must like something or other somewhere, but what do you suppose it is? What does he do with his time?"

"Why, the poor boy's at Lamb and Company's all day. He doesn't get through until five in the afternoon; he doesn't *have* much time."

"Well, we never have dinner until about seven, and he's always late for dinner, and goes out, heaven knows where, right afterward!" Alice shook her head. "He used to go with our friends' boys, but I don't think he does now."

"Why, how could he?" Mrs. Adams protested. "That isn't *his* fault, poor child! The boys he knew when he was younger are nearly all away at college."

"Yes, but he doesn't see anything of 'em when they're here at holiday-time or vacation. None of 'em come to the house any more."

"I suppose he's made other friends. It's natural for him to want companions, at his age."

"Yes," Alice said, with disapproving emphasis. "But who are they? I've got an idea he plays pool at some rough place down-town."

"Oh, no; I'm sure he's a steady boy," Mrs. Adams protested, but her tone was not that of thoroughgoing conviction, and she added, "Life might be a very different thing for him if only your father can be brought to see——"

"Never mind, mama! It isn't me that has to be convinced, you know; and we can do a lot more with papa if we just let him alone about it for a day or two. Promise me you won't say any more to him until—well, until he's able to come downstairs to table. Will you?"

Mrs. Adams bit her lip, which had begun to tremble. "I think you can trust me to know a *few* things, Alice," she said. "I'm a little older than you, you know."

"That's a good girl!" Alice jumped up, laughing. "Don't forget it's the same as a promise, and do just cheer him up a little. I'll say good-bye to him before I go out."

"Where are you going?"

"Oh, I've got lots to do. I thought I'd run out to Mildred's to see what she's going to wear to-night, and then I want to go down and buy a yard of chiffon and some narrow ribbon to make new bows for my slippers—you'll have to give me some money——"

"If he'll give it to me!" her mother lamented, as they went toward the front stairs together; but an hour later she came into Alice's room with a bill in her hand.

"He has some money in his bureau drawer," she said. "He finally told me where it was."

There were traces of emotion in her voice, and Alice, looking shrewdly at her, saw moisture in her eyes.

"Mama!" she cried. "You didn't do what you promised me you wouldn't, did you—*not* before Miss Perry!"

"Miss Perry's getting him some broth," Mrs. Adams returned, calmly. "Besides, you're mistaken in saying I promised you anything; I said I thought you could trust me to know what is right."

"So you did bring it up again!" And Alice swung away from her, strode to her father's door, flung it open, went to him, and put a light hand soothingly over his unrelaxed forehead.

"Poor old papa!" she said. "It's a shame how everybody wants to trouble him. He shan't be bothered any more at all! He doesn't need to have everybody telling him how to get away from that old hole he's worked in so long and begin to make us all nice and rich. *He* knows how!"

Thereupon she kissed him a consoling good-bye, and made another gay departure, the charming hand again fluttering like a white butterfly in the shadow of the closing door.

Chapter III

MRS. ADAMS had remained in Alice's room, but her mood seemed to have changed, during her daughter's little more than momentary absence.

"What did he *say*?" she asked, quickly, and her tone was hopeful.

"'Say?'" Alice repeated, impatiently. "Why, nothing. I didn't let him. Really, mama, I think the best thing for you to do would be to just keep out of his room, because I don't believe you can go in there and not talk to him about it, and if you do talk we'll never get him to do the right thing. Never!"

The mother's response was a grieving silence; she turned from her daughter and walked to the door.

"Now, for goodness' sake!" Alice cried. "Don't go making tragedy out of my offering you a little practical advice!"

"I'm not," Mrs. Adams gulped, halting. "I'm just—just going to dust the downstairs, Alice." And with her face still averted, she went out into the little hallway, closing the door behind her. A moment later she could be heard descending the stairs, the sound of her footsteps carrying somehow an effect of resignation.

Alice listened, sighed, and, breathing the words, "Oh, murder!" turned to cheerier matters. She put on a little apple-green turban with a dim gold band round it, and then, having shrouded the turban in a white veil, which she kept pushed up above her forehead, she got herself into a tan coat of soft cloth fashioned with rakish severity. After that, having studied herself gravely in a long glass, she took from one of the drawers of her dressing-table a black leather card-case cornered in silver filigree, but found it empty.

She opened another drawer wherein were two white pasteboard boxes of cards, the one set showing simply "Miss Adams," the other engraved in Gothic characters, "Miss Alys Tuttle Adams." The latter belonged to Alice's "Alys" period—most girls go through it; and Alice must have felt that she had graduated, for, after frowning thoughtfully at the exhibit this morning, she took the box with its contents, and let the white shower fall from her fingers into the waste-basket beside her small desk. She replenished the card-case from the "Miss Adams" box; then, having found a pair of fresh white gloves, she tucked an ivory-topped Malacca walking-stick under her arm and set forth.

She went down the stairs, buttoning her gloves and still wearing the frown with which she had put "Alys" finally out of her life. She descended slowly, and paused on the lowest step, looking about her with an expression that needed but a slight deepening to betoken bitterness. Its connection with her dropping "Alys" forever was slight, however.

The small frame house, about fifteen years old, was already inclining to become a new Colonial relic. The Adamses had built it, moving into it from the "Queen Anne" house they had rented until they took this step in fashion. But fifteen years is a long time to stand still in the midland country, even for a house, and this one was lightly made, though the Adamses had not realized how flimsily until they had lived in it for some time. "Solid, compact, and convenient" were the instructions to the architect; and he had made it compact successfully. Alice, pausing at the foot of the stairway, was at the same time fairly in the "living-room," for the only separation between the "living-room" and the hall was a demarcation suggested to willing imaginations by a pair of wooden columns painted white. These columns, pine under the paint, were bruised and chipped at the base; one of them showed a crack that threatened to become a split; the "hard-wood" floor had become uneven; and in a corner the walls apparently failed of solidity, where the wall-paper had declined to accompany some staggerings of the plaster beneath it.

The furniture was in great part an accumulation begun with the wedding gifts; though some of it was older, two large patent rocking-chairs and a foot-stool having belonged to Mrs. Adams's mother in the days of hard brown plush and veneer. For decoration there were pictures and vases. Mrs. Adams had always been fond of vases, she said, and every year her husband's Christmas present to her was a vase of one sort or another —whatever the clerk showed him, marked at about twelve or fourteen dollars. The pictures were some of them etchings framed in gilt: Rheims, Canterbury, schooners grouped against a wharf; and Alice could remember how, in her childhood, her father sometimes pointed out the watery reflections in this last as very fine. But it was a long time since he had shown interest in such things—"or in anything much," as she thought.

Other pictures were two water-colours in baroque frames; one being the Amalfi monk on a pergola wall, while the second was a yard-wide display of iris blossoms, painted by Alice herself at fourteen, as a birthday gift to her mother. Alice's glance paused upon it now with no great pride, but showed more approval of an enormous photograph of the Colosseum. This she thought of as "the only good thing in the room"; it possessed and bestowed distinction, she felt; and she did not regret having won her struggle to get it hung in its conspicuous place of honour over the mantelpiece. Formerly that place had been held for years by a steel-engraving, an accurate representation of the Suspension Bridge at Niagara Falls. It was almost as large as its successor, the "Colosseum," and it had been presented to Mr. Adams by colleagues in his department at Lamb and Company's. Adams had shown some feeling when Alice began to urge its removal to obscurity in the "upstairs hall"; he even resisted for several days after she had the "Colosseum" charged to him, framed in oak, and sent to the house. She cheered him up, of course, when he gave way; and her heart never misgave her that there might be a doubt which of the two pictures was the more dismaying.

Over the pictures, the vases, the old brown plush rocking-chairs and the stool, over the three gilt chairs, over the new chintz-covered easy chair and the gray velure sofa—over everything everywhere, was the familiar coating of smoke grime. It had worked into every fibre of the lace curtains, dingying them to an unpleasant gray; it lay on the window-sills and it dimmed the glass panes; it covered the walls, covered the ceiling, and was smeared darker and thicker in all corners. Yet here was no fault of housewifery; the curse could not be lifted, as the ingrained smudges permanent on the once white woodwork proved. The grime was perpetually renewed; scrubbing only ground it in.

This particular ugliness was small part of Alice's discontent, for though the coating grew a little deeper each year she was used to it. Moreover, she knew that she was not likely to find anything better in a thousand miles, so long as she kept to cities, and that none of her friends, however opulent, had any advantage of her here. Indeed, throughout all the great soft-coal country, people who consider themselves comparatively poor may find this consolation: cleanliness has been added to the virtues and beatitudes that money can not buy.

Alice brightened a little as she went forward to the front door, and she brightened more when the spring breeze met her there. Then all depression left her as she walked down the short brick path to the sidewalk, looked up and down the street, and saw how bravely the maple shade-trees, in spite of the black powder they breathed, were flinging out their thousands of young green particles overhead.

She turned north, treading the new little shadows on the pavement briskly, and, having finished buttoning her gloves, swung down her Malacca stick from under her arm to let it tap a more leisurely accompaniment to her quick, short step. She had to step quickly if she was to get anywhere; for the closeness of her skirt, in spite of its little length, permitted no natural stride; but she was pleased to be impeded, these brevities forming part of her show of fashion.

Other pedestrians found them not without charm, though approval may have been lacking here and there; and at the first crossing Alice suffered what she might have accounted an actual injury, had she allowed herself to be so sensitive. An elderly woman in fussy black silk stood there, waiting for a street-car; she was all of a globular modelling, with a face patterned like a frost-bitten peach; and that the approaching gracefulness was uncongenial she naïvely made too evident. Her round, wan eyes seemed roused to bitter life as they rose from the curved high heels of the buckled slippers to the tight little skirt, and thence with startled ferocity to the Malacca cane, which plainly appeared to her as a decoration not more astounding than it was insulting.

Perceiving that the girl was bowing to her, the globular lady hurriedly made shift to alter her injurious expression. "Good morning, Mrs. Dowling," Alice said, gravely. Mrs. Dowling returned the salutation with a smile as convincingly benevolent as the ghastly smile upon a Santa Claus face; and then, while Alice passed on, exploded toward her a single compacted breath through tightened lips.

The sound was eloquently audible, though Mrs. Dowling remained unaware that in this or any manner whatever she had shed a light upon her thoughts; for it was her lifelong innocent conviction that other people saw her only as she wished to be seen, and heard from her only what she intended to be heard. At home it was always her husband who pulled down the shades of their bedroom window.

Alice looked serious for a few moments after the little encounter, then found some consolation in the behaviour of a gentleman of forty or so who was coming toward her. Like Mrs. Dowling, he had begun to show consciousness of Alice's approach while she was yet afar off; but his tokens were of a kind pleasanter to her. He was like Mrs. Dowling again, however, in his conception that Alice would not realize the significance of what he did. He passed his hand over his neck-scarf to see that it lay neatly to his collar, smoothed a lapel of his coat, and adjusted his hat, seeming to be preoccupied the while with problems that kept his eyes to the pavement; then, as he came within a few feet of her, he looked up, as in a surprised recognition almost dramatic, smiled winningly, lifted his hat decisively, and carried it to the full arm's length.

Alice's response was all he could have asked. The cane in her right hand stopped short in its swing, while her left hand moved in a pretty gesture as if an impulse carried it toward the heart; and she smiled, with her under lip caught suddenly between her teeth. Months ago she had seen an actress use this smile in a play, and it came perfectly to Alice now, without conscious direction, it had been so well acquired; but the pretty hand's little impulse toward the heart was an original bit all her own, on the spur of the moment.

The gentleman went on, passing from her forward vision as he replaced his hat. Of himself he was nothing to Alice, except for the gracious circumstance that he had shown strong consciousness of a pretty girl. He was middle-aged, substantial, a family man, securely married; and Alice had with him one of those long acquaintances that never become emphasized by so much as five minutes of talk; yet for this inconsequent meeting she had enacted a little part like a fragment in a pantomime of Spanish wooing.

It was not for him—not even to impress him, except as a messenger. Alice was herself almost unaware of her thought, which was one of the running thousands of her thoughts that took no deliberate form in words. Nevertheless, she had it, and it was the impulse of all her pretty bits of pantomime when she met other acquaintances who made their appreciation visible, as this substantial gentleman did. In Alice's unworded thought, he was to be thus encouraged as in some measure a champion to speak well of her to the world; but more than this: he was to tell some magnificent unknown bachelor how wonderful, how mysterious, she was.

She hastened on gravely, a little stirred reciprocally with the supposed stirrings in the breast of that shadowy ducal mate, who must be somewhere "waiting," or perhaps already seeking her; for she more often thought of herself as "waiting" while he sought her; and sometimes this view of things became so definite that it shaped into a murmur on her lips. "Waiting. Just waiting." And she might add, "For him!" Then, being twenty-two, she was apt to conclude the mystic interview by laughing at herself, though not without a continued wistfulness.

She came to a group of small coloured children playing waywardly in a puddle at the mouth of a muddy alley; and at sight of her they gave over their pastime in order to stare. She smiled brilliantly upon them, but they were too struck with wonder to comprehend that the manifestation was friendly; and as Alice picked her way in a little detour to keep from the mud, she heard one of them say, "Lady got cane! Jeez'!"

She knew that many coloured children use impieties familiarly, and she was not startled. She was disturbed, however, by an unfavourable hint in the speaker's tone. He was six, probably, but the sting of a criticism is not necessarily allayed by knowledge of its ignoble source, and Alice had already begun to feel a slight uneasiness about her cane. Mrs. Dowling's stare had been strikingly projected at it; other women more than merely glanced, their brows and lips contracting impulsively; and Alice was aware that one or two of them frankly halted as soon as she had passed.

She had seen in several magazines pictures of ladies with

canes, and on that account she had bought this one, never questioning that fashion is recognized, even in the provinces, as soon as beheld. On the contrary, these staring women obviously failed to realize that what they were being shown was not an eccentric outburst, but the bright harbinger of an illustrious mode. Alice had applied a bit of artificial pigment to her lips and cheeks before she set forth this morning; she did not need it, having a ready colour of her own, which now mounted high with annoyance.

Then a splendidly shining closed black automobile, with windows of polished glass, came silently down the street toward her. Within it, as in a luxurious little apartment, three comely ladies in mourning sat and gossiped; but when they saw Alice they clutched one another. They instantly recovered, bowing to her solemnly as they were borne by, yet were not gone from her sight so swiftly but the edge of her side glance caught a flash of teeth in mouths suddenly opened, and the dark glisten of black gloves again clutching to share mirth.

The colour that outdid the rouge on Alice's cheek extended its area and grew warmer as she realized how all too cordial had been her nod and smile to these humorous ladies. But in their identity lay a significance causing her a sharper smart, for they were of the family of that Lamb, chief of Lamb and Company, who had employed her father since before she was born.

"And know his salary! They'd be *sure* to find out about that!" was her thought, coupled with another bitter one to the effect that they had probably made instantaneous financial estimates of what she wore—though certainly her walking-stick had most fed their hilarity.

She tucked it under her arm, not swinging it again; and her breath became quick and irregular as emotion beset her. She had been enjoying her walk, but within the space of the few blocks she had gone since she met the substantial gentleman, she found that more than the walk was spoiled: suddenly her life seemed to be spoiled, too; though she did not view the ruin with complaisance. These Lamb women thought her and her cane ridiculous, did they? she said to herself. That was their parvenu blood: to think because a girl's father worked for their grandfather she had no right to be rather striking in style, especially when the striking *was* her style. Probably all the other girls and women would agree with them and would laugh at her when they got together, and, what might be fatal, would try to make all the men think her a silly pretender. Men were just like sheep, and nothing was easier than for women to set up as shepherds and pen them in a fold. "To keep out outsiders," Alice thought. "And make 'em believe I *am* an outsider. What's the use of living?"

All seemed lost when a trim young man appeared, striding out of a cross-street not far before her, and, turning at the corner, came toward her. Visibly, he slackened his gait to lengthen the time of his approach, and, as he was a stranger to her, no motive could be ascribed to him other than a wish to have a longer time to look at her.

She lifted a pretty hand to a pin at her throat, bit her lip—not with the smile, but mysteriously—and at the last instant before her shadow touched the stranger, let her eyes gravely meet his. A moment later, having arrived before the house which was her destination, she halted at the entrance to a driveway leading through fine lawns to the intentionally important mansion. It was a pleasant and impressive place to be seen entering, but Alice did not enter at once. She paused, examining a tiny bit of mortar which the masons had forgotten to scrape from a brick in one of the massive gate-posts. She frowned at this tiny defacement, and with an air of annoyance scraped it away, using the ferrule of her cane—an act of fastidious proprietorship. If any one had looked back over his shoulder he would not have doubted that she lived there.

Alice did not turn to see whether anything of the sort happened or not, but she may have surmised that it did. At all events, it was with an invigorated step that she left the gateway behind her and went cheerfully up the drive to the house of her friend Mildred.

Chapter IV

ADAMS HAD a restless morning, and toward noon he asked Miss Perry to call his daughter; he wished to say something to her.

"I thought I heard her leaving the house a couple of hours ago—maybe longer," the nurse told him. "I'll go see." And she returned from the brief errand, her impression confirmed by information from Mrs. Adams. "Yes. She went up to Miss Mildred Palmer's to see what she's going to wear to-night."

Adams looked at Miss Perry wearily, but remained passive, making no inquiries; for he was long accustomed to what seemed to him a kind of jargon among ladies, which became the more incomprehensible when they tried to explain it. A man's best course, he had found, was just to let it go as so much sound. His sorrowful eyes followed the nurse as she went back to her rocking-chair by the window; and her placidity showed him that there was no mystery for her in the fact that Alice walked two miles to ask so simple a question when there was a telephone in the house. Obviously Miss Perry also comprehended why Alice thought it important to know what Mildred meant to wear. Adams understood why Alice should be concerned with what she herself wore—"to look neat and tidy and at her best, why, of course she'd want to," he thought —but he realized that it was forever beyond him to understand why the clothing of other people had long since become an absorbing part of her life.

Her excursion this morning was no novelty; she was continually going to see what Mildred meant to wear, or what some other girl meant to wear; and when Alice came home from wherever other girls or women had been gathered, she always hurried to her mother with earnest descriptions of the clothing she had seen. At such times, if Adams was present, he might recognize "organdie," or "taffeta," or "chiffon," as words defining certain textiles, but the rest was too technical for him, and he was like a dismal boy at a sermon, just waiting for it to get itself finished. Not the least of the mystery was his wife's interest: she was almost indifferent about her own clothes, and when she consulted Alice about them spoke hurriedly and with an air of apology; but when Alice described other people's clothes, Mrs. Adams listened as eagerly as the daughter talked.

"There they go!" he muttered to-day, a moment after he heard the front door closing, a sound recognizable throughout most of the thinly built house. Alice had just returned, and Mrs. Adams called to her from the upper hallway, not far from Adams's door.

"What did she *say*?"

"She was sort of snippy about it," Alice returned, ascending the stairs. "She gets that way sometimes, and pretended she hadn't made up her mind, but I'm pretty sure it'll be the maize Georgette with Malines flounces."

"Didn't you say she wore that at the Pattersons'?" Mrs. Adams inquired, as Alice arrived at the top of the stairs. "And didn't you tell me she wore it again at the——"

"Certainly not," Alice interrupted, rather petulantly. "She's never worn it but once, and of course she wouldn't want to wear anything to-night that people have seen her in a lot."

Miss Perry opened the door of Adams's room and stepped out. "Your father wants to know if you'll come and see him a minute, Miss Adams."

"Poor old thing! Of course!" Alice exclaimed, and went quickly into the room, Miss Perry remaining outside. "What's the matter, papa? Getting awful sick of lying on his tired old back, I expect."

"I've had kind of a poor morning," Adams said, as she patted his hand comfortingly. "I been thinking——"

"Didn't I tell you not to?" she cried, gaily. "Of course you'll have poor times when you go and do just exactly what I say you mustn't. You stop thinking this very minute!"

He smiled ruefully, closing his eyes; was silent for a moment, then asked her to sit beside the bed. "I been thinking of something I wanted to say," he added.

"What like, papa?"

"Well, it's nothing—much," he said, with something deprecatory in his tone, as if he felt vague impulses toward both humour and apology. "I just thought maybe I ought to've said more to you some time or other about—well, about the way things *are*, down at Lamb and Company's, for instance."

"Now, papa!" She leaned forward in the chair she had taken, and pretended to slap his hand crossly. "Isn't that exactly what I said you couldn't think one single think about till you get *all* well?"

"Well——" he said, and went on slowly, not looking at her, but at the ceiling. "I just thought maybe it wouldn't been any harm if some time or other I told you something about the way they sort of depend on me down there."

"Why don't they show it, then?" she asked, quickly. "That's just what mama and I have been feeling so much; they don't appreciate you."

"Why, yes, they do," he said. "Yes, they do. They began h'isting my salary the second year I went in there, and they've h'isted it a little every two years all the time I've worked for 'em. I've been head of the sundries department for seven years now, and I could hardly have more authority in that department unless I was a member of the firm itself."

"Well, why don't they make you a member of the firm? That's what they ought to've done! Yes, and long ago!"

Adams laughed, but sighed with more heartiness than he had laughed. "They call me their 'oldest stand-by' down there." He laughed again, apologetically, as if to excuse himself for taking a little pride in this title. "Yes, sir; they say I'm their 'oldest stand-by'; and I guess they know they can count on my department's turning in as good a report as they look for, at the end of every month; but they don't have to take a man into the firm to get him to do my work, dearie."

"But you said they depended on you, papa."

"So they do; but of course not so's they couldn't get along without me." He paused, reflecting. "I don't just seem to know how to put it—I mean how to put what I started out to say. I kind of wanted to tell you—well, it seems funny to me, these last few years, the way your mother's taken to feeling about it. I'd like to see a better established wholesale drug business than Lamb and Company this side the Alleghanies—I don't say bigger, I say better established—and it's kind of funny for a man that's been with a business like that as long as I have to hear it called a 'hole.' It's kind of funny when you think, yourself, you've done pretty fairly well in a business like that, and the men at the head of it seem to think so, too, and put your salary just about as high as anybody could consider customary—well, what I mean, Alice, it's kind of funny to have your mother think it's mostly just—mostly just a failure, so to speak."

His voice had become tremulous in spite of him; and this sign of weakness and emotion had sufficient effect upon Alice. She bent over him suddenly, with her arm about him and her cheek against his. "Poor papa!" she murmured. "Poor papa!"

"No, no," he said. "I didn't mean anything to trouble you. I just thought——" He hesitated. "I just wondered—I thought maybe it wouldn't be any harm if I said something about how things *are* down there. I got to thinking maybe you didn't understand it's a pretty good place. They're fine people to work for; and they've always seemed to think something of me;—the way they took Walter on, for instance, soon as I asked 'em, last year. Don't you think that looked a good deal as if they thought something of me, Alice?"

"Yes, papa," she said, not moving.

"And the work's right pleasant," he went on. "Mighty nice boys in our department, Alice. Well, they are in all the departments, for that matter. We have a good deal of fun down there some days."

She lifted her head. "More than you do at home 'some days,' I expect, papa!" she said.

He protested feebly. "Now, I didn't mean that—I didn't want to trouble you——"

She looked at him through winking eyelashes. "I'm sorry I called it a 'hole,' papa."

"No, no," he protested, gently. "It was your mother said that."

"No. I did, too."

"Well, if you did, it was only because you'd heard her."

She shook her head, then kissed him. "I'm going to talk to her," she said, and rose decisively.

But at this, her father's troubled voice became quickly louder: "You better let her alone. I just wanted to have a little talk with you. I didn't mean to start any—your mother won't——"

"Now, papa!" Alice spoke cheerfully again, and smiled upon

him. "I want you to quit worrying! Everything's going to be all right and nobody's going to bother you any more about anything. You'll see!"

She carried her smile out into the hall, but after she had closed the door her face was all pity; and her mother, waiting for her in the opposite room, spoke sympathetically.

"What's the matter, Alice? What did he say that's upset you?"

"Wait a minute, mama." Alice found a handkerchief, used it for eyes and suffused nose, gulped, then suddenly and desolately sat upon the bed. "Poor, poor, *poor* papa!" she whispered.

"Why?" Mrs. Adams inquired, mildly. "What's the matter with him? Sometimes you act as if he weren't getting well. What's he been talking about?"

"Mama—well, I think I'm pretty selfish. Oh, I do!"

"Did he say you were?"

"Papa? No, indeed! What I mean is, maybe we're both a little selfish to try to make him go out and hunt around for something new."

Mrs. Adams looked thoughtful. "Oh, that's what he was up to!"

"Mama, I think we ought to give it up. I didn't dream it had really hurt him."

"Well, doesn't he hurt us?"

"Never that I know of, mama."

"I don't mean by *saying* things," Mrs. Adams explained, impatiently. "There are more ways than that of hurting people. When a man sticks to a salary that doesn't provide for his family, isn't that hurting them?"

"Oh, it 'provides' for us well enough, mama. We have what we need—if I weren't so extravagant. Oh, *I* know I am!"

But at this admission her mother cried out sharply. "'Extravagant!' You haven't one tenth of what the other girls you go with have. And you *can't* have what you ought to as long as he doesn't get out of that horrible place. It provides bare food and shelter for us, but what's that?"

"I don't think we ought to try any more to change him."

"You don't?" Mrs. Adams came and stood before her. "Listen, Alice: your father's asleep; that's his trouble, and he's got to be waked up. He doesn't know that things have changed. When you and Walter were little children we did have enough

—at least it seemed to be about as much as most of the people we knew. But the town isn't what it was in those days, and times aren't what they were then, and these fearful *prices* aren't the old prices. Everything else but your father has changed, and all the time he's stood still. He doesn't know it; he thinks because they've given him a hundred dollars more every two years he's quite a prosperous man! And he thinks that because his children cost him more than he and I cost our parents he gives them—enough!"

"But Walter——" Alice faltered. "Walter doesn't cost him anything at all any more." And she concluded, in a stricken voice, "It's all—me!"

"Why shouldn't it be?" her mother cried. "You're young—you're just at the time when your life should be fullest of good things and happiness. Yet what do you get?"

Alice's lip quivered; she was not unsusceptible to such an appeal, but she contrived the semblance of a protest. "I don't have such a bad time—not a good *deal* of the time, anyhow. I've got a good *many* of the things other girls have——"

"You have?" Mrs. Adams was piteously satirical. "I suppose you've got a limousine to go to that dance to-night? I suppose you've only got to call a florist and tell him to send you some orchids? I suppose you've——"

But Alice interrupted this list. Apparently in a single instant all emotion left her, and she became businesslike, as one in the midst of trifles reminded of really serious matters. She got up from the bed and went to the door of the closet where she kept her dresses. "Oh, see here," she said, briskly. "I've decided to wear my white organdie if you could put in a new lining for me. I'm afraid it'll take you nearly all afternoon."

She brought forth the dress, displayed it upon the bed, and Mrs. Adams examined it attentively.

"Do you think you could get it done, mama?"

"I don't see why not," Mrs. Adams answered, passing a thoughtful hand over the fabric. "It oughtn't to take more than four or five hours."

"It's a shame to have you sit at the machine that long," Alice said, absently, adding, "And I'm sure we ought to let papa alone. Let's just give it up, mama."

Mrs. Adams continued her thoughtful examination of the dress. "Did you buy the chiffon and ribbon, Alice?"

"Yes. I'm sure we oughtn't to talk to him about it any more, mama."

"Well, we'll see."

"Let's both agree that we'll *never* say another single word to him about it," said Alice. "It'll be a great deal better if we just let him make up his mind for himself."

Chapter V

WITH THIS, having more immediately practical questions before them, they dropped the subject, to bend their entire attention upon the dress; and when the lunch-gong sounded downstairs Alice was still sketching repairs and alterations. She continued to sketch them, not heeding the summons.

"I suppose we'd better go down to lunch," Mrs. Adams said, absently. "She's at the gong again."

"In a minute, mama. Now about the sleeves——" And she went on with her planning. Unfortunately the gong was inexpressive of the mood of the person who beat upon it. It consisted of three little metal bowls upon a string; they were unequal in size, and, upon being tapped with a padded stick, gave forth vibrations almost musically pleasant. It was Alice who had substituted this contrivance for the brass "dinner-bell" in use throughout her childhood; and neither she nor the others of her family realized that the substitution of sweeter sounds had made the life of that household more difficult. In spite of dismaying increases in wages, the Adamses still strove to keep a cook; and, as they were unable to pay the higher rates demanded by a good one, what they usually had was a whimsical coloured woman of nomadic impulses. In the hands of such a person the old-fashioned "dinner-bell" was satisfying; life could instantly be made intolerable for any one dawdling on his way to a meal; the bell was capable of every desirable profanity and left nothing bottled up in the breast of the ringer. But the chamois-covered stick might whack upon Alice's little Chinese bowls for a considerable length of time and produce no great effect of urgency upon a hearer, nor any other effect, except fury in the cook. The ironical impossibility of expressing indignation otherwise than by sounds of gentle harmony proved exasperating; the cook was apt to become surcharged, so that explosive resignations, never rare, were somewhat more frequent after the introduction of the gong.

Mrs. Adams took this increased frequency to be only another manifestation of the inexplicable new difficulties that beset all housekeeping. You paid a cook double what you had paid one a few years before; and the cook knew half as much of cookery, and had no gratitude. The more you gave these people, it seemed, the worse they behaved—a condition not to be remedied by simply giving them less, because you couldn't even get the worst unless you paid her what she demanded. Nevertheless, Mrs. Adams remained fitfully an optimist in the matter. Brought up by her mother to speak of a female cook as "the girl," she had been instructed by Alice to drop that definition in favour of one not an improvement in accuracy: "the maid." Almost always, during the first day or so after every cook came, Mrs. Adams would say, at intervals, with an air of triumph: "I believe—of course it's a little soon to be sure—but I do really believe this new maid is the treasure we've been looking for so long!" Much in the same way that Alice dreamed of a mysterious perfect mate for whom she "waited," her mother had a fairy theory that hidden somewhere in the universe there was the treasure, the perfect "maid," who would come and cook in the Adamses' kitchen, not four days or four weeks, but forever.

The present incumbent was not she. Alice, profoundly interested herself, kept her mother likewise so preoccupied with the dress that they were but vaguely conscious of the gong's soft warnings, though these were repeated and protracted unusually. Finally the sound of a hearty voice, independent and enraged, reached the pair. It came from the hall below.

"I says goo'-*bye*!" it called. "Da'ss all!"

Then the front door slammed.

"Why, what——" Mrs. Adams began.

They went down hurriedly to find out. Miss Perry informed them.

"I couldn't make her listen to reason," she said. "She rang the gong four or five times and got to talking to herself; and then she went up to her room and packed her bag. I told her she had no business to go out the front door, anyhow."

Mrs. Adams took the news philosophically. "I thought she had something like that in her eye when I paid her this morning, and I'm not surprised. Well, we won't let Mr. Adams know anything's the matter till I get a new one."

They lunched upon what the late incumbent had left chilling on the table, and then Mrs. Adams prepared to wash the dishes; she would "have them done in a jiffy," she said, cheerfully. But it was Alice who washed the dishes.

"I *don't* like to have you do that, Alice," her mother protested, following her into the kitchen. "It roughens the hands, and when a girl has hands like yours——"

"I know, mama." Alice looked troubled, but shook her head. "It can't be helped this time; you'll need every minute to get that dress done."

Mrs. Adams went away lamenting, while Alice, no expert, began to splash the plates and cups and saucers in the warm water. After a while, as she worked, her eyes grew dreamy: she was making little gay-coloured pictures of herself, unfounded prophecies of how she would look and what would happen to her that evening. She saw herself, charming and demure, wearing a fluffy idealization of the dress her mother now determinedly struggled with upstairs; she saw herself framed in a garlanded archway, the entrance to a ballroom, and saw the people on the shining floor turning dramatically to look at her; then from all points a rush of young men shouting for dances with her; and she constructed a superb stranger, tall, dark, masterfully smiling, who swung her out of the clamouring group as the music began. She saw herself dancing with him, saw the half-troubled smile she would give him; and she accurately smiled that smile as she rinsed the knives and forks.

These hopeful fragments of drama were not to be realized, she knew; but she played that they were true, and went on creating them. In all of them she wore or carried flowers—her mother's sorrow for her in this detail but made it the more important—and she saw herself glamorous with orchids; discarded these for an armful of long-stemmed, heavy roses; tossed them away for a great bouquet of white camellias; and so wandered down a lengthening hothouse gallery of floral beauty, all costly and beyond her reach except in such a wistful day-dream. And upon her present whole horizon, though she searched it earnestly, she could discover no figure of a sender of flowers.

Out of her fancies the desire for flowers to wear that night emerged definitely and became poignant; she began to feel that it might be particularly important to have them. "This might be the night!" She was still at the age to dream that the night of any dance may be the vital point in destiny. No matter how commonplace or disappointing other dance nights have been this one may bring the great meeting. The unknown magnifico may be there.

Alice was almost unaware of her own reveries in which this being appeared—reveries often so transitory that they developed and passed in a few seconds. And in some of them the being was not wholly a stranger; there were moments when he seemed to be composed of recognizable fragments of young men she knew—a smile she had liked, from one; the figure of another, the hair of another—and sometimes she thought he might be concealed, so to say, within the person of an actual acquaintance, someone she had never suspected of being the right seeker for her, someone who had never suspected that it was she who "waited" for him. Anything might reveal them to each other: a look, a turn of the head, a singular word—perhaps some flowers upon her breast or in her hand.

She wiped the dishes slowly, concluding the operation by dropping a saucer upon the floor and dreamily sweeping the fragments under the stove. She sighed and replaced the broom near a window, letting her glance wander over the small yard outside. The grass, repulsively besooted to the colour of coal-smoke all winter, had lately come to life again and now sparkled with green, in the midst of which a tiny shot of blue suddenly fixed her absent eyes. They remained upon it for several moments, becoming less absent.

It was a violet.

Alice ran upstairs, put on her hat, went outdoors and began to search out the violets. She found twenty-two, a bright omen —since the number was that of her years—but not enough violets. There were no more; she had ransacked every foot of the yard.

She looked dubiously at the little bunch in her hand, glanced at the lawn next door, which offered no favourable prospect; then went thoughtfully into the house, left her twenty-two violets in a bowl of water, and came quickly out again, her brow marked with a frown of decision. She went to a trolley-line and took a car to the outskirts of the city where a new park had been opened.

Here she resumed her search, but it was not an easily

rewarded one, and for an hour after her arrival she found no violets. She walked conscientiously over the whole stretch of meadow, her eyes roving discontentedly; there was never a blue dot in the groomed expanse; but at last, as she came near the borders of an old grove of trees, left untouched by the municipal landscapers, the little flowers appeared, and she began to gather them. She picked them carefully, loosening the earth round each tiny plant, so as to bring the roots up with it, that it might live the longer; and she had brought a napkin, which she drenched at a hydrant, and kept loosely wrapped about the stems of her collection.

The turf was too damp for her to kneel; she worked patiently, stooping from the waist; and when she got home in a drizzle of rain at five o'clock her knees were tremulous with strain, her back ached, and she was tired all over, but she had three hundred violets. Her mother moaned when Alice showed them to her, fragrant in a basin of water.

"Oh, you *poor* child! To think of your having to work so hard to get things that other girls only need lift their little fingers for!"

"Never mind," said Alice, huskily. "I've got 'em and I *am* going to have a good time to-night!"

"You've just got to!" Mrs. Adams agreed, intensely sympathetic. "The Lord knows you deserve to, after picking all these violets, poor thing, and He wouldn't be mean enough to keep you from it. I may have to get dinner before I finish the dress, but I can get it done in a few minutes afterward, and it's going to look right pretty. Don't you worry about *that*! And with all these lovely violets——"

"I wonder——" Alice began, paused, then went on, fragmentarily: "I suppose—well, I wonder—do you suppose it would have been better policy to have told Walter before——"

"No," said her mother. "It would only have given him longer to grumble."

"But he might——"

"Don't worry," Mrs. Adams reassured her. "He'll be a little cross, but he won't be stubborn; just let me talk to him and don't you say anything at all, no matter what *he* says."

These references to Walter concerned some necessary manœuvres which took place at dinner, and were conducted by the mother, Alice having accepted her advice to sit in silence. Mrs. Adams began by laughing cheerfully. "I wonder how much longer it took me to cook this dinner than it does Walter to eat it?" she said. "Don't gobble, child! There's no hurry."

In contact with his own family Walter was no squanderer of words. "Is for me," he said. "Got date."

"I know you have, but there's plenty of time."

He smiled in benevolent pity. "*You* know, do you? If you made any coffee—don't bother if you didn't. Get some downtown." He seemed about to rise and depart; whereupon Alice, biting her lip, sent a panic-stricken glance at her mother.

But Mrs. Adams seemed not at all disturbed; and laughed again. "Why, what nonsense, Walter! I'll bring your coffee in a few minutes, but we're going to have dessert first."

"What sort?"

"Some lovely peaches."

"Doe' want 'ny canned peaches," said the frank Walter, moving back his chair. "G'-night."

"Walter! It doesn't begin till about nine o'clock at the earliest."

He paused, mystified. "What doesn't?"

"The dance."

"What dance?"

"Why, Mildred Palmer's dance, of course."

Walter laughed briefly. "What's that to me?"

"Why, you haven't forgotten it's *to-night*, have you?" Mrs. Adams cried. "What a boy!"

"I told you a week ago I wasn't going to that ole dance," he returned, frowning. "You heard me."

"Walter!" she exclaimed. "Of *course* you're going. I got your clothes all out this afternoon, and brushed them for you. They'll look very nice, and——"

"They won't look nice on *me*," he interrupted. "Got date down-town, I tell you."

"But of course you'll——"

"See here!" Walter said, decisively. "Don't get any wrong ideas in your head. I'm just as liable to go up to that ole dance at the Palmers' as I am to eat a couple of barrels of broken glass."

"But, Walter——"

Walter was beginning to be seriously annoyed. "Don't 'Walter' me! I'm no s'ciety snake. I wouldn't jazz with that Palmer crowd if they coaxed me with diamonds."

"Walter——"

"Didn't I tell you it's no use to 'Walter' me?" he demanded.

"My dear child——"

"Oh, Glory!"

At this Mrs. Adams abandoned her air of amusement, looked hurt, and glanced at the demure Miss Perry across the table. "I'm afraid Miss Perry won't think you have very good manners, Walter."

"You're right she won't," he agreed, grimly. "Not if I haf to hear any more about me goin' to——"

But his mother interrupted him with some asperity: "It seems very strange that you always object to going anywhere among *our* friends, Walter."

"*Your* friends!" he said, and, rising from his chair, gave utterance to an ironical laugh strictly monosyllabic. "*Your* friends!" he repeated, going to the door. "Oh, yes! Certainly! Good-*night*!"

And looking back over his shoulder to offer a final brief view of his derisive face, he took himself out of the room.

Alice gasped: "Mama——"

"I'll stop him!" her mother responded, sharply; and hurried after the truant, catching him at the front door with his hat and raincoat on.

"Walter——"

"Told you had a date down-town," he said, gruffly; and would have opened the door, but she caught his arm and detained him.

"Walter, please come back and finish your dinner. When I take all the trouble to cook it for you, I think you might at least——"

"Now, now!" he said. "That isn't what you're up to. You don't want to make me eat; you want to make me listen."

"Well, you *must* listen!" She retained her grasp upon his arm, and made it tighter. "Walter, please!" she entreated, her voice becoming tremulous. "*Please* don't make me so much trouble!"

He drew back from her as far as her hold upon him permitted, and looked at her sharply. "Look here!" he said. "I *get* you, all right! What's the matter of Alice goin' to that party by herself?"

"She just *can't*!"

"Why not?"

"It makes things too *mean* for her, Walter. All the other girls have somebody to depend on after they get there."

"Well, why doesn't she have somebody?" he asked, testily. "Somebody besides *me*, I mean! Why hasn't somebody asked her to go? She ought to be *that* popular, anyhow, I sh'd think —she *tries* enough!"

"I don't understand how you can be so hard," his mother wailed, huskily. "You know why they don't run after her the way they do the other girls she goes with, Walter. It's because we're poor, and she hasn't got any background."

"'Background?'" Walter repeated. "'Background?' What kind of talk is that?"

"You *will* go with her to-night, Walter?" his mother pleaded, not stopping to enlighten him. "You don't understand how hard things are for her and how brave she is about them, or you *couldn't* be so selfish! It'd be more than I can bear to see her disappointed to-night! She went clear out to Belleview Park this afternoon, Walter, and spent hours and hours picking violets to wear. You *will*——"

Walter's heart was not iron, and the episode of the violets may have reached it. "Oh, *blub*!" he said, and flung his soft hat violently at the wall.

His mother beamed with delight. "*That's* a good boy, darling! You'll never be sorry you——"

"Cut it out," he requested. "If I take her, will you pay for a taxi?"

"Oh, Walter!" And again Mrs. Adams showed distress. "Couldn't you?"

"No, I couldn't; I'm not goin' to throw away my good money like that, and you can't tell what time o' night it'll be before she's willin' to come home. What's the matter you payin' for one?"

"I haven't any money."

"Well, father——"

She shook her head dolefully. “I got some from him this morning, and I can’t bother him for any more; it upsets him. He’s *always* been so terribly close with money——”

“I guess he couldn’t help that,” Walter observed. “We’re liable to go to the poorhouse the way it is. Well, what’s the matter our walkin’ to this rotten party?”

“In the rain, Walter?”

“Well, it’s only a drizzle and we can take a streetcar to within a block of the house.”

Again his mother shook her head. “It wouldn’t do.”

“Well, darn the luck, all *right*!” he consented, explosively. “I’ll get her something to ride in. It means seventy-five cents.”

“Why, Walter!” Mrs. Adams cried, much pleased. “Do you know how to get a cab for that little? How splendid!”

“Tain’t a cab,” Walter informed her crossly. “It’s a tin Lizzie, but you don’t haf’ to tell her what it is till I get her into it, do you?”

Mrs. Adams agreed that she didn’t.

Chapter VI

ALICE WAS busy with herself for two hours after dinner; but a little before nine o'clock she stood in front of her long mirror, completed, bright-eyed and solemn. Her hair, exquisitely arranged, gave all she asked of it; what artificialities in colour she had used upon her face were only bits of emphasis that made her prettiness the more distinct; and the dress, not rumpled by her mother's careful hours of work, was a white cloud of loveliness. Finally there were two triumphant bouquets of violets, each with the stems wrapped in tin-foil shrouded by a bow of purple chiffon; and one bouquet she wore at her waist and the other she carried in her hand.

Miss Perry, called in by a rapturous mother for the free treat of a look at this radiance, insisted that Alice was a vision. "Purely and simply a vision!" she said, meaning that no other definition whatever would satisfy her. "I never saw anybody look a vision if she don't look one to-night," the admiring nurse declared. "Her papa'll think the same I do about it. You see if he doesn't say she's purely and simply a vision."

Adams did not fulfil the prediction quite literally when Alice paid a brief visit to his room to "show" him and bid him good-night; but he chuckled feebly. "Well, well, well!" he said. "You look mighty fine—*mighty* fine!" And he waggled a bony finger at her two bouquets. "Why, Alice, who's your beau?"

"Never you mind!" she laughed, archly brushing his nose with the violets in her hand. "He treats me pretty well, doesn't he?"

"Must like to throw his money around! These violets smell mighty sweet, and they ought to, if they're going to a party with *you*. Have a good time, dearie."

"I mean to!" she cried; and she repeated this gaily, but with an emphasis expressing sharp determination as she left him. "I *mean* to!"

"What was he talking about?" her mother inquired, smoothing the rather worn and old evening wrap she had placed on Alice's bed. "What were you telling him you 'mean to?'"

Alice went back to her triple mirror for the last time, then stood before the long one. "That I mean to have a good time to-night," she said; and as she turned from her reflection to the wrap Mrs. Adams held up for her, "It looks as though I *could*, don't you think so?"

"You'll just be a queen to-night," her mother whispered in fond emotion. "You mustn't doubt yourself."

"Well, there's one thing," said Alice. "I think I do look nice enough to get along without having to dance with that Frank Dowling! All I ask is for it to happen just *once*; and if he comes near me to-night I'm going to treat him the way the other girls do. Do you suppose Walter's got the taxi out in front?"

"He—he's waiting down in the hall," Mrs. Adams answered, nervously; and she held up another garment to go over the wrap.

Alice frowned at it. "What's that, mama?"

"It's—it's your father's raincoat. I thought you'd put it on over——"

"But I won't need it in a taxicab."

"You will to get in and out, and you needn't take it into the Palmers'. You can leave it in the—in the—— It's drizzling, and you'll need it."

"Oh, well," Alice consented; and a few minutes later, as with Walter's assistance she climbed into the vehicle he had provided, she better understood her mother's solicitude.

"What on earth *is* this, Walter?" she asked.

"Never mind; it'll keep you dry enough with the top up," he returned, taking his seat beside her. Then for a time, as they went rather jerkily up the street, she was silent; but finally she repeated her question: "What *is* it, Walter?"

"What's what?"

"This—this *car*?"

"It's a ottomobile."

"I mean—what kind is it?"

"Haven't you got eyes?"

"It's too dark."

"It's a second-hand tin Lizzie," said Walter. "D'you know what that means? It means a flivver."

"Yes, Walter."

"Got 'ny 'bjections?"

"Why, no, dear," she said, placatively. "Is it yours, Walter? Have you bought it?"

"Me?" he laughed. "*I* couldn't buy a used wheelbarrow. I rent this sometimes when I'm goin' out among 'em. Costs me seventy-five cents and the price o' the gas."

"That seems very moderate."

"I guess it is! The feller owes me some money, and this is the only way I'd ever get it off him."

"Is he a garage-keeper?"

"Not exactly!" Walter uttered husky sounds of amusement. "You'll be just as happy, I guess, if you don't know who he is," he said.

His tone misgave her; and she said truthfully that she was content not to know who owned the car. "I joke sometimes about how you keep things to yourself," she added, "but I really never do pry in your affairs, Walter."

"Oh, no, you don't!"

"Indeed, I don't."

"Yes, you're mighty nice and cooing when you got me where you want me," he jeered. "Well, *I* just as soon tell you where I get this car."

"I'd just as soon you wouldn't, Walter," she said, hurriedly. "Please don't."

But Walter meant to tell her. "Why, there's nothin' exactly *criminal* about it," he said. "It belongs to old J. A. Lamb himself. He keeps it for their coon chauffeur. I rent it from him."

"From Mr. *Lamb*?"

"No; from the coon chauffeur."

"Walter!" she gasped.

"Sure I do! I can get it any night when the coon isn't goin' to use it himself. He's drivin' their limousine to-night—that little Henrietta Lamb's goin' to the party, no matter if her father *has* only been dead less'n a year!" He paused, then inquired: "Well, how d'you like it?"

She did not speak, and he began to be remorseful for having imparted so much information, though his way of expressing regret was his own. "Well, you *will* make the folks make me take you to parties!" he said. "I got to do it the best way I *can*, don't I?"

Then as she made no response, "Oh, the car's *clean* enough," he said. "This coon, he's as particular as any white man; you needn't worry about that." And as she still said nothing, he added gruffly, "I'd of had a better car if I could afforded it. You needn't get so upset about it."

"I don't understand—" she said in a low voice—"I don't understand how you know such people."

"Such people as who?"

"As—coloured chauffeurs."

"Oh, look here, now!" he protested, loudly. "Don't you know this is a democratic country?"

"Not quite that democratic, is it, Walter?"

"The trouble with you," he retorted, "you don't know there's anybody in town except just this silk-shirt crowd." He paused, seeming to await a refutation; but as none came, he expressed himself definitely: "They make me sick."

They were coming near their destination, and the glow of the big, brightly lighted house was seen before them in the wet night. Other cars, not like theirs, were approaching this center of brilliance; long triangles of light near the ground swept through the fine drizzle; small red tail-lights gleamed again from the moist pavement of the street; and, through the myriads of little glistening leaves along the curving driveway, glimpses were caught of lively colours moving in a white glare as the limousines released their occupants under the shelter of the porte-cochère.

Alice clutched Walter's arm in a panic; they were just at the driveway entrance. "Walter, we mustn't go in there."

"What's the matter?"

"Leave this awful car outside."

"Why, I——"

"Stop!" she insisted, vehemently. "You've got to! Go back!"

"Oh, Glory!"

The little car was between the entrance posts; but Walter backed it out, avoiding a collision with an impressive machine which swerved away from them and passed on toward the porte-cochère, showing a man's face grinning at the window as it went by. "Flivver runabout got the wrong number!" he said.

"Did he *see* us?" Alice cried.

"Did who see us?"

"Harvey Malone—in that foreign coupé."

"No; he couldn't tell who we were under this top," Walter assured her as he brought the little car to a standstill beside the curbstone, out in the street. "What's it matter if he did, the big fish?"

Alice responded with a loud sigh, and sat still.

"Well, want to go on back?" Walter inquired. "You bet I'm willing!"

"No."

"Well, then, what's the matter our drivin' on up to the porte-cochère? There's room for me to park just the other side of it."

"No, *no*!"

"What you expect to do? Sit *here* all night?"

"No, leave the car here."

"*I* don't care where we leave it," he said. "Sit still till I lock her, so none o' these millionaires around here'll run off with her." He got out with a padlock and chain; and, having put these in place, offered Alice his hand. "Come on, if you're ready."

"Wait," she said, and, divesting herself of the raincoat, handed it to Walter. "Please leave this with your things in the men's dressing-room, as if it were an extra one of your own, Walter."

He nodded; she jumped out; and they scurried through the drizzle. As they reached the porte-cochère she began to laugh airily, and spoke to the impassive man in livery who stood there. "Joke on us!" she said, hurrying by him toward the door of the house. "Our car broke down outside the gate."

The man remained impassive, though he responded with a faint gleam as Walter, looking back at him, produced for his benefit a cynical distortion of countenance which offered little confirmation of Alice's account of things. Then the door was swiftly opened to the brother and sister; and they came into a marble-floored hall, where a dozen sleeked young men lounged, smoked cigarettes and fastened their gloves, as they waited for their ladies. Alice nodded to one or another of these, and went quickly on, her face uplifted and smiling; but Walter detained her at the door to which she hastened.

"Listen here," he said. "I suppose you want me to dance the first dance with you——"

"If you please, Walter," she said, meekly.

"How long you goin' to hang around fixin' up in that dressin'-room?"

"I'll be out before you're ready yourself," she promised him; and kept her word, she was so eager for her good time to begin. When he came for her, they went down the hall to a corridor opening upon three great rooms which had been thrown open together, with the furniture removed and the broad floors waxed. At one end of the corridor musicians sat in a green grove, and Walter, with some interest, turned toward these; but his sister, pressing his arm, impelled him in the opposite direction.

"What's the matter now?" he asked. "That's Jazz Louie and his half-breed bunch—three white and four mulatto. Let's——?"

"No, no," she whispered. "We must speak to Mildred and Mr. and Mrs. Palmer."

"'Speak' to 'em? I haven't got a thing to say to *those* berries!"

"Walter, won't you *please* behave?"

He seemed to consent, for the moment, at least, and suffered her to take him down the corridor toward a floral bower where the hostess stood with her father and mother. Other couples and groups were moving in the same direction, carrying with them a hubbub of laughter and fragmentary chatterings; and Alice, smiling all the time, greeted people on every side of her eagerly—a little more eagerly than most of them responded—while Walter nodded in a non-committal manner to one or two, said nothing, and yawned audibly, the last resource of a person who finds himself nervous in a false situation. He repeated his yawn and was beginning another when a convulsive pressure upon his arm made him understand that he must abandon this method of reassuring himself. They were close upon the floral bower.

Mildred was giving her hand to one and another of her guests as rapidly as she could, passing them on to her father and mother, and at the same time resisting the efforts of three or four detached bachelors who besought her to give over her duty in favour of the dance-music just beginning to blare.

She was a large, fair girl, with a kindness of eye somewhat withheld by an expression of fastidiousness; at first sight of her it was clear that she would never in her life do anything "incorrect," or wear anything "incorrect." But her correctness was of the finer sort, and had no air of being studied or achieved; conduct would never offer her a problem to be settled from a book of rules, for the rules were so deep within her that she was unconscious of them. And behind this perfection there was an even ampler perfection of what Mrs. Adams called "background." The big, rich, simple house was part of it, and Mildred's father and mother were part of it. They stood beside her, large, serene people, murmuring graciously and gently inclining their handsome heads as they gave their hands to the guests; and even the youngest and most ebullient of these took on a hushed mannerliness with a closer approach to the bower.

When the opportunity came for Alice and Walter to pass within this precinct, Alice, going first, leaned forward and whispered in Mildred's ear. "You *didn't* wear the maize georgette! That's what I thought you were going to. But you look simply *darling*! And those *pearls*——"

Others were crowding decorously forward, anxious to be done with ceremony and get to the dancing; and Mildred did not prolong the intimacy of Alice's enthusiastic whispering. With a faint accession of colour and a smile tending somewhat in the direction of rigidity, she carried Alice's hand immediately onward to Mrs. Palmer's. Alice's own colour showed a little heightening as she accepted the suggestion thus implied; nor was that emotional tint in any wise decreased, a moment later, by an impression that Walter, in concluding the brief exchange of courtesies between himself and the stately Mr. Palmer, had again reassured himself with a yawn.

But she did not speak of it to Walter; she preferred not to confirm the impression and to leave in her mind a possible doubt that he had done it. He followed her out upon the waxed floor, said resignedly: "Well, come on," put his arm about her, and they began to dance.

Alice danced gracefully and well, but not so well as Walter. Of all the steps and runs, of all the whimsical turns and twirlings, of all the rhythmic swayings and dips commanded that season by such blarings as were the barbaric product, loud and wild, of the Jazz Louies and their half-breed bunches, the thin and sallow youth was a master. Upon his face could be seen contempt of the easy marvels he performed as he moved in swift precision from one smooth agility to another; and if some too-dainty or jealous cavalier complained that to be so much a stylist in dancing was "not quite like a gentleman," at least Walter's style was what the music called for. No other dancer in the room could be thought comparable to him. Alice told him so.

"It's wonderful!" she said. "And the mystery is, where you ever learned to *do* it! You never went to dancing-school, but there isn't a man in the room who can dance half so well. I don't see why, when you dance like this, you always make such a fuss about coming to parties."

He sounded his brief laugh, a jeering bark out of one side of the mouth, and swung her miraculously through a closing space between two other couples. "You know a lot about what goes on, don't you? You prob'ly think there's no other place to dance in this town except these frozen-face joints."

"'Frozen face?'" she echoed, laughing. "Why, everybody's having a splendid time. Look at them."

"Oh, they holler loud enough," he said. "They do it to make each other think they're havin' a good time. You don't call that Palmer family frozen-face berries, I s'pose. No?"

"Certainly not. They're just dignified and——"

"Yeuh!" said Walter. "They're dignified, 'specially when you tried to whisper to Mildred to show how *in* with her you were, and she moved you on that way. *She's* a hot friend, isn't she!"

"She didn't mean anything by it. She——"

"Ole Palmer's a hearty, slap-you-on-the-back ole berry," Walter interrupted; adding in a casual tone, "All I'd like, I'd like to hit him."

"Walter! By the way, you mustn't forget to ask Mildred for a dance before the evening is over."

"Me?" He produced the lop-sided appearance of his laugh, but without making it vocal. "You watch me do it!"

"She probably won't have one left, but you must ask her, anyway."

"Why must I?"

"Because, in the first place, you're supposed to, and, in the second place, she's my most intimate friend."

"Yeuh? Is she? I've heard you pull that 'most-intimate-friend' stuff often enough about her. What's *she* ever do to show she is?"

"Never mind. You really must ask her, Walter. I want you to; and I want you to ask several other girls afterwhile; I'll tell you who."

"Keep on wanting; it'll do you good."

"Oh, but you really——"

"Listen!" he said. "I'm just as liable to dance with any of these fairies as I am to buy a bucket o' rusty tacks and eat 'em. Forget it! Soon as I get rid of you I'm goin' back to that room where I left my hat and overcoat and smoke myself to death."

"Well," she said, a little ruefully, as the frenzy of Jazz Louie and his half-breeds was suddenly abated to silence, "you mustn't—you mustn't get rid of me *too* soon, Walter."

They stood near one of the wide doorways, remaining where they had stopped. Other couples, everywhere, joined one another, forming vivacious clusters, but none of these groups adopted the brother and sister, nor did any one appear to be hurrying in Alice's direction to ask her for the next dance. She looked about her, still maintaining that jubilance of look and manner she felt so necessary—for it is to the girls who are "having a good time" that partners are attracted—and, in order to lend greater colour to her impersonation of a lively belle, she began to chatter loudly, bringing into play an accompaniment of frolicsome gesture. She brushed Walter's nose saucily with the bunch of violets in her hand, tapped him on the shoulder, shook her pretty forefinger in his face, flourished her arms, kept her shoulders moving, and laughed continuously as she spoke.

"You *naughty* old Walter!" she cried. "*Aren't* you ashamed to be such a wonderful dancer and then only dance with your own little sister! You could dance on the stage if you wanted to. Why, you could make your *fortune* that way! Why don't you? Wouldn't it be just lovely to have all the rows and rows of people clapping their hands and shouting, 'Hurrah! Hurrah, for Walter Adams! Hurrah! Hurrah! Hurrah!'"

He stood looking at her in stolid pity.

"Cut it out," he said. "You better be givin' some of these berries the eye so they'll ask you to dance."

She was not to be so easily checked, and laughed loudly, flourishing her violets in his face again. "You *would* like it; you know you would; you needn't pretend! Just think! A whole big audience shouting, 'Hurrah! *Hurrah! Hur*——'"

"The place 'll be pulled if you get any noisier," he interrupted, not ungently. "Besides, I'm no muley cow."

"A '*cow?*'" she laughed. "What on earth——"

"I can't eat dead violets," he explained. "So don't keep tryin' to make me do it."

This had the effect he desired, and subdued her; she abandoned her unsisterly coquetries, and looked beamingly about her, but her smile was more mechanical than it had been at first.

At home she had seemed beautiful; but here, where the other girls competed, things were not as they had been there, with only her mother and Miss Perry to give contrast. These crowds of other girls had all done their best, also, to look beautiful, though not one of them had worked so hard for such a consummation as Alice had. They did not need to; they did not need to get their mothers to make old dresses over; they did not need to hunt violets in the rain.

At home her dress had seemed beautiful; but that was different, too, where there were dozens of brilliant fabrics, fashioned in new ways—some of these new ways startling, which only made the wearers centers of interest and shocked no one. And Alice remembered that she had heard a girl say, not long before, "Oh, *organdie*! Nobody wears organdie for evening gowns except in midsummer." Alice had thought little of this; but as she looked about her and saw no organdie except her own, she found greater difficulty in keeping her smile as arch and spontaneous as she wished it. In fact, it was beginning to make her face ache a little.

Mildred came in from the corridor, heavily attended. She carried a great bouquet of violets laced with lilies-of-the-valley; and the violets were lusty, big purple things, their stems wrapped in cloth of gold, with silken cords dependent, ending in long tassels. She and her convoy passed near the two young Adamses; and it appeared that one of the convoy besought his hostess to permit "cutting in"; they were "doing it other places" of late, he urged; but he was denied and told to console himself by holding the bouquet, at intervals, until his third of the sixteenth dance should come. Alice looked dubiously at her own bouquet.

Suddenly she felt that the violets betrayed her; that any one who looked at them could see how rustic, how innocent of any florist's craft they were. "I can't eat dead violets," Walter said. The little wild flowers, dying indeed in the warm air, were drooping in a forlorn mass; and it seemed to her that whoever noticed them would guess that she had picked them herself. She decided to get rid of them.

Walter was becoming restive. "Look here!" he said. "Can't you flag one o' these long-tailed birds to take you on for the next dance? You came to have a good time; why don't you get busy and have it? I want to get out and smoke."

"You *mustn't* leave me, Walter," she whispered, hastily. "Somebody'll come for me before long, but until they do——"

"Well, couldn't you sit somewhere?"

"No, no! There isn't any one I could sit with."

"Well, why not? Look at those ole dames in the corners. What's the matter your tyin' up with some o' them for a while?"

"*Please*, Walter; no!"

In fact, that indomitable smile of hers was the more difficult to maintain because of these very elders to whom Walter referred. They were mothers of girls among the dancers, and they were there to fend and contrive for their offspring; to keep them in countenance through any trial; to lend them diplomacy in the carrying out of all enterprises; to be "background" for them; and in these essentially biological functionings to imitate their own matings and renew the excitement of their nuptial periods. Older men, husbands of these ladies and fathers of eligible girls, were also to be seen, most of them with Mr. Palmer in a billiard-room across the corridor.

Mr. and Mrs. Adams had not been invited. "Of course papa and mama just barely know Mildred Palmer," Alice thought, "and most of the other girls' fathers and mothers are old friends of Mr. and Mrs. Palmer, but I do think she might have *asked* papa and mama, anyway—she needn't have been afraid just to ask them; she knew they couldn't come." And her smiling lip twitched a little threateningly, as she concluded the silent monologue. "I suppose she thinks I ought to be glad enough she asked Walter!"

Walter was, in fact, rather noticeable. He was not Mildred's only guest to wear a short coat and to appear without gloves; but he was singular (at least in his present surroundings) on account of a kind of coiffuring he favoured, his hair having been shaped after what seemed a Mongol inspiration. Only upon the top of the head was actual hair perceived, the rest appearing to be nudity. And even more than by any difference in mode he was set apart by his look and manner, in which there seemed to be a brooding, secretive and jeering superiority; and this was most vividly expressed when he felt called upon for his loud, short, lop-sided laugh. Whenever he uttered it Alice laughed, too, as loudly as she could, to cover it.

"Well," he said. "How long we goin' to stand here? My feet are sproutin' roots."

Alice took his arm, and they began to walk aimlessly through the rooms, though she tried to look as if they had a definite destination, keeping her eyes eager and her lips parted;—people had called jovially to them from the distance, she meant to imply, and they were going to join these merry friends. She was still upon this ghostly errand when a furious outbreak of drums and saxophones sounded a prelude for the second dance.

Walter danced with her again, but he gave her a warning. "I don't want to leave you high and dry," he told her, "but I can't stand it. I got to get somewhere I don't haf' to hurt my eyes with these berries; I'll go blind if I got to look at any more of 'em. I'm goin' out to smoke as soon as the music begins the next time, and you better get fixed for it."

Alice tried to get fixed for it. As they danced she nodded sunnily to every man whose eye she caught, smiled her smile with the under lip caught between her teeth; but it was not until the end of the intermission after the dance that she saw help coming.

Across the room sat the globular lady she had encountered that morning, and beside the globular lady sat a round-headed, round-bodied girl; her daughter, at first glance. The family contour was also as evident a characteristic of the short young man who stood in front of Mrs. Dowling, engaged with her in a discussion which was not without evidences of an earnestness almost impassioned. Like Walter, he was declining to dance a third time with sister; he wished to go elsewhere.

Alice from a sidelong eye watched the controversy: she saw the globular young man glance toward her, over his shoulder; whereupon Mrs. Dowling, following this glance, gave Alice a look of open fury, became much more vehement in the argument, and even struck her knee with a round, fat fist for emphasis.

"I'm on my way," said Walter. "There's the music startin' up again, and I told you——"

She nodded gratefully. "It's all right—but come back before long, Walter."

The globular young man, red with annoyance, had torn himself from his family and was hastening across the room to her. "C'n I have this dance?"

"Why, you nice Frank Dowling!" Alice cried. "How lovely!"

Chapter VII

THEY DANCED. Mr. Dowling should have found other forms of exercise and pastime. Nature has not designed everyone for dancing, though sometimes those she has denied are the last to discover her niggardliness. But the round young man was at least vigorous enough—too much so, when his knees collided with Alice's—and he was too sturdy to be thrown off his feet, himself, or to allow his partner to fall when he tripped her. He held her up valiantly, and continued to beat a path through the crowd of other dancers by main force.

He paid no attention to anything suggested by the efforts of the musicians, and appeared to be unaware that there should have been some connection between what they were doing and what he was doing; but he may have listened to other music of his own, for his expression was of high content; he seemed to feel no doubt whatever that he was dancing. Alice kept as far away from him as under the circumstances she could; and when they stopped she glanced down, and found the execution of unseen manœuvres, within the protection of her skirt, helpful to one of her insteps and to the toes of both of her slippers.

Her cheery partner was paddling his rosy brows with a fine handkerchief. "That was great!" he said. "Let's go out and sit in the corridor; they've got some comfortable chairs out there."

"Well—let's not," she returned. "I believe I'd rather stay in here and look at the crowd."

"No; that isn't it," he said, chiding her with a waggish forefinger. "You think if you go out there you'll miss a chance of someone else asking you for the next dance, and so you'll have to give it to me."

"How absurd!" Then, after a look about her that revealed nothing encouraging, she added graciously, "You can have the next if you want it."

"Great!" he exclaimed, mechanically. "Now let's get out of here—out of *this* room, anyhow."

"Why? What's the matter with——"

"My mother," Mr. Dowling explained. "But don't look at her. She keeps motioning me to come and see after Ella, and I'm simply *not* going to do it, you see!"

Alice laughed. "I don't believe it's so much that," she said, and consented to walk with him to a point in the next room from which Mrs. Dowling's continuous signalling could not be seen. "Your mother hates me."

"Oh, no; I wouldn't say that. No, she don't," he protested, innocently. "She don't know you more than just to speak to, you see. So how could she?"

"Well, she does. I can tell."

A frown appeared upon his rounded brow. "No; I'll tell you the way she feels. It's like this: Ella isn't *too* popular, you know—it's hard to see why, because she's a right nice girl, in her way—and mother thinks I ought to look after her, you see. She thinks I ought to dance a whole lot with her myself, and stir up other fellows to dance with her—it's simply impossible to make mother understand you *can't* do that, you see. And then about me, you see, if she had her way I wouldn't get to dance with anybody at all except girls like Mildred Palmer and Henrietta Lamb. Mother wants to run my whole programme for me, you understand, but the trouble of it is—about girls like that, you see—well, I couldn't do what she wants, even if I wanted to myself, because you take those girls, and by the time I get Ella off my hands for a minute, why, their dances are always every last one taken, and where do I come in?"

Alice nodded, her amiability undamaged. "I see. So that's why you dance with me."

"No, I like to," he protested. "I rather dance with you than I do with those girls." And he added with a retrospective determination which showed that he had been through quite an experience with Mrs. Dowling in this matter, "I *told* mother I would, too!"

"Did it take all your courage, Frank?"

He looked at her shrewdly. "Now you're trying to tease me," he said. "I don't care; I *would* rather dance with you! In the first place, you're a perfectly beautiful dancer, you see, and in the second, a man feels a lot more comfortable with you than he does with them. Of course I know almost all the other fellows get along with those girls all right; but I don't waste any time on 'em I don't have to. *I* like people that are always cordial to everybody, you see—the way you are."

"Thank you," she said, thoughtfully.

"Oh, I *mean* it," he insisted. "There goes the band again. Shall we——?"

"Suppose we sit it out?" she suggested. "I believe I'd like to go out in the corridor, after all—it's pretty warm in here."

Assenting cheerfully, Dowling conducted her to a pair of easy-chairs within a secluding grove of box-trees, and when they came to this retreat they found Mildred Palmer just departing, under escort of a well-favoured gentleman about thirty. As these two walked slowly away, in the direction of the dancing-floor, they left it not to be doubted that they were on excellent terms with each other; Mildred was evidently willing to make their progress even slower, for she halted momentarily, once or twice; and her upward glances to her tall companion's face were of a gentle, almost blushing deference. Never before had Alice seen anything like this in her friend's manner.

"How queer!" she murmured.

"What's queer?" Dowling inquired as they sat down.

"Who was that man?"

"Haven't you met him?"

"I never saw him before. Who is he?"

"Why, it's this Arthur Russell."

"What Arthur Russell? I never heard of him."

Mr. Dowling was puzzled. "Why, *that's* funny! Only the last time I saw you, you were telling me how awfully well you knew Mildred Palmer."

"Why, certainly I do," Alice informed him. "She's my most intimate friend."

"That's what makes it seem so funny you haven't heard anything about this Russell, because everybody says even if she isn't engaged to him right now, she most likely will be before very long. I must say it looks a good deal that way to me, myself."

"What nonsense!" Alice exclaimed. "She's never even mentioned him to me."

The young man glanced at her dubiously and passed a finger over the tiny prong that dashingly composed the whole substance of his moustache.

"Well, you see, Mildred *is* pretty reserved," he remarked. "This Russell is some kind of cousin of the Palmer family, I understand."

"He is?"

"Yes—second or third or something, the girls say. You see, my sister Ella hasn't got much to do at home, and don't read anything, or sew, or play solitaire, you see; and she hears about pretty much everything that goes on, you see. Well, Ella says a lot of the girls have been talking about Mildred and this Arthur Russell for quite a while back, you see. They were all wondering what he was going to look like, you see; because he only got here yesterday; and that proves she must have been talking to some of 'em, or else how——"

Alice laughed airily, but the pretty sound ended abruptly with an audible intake of breath. "Of course, while Mildred *is* my most intimate friend," she said, "I don't mean she tells me everything—and naturally she has other friends besides. What else did your sister say she told them about this Mr. Russell?"

"Well, it seems he's *very* well off; at least Henrietta Lamb told Ella he was. Ella says——"

Alice interrupted again, with an increased irritability. "Oh, never mind what Ella says! Let's find something better to talk about than Mr. Russell!"

"Well, *I'm* willing," Mr. Dowling assented, ruefully. "What you want to talk about?"

But this liberal offer found her unresponsive; she sat leaning back, silent, her arms along the arms of her chair, and her eyes, moist and bright, fixed upon a wide doorway where the dancers fluctuated. She was disquieted by more than Mildred's reserve, though reserve so marked had certainly the significance of a warning that Alice's definition, "my most intimate friend," lacked sanction. Indirect notice to this effect could not well have been more emphatic, but the sting of it was left for a later moment. Something else preoccupied Alice: she had just been surprised by an odd experience. At first sight of this Mr. Arthur Russell, she had said to herself instantly, in words as definite as if she spoke them aloud, though they seemed more like words spoken to her by some unknown person within her: "There! That's exactly the kind of looking man I'd like to marry!"

In the eyes of the restless and the longing, Providence often appears to be worse than inscrutable: an unreliable Omnipotence given to haphazard whimsies in dealing with its own creatures, choosing at random some among them to be rent with tragic deprivations and others to be petted with blessing upon blessing. In Alice's eyes, Mildred had been blessed enough; something ought to be left over, by this time, for another girl. The final touch to the heaping perfection of Christmas-in-everything for Mildred was that this Mr. Arthur Russell, good-looking, kind-looking, graceful, the perfect fiancé, should be also "*very* well off." Of course! These rich always married one another. And while the Mildreds danced with their Arthur Russells the best an outsider could do for herself was to sit with Frank Dowling—the one last course left her that was better than dancing with him.

"Well, what *do* you want to talk about?" he inquired.

"Nothing," she said. "Suppose we just sit, Frank." But a moment later she remembered something, and, with a sudden animation, began to prattle. She pointed to the musicians down the corridor. "Oh, look at them! Look at the leader! Aren't they *funny*? Someone told me they're called 'Jazz Louie and his half-breed bunch.' Isn't that just crazy? Don't you *love* it? Do watch them, Frank."

She continued to chatter, and, while thus keeping his glance away from herself, she detached the forlorn bouquet of dead violets from her dress and laid it gently beside the one she had carried. The latter already reposed in the obscurity selected for it at the base of one of the box-trees.

Then she was abruptly silent.

"You certainly are a funny girl," Dowling remarked. "You say you don't want to talk about anything at all, and all of a sudden you break out and talk a blue streak; and just about the time I begin to get interested in what you're saying you shut off! What's the matter with girls, anyhow, when they do things like that?"

"I don't know; we're just queer, I guess."

"I say so! Well, what'll we do *now*? Talk, or just sit?"

"Suppose we just sit some more."

"Anything to oblige," he assented. "I'm willing to sit as long as you like."

But even as he made his amiability clear in this matter, the peace was threatened—his mother came down the corridor like a rolling, ominous cloud. She was looking about her on all sides, in a fidget of annoyance, searching for him, and to his dismay she saw him. She immediately made a horrible face at his companion, beckoned to him imperiously with a dumpy arm, and shook her head reprovingly. The unfortunate young man tried to repulse her with an icy stare, but this effort having obtained little to encourage his feeble hope of driving her away, he shifted his chair so that his back was toward her discomfiting pantomime. He should have known better, the instant result was Mrs. Dowling in motion at an impetuous waddle.

She entered the box-tree seclusion with the lower rotundities of her face hastily modelled into the resemblance of an over-benevolent smile—a contortion which neglected to spread its intended geniality upward to the exasperated eyes and anxious forehead.

"I think your mother wants to speak to you, Frank," Alice said, upon this advent.

Mrs. Dowling nodded to her. "Good evening, Miss Adams," she said. "I just thought as you and Frank weren't dancing you wouldn't mind my disturbing you——"

"Not at all," Alice murmured.

Mr. Dowling seemed of a different mind. "Well, what *do* you want?" he inquired, whereupon his mother struck him roguishly with her fan.

"Bad fellow!" She turned to Alice. "I'm sure you won't mind excusing him to let him do something for his old mother, Miss Adams."

"What *do* you want?" the son repeated.

"Two very nice things," Mrs. Dowling informed him. "Everybody is so anxious for Henrietta Lamb to have a pleasant evening, because it's the very first time she's been anywhere since her father's death, and of course her dear grandfather's an old friend of ours, and——"

"Well, well!" her son interrupted. "Miss Adams isn't interested in all this, mother."

"But Henrietta came to speak to Ella and me, and I told her you were so anxious to dance with her——"

"Here!" he cried. "Look here! I'd rather do my own——"

"Yes; that's just it," Mrs. Dowling explained. "I just thought it was such a good opportunity; and Henrietta said she had most of her dances taken, but she'd give you one if you asked her before they were all gone. So I thought you'd better see her as soon as possible."

Dowling's face had become rosy. "I refuse to do anything of the kind."

"Bad fellow!" said his mother, gaily. "I thought this would be the best time for you to see Henrietta, because it won't be long till all her dances are gone, and you've promised on your *word* to dance the next with Ella, and you mightn't have a chance to do it then. I'm sure Miss Adams won't mind if you——"

"Not at all," Alice said.

"Well, *I* mind!" he said. "I wish you *could* understand that when I want to dance with any girl I don't need my mother to ask her for me. I really *am* more than six years old!"

He spoke with too much vehemence, and Mrs. Dowling at once saw how to have her way. As with husbands and wives, so with many fathers and daughters, and so with some sons and mothers: the man will himself be cross in public and think nothing of it, nor will he greatly mind a little crossness on the part of the woman; but let her show agitation before any spectator, he is instantly reduced to a coward's slavery. Women understand that ancient weakness, of course; for it is one of their most important means of defense, but can be used ignobly.

Mrs. Dowling permitted a tremulousness to become audible in her voice. "It isn't very—very pleasant—to be talked to like that by your own son—before strangers!"

"Oh, my! Look here!" the stricken Dowling protested. "*I* didn't say anything, mother. I was just joking about how you never get over thinking I'm a little boy. I only——"

Mrs. Dowling continued: "I just thought I was doing you a little favour. I didn't think it would make you so angry."

"Mother, for goodness' sake! Miss Adams'll think——"

"I suppose," Mrs. Dowling interrupted, piteously, "I suppose it doesn't matter what *I* think!"

"Oh, gracious!"

Alice interfered; she perceived that the ruthless Mrs. Dowling meant to have her way. "I think you'd better go, Frank. Really."

"There!" his mother cried. "Miss Adams says so, herself! What more do you want?"

"Oh, gracious!" he lamented again, and, with a sick look over his shoulder at Alice, permitted his mother to take his arm and propel him away. Mrs. Dowling's spirits had strikingly recovered even before the pair passed from the corridor: she moved almost bouncingly beside her embittered son, and her eyes and all the convolutions of her abundant face were blithe.

Alice went in search of Walter, but without much hope of finding him. What he did with himself at frozen-face dances was one of his most successful mysteries, and her present excursion gave her no clue leading to its solution. When the musicians again lowered their instruments for an interval she had returned, alone, to her former seat within the partial shelter of the box-trees.

She had now to practise an art that affords but a limited variety of methods, even to the expert: the art of seeming to have an escort or partner when there is none. The practitioner must imply, merely by expression and attitude, that the supposed companion has left her for only a few moments, that she herself has sent him upon an errand; and, if possible, the minds of observers must be directed toward a conclusion that this errand of her devising is an amusing one; at all events, she is alone temporarily and of choice, not deserted. She awaits a devoted man who may return at any instant.

Other people desired to sit in Alice's nook, but discovered her in occupancy. She had moved the vacant chair closer to her own, and she sat with her arm extended so that her hand, holding her lace kerchief, rested upon the back of this second chair, claiming it. Such a preëmption, like that of a traveller's bag in the rack, was unquestionable; and, for additional evidence, sitting with her knees crossed, she kept one foot continuously moving a little, in cadence with the other, which tapped the floor. Moreover, she added a fine detail: her half-smile, with the under lip caught, seemed to struggle against repression, as if she found the service engaging her absent companion even more amusing than she would let him see when he returned: there was jovial intrigue of some sort afoot, evidently. Her eyes, beaming with secret fun, were averted from intruders, but sometimes, when couples approached, seeking possession of the nook, her thoughts about the absentee appeared to threaten her with outright laughter; and though one or two girls looked at her skeptically, as they turned away, their escorts felt no such doubts, and merely wondered what importantly funny affair Alice Adams was engaged in. She had learned to do it perfectly.

She had learned it during the last two years; she was twenty when for the first time she had the shock of finding herself without an applicant for one of her dances. When she was sixteen "all the nice boys in town," as her mother said, crowded the Adamses' small veranda and steps, or sat near by, cross-legged on the lawn, on summer evenings; and at eighteen she had replaced the boys with "the older men." By this time most of "the other girls," her contemporaries, were away at school or college, and when they came home to stay, they "came out" —that feeble revival of an ancient custom offering the maiden to the ceremonial inspection of the tribe. Alice neither went away nor "came out," and, in contrast with those who did, she may have seemed to lack freshness of lustre—jewels are richest when revealed all new in a white velvet box. And Alice may have been too eager to secure new retainers, too kind in her efforts to keep the old ones. She had been a belle too soon.

Chapter VIII

THE DEVICE of the absentee partner has the defect that it cannot be employed for longer than ten or fifteen minutes at a time, and it may not be repeated more than twice in one evening: a single repetition, indeed, is weak, and may prove a betrayal. Alice knew that her present performance could be effective during only this interval between dances; and though her eyes were guarded, she anxiously counted over the partnerless young men who lounged together in the doorways within her view. Every one of them ought to have asked her for dances, she thought, and although she might have been put to it to give a reason why any of them "ought," her heart was hot with resentment against them.

For a girl who has been a belle, it is harder to live through these bad times than it is for one who has never known anything better. Like a figure of painted and brightly varnished wood, Ella Dowling sat against the wall through dance after dance with glassy imperturbability; it was easier to be wooden, Alice thought, if you had your mother with you, as Ella had. You were left with at least the shred of a pretense that you came to sit with your mother as a spectator, and not to offer yourself to be danced with by men who looked you over and rejected you—not for the first time. "Not for the first time": there lay a sting! Why had you thought this time might be different from the other times? Why had you broken your back picking those hundreds of violets?

Hating the fatuous young men in the doorways more bitterly for every instant that she had to maintain her tableau, the smiling Alice knew fierce impulses to spring to her feet and shout at them, "You *idiots*!" Hands in pockets, they lounged against the pilasters, or faced one another, laughing vaguely, each one of them seeming to Alice no more than so much mean beef in clothes. She wanted to tell them they were no better than that; and it seemed a cruel thing of heaven to let them go on believing themselves young lords. They were doing nothing, killing time. Wasn't she at her lowest value at least a means of killing time? Evidently the mean beeves thought not. And when one of them finally lounged across the corridor and spoke to her, he was the very one to whom she preferred her loneliness.

"Waiting for somebody, Lady Alicia?" he asked, negligently; and his easy burlesque of her name was like the familiarity of the rest of him. He was one of those full-bodied, grossly handsome men who are powerful and active, but never submit themselves to the rigour of becoming athletes, though they shoot and fish from expensive camps. Gloss is the most shining outward mark of the type. Nowadays these men no longer use brilliantine on their moustaches, but they have gloss bought from manicure-girls, from masseurs, and from automobile-makers; and their eyes, usually large, are glossy. None of this is allowed to interfere with business; these are "good business men," and often make large fortunes. They are men of imagination about two things—women and money, and, combining their imaginings about both, usually make a wise first marriage. Later, however, they are apt to imagine too much about some little woman without whom life seems duller than need be. They run away, leaving the first wife well enough dowered. They are never intentionally unkind to women, and in the end they usually make the mistake of thinking they have had their money's worth of life. Here was Mr. Harvey Malone, a young specimen in an earlier stage of development, trying to marry Henrietta Lamb, and now sauntering over to speak to Alice, as a time-killer before his next dance with Henrietta.

Alice made no response to his question, and he dropped lazily into the vacant chair, from which she sharply withdrew her hand. "I might as well use his chair till he comes, don't you think? You don't *mind*, do you, old girl?"

"Oh, no," Alice said. "It doesn't matter one way or the other. Please don't call me that."

"So that's how you feel?" Mr. Malone laughed indulgently, without much interest. "I've been meaning to come to see you for a long time—honestly I have—because I wanted to have a good talk with you about old times. I know you think it was funny, after the way I used to come to your house two or three times a week, and sometimes oftener—well, I don't blame you for being hurt, the way I stopped without explaining or anything. The truth is there wasn't any reason: I just happened to have a lot of important things to do and couldn't find the time. But I *am* going to call on you some evening—honestly I am. I don't wonder you think——"

"You're mistaken," Alice said. "I've never thought anything about it at all."

"Well, well!" he said, and looked at her languidly. "What's the use of being cross with this old man? He always means well." And, extending his arm, he would have given her a friendly pat upon the shoulder but she evaded it. "Well, well!" he said. "Seems to me you're getting awful tetchy! Don't you like your old friends any more?"

"Not all of them."

"Who's the new one?" he asked, teasingly. "Come on and tell us, Alice. Who is it you were holding this chair for?"

"Never mind."

"Well, all I've got to do is to sit here till he comes back; then I'll see who it is."

"He may not come back before you have to go."

"Guess you got me *that* time," Malone admitted, laughing as he rose. "They're tuning up, and I've got this dance. I *am* coming around to see you some evening." He moved away, calling back over his shoulder, "Honestly, I am!"

Alice did not look at him.

She had held her tableau as long as she could; it was time for her to abandon the box-trees; and she stepped forth frowning, as if a little annoyed with the absentee for being such a time upon her errand; whereupon the two chairs were instantly seized by a coquetting pair who intended to "sit out" the dance. She walked quickly down the broad corridor, turned into the broader hall, and hurriedly entered the dressing-room where she had left her wraps.

She stayed here as long as she could, pretending to arrange her hair at a mirror, then fidgeting with one of her slipper-buckles; but the intelligent elderly woman in charge of the room made an indefinite sojourn impracticable. "Perhaps I could help you with that buckle, Miss," she suggested, approaching. "Has it come loose?" Alice wrenched desperately; then it was loose. The competent woman, producing needle and thread, deftly made the buckle fast; and there was nothing for Alice to do but to express her gratitude and go.

She went to the door of the cloak-room opposite, where a coloured man stood watchfully in the doorway. "I wonder if you know which of the gentlemen is my brother, Mr. Walter Adams," she said.

"Yes'm; I know him."

"Could you tell me where he is?"

"No'm; I couldn't say."

"Well, if you see him, would you please tell him that his sister, Miss Adams, is looking for him and very anxious to speak to him?"

"Yes'm. Sho'ly, sho'ly!"

As she went away he stared after her and seemed to swell with some bursting emotion. In fact, it was too much for him, and he suddenly retired within the room, releasing strangulated laughter.

Walter remonstrated. Behind an excellent screen of coats and hats, in a remote part of the room, he was kneeling on the floor, engaged in a game of chance with a second coloured attendant; and the laughter became so vehement that it not only interfered with the pastime in hand, but threatened to attract frozen-face attention.

"I cain' he'p it, man," the laughter explained. "I cain' he'p it! You sut'n'y the beatin'es' white boy 'n 'is city!"

The dancers were swinging into an "encore" as Alice halted for an irresolute moment in a doorway. Across the room, a cluster of matrons sat chatting absently, their eyes on their dancing daughters; and Alice, finding a refugee's courage, dodged through the scurrying couples, seated herself in a chair on the outskirts of this colony of elders, and began to talk eagerly to the matron nearest her. The matron seemed unaccustomed to so much vivacity, and responded but dryly, whereupon Alice was more vivacious than ever; for she meant now to present the picture of a jolly girl too much interested in these wise older women to bother about every foolish young man who asked her for a dance.

Her matron was constrained to go so far as to supply a tolerant nod, now and then, in complement to the girl's animation, and Alice was grateful for the nods. In this fashion she supplemented the exhausted resources of the dressing-room and the box-tree nook; and lived through two more dances, when again Mr. Frank Dowling presented himself as a partner.

She needed no pretense to seek the dressing-room for repairs after that number; this time they were necessary and genuine. Dowling waited for her, and when she came out he explained for the fourth or fifth time how the accident had happened. "It was entirely those other people's fault," he said. "They got me in a kind of a corner, because neither of those fellows knows the least thing about guiding; they just jam ahead and expect everybody to get out of *their* way. It was Charlotte Thom's diamond crescent pin that got caught on your dress in the back and made such a——"

"Never mind," Alice said in a tired voice. "The maid fixed it so that she says it isn't very noticeable."

"Well, it isn't," he returned. "You could hardly tell there'd been anything the matter. Where do you want to go? Mother's been interfering in my affairs some more and I've got the next taken."

"I was sitting with Mrs. George Dresser. You might take me back there."

He left her with the matron, and Alice returned to her picture-making, so that once more, while two numbers passed, whoever cared to look was offered the sketch of a jolly, clever girl preoccupied with her elders. Then she found her friend Mildred standing before her, presenting Mr. Arthur Russell, who asked her to dance with him.

Alice looked uncertain, as though not sure what her engagements were; but her perplexity cleared; she nodded, and swung rhythmically away with the tall applicant. She was not grateful to her hostess for this alms. What a young hostess does with a fiancé, Alice thought, is to make him dance with the unpopular girls. She supposed that Mr. Arthur Russell had already danced with Ella Dowling.

The loan of a lover, under these circumstances, may be painful to the lessee, and Alice, smiling never more brightly, found nothing to say to Mr. Russell, though she thought he might have found something to say to her. "I wonder what Mildred told him," she thought. "Probably she said, 'Dearest, there's one more girl you've got to help me out with. You wouldn't like her much, but she dances well enough and she's having a rotten time. Nobody ever goes near her any more.'"

When the music stopped, Russell added his applause to the hand-clapping that encouraged the uproarious instruments to continue, and as they renewed the tumult, he said heartily, "That's splendid!"

Alice gave him a glance, necessarily at short range, and found his eyes kindly and pleased. Here was a friendly soul, it appeared, who probably "liked everybody." No doubt he had applauded for an "encore" when he danced with Ella Dowling, gave Ella the same genial look, and said, "That's splendid!"

When the "encore" was over, Alice spoke to him for the first time.

"Mildred will be looking for you," she said. "I think you'd better take me back to where you found me."

He looked surprised. "Oh, if you——"

"I'm sure Mildred will be needing you," Alice said, and as she took his arm and they walked toward Mrs. Dresser, she thought it might be just possible to make a further use of the loan. "Oh, I wonder if you——" she began.

"Yes?" he said, quickly.

"You don't know my brother, Walter Adams," she said. "But he's somewhere—I think possibly he's in a smoking-room or some place where girls aren't expected, and if you wouldn't think it too much trouble to inquire——"

"I'll find him," Russell said, promptly. "Thank you so much for that dance. I'll bring your brother in a moment."

It was to be a long moment, Alice decided, presently. Mrs. Dresser had grown restive; and her nods and vague responses to her young dependent's gaieties were as meager as they could well be. Evidently the matron had no intention of appearing to her world in the light of a chaperone for Alice Adams; and she finally made this clear. With a word or two of excuse, breaking into something Alice was saying, she rose and went to sit next to Mildred's mother, who had become the nucleus of the cluster. So Alice was left very much against the wall, with short stretches of vacant chairs on each side of her. She had come to the end of her picture-making, and could only pretend that there was something amusing the matter with the arm of her chair.

She supposed that Mildred's Mr. Russell had forgotten Walter by this time. "I'm not even an intimate enough friend of Mildred's for him to have thought he ought to bother to tell me he couldn't find him," she thought. And then she saw Russell coming across the room toward her, with Walter beside him. She jumped up gaily.

"Oh, thank you!" she cried. "I know this naughty boy must have been terribly hard to find. Mildred'll *never* forgive me! I've put you to so much——"

"Not at all," he said, amiably, and went away, leaving the brother and sister together.

"Walter, let's dance just once more," Alice said, touching his arm placatively. "I thought—well, perhaps we might go home then."

But Walter's expression was that of a person upon whom an outrage has just been perpetrated. "No," he said. "We've stayed *this* long, I'm goin' to wait and see what they got to eat. And you look here!" He turned upon her angrily. "Don't you ever do that again!"

"Do what?"

"Send somebody after me that pokes his nose into every corner of the house till he finds me! 'Are you Mr. Walter Adams?' he says. I guess he must asked everybody in the place if they were Mr. Walter Adams! Well, I'll bet a few iron men you wouldn't send anybody to hunt for me again if you knew where he found me!"

"Where was it?"

Walter decided that her fit punishment was to know. "I was shootin' dice with those coons in the cloak-room."

"And he *saw* you?"

"Unless he was blind!" said Walter. "Come on, I'll dance this one more dance with you. Supper comes after that, and *then* we'll go home."

Mrs. Adams heard Alice's key turning in the front door and hurried down the stairs to meet her.

"Did you get wet coming in, darling?" she asked. "Did you have a good time?"

"Just lovely!" Alice said, cheerily; and after she had arranged the latch for Walter, who had gone to return the little car, she followed her mother upstairs and hummed a dance-tune on the way.

"Oh, I'm so glad you had a nice time," Mrs. Adams said, as they reached the door of her daughter's room together. "You *deserved* to, and it's lovely to think——"

But at this, without warning, Alice threw herself into her mother's arms, sobbing so loudly that in his room, close by, her father, half drowsing through the night, started to full wakefulness.

Chapter IX

ON A morning, a week after this collapse of festal hopes, Mrs. Adams and her daughter were concluding a three-days' disturbance, the "Spring house-cleaning"—postponed until now by Adams's long illness—and Alice, on her knees before a chest of drawers, in her mother's room, paused thoughtfully after dusting a packet of letters wrapped in worn muslin. She called to her mother, who was scrubbing the floor of the hallway just beyond the open door,

"These old letters you had in the bottom drawer, weren't they some papa wrote you before you were married?"

Mrs. Adams laughed and said, "Yes. Just put 'em back where they were—or else up in the attic—anywhere you want to."

"Do you mind if I read one, mama?"

Mrs. Adams laughed again. "Oh, I guess you can if you want to. I expect they're pretty funny!"

Alice laughed in response, and chose the topmost letter of the packet. "My dear, beautiful girl," it began; and she stared at these singular words. They gave her a shock like that caused by overhearing some bewildering impropriety; and, having read them over to herself several times, she went on to experience other shocks.

MY DEAR, BEAUTIFUL GIRL:

This time yesterday I had a mighty bad case of blues because I had not had a word from you in two whole long days and when I do not hear from you every day things look mighty down in the mouth to me. Now it is all so different because your letter has arrived and besides I have got a piece of news I believe you will think as fine as I do. Darling, you will be surprised, so get ready to hear about a big effect on our future. It is this way. I had sort of a suspicion the head of the firm kind of took a fancy to me from the first when I went in there, and liked the way I attended to my work and so when he took me on this business trip with him I felt pretty sure of it and now it turns out I was about right. In return I guess I have got about the best boss in this world and I believe you will think so too. Yes, sweetheart, after the talk I have just had with him if J. A. Lamb asked me to cut my hand off for him I guess I would come pretty near doing it because what he says means the end of our waiting to be together. From New Years on he is going to put me in entire charge of the sundries dept. and what do you think is going to be my salary? Eleven hundred cool dollars a year ($1,100.00). That's all! Just only a cool eleven hundred per annum! Well, I guess that will show your mother whether I can take care of you or not. And oh how I would like to see your dear, beautiful, loving face when you get this news.

I would like to go out on the public streets and just dance and shout and it is all I can do to help doing it, especially when I know we will be talking it all over together this time next week, and oh my darling, now that your folks have no excuse for putting it off any longer we might be in our own little home before Xmas. Would you be glad?

Well, darling, this settles everything and makes our future just about as smooth for us as anybody could ask. I can hardly realize after all this waiting life's troubles are over for you and me and we have nothing to do but to enjoy the happiness granted us by this wonderful, beautiful thing we call life. I know I am not any poet and the one I tried to write about you the day of the picnic was fearful but the way I *think* about you is a poem.

Write me what you think of the news. I know but write me anyhow. I'll get it before we start home and I can be reading it over all the time on the train.

Your always loving
VIRGIL.

The sound of her mother's diligent scrubbing in the hall came back slowly to Alice's hearing, as she restored the letter to the packet, wrapped the packet in its muslin covering, and returned it to the drawer. She had remained upon her knees while she read the letter; now she sank backward, sitting upon the floor with her hands behind her, an unconscious relaxing for better ease to think. Upon her face there had fallen a look of wonder.

For the first time she was vaguely perceiving that life is everlasting movement. Youth really believes what is running water to be a permanent crystallization and sees time fixed to a point: some people have dark hair, some people have blond hair, some people have gray hair. Until this moment, Alice had no conviction that there was a universe before she came into it. She had always thought of it as the background of herself: the moon was something to make her prettier on a summer night.

But this old letter, through which she saw still flickering an ancient starlight of young love, astounded her. Faintly before her it revealed the whole lives of her father and mother, who had been young, after all—they *really* had—and their youth was now so utterly passed from them that the picture of it, in the letter, was like a burlesque of them. And so she, herself, must pass to such changes, too, and all that now seemed vital to her would be nothing.

When her work was finished, that afternoon, she went into her father's room. His recovery had progressed well enough to permit the departure of Miss Perry; and Adams, wearing one of Mrs. Adams's wrappers over his night-gown, sat in a high-backed chair by a closed window. The weather was warm, but the closed window and the flannel wrapper had not sufficed him: round his shoulders he had an old crocheted scarf of Alice's; his legs were wrapped in a heavy comfort; and, with these swathings about him, and his eyes closed, his thin and grizzled head making but a slight indentation in the pillow supporting it, he looked old and little and queer.

Alice would have gone out softly, but without opening his eyes, he spoke to her: "Don't go, dearie. Come sit with the old man a little while."

She brought a chair near his. "I thought you were napping."

"No. I don't hardly ever do that. I just drift a little sometimes."

"How do you mean you drift, papa?"

He looked at her vaguely. "Oh, I don't know. Kind of pictures. They get a little mixed up—old times with times still ahead, like planning what to do, you know. That's as near a nap as I get—when the pictures mix up some. I suppose it's sort of drowsing."

She took one of his hands and stroked it. "What do you mean when you say you have pictures like 'planning what to do'?" she asked.

"I mean planning what to do when I get out and able to go to work again."

"But that doesn't need any planning," Alice said, quickly. "You're going back to your old place at Lamb's, of course."

Adams closed his eyes again, sighing heavily, but made no other response.

"Why, of *course* you are!" she cried. "What are you talking about?"

His head turned slowly toward her, revealing the eyes, open in a haggard stare. "I heard you the other night when you came from the party," he said. "I know what was the matter."

"Indeed, you don't," she assured him. "You don't know anything about it, because there wasn't anything the matter at all."

"Don't you suppose I heard you crying? What'd you cry for if there wasn't anything the matter?"

"Just nerves, papa. It wasn't anything else in the world."

"Never mind," he said. "Your mother told me."

"She promised me not to!"

At that Adams laughed mournfully. "It wouldn't be very likely I'd hear you so upset and not ask about it, even if she didn't come and tell me on her own hook. You needn't try to fool me; I tell you I know what was the matter."

"The only matter was I had a silly fit," Alice protested. "It did me good, too."

"How's that?"

"Because I've decided to do something about it, papa."

"That isn't the way your mother looks at it," Adams said, ruefully. "She thinks it's our place to do something about it. Well, I don't know—I don't know; everything seems so changed these days. You've always been a good daughter, Alice, and you ought to have as much as any of these girls you go with; she's convinced me she's right about *that*. The trouble is——" He faltered, apologetically, then went on, "I mean the question is—how to get it for you."

"No!" she cried. "I had no business to make such a fuss just because a lot of idiots didn't break their necks to get dances with me and because I got mortified about Walter—Walter *was* pretty terrible——"

"Oh, me, my!" Adams lamented. "I guess that's something we just have to leave work out itself. What you going to do with a boy nineteen or twenty years old that makes his own living? Can't whip him. Can't keep him locked up in the house. Just got to hope he'll learn better, I suppose."

"Of course he didn't want to go to the Palmers'," Alice explained, tolerantly—"and as mama and I made him take me, and he thought that was pretty selfish in me, why, he felt he had a right to amuse himself any way he could. Of course it was awful that this—that this Mr. Russell should——" In spite of her, the recollection choked her.

"Yes, it was awful," Adams agreed. "Just awful. Oh, me, my!"

But Alice recovered herself at once, and showed him a cheerful face. "Well, just a few years from now I probably won't even remember it! I believe hardly anything amounts to as much as we think it does at the time."

"Well—sometimes it don't."

"What I've been thinking, papa: it seems to me I ought to *do* something."

"What like?"

She looked dreamy, but was obviously serious as she told him: "Well, I mean I ought to be something besides just a kind of nobody. I ought to——" She paused.

"What, dearie?"

"Well—there's one thing I'd like to do. I'm sure I *could* do it, too."

"What?"

"I want to go on the stage: I know I could act."

At this, her father abruptly gave utterance to a feeble cackling of laughter; and when Alice, surprised and a little offended, pressed him for his reason, he tried to evade, saying, "Nothing, dearie. I just thought of something." But she persisted until he had to explain.

"It made me think of your mother's sister, your Aunt Flora, that died when you were little," he said. "She was always telling how she was going on the stage, and talking about how she was certain she'd make a great actress, and all so on; and one day your mother broke out and said *she* ought 'a' gone on the stage, herself, because she always knew she had the talent for it—and, well, they got into kind of a spat about which one'd make the best actress. I had to go out in the hall to laugh!"

"Maybe you were wrong," Alice said, gravely. "If they both felt it, why wouldn't that look as if there was talent in the family? I've *always* thought——"

"No, dearie," he said, with a final chuckle. "Your mother and Flora weren't different from a good many others. I expect ninety per cent. of all the women I ever knew were just sure they'd be mighty fine actresses if they ever got the chance. Well, I guess it's a good thing; they enjoy thinking about it and it don't do anybody any harm."

Alice was piqued. For several days she had thought almost continuously of a career to be won by her own genius. Not that she planned details, or concerned herself with first steps; her picturings overleaped all that. Principally, she saw her name great on all the bill-boards of that unkind city, and herself, unchanged in age but glamorous with fame and Paris clothes, returning in a private car. No doubt the pleasantest development of her vision was a dialogue with Mildred; and this became so real that, as she projected it, Alice assumed the proper expressions for both parties to it, formed words with her lips, and even spoke some of them aloud. "No, I haven't forgotten you, Mrs. Russell. I remember you quite pleasantly, in fact. You were a Miss Palmer, I recall, in those funny old days. Very kind of you, I'm shaw. I appreciate your eagerness to do something for me in your own little home. As you say, a reception *would* renew my acquaintanceship with many old friends—but I'm shaw you won't mind my mentioning that I don't find much inspiration in these provincials. I really must ask you not to press me. An artist's time is not her own, though of course I could hardly expect you to understand——"

Thus Alice illuminated the dull time; but she retired from the interview with her father still manfully displaying an outward cheerfulness, while depression grew heavier within, as if she had eaten soggy cake. Her father knew nothing whatever of the stage, and she was aware of his ignorance, yet for some reason his innocently skeptical amusement reduced her bright project almost to nothing. Something like this always happened, it seemed; she was continually making these illuminations, all gay with gildings and colourings; and then as soon as anybody else so much as glanced at them—even her father, who loved her—the pretty designs were stricken with a desolating pallor. "Is this *life*?" Alice wondered, not doubting that the question was original and all her own. "Is it life to spend your time imagining things that aren't so, and never will be? Beautiful things happen to other people; why should I be the only one they never *can* happen to?"

The mood lasted overnight; and was still upon her the next afternoon when an errand for her father took her down-town. Adams had decided to begin smoking again, and Alice felt rather degraded, as well as embarrassed, when she went into the large shop her father had named, and asked for the cheap tobacco he used in his pipe. She fell back upon an air of amused indulgence, hoping thus to suggest that her purchase was made for some faithful old retainer, now infirm; and although the calmness of the clerk who served her called for no such elaboration of her sketch, she ornamented it with a little laugh and with the remark, as she dropped the package into her coat-pocket, "I'm sure it'll please him; they tell me it's the kind he likes."

Still playing Lady Bountiful, smiling to herself in anticipation of the joy she was bringing to the simple old negro or Irish follower of the family, she left the shop; but as she came out upon the crowded pavement her smile vanished quickly.

Next to the door of the tobacco-shop, there was the open entrance to a stairway, and, above this rather bleak and dark aperture, a sign-board displayed in begrimed gilt letters the information that Frincke's Business College occupied the upper floors of the building. Furthermore, Frincke here publicly offered "personal instruction and training in practical mathematics, bookkeeping, and all branches of the business life, including stenography, typewriting, etc."

Alice halted for a moment, frowning at this sign-board as though it were something surprising and distasteful which she had never seen before. Yet it was conspicuous in a busy quarter; she almost always passed it when she came down-town, and never without noticing it. Nor was this the first time she had paused to lift toward it that same glance of vague misgiving.

The building was not what the changeful city defined as a modern one, and the dusty wooden stairway, as seen from the pavement, disappeared upward into a smoky darkness. So would the footsteps of a girl ascending there lead to a hideous obscurity, Alice thought; an obscurity as dreary and as permanent as death. And like dry leaves falling about her she saw her wintry imaginings in the May air: pretty girls turning into withered creatures as they worked at typing-machines; old maids "taking dictation" from men with double chins; Alice saw old maids of a dozen different kinds "taking dictation." Her mind's eye was crowded with them, as it always was when she passed that stairway entrance; and though they were all different from one another, all of them looked a little like herself.

She hated the place, and yet she seldom hurried by it or averted her eyes. It had an unpleasant fascination for her, and a mysterious reproach, which she did not seek to fathom. She walked on thoughtfully to-day; and when, at the next corner, she turned into the street that led toward home, she was given a surprise. Arthur Russell came rapidly from behind her, lifting his hat as she saw him.

"Are you walking north, Miss Adams?" he asked. "Do you mind if I walk with you?"

She was not delighted, but seemed so. "How charming!" she cried, giving him a little flourish of the shapely hands; and then, because she wondered if he had seen her coming out of the tobacco-shop, she laughed and added, "I've just been on the most ridiculous errand!"

"What was that?"

"To order some cigars for my father. He's been quite ill, poor man, and he's so particular—but what in the world do *I* know about cigars?"

Russell laughed. "Well, what *do* you know about 'em? Did you select by the price?"

"Mercy, no!" she exclaimed, and added, with an afterthought, "Of course he wrote down the name of the kind he wanted and I gave it to the shopman. I could never have pronounced it."

Chapter X

IN HER pocket as she spoke her hand rested upon the little sack of tobacco, which responded accusingly to the touch of her restless fingers; and she found time to wonder why she was building up this fiction for Mr. Arthur Russell. His discovery of Walter's device for whiling away the dull evening had shamed and distressed her; but she would have suffered no less if almost any other had been the discoverer. In this gentleman, after hearing that he was Mildred's Mr. Arthur Russell, Alice felt not the slightest "personal interest"; and there was yet to develop in her life such a thing as an interest not personal. At twenty-two this state of affairs is not unique.

So far as Alice was concerned Russell might have worn a placard, "Engaged." She looked upon him as diners entering a restaurant look upon tables marked "Reserved": the glance, slightly discontented, passes on at once. Or so the eye of a prospector wanders querulously over staked and established claims on the mountainside, and seeks the virgin land beyond; unless, indeed, the prospector be dishonest. But Alice was no claim-jumper—so long as the notice of ownership was plainly posted.

Though she was indifferent now, habit ruled her: and, at the very time she wondered why she created fictitious cigars for her father, she was also regretting that she had not boldly carried her Malacca stick down-town with her. Her vivacity increased automatically.

"Perhaps the clerk thought you wanted the cigars for yourself," Russell suggested. "He may have taken you for a Spanish countess."

"I'm sure he did!" Alice agreed, gaily; and she hummed a bar or two of "La Paloma," snapping her fingers as castanets, and swaying her body a little, to suggest the accepted stencil of a "Spanish Dancer." "Would you have taken me for one, Mr. Russell?" she asked, as she concluded the impersonation.

"I? Why, yes," he said. "*I'd* take you for anything you wanted me to."

"Why, what a speech!" she cried, and, laughing, gave him a

quick glance in which there glimmered some real surprise. He was looking at her quizzically, but with the liveliest appreciation. Her surprise increased; and she was glad that he had joined her.

To be seen walking with such a companion added to her pleasure. She would have described him as "altogether quite stunning-looking"; and she liked his tall, dark thinness, his gray clothes, his soft hat, and his clean brown shoes; she liked his easy swing of the stick he carried.

"Shouldn't I have said it?" he asked. "Would you rather not be taken for a Spanish countess?"

"That isn't it," she explained. "You said——"

"I said I'd take you for whatever you wanted me to. Isn't that all right?"

"It would all depend, wouldn't it?"

"Of course it would depend on what you wanted."

"Oh, no!" she laughed. "It might depend on a lot of things."

"Such as?"

"Well——" She hesitated, having the mischievous impulse to say, "Such as Mildred!" But she decided to omit this reference, and became serious, remembering Russell's service to her at Mildred's house. "Speaking of what I want to be taken for," she said;—"I've been wondering ever since the other night what you did take me for! You must have taken me for the sister of a professional gambler, I'm afraid!"

Russell's look of kindness was the truth about him, she was to discover; and he reassured her now by the promptness of his friendly chuckle. "Then your young brother told you where I found him, did he? I kept my face straight at the time, but I laughed afterward—to myself. It struck me as original, to say the least: his amusing himself with those darkies."

"Walter *is* original," Alice said; and, having adopted this new view of her brother's eccentricities, she impulsively went on to make it more plausible. "He's a very odd boy, and I was afraid you'd misunderstand. He tells wonderful 'darky stories,' and he'll do anything to draw coloured people out and make them talk; and that's what he was doing at Mildred's when you found him for me—he says he wins their confidence by playing dice with them. In the family we think he'll probably write about them some day. He's rather literary."

"Are you?" Russell asked, smiling.

"I? Oh——" She paused, lifting both hands in a charming gesture of helplessness. "Oh, I'm just—me!"

His glance followed the lightly waved hands with keen approval, then rose to the lively and colourful face, with its hazel eyes, its small and pretty nose, and the lip-caught smile which seemed the climax of her decorative transition. Never had he seen a creature so plastic or so wistful.

Here was a contrast to his cousin Mildred, who was not wistful, and controlled any impulses toward plasticity, if she had them. "By George!" he said. "But you *are* different!"

With that, there leaped in her such an impulse of roguish gallantry as she could never resist. She turned her head, and, laughing and bright-eyed, looked him full in the face.

"From whom?" she cried.

"From—everybody!" he said. "Are you a mind-reader?"

"Why?"

"How did you know I was thinking you were different from my cousin, Mildred Palmer?"

"What makes you think I *did* know it?"

"Nonsense!" he said. "You knew what I was thinking and I knew you knew."

"Yes," she said with cool humour. "How intimate that seems to make us all at once!"

Russell left no doubt that he was delighted with these gaieties of hers. "By George!" he exclaimed again. "I thought you were this sort of girl the first moment I saw you!"

"What sort of girl? Didn't Mildred tell you what sort of girl I am when she asked you to dance with me?"

"She didn't ask me to dance with you—I'd been looking at you. You were talking to some old ladies, and I asked Mildred who you were."

"Oh, so Mildred *didn't*——" Alice checked herself. "Who did she tell you I was?"

"She just said you were a Miss Adams, so I——"

"'A' Miss Adams?" Alice interrupted.

"Yes. Then I said I'd like to meet you."

"I see. You thought you'd save me from the old ladies."

"No. I thought I'd save myself from some of the girls Mildred was getting me to dance with. There was a Miss Dowling——"

"Poor man!" Alice said, gently, and her impulsive thought was that Mildred had taken few chances, and that as a matter of self-defense her carefulness might have been well founded. This Mr. Arthur Russell was a much more responsive person than one had supposed.

"So, Mr. Russell, you don't know anything about me except what you thought when you first saw me?"

"Yes, I know I was right when I thought it."

"You haven't told me what you thought."

"I thought you were like what you *are* like."

"Not very definite, is it? I'm afraid you shed more light a minute or so ago, when you said how different from Mildred you thought I was. That *was* definite, unfortunately!"

"I didn't say it," Russell explained. "I thought it, and you read my mind. That's the sort of girl I thought you were—one that could read a man's mind. Why do you say 'unfortunately' you're not like Mildred?"

Alice's smooth gesture seemed to sketch Mildred. "Because she's perfect—why, she's *perfectly* perfect! She never makes a mistake, and everybody looks up to her—oh, yes, we all fairly adore her! She's like some big, noble, cold statue—'way above the rest of us—and she hardly ever does anything mean or treacherous. Of all the girls I know I believe she's played the fewest really petty tricks. She's——"

Russell interrupted; he looked perplexed. "You say she's perfectly perfect, but that she does play *some*——"

Alice laughed, as if at his sweet innocence. "Men are so funny!" she informed him. "Of course girls *all* do mean things sometimes. My own career's just one long brazen smirch of 'em! What I mean is, Mildred's perfectly perfect compared to the rest of us."

"I see," he said, and seemed to need a moment or two of thoughtfulness. Then he inquired, "What sort of treacherous things do *you* do?"

"I? Oh, the very worst kind! Most people bore me—particularly the men in this town—and I show it."

"But I shouldn't call that treacherous, exactly."

"Well, *they* do," Alice laughed. "It's made me a terribly unpopular character! I do a lot of things they hate. For instance, at a dance I'd a lot rather find some clever old woman and talk to her than dance with nine-tenths of these nonentities. I usually do it, too."

"But you danced as if you liked it. You danced better than any other girl I——"

"This flattery of yours doesn't quite turn my head, Mr. Russell," Alice interrupted. "Particularly since Mildred only gave you Ella Dowling to compare with me!"

"Oh, no," he insisted. "There were others—and of course Mildred, herself."

"Oh, of course, yes. I forgot that. Well——" She paused, then added, "I certainly *ought* to dance well."

"Why is it so much a duty?"

"When I think of the dancing-teachers and the expense to papa! All sorts of fancy instructors—I suppose that's what daughters have fathers for, though, isn't it? To throw money away on them?"

"You don't——" Russell began, and his look was one of alarm. "You haven't taken up——"

She understood his apprehension and responded merrily, "Oh, murder, no! You mean you're afraid I break out sometimes in a piece of cheesecloth and run around a fountain thirty times, and then, for an encore, show how much like snakes I can make my arms look."

"I *said* you were a mind-reader!" he exclaimed. "That's exactly what I was pretending to be afraid you might do."

"'Pretending?' That's nicer of you. No; it's not my mania."

"What is?"

"Oh, nothing in particular that I know of just now. Of course I've had the usual one: the one that every girl goes through."

"What's that?"

"Good heavens, Mr. Russell, you can't expect me to believe you're really a man of the world if you don't know that every girl has a time in her life when she's positive she's divinely talented for the stage! It's the only universal rule about women that hasn't got an exception. I don't mean we all want to go on the stage, but we all think we'd be wonderful if we did. Even Mildred. Oh, she wouldn't confess it to you: you'd have to know her a great deal better than any man can ever know her to find out."

"I see," he said. "Girls are always telling us we can't know them. I wonder if you——"

She took up his thought before he expressed it, and again he was fascinated by her quickness, which indeed seemed to him almost telepathic. "Oh, but *don't* we know one another, though!" she cried. "Such things we have to keep secret—things that go on right before *your* eyes!"

"Why don't some of you tell us?" he asked.

"We can't tell you."

"Too much honour?"

"No. Not even too much honour among thieves, Mr. Russell. We don't tell you about our tricks against one another because we know it wouldn't make any impression on you. The tricks aren't played against you, and you have a soft side for cats with lovely manners!"

"What about your tricks against us?"

"Oh, those!" Alice laughed. "We think they're rather cute!"

"Bravo!" he cried, and hammered the ferrule of his stick upon the pavement.

"What's the applause for?"

"For you. What you said was like running up the black flag to the masthead."

"Oh, no. It was just a modest little sign in a pretty flower-bed: 'Gentlemen, beware!'"

"I see I must," he said, gallantly.

"Thanks! But I mean, beware of the whole bloomin' garden!" Then, picking up a thread that had almost disappeared: "You needn't think you'll ever find out whether I'm right about Mildred's not being an exception by asking her," she said. "She won't tell you: she's not the sort that ever makes a confession."

But Russell had not followed her shift to the former topic. "'Mildred's not being an exception?'" he said, vaguely. "I don't——"

"An exception about thinking she could be a wonderful thing on the stage if she only cared to. If you asked her I'm pretty sure she'd say, 'What nonsense!' Mildred's the dearest, finest thing anywhere, but you won't find out many things about her by asking her."

Russell's expression became more serious, as it did whenever his cousin was made their topic. "You think not?" he said. "You think she's——"

"No. But it's not because she isn't sincere exactly. It's only because she has such a lot to live up to. She has to live up to being a girl on the grand style—to herself, I mean, of course." And without pausing Alice rippled on, "You ought to have seen *me* when I had the stage-fever! I used to play 'Juliet' all alone in my room." She lifted her arms in graceful entreaty, pleading musically,

> "O, swear not by the moon, the inconstant moon,
> That monthly changes in her circled orb,
> Lest thy love prove——"

She broke off abruptly with a little flourish, snapping thumb and finger of each outstretched hand, then laughed and said, "Papa used to make such fun of me! Thank heaven, I was only fifteen; I was all over it by the next year."

"No wonder you had the fever," Russell observed. "You do it beautifully. Why didn't you finish the line?"

"Which one? 'Lest thy love prove likewise variable'? Juliet was saying it to a *man*, you know. She seems to have been ready to worry about his constancy pretty early in their affair!"

Her companion was again thoughtful. "Yes," he said, seeming to be rather irksomely impressed with Alice's suggestion. "Yes; it does appear so."

Alice glanced at his serious face, and yielded to an audacious temptation. "You mustn't take it so hard," she said, flippantly. "It isn't about you: it's only about Romeo and Juliet."

"See here!" he exclaimed. "You aren't at your mind-reading again, are you? There are times when it won't do, you know!"

She leaned toward him a little, as if companionably: they were walking slowly, and this geniality of hers brought her shoulder in light contact with his for a moment. "Do you dislike my mind-reading?" she asked, and, across their two just touching shoulders, gave him her sudden look of smiling wistfulness. "Do you hate it?"

He shook his head. "No, I don't," he said, gravely. "It's quite —pleasant. But I think it says, 'Gentlemen, beware!'"

She instantly moved away from him, with the lawless and frank laugh of one who is delighted to be caught in a piece of hypocrisy. "How lovely!" she cried. Then she pointed ahead.

"Our walk is nearly over. We're coming to the foolish little house where I live. It's a queer little place, but my father's so attached to it the family have about given up hope of getting him to build a real house farther out. He doesn't mind our being extravagant about anything else, but he won't let us alter one single thing about his precious little old house. Well!" She halted, and gave him her hand. "Adieu!"

"I couldn't," he began; hesitated, then asked: "I couldn't come in with you for a little while?"

"Not now," she said, quickly. "You can come——" She paused.

"When?"

"Almost any time." She turned and walked slowly up the path, but he waited. "You can come in the evening if you like," she called back to him over her shoulder.

"Soon?"

"As soon as you like!" She waved her hand; then ran indoors and watched him from a window as he went up the street. He walked rapidly, a fine, easy figure, swinging his stick in a way that suggested exhilaration. Alice, staring after him through the irregular apertures of a lace curtain, showed no similar buoyancy. Upon the instant she closed the door all sparkle left her: she had become at once the simple and sometimes troubled girl her family knew.

"What's going on out there?" her mother asked, approaching from the dining-room.

"Oh, nothing," Alice said, indifferently, as she turned away. "That Mr. Russell met me down-town and walked up with me."

"Mr. Russell? Oh, the one that's engaged to Mildred?"

"Well—I don't know for certain. He didn't seem so much like an engaged man to me." And she added, in the tone of thoughtful preoccupation: "Anyhow—not so terribly!"

Then she ran upstairs, gave her father his tobacco, filled his pipe for him, and petted him as he lighted it.

Chapter XI

AFTER THAT, she went to her room and sat down before her three-leaved mirror. There was where she nearly always sat when she came into her room, if she had nothing in mind to do. She went to that chair as naturally as a dog goes to his corner.

She leaned forward, observing her profile; gravity seemed to be her mood. But after a long, almost motionless scrutiny, she began to produce dramatic sketches upon that ever-ready stage, her countenance: she showed gaiety, satire, doubt, gentleness, appreciation of a companion and love-in-hiding—all studied in profile first, then repeated for a "three-quarter view." Subsequently she ran through them, facing herself in full.

In this manner she outlined a playful scenario for her next interview with Arthur Russell; but grew solemn again, thinking of the impression she had already sought to give him. She had no twinges for any underminings of her "most intimate friend"—in fact, she felt that her work on a new portrait of Mildred for Mr. Russell had been honest and accurate. But why had it been her instinct to show him an Alice Adams who didn't exist?

Almost everything she had said to him was upon spontaneous impulse, springing to her lips on the instant; yet it all seemed to have been founded upon a careful design, as if some hidden self kept such designs in stock and handed them up to her, ready-made, to be used for its own purpose. What appeared to be the desired result was a false-coloured image in Russell's mind; but if he liked that image he wouldn't be liking Alice Adams; nor would anything he thought about the image be a thought about her. Nevertheless, she knew she would go on with her false, fancy colourings of this nothing as soon as she saw him again; she had just been practising them. "What's the idea?" she wondered. "What makes me tell such lies? Why shouldn't I be just myself?" And then she thought, "But which one is myself?"

Her eyes dwelt on the solemn eyes in the mirror; and her lips, disquieted by a deepening wonder, parted to whisper:

"Who in the world are you?"

The apparition before her had obeyed her like an alert slave, but now, as she subsided to a complete stillness, that aspect changed to the old mockery with which mirrors avenge their wrongs. The nucleus of some queer thing seemed to gather and shape itself behind the nothingness of the reflected eyes until it became almost an actual strange presence. If it could be identified, perhaps the presence was that of the hidden designer who handed up the false, ready-made pictures, and, for unknown purposes, made Alice exhibit them; but whatever it was, she suddenly found it monkey-like and terrifying. In a flutter she jumped up and went to another part of the room.

A moment or two later she was whistling softly as she hung her light coat over a wooden triangle in her closet, and her musing now was quainter than the experience that led to it; for what she thought was this, "I certainly am a queer girl!" She took a little pride in so much originality, believing herself probably the only person in the world to have such thoughts as had been hers since she entered the room, and the first to be disturbed by a strange presence in the mirror. In fact, the effect of the tiny episode became apparent in that look of preoccupied complacency to be seen for a time upon any girl who has found reason to suspect that she is a being without counterpart.

This slight glow, still faintly radiant, was observed across the dinner-table by Walter, but he misinterpreted it. "What *you* lookin' so self-satisfied about?" he inquired, and added in his knowing way, "I saw you, all right, cutie!"

"Where'd you see me?"

"Down-town."

"This afternoon, you mean, Walter?"

"Yes, 'this afternoon, I mean, Walter,'" he returned, burlesquing her voice at least happily enough to please himself; for he laughed applausively. "Oh, you never saw me! I passed you close enough to pull a tooth, but you were awful busy. I never did see anybody as busy as you get, Alice, when you're towin' a barge. My, but you keep your hands goin'! Looked like the air was full of 'em! That's why I'm onto why you look so tickled this evening; I saw you with that big fish."

Mrs. Adams laughed benevolently; she was not displeased with this rallying. "Well, what of it, Walter?" she asked. "If you happen to see your sister on the street when some nice young man is being attentive to her——"

Walter barked and then cackled. "Whoa, Sal!" he said. "You got the parts mixed. It's little Alice that was 'being attentive.' I know the big fish she was attentive to, all right, too."

"Yes," his sister retorted, quietly. "I should think you might have recognized him, Walter."

Walter looked annoyed. "Still harpin' on *that*!" he complained. "The kind of women I like, if they get sore they just hit you somewhere on the face and then they're through. By the way, I heard this Russell was supposed to be your dear, old, sweet friend Mildred's steady. What you doin' walkin' as close to him as all that?"

Mrs. Adams addressed her son in gentle reproof, "Why Walter!"

"Oh, never mind, mama," Alice said. "To the horrid all things are horrid."

"Get out!" Walter protested, carelessly. "I heard all about this Russell down at the shop. Young Joe Lamb's such a talker I wonder he don't ruin his grandfather's business; he keeps all us cheap help standin' round listening to him nine-tenths of our time. Well, Joe told me this Russell's some kin or other to the Palmer family, and he's got some little money of his own, and he's puttin' it into ole Palmer's trust company and Palmer's goin' to make him a vice-president of the company. Sort of a keep-the-money-in-the-family arrangement, Joe Lamb says."

Mrs. Adams looked thoughtful. "I don't see——" she began.

"Why, this Russell's supposed to be tied up to Mildred," her son explained. "When ole Palmer dies this Russell will be his son-in-law, and all he'll haf' to do'll be to barely lift his feet and step into the ole man's shoes. It's certainly a mighty fat hand-me-out for this Russell! You better lay off o' there, Alice. Pick somebody that's got less to lose and you'll make a better showing."

Mrs. Adams's air of thoughtfulness had not departed. "But you say this Mr. Russell is well off on his own account, Walter."

"Oh, Joe Lamb says he's got some little of his own. Didn't know how much."

"Well, then——"

Walter laughed his laugh. "Cut it out," he bade her. "Alice wouldn't run in fourth place."

Alice had been looking at him in a detached way, as though estimating the value of a specimen in a collection not her own. "Yes," she said, indifferently. "You *really* are vulgar, Walter."

He had finished his meal; and, rising, he came round the table to her and patted her good-naturedly on the shoulder. "Good ole Allie!" he said. "*Honest*, you wouldn't run in fourth place. If I was you I'd never even start in the class. That frozen-face gang will rule you off the track soon as they see your colours."

"Walter!" his mother said again.

"Well, ain't I her brother?" he returned, seeming to be entirely serious and direct, for the moment, at least. "*I* like the ole girl all right. Fact is, sometimes I'm kind of sorry for her."

"But what's it all *about*?" Alice cried. "Simply because you met me down-town with a man I never saw but once before and just barely know! Why all this palaver?"

"'Why?'" he repeated, grinning. "Well, I've seen you start before, you know!" He went to the door, and paused. "I got no date to-night. Take you to the movies, you care to go."

She declined crisply. "No, thanks!"

"Come on," he said, as pleasantly as he knew how. "Give me a chance to show you a better time than we had up at that frozen-face joint. I'll get you some chop suey afterward."

"No, thanks!"

"All right," he responded and waved a flippant adieu. "As the barber says, 'The better the advice, the worse it's wasted!' Good-*night*!"

Alice shrugged her shoulders; but a moment or two later, as the jar of the carelessly slammed front door went through the house, she shook her head, reconsidering. "Perhaps I ought to have gone with him. It might have kept him away from whatever dreadful people are his friends—at least for one night."

"Oh, I'm sure Walter's a *good* boy," Mrs. Adams said, soothingly; and this was what she almost always said when either her husband or Alice expressed such misgivings. "He's odd, and he's picked up right queer manners; but that's only because we haven't given him advantages like the other young men. But I'm sure he's a *good* boy."

She reverted to the subject a little later, while she washed the dishes and Alice wiped them. "Of course Walter could take his place with the other nice boys of the town even yet," she said. "I mean, if we could afford to help him financially. They all belong to the country clubs and have cars and——"

"Let's don't go into that any more, mama," the daughter begged her. "What's the use?"

"It *could* be of use," Mrs. Adams insisted. "It could if your father——"

"But papa *can't*."

"Yes, he can."

"But how can he? He told me a man of his age *can't* give up a business he's been in practically all his life, and just go groping about for something that might never turn up at all. I think he's right about it, too, of course!"

Mrs. Adams splashed among the plates with a new vigour heightened by an old bitterness. "Oh, yes," she said. "He talks that way; but he knows better."

"How could he 'know better,' mama?"

"*He* knows how!"

"But what does he know?"

Mrs. Adams tossed her head. "You don't suppose I'm such a fool I'd be urging him to give up something for nothing, do you, Alice? Do you suppose I'd want him to just go 'groping around' like he was telling you? That would be crazy, of course. Little as his work at Lamb's brings in, I wouldn't be so silly as to ask him to give it up just on a *chance* he could find something else. Good gracious, Alice, you must give me credit for a little intelligence once in a while!"

Alice was puzzled. "But what else could there be except a chance? I don't see——"

"Well, *I* do," her mother interrupted, decisively. "That man could make us all well off right now if he wanted to. We could have been rich long ago if he'd ever really felt as he ought to about his family."

"What! Why, how could——"

"You know how as well as I do," Mrs. Adams said, crossly. "I guess you haven't forgotten how he treated me about it the Sunday before he got sick."

She went on with her work, putting into it a sudden violence inspired by the recollection; but Alice, enlightened, gave utterance to a laugh of lugubrious derision. "Oh, the *glue* factory again!" she cried. "How silly!" And she renewed her laughter.

So often do the great projects of parents appear ignominious to their children. Mrs. Adams's conception of a glue factory as a fairy godmother of this family was an absurd old story which Alice had never taken seriously. She remembered that when she was about fifteen her mother began now and then to say something to Adams about a "glue factory," rather timidly, and as a vague suggestion, but never without irritating him. Then, for years, the preposterous subject had not been mentioned; possibly because of some explosion on the part of Adams, when his daughter had not been present. But during the last year Mrs. Adams had quietly gone back to these old hints, reviving them at intervals and also reviving her husband's irritation. Alice's bored impression was that her mother wanted him to found, or buy, or do something, or other, about a glue factory; and that he considered the proposal so impracticable as to be insulting. The parental conversations took place when neither Alice nor Walter was at hand, but sometimes Alice had come in upon the conclusion of one, to find her father in a shouting mood, and shocking the air behind him with profane monosyllables as he departed. Mrs. Adams would be left quiet and troubled; and when Alice, sympathizing with the goaded man, inquired of her mother why these tiresome bickerings had been renewed, she always got the brooding and cryptic answer, "He *could* do it—if he wanted to." Alice failed to comprehend the desirability of a glue factory—to her mind a father engaged in a glue factory lacked impressiveness; had no advantage over a father employed by Lamb and Company; and she supposed that Adams knew better than her mother whether such an enterprise would be profitable or not. Emphatically, he thought it would not, for she had heard him shouting at the end of one of these painful interviews, "You can keep up your dang talk till *you* die and *I* die, but I'll never make one God's cent that way!"

There had been a culmination. Returning from church on the Sunday preceding the collapse with which Adams's illness had begun, Alice found her mother downstairs, weeping and intimidated, while her father's stamping footsteps were loudly audible as he strode up and down his room overhead. So were his endless repetitions of invective loudly audible: "That woman! Oh, that woman! Oh, that danged woman!"

Mrs. Adams admitted to her daughter that it was "the old glue factory" and that her husband's wildness had frightened her into a "solemn promise" never to mention the subject again so long as she had breath. Alice laughed. The "glue factory" idea was not only a bore, but ridiculous, and her mother's evident seriousness about it one of those inexplicable vagaries we sometimes discover in the people we know best. But this Sunday rampage appeared to be the end of it, and when Adams came down to dinner, an hour later, he was unusually cheerful. Alice was glad he had gone wild enough to settle the glue factory once and for all; and she had ceased to think of the episode long before Friday of that week, when Adams was brought home in the middle of the afternoon by his old employer, the "great J. A. Lamb," in the latter's car.

During the long illness the "glue factory" was completely forgotten, by Alice at least; and her laugh was rueful as well as derisive now, in the kitchen, when she realized that her mother's mind again dwelt upon this abandoned nuisance. "I thought you'd got over all that nonsense, mama," she said.

Mrs. Adams smiled, pathetically. "Of course you think it's nonsense, dearie. Young people think everything's nonsense that they don't know anything about."

"Good gracious!" Alice cried. "I should think I used to hear enough about that horrible old glue factory to know something about it!"

"No," her mother returned patiently. "You've never heard anything about it at all."

"I haven't?"

"No. Your father and I didn't discuss it before you children. All you ever heard was when he'd get in such a rage, after we'd been speaking of it, that he couldn't control himself when you came in. Wasn't *I* always quiet? Did *I* ever go on talking about it?"

"No; perhaps not. But you're talking about it now, mama, after you promised never to mention it again."

"I promised not to mention it to your father," said Mrs. Adams, gently. "I haven't mentioned it to him, have I?"

"Ah, but if you mention it to me I'm afraid you *will* mention it to him. You always do speak of things that you have on your mind, and you might get papa all stirred up again about——" Alice paused, a light of divination flickering in her eyes. "Oh!" she cried. "I *see*!"

"What do you see?"

"You *have* been at him about it!"

"Not one single word!"

"No!" Alice cried. "Not a *word*, but that's what you've meant all along! You haven't spoken the words to him, but all this urging him to change, to 'find something better to go into'—it's all been about nothing on earth but your foolish old glue factory that you know upsets him, and you gave your solemn word never to speak to him about again! You didn't say it, but you meant it—and he *knows* that's what you meant! Oh, mama!"

Mrs. Adams, with her hands still automatically at work in the flooded dishpan, turned to face her daughter. "Alice," she said, tremulously, "what do I ask for myself?"

"What?"

"I say, What do I ask for myself? Do you suppose *I* want anything? Don't you know I'd be perfectly content on your father's present income if I were the only person to be considered? What do I care about any pleasure for myself? I'd be willing never to have a maid again; *I* don't mind doing the work. If we didn't have any children I'd be glad to do your father's cooking and the housework and the washing and ironing, too, for the rest of my life. I wouldn't care. I'm a poor cook and a poor housekeeper; I don't do anything well; but it would be good enough for just him and me. I wouldn't ever utter one word of com——"

"Oh, goodness!" Alice lamented. "What *is* it all about?"

"It's about this," said Mrs. Adams, swallowing. "You and Walter are a new generation and you ought to have the same as the rest of the new generation get. Poor Walter—asking you to go to the movies and a Chinese restaurant: the best he had to offer! Don't you suppose *I* see how the poor boy is deteriorating? Don't you suppose I know what *you* have to go through, Alice? And when I think of that man upstairs——" The agitated voice grew louder. "When I think of him and know that nothing in the world but his *stubbornness* keeps my children from having all they want and what they *ought* to have, do you suppose I'm going to hold myself bound to keep to the absolute letter of a silly promise he got from me by behaving like a crazy man? I can't! I can't do it! No mother could sit by and see him lock up a horn of plenty like that in his closet when the children were starving!"

"Oh, goodness, goodness me!" Alice protested. "We aren't precisely 'starving,' are we?"

Mrs. Adams began to weep. "It's just the same. Didn't I see how flushed and pretty you looked, this afternoon, after you'd been walking with this young man that's come here? Do you suppose he'd *look* at a girl like Mildred Palmer if you had what you ought to have? Do you suppose he'd be going into business with her father if *your* father——"

"Good heavens, mama; you're worse than Walter: I just barely know the man! *Don't* be so absurd!"

"Yes, I'm always 'absurd,'" Mrs. Adams moaned. "All I can do is cry, while your father sits upstairs, and his horn of plenty——"

But Alice interrupted with a peal of desperate laughter. "Oh, that 'horn of plenty!' Do come down to earth, mama. How can you call a *glue* factory, that doesn't exist except in your mind, a 'horn of plenty'? Do let's be a little rational!"

"It *could* be a horn of plenty," the tearful Mrs. Adams insisted. "It could! You don't understand a thing about it."

"Well, I'm willing," Alice said, with tired skepticism. "Make me understand, then. Where'd you ever get the idea?"

Mrs. Adams withdrew her hands from the water, dried them on a towel, and then wiped her eyes with a handkerchief. "Your father could make a fortune if he wanted to," she said, quietly. "At least, I don't say a fortune, but anyhow a great deal more than he does make."

"Yes, I've heard that before, mama, and you think he could make it out of a glue factory. What I'm asking is: How?"

"How? Why, by making glue and selling it. Don't you know how bad most glue is when you try to mend anything? A good glue is one of the rarest things there is; and it would just sell itself, once it got started. Well, your father knows how to make as good a glue as there is in the world."

Alice was not interested. "What of it? I suppose probably anybody could make it if they wanted to."

"I *said* you didn't know anything about it. Nobody else could make it. Your father knows a formula for making it."

"What of that?"

"It's a secret formula. It isn't even down on paper. It's worth any amount of money."

"'Any amount?'" Alice said, remaining incredulous. "Why hasn't papa sold it then?"

"Just because he's too stubborn to do anything with it at all!"

"How did papa get it?"

"He got it before you were born, just after we were married. I didn't think much about it then: it wasn't till you were growing up and I saw how much we needed money that I——"

"Yes, but how did papa get it?" Alice began to feel a little more curious about this possible buried treasure. "Did he invent it?"

"Partly," Mrs. Adams said, looking somewhat preoccupied. "He and another man invented it."

"Then maybe the other man——"

"He's dead."

"Then his family——"

"I don't think he left any family," Mrs. Adams said. "Anyhow, it belongs to your father. At least it belongs to him as much as it does to any one else. He's got an absolutely perfect right to do anything he wants to with it, and it would make us all comfortable if he'd do what I want him to—and he *knows* it would, too!"

Alice shook her head pityingly. "Poor mama!" she said. "Of course he knows it wouldn't do anything of the kind, or else he'd have done it long ago."

"He would, you say?" her mother cried. "That only shows how little you know him!"

"Poor mama!" Alice said again, soothingly. "If papa were like what you say he is, he'd be—why, he'd be crazy!"

Mrs. Adams agreed with a vehemence near passion. "You're right about him for once: that's just what he is! He sits up there in his stubbornness and—lets us slave here in the kitchen when if he wanted to—if he'd so much as lift his little finger——"

"Oh, come, now!" Alice laughed. "You can't build even a glue factory with just one little finger."

Mrs. Adams seemed about to reply that finding fault with a figure of speech was beside the point; but a ringing of the front door bell forestalled the retort. "Now, who do you suppose that is?" she wondered aloud; then her face brightened. "Ah —did Mr. Russell ask if he could——"

"No, he wouldn't be coming this evening," Alice said. "Probably it's the great J. A. Lamb: he usually stops for a minute on Thursdays to ask how papa's getting along. I'll go."

She tossed her apron off, and as she went through the house her expression was thoughtful. She was thinking vaguely about the glue factory and wondering if there might be "something in it" after all. If her mother was right about the rich possibilities of Adams's secret—but that was as far as Alice's speculations upon the matter went at this time: they were checked, partly by the thought that her father probably hadn't enough money for such an enterprise, and partly by the fact that she had arrived at the front door.

Chapter XII

THE FINE old gentleman revealed when she opened the door was probably the last great merchant in America to wear the chin beard. White as white frost, it was trimmed short with exquisite precision, while his upper lip and the lower expanses of his cheeks were clean and rosy from fresh shaving. With this trim white chin beard, the white waistcoat, the white tie, the suit of fine gray cloth, the broad and brilliantly polished black shoes, and the wide-brimmed gray felt hat, here was a man who had found his style in the seventies of the last century, and thenceforth kept it. Files of old magazines of that period might show him, in woodcut, as, "Type of Boston Merchant"; Nast might have drawn him as an honest statesman. He was eighty, hale and sturdy, not aged; and his quick blue eyes, still unflecked, and as brisk as a boy's, saw everything.

"Well, well, well!" he said, heartily. "You haven't lost any of your good looks since last week, I see, Miss Alice, so I guess I'm to take it you haven't been worrying over your daddy. The young feller's getting along all right, is he?"

"He's much better; he's sitting up, Mr. Lamb. Won't you come in?"

"Well, I don't know but I might." He turned to call toward twin disks of light at the curb, "Be out in a minute, Billy"; and the silhouette of a chauffeur standing beside a car could be seen to salute in response, as the old gentleman stepped into the hall. "You don't suppose your daddy's receiving callers yet, is he?"

"He's a good deal stronger than he was when you were here last week, but I'm afraid he's not very presentable, though."

"'Presentable?'" The old man echoed her jovially. "Pshaw! I've seen lots of sick folks. *I* know what they look like and how they love to kind of nest in among a pile of old blankets and wrappers. Don't you worry about *that*, Miss Alice, if you think he'd like to see me."

"Of course he would—if——" Alice hesitated; then said quickly, "Of course he'd love to see you and he's quite able to, if you care to come up."

She ran up the stairs ahead of him, and had time to snatch the crocheted wrap from her father's shoulders. Swathed as usual, he was sitting beside a table, reading the evening paper; but when his employer appeared in the doorway he half rose as if to come forward in greeting.

"Sit still!" the old gentleman shouted. "What do you mean? Don't you know you're weak as a cat? D'you think a man can be sick as long as you have and *not* be weak as a cat? What you trying to do the polite with *me* for?"

Adams gratefully protracted the handshake that accompanied these inquiries. "This is certainly mighty fine of you, Mr. Lamb," he said. "I guess Alice has told you how much our whole family appreciate your coming here so regularly to see how this old bag o' bones was getting along. Haven't you, Alice?"

"Yes, papa," she said; and turned to go out, but Lamb checked her.

"Stay right here, Miss Alice; I'm not even going to sit down. I know how it upsets sick folks when people outside the family come in for the first time."

"*You* don't upset me," Adams said. "I'll feel a lot better for getting a glimpse of you, Mr. Lamb."

The visitor's laugh was husky, but hearty and reassuring, like his voice in speaking. "That's the way all my boys blarney me, Miss Alice," he said. "They think I'll make the work lighter on 'em if they can get me kind of flattered up. You just tell your daddy it's no use; he doesn't get on *my* soft side, pretending he likes to see me even when he's sick."

"Oh, I'm not so sick any more," Adams said. "I expect to be back in my place ten days from now at the longest."

"Well, now, don't hurry it, Virgil; don't hurry it. You take your time; take your time."

This brought to Adams's lips a feeble smile not lacking in a kind of vanity, as feeble. "Why?" he asked. "I suppose you think my department runs itself down there, do you?"

His employer's response was another husky laugh. "Well, well, well!" he cried, and patted Adams's shoulder with a strong pink hand. "Listen to this young feller, Miss Alice, will you! He thinks we can't get along without him a minute! Yes, sir, this daddy of yours believes the whole works'll just take and run down if he isn't there to keep 'em wound up. I always suspected he thought a good deal of himself, and now I know he does!"

Adams looked troubled. "Well, I don't like to feel that my salary's going on with me not earning it."

"Listen to him, Miss Alice! Wouldn't you think, now, he'd let me be the one to worry about that? Why, on my word, if your daddy had his way, *I* wouldn't be anywhere. He'd take all my worrying and everything else off my shoulders and shove me right out of Lamb and Company! He would!"

"It seems to me I've been soldiering on you a pretty long while, Mr. Lamb," the convalescent said, querulously. "I don't feel right about it; but I'll be back in ten days. You'll see."

The old man took his hand in parting. "All right; we'll see, Virgil. Of course we do need you, seriously speaking; but we don't need you so bad we'll let you come down there before you're fully fit and able." He went to the door. "You hear, Miss Alice? That's what I wanted to make the old feller understand, and what I want you to kind of enforce on him. The old place is there waiting for him, and it'd wait ten years if it took him that long to get good and well. You see that he remembers it, Miss Alice!"

She went down the stairs with him, and he continued to impress this upon her until he had gone out of the front door. And even after that, the husky voice called back from the darkness, as he went to his car, "Don't forget, Miss Alice; let him take his own time. We always want him, but we want him to get good and well first. Good-night, good-night, young lady!"

When she closed the door her mother came from the farther end of the "living-room," where there was no light; and Alice turned to her.

"I can't help liking that old man, mama," she said. "He always sounds so—well, so solid and honest and friendly! I do like him."

But Mrs. Adams failed in sympathy upon this point. "He didn't say anything about raising your father's salary, did he?" she asked, dryly.

"No."

"No. I thought not."

She would have said more, but Alice, indisposed to listen, began to whistle, ran up the stairs, and went to sit with her father. She found him bright-eyed with the excitement a first caller brings into a slow convalescence: his cheeks showed actual hints of colour; and he was smiling tremulously as he filled and lit his pipe. She brought the crocheted scarf and put it about his shoulders again, then took a chair near him.

"I believe seeing Mr. Lamb did do you good, papa," she said. "I sort of thought it might, and that's why I let him come up. You really look a little like your old self again."

Adams exhaled a breathy "Ha!" with the smoke from his pipe as he waved the match to extinguish it. "That's fine," he said. "The smoke I had before dinner didn't taste the way it used to, and I kind of wondered if I'd lost my liking for tobacco, but this one seems to be all right. You bet it did me good to see J. A. Lamb! He's the biggest man that's ever lived in this town or ever will live here; and you can take all the Governors and Senators or anything they've raised here, and put 'em in a pot with him, and they won't come out one-two-three alongside o' him! And to think as big a man as that, with all his interests and everything he's got on his mind—to think he'd never let anything prevent him from coming here once every week to ask how I was getting along, and then walk right upstairs and kind of *call* on me, as it were—well, it makes me sort of feel as if I wasn't so much of a nobody, so to speak, as your mother seems to like to make out sometimes."

"How foolish, papa! Of *course* you're not 'a nobody.'"

Adams chuckled faintly upon his pipe-stem, what vanity he had seeming to be further stimulated by his daughter's applause. "I guess there aren't a whole lot of people in this town that could claim J. A. showed that much interest in 'em," he said. "Of course I don't set up to believe it's all because of merit, or anything like that. He'd do the same for anybody else that'd been with the company as long as I have, but still it *is* something to be with the company that long and have him show he appreciates it."

"Yes, indeed, it is, papa."

"Yes, sir," Adams said, reflectively. "Yes, sir, I guess that's so. And besides, it all goes to show the kind of a man he is. Simon pure, that's what that man is, Alice. Simon pure! There's never been anybody work for him that didn't respect him more than they did any other man in the world, I guess. And when you work for him you know he respects you, too. Right from the start you get the feeling that J. A. puts absolute confidence in you; and that's mighty stimulating: it makes you want to show him he hasn't misplaced it. There's great big moral values to the way a man like him gets you to feeling about your relations with the business: it ain't all just dollars and cents—not by any means!"

He was silent for a time, then returned with increasing enthusiasm to this theme, and Alice was glad to see so much renewal of life in him; he had not spoken with a like cheerful vigour since before his illness. The visit of his idolized great man had indeed been good for him, putting new spirit into him; and liveliness of the body followed that of the spirit. His improvement carried over the night: he slept well and awoke late, declaring that he was "pretty near a well man and ready for business right now." Moreover, having slept again in the afternoon, he dressed and went down to dinner, leaning but lightly on Alice, who conducted him.

"My! but you and your mother have been at it with your scrubbing and dusting!" he said, as they came through the "living-room." "I don't know I ever did see the house so spick and span before!" His glance fell upon a few carnations in a vase, and he chuckled admiringly. "Flowers, too! So *that's* what you coaxed that dollar and a half out o' me for, this morning!"

Other embellishments brought forth his comment when he had taken his old seat at the head of the small dinner-table. "Why, I declare, Alice!" he exclaimed. "I been so busy looking at all the spick-and-spanishness after the house-cleaning, and the flowers out in the parlour—'living-room' I suppose you want me to call it, if I just *got* to be fashionable—I been so busy studying over all this so-and-so, I declare I never noticed *you* till this minute! My, but you *are* all dressed up! What's goin' on? What's it about: you so all dressed up, and flowers in the parlour and everything?"

"Don't you see, papa? It's in honour of your coming downstairs again, of course."

"Oh, so that's it," he said. "I never would 'a' thought of that, I guess."

But Walter looked sidelong at his father, and gave forth his sly and knowing laugh. "Neither would I!" he said.

Adams lifted his eyebrows jocosely. "You're jealous, are you, sonny? You don't want the old man to think our young lady'd make so much fuss over him, do you?"

"Go on thinkin' it's over you," Walter retorted, amused. "Go on and think it. It'll do you good."

"Of course I'll think it," Adams said. "It isn't anybody's birthday. Certainly the decorations are on account of me coming downstairs. Didn't you hear Alice say so?"

"Sure, I heard her say so."

"Well, then——"

Walter interrupted him with a little music. Looking shrewdly at Alice, he sang:

> "I was walkin' out on Monday with my sweet thing.
> She's my neat thing,
> My sweet thing:
> I'll go round on Tuesday night to see her.
> Oh, how we'll spoon——"

"Walter!" his mother cried. "*Where* do you learn such vulgar songs?" However, she seemed not greatly displeased with him, and laughed as she spoke.

"So that's it, Alice!" said Adams. "Playing the hypocrite with your old man, are you? It's some new beau, is it?"

"I only wish it were," she said, calmly. "No. It's just what I said: it's all for you, dear."

"Don't let her con you," Walter advised his father. "She's got expectations. You hang around downstairs a while after dinner and you'll see."

But the prophecy failed, though Adams went to his own room without waiting to test it. No one came.

Alice stayed in the "living-room" until half-past nine, when she went slowly upstairs. Her mother, almost tearful, met her at the top, and whispered, "You mustn't mind, dearie."

"Mustn't mind what?" Alice asked, and then, as she went on her way, laughed scornfully. "What utter nonsense!" she said.

Next day she cut the stems of the rather scant show of carnations and refreshed them with new water. At dinner, her father, still in high spirits, observed that she had again "dressed up" in honour of his second descent of the stairs; and Walter repeated his fragment of objectionable song; but these jocularities were rendered pointless by the eventless evening that followed; and in the morning the carnations began to appear tarnished and flaccid. Alice gave them a long look, then threw them away; and neither Walter nor her father was inspired to any rallying by her plain costume for that evening. Mrs. Adams was visibly depressed.

When Alice finished helping her mother with the dishes, she went outdoors and sat upon the steps of the little front veranda. The night, gentle with warm air from the south, surrounded her pleasantly, and the perpetual smoke was thinner. Now that the furnaces of dwelling-houses were no longer fired, life in that city had begun to be less like life in a railway tunnel; people were aware of summer in the air, and in the thickened foliage of the shade-trees, and in the sky. Stars were unveiled by the passing of the denser smoke fogs, and to-night they could be seen clearly; they looked warm and near. Other girls sat upon verandas and stoops in Alice's street, cheerful as young fishermen along the banks of a stream.

Alice could hear them from time to time; thin sopranos persistent in laughter that fell dismally upon her ears. She had set no lines or nets herself, and what she had of "expectations," as Walter called them, were vanished. For Alice was experienced; and one of the conclusions she drew from her experience was that when a man says, "I'd take you for anything you wanted me to," he may mean it or he may not; but, if he does, he will not postpone the first opportunity to say something more. Little affairs, once begun, must be warmed quickly; for if they cool they are dead.

But Alice was not thinking of Arthur Russell. When she tossed away the carnations she likewise tossed away her thoughts of that young man. She had been like a boy who sees upon the street, some distance before him, a bit of something round and glittering, a possible dime. He hopes it is a dime, and, until he comes near enough to make sure, he plays that it is a dime. In his mind he has an adventure with it: he buys something delightful. If he picks it up, discovering only some tin-foil which has happened upon a round shape, he feels a sinking. A dulness falls upon him.

So Alice was dull with the loss of an adventure; and when the laughter of other girls reached her, intermittently, she had not sprightliness enough left in her to be envious of their gaiety. Besides, these neighbours were ineligible even for her envy, being of another caste; they could never know a dance at the Palmers', except remotely, through a newspaper. Their laughter was for the encouragement of snappy young men of the stores and offices down-town, clerks, bookkeepers, what not—some of them probably graduates of Frincke's Business College.

Then, as she recalled that dark portal, with its dusty stairway mounting between close walls to disappear in the upper shadows, her mind drew back as from a doorway to Purgatory. Nevertheless, it was a picture often in her reverie; and sometimes it came suddenly, without sequence, into the midst of her other thoughts, as if it leaped up among them from a lower darkness; and when it arrived it wanted to stay. So a traveller, still roaming the world afar, sometimes broods without apparent reason upon his family burial lot: "I wonder if I shall end there."

The foreboding passed abruptly, with a jerk of her breath, as the street-lamp revealed a tall and easy figure approaching from the north, swinging a stick in time to its stride. She had given Russell up—and he came.

"What luck for me!" he exclaimed. "To find you alone!"

Alice gave him her hand for an instant, not otherwise moving. "I'm glad it happened so," she said. "Let's stay out here, shall we? Do you think it's too provincial to sit on a girl's front steps with her?"

"'Provincial?' Why, it's the very best of our institutions," he returned, taking his place beside her. "At least, I think so to-night."

"Thanks! Is that practise for other nights somewhere else?"

"No," he laughed. "The practising all led up to this. Did I come too soon?"

"No," she replied, gravely. "Just in time!"

"I'm glad to be so accurate; I've spent two evenings wanting to come, Miss Adams, instead of doing what I was doing."

"What was that?"

"Dinners. Large and long dinners. Your fellow-citizens are immensely hospitable to a newcomer."

"Oh, no," Alice said. "We don't do it for everybody. Didn't you find yourself charmed?"

"One was a men's dinner," he explained. "Mr. Palmer seemed to think I ought to be shown to the principal business men."

"What was the other dinner?"

"My cousin Mildred gave it."

"Oh, *did* she!" Alice said, sharply, but she recovered herself in the same instant, and laughed. "She wanted to show you to the principal business women, I suppose."

"I don't know. At all events, I shouldn't give myself out to be so much fêted by your 'fellow-citizens,' after all, seeing these were both done by my relatives, the Palmers. However, there are others to follow, I'm afraid. I was wondering—I hoped maybe you'd be coming to some of them. Aren't you?"

"I rather doubt it," Alice said, slowly. "Mildred's dance was almost the only evening I've gone out since my father's illness began. He seemed better that day; so I went. He was better the other day when he wanted those cigars. He's very much up and down." She paused. "I'd almost forgotten that Mildred is your cousin."

"Not a very near one," he explained. "Mr. Palmer's father was my great-uncle."

"Still, of course you are related."

"Yes; that distantly."

Alice said placidly, "It's quite an advantage."

He agreed. "Yes. It is."

"No," she said, in the same placid tone. "I mean for Mildred."

"I don't see——"

She laughed. "No. You wouldn't. I mean it's an advantage over the rest of us who might like to compete for some of your time; and the worst of it is we can't accuse her of being unfair about it. We can't prove she showed any trickiness in having you for a cousin. Whatever else she might plan to do with you, she didn't plan that. So the rest of us must just bear it!"

"The 'rest of you!'" he laughed. "It's going to mean a great deal of suffering!"

Alice resumed her placid tone. "You're staying at the Palmers', aren't you?"

"No, not now. I've taken an apartment. I'm going to live here; I'm permanent. Didn't I tell you?"

"I think I'd heard somewhere that you were," she said. "Do you think you'll like living here?"

"How can one tell?"

"If I were in your place I think I should be able to tell, Mr. Russell."

"How?"

"Why, good gracious!" she cried. "Haven't you got the most perfect creature in town for your—your cousin? *She* expects to make you like living here, doesn't she? How could you keep from liking it, even if you tried not to, under the circumstances?"

"Well, you see, there's such a lot of circumstances," he explained; "I'm not sure I'll like getting back into a business again. I suppose most of the men of my age in the country have been going through the same experience: the War left us with a considerable restlessness of spirit."

"You were in the War?" she asked, quickly, and as quickly answered herself, "Of course you were!"

"I was a left-over; they only let me out about four months ago," he said. "It's quite a shake-up trying to settle down again."

"You were in France, then?"

"Oh, yes; but I didn't get up to the front much—only two or three times, and then just for a day or so. I was in the transportation service."

"You were an officer, of course."

"Yes," he said. "They let me play I was a major."

"I guessed a major," she said. "You'd always be pretty grand, of course."

Russell was amused. "Well, you see," he informed her, "as it happened, we had at least several other majors in our army. Why would I always be something 'pretty grand?'"

"You're related to the Palmers. Don't you notice they always affect the pretty grand?"

"Then you think I'm only one of their affectations, I take it."

"Yes, you seem to be the most successful one they've got!" Alice said, lightly. "You certainly do belong to them." And she laughed as if at something hidden from him. "Don't you?"

"But you've just excused me for that," he protested. "You said nobody could be blamed for my being their third cousin. What a contradictory girl you are!"

Alice shook her head. "Let's keep away from the kind of girl I am."

"No," he said. "That's just what I came here to talk about."

She shook her head again. "Let's keep first to the kind of man you are. I'm glad you were in the War."

"Why?"

"Oh, I don't know." She was quiet a moment, for she was thinking that here she spoke the truth: his service put about him a little glamour that helped to please her with him. She had been pleased with him during their walk; pleased with him on his own account; and now that pleasure was growing keener. She looked at him, and though the light in which she saw him was little more than starlight, she saw that he was looking steadily at her with a kindly and smiling seriousness. All at once it seemed to her that the night air was sweeter to breathe, as if a distant fragrance of new blossoms had been blown to her. She smiled back to him, and said, "Well, what kind of man are you?"

"I don't know; I've often wondered," he replied. "What kind of girl are you?"

"Don't you remember? I told you the other day. I'm just me!"

"But who is that?"

"You forget everything," said Alice. "You told me what kind of a girl I am. You seemed to think you'd taken quite a fancy to me from the very first."

"So I did," he agreed, heartily.

"But how quickly you forgot it!"

"Oh, no. I only want *you* to say what kind of a girl you are."

She mocked him. "'I don't know; I've often wondered!' What kind of a girl does Mildred tell you I am? What has she said about me since she told you I was 'a Miss Adams?'"

"I don't know; I haven't asked her."

"Then *don't* ask her," Alice said, quickly.

"Why?"

"Because she's such a perfect creature and I'm such an imperfect one. Perfect creatures have the most perfect way of ruining the imperfect ones."

"But then they wouldn't be perfect. Not if they——"

"Oh, yes, they remain perfectly perfect," she assured him. "That's because they never go into details. They're not so vulgar as to come right out and *tell* that you've been in jail for stealing chickens. They just look absent-minded and say in a low voice, 'Oh, very; but I scarcely think you'd like her particularly'; and then begin to talk of something else right away."

His smile had disappeared. "Yes," he said, somewhat ruefully. "That does sound like Mildred. You certainly do seem to know her! Do you know everybody as well as that?"

"Not myself," Alice said. "I don't know myself at all. I got to wondering about that—about who I was—the other day after you walked home with me."

He uttered an exclamation, and added, explaining it, "You do give a man a chance to be fatuous, though! As if it were walking home with me that made you wonder about yourself!"

"It was," Alice informed him, coolly. "I was wondering what I wanted to make you think of me, in case I should ever happen to see you again."

This audacity appeared to take his breath. "By George!" he cried.

"You mustn't be astonished," she said. "What I decided then was that I would probably never dare to be just myself with you—not if I cared to have you want to see me again—and yet here I am, just being myself after all!"

"You *are* the cheeriest series of shocks," Russell exclaimed, whereupon Alice added to the series.

"Tell me: Is it a good policy for me to follow with you?" she asked, and he found the mockery in her voice delightful. "Would you advise me to offer you shocks as a sort of vacation from suavity?"

"Suavity" was yet another sketch of Mildred; a recognizable one, or it would not have been humorous. In Alice's hands, so dexterous in this work, her statuesque friend was becoming as ridiculous as a fine figure of wax left to the mercies of a satirist.

But the lively young sculptress knew better than to overdo: what she did must appear to spring all from mirth; so she laughed as if unwillingly, and said, "I *mustn't* laugh at Mildred! In the first place, she's your—your cousin. And in the second place, she's not meant to be funny; it isn't right to laugh at really splendid people who take themselves seriously. In the third place, you won't come again if I do."

"Don't be sure of that," Russell said, "whatever you do."

"'Whatever I do?'" she echoed. "That sounds as if you thought I *could* be terrific! Be careful; there's one thing I could do that would keep you away."

"What's that?"

"I could tell you not to come," she said. "I wonder if I ought to."

"Why do you wonder if you 'ought to?'"

"Don't you guess?"

"No."

"Then let's both be mysteries to each other," she suggested. "I mystify you because I wonder, and you mystify me because you don't guess why I wonder. We'll let it go at that, shall we?"

"Very well; so long as it's certain that you *don't* tell me not to come again."

"I'll not tell you that—yet," she said. "In fact——" She paused, reflecting, with her head to one side. "In fact, I won't tell you not to come, probably, until I see that's what you want me to tell you. I'll let you out easily—and I'll be sure to see it. Even before you do, perhaps."

"That arrangement suits me," Russell returned, and his voice held no trace of jocularity: he had become serious. "It suits me better if you're enough in earnest to mean that I can come —oh, not whenever I want to; I don't expect so much!—but if you mean that I can see you pretty often."

"Of course I'm in earnest," she said. "But before I say you can come 'pretty often,' I'd like to know how much of my time you'd need if you did come 'whenever you want to'; and of course you wouldn't dare make any answer to that question except one. Wouldn't you let me have Thursdays out?"

"No, no," he protested. "I want to know. Will you let me come pretty often?"

"Lean toward me a little," Alice said. "I want you to understand." And as he obediently bent his head near hers, she inclined toward him as if to whisper; then, in a half-shout, she cried,

"*Yes!*"

He clapped his hands. "By George!" he said. "What a girl you are!"

"Why?"

"Well, for the first reason, because you have such gaieties as that one. I should think your father would actually like being ill, just to be in the house with you all the time."

"You mean by that," Alice inquired, "I keep my family cheerful with my amusing little ways?"

"Yes. Don't you?"

"There were only boys in your family, weren't there, Mr. Russell?"

"I was an only child, unfortunately."

"Yes," she said. "I see you hadn't any sisters."

For a moment he puzzled over her meaning, then saw it, and was more delighted with her than ever. "I can answer a question of yours, now, that I couldn't a while ago."

"Yes, I know," she returned, quietly.

"But how could you know?"

"It's the question I asked you about whether you were going to like living here," she said. "You're about to tell me that now you know you *will* like it."

"More telepathy!" he exclaimed. "Yes, that was it, precisely. I suppose the same thing's been said to you so many times that you——"

"No, it hasn't," Alice said, a little confused for the moment. "Not at all. I meant——" She paused, then asked in a gentle voice, "Would you really like to know?"

"Yes."

"Well, then, I was only afraid you didn't mean it."

"See here," he said. "I did mean it. I told you it was being pretty difficult for me to settle down to things again. Well, it's more difficult than you know, but I think I can pull through in fair spirits if I can see a girl like you 'pretty often.'"

"All right," she said, in a business-like tone. "I've told you that you can if you want to."

"I do want to," he assured her. "I do, indeed!"

"How often is 'pretty often,' Mr. Russell?"

"Would you walk with me sometimes? To-morrow?"

"Sometimes. Not to-morrow. The day after."

"That's splendid!" he said. "You'll walk with me day after to-morrow, and the night after that I'll see you at Miss Lamb's dance, won't I?"

But this fell rather chillingly upon Alice. "Miss Lamb's dance? Which Miss Lamb?" she asked.

"I don't know—it's the one that's just coming out of mourning."

"Oh, Henrietta—yes. Is her dance so soon? I'd forgotten."

"You'll be there, won't you?" he asked. "Please say you're going."

Alice did not respond at once, and he urged her again: "Please do promise you'll be there."

"No, I can't promise anything," she said, slowly. "You see, for one thing, papa might not be well enough."

"But if he is?" said Russell. "If he is you'll surely come, won't you? Or, perhaps——" He hesitated, then went on quickly, "I don't know the rules in this place yet, and different places have different rules; but do you have to have a chaperone, or don't girls just go to dances with the men sometimes? If they do, would you—would you let me take you?"

Alice was startled. "Good gracious!"

"What's the matter?"

"Don't you think your relatives—— Aren't you expected to go with Mildred—and Mrs. Palmer?"

"Not necessarily. It doesn't matter what I might be expected to do," he said. "Will you go with me?"

"I—— No; I couldn't."

"Why not?"

"I can't. I'm not going."

"But why?"

"Papa's not really any better," Alice said, huskily. "I'm too worried about him to go to a dance." Her voice sounded emotional, genuinely enough; there was something almost like a sob in it. "Let's talk of other things, please."

He acquiesced gently; but Mrs. Adams, who had been listening to the conversation at the open window, just overhead, did not hear him. She had correctly interpreted the sob in Alice's voice, and, trembling with sudden anger, she rose from her knees, and went fiercely to her husband's room.

Chapter XIII

HE HAD not undressed, and he sat beside the table, smoking his pipe and reading his newspaper. Upon his forehead the lines in that old pattern, the historical map of his troubles, had grown a little vaguer lately; relaxed by the complacency of a man who not only finds his health restored, but sees the days before him promising once more a familiar routine that he has always liked to follow.

As his wife came in, closing the door behind her, he looked up cheerfully, "Well, mother," he said, "what's the news downstairs?"

"That's what I came to tell you," she informed him, grimly.

Adams lowered his newspaper to his knee and peered over his spectacles at her. She had remained by the door, standing, and the great greenish shadow of the small lamp-shade upon his table revealed her but dubiously. "Isn't everything all right?" he asked. "What's the matter?"

"Don't worry: I'm going to tell you," she said, her grimness not relaxed. "There's matter enough, Virgil Adams. Matter enough to make me sick of being alive!"

With that, the markings on his brows began to emerge again in all their sharpness; the old pattern reappeared. "Oh, my, my!" he lamented. "I thought maybe we were all going to settle down to a little peace for a while. What's it about now?"

"It's about Alice. Did you think it was about *me* or anything for *myself*?"

Like some ready old machine, always in order, his irritability responded immediately and automatically to her emotion. "How in thunder could I think what it's about, or who it's for? *Say* it, and get it over!"

"Oh, I'll 'say' it," she promised, ominously. "What I've come to ask you is, How much longer do you expect me to put up with that old man and his doings?"

"Whose doings? What old man?"

She came at him, fiercely accusing. "You know well enough what old man, Virgil Adams! That old man who was here the other night."

"Mr. Lamb?"

"Yes; 'Mister Lamb!'" She mocked his voice. "What other old man would I be likely to mean, except J. A. Lamb?"

"What's he been doing now?" her husband inquired, satirically. "Where'd you get something new against him since the last time you——"

"Just this!" she cried. "The other night when that man was here, if I'd known how he was going to make my child suffer, I'd never have let him set his foot in my house."

Adams leaned back in his chair as though her absurdity had eased his mind. "Oh, I see," he said. "You've just gone plain crazy. That's the only explanation of such talk, and it suits the case."

"Hasn't that man made us all suffer every day of our lives?" she demanded. "I'd like to know why it is that my life and my children's lives have to be sacrificed to him?"

"How are they 'sacrificed' to him?"

"Because you keep on working for him! Because you keep on letting him hand out whatever miserable little pittance he chooses to give you; that's why! It's as if he were some horrible old Juggernaut and I had to see my children's own father throwing them under the wheels to keep him satisfied."

"I won't hear any more such stuff!" Lifting his paper, Adams affected to read.

"You'd better listen to me," she admonished him. "You might be sorry you didn't, in case he ever tried to set foot in my house again! I might tell him to his face what I think of him."

At this, Adams slapped the newspaper down upon his knee. "Oh, the devil! What's it matter what you think of him?"

"It had better matter to you!" she cried. "Do you suppose I'm going to submit forever to him and his family and what they're doing to my child?"

"What are he and his family doing to 'your child?'"

Mrs. Adams came out with it. "That snippy little Henrietta Lamb has always snubbed Alice every time she's ever had the chance. She's followed the lead of the other girls; they've always all of 'em been jealous of Alice because she dared to try and be happy, and because she's showier and better-looking than they are, even though you do give her only about thirty-five cents a year to do it on! They've all done everything on earth they could to drive the young men away from her and belittle her to 'em; and this mean little Henrietta Lamb's been the worst of the whole crowd to Alice, every time she could see a chance."

"What for?" Adams asked, incredulously. "Why should she or anybody else pick on Alice?"

"'Why?' 'What for?'" his wife repeated with a greater vehemence. "Do *you* ask me such a thing as that? Do *you* really want to know?"

"Yes; I'd want to know—I would if I believed it."

"Then I'll tell you," she said in a cold fury. "It's on account of *you*, Virgil, and nothing else in the world."

He hooted at her. "Oh, yes! These girls don't like *me*, so they pick on Alice."

"Quit your palavering and evading," she said. "A crowd of girls like that, when they get a pretty girl like Alice among them, they act just like wild beasts. They'll tear her to pieces, or else they'll chase her and run her out, because they know if she had half a chance she'd outshine 'em. They can't do that to a girl like Mildred Palmer because she's got money and family to back her. Now you listen to me, Virgil Adams: the way the world is now, money *is* family. Alice would have just as much 'family' as any of 'em—every single bit—if you hadn't fallen behind in the race."

"How did I——"

"Yes, you did!" she cried. "Twenty-five years ago when we were starting and this town was smaller, you and I could have gone with any of 'em if we'd tried hard enough. Look at the people we knew then that do hold their heads up alongside of anybody in this town! *Why* can they? Because the men of those families made money and gave their children everything that makes life worth living! Why can't we hold *our* heads up? Because those men passed you in the race. They went up the ladder, and you—you're still a clerk down at that old hole!"

"You leave that out, please," he said. "I thought you were going to tell me something Henrietta Lamb had done to our Alice."

"You *bet* I'm going to tell you," she assured him, vehemently. "But first I'm telling *why* she does it. It's because you've never given Alice any backing nor any background, and they all know they can do anything they like to her with perfect impunity. If she had the hundredth part of what *they* have to fall back on she'd have made 'em sing a mighty different song long ago!"

"How would she?"

"Oh, my heavens, but you're slow!" Mrs. Adams moaned. "Look here! You remember how practically all the nicest boys in this town used to come here a few years ago. Why, they were all crazy over her; and the girls *had* to be nice to her then. Look at the difference now! There'll be a whole month go by and not a young man come to call on her, let alone send her candy or flowers, or ever think of *taking* her any place—and yet she's prettier and brighter than she was when they used to come. It isn't the child's fault she couldn't hold 'em, is it? Poor thing, *she* tried hard enough! I suppose you'd say it was her fault, though."

"No; I wouldn't."

"Then whose fault is it?"

"Oh, mine, mine," he said, wearily. "I drove the young men away, of course."

"You might as well have driven 'em, Virgil. It amounts to just the same thing."

"How does it?"

"Because as they got older a good many of 'em began to think more about money; that's one thing. Money's at the bottom of it all, for that matter. Look at these country clubs and all such things: the other girls' families belong and we don't, and Alice don't; and she can't go unless somebody takes her, and nobody does any more. Look at the other girls' houses, and then look at our house, so shabby and old-fashioned she'd be pretty near ashamed to ask anybody to come in and sit down nowadays! Look at her clothes—oh, yes; you think you shelled out a lot for that little coat of hers and the hat and skirt she got last March; but it's nothing. Some of these girls nowadays spend more than your whole salary on their clothes. And what jewellery has she got? A plated watch and two or three little pins and rings of the kind people's maids wouldn't wear now. Good Lord, Virgil Adams, wake up! Don't sit there and tell me you don't know things like this mean *suffering* for the child!"

He had begun to rub his hands wretchedly back and forth over his bony knees, as if in that way he somewhat alleviated the tedium caused by her racking voice. "Oh, my, my!" he muttered. "*Oh*, my, my!"

"Yes, I should think you *would* say 'Oh, my, my!'" she took him up, loudly. "That doesn't help things much! If you ever wanted to *do* anything about it, the poor child might see some gleam of hope in her life. You don't *care* for her, that's the trouble; you don't care a single thing about her."

"I don't?"

"No; you don't. Why, even with your miserable little salary you could have given her more than you have. You're the closest man I ever knew: it's like pulling teeth to get a dollar out of you for her, now and then, and yet you hide some away, every month or so, in some wretched little investment or other. You——"

"Look here, now," he interrupted, angrily. "You look here! If I didn't put a little by whenever I could, in a bond or something, where would you be if anything happened to me? The insurance doctors never passed me; *you* know that. Haven't we got to have *something* to fall back on?"

"Yes, we have!" she cried. "We ought to have something to go on with right now, too, when we need it. Do you suppose these snippets would treat Alice the way they do if she could afford to *entertain*? They leave her out of their dinners and dances simply because they know she can't give any dinners and dances to leave them out of! They know she can't get *even*, and that's the whole story! That's why Henrietta Lamb's done this thing to her now."

Adams had gone back to his rubbing of his knees. "Oh, my, my!" he said. "*What* thing?"

She told him. "Your dear, grand, old Mister Lamb's Henrietta has sent out invitations for a large party—a *large* one. Everybody that is anybody in this town is asked, you can be sure. There's a very fine young man, a Mr. Russell, has just come to town, and he's interested in Alice, and he's asked her to go to this dance with him. Well, Alice can't accept. She can't go with him, though she'd give anything in the world to do it. Do you understand? The reason she can't is because Henrietta

Lamb hasn't invited her. Do you want to know why Henrietta hasn't invited her? It's because she knows Alice can't get even, and because she thinks Alice ought to be snubbed like this on account of only being the daughter of one of her grandfather's clerks. I *hope* you understand!"

"Oh, my, my!" he said. "*Oh*, my, my!"

"That's your sweet old employer," his wife cried, tauntingly. "That's your dear, kind, grand old Mister Lamb! Alice has been left out of a good many smaller things, like big dinners and little dances, but this is just the same as serving her notice that she's out of everything! And it's all done by your dear, grand old——"

"Look here!" Adams exclaimed. "I don't want to hear any more of that! You can't hold him responsible for everything his grandchildren do, I guess! He probably doesn't know a thing about it. You don't suppose he's troubling *his* head over——"

But she burst out at him passionately. "Suppose *you* trouble *your* head about it! You'd better, Virgil Adams! You'd better, unless you want to see your child just dry up into a miserable old maid! She's still young and she has a chance for happiness, if she had a father that didn't bring a millstone to hang around her neck, instead of what he ought to give her! You just wait till you die and God asks you what you had in your breast instead of a heart!"

"Oh, my, my!" he groaned. "What's my heart got to do with it?"

"Nothing! You haven't got one or you'd give her what she needed. Am I asking anything you *can't* do? You know better; you know I'm not!"

At this he sat suddenly rigid, his troubled hands ceasing to rub his knees; and he looked at her fixedly. "Now, tell me," he said, slowly. "Just what *are* you asking?"

"You know!" she sobbed.

"You mean you've broken your word never to speak of *that* to me again?"

"What do *I* care for my word?" she cried, and, sinking to the floor at his feet, rocked herself back and forth there. "Do you suppose I'll let my 'word' keep me from struggling for a little happiness for my children? It won't, I tell you; it won't! I'll struggle for that till I die! I will, till I die—till I die!"

He rubbed his head now instead of his knees, and, shaking all over, he got up and began with uncertain steps to pace the floor. “Hell, hell, hell!” he said. “I’ve got to go through *that* again!”

“Yes, you have!” she sobbed. “Till I die.”

“Yes; that’s what you been after all the time I was getting well.”

“Yes, I have, and I’ll keep on till I die!”

“A fine wife for a man,” he said. “Beggin’ a man to be a dirty dog!”

“No! To be a *man*—and I’ll keep on till I die!”

Adams again fell back upon his last solace: he walked, half staggering, up and down the room, swearing in a rhythmic repetition.

His wife had repetitions of her own, and she kept at them in a voice that rose to a higher and higher pitch, like the sound of an old well-pump. “Till I die! Till I die! Till I *die*!”

She ended in a scream; and Alice, coming up the stairs, thanked heaven that Russell had gone. She ran to her father’s door and went in.

Adams looked at her, and gesticulated shakily at the convulsive figure on the floor. “Can you get her out of here?”

Alice helped Mrs. Adams to her feet; and the stricken woman threw her arms passionately about her daughter.

“Get her out!” Adams said, harshly; then cried, “Wait!”

Alice, moving toward the door, halted, and looked at him blankly, over her mother’s shoulder. “What is it, papa?”

He stretched out his arm and pointed at her. “She says—she says you have a mean life, Alice.”

“No, papa.”

Mrs. Adams turned in her daughter’s arms. “Do you hear her lie? Couldn’t you be as brave as she is, Virgil?”

“Are you lying, Alice?” he asked. “Do you have a mean time?”

“No, papa.”

He came toward her. “Look at me!” he said. “Things like this dance now—is that so hard to bear?”

Alice tried to say, “No, papa,” again, but she couldn’t. Suddenly and in spite of herself she began to cry.

“Do you hear her?” his wife sobbed. “Now do you——”

He waved at them fiercely. "Get out of here!" he said. "Both of you! Get out of here!"

As they went, he dropped in his chair and bent far forward, so that his haggard face was concealed from them. Then, as Alice closed the door, he began to rub his knees again, muttering, "Oh, my, my! *Oh*, my, my!"

Chapter XIV

THERE SHONE a jovial sun overhead on the appointed "day after to-morrow"; a day not cool yet of a temperature friendly to walkers; and the air, powdered with sunshine, had so much life in it that it seemed to sparkle. To Arthur Russell this was a day like a gay companion who pleased him well; but the gay companion at his side pleased him even better. She looked her prettiest, chattered her wittiest, smiled her wistfulest, and delighted him with all together.

"You look so happy it's easy to see your father's taken a good turn," he told her.

"Yes; he has this afternoon, at least," she said. "I might have other reasons for looking cheerful, though."

"For instance?"

"Exactly!" she said, giving him a sweet look just enough mocked by her laughter. "For instance!"

"Well, go on," he begged.

"Isn't it expected?" she asked.

"Of you, you mean?"

"No," she returned. "For you, I mean!"

In this style, which uses a word for any meaning that quick look and colourful gesture care to endow it with, she was an expert; and she carried it merrily on, leaving him at liberty (one of the great values of the style) to choose as he would how much or how little she meant. He was content to supply mere cues, for although he had little coquetry of his own, he had lately begun to find that the only interesting moments in his life were those during which Alice Adams coquetted with him. Happily, these obliging moments extended themselves to cover all the time he spent with her. However serious she might seem, whatever appeared to be her topic, all was thou-and-I.

He planned for more of it, seeing otherwise a dull evening ahead; and reverted, afterwhile, to a forbidden subject. "About that dance at Miss Lamb's—since your father's so much better——"

She flushed a little. "Now, now!" she chided him. "We agreed not to say any more about that."

"Yes, but since he *is* better——"

Alice shook her head. "He won't be better to-morrow. He always has a bad day after a good one—especially after such a good one as this is."

"But if this time it should be different," Russell persisted; "wouldn't you be willing to come—if he's better by to-morrow evening? Why not wait and decide at the last minute?"

She waved her hands airily. "What a pother!" she cried. "What does it matter whether poor little Alice Adams goes to a dance or not?"

"Well, I thought I'd made it clear that it looks fairly bleak to me if you don't go."

"Oh, yes!" she jeered.

"It's the simple truth," he insisted. "I don't care a great deal about dances these days; and if you aren't going to be there——"

"You could stay away," she suggested. "You wouldn't!"

"Unfortunately, I can't. I'm afraid I'm supposed to be the excuse. Miss Lamb, in her capacity as a friend of my relatives——"

"Oh, she's giving it for *you*! I see! On Mildred's account you mean?"

At that his face showed an increase of colour. "I suppose just on account of my being a cousin of Mildred's and of——"

"Of course! You'll have a beautiful time, too. Henrietta'll see that you have somebody to dance with besides Miss Dowling, poor man!"

"But what I want somebody to see is that I dance with you! And perhaps your father——"

"Wait!" she said, frowning as if she debated whether or not to tell him something of import; then, seeming to decide affirmatively, she asked: "Would you really like to know the truth about it?"

"If it isn't too unflattering."

"It hasn't anything to do with you at all," she said. "Of course I'd like to go with you and to dance with you—though you don't seem to realize that you wouldn't be permitted much time with me."

"Oh, yes, I——"

"Never mind!" she laughed. "Of course you wouldn't. But even if papa should be better to-morrow, I doubt if I'd go. In fact, I know I wouldn't. There's another reason besides papa."

"Is there?"

"Yes. The truth is, I don't get on with Henrietta Lamb. As a matter of fact, I dislike her, and of course that means she dislikes me. I should never think of asking her to anything *I* gave, and I really wonder she asks me to things *she* gives." This was a new inspiration; and Alice, beginning to see her way out of a perplexity, wished that she had thought of it earlier: she should have told him from the first that she and Henrietta had a feud, and consequently exchanged no invitations. Moreover, there was another thing to beset her with little anxieties: she might better not have told him from the first, as she had indeed told him by intimation, that she was the pampered daughter of an indulgent father, presumably able to indulge her; for now she must elaborately keep to the part. Veracity is usually simple; and its opposite, to be successful, should be as simple; but practitioners of the opposite are most often impulsive, like Alice; and, like her, they become enmeshed in elaborations.

"It wouldn't be very nice for me to go to her house," Alice went on, "when I wouldn't want her in mine. I've never admired her. I've always thought she was lacking in some things most people are supposed to be equipped with—for instance, a certain feeling about the death of a father who was always pretty decent to his daughter. Henrietta's father died just eleven months and twenty-seven days before your cousin's dance, but she couldn't stick out those few last days and make it a year; she was there." Alice stopped, then laughed ruefully, exclaiming, "But this is dreadful of me!"

"Is it?"

"Blackguarding her to you when she's giving a big party for you! Just the way Henrietta would blackguard me to you—heaven knows what she *wouldn't* say if she talked about me to you! It would be fair, of course, but—well, I'd rather she didn't!" And with that, Alice let her pretty hand, in its white glove, rest upon his arm for a moment; and he looked down at it, not unmoved to see it there. "I want to be unfair about just this," she said, letting a troubled laughter tremble through her appealing voice as she spoke. "I won't take advantage of her with anybody, except just—you! I'd a little rather you didn't hear anybody blackguard me, and, if you don't mind—could you promise not to give Henrietta the chance?"

It was charmingly done, with a humorous, faint pathos altogether genuine; and Russell found himself suddenly wanting to shout at her, "Oh, you *dear*!" Nothing else seemed adequate; but he controlled the impulse in favour of something more conservative. "Imagine any one speaking unkindly of you—not praising you!"

"Who *has* praised me to you?" she asked, quickly.

"I haven't talked about you with any one; but if I did, I know they'd——"

"No, no!" she cried, and went on, again accompanying her words with little tremulous runs of laughter. "You don't understand this town yet. You'll be surprised when you do; we're different. We talk about one another fearfully! Haven't I just proved it, the way I've been going for Henrietta? Of course I didn't say anything really very terrible about her, but that's only because I don't follow that practise the way most of the others do. They don't stop with the worst of the truth they can find: they make *up* things—yes, they really do! And, oh, I'd *rather* they didn't make up things about me—to you!"

"What difference would it make if they did?" he inquired, cheerfully. "I'd know they weren't true."

"Even if you did know that, they'd make a difference," she said. "Oh, yes, they would! It's too bad, but we don't like anything quite so well that's had specks on it, even if we've wiped the specks off;—it's just that much spoiled, and some things are all spoiled the instant they're the least bit spoiled. What a man thinks about a girl, for instance. Do you want to have what you think about me spoiled, Mr. Russell?"

"Oh, but that's already far beyond reach," he said, lightly.

"But it can't be!" she protested.

"Why not?"

"Because it never can be. Men don't change their minds about one another often: they make it quite an event when they do, and talk about it as if something important had happened. But a girl only has to go down-town with a shoe-string unfastened, and every man who sees her will change his mind about her. Don't you know that's true?"

"Not of myself, I think."

"There!" she cried. "That's precisely what every man in the world would say!"

"So you wouldn't trust me?"

"Well—I'll be awfully worried if you give 'em a chance to tell you that I'm too lazy to tie my shoe-strings!"

He laughed delightedly. "Is that what they do say?" he asked.

"Just about! Whatever they hope will get results." She shook her head wisely. "Oh, yes; we do that here!"

"But I don't mind loose shoe-strings," he said. "Not if they're yours."

"They'll find out what you do mind."

"But suppose," he said, looking at her whimsically; "suppose I wouldn't mind anything—so long as it's yours?"

She courtesied. "Oh, pretty enough! But a girl who's talked about has a weakness that's often a fatal one."

"What is it?"

"It's this: when she's talked about she isn't *there*. That's how they kill her."

"I'm afraid I don't follow you."

"Don't you see? If Henrietta—or Mildred—or any of 'em—or some of their mothers—oh, we *all* do it! Well, if any of 'em told you I didn't tie my shoe-strings, and if I were there, so that you could see me, you'd know it wasn't true. Even if I were sitting so that you couldn't see my feet, and couldn't tell whether the strings were tied or not just then, still you could look at me, and see that I wasn't the sort of girl to neglect my shoe-strings. But that isn't the way it happens: they'll get at you when I'm nowhere around and can't remind you of the sort of girl I really am."

"But you don't do that," he complained. "You don't remind me—you don't even tell me—the sort of girl you really are! I'd like to know."

"Let's be serious then," she said, and looked serious enough herself. "Would you honestly like to know?"

"Yes."

"Well, then, you must be careful."

"'Careful?'" The word amused him.

"I mean careful not to get me mixed up," she said. "Careful not to mix up the girl you might hear somebody talking about with the me I honestly try to make you see. If you do get those two mixed up—well, the whole show'll be spoiled!"

"What makes you think so?"

"Because it's——" She checked herself, having begun to speak too impulsively; and she was disturbed, realizing in what tricky stuff she dealt. What had been on her lips to say was, "Because it's happened before!" She changed to, "Because it's so easy to spoil anything—easiest of all to spoil anything that's pleasant."

"That might depend."

"No; it's so. And if you care at all about—about knowing a girl who'd like someone to know her——"

"Just 'someone?' That's disappointing."

"Well—you," she said.

"Tell me how 'careful' you want me to be, then!"

"Well, don't you think it would be nice if you didn't give anybody the chance to talk about me the way—the way I've just been talking about Henrietta Lamb?"

With that they laughed together, and he said, "You may be cutting me off from a great deal of information, you know."

"Yes," Alice admitted. "Somebody might begin to praise me to you, too; so it's dangerous to ask you to change the subject if I ever happen to be mentioned. But after all——" She paused.

"'After all' isn't the end of a thought, is it?"

"Sometimes it is of a girl's thought; I suppose men are neater about their thoughts, and always finish 'em. It isn't the end of the thought I had then, though."

"What is the end of it?"

She looked at him impulsively. "Oh, it's foolish," she said, and she laughed as laughs one who proposes something probably impossible. "But *wouldn't* it be pleasant if two people could ever just keep themselves *to* themselves, so far as they two were concerned? I mean, if they could just manage to be friends without people talking about it, or talking to *them* about it?"

"I suppose that might be rather difficult," he said, more amused than impressed by her idea.

"I don't know: it might be done," she returned, hopefully. "Especially in a town of this size; it's grown so it's quite a huge place these days. People can keep themselves to themselves in a big place better, you know. For instance, nobody knows that you and I are taking a walk together to-day."

"How absurd, when here we are on exhibition!"

"No; we aren't."

"We aren't?"

"Not a bit of it!" she laughed. "We were the other day, when you walked home with me, but anybody could tell that had just happened by chance, on account of your overtaking me; people can always see things like that. But we're not on exhibition now. Look where I've led you!"

Amused and a little bewildered, he looked up and down the street, which was one of gaunt-faced apartment-houses, old, sooty, frame boarding-houses, small groceries and drug-stores, laundries and one-room plumbers' shops, with the sign of a clairvoyant here and there.

"You see?" she said. "I've been leading you without your knowing it. Of course that's because you're new to the town, and you give yourself up to the guidance of an old citizen."

"I'm not so sure, Miss Adams. It might mean that I don't care where I follow so long as I follow you."

"Very well," she said. "I'd like you to keep on following me—at least long enough for me to show you that there's something nicer ahead of us than this dingy street."

"Is that figurative?" he asked.

"Might be!" she returned, gaily. "There's a pretty little park at the end, but it's very proletarian, and nobody you and I know will be more likely to see us there than on this street."

"What an imagination you have!" he exclaimed. "You turn our proper little walk into a Parisian adventure."

She looked at him in what seemed to be a momentary grave puzzlement. "Perhaps you feel that a Parisian adventure mightn't please your—your relatives?"

"Why, no," he returned. "You seem to think of them oftener than I do."

This appeared to amuse Alice, or at least to please her, for she laughed. "Then I can afford to quit thinking of them, I suppose. It's only that I used to be quite a friend of Mildred's—but there! we needn't to go into that. I've never been a friend of Henrietta Lamb's, though, and I almost wish she weren't taking such pains to be a friend of yours."

"Oh, but she's not. It's all on account of——"

"On Mildred's account," Alice finished this for him, coolly. "Yes, of course."

"It's on account of the two families," he was at pains to explain, a little awkwardly. "It's because I'm a relative of the Palmers, and the Palmers and the Lambs seem to be old family friends."

"Something the Adamses certainly are not," Alice said. "Not with either of 'em; particularly not with the Lambs!" And here, scarce aware of what impelled her, she returned to her former elaborations and colourings. "You see, the differences between Henrietta and me aren't entirely personal: I couldn't go to her house even if I liked her. The Lambs and Adamses don't get on with each other, and we've just about come to the breaking-point as it happens."

"I hope it's nothing to bother you."

"Why? A lot of things bother me."

"I'm sorry they do," he said, and seemed simply to mean it.

She nodded gratefully. "That's nice of you, Mr. Russell. It helps. The break between the Adamses and the Lambs is a pretty bothersome thing. It's been coming on a long time." She sighed deeply, and the sigh was half genuine; this half being for her father, but the other half probably belonged to her instinctive rendering of Juliet Capulet, daughter to a warring house. "I hate it all so!" she added.

"Of course you must."

"I suppose most quarrels between families are on account of business," she said. "That's why they're so sordid. Certainly the Lambs seem a sordid lot to me, though of course I'm biased." And with that she began to sketch a history of the commercial antagonism that had risen between the Adamses and the Lambs.

The sketching was spontaneous and dramatic. Mathematics had no part in it; nor was there accurate definition of Mr. Adams's relation to the institution of Lamb and Company. The point was clouded, in fact; though that might easily be set down to the general haziness of young ladies confronted with the mysteries of trade or commerce. Mr. Adams either had been a vague sort of junior member of the firm, it appeared, or else he should have been made some such thing; at all events, he was an old mainstay of the business; and he, as much as any Lamb, had helped to build up the prosperity of the company. But at last, tired of providing so much intelligence and energy for which other people took profit greater than his own, he had decided to leave the company and found a business entirely for himself. The Lambs were going to be enraged when they learned what was afoot.

Such was the impression, a little misted, wrought by Alice's quick narrative. But there was dolorous fact behind it: Adams had succumbed.

His wife, grave and nervous, rather than triumphant, in success, had told their daughter that the great J. A. would be furious and possibly vindictive. Adams was afraid of him, she said.

"But what for, mama?" Alice asked, since this seemed a turn of affairs out of reason. "What in the world has Mr. Lamb to do with papa's leaving the company to set up for himself? What right has he to be angry about it? If he's such a friend as he claims to be, I should think he'd be glad—that is, if the glue factory turns out well. What will he be angry for?"

Mrs. Adams gave Alice an uneasy glance, hesitated, and then explained that a resignation from Lamb's had always been looked upon, especially by "that old man," as treachery. You were supposed to die in the service, she said bitterly, and her daughter, a little mystified, accepted this explanation. Adams had not spoken to her of his surrender; he seemed not inclined to speak to her at all, or to any one.

Alice was not serious too long, and she began to laugh as she came to the end of her decorative sketch. "After all, the whole thing is perfectly ridiculous," she said. "In fact, it's *funny*! That's on account of what papa's going to throw over the Lamb business *for*! To save your life you couldn't imagine what he's going to do!"

"I won't try, then," Russell assented.

"It takes all the romance out of *me*," she laughed. "You'll never go for a Parisian walk with me again, after I tell you what I'll be heiress to." They had come to the entrance of the little park; and, as Alice had said, it was a pretty place, especially on a day so radiant. Trees of the oldest forest stood there, hale and serene over the trim, bright grass; and the proletarians had not come from their factories at this hour; only a few mothers and their babies were to be seen, here and there, in the shade. "I think I'll postpone telling you about it till we get nearly home again," Alice said, as they began to saunter down one of the gravelled paths. "There's a bench beside a spring farther on; we can sit there and talk about a lot of things—things not so sticky as my dowry's going to be."

"'Sticky?'" he echoed. "What in the world——"

She laughed despairingly.

"A glue factory!"

Then he laughed, too, as much from friendliness as from amusement; and she remembered to tell him that the project of a glue factory was still "an Adams secret." It would be known soon, however, she added; and the whole Lamb connection would probably begin saying all sorts of things, heaven knew what!

Thus Alice built her walls of flimsy, working always gaily, or with at least the air of gaiety; and even as she rattled on, there was somewhere in her mind a constant little wonder. Everything she said seemed to be necessary to support something else she had said. How had it happened? She found herself telling him that since her father had decided on making so great a change in his ways, she and her mother hoped at last to persuade him to give up that "foolish little house" he had been so obstinate about; and she checked herself abruptly on this declivity just as she was about to slide into a remark concerning her own preference for a "country place." Discretion caught her in time; and something else, in company with discretion, caught her, for she stopped short in her talk and blushed.

They had taken possession of the bench beside the spring, by this time; and Russell, his elbow on the back of the bench and his chin on his hand, the better to look at her, had no guess at the cause of the blush, but was content to find it lovely. At his first sight of Alice she had seemed pretty in the particular way of being pretty that he happened to like best; and, with every moment he spent with her, this prettiness appeared to increase. He felt that he could not look at her enough: his gaze followed the fluttering of the graceful hands in almost continual gesture as she talked; then lifted happily to the vivacious face again. She charmed him.

After her abrupt pause, she sighed, then looked at him with her eyebrows lifted in a comedy appeal. "You haven't said you wouldn't give Henrietta the chance," she said, in the softest voice that can still have a little laugh running in it.

He was puzzled. "Give Henrietta the chance?"

"*You* know! You'll let me keep on being unfair, won't you? Not give the other girls a chance to get even?"

He promised, heartily.

Chapter XV

ALICE HAD said that no one who knew either Russell or herself would be likely to see them in the park or upon the dingy street; but although they returned by that same ungenteel thoroughfare they were seen by a person who knew them both. Also, with some surprise on the part of Russell, and something more poignant than surprise for Alice, they saw this person.

All of the dingy street was ugly, but the greater part of it appeared to be honest. The two pedestrians came upon a block or two, however, where it offered suggestions of a less upright character, like a steady enough workingman with a naughty book sticking out of his pocket. Three or four dim shops, a single story in height, exhibited foul signboards, yet fair enough so far as the wording went; one proclaiming a tobacconist, one a junk-dealer, one a dispenser of "soft drinks and cigars." The most credulous would have doubted these signboards; for the craft of the modern tradesman is exerted to lure indoors the passing glance, since if the glance is pleased the feet may follow; but this alleged tobacconist and his neighbours had long been fond of dust on their windows, evidently, and shades were pulled far down on the glass of their doors. Thus the public eye, small of pupil in the light of the open street, was intentionally not invited to the dusky interiors. Something different from mere lack of enterprise was apparent; and the signboards might have been omitted; they were pains thrown away, since it was plain to the world that the business parts of these shops were the brighter back rooms implied by the dark front rooms, and that the commerce there was in perilous new liquors and in dice and rough girls.

Nothing could have been more innocent than the serenity with which these wicked little places revealed themselves for what they were; and, bound by this final tie of guilelessness, they stood together in a row which ended with a companionable barber-shop, much like them. Beyond was a series of soot-harried frame two-story houses, once part of a cheerful neighbourhood when the town was middle-aged and settled, and not old and growing. These houses, all carrying the label, "Rooms," had the worried look of vacancy that houses have when they are too full of everybody without being anybody's home; and there was, too, a surreptitious air about them, as if, like the false little shops, they advertised something by concealing it.

One of them—the one next to the barber-shop—had across its front an ample, jig-sawed veranda, where aforetime, no doubt, the father of a family had fanned himself with a palm-leaf fan on Sunday afternoons, watching the surreys go by, and where his daughter listened to mandolins and badinage on starlit evenings; but, although youth still held the veranda, both the youth and the veranda were in decay. The four or five young men who lounged there this afternoon were of a type known to shady pool-parlours. Hats found no favour with them; all of them wore caps; and their tight clothes, apparently from a common source, showed a vivacious fancy for oblique pockets, false belts, and Easter-egg colourings. Another thing common to the group was the expression of eye and mouth; and Alice, in the midst of her other thoughts, had a distasteful thought about this.

The veranda was within a dozen feet of the sidewalk, and as she and her escort came nearer, she took note of the young men, her face hardening a little, even before she suspected there might be a resemblance between them and any one she knew. Then she observed that each of these loungers wore not for the occasion, but as of habit, a look of furtively amused contempt; the mouth smiled to one side as if not to dislodge a cigarette, while the eyes kept languidly superior. All at once Alice was reminded of Walter; and the slight frown caused by this idea had just begun to darken her forehead when Walter himself stepped out of the open door of the house and appeared upon the veranda. Upon his head was a new straw hat, and in his hand was a Malacca stick with an ivory top, for Alice had finally decided against it for herself and had given it to him. His mood was lively: he twirled the stick through his fingers like a drum-major's baton, and whistled loudly.

Moreover, he was indeed accompanied. With him was a thin girl who had made a violent black-and-white poster of herself: black dress, black flimsy boa, black stockings, white slippers, great black hat down upon the black eyes; and beneath the hat a curve of cheek and chin made white as whitewash, and in strong bilateral motion with gum.

The loungers on the veranda were familiars of the pair; hailed them with cacklings; and one began to sing, in a voice all tin:

> "Then my skirt, Sal, and me did go
> Right straight to the moving-pitcher show.
> *Oh*, you bashful vamp!"

The girl laughed airily. "God, but you guys are wise!" she said. "Come on, Wallie."

Walter stared at his sister; then grinned faintly, and nodded at Russell as the latter lifted his hat in salutation. Alice uttered an incoherent syllable of exclamation, and, as she began to walk faster, she bit her lip hard, not in order to look wistful, this time, but to help her keep tears of anger from her eyes.

Russell laughed cheerfully. "Your brother certainly seems to have found the place for 'colour' to-day," he said. "That girl's talk must be full of it."

But Alice had forgotten the colour she herself had used in accounting for Walter's peculiarities, and she did not understand. "What?" she said, huskily.

"Don't you remember telling me about him? How he was going to write, probably, and would go anywhere to pick up types and get them to talk?"

She kept her eyes ahead, and said sharply, "I think his literary tastes scarcely cover *this* case!"

"Don't be too sure. He didn't look at all disconcerted. He didn't seem to mind your seeing him."

"That's all the worse, isn't it?"

"Why, no," her friend said, genially. "It means he didn't consider that he was engaged in anything out of the way. You can't expect to understand everything boys do at his age; they do all sorts of queer things, and outgrow them. Your brother evidently has a taste for queer people, and very likely he's been at least half sincere when he's made you believe he had a literary motive behind it. We all go through——"

"Thanks, Mr. Russell," she interrupted. "Let's don't say any more."

He looked at her flushed face and enlarged eyes; and he liked her all the better for her indignation: this was how good sisters ought to feel, he thought, failing to understand that most of what she felt was not about Walter. He ventured only a word more. "Try not to mind it so much; it really doesn't amount to anything."

She shook her head, and they went on in silence; she did not look at him again until they stopped before her own house. Then she gave him only one glimpse of her eyes before she looked down. "It's spoiled, isn't it?" she said, in a low voice.

"What's 'spoiled?'"

"Our walk—well, everything. Somehow it always—is."

"'Always is' what?" he asked.

"Spoiled," she said.

He laughed at that; but without looking at him she suddenly offered him her hand, and, as he took it, he felt a hurried, violent pressure upon his fingers, as if she meant to thank him almost passionately for being kind. She was gone before he could speak to her again.

In her room, with the door locked, she did not go to her mirror, but to her bed, flinging herself face down, not caring how far the pillows put her hat awry. Sheer grief had followed her anger; grief for the calamitous end of her bright afternoon, grief for the "end of everything," as she thought then. Nevertheless, she gradually grew more composed, and, when her mother tapped on the door presently, let her in. Mrs. Adams looked at her with quick apprehension.

"Oh, poor child! Wasn't he——"

Alice told her. "You see how it—how it made me look, mama," she quavered, having concluded her narrative. "I'd tried to cover up Walter's awfulness at the dance with that story about his being 'literary,' but no story was big enough to cover this up—and oh! it must make him think I tell stories about other things!"

"No, no, no!" Mrs. Adams protested. "Don't you see? At the worst, all *he* could think is that Walter told stories to you about why he likes to be with such dreadful people, and you believed them. That's all *he'd* think; don't you see?"

Alice's wet eyes began to show a little hopefulness. "You honestly think it might be that way, mama?"

"Why, from what you've told me he said, I *know* it's that way. Didn't he say he wanted to come again?"

"N-no," Alice said, uncertainly. "But I think he will. At least I begin to think so now. He——" She stopped.

"From all you tell me, he seems to be a very desirable young man," Mrs. Adams said, primly.

Her daughter was silent for several moments; then new tears gathered upon her downcast lashes. "He's just—dear!" she faltered.

Mrs. Adams nodded. "He's told you he isn't engaged, hasn't he?"

"No. But I know he isn't. Maybe when he first came here he was near it, but I know he's not."

"I guess Mildred Palmer would *like* him to be, all right!" Mrs. Adams was frank enough to say, rather triumphantly; and Alice, with a lowered head, murmured:

"Anybody—would."

The words were all but inaudible.

"Don't you worry," her mother said, and patted her on the shoulder. "Everything will come out all right; don't you fear, Alice. Can't you see that beside any other girl in town you're just a perfect *queen*? Do you think any young man that wasn't prejudiced, or something, would need more than just one look to——"

But Alice moved away from the caressing hand. "Never mind, mama. I wonder he looks at me at all. And if he does again, after seeing my brother with those horrible people——"

"Now, now!" Mrs. Adams interrupted, expostulating mournfully. "I'm sure Walter's a *good* boy——"

"You are?" Alice cried, with a sudden vigour. "You *are*?"

"I'm sure he's *good*, yes—and if he isn't, it's not his fault. It's mine."

"What nonsense!"

"No, it's true," Mrs. Adams lamented. "I tried to bring him up to be good, God knows; and when he was little he was the best boy I ever saw. When he came from Sunday-school he'd always run to me and we'd go over the lesson together; and he let me come in his room at night to hear his prayers almost until he was sixteen. Most boys won't do that with their mothers

—not nearly that long. I tried so hard to bring him up right—but if anything's gone wrong it's my fault."

"How could it be? You've just said——"

"It's because I didn't make your father take this—this new step earlier. Then Walter might have had all the advantages that other——"

"Oh, mama, *please*!" Alice begged her. "Let's don't go over all that again. Isn't it more important to think what's to be done about him? Is he going to be allowed to go on disgracing us as he does?"

Mrs. Adams sighed profoundly. "I don't know what to do," she confessed, unhappily. "Your father's so upset about—about this new step he's taking—I don't feel as if we ought to——"

"No, no!" Alice cried. "Papa mustn't be distressed with this, on top of everything else. But *something's* got to be done about Walter."

"What can be?" her mother asked, helplessly. "What can be?"

Alice admitted that she didn't know.

At dinner, an hour later, Walter's habitually veiled glance lifted, now and then, to touch her furtively;—he was waiting, as he would have said, for her to "spring it"; and he had prepared a brief and sincere defense to the effect that he made his own living, and would like to inquire whose business it was to offer intrusive comment upon his private conduct. But she said nothing, while his father and mother were as silent as she. Walter concluded that there was to be no attack, but changed his mind when his father, who ate only a little, and broodingly at that, rose to leave the table and spoke to him.

"Walter," he said, "when you've finished I wish you'd come up to my room. I got something I want to say to you."

Walter shot a hard look at his apathetic sister, then turned to his father. "Make it to-morrow," he said. "This is Satad'y night and I got a date."

"No," Adams said, frowning. "You come up before you go out. It's important."

"All right; I've had all I want to eat," Walter returned. "I got a few minutes. Make it quick."

He followed his father upstairs, and when they were in the room together Adams shut the door, sat down, and began to rub his knees.

"Rheumatism?" the boy inquired, slyly. "That what you want to talk to me about?"

"No." But Adams did not go on; he seemed to be in difficulties for words, and Walter decided to help him.

"Hop ahead and spring it," he said. "Get it off your mind: I'll tell the world *I* should worry! You aren't goin' to bother *me* any, so why bother yourself? Alice hopped home and told you she saw me playin' around with some pretty gay-lookin' berries and you——"

"Alice?" his father said, obviously surprised. "It's nothing about Alice."

"Didn't she tell you——"

"I haven't talked with her all day."

"Oh, I see," Walter said. "She told mother and mother told you."

"No, neither of 'em have told me anything. What was there to tell?"

Walter laughed. "Oh, it's nothin'," he said. "I was just startin' out to buy a girl friend o' mine a rhinestone buckle I lost to her on a bet, this afternoon, and Alice came along with that big Russell fish; and I thought she looked sore. She expects me to like the kind she likes, and I don't like 'em. I thought she'd prob'ly got you all stirred up about it."

"No, no," his father said, peevishly. "I don't know anything about it, and I don't care to know anything about it. I want to talk to you about something important."

Then, as he was again silent, Walter said, "Well, *talk* about it; I'm listening."

"It's this," Adams began, heavily. "It's about me going into this glue business. Your mother's told you, hasn't she?"

"She said you were goin' to leave the old place down-town and start a glue factory. That's all I know about it; I got my own affairs to 'tend to."

"Well, this is your affair," his father said, frowning. "You can't stay with Lamb and Company."

Walter looked a little startled. "What you mean, I can't? Why not?"

"You've got to help me," Adams explained slowly; and he frowned more deeply, as if the interview were growing increasingly laborious for him. "It's going to be a big pull to get this business on its feet."

"Yes!" Walter exclaimed with a sharp skepticism. "I should say it was!" He stared at his father incredulously. "Look here; aren't you just a little bit sudden, the way you're goin' about things? You've let mother shove you a little too fast, haven't you? Do you know anything about what it means to set up a new business these days?"

"Yes, I know all about it," Adams said. "About this business, I do."

"How do you?"

"Because I made a long study of it. I'm not afraid of going about it the wrong way; but it's a hard job and you'll have to put in all whatever sense and strength you've got."

Walter began to breathe quickly, and his lips were agitated; then he set them obstinately. "Oh, I will," he said.

"Yes, you will," Adams returned, not noticing that his son's inflection was satiric. "It's going to take every bit of energy in your body, and all the energy I got left in mine, and every cent of the little I've saved, besides something I'll have to raise on this house. I'm going right at it, now I've got to; and you'll have to quit Lamb's by the end of next week."

"Oh, I will?" Walter's voice grew louder, and there was a shrillness in it. "I got to quit Lamb's the end of next week, have I?" He stepped forward, angrily. "Listen!" he said. "I'm not walkin' out o' Lamb's, see? I'm not quittin' down there: I stay with 'em, see?"

Adams looked up at him, astonished. "You'll leave there next Saturday," he said. "I've got to have you."

"You don't anything o' the kind," Walter told him, sharply. "Do you expect to pay me anything?"

"I'd pay you about what you been getting down there."

"Then pay somebody else; *I* don't know anything about glue. You get somebody else."

"No. You've got to——"

Walter cut him off with the utmost vehemence. "Don't tell me what I got to do! *I* know what I got to do better'n you, I guess! I stay at Lamb's, see?"

Adams rose angrily. "You'll do what I tell you. You can't stay down there."

"Why can't I?"

"Because I won't let you."

"Listen! Keep on not lettin' me: I'll be there just the same."

At that his father broke into a sour laughter. "*They* won't let you, Walter! They won't have you down there after they find out I'm going."

"Why won't they? You don't think they're goin' to be all shot to pieces over losin' *you*, do you?"

"I tell you they won't let you stay," his father insisted, loudly.

"Why, what do they care whether you go or not?"

"They'll care enough to fire *you*, my boy!"

"Look here, then; show me why."

"They'll do it!"

"Yes," Walter jeered; "you keep sayin' they will, but when I ask you to show me why, you keep sayin' they will! That makes little headway with *me*, I can tell you!"

Adams groaned, and, rubbing his head, began to pace the floor. Walter's refusal was something he had not anticipated; and he felt the weakness of his own attempt to meet it: he seemed powerless to do anything but utter angry words, which, as Walter said, made little headway. "Oh, my, my!" he muttered, "*Oh*, my, my!"

Walter, usually sallow, had grown pale: he watched his father narrowly, and now took a sudden resolution. "Look here," he said. "When you say Lamb's is likely to fire me because you're goin' to quit, you talk like the people that have to be locked up. I don't know where you get such things in your head; Lamb and Company won't know you're gone. Listen: I can stay there long as I want to. But I'll tell you what I'll do: make it worth my while and I'll hook up with your old glue factory, after all."

Adams stopped his pacing abruptly, and stared at him. "'Make it worth your while?' What you mean?"

"I got a good use for three hundred dollars right now," Walter said. "Let me have it and I'll quit Lamb's to work for you. Don't let me have it and I *swear* I won't!"

"Are you crazy?"

"Is everybody crazy that needs three hundred dollars?"

"Yes," Adams said. "They are if they ask *me* for it, when I got to stretch every cent I can lay my hands on to make it look like a dollar!"

"You won't do it?"

Adams burst out at him. "You little fool! If I had three hundred dollars to throw away, besides the pay I expected to give you, haven't you got sense enough to see I could hire a man worth three hundred dollars more to me than you'd be? It's a *fine* time to ask me for three hundred dollars, isn't it! What *for*? Rhinestone buckles to throw around on your 'girl friends?' Shame on you! Ask me to *bribe* you to help yourself and your own family!"

"I'll give you a last chance," Walter said. "Either you do what I want, or I won't do what you want. Don't ask me again after this, because——"

Adams interrupted him fiercely. "'Ask you again!' Don't worry about that, my boy! All I ask you is to get out o' my room."

"Look here," Walter said, quietly; and his lopsided smile distorted his livid cheek. "Look here: I expect *you* wouldn't give me three hundred dollars to save my life, would you?"

"You make me sick," Adams said, in his bitterness. "Get out of here."

Walter went out, whistling; and Adams drooped into his old chair again as the door closed. "*Oh*, my, my!" he groaned. "Oh, Lordy, Lordy! The way of the transgressor——"

Chapter XVI

HE MEANT his own transgression and his own way; for Walter's stubborn refusal appeared to Adams just then as one of the inexplicable but righteous besettings he must encounter in following that way. "Oh, Lordy, Lord!" he groaned, and then, as resentment moved him—"That dang boy! Dang idiot!" Yet he knew himself for a greater idiot because he had not been able to tell Walter the truth. He could not bring himself to do it, nor even to state his case in its best terms; and that was because he felt that even in its best terms the case was a bad one.

Of all his regrets the greatest was that in a moment of vanity and tenderness, twenty-five years ago, he had told his young wife a business secret. He had wanted to show how important her husband was becoming, and how much the head of the universe, J. A. Lamb, trusted to his integrity and ability. The great man had an idea: he thought of "branching out a little," he told Adams confidentially, and there were possibilities of profit in glue.

What he wanted was a liquid glue to be put into little bottles and sold cheaply. "The kind of thing that sells itself," he said; "the kind of thing that pays its own small way as it goes along, until it has profits enough to begin advertising it right. Everybody has to use glue, and if I make mine convenient and cheap, everybody'll buy mine. But it's got to be glue that'll *stick*; it's got to be the best; and if we find how to make it we've got to keep it a big secret, of course, or anybody can steal it from us. There was a man here last month; he knew a formula he wanted to sell me, 'sight unseen'; but he was in such a hurry I got suspicious, and I found he'd managed to steal it, working for the big packers in their glue-works. We've got to find a better glue than that, anyhow. I'm going to set you and Campbell at it. You're a practical, wide-awake young feller, and Campbell's a mighty good chemist; I guess you two boys ought to make something happen."

His guess was shrewd enough. Working in a shed a little way outside the town, where their cheery employer visited them sometimes to study their malodorous stews, the two young men found what Lamb had set them to find. But Campbell was thoughtful over the discovery. "Look here," he said. "Why ain't this just about yours and mine? After all, it may be Lamb's money that's paid for the stuff we've used, but it hasn't cost much."

"But he pays *us*," Adams remonstrated, horrified by his companion's idea. "He paid us to do it. It belongs absolutely to him."

"Oh, I know he *thinks* it does," Campbell admitted, plaintively. "I suppose we've got to let him take it. It's not patentable, and he'll have to do pretty well by us when he starts his factory, because he's got to depend on us to run the making of the stuff so that the workmen can't get onto the process. You better ask him the same salary I do, and mine's going to be high."

But the high salary, thus pleasantly imagined, was never paid. Campbell died of typhoid fever, that summer, leaving Adams and his employer the only possessors of the formula, an unwritten one; and Adams, pleased to think himself more important to the great man than ever, told his wife that there could be little doubt of his being put in sole charge of the prospective glue-works. Unfortunately, the enterprise remained prospective.

Its projector had already become "inveigled into another side-line," as he told Adams. One of his sons had persuaded him to take up a "cough-lozenge," to be called the "Jalamb Balm Trochee"; and the lozenge did well enough to amuse Mr. Lamb and occupy his spare time, which was really about all he had asked of the glue project. He had "all the *money* anybody ought to want," he said, when Adams urged him; and he could "start up this little glue side-line" at any time; the formula was safe in their two heads.

At intervals Adams would seek opportunity to speak of "the little glue side-line" to his patron, and to suggest that the years were passing; but Lamb, petting other hobbies, had lost interest. "Oh, I'll start it up some day, maybe. If I don't, I may turn it over to my heirs: it's always an asset, worth something or other, of course. We'll probably take it up some day, though, you and I."

The sun persistently declined to rise on that day, and, as time went on, Adams saw that his rather timid urgings bored his employer, and he ceased to bring up the subject. Lamb apparently forgot all about glue, but Adams discovered that unfortunately there was someone else who remembered it.

"It's really *yours*," she argued, that painful day when for the first time she suggested his using his knowledge for the benefit of himself and his family. "Mr. Campbell might have had a right to part of it, but he died and didn't leave any kin, so it belongs to you."

"Suppose J. A. Lamb hired me to saw some wood," Adams said. "Would the sticks belong to me?"

"He hasn't got any right to take your invention and bury it," she protested. "What good is it doing him if he doesn't *do* anything with it? What good is it doing *anybody*? None in the world! And what harm would it do him if you went ahead and did this for yourself and for your children? None in the world! And what could he do to you if he *was* old pig enough to get angry with you for doing it? He couldn't do a single thing, and you've admitted he couldn't, yourself. So what's your reason for depriving your children and your wife of the benefits you know you could give 'em?"

"Nothing but decency," he answered; and she had her reply ready for that. It seemed to him that, strive as he would, he could not reach her mind with even the plainest language; while everything that she said to him, with such vehemence, sounded like so much obstinate gibberish. Over and over he pressed her with the same illustration, on the point of ownership, though he thought he was varying it.

"Suppose he hired me to build him a house: would that be *my* house?"

"He didn't hire you to build him a house. You and Campbell invented——"

"Look here: suppose you give a cook a soup-bone and some vegetables, and pay her to make you a soup: has she got a right to take and sell it? You know better!"

"I know *one* thing: if that old man tried to keep your own invention from you he's no better than a robber!"

They never found any point of contact in all their passionate discussions of this ethical question; and the question was no more settled between them, now that Adams had succumbed, than it had ever been. But at least the wrangling about it was over: they were grave together, almost silent, and an uneasiness prevailed with her as much as with him.

He had already been out of the house, to walk about the small green yard; and on Monday afternoon he sent for a taxicab and went down-town, but kept a long way from the "wholesale section," where stood the formidable old oblong pile of Lamb and Company. He arranged for the sale of the bonds he had laid away, and for placing a mortgage upon his house; and on his way home, after five o'clock, he went to see an old friend, a man whose term of service with Lamb and Company was even a little longer than his own.

This veteran, returned from the day's work, was sitting in front of the apartment house where he lived, but when the cab stopped at the curb he rose and came forward, offering a jocular greeting. "Well, well, Virgil Adams! I always thought you had a sporty streak in you. Travel in your own hired private automobile nowadays, do you? Pamperin' yourself because you're still layin' off sick, I expect."

"Oh, I'm well enough again, Charley Lohr," Adams said, as he got out and shook hands. Then, telling the driver to wait, he took his friend's arm, walked to the bench with him, and sat down. "I been practically well for some time," he said. "I'm fixin' to get into harness again."

"Bein' sick has certainly produced a change of heart in you," his friend laughed. "You're the last man I ever expected to see blowin' yourself—or anybody else—to a taxicab! For that matter, I never heard of you bein' in *any* kind of a cab, 'less'n it might be when you been pall-bearer for somebody. What's come over you?"

"Well, I got to turn over a new leaf, and that's a fact," Adams said. "I got a lot to do, and the only way to accomplish it, it's got to be done soon, or I won't have anything to live on while I'm doing it."

"What you talkin' about? What you got to do except to get strong enough to come back to the old place?"

"Well——" Adams paused, then coughed, and said slowly, "Fact is, Charley Lohr, I been thinking likely I wouldn't come back."

"What! What you talkin' about?"

"No," said Adams. "I been thinking I might likely kind of branch out on my own account."

"Well, I'll be doggoned!" Old Charley Lohr was amazed; he ruffled up his gray moustache with thumb and forefinger, leaving his mouth open beneath, like a dark cave under a tangled wintry thicket. "Why, that's the doggonedest thing I ever heard!" he said. "I already am the oldest inhabitant down there, but if you go, there won't be anybody else of the old generation at all. What on earth you thinkin' of goin' into?"

"Well," said Adams, "I rather you didn't mention it till I get started—of course anybody'll know what it is by then—but I *have* been kind of planning to put a liquid glue on the market."

His friend, still ruffling the gray moustache upward, stared at him in frowning perplexity. "Glue?" he said. "*Glue!*"

"Yes. I been sort of milling over the idea of taking up something like that."

"Handlin' it for some firm, you mean?"

"No. Making it. Sort of a glue-works likely."

Lohr continued to frown. "Let me think," he said. "Didn't the ole man have some such idea once, himself?"

Adams leaned forward, rubbing his knees; and he coughed again before he spoke. "Well, yes. Fact is, he did. That is to say, a mighty long while ago he did."

"I remember," said Lohr. "He never said anything about it that I know of; but seems to me I recollect we had sort of a rumour around the place how you and that man—le's see, wasn't his name Campbell, that died of typhoid fever? Yes, that was it, Campbell. Didn't the ole man have you and Campbell workin' sort of private on some glue proposition or other?"

"Yes, he did." Adams nodded. "I found out a good deal about glue then, too."

"Been workin' on it since, I suppose?"

"Yes. Kept it in my mind and studied out new things about it."

Lohr looked serious. "Well, but see here," he said. "I hope it ain't anything the ole man'll think might infringe on whatever he had you doin' for *him*. You know how he is: broad-minded, liberal, free-handed man as walks this earth, and if he thought he owed you a cent he'd sell his right hand for a pork-chop to pay it, if that was the only way; but if he got the idea anybody was tryin' to get the better of him, he'd sell *both* his hands, if he had to, to keep 'em from doin' it. Yes, at eighty, he would! Not that I mean I think you might be tryin' to get the better of him, Virg. You're a mighty close ole codger, but such a thing ain't in you. What I mean: I hope there ain't any chance for the ole man to *think* you might be——"

"Oh, no," Adams interrupted. "As a matter of fact, I don't believe he'll ever think about it at all, and if he did he wouldn't have any real right to feel offended at me: the process I'm going to use is one I expect to change and improve a lot different from the one Campbell and I worked on for him."

"Well, that's good," said Lohr. "Of course you know what you're up to: you're old enough, God knows!" He laughed ruefully. "My, but it will seem funny to me—down there with you gone! I expect you and I both been gettin' to be pretty much dead-wood in the place, the way the young fellows look at it, and the only one that'd miss either of us would be the other one! Have you told the ole man yet?"

"Well——" Adams spoke laboriously. "No. No, I haven't. I thought—well, that's what I wanted to see you about."

"What can I do?"

"I thought I'd write him a letter and get you to hand it to him for me."

"My soul!" his friend exclaimed. "Why on earth don't you just go down there and tell him?"

Adams became pitiably embarrassed. He stammered, coughed, stammered again, wrinkling his face so deeply he seemed about to weep; but finally he contrived to utter an apologetic laugh. "I ought to do that, of course; but in some way or other I just don't seem to be able to—to manage it."

"Why in the world not?" the mystified Lohr inquired.

"I could hardly tell you—'less'n it is to say that when you been with one boss all your life it's so—so kind of embarrassing—to quit him, I just can't make up my mind to go and speak to him about it. No; I got it in my head a letter's the only satisfactory way to do it, and I thought I'd ask you to hand it to him."

"Well, of course I don't mind doin' that for you," Lohr said, mildly. "But why in the world don't you just mail it to him?"

"Well, I'll tell you," Adams returned. "You know, like that, it'd have to go through a clerk and that secretary of his, and I don't know who all. There's a couple of kind of delicate points I want to put in it: for instance, I want to explain to him how much improvement and so on I'm going to introduce on the old process I helped to work out with Campbell when we were working for him, so't he'll understand it's a different article and no infringement at all. Then there's another thing: you see all during while I was sick he had my salary paid to me—it amounts to considerable, I was on my back so long. Under the circumstances, because I'm quitting, I don't feel as if I ought to accept it, and so I'll have a check for him in the letter to cover it, and I want to be sure he knows it, and gets it personally. If it had to go through a lot of other people, the way it would if I put it in the mail, why, you can't tell. So what I thought: if you'd hand it to him for me, and maybe if he happened to read it right then, or anything, it might be you'd notice whatever he'd happen to say about it—and you could tell me afterward."

"All right," Lohr said. "Certainly if you'd rather do it that way, I'll hand it to him and tell you what he says; that is, if he says anything and I hear him. Got it written?"

"No; I'll send it around to you last of the week." Adams moved toward his taxicab. "Don't say anything to anybody about it, Charley, especially till after that."

"All right."

"And, Charley, I'll be mighty obliged to you," Adams said, and came back to shake hands in farewell. "There's one thing more you might do—if you'd ever happen to feel like it." He kept his eyes rather vaguely fixed on a point above his friend's head as he spoke, and his voice was not well controlled. "I been —I been down there a good many years and I may not 'a' been so much use lately as I was at first, but I always *tried* to do my best for the old firm. If anything turned out so's they *did* kind of take offense with me, down there, why, just say a good word for me—if you'd happen to feel like it, maybe."

Old Charley Lohr assured him that he would speak a good word if opportunity became available; then, after the cab had driven away, he went up to his small apartment on the third floor and muttered ruminatively until his wife inquired what he was talking to himself about.

"Ole Virg Adams," he told her. "He's out again after his long spell of sickness, and the way it looks to me he'd better stayed in bed."

"You mean he still looks too bad to be out?"

"Oh, I expect he's gettin' his *health* back," Lohr said, frowning.

"Then what's the matter with him? You mean he's lost his mind?"

"My goodness, but women do jump at conclusions!" he exclaimed.

"Well," said Mrs. Lohr, "what other conclusion did you leave me to jump at?"

Her husband explained with a little heat: "People can have a sickness that *affects* their mind, can't they? Their mind can get some affected without bein' *lost*, can't it?"

"Then you mean the poor man's mind does seem affected?"

"Why, no; I'd scarcely go as far as that," Lohr said, inconsistently, and declined to be more definite.

Adams devoted the latter part of that evening to the composition of his letter—a disquieting task not completed when, at eleven o'clock, he heard his daughter coming up the stairs. She was singing to herself in a low, sweet voice, and Adams paused to listen incredulously, with his pen lifted and his mouth open, as if he heard the strangest sound in the world. Then he set down the pen upon a blotter, went to his door, and opened it, looking out at her as she came.

"Well, dearie, you seem to be feeling pretty good," he said. "What you been doing?"

"Just sitting out on the front steps, papa."

"All alone, I suppose."

"No. Mr. Russell called."

"Oh, he did?" Adams pretended to be surprised. "What all could you and he find to talk about till this hour o' the night?"

She laughed gaily. "You don't know me, papa!"

"How's that?"

"You've never found out that I always do all the talking."

"Didn't you let him get a word in all evening?"

"Oh, yes; every now and then."

Adams took her hand and petted it. "Well, what did he say?"

Alice gave him a radiant look and kissed him. "Not what you think!" she laughed; then slapped his cheek with saucy affection, pirouetted across the narrow hall and into her own room, and curtsied to him as she closed her door.

Adams went back to his writing with a lighter heart; for since Alice was born she had been to him the apple of his eye, his own phrase in thinking of her; and what he was doing now was for her. He smiled as he picked up his pen to begin a new draft of the painful letter; but presently he looked puzzled. After all, she could be happy just as things were, it seemed. Then why had he taken what his wife called "this new step," which he had so long resisted?

He could only sigh and wonder. "Life works out pretty peculiarly," he thought; for he couldn't go back now, though the reason he couldn't was not clearly apparent. He had to go ahead.

Chapter XVII

HE WAS out in his taxicab again the next morning, and by noon he had secured what he wanted.

It was curiously significant that he worked so quickly. All the years during which his wife had pressed him toward his present shift he had sworn to himself, as well as to her, that he would never yield; and yet when he did yield he had no plans to make, because he found them already prepared and worked out in detail in his mind; as if he had long contemplated the "step" he believed himself incapable of taking.

Sometimes he had thought of improving his income by exchanging his little collection of bonds for a "small rental property," if he could find "a good buy"; and he had spent many of his spare hours rambling over the enormously spreading city and its purlieus, looking for the ideal "buy." It remained unattainable, so far as he was concerned; but he found other things.

Not twice a crow's mile from his own house there was a dismal and slummish quarter, a decayed "industrial district" of earlier days. Most of the industries were small; some of them died, perishing of bankruptcy or fire; and a few had moved, leaving their shells. Of the relics, the best was a brick building which had been the largest and most important factory in the quarter: it had been injured by a long vacancy almost as serious as a fire, in effect, and Adams had often guessed at the sum needed to put it in repair.

When he passed it, he would look at it with an interest which he supposed detached and idly speculative. "That'd be just the thing," he thought. "If a fellow had money enough, and took a notion to set up some new business on a big scale, this would be a pretty good place—to make glue, for instance, if that wasn't out of the question, of course. It would take a lot of money, though; a great deal too much for *me* to expect to handle—even if I'd ever dream of doing such a thing."

Opposite the dismantled factory was a muddy, open lot of two acres or so, and near the middle of the lot, a long brick shed stood in a desolate abandonment, not happily decorated by old coatings of theatrical and medicinal advertisements. But the brick shed had two wooden ells, and, though both shed and ells were of a single story, here was empty space enough for a modest enterprise—"space enough for almost anything, to start with," Adams thought, as he walked through the low buildings, one day, when he was prospecting in that section. "Yes, I suppose I *could* swing this," he thought. "If the process belonged to me, say, instead of being out of the question because it isn't my property—or if I was the kind of man to do such a thing anyhow, here would be something I could probably get hold of pretty cheap. They'd want a lot of money for a lease on that big building over the way—but this, why, I should think it'd be practically nothing at all."

Then, by chance, meeting an agent he knew, he made inquiries—merely to satisfy a casual curiosity, he thought—and he found matters much as he had supposed, except that the owners of the big building did not wish to let, but to sell it, and this at a price so exorbitant that Adams laughed. But the long brick shed in the great muddy lot was for sale or to let, or "pretty near to be given away," he learned, if anybody would take it.

Adams took it now, though without seeing that he had been destined to take it, and that some dreary wizard in the back of his head had foreseen all along that he would take it, and planned to be ready. He drove in his taxicab to look the place over again, then down-town to arrange for a lease; and came home to lunch with his wife and daughter. Things were "moving," he told them.

He boasted a little of having acted so decisively, and said that since the dang thing had to be done, it was "going to be done *right*!" He was almost cheerful, in a feverish way, and when the cab came for him again, soon after lunch, he explained that he intended not only to get things done right, but also to "get 'em done quick!" Alice, following him to the front door, looked at him anxiously and asked if she couldn't help. He laughed at her grimly.

"Then let me go along with you in the cab," she begged. "You don't look able to start in so hard, papa, just when you're barely beginning to get your strength back. Do let me go with you and see if I can't help—or at least take care of you if you should get to feeling badly."

He declined, but upon pressure let her put a tiny bottle of spirits of ammonia in his pocket, and promised to make use of it if he "felt faint or anything." Then he was off again; and the next morning had men at work in his sheds, though the wages he had to pay frightened him.

He directed the workmen in every detail, hurrying them by example and exhortations, and receiving, in consequence, several declarations of independence, as well as one resignation, which took effect immediately. "Yous capitalusts seem to think a man's got nothin' to do but break his back p'doosin' wealth fer yous to squander," the resigning person loudly complained. "You look out: the toiler's day is a-comin', and it ain't so fur off, neither!" But the capitalist was already out of hearing, gone to find a man to take this orator's place.

By the end of the week, Adams felt that he had moved satisfactorily forward in his preparations for the simple equipment he needed; but he hated the pause of Sunday. He didn't *want* any rest, he told Alice impatiently, when she suggested that the idle day might be good for him.

Late that afternoon he walked over to the apartment house where old Charley Lohr lived, and gave his friend the letter he wanted the head of Lamb and Company to receive "personally." "I'll take it as a mighty great favour in you to hand it to him personally, Charley," he said, in parting. "And you won't forget, in case he says anything about it—and remember if you ever do get a chance to put in a good word for me later, you know——"

Old Charley promised to remember, and, when Mrs. Lohr came out of the "kitchenette," after the door closed, he said thoughtfully, "Just skin and bones."

"You mean Mr. Adams is?" Mrs. Lohr inquired.

"Who'd you think I meant?" he returned. "One o' these partridges in the wall-paper?"

"Did he look so badly?"

"Looked kind of distracted to *me*," her husband replied. "These little thin fellers can stand a heap sometimes, though. He'll be over here again Monday."

"Did he say he would?"

"No," said Lohr. "But he will. You'll see. He'll be over to find out what the big boss says when I give him this letter. Expect I'd be kind of anxious, myself, if I was him."

"Why would you? What's Mr. Adams doing to be so anxious about?"

Lohr's expression became one of reserve, the look of a man who has found that when he speaks his inner thoughts his wife jumps too far to conclusions. "Oh, nothing," he said. "Of course any man starting up a new business is bound to be pretty nervous a while. He'll be over here to-morrow evening, all right; you'll see."

The prediction was fulfilled: Adams arrived just after Mrs. Lohr had removed the dinner dishes to her "kitchenette"; but Lohr had little information to give his caller.

"He didn't say a word, Virgil; nary a word. I took it into his office and handed it to him, and he just sat and read it; that's all. I kind of stood around as long as I could, but he was sittin' at his desk with his side to me, and he never turned around full toward me, as it were, so I couldn't hardly even tell anything. All I know: he just read it."

"Well, but see here," Adams began, nervously. "Well——"

"Well what, Virg?"

"Well, but what did he say when he *did* speak?"

"He didn't speak. Not so long I was in there, anyhow. He just sat there and read it. Read kind of slow. Then, when he came to the end, he turned back and started to read it all over again. By that time there was three or four other men standin' around in the office waitin' to speak to him, and I had to go."

Adams sighed, and stared at the floor, irresolute. "Well, I'll be getting along back home then, I guess, Charley. So you're sure you couldn't tell anything what he might have thought about it, then?"

"Not a thing in the world. I've told you all I know, Virg."

"I guess so, I guess so," Adams said, mournfully. "I feel mighty obliged to you, Charley Lohr; mighty obliged. Good-night to you." And he departed, sighing in perplexity.

On his way home, preoccupied with many thoughts, he walked so slowly that once or twice he stopped and stood motionless for a few moments, without being aware of it; and when he reached the juncture of the sidewalk with the short brick path that led to his own front door, he stopped again, and stood for more than a minute. "Ah, I wish I knew," he whispered, plaintively. "I do wish I knew what he thought about it."

He was roused by a laugh that came lightly from the little veranda near by. "Papa!" Alice called gaily. "What *are* you standing there muttering to yourself about?"

"Oh, are you there, dearie?" he said, and came up the path. A tall figure rose from a chair on the veranda.

"Papa, this is Mr. Russell."

The two men shook hands, Adams saying, "Pleased to make your acquaintance," as they looked at each other in the faint light diffused through the opaque glass in the upper part of the door. Adams's impression was of a strong and tall young man, fashionable but gentle; and Russell's was of a dried, little old business man with a grizzled moustache, worried bright eyes, shapeless dark clothes, and a homely manner.

"Nice evening," Adams said further, as their hands parted. "Nice time o' year it is, but we don't always have as good weather as this; that's the trouble of it. Well——" He went to the door. "Well—I bid you good evening," he said, and retired within the house.

Alice laughed. "He's the old-fashionedest man in town, I suppose—and frightfully impressed with *you*, I could see!"

"What nonsense!" said Russell. "How could anybody be impressed with me?"

"Why not? Because you're quiet? Good gracious! Don't you know that you're the *most* impressive sort? We chatterers spend all our time playing to you quiet people."

"Yes; we're only the audience."

"'Only!'" she echoed. "Why, we live for you, and we can't live without you."

"I wish you couldn't," said Russell. "That would be a new experience for both of us, wouldn't it?"

"It might be a rather bleak one for me," she answered, lightly. "I'm afraid I'll miss these summer evenings with you when they're over. I'll miss them enough, thanks!"

"Do they have to be over some time?" he asked.

"Oh, everything's over *some* time, isn't it?"

Russell laughed at her. "Don't let's look so far ahead as that," he said. "We don't need to be already thinking of the cemetery, do we?"

"I didn't," she said, shaking her head. "Our summer evenings will be over before then, Mr. Russell."

"Why?" he asked.

"Good heavens!" she said. "*There's* laconic eloquence: almost a proposal in a single word! Never mind, I shan't hold you to it. But to answer you: well, I'm always looking ahead, and somehow I usually see about how things are coming out."

"Yes," he said. "I suppose most of us do; at least it seems as if we did, because we so seldom feel surprised by the way they do come out. But maybe that's only because life isn't like a play in a theatre, and most things come about so gradually we get used to them."

"No, I'm sure I can see quite a long way ahead," she insisted, gravely. "And it doesn't seem to me as if our summer evenings could last very long. Something'll interfere—somebody will, I mean—they'll *say* something——"

"What if they do?"

She moved her shoulders in a little apprehensive shiver. "It'll change you," she said. "I'm just sure something spiteful's going to happen to me. You'll feel differently about—things."

"Now, isn't that an idea!" he exclaimed.

"It will," she insisted. "I know something spiteful's going to happen!"

"You seem possessed by a notion not a bit flattering to me," he remarked.

"Oh, but isn't it? That's just what it is! Why isn't it?"

"Because it implies that I'm made of such soft material the slightest breeze will mess me all up. I'm not so like that as I evidently appear; and if it's true that we're afraid other people will do the things we'd be most likely to do ourselves, it seems to me that I ought to be the one to be afraid. I ought to be afraid that somebody may say something about me to you that will make you believe I'm a professional forger."

"No. We both know they won't," she said. "We both know you're the sort of person everybody in the world says nice things about." She lifted her hand to silence him as he laughed at this. "Oh, of course you are! I think perhaps you're a little flirtatious—most quiet men have that one sly way with 'em—oh, yes, they do! But you happen to be the kind of man everybody loves to praise. And if you weren't, *I* shouldn't hear anything terrible about you. I told you I was unpopular: I don't see anybody at all any more. The only man except you who's been to see me in a month is that fearful little fat Frank Dowling, and I sent word to *him* I wasn't home. Nobody'd tell me of your wickedness, you see."

"Then let me break some news to you," Russell said. "Nobody would tell me of yours, either. Nobody's even mentioned you to me."

She burlesqued a cry of anguish. "That *is* obscurity! I suppose I'm too apt to forget that they say the population's about half a million nowadays. There *are* other people to talk about, you feel, then?"

"None that I want to," he said. "But I should think the size of the place might relieve your mind of what seems to insist on burdening it. Besides, I'd rather you thought me a better man than you do."

"What kind of a man do I think you are?"

"The kind affected by what's said about people instead of by what they do themselves."

"Aren't you?"

"No, I'm not," he said. "If you want our summer evenings to be over you'll have to drive me away yourself."

"Nobody else could?"

"No."

She was silent, leaning forward, with her elbows on her knees and her clasped hands against her lips. Then, not moving, she said softly:

"Well—I won't!"

She was silent again, and he said nothing, but looked at her, seeming to be content with looking. Her attitude was one only a graceful person should assume, but she was graceful; and, in the wan light, which made a prettily shaped mist of her, she had beauty. Perhaps it was beauty of the hour, and of the love scene almost made into form by what they had both just said, but she had it; and though beauty of the hour passes, he who sees it will long remember it and the hour when it came.

"What are you thinking of?" he asked.

She leaned back in her chair and did not answer at once. Then she said:

"I don't know; I doubt if I was thinking of anything. It seems to me I wasn't. I think I was just being sort of sadly happy just then."

"Were you? Was it 'sadly,' too?"

"Don't you know?" she said. "It seems to me that only little children can be just happily happy. I think when we get older our happiest moments are like the one I had just then: it's as if we heard strains of minor music running through them—oh, so sweet, but oh, so sad!"

"But what makes it sad for *you*?"

"I don't know," she said, in a lighter tone. "Perhaps it's a kind of useless foreboding I seem to have pretty often. It may be that—or it may be poor papa."

"You *are* a funny, delightful girl, though!" Russell laughed. "When your father's so well again that he goes out walking in the evenings!"

"He does too much walking," Alice said. "Too much altogether, over at his new plant. But there isn't any stopping him." She laughed and shook her head. "When a man gets an ambition to be a multi-millionaire his family don't appear to have much weight with him. He'll walk all he wants to, in spite of them."

"I suppose so," Russell said, absently; then he leaned forward. "I wish I could understand better why you were 'sadly' happy."

Meanwhile, as Alice shed what further light she could on this point, the man ambitious to be a "multi-millionaire" was indeed walking too much for his own good. He had gone to bed, hoping to sleep well and rise early for a long day's work, but he could not rest, and now, in his nightgown and slippers, he was pacing the floor of his room.

"I wish I *did* know," he thought, over and over. "I *do* wish I knew how he feels about it."

Chapter XVIII

THAT WAS a thought almost continuously in his mind, even when he was hardest at work; and, as the days went on and he could not free himself, he became querulous about it. "I guess I'm the biggest dang fool alive," he told his wife as they sat together one evening. "I got plenty else to bother me, without worrying my head off about what *he* thinks. I can't help what he thinks; it's too late for that. So why should I keep pestering myself about it?"

"It'll wear off, Virgil," Mrs. Adams said, reassuringly. She was gentle and sympathetic with him, and for the first time in many years he would come to sit with her and talk, when he had finished his day's work. He had told her, evading her eye, "Oh, I don't blame you. You didn't get after me to do this on your own account; you couldn't help it."

"Yes; but it don't wear off," he complained. "This afternoon I was showing the men how I wanted my vats to go, and I caught my fool self standing there saying to my fool self, 'It's funny I don't hear how he feels about it from *some*-*body*.' I was saying it aloud, almost—and it *is* funny I don't hear anything!"

"Well, you see what it means, don't you, Virgil? It only means he hasn't said anything to anybody about it. Don't you think you're getting kind of morbid over it?"

"Maybe, maybe," he muttered.

"Why, yes," she said, briskly. "You don't realize what a little bit of a thing all this is to him. It's been a long, long while since the last time you even mentioned glue to him, and he's probably forgotten everything about it."

"You're off your base; it isn't like him to forget things," Adams returned, peevishly. "He may seem to forget 'em, but he don't."

"But he's not thinking about this, or you'd have heard from him before now."

Her husband shook his head. "Ah, that's just it!" he said. "Why *haven't* I heard from him?"

"It's all your morbidness, Virgil. Look at Walter: if Mr. Lamb held this up against you, would he still let Walter stay there? Wouldn't he have discharged Walter if he felt angry with you?"

"That dang boy!" Adams said. "If he *wanted* to come with me now, I wouldn't hardly let him. What do you suppose makes him so bull-headed?"

"But hasn't he a right to choose for himself?" she asked. "I suppose he feels he ought to stick to what he thinks is sure pay. As soon as he sees that you're going to succeed with the glue-works he'll want to be with you quick enough."

"Well, he better get a little sense in his head," Adams returned, crossly. "He wanted me to pay him a three-hundred-dollar bonus in advance, when anybody with a grain of common sense knows I need every penny I can lay my hands on!"

"Never mind," she said. "He'll come around later and be glad of the chance."

"He'll have to beg for it then! *I* won't ask him again."

"Oh, Walter will come out all right; you needn't worry. And don't you see that Mr. Lamb's not discharging him means there's no hard feeling against you, Virgil?"

"I can't make it out at all," he said, frowning. "The only thing I can *think* it means is that J. A. Lamb is so fair-minded—and of course he *is* one of the fair-mindedest men alive—I suppose that's the reason he hasn't fired Walter. He may know," Adams concluded, morosely—"he may know that's just another thing to make me feel all the meaner: keeping my boy there on a salary after I've done him an injury."

"Now, now!" she said, trying to comfort him. "You couldn't do anybody an injury to save your life, and everybody knows it."

"Well, anybody ought to know I wouldn't *want* to do an injury, but this world isn't built so't we can do just what we want." He paused, reflecting. "Of course there may be one explanation of why Walter's still there: J. A. maybe hasn't noticed that he *is* there. There's so many I expect he hardly knows him by sight."

"Well, just do quit thinking about it," she urged him. "It only bothers you without doing any good. Don't you know that?"

"Don't I, though!" he laughed, feebly. "I know it better'n anybody! How funny that is: when you know thinking about a thing only pesters you without helping anything at all, and yet you keep right on pestering yourself with it!"

"But *why?*" she said. "What's the use when you know you haven't done anything wrong, Virgil? You said yourself you were going to improve the process so much it would be different from the old one, and you'd *really* have a right to it."

Adams had persuaded himself of this when he yielded; he had found it necessary to persuade himself of it—though there was a part of him, of course, that remained unpersuaded; and this discomfiting part of him was what made his present trouble. "Yes, I know," he said. "That's true, but I can't quite seem to get away from the fact that the principle of the process is a good deal the same—well, it's more'n that; it's just *about* the same as the one he hired Campbell and me to work out for him. Truth is, nobody could tell the difference, and I don't know as there *is* any difference except in these improvements I'm making. Of course, the improvements do give me pretty near a perfect right to it, as a person might say; and that's one of the things I thought of putting in my letter to him; but I was afraid he'd just think I was trying to make up excuses, so I left it out. I kind of worried all the time I was writing that letter, because if he thought I *was* just making up excuses, why, it might set him just so much more against me."

Ever since Mrs. Adams had found that she was to have her way, the depths of her eyes had been troubled by a continuous uneasiness; and, although she knew it was there, and sometimes veiled it by keeping the revealing eyes averted from her husband and children, she could not always cover it under that assumption of absent-mindedness. The uneasy look became vivid, and her voice was slightly tremulous now, as she said, "But what if he *should* be against you—although I don't believe he is, of course—you told me he couldn't *do* anything to you, Virgil."

"No," he said, slowly. "I can't see how he could do anything. It was just a secret, not a patent; the thing ain't patentable. I've tried to think what he could do—supposing he was to want to—but I can't figure out anything at all that would be any harm to me. There isn't any way in the world it could be made a question of law. Only thing he could do'd be to *tell* people his side of it, and set 'em against me. I been kind of waiting for that to happen, all along."

She looked somewhat relieved. "So did I expect it," she said. "I was dreading it most on Alice's account: it might have—well, young men are so easily influenced and all. But so far as the business is concerned, what if Mr. Lamb did talk? That wouldn't amount to much. It wouldn't affect the business; not to hurt. And, besides, he isn't even doing that."

"No; anyhow not yet, it seems." And Adams sighed again, wistfully. "But I *would* give a good deal to know what he thinks!"

Before his surrender he had always supposed that if he did such an unthinkable thing as to seize upon the glue process for himself, what he would feel must be an overpowering shame. But shame is the rarest thing in the world: what he felt was this unremittent curiosity about his old employer's thoughts. It was an obsession, yet he did not want to hear what Lamb "thought" from Lamb himself, for Adams had a second obsession, and this was his dread of meeting the old man face to face. Such an encounter could happen only by chance and unexpectedly; since Adams would have avoided any deliberate meeting, so long as his legs had strength to carry him, even if Lamb came to the house to see him. But people do meet unexpectedly; and when Adams had to be down-town he kept away from the "wholesale district." One day he did see Lamb, as the latter went by in his car, impassive, going home to lunch; and Adams, in the crowd at a corner, knew that the old man had not seen him. Nevertheless, in a street-car, on the way back to his sheds, an hour later, he was still subject to little shivering seizures of horror.

He worked unceasingly, seeming to keep at it even in his sleep, for he always woke in the midst of a planning and estimating that must have been going on in his mind before consciousness of himself returned. Moreover, the work, thus urged, went rapidly, in spite of the high wages he had to pay his labourers for their short hours. "It eats money," he complained, and, in fact, by the time his vats and boilers were in place it had eaten almost all he could supply; but in addition to his equipment he now owned a stock of "raw material," raw indeed; and when operations should be a little further along he was confident his banker would be willing to "carry" him.

Six weeks from the day he had obtained his lease he began his glue-making. The terrible smells came out of the sheds and went writhing like snakes all through that quarter of the town. A smiling man, strolling and breathing the air with satisfaction, would turn a corner and smile no more, but hurry. However, coloured people had almost all the dwellings of this old section to themselves; and although even they were troubled, there was recompense for them. Being philosophic about what appeared to them as in the order of nature, they sought neither escape nor redress, and soon learned to bear what the wind brought them. They even made use of it to enrich those figures of speech with which the native impulses of coloured people decorate their communications: they flavoured metaphor, simile, and invective with it; and thus may be said to have enjoyed it. But the man who produced it took a hot bath as soon as he reached his home the evening of that first day when his manufacturing began. Then he put on fresh clothes; but after dinner he seemed to be haunted, and asked his wife if she "noticed anything."

She laughed and inquired what he meant.

"Seems to me as if that glue-works smell hadn't quit hanging to me," he explained. "Don't you notice it?"

"No! What an idea!"

He laughed, too, but uneasily; and told her he was sure "the dang glue smell" was somehow sticking to him. Later, he went outdoors and walked up and down the small yard in the dusk; but now and then he stood still, with his head lifted, and sniffed the air suspiciously. "Can *you* smell it?" he called to Alice, who sat upon the veranda, prettily dressed and waiting in a reverie.

"Smell what, papa?"

"That dang glue-works."

She did the same thing her mother had done: laughed, and said, "No! How foolish! Why, papa, it's over two miles from here!"

"You don't get it at all?" he insisted.

"The idea! The air is lovely to-night, papa."

The air did not seem lovely to him, for he was positive that he detected the taint. He wondered how far it carried, and if

J. A. Lamb would smell it, too, out on his own lawn a mile to the north; and if he did, would he guess what it was? Then Adams laughed at himself for such nonsense; but could not rid his nostrils of their disgust. To him the whole town seemed to smell of his glue-works.

Nevertheless, the glue was making, and his sheds were busy. "Guess we're stirrin' up this ole neighbourhood with more than the smell," his foreman remarked one morning.

"How's that?" Adams inquired.

"That great big, enormous ole dead butterine factory across the street from our lot," the man said. "Nothin' like settin' an example to bring real estate to life. That place is full o' carpenters startin' in to make a regular buildin' of it again. Guess you ought to have the credit of it, because you was the first man in ten years to see any possibilities in this neighbourhood."

Adams was pleased, and, going out to see for himself, heard a great hammering and sawing from within the building; while carpenters were just emerging gingerly upon the dangerous roof. He walked out over the dried mud of his deep lot, crossed the street, and spoke genially to a workman who was removing the broken glass of a window on the ground floor.

"Here! What's all this howdy-do over here?"

"Goin' to fix her all up, I guess," the workman said. "Big job it is, too."

"Sh' think it would be."

"Yes, sir; a pretty big job—a pretty big job. Got men at it on all four floors and on the roof. They're doin' it *right*."

"Who's doing it?"

"Lord! I d' know. Some o' these here big manufacturing corporations, I guess."

"What's it going to be?"

"They tell *me*," the workman answered—"they tell *me* she's goin' to be a butterine factory again. Anyways, I hope she won't be anything to smell like that glue-works you got over there—not while *I'm* workin' around her, anyways!"

"That smell's all right," Adams said. "You soon get used to it."

"You do?" The man appeared incredulous. "Listen! I was over in France: it's a good thing them Dutchmen never thought of it; we'd of had to quit!"

Adams laughed, and went back to his sheds. "I guess my foreman was right," he told his wife, that evening, with a little satisfaction. "As soon as one man shows enterprise enough to found an industry in a broken-down neighbourhood, somebody else is sure to follow. I kind of like the look of it: it'll help make our place seem sort of more busy and prosperous when it comes to getting a loan from the bank—and I got to get one mighty soon, too. I did think some that if things go as well as there's every reason to think they *ought* to, I might want to spread out and maybe get hold of that old factory myself; but I hardly expected to be able to handle a proposition of that size before two or three years from now, and anyhow there's room enough on the lot I got, if we need more buildings some day. Things are going about as fine as I could ask: I hired some girls to-day to do the bottling—coloured girls along about sixteen to twenty years old. Afterwhile, I expect to get a machine to put the stuff in the little bottles, when we begin to get good returns; but half a dozen of these coloured girls can do it all right now, by hand. We're getting to have really quite a little plant over there: yes, sir, quite a regular little plant!"

He chuckled, and at this cheerful sound, of a kind his wife had almost forgotten he was capable of producing, she ventured to put her hand upon his arm. They had gone outdoors, after dinner, taking two chairs with them, and were sitting through the late twilight together, keeping well away from the "front porch," which was not yet occupied, however. Alice was in her room changing her dress.

"Well, honey," Mrs. Adams said, taking confidence not only to put her hand upon his arm, but to revive this disused endearment;—"it's grand to have you so optimistic. Maybe some time you'll admit I was right, after all. Everything's going so well, it seems a pity you didn't take this—this step—long ago. Don't you think maybe so, Virgil?"

"Well—if I was ever going to, I don't know but I might as well of. I got to admit the proposition begins to look pretty good: I know the stuff'll sell, and I can't see a thing in the world to stop it. It does look good, and if—if——" He paused.

"If what?" she said, suddenly anxious.

He laughed plaintively, as if confessing a superstition. "It's funny—well, it's mighty funny about that smell. I've got so used to it at the plant I never seem to notice it at all over there. It's only when I get away. Honestly, can't you notice——?"

"Virgil!" She lifted her hand to strike his arm chidingly. "Do quit harping on that nonsense!"

"Oh, of course it don't amount to anything," he said. "A person can stand a good deal of just smell. It don't *worry* me any."

"I should think not—especially as there isn't any."

"Well," he said, "I feel pretty fair over the whole thing—a lot better'n I ever expected to, anyhow. I don't know as there's any reason I shouldn't tell you so."

She was deeply pleased with this acknowledgment, and her voice had tenderness in it as she responded: "There, honey! Didn't I always say you'd be glad if you did it?"

Embarrassed, he coughed loudly, then filled his pipe and lit it. "Well," he said, slowly, "it's a puzzle. Yes, sir, it's a puzzle."

"What is?"

"Pretty much everything, I guess."

As he spoke, a song came to them from a lighted window over their heads. Then the window darkened abruptly, but the song continued as Alice went down through the house to wait on the little veranda. "*Mi chiamano Mimi*," she sang, and in her voice throbbed something almost startling in its sweetness. Her father and mother listened, not speaking until the song stopped with the click of the wire screen at the front door as Alice came out.

"My!" said her father. "How sweet she does sing! I don't know as I ever heard her voice sound nicer than it did just then."

"There's something that makes it sound that way," his wife told him.

"I suppose so," he said, sighing. "I suppose so. You think——"

"She's just terribly in love with him!"

"I expect that's the way it ought to be," he said, then drew upon his pipe for reflection, and became murmurous with the symptoms of melancholy laughter. "It don't make things less of a puzzle, though, does it?"

"In what way, Virgil?"

"Why, here," he said—"here we go through all this muck and moil to help fix things nicer for her at home, and what's it all amount to? Seems like she's just gone ahead the way she'd 'a' gone anyhow; and *now*, I suppose, getting ready to up and leave us! Ain't that a puzzle to you? It is to me."

"Oh, but things haven't gone that far yet."

"Why, you just said——"

She gave a little cry of protest. "Oh, they aren't *engaged* yet. Of course they *will* be; he's just as much interested in her as she is in him, but——"

"Well, what's the trouble then?"

"You *are* a simple old fellow!" his wife exclaimed, and then rose from her chair. "That reminds me," she said.

"What of?" he asked. "What's my being simple remind you of?"

"Nothing!" she laughed. "It wasn't you that reminded me. It was just something that's been on my mind. I don't believe he's actually ever been inside our house!"

"Hasn't he?"

"I actually don't believe he ever has," she said. "Of course we must——" She paused, debating.

"We must what?"

"I guess I better talk to Alice about it right now," she said. "He don't usually come for about half an hour yet; I guess I've got time." And with that she walked away, leaving him to his puzzles.

Chapter XIX

ALICE WAS softly crooning to herself as her mother turned the corner of the house and approached through the dusk.

"Isn't it the most *beautiful* evening!" the daughter said. "*Why* can't summer last all year? Did you ever know a lovelier twilight than this, mama?"

Mrs. Adams laughed, and answered, "Not since I was your age, I expect."

Alice was wistful at once. "Don't they stay beautiful after my age?"

"Well, it's not the same thing."

"Isn't it? Not—ever?"

"You may have a different kind from mine," the mother said, a little sadly. "I think you will, Alice. You deserve——"

"No, I don't. I don't deserve anything, and I know it. But I'm getting a great deal these days—more than I ever dreamed *could* come to me. I'm—I'm pretty happy, mama!"

"Dearie!" Her mother would have kissed her, but Alice drew away.

"Oh, I don't mean——" She laughed nervously. "I wasn't meaning to tell you I'm *engaged*, mama. We're not. I mean —oh! things seem pretty beautiful in spite of all I've done to spoil 'em."

"You?" Mrs. Adams cried, incredulously. "What have you done to spoil anything?"

"Little things," Alice said. "A thousand little silly—oh, what's the use? He's so honestly what he is—just simple and good and intelligent—I feel a tricky mess beside him! I don't see why he likes me; and sometimes I'm afraid he wouldn't if he knew me."

"He'd just worship you," said the fond mother. "And the more he knew you, the more he'd worship you."

Alice shook her head. "He's not the worshiping kind. Not like that at all. He's more——"

But Mrs. Adams was not interested in this analysis, and she interrupted briskly, "Of course it's time your father and I showed some interest in him. I was just saying I actually don't believe he's ever been inside the house."

"No," Alice said, musingly; "that's true: I don't believe he has. Except when we've walked in the evening we've always sat out here, even those two times when it was drizzly. It's so much nicer."

"We'll have to do *something* or other, of course," her mother said.

"What like?"

"I was thinking——" Mrs. Adams paused. "Well, of course we could hardly put off asking him to dinner, or something, much longer."

Alice was not enthusiastic; so far from it, indeed, that there was a melancholy alarm in her voice. "Oh, mama, must we? Do you think so?"

"Yes, I do. I really do."

"Couldn't we—well, couldn't we wait?"

"It looks queer," Mrs. Adams said. "It isn't the thing at all for a young man to come as much as he does, and never more than just barely meet your father and mother. No. We ought to do something."

"But a dinner!" Alice objected. "In the first place, there isn't anybody I want to ask. There isn't anybody I *would* ask."

"I didn't mean trying to give a big dinner," her mother explained. "I just mean having him to dinner. That mulatto woman, Malena Burns, goes out by the day, and she could bring a waitress. We can get some flowers for the table and some to put in the living-room. We might just as well go ahead and do it to-morrow as any other time; because your father's in a fine mood, and I saw Malena this afternoon and told her I might want her soon. She said she didn't have any engagements this week, and I can let her know to-night. Suppose when he comes you ask him for to-morrow, Alice. Everything'll be very nice, I'm sure. Don't worry about it."

"Well—but——" Alice was uncertain.

"But don't you see, it looks so queer, not to do *something*?" her mother urged. "It looks so kind of poverty-stricken. We really oughtn't to wait any longer."

Alice assented, though not with a good heart. "Very well, I'll ask him, if you think we've got to."

"That matter's settled then," Mrs. Adams said. "I'll go telephone Malena, and then I'll tell your father about it."

But when she went back to her husband, she found him in an excited state of mind, and Walter standing before him in the darkness. Adams was almost shouting, so great was his vehemence.

"Hush, hush!" his wife implored, as she came near them. "They'll hear you out on the front porch!"

"I don't care who hears me," Adams said, harshly, though he tempered his loudness. "Do you want to know what this boy's asking me for? I thought he'd maybe come to tell me he'd got a little sense in his head at last, and a little decency about what's due his family! I thought he was going to ask me to take him into my plant. No, ma'am; *that's* not what he wants!"

"No, it isn't," Walter said. In the darkness his face could not be seen; he stood motionless, in what seemed an apathetic attitude; and he spoke quietly, "No," he repeated. "That isn't what I want."

"You stay down at that place," Adams went on, hotly, "instead of trying to be a little use to your family; and the only reason you're *allowed* to stay there is because Mr. Lamb's never happened to notice you *are* still there! You just wait——"

"You're off," Walter said, in the same quiet way. "He knows I'm there. He spoke to me yesterday: he asked me how I was getting along with my work."

"He did?" Adams said, seeming not to believe him.

"Yes. He did."

"What else did he say, Walter?" Mrs. Adams asked quickly.

"Nothin'. Just walked on."

"I don't believe he knew who you were," Adams declared.

"Think not? He called me 'Walter Adams.'"

At this Adams was silent; and Walter, after waiting a moment, said:

"Well, are you going to do anything about me? About what I told you I got to have?"

"What is it, Walter?" his mother asked, since Adams did not speak.

Walter cleared his throat, and replied in a tone as quiet as that he had used before, though with a slight huskiness, "I got to have three hundred and fifty dollars. You better get him to give it to me if you can."

Adams found his voice. "Yes," he said, bitterly. "That's all he asks! He won't do anything I ask *him* to, and in return he asks me for three hundred and fifty dollars! That's all!"

"What in the world!" Mrs. Adams exclaimed. "What *for*, Walter?"

"I got to have it," Walter said.

"But what *for*?"

His quiet huskiness did not alter. "I got to have it."

"But can't you tell us——"

"I got to have it."

"That's all you can get out of him," Adams said. "He seems to think it'll bring him in three hundred and fifty dollars!"

A faint tremulousness became evident in the husky voice. "Haven't you got it?"

"*No*, I haven't got it!" his father answered. "And I've got to go to a bank for more than my pay-roll next week. Do you think I'm a mint?"

"I don't understand what you mean, Walter," Mrs. Adams interposed, perplexed and distressed. "If your father had the money, of course he'd need every cent of it, especially just now, and, anyhow, you could scarcely expect him to give it to you, unless you told us what you want with it. But he hasn't got it."

"All right," Walter said; and after standing a moment more, in silence, he added, impersonally, "I don't see as you ever did anything much for me, anyhow—either of you."

Then, as if this were his valedictory, he turned his back upon them, walked away quickly, and was at once lost to their sight in the darkness.

"There's a fine boy to've had the trouble of raising!" Adams grumbled. "Just crazy, that's all."

"What in the world do you suppose he wants all that money for?" his wife said, wonderingly. "I can't imagine what he could *do* with it. I wonder——" She paused. "I wonder if he——"

"If he what?" Adams prompted her irritably.

"If he *could* have bad—associates."

"God knows!" said Adams. "*I* don't! It just looks to me like he had something in him I don't understand. You can't keep your eye on a boy all the time in a city this size, not a boy Walter's age. You got a girl pretty much in the house, but a boy'll follow his nature. *I* don't know what to do with him!"

Mrs. Adams brightened a little. "He'll come *out* all right," she said. "I'm sure he will. I'm sure he'd never be anything really bad: and he'll come around all right about the glue-works, too; you'll see. Of course every young man wants money—it doesn't prove he's doing anything wrong just because he asks you for it."

"No. All it proves to me is that he hasn't got good sense—asking me for three hundred and fifty dollars, when he knows as well as you do the position I'm in! If I wanted to, I couldn't hardly let him have three hundred and fifty cents, let alone dollars!"

"I'm afraid you'll have to let *me* have that much—and maybe a little more," she ventured, timidly; and she told him of her plans for the morrow. He objected vehemently.

"Oh, but Alice has probably asked him by this time," Mrs. Adams said. "It really must be done, Virgil: you don't want him to think she's ashamed of us, do you?"

"Well, go ahead, but just let me stay away," he begged. "Of course I expect to undergo a kind of talk with him, when he gets ready to say something to us about Alice, but I do hate to have to sit through a fashionable dinner."

"Why, it isn't going to bother you," she said; "just one young man as a guest."

"Yes, I know; but you want to have all this fancy cookin'; and I see well enough you're going to get that old dress suit out of the cedar chest in the attic, and try to make me put it on me."

"I do think you better, Virgil."

"I hope the moths have got in it," he said. "Last time I wore it was to the banquet, and it was pretty old then. Of course I didn't mind wearing it to the banquet so much, because that was what you might call quite an occasion." He spoke with some reminiscent complacency; "the banquet," an affair now five years past, having provided the one time in his life when he had been so distinguished among his fellow-citizens as to receive an invitation to be present, with some seven hundred others, at the annual eating and speech-making of the city's Chamber of Commerce. "Anyhow, as you say, I think it would look foolish of me to wear a dress suit for just one young man," he went on protesting, feebly. "What's the use of all so much howdy-do, anyway? You don't expect him to believe we put on all that style every night, do you? Is that what you're after?"

"Well, we want him to think we live nicely," she admitted.

"So that's it!" he said, querulously. "You want him to think that's our regular gait, do you? Well, he'll know better about me, no matter how you fix me up, because he saw me in my regular suit the evening she introduced me to him, and he could tell anyway I'm not one of these moving-picture sporting-men that's always got a dress suit on. Besides, you and Alice certainly have some idea he'll come *again*, haven't you? If they get things settled between 'em he'll be around the house and to meals most any time, won't he? You don't hardly expect to put on style all the time, I guess. Well, he'll see then that this kind of thing was all show-off and bluff, won't he? What about it?"

"Oh, well, by *that* time——" She left the sentence unfinished, as if absently. "You could let us have a little money for to-morrow, couldn't you, honey?"

"Oh, I reckon, I reckon," he mumbled. "A girl like Alice is some comfort: she don't come around acting as if she'd commit suicide if she didn't get three hundred and fifty dollars in the next five minutes. I expect I can spare five or six dollars for your show-off if I got to."

However, she finally obtained fifteen before his bedtime; and the next morning "went to market" after breakfast, leaving Alice to make the beds. Walter had not yet come downstairs. "You had better call him," Mrs. Adams said, as she departed with a big basket on her arm. "I expect he's pretty sleepy; he was out so late last night I didn't hear him come in, though I kept awake till after midnight, listening for him. Tell him he'll be late to work if he doesn't hurry; and see that he drinks his coffee, even if he hasn't time for anything else. And when Malena comes, get her started in the kitchen: show her where everything is." She waved her hand, as she set out for a corner where the cars stopped. "Everything'll be lovely. Don't forget about Walter."

Nevertheless, Alice forgot about Walter for a few minutes. She closed the door, went into the "living-room" absently, and stared vaguely at one of the old brown-plush rocking-chairs there. Upon her forehead were the little shadows of an apprehensive reverie, and her thoughts overlapped one another in a fretful jumble. "What will he think? These old chairs—they're hideous. I'll scrub those soot-streaks on the columns: it won't do any good, though. That long crack in the column—nothing can help it. What will he think of papa? I hope mama won't talk too much. When he thinks of Mildred's house, or of Henrietta's, or any of 'em, beside this—— She said she'd buy plenty of roses; that ought to help some. Nothing could be done about these horrible chairs: can't take 'em up in the attic—a room's got to have chairs! Might have rented some. No; if he ever comes again he'd see they weren't here. 'If he ever comes again'—oh, it won't be *that* bad! But it won't be what he expects. I'm responsible for what he expects: he expects just what the airs I've put on have made him expect. What did I want to pose so to him for—as if papa were a wealthy man and all that? What *will* he think? The photograph of the Colosseum's a rather good thing, though. It helps some—as if we'd bought it in Rome perhaps. I hope he'll think so; he believes I've been abroad, of course. The other night he said, 'You remember the feeling you get in the Sainte-Chapelle'—— There's another lie of mine, not saying I didn't remember because I'd never been there. What makes me do it? Papa *must* wear his evening clothes. But Walter——"

With that she recalled her mother's admonition, and went upstairs to Walter's door. She tapped upon it with her fingers.

"Time to get up, Walter. The rest of us had breakfast over half an hour ago, and it's nearly eight o'clock. You'll be late. Hurry down and I'll have some coffee and toast ready for you." There came no sound from within the room, so she rapped louder.

"Wake up, Walter!"

She called and rapped again, without getting any response, and then, finding that the door yielded to her, opened it and went in. Walter was not there.

He had been there, however; had slept upon the bed, though not inside the covers; and Alice supposed he must have come home so late that he had been too sleepy to take off his clothes. Near the foot of the bed was a shallow closet where he kept his "other suit" and his evening clothes; and the door stood open, showing a bare wall. Nothing whatever was in the closet, and Alice was rather surprised at this for a moment. "That's queer," she murmured; and then she decided that when he woke he found the clothes he had slept in "so mussy" he had put on his "other suit," and had gone out before breakfast with the mussed clothes to have them pressed, taking his evening things with them. Satisfied with this explanation, and failing to observe that it did not account for the absence of shoes from the closet floor, she nodded absently, "Yes, that must be it"; and, when her mother returned, told her that Walter had probably breakfasted down-town. They did not delay over this; the coloured woman had arrived, and the basket's disclosures were important.

"I stopped at Worlig's on the way back," said Mrs. Adams, flushed with hurry and excitement. "I bought a can of caviar there. I thought we'd have little sandwiches brought into the 'living-room' before dinner, the way you said they did when you went to that dinner at the——"

"But I think that was to go with cocktails, mama, and of course we haven't——"

"No," Mrs. Adams said. "Still, I think it would be nice. We can make them look very dainty, on a tray, and the waitress can bring them in. I thought we'd have the soup already on the table; and we can walk right out as soon as we have the sandwiches, so it won't get cold. Then, after the soup, Malena says she can make sweetbread patés with mushrooms: and for the meat course we'll have larded fillet. Malena's really a fancy cook, you know, and she says she can do anything like that to perfection. We'll have peas with the fillet, and potato balls and Brussels sprouts. Brussels sprouts are fashionable now, they told me at market. Then will come the chicken salad, and after that the ice-cream—she's going to make an angel-food cake to go with it—and then coffee and crackers and a new kind of cheese I got at Worlig's, he says is very fine."

Alice was alarmed. "Don't you think perhaps it's too much, mama?"

"It's better to have too much than too little," her mother said, cheerfully. "We don't want him to think we're the kind that skimp. Lord knows we have to enough, though, most of the time! Get the flowers in water, child. I bought 'em at market because they're so much cheaper there, but they'll keep fresh and nice. You fix 'em any way you want. Hurry! It's got to be a busy day."

She had bought three dozen little roses. Alice took them and began to arrange them in vases, keeping the stems separated as far as possible so that the clumps would look larger. She put half a dozen in each of three vases in the "living-room," placing one vase on the table in the center of the room, and one at each end of the mantelpiece. Then she took the rest of the roses to the dining-room; but she postponed the arrangement of them until the table should be set, just before dinner. She was thoughtful; planning to dry the stems and lay them on the tablecloth like a vine of roses running in a delicate design, if she found that the dozen and a half she had left were enough for that. If they weren't she would arrange them in a vase.

She looked a long time at the little roses in the basin of water, where she had put them; then she sighed, and went away to heavier tasks, while her mother worked in the kitchen with Malena. Alice dusted the "living-room" and the dining-room vigorously, though all the time with a look that grew more and more pensive; and having dusted everything, she wiped the furniture; rubbed it hard. After that, she washed the floors and the woodwork.

Emerging from the kitchen at noon, Mrs. Adams found her daughter on hands and knees, scrubbing the bases of the columns between the hall and the "living-room."

"Now, dearie," she said, "you mustn't tire yourself out, and you'd better come and eat something. Your father said he'd get a bite down-town to-day—he was going down to the bank—and Walter eats down-town all the time lately, so I thought we wouldn't bother to set the table for lunch. Come on and we'll have something in the kitchen."

"No," Alice said, dully, as she went on with her work. "I don't want anything."

Her mother came closer to her. "Why, what's the matter?" she asked, briskly. "You seem kind of pale, to me; and you don't look—you don't look *happy*."

"Well——" Alice began, uncertainly, but said no more.

"See here!" Mrs. Adams exclaimed. "This is all just for you! You ought to be *enjoying* it. Why, it's the first time we've

—we've entertained in I don't know how long! I guess it's almost since we had that little party when you were eighteen. What's the matter with you?"

"Nothing. I don't know."

"But, dearie, aren't you looking *forward* to this evening?"

The girl looked up, showing a pallid and solemn face. "Oh, yes, of course," she said, and tried to smile. "Of course we had to do it—I do think it'll be nice. Of course I'm looking forward to it."

Chapter XX

SHE WAS indeed "looking forward" to that evening, but in a cloud of apprehension; and, although she could never have guessed it, this was the simultaneous condition of another person—none other than the guest for whose pleasure so much cooking and scrubbing seemed to be necessary. Moreover, Mr. Arthur Russell's premonitions were no product of mere coincidence; neither had any magical sympathy produced them. His state of mind was rather the result of rougher undercurrents which had all the time been running beneath the surface of a romantic friendship.

Never shrewder than when she analyzed the gentlemen, Alice did not libel him when she said he was one of those quiet men who are a bit flirtatious, by which she meant that he was a bit "susceptible," the same thing—and he had proved himself susceptible to Alice upon his first sight of her. "There!" he said to himself. "Who's that?" And in the crowd of girls at his cousin's dance, all strangers to him, she was the one he wanted to know.

Since then, his summer evenings with her had been as secluded as if, for three hours after the falling of dusk, they two had drawn apart from the world to some dear bower of their own. The little veranda was that glamorous nook, with a faint golden light falling through the glass of the closed door upon Alice, and darkness elsewhere, except for the one round globe of the street lamp at the corner. The people who passed along the sidewalk, now and then, were only shadows with voices, moving vaguely under the maple trees that loomed in obscure contours against the stars. So, as the two sat together, the back of the world was the wall and closed door behind them; and Russell, when he was away from Alice, always thought of her as sitting there before the closed door. A glamour was about her thus, and a spell upon him; but he had a formless anxiety never put into words: all the pictures of her in his mind stopped at the closed door.

He had another anxiety; and, for the greater part, this was of her own creating. She had too often asked him (no matter how gaily) what he heard about her; too often begged him not to hear anything. Then, hoping to forestall whatever he might hear, she had been at too great pains to account for it, to discredit and mock it; and, though he laughed at her for this, telling her truthfully he did not even hear her mentioned, the everlasting irony that deals with all such human forefendings prevailed.

Lately, he had half confessed to her what a nervousness she had produced. "You make me dread the day when I'll hear somebody speaking of you. You're getting me so upset about it that if I ever hear anybody so much as say the name 'Alice Adams,' I'll run!" The confession was but half of one because he laughed; and she took it for an assurance of loyalty in the form of burlesque. She misunderstood: he laughed, but his nervousness was genuine.

After any stroke of events, whether a happy one or a catastrophe, we see that the materials for it were a long time gathering, and the only marvel is that the stroke was not prophesied. What bore the air of fatal coincidence may remain fatal indeed, to this later view; but, with the haphazard aspect dispelled, there is left for scrutiny the same ancient hint from the Infinite to the effect that since events have never yet failed to be law-abiding, perhaps it were well for us to deduce that they will continue to be so until further notice.

. . . On the day that was to open the closed door in the background of his pictures of Alice, Russell lunched with his relatives. There were but the four people, Russell and Mildred and her mother and father, in the great, cool dining-room. Arched French windows, shaded by awnings, admitted a mellow light and looked out upon a green lawn ending in a long conservatory, which revealed through its glass panes a carnival of plants in luxuriant blossom. From his seat at the table, Russell glanced out at this pretty display, and informed his cousins that he was surprised. "You have such a glorious spread of flowers all over the house," he said, "I didn't suppose you'd have any left out yonder. In fact, I didn't know there were so many splendid flowers in the world."

Mrs. Palmer, large, calm, fair, like her daughter, responded with a mild reproach: "That's because you haven't been cousinly enough to get used to them, Arthur. You've almost taught us to forget what you look like."

In defense Russell waved a hand toward her husband. "You see, he's begun to keep me so hard at work——"

But Mr. Palmer declined the responsibility. "Up to four or five in the afternoon, perhaps," he said. "After that, the young gentleman is as much a stranger to me as he is to my family. I've been wondering who she could be."

"When a man's preoccupied there must be a lady then?" Russell inquired.

"That seems to be the view of your sex," Mrs. Palmer suggested. "It was my husband who said it, not Mildred or I."

Mildred smiled faintly. "Papa may be singular in his ideas; they may come entirely from his own experience, and have nothing to do with Arthur."

"Thank you, Mildred," her cousin said, bowing to her gratefully. "You seem to understand my character—and your father's quite as well!"

However, Mildred remained grave in the face of this customary pleasantry, not because the old jest, worn round, like what preceded it, rolled in an old groove, but because of some preoccupation of her own. Her faint smile had disappeared, and, as her cousin's glance met hers, she looked down; yet not before he had seen in her eyes the flicker of something like a question—a question both poignant and dismayed. He may have understood it; for his own smile vanished at once in favour of a reciprocal solemnity.

"You see, Arthur," Mrs. Palmer said, "Mildred is always a good cousin. She and I stand by you, even if you do stay away from us for weeks and weeks." Then, observing that he appeared to be so occupied with a bunch of iced grapes upon his plate that he had not heard her, she began to talk to her husband, asking him what was "going on down-town."

Arthur continued to eat his grapes, but he ventured to look again at Mildred after a few moments. She, also, appeared to be occupied with a bunch of grapes though she ate none, and only pulled them from their stems. She sat straight, her features as composed and pure as those of a new marble saint in a cathedral niche; yet her downcast eyes seemed to conceal many thoughts; and her cousin, against his will, was more aware of what these thoughts might be than of the leisurely conversation between her father and mother. All at once, however, he heard something that startled him, and he listened—and here was the effect of all Alice's forefendings; he listened from the first with a sinking heart.

Mr. Palmer, mildly amused by what he was telling his wife, had just spoken the words, "this Virgil Adams." What he had said was, "this Virgil Adams—that's the man's name. Queer case."

"Who told you?" Mrs. Palmer inquired, not much interested.

"Alfred Lamb," her husband answered. "He was laughing about his father, at the club. You see the old gentleman takes a great pride in his judgment of men, and always boasted to his sons that he'd never in his life made a mistake in trusting the wrong man. Now Alfred and James Albert, Junior, think they have a great joke on him; and they've twitted him so much about it he'll scarcely speak to them. From the first, Alfred says, the old chap's only repartee was, 'You wait and you'll see!' And they've asked him so often to show them what they're going to see that he won't say anything at all!"

"He's a funny old fellow," Mrs. Palmer observed. "But he's so shrewd I can't imagine his being deceived for such a long time. Twenty years, you said?"

"Yes, longer than that, I understand. It appears when this man—this Adams—was a young clerk, the old gentleman trusted him with one of his business secrets, a glue process that Mr. Lamb had spent some money to get hold of. The old chap thought this Adams was going to have quite a future with the Lamb concern, and of course never dreamed he was dishonest. Alfred says this Adams hasn't been of any real use for years, and they should have let him go as dead wood, but the old gentleman wouldn't hear of it, and insisted on his being kept on the payroll; so they just decided to look on it as a sort of pension. Well, one morning last March the man had an attack of some sort down there, and Mr. Lamb got his own car out and went home with him, himself, and worried about him and went to see him no end, all the time he was ill."

"He would," Mrs. Palmer said, approvingly. "He's a kind-hearted creature, that old man."

Her husband laughed. "Alfred says he thinks his kind-heartedness is about cured! It seems that as soon as the man got well again he deliberately walked off with the old gentleman's glue secret. Just calmly stole it! Alfred says he believes that if he had a stroke in the office now, himself, his father wouldn't lift a finger to help him!"

Mrs. Palmer repeated the name to herself thoughtfully. "'Adams'—'Virgil Adams.' You said his name was Virgil Adams?"

"Yes."

She looked at her daughter. "Why, you know who that is, Mildred," she said, casually. "It's that Alice Adams's father, isn't it? Wasn't his name Virgil Adams?"

"I think it is," Mildred said.

Mrs. Palmer turned toward her husband. "You've seen this Alice Adams here. Mr. Lamb's pet swindler must be her father."

Mr. Palmer passed a smooth hand over his neat gray hair, which was not disturbed by this effort to stimulate recollection. "Oh, yes," he said. "Of course—certainly. Quite a good-looking girl—one of Mildred's friends. How queer!"

Mildred looked up, as if in a little alarm, but did not speak. Her mother set matters straight. "Fathers *are* amusing," she said smilingly to Russell, who was looking at her, though how fixedly she did not notice; for she turned from him at once to enlighten her husband. "Every girl who meets Mildred, and tries to push the acquaintance by coming here until the poor child has to hide, isn't a *friend* of hers, my dear!"

Mildred's eyes were downcast again, and a faint colour rose in her cheeks. "Oh, I shouldn't put it quite that way about Alice Adams," she said, in a low voice. "I saw something of her for a time. She's not unattractive—in a way."

Mrs. Palmer settled the whole case of Alice carelessly. "A pushing sort of girl," she said. "A very pushing little person."

"I——" Mildred began; and, after hesitating, concluded, "I rather dropped her."

"Fortunate you've done so," her father remarked, cheerfully. "Especially since various members of the Lamb connection are here frequently. They mightn't think you'd show great tact in having her about the place." He laughed, and turned to his cousin. "All this isn't very interesting to poor Arthur. How terrible people are with a newcomer in a town; they talk as if he knew all about everybody!"

"But we don't know anything about these queer people, ourselves," said Mrs. Palmer. "We know something about the girl, of course—she used to be a bit *too* conspicuous, in fact! However, as you say, we might find a subject more interesting for Arthur." She smiled whimsically upon the young man. "Tell the truth," she said. "Don't you fairly detest going into business with that tyrant yonder?"

"What? Yes—I beg your pardon!" he stammered.

"You were right," Mrs. Palmer said to her husband. "You've bored him so, talking about thievish clerks, he can't even answer an honest question."

But Russell was beginning to recover his outward composure. "Try me again," he said. "I'm afraid I was thinking of something else."

This was the best he found to say. There was a part of him that wanted to protest and deny, but he had not heat enough, in the chill that had come upon him. Here was the first "mention" of Alice, and with it the reason why it was the first: Mr. Palmer had difficulty in recalling her, and she happened to be spoken of, only because her father's betrayal of a benefactor's trust had been so peculiarly atrocious that, in the view of the benefactor's family, it contained enough of the element of humour to warrant a mild laugh at a club. There was the deadliness of the story: its lack of malice, even of resentment. Deadlier still were Mrs. Palmer's phrases: "a pushing sort of girl," "a very pushing little person," and "used to be a bit *too* conspicuous, in fact." But she spoke placidly and by chance; being as obviously without unkindly motive as Mr. Palmer was when he related the cause of Alfred Lamb's amusement. Her opinion of the obscure young lady momentarily her topic had been expressed, moreover, to her husband, and at her own table. She sat there, large, kind, serene—a protest might astonish but could not change her; and Russell, crumpling in his strained fingers the lace-edged little web of a napkin on his knee, found heart enough to grow red, but not enough to challenge her.

She noticed his colour, and attributed it to the embarrassment of a scrupulously gallant gentleman caught in a lapse of attention to a lady. "Don't be disturbed," she said, benevolently. "People aren't expected to listen all the time to their relatives. A high colour's very becoming to you, Arthur; but it really isn't necessary between cousins. You can always be informal enough with us to listen only when you care to."

His complexion continued to be ruddier than usual, however, throughout the meal, and was still somewhat tinted when Mrs. Palmer rose. "The man's bringing you cigarettes here," she said, nodding to the two gentlemen. "We'll give you a chance to do the sordid kind of talking we know you really like. Afterwhile, Mildred will show you what's in bloom in the hothouse, if you wish, Arthur."

Mildred followed her, and, when they were alone in another of the spacious rooms, went to a window and looked out, while her mother seated herself near the center of the room in a gilt armchair, mellowed with old Aubusson tapestry. Mrs. Palmer looked thoughtfully at her daughter's back, but did not speak to her until coffee had been brought for them.

"Thanks," Mildred said, not turning, "I don't care for any coffee, I believe."

"No?" Mrs. Palmer said, gently. "I'm afraid our good-looking cousin won't think you're very talkative, Mildred. You spoke only about twice at lunch. I shouldn't care for him to get the idea you're piqued because he's come here so little lately, should you?"

"No, I shouldn't," Mildred answered in a low voice, and with that she turned quickly, and came to sit near her mother. "But it's what I am afraid of! Mama, did you notice how red he got?"

"You mean when he was caught not listening to a question of mine? Yes; it's very becoming to him."

"Mama, I don't think that was the reason. I don't think it was because he wasn't listening, I mean."

"No?"

"I think his colour and his not listening came from the same reason," Mildred said, and although she had come to sit near her mother, she did not look at her. "I think it happened because you and papa——" She stopped.

"Yes?" Mrs. Palmer said, good-naturedly, to prompt her. "Your father and I did something embarrassing?"

"Mama, it was because of those things that came out about Alice Adams."

"How could that bother Arthur? Does he know her?"

"Don't you remember?" the daughter asked. "The day after my dance I mentioned how odd I thought it was in him—I was a little disappointed in him. I'd been seeing that he met everybody, of course, but she was the only girl *he* asked to meet; and he did it as soon as he noticed her. I hadn't meant to have him meet her—in fact, I was rather sorry I'd felt I had to ask her, because she—oh, well, she's the sort that 'tries for the new man,' if she has half a chance; and sometimes they seem quite fascinated—for a time, that is. I thought Arthur was above all that; or at the very least I gave him credit for being too sophisticated."

"I see," Mrs. Palmer said, thoughtfully. "I remember now that you spoke of it. You said it seemed a little peculiar, but of course it really wasn't: a 'new man' has nothing to go by, except his own first impressions. You can't blame poor Arthur—she's quite a piquant looking little person. You think he's seen something of her since then?"

Mildred nodded slowly. "I never dreamed such a thing till yesterday, and even then I rather doubted it—till he got so red, just now! I was surprised when he asked to meet her, but he just danced with her once and didn't mention her afterward; I forgot all about it—in fact, I virtually forgot all about *her*. I'd seen quite a little of her——"

"Yes," said Mrs. Palmer. "She did keep coming here!"

"But I'd just about decided that it really wouldn't do," Mildred went on. "She isn't—well, I didn't admire her."

"No," her mother assented, and evidently followed a direct connection of thought in a speech apparently irrelevant. "I understand the young Malone wants to marry Henrietta. I hope she won't; he seems rather a gross type of person."

"Oh, he's just one," Mildred said. "I don't know that he and Alice Adams were ever engaged—she never told me so. She may not have been engaged to any of them; she was just enough among the other girls to get talked about—and one of the reasons I felt a little inclined to be nice to her was that they seemed to be rather edging her out of the circle. It wasn't long before I saw they were right, though. I happened to mention I was going to give a dance and she pretended to take it as a matter of course that I meant to invite her brother—at least, I thought she pretended; she may have really believed it. At any rate, I had to send him a card; but I didn't intend to be let in for that sort of thing again, of course. She's what you said, 'pushing'; though I'm awfully sorry you said it."

"Why shouldn't I have said it, my dear?"

"Of course I didn't say 'shouldn't,'" Mildred explained, gravely. "I meant only that I'm sorry it happened."

"Yes; but why?"

"Mama"— Mildred turned to her, leaning forward and speaking in a lowered voice—"Mama, at first the change was so little it seemed as if Arthur hardly knew it himself. He'd been lovely to me always, and he was still lovely to me—but —oh, well, you've understood—after my dance it was more as if it was just his nature and his training to be lovely to me, as he would be to everyone—a kind of politeness. He'd never said he *cared* for me, but after that I could see he didn't. It was clear —after that. I didn't know what had happened; I couldn't think of anything I'd done. Mama—it was Alice Adams."

Mrs. Palmer set her little coffee-cup upon the table beside her, calmly following her own motion with her eyes, and not seeming to realize with what serious entreaty her daughter's gaze was fixed upon her. Mildred repeated the last sentence of her revelation, and introduced a stress of insistence.

"Mama, it *was* Alice Adams!"

But Mrs. Palmer declined to be greatly impressed, so far as her appearance went, at least; and to emphasize her refusal, she smiled indulgently. "What makes you think so?"

"Henrietta told me yesterday."

At this Mrs. Palmer permitted herself to laugh softly aloud. "Good heavens! Is Henrietta a sooth-sayer? Or is she Arthur's particular *confidante*?"

"No. Ella Dowling told her."

Mrs. Palmer's laughter continued. "Now we have it!" she exclaimed. "It's a game of gossip: Arthur tells Ella, Ella tells Henrietta, and Henrietta tells——"

"Don't laugh, please, mama," Mildred begged. "Of course Arthur didn't tell anybody. It's roundabout enough, but it's true. I know it! I hadn't quite believed it, but I knew it was true when he got so red. He looked—oh, for a second or so he looked—stricken! He thought I didn't notice it. Mama, he's been to see her almost every evening lately. They take long walks together. That's why he hasn't been here."

Of Mrs. Palmer's laughter there was left only her indulgent smile, which she had not allowed to vanish. "Well, what of it?" she said.

"Mama!"

"Yes," said Mrs. Palmer. "What of it?"

"But don't you see?" Mildred's well-tutored voice, though modulated and repressed even in her present emotion, nevertheless had a tendency to quaver. "It's true. Frank Dowling was going to see her one evening and he saw Arthur sitting on the stoop with her, and didn't go in. And Ella used to go to school with a girl who lives across the street from her. She told Ella——"

"Oh, I understand," Mrs. Palmer interrupted. "Suppose he does go there. My dear, I said, 'What of it?'"

"I don't see what you mean, mama. I'm so afraid he might think we knew about it, and that you and papa said those things about her and her father on that account—as if we abused them because he goes there instead of coming here."

"Nonsense!" Mrs. Palmer rose, went to a window, and, turning there, stood with her back to it, facing her daughter and looking at her cheerfully. "Nonsense, my dear! It was perfectly clear that she was mentioned by accident, and so was her father. What an extraordinary man! If Arthur makes friends with people like that, he certainly knows better than to expect to hear favourable opinions of them. Besides, it's only a little passing thing with him."

"Mama! When he goes there almost every——"

"Yes," Mrs. Palmer said, dryly. "It seems to me I've heard somewhere that other young men have gone there 'almost every!' She doesn't last, apparently. Arthur's gallant, and he's impressionable—but he's fastidious, and fastidiousness is always the check on impressionableness. A girl belongs to her family, too—and this one does especially, it strikes me! Arthur's very sensible; he sees more than you'd think."

Mildred looked at her hopefully. "Then you don't believe he's likely to imagine we said those things of her in any meaning way?"

At this, Mrs. Palmer laughed again. "There's one thing you seem not to have noticed, Mildred."

"What's that?"

"It seems to have escaped your attention that he never said a word."

"Mightn't that mean——?" Mildred began, but she stopped.

"No, it mightn't," her mother replied, comprehending easily. "On the contrary, it might mean that instead of his feeling it too deeply to speak, he was getting a little illumination."

Mildred rose and came to her. "*Why* do you suppose he never told us he went there? Do you think he's—do you think he's pleased with her, and yet ashamed of it? *Why* do you suppose he's never spoken of it?"

"Ah, that," Mrs. Palmer said;—"that might possibly be her own doing. If it is, she's well paid by what your father and I said, because we wouldn't have said it if we'd known that Arthur——" She checked herself quickly. Looking over her daughter's shoulder, she saw the two gentlemen coming from the corridor toward the wide doorway of the room; and she greeted them cheerfully. "If you've finished with each other for a while," she added, "Arthur may find it a relief to put his thoughts on something prettier than a trust company—and more fragrant."

Arthur came to Mildred.

"Your mother said at lunch that perhaps you'd——"

"I didn't say 'perhaps,' Arthur," Mrs. Palmer interrupted, to correct him. "I said she would. If you care to see and smell those lovely things out yonder, she'll show them to you. Run along, children!"

Half an hour later, glancing from a window, she saw them come from the hothouses and slowly cross the lawn. Arthur had a fine rose in his buttonhole and looked profoundly thoughtful.

Chapter XXI

THAT MORNING and noon had been warm, though the stirrings of a feeble breeze made weather not flagrantly intemperate; but at about three o'clock in the afternoon there came out of the southwest a heat like an affliction sent upon an accursed people, and the air was soon dead of it. Dripping negro ditch-diggers whooped with satires praising hell and hot weather, as the tossing shovels flickered up to the street level, where sluggish male pedestrians carried coats upon hot arms, and fanned themselves with straw hats, or, remaining covered, wore soaked handkerchiefs between scalp and straw. Clerks drooped in silent, big department stores; stenographers in offices kept as close to electric fans as the intervening bulk of their employers would let them; guests in hotels left the lobbies and went to lie unclad upon their beds; while in hospitals the patients murmured querulously against the heat, and perhaps against some noisy motorist who strove to feel the air by splitting it, not troubled by any foreboding that he, too, that hour next week, might need quiet near a hospital. The "hot spell" was a true spell, one upon men's spirits; for it was so hot that, in suburban outskirts, golfers crept slowly back over the low undulations of their club lands, abandoning their matches and returning to shelter.

Even on such a day, sizzling work had to be done, as in winter. There were glowing furnaces to be stoked, liquid metals to be poured; but such tasks found seasoned men standing to them; and in all the city probably no brave soul challenged the heat more gamely than Mrs. Adams did, when, in a corner of her small and fiery kitchen, where all day long her hired African immune cooked fiercely, she pressed her husband's evening clothes with a hot iron. No doubt she risked her life, but she risked it cheerfully in so good and necessary a service for him. She would have given her life for him at any time, and both his and her own for her children.

Unconscious of her own heroism, she was surprised to find herself rather faint when she finished her ironing. However, she took heart to believe that the clothes looked better, in spite of one or two scorched places; and she carried them upstairs to her husband's room before increasing blindness forced her to grope for the nearest chair. Then, trying to rise and walk, without having sufficiently recovered, she had to sit down again; but after a little while she was able to get upon her feet; and, keeping her hand against the wall, moved successfully to the door of her own room. Here she wavered; might have gone down, had she not been stimulated by the thought of how much depended upon her;—she made a final great effort, and floundered across the room to her bureau, where she kept some simple restoratives. They served her need, or her faith in them did; and she returned to her work.

She went down the stairs, keeping a still tremulous hand upon the rail; but she smiled brightly when Alice looked up from below, where the woodwork was again being tormented with superfluous attentions.

"Alice, *don't*!" her mother said, commiseratingly. "You did all that this morning and it looks lovely. What's the use of wearing yourself out on it? You ought to be lying down, so's to look fresh for to-night."

"Hadn't you better lie down yourself?" the daughter returned. " Are you ill, mama?"

"Certainly not. What in the world makes you think so?"

"You look pretty pale," Alice said, and sighed heavily. "It makes me ashamed, having you work so hard—for me."

"How foolish! I think it's fun, getting ready to entertain a little again, like this. I only wish it hadn't turned so hot: I'm afraid your poor father'll suffer—his things are pretty heavy, I noticed. Well, it'll do him good to bear something for style's sake this once, anyhow!" She laughed, and coming to Alice, bent down and kissed her. "Dearie," she said, tenderly, "wouldn't you please slip upstairs now and take just a little teeny nap to please your mother?"

But Alice responded only by moving her head slowly, in token of refusal.

"Do!" Mrs. Adams urged. "You don't want to look worn out, do you?"

"I'll *look* all right," Alice said, huskily. "Do you like the way I've arranged the furniture now? I've tried all the different ways it'll go."

"It's lovely," her mother said, admiringly. "I thought the last way you had it was pretty, too. But you know best; I never knew anybody with so much taste. If you'd only just quit now, and take a little rest——"

"There'd hardly be time, even if I wanted to; it's after five —but I couldn't; really, I couldn't. How do you think we can manage about Walter—to see that he wears his evening things, I mean?"

Mrs. Adams pondered. "I'm afraid he'll make a lot of objections, on account of the weather and everything. I wish we'd had a chance to tell him last night or this morning. I'd have telephoned to him this afternoon except—well, I scarcely like to call him up at that place, since your father——"

"No, of course not, mama."

"If Walter gets home late," Mrs. Adams went on, "I'll just slip out and speak to him, in case Mr. Russell's here before he comes. I'll just tell him he's *got* to hurry and get his things on."

"Maybe he won't come home to dinner," Alice suggested, rather hopefully. "Sometimes he doesn't."

"No; I think he'll be here. When he doesn't come he usually telephones by this time to say not to wait for him; he's very thoughtful about that. Well, it really is getting late: I must go and tell her she ought to be preparing her fillet. Dearie, *do* rest a little."

"You'd much better do that yourself," Alice called after her, but Mrs. Adams shook her head cheerily, not pausing on her way to the fiery kitchen.

Alice continued her useless labours for a time; then carried her bucket to the head of the cellar stairway, where she left it upon the top step; and, closing the door, returned to the "living-room." Again she changed the positions of the old plush rocking-chairs, moving them into the corners where she thought they might be least noticeable; and while thus engaged she was startled by a loud ringing of the door-bell. For a moment her face was panic-stricken, and she stood staring; then she realized that Russell would not arrive for another hour, at the earliest, and recovering her equipoise, went to the door.

Waiting there, in a languid attitude, was a young coloured woman, with a small bundle under her arm and something malleable in her mouth. "Listen," she said. "You folks expectin' a coloured lady?"

"No," said Alice. "Especially not at the front door."

"Listen," the coloured woman said again. "Listen. Say, listen. Ain't they another coloured lady awready here by the day? Listen. Ain't Miz Malena Burns here by the day this evenin'? Say, listen. This the number house she give *me*."

"Are you the waitress?" Alice asked, dismally.

"Yes'm, if Malena here."

"Malena is here," Alice said, and hesitated; but she decided not to send the waitress to the back door; it might be a risk. She let her in. "What's your name?"

"Me? I'm name' Gertrude. Miss Gertrude Collamus."

"Did you bring a cap and apron?"

Gertrude took the little bundle from under her arm. "Yes'm. I'm all fix'."

"I've already set the table," Alice said. "I'll show you what we want done."

She led the way to the dining-room, and, after offering some instruction there, received by Gertrude with languor and a slowly moving jaw, she took her into the kitchen, where the cap and apron were put on. The effect was not fortunate; Gertrude's eyes were noticeably bloodshot, an affliction made more apparent by the white cap; and Alice drew her mother apart, whispering anxiously,

"Do you suppose it's too late to get someone else?"

"I'm afraid it is," Mrs. Adams said. "Malena says it was hard enough to get *her*! You have to pay them so much that they only work when they feel like it."

"Mama, could you ask her to wear her cap straighter? Every time she moves her head she gets it on one side, and her skirt's too long behind and too short in front—and oh, I've *never* seen such *feet*!" Alice laughed desolately. "And she *must* quit that terrible chewing!"

"Never mind; I'll get to work with her. I'll straighten her out all I can, dearie; don't worry." Mrs. Adams patted her daughter's shoulder encouragingly. "Now *you* can't do another thing, and if you don't run and begin dressing you won't be ready. It'll only take me a minute to dress, myself, and I'll be down long before you will. Run, darling! I'll look after everything."

Alice nodded vaguely, went up to her room, and, after only a moment with her mirror, brought from her closet the dress of white organdie she had worn the night when she met Russell for the first time. She laid it carefully upon her bed, and began to make ready to put it on. Her mother came in, half an hour later, to "fasten" her.

"*I'm* all dressed," Mrs. Adams said, briskly. "Of course it doesn't matter. He won't know what the rest of us even look like: How could he? I know I'm an old *sight*, but all I want is to look respectable. Do I?"

"You look like the best woman in the world; that's all!" Alice said, with a little gulp.

Her mother laughed and gave her a final scrutiny. "You might use just a tiny bit more colour, dearie—I'm afraid the excitement's made you a little pale. And you *must* brighten up! There's sort of a look in your eyes as if you'd got in a trance and couldn't get out. You've had it all day. I must run: your father wants me to help him with his studs. Walter hasn't come yet, but I'll look after him; don't worry. And you better *hurry*, dearie, if you're going to take any time fixing the flowers on the table."

She departed, while Alice sat at the mirror again, to follow her advice concerning a "tiny bit more colour." Before she had finished, her father knocked at the door, and, when she responded, came in. He was dressed in the clothes his wife had pressed; but he had lost substantially in weight since they were made for him; no one would have thought that they had been pressed. They hung from him voluminously, seeming to be the clothes of a larger man.

"Your mother's gone downstairs," he said, in a voice of distress. "One of the buttonholes in my shirt is too large and I can't keep the dang thing fastened. *I* don't know what to do about it! I only got one other white shirt, and it's kind of ruined: I tried it before I did this one. Do you s'pose you could do anything?"

"I'll see," she said.

"My collar's got a frayed edge," he complained, as she examined his troublesome shirt. "It's a good deal like wearing a saw; but I expect it'll wilt down flat pretty soon, and not bother me long. I'm liable to wilt down flat, myself, I expect;

I don't know as I remember any such hot night in the last ten or twelve years." He lifted his head and sniffed the flaccid air, which was laden with a heavy odour. "My, but that smell is pretty strong!" he said.

"Stand still, please, papa," Alice begged him. "I can't see what's the matter if you move around. How absurd you are about your old glue smell, papa! There isn't a vestige of it, of course."

"I didn't mean glue," he informed her. "I mean cabbage. Is that fashionable now, to have cabbage when there's company for dinner?"

"That isn't cabbage, papa. It's Brussels sprouts."

"Oh, is it? I don't mind it much, because it keeps that glue smell off me, but it's fairly strong. I expect you don't notice it so much because you been in the house with it all along, and got used to it while it was growing."

"It is pretty dreadful," Alice said. "Are all the windows open downstairs?"

"I'll go down and see, if you'll just fix that hole up for me."

"I'm afraid I can't," she said. "Not unless you take your shirt off and bring it to me. I'll have to sew the hole smaller."

"Oh, well, I'll go ask your mother to——"

"No," said Alice. "She's got everything on her hands. Run and take it off. Hurry, papa; I've got to arrange the flowers on the table before he comes."

He went away, and came back presently, half undressed, bringing the shirt. "There's *one* comfort," he remarked, pensively, as she worked. "I've got that collar off—for a while, anyway. I wish I could go to table like this; I could stand it a good deal better. Do you seem to be making any headway with the dang thing?"

"I think probably I can——"

Downstairs the door-bell rang, and Alice's arms jerked with the shock.

"Golly!" her father said. "Did you stick your finger with that fool needle?"

She gave him a blank stare. "He's come!"

She was not mistaken, for, upon the little veranda, Russell stood facing the closed door at last. However, it remained closed for a considerable time after he rang. Inside the house the warning summons of the bell was immediately followed by another sound, audible to Alice and her father as a crash preceding a series of muffled falls. Then came a distant voice, bitter in complaint.

"Oh, Lord!" said Adams. "What's that?"

Alice went to the top of the front stairs, and her mother appeared in the hall below.

"Mama!"

Mrs. Adams looked up. "It's all right," she said, in a loud whisper. "Gertrude fell down the cellar stairs. Somebody left a bucket there, and——" She was interrupted by a gasp from Alice, and hastened to reassure her. "Don't worry, dearie. She may limp a little, but——"

Adams leaned over the banisters. "Did she break anything?" he asked.

"Hush!" his wife whispered. "No. She seems upset and angry about it, more than anything else; but she's rubbing herself, and she'll be all right in time to bring in the little sandwiches. Alice! Those flowers!"

"I know, mama. But——"

"Hurry!" Mrs. Adams warned her. "Both of you hurry! I *must* let him in!"

She turned to the door, smiling cordially, even before she opened it. "Do come right in, Mr. Russell," she said, loudly, lifting her voice for additional warning to those above. "I'm *so* glad to receive you informally, this way, in our own little home. There's a hat-rack here under the stairway," she continued, as Russell, murmuring some response, came into the hall. "I'm afraid you'll think it's almost *too* informal, my coming to the door, but unfortunately our housemaid's just had a little accident—oh, nothing to mention! I just thought we better not keep you waiting any longer. Will you step into our living-room, please?"

She led the way between the two small columns, and seated herself in one of the plush rocking-chairs, selecting it because Alice had once pointed out that the chairs, themselves, were less noticeable when they had people sitting in them. "Do sit down, Mr. Russell; it's so very warm it's really quite a trial just to stand up!"

"Thank you," he said, as he took a seat. "Yes. It is quite

warm." And this seemed to be the extent of his responsiveness for the moment. He was grave, rather pale; and Mrs. Adams's impression of him, as she formed it then, was of "a distinguished-looking young man, really elegant in the best sense of the word, but timid and formal when he first meets you." She beamed upon him, and used with everything she said a continuous accompaniment of laughter, meaningless except that it was meant to convey cordiality. "Of course we *do* have a great deal of warm weather," she informed him. "I'm glad it's so much cooler in the house than it is outdoors."

"Yes," he said. "It is pleasanter indoors." And, stopping with this single untruth, he permitted himself the briefest glance about the room; then his eyes returned to his smiling hostess.

"Most people make a great fuss about hot weather," she said. "The only person I know who doesn't mind the heat the way other people do is Alice. She always seems as cool as if we had a breeze blowing, no matter how hot it is. But then she's so amiable she never minds anything. It's just her character. She's always been that way since she was a little child; always the same to everybody, high and low. I think character's the most important thing in the world, after all, don't you, Mr. Russell?"

"Yes," he said, solemnly; and touched his bedewed white forehead with a handkerchief.

"Indeed it is," she agreed with herself, never failing to continue her murmur of laughter. "That's what I've always told Alice; but she never sees anything good in herself, and she just laughs at me when I praise her. She sees good in everybody *else* in the world, no matter how unworthy they are, or how they behave toward *her*; but she always underestimates herself. From the time she was a little child she was always that way. When some other little girl would behave selfishly or meanly toward her, do you think she'd come and tell me? Never a word to anybody! The little thing was too proud! She was the same way about school. The teachers had to tell me when she took a prize; she'd bring it home and keep it in her room without a word about it to her father and mother. Now, Walter was just the other way. Walter would——" But here Mrs. Adams checked herself, though she increased the volume of her laughter. "How silly of me!" she exclaimed. "I expect you know how mothers *are*, though, Mr. Russell. Give us a chance and we'll talk about our children forever! Alice would feel terribly if she knew how I've been going on about her to you."

In this Mrs. Adams was right, though she did not herself suspect it, and upon an almost inaudible word or two from him she went on with her topic. "Of course my excuse is that few mothers have a daughter like Alice. I suppose we all think the same way about our children, but *some* of us must be right when we feel we've got the best. Don't you think so?"

"Yes. Yes, indeed."

"I'm sure *I* am!" she laughed. "I'll let the others speak for themselves." She paused reflectively. "No; I think a mother knows when she's got a treasure in her family. If she *hasn't* got one, she'll pretend she has, maybe; but if she has, she knows it. I certainly know *I* have. She's always been what people call 'the joy of the household'—always cheerful, no matter what went wrong, and always ready to smooth things over with some bright, witty saying. You must be sure not to *tell* we've had this little chat about her—she'd just be furious with me—but she *is* such a dear child! You won't tell her, will you?"

"No," he said, and again applied the handkerchief to his forehead for an instant. "No, I'll——" He paused, and finished lamely: "I'll—not tell her."

Thus reassured, Mrs. Adams set before him some details of her daughter's popularity at sixteen, dwelling upon Alice's impartiality among her young suitors: "She never could *bear* to hurt their feelings, and always treated all of them just alike. About half a dozen of them were just *bound* to marry her! Naturally, her father and I considered any such idea ridiculous; she was too young, of course."

Thus the mother went on with her biographical sketches, while the pale young man sat facing her under the hard overhead light of a white globe, set to the ceiling; and listened without interrupting. She was glad to have the chance to tell him a few things about Alice he might not have guessed for himself, and, indeed, she had planned to find such an opportunity, if she could; but this was getting to be altogether too much of one, she felt. As time passed, she was like an actor who must improvise to keep the audience from perceiving that his fellow-players have missed their cues; but her anxiety was not betrayed to the still listener; she had a valiant soul.

Alice, meanwhile, had arranged her little roses on the table in as many ways, probably, as there were blossoms; and she was still at it when her father arrived in the dining-room by way of the back stairs and the kitchen.

"It's pulled out again," he said. "But I guess there's no help for it now; it's too late, and anyway it lets some air into me when it bulges. I can sit so's it won't be noticed much, I expect. Isn't it time you quit bothering about the looks of the table? Your mother's been talking to him about half an hour now, and I had the idea he came on your account, not hers. Hadn't you better go and——"

"Just a minute," Alice said, piteously. "Do *you* think it looks all right?"

"The flowers? Fine! Hadn't you better leave 'em the way they are, though?"

"Just a minute," she begged again. "Just *one* minute, papa!" And she exchanged a rose in front of Russell's plate for one that seemed to her a little larger.

"You better come on," Adams said, moving to the door.

"Just *one* more second, papa." She shook her head, lamenting. "Oh, I wish we'd rented some silver!"

"Why?"

"Because so much of the plating has rubbed off a lot of it. *Just* a second, papa." And as she spoke she hastily went round the table, gathering the knives and forks and spoons that she thought had their plating best preserved, and exchanging them for more damaged pieces at Russell's place. "There!" she sighed, finally. "Now I'll come." But at the door she paused to look back dubiously, over her shoulder.

"What's the matter now?"

"The roses. I believe after all I shouldn't have tried that vine effect; I ought to have kept them in water, in the vase. It's so hot, they already begin to look a little wilted, out on the dry tablecloth like that. I believe I'll——"

"Why, look here, Alice!" he remonstrated, as she seemed disposed to turn back. "Everything'll burn up on the stove if you keep on——"

"Oh, well," she said, "the vase was terribly ugly; I can't do any better. We'll go in." But with her hand on the door-knob she paused. "No, papa. We mustn't go in by this door. It might look as if——"

"As if what?"

"Never mind," she said. "Let's go the other way."

"I don't see what difference it makes," he grumbled, but nevertheless followed her through the kitchen, and up the back stairs then through the upper hallway. At the top of the front stairs she paused for a moment, drawing a deep breath; and then, before her father's puzzled eyes, a transformation came upon her. Her shoulders, like her eyelids, had been drooping, but now she threw her head back: the shoulders straightened, and the lashes lifted over sparkling eyes; vivacity came to her whole body in a flash; and she tripped down the steps, with her pretty hands rising in time to the lilting little tune she had begun to hum.

At the foot of the stairs, one of those pretty hands extended itself at full arm's length toward Russell, and continued to be extended until it reached his own hand as he came to meet her. "How terrible of me!" she exclaimed. "To be so late coming down! And papa, too—I think you know each other."

Her father was advancing toward the young man, expecting to shake hands with him, but Alice stood between them, and Russell, a little flushed, bowed to him gravely over her shoulder, without looking at him; whereupon Adams, slightly disconcerted, put his hands in his pockets and turned to his wife.

"I guess dinner's more'n ready," he said. "We better go sit down."

But she shook her head at him fiercely. "Wait!" she whispered.

"What for? For Walter?"

"No; he can't be coming," she returned, hurriedly, and again warned him by a shake of her head. "Be quiet!"

"Oh, well——" he muttered.

"Sit down!"

He was thoroughly mystified, but obeyed her gesture and went to the rocking-chair in the opposite corner, where he sat down, and, with an expression of meek inquiry, awaited events.

Meanwhile, Alice prattled on: "It's really not a fault of mine, being tardy. The shameful truth is I was trying to hurry papa. He's incorrigible: he stays so late at his terrible old factory

—terrible *new* factory, I should say. I hope you don't *hate* us for making you dine with us in such fearful weather! I'm nearly dying of the heat, myself, so you have a fellow-sufferer, if that pleases you. Why is it we always bear things better if we think other people have to stand them, too?" And she added, with an excited laugh: "*Silly* of us, don't you think?"

Gertrude had just made her entrance from the dining-room, bearing a tray. She came slowly, with an air of resentment; and her skirt still needed adjusting, while her lower jaw moved at intervals, though not now upon any substance, but reminiscently, of habit. She halted before Adams, facing him.

He looked plaintive. "What you want o' me?" he asked.

For response, she extended the tray toward him with a gesture of indifference; but he still appeared to be puzzled. "What in the world——?" he began, then caught his wife's eye, and had presence of mind enough to take a damp and plastic sandwich from the tray. "Well, I'll *try* one," he said, but a moment later, as he fulfilled this promise, an expression of intense dislike came upon his features, and he would have returned the sandwich to Gertrude. However, as she had crossed the room to Mrs. Adams he checked the gesture, and sat helplessly, with the sandwich in his hand. He made another effort to get rid of it as the waitress passed him, on her way back to the dining-room, but she appeared not to observe him, and he continued to be troubled by it.

Alice was a loyal daughter. "These are delicious, mama," she said; and turning to Russell, "You missed it; you should have taken one. Too bad we couldn't have offered you what ought to go with it, of course, but——"

She was interrupted by the second entrance of Gertrude, who announced, "Dinner serve'," and retired from view.

"Well, well!" Adams said, rising from his chair, with relief. "That's good! Let's go see if we can eat it." And as the little group moved toward the open door of the dining-room he disposed of his sandwich by dropping it in the empty fireplace.

Alice, glancing back over her shoulder, was the only one who saw him, and she shuddered in spite of herself. Then, seeing that he looked at her entreatingly, as if he wanted to explain that he was doing the best he could, she smiled upon him sunnily, and began to chatter to Russell again.

Chapter XXII

ALICE KEPT her sprightly chatter going when they sat down, though the temperature of the room and the sight of hot soup might have discouraged a less determined gayety. Moreover, there were details as unpropitious as the heat: the expiring roses expressed not beauty but pathos, and what faint odour they exhaled was no rival to the lusty emanations of the Brussels sprouts; at the head of the table, Adams, sitting low in his chair, appeared to be unable to flatten the uprising wave of his starched bosom; and Gertrude's manner and expression were of a recognizable hostility during the long period of vain waiting for the cups of soup to be emptied. Only Mrs. Adams made any progress in this direction; the others merely feinting, now and then lifting their spoons as if they intended to do something with them.

Alice's talk was little more than cheerful sound, but, to fill a desolate interval, served its purpose; and her mother supported her with ever-faithful cooings of applausive laughter. "What a funny thing weather is!" the girl ran on. "Yesterday it was cool—angels had charge of it—and to-day they had an engagement somewhere else, so the devil saw his chance and started to move the equator to the North Pole; but by the time he got half-way, he thought of something else he wanted to do, and went off; and left the equator here, right on top of *us*! I wish he'd come back and get it!"

"Why, Alice dear!" her mother cried, fondly. "What an imagination! Not a very pious one, I'm afraid Mr. Russell might think, though!" Here she gave Gertrude a hidden signal to remove the soup; but, as there was no response, she had to make the signal more conspicuous. Gertrude was leaning against the wall, her chin moving like a slow pendulum, her streaked eyes fixed mutinously upon Russell. Mrs. Adams nodded several times, increasing the emphasis of her gesture, while Alice talked briskly; but the brooding waitress continued to brood. A faint snap of the fingers failed to disturb her; nor was a covert hissing whisper of avail, and Mrs. Adams was beginning to show signs of strain when her daughter relieved her.

"Imagine our trying to eat anything so hot as soup on a night like this!" Alice laughed. "What *could* have been in the cook's mind not to give us something iced and jellied instead? Of course it's because she's equatorial, herself, originally, and only feels at home when Mr. Satan moves it north." She looked round at Gertrude, who stood behind her. "Do take this dreadful soup away!"

Thus directly addressed, Gertrude yielded her attention, though unwillingly, and as if she decided only by a hair's weight not to revolt, instead. However, she finally set herself in slow motion; but overlooked the supposed head of the table, seeming to be unaware of the sweltering little man who sat there. As she disappeared toward the kitchen with but three of the cups upon her tray he turned to look plaintively after her, and ventured an attempt to recall her.

"Here!" he said, in a low voice. "Here, you!"

"What is it, Virgil?" his wife asked.

"What's her name?"

Mrs. Adams gave him a glance of sudden panic, and, seeing that the guest of the evening was not looking at her, but down at the white cloth before him, she frowned hard, and shook her head.

Unfortunately Alice was not observing her mother, and asked, innocently: "What's whose name, papa?"

"Why, this young darky woman," he explained. "She left mine."

"Never mind," Alice laughed. "There's hope for you, papa. She hasn't gone forever!"

"I don't know about that," he said, not content with this impulsive assurance. "She *looked* like she is." And his remark, considered as a prediction, had begun to seem warranted before Gertrude's return with china preliminary to the next stage of the banquet.

Alice proved herself equal to the long gap, and rattled on through it with a spirit richly justifying her mother's praise of her as "always ready to smooth things over"; for here was more than long delay to be smoothed over. She smoothed over her father and mother for Russell; and she smoothed over him for them, though he did not know it, and remained unaware of what he owed her. With all this, throughout her prattlings, the girl's bright eyes kept seeking his with an eager gayety, which but little veiled both interrogation and entreaty—as if she asked: "Is it too much for you? Can't you bear it? Won't you *please* bear it? I would for you. Won't you give me a sign that it's all right?"

He looked at her but fleetingly, and seemed to suffer from the heat, in spite of every manly effort not to wipe his brow too often. His colour, after rising when he greeted Alice and her father, had departed, leaving him again moistly pallid; a condition arising from discomfort, no doubt, but, considered as a decoration, almost poetically becoming to him. Not less becoming was the faint, kindly smile, which showed his wish to express amusement and approval; and yet it was a smile rather strained and plaintive, as if he, like Adams, could only do the best he could.

He pleased Adams, who thought him a fine young man, and decidedly the quietest that Alice had ever shown to her family. In her father's opinion this was no small merit; and it was to Russell's credit, too, that he showed embarrassment upon this first intimate presentation; here was an applicant with both reserve and modesty. "So far, he seems to be first rate—a mighty fine young man," Adams thought; and, prompted by no wish to part from Alice but by reminiscences of apparent candidates less pleasing, he added, "At last!"

Alice's liveliness never flagged. Her smoothing over of things was an almost continuous performance, and had to be. Yet, while she chattered through the hot and heavy courses, the questions she asked herself were as continuous as the performance, and as poignant as what her eyes seemed to be asking Russell. Why had she not prevailed over her mother's fear of being "skimpy?" Had she been, indeed, as her mother said she looked, "in a trance?" But above all: What was the matter with *him*? What had happened? For she told herself with painful humour that something even worse than this dinner must be "the matter with him."

The small room, suffocated with the odour of boiled sprouts, grew hotter and hotter as more and more food appeared, slowly borne in, between deathly long waits, by the resentful, loud-breathing Gertrude. And while Alice still sought Russell's glance, and read the look upon his face a dozen different ways, fearing all of them; and while the straggling little flowers died upon the stained cloth, she felt her heart grow as heavy as the food, and wondered that it did not die like the roses.

With the arrival of coffee, the host bestirred himself to make known a hospitable regret, "By George!" he said. "I meant to buy some cigars." He addressed himself apologetically to the guest. "I don't know what I was thinking about, to forget to bring some home with me. I don't use 'em myself—unless somebody hands me one, you might say. I've always been a pipe-smoker, pure and simple, but I ought to remembered for kind of an occasion like this."

"Not at all," Russell said. "I'm not smoking at all lately; but when I do, I'm like you, and smoke a pipe."

Alice started, remembering what she had told him when he overtook her on her way from the tobacconist's; but, after a moment, looking at him, she decided that he must have forgotten it. If he had remembered, she thought, he could not have helped glancing at her. On the contrary, he seemed more at ease, just then, than he had since they sat down, for he was favouring her father with a thoughtful attention as Adams responded to the introduction of a man's topic into the conversation at last. "Well, Mr. Russell, I guess you're right, at that. I don't say but what cigars may be all right for a man that can afford 'em, if he likes 'em better than a pipe, but you take a good old pipe now——"

He continued, and was getting well into the eulogium customarily provoked by this theme, when there came an interruption: the door-bell rang, and he paused inquiringly, rather surprised.

Mrs. Adams spoke to Gertrude in an undertone:

"Just say, 'Not at home.'"

"What?"

"If it's callers, just say we're not at home."

Gertrude spoke out freely: "You mean you astin' me to 'tend you' front do' fer you?"

She seemed both incredulous and affronted, but Mrs. Adams persisted, though somewhat apprehensively. "Yes. Hurry —uh—please. Just say we're not at home—if you please."

Again Gertrude obviously hesitated between compliance and revolt, and again the meeker course fortunately prevailed with her. She gave Mrs. Adams a stare, grimly derisive, then departed. When she came back she said:

"He say he wait."

"But I told you to tell anybody we were not at home," Mrs. Adams returned. "Who is it?"

"Say he name Mr. Law."

"We don't know any Mr. Law."

"Yes'm; he know you. Say he anxious to speak Mr. Adams. Say he wait."

"Tell him Mr. Adams is engaged."

"Hold on a minute," Adams intervened. "Law? No. I don't know any Mr. Law. You sure you got the name right?"

"Say he name Law," Gertrude replied, looking at the ceiling to express her fatigue. "Law. 'S all he tell me; 's all I know."

Adams frowned. "Law," he said. "Wasn't it maybe 'Lohr?'"

"Law," Gertrude repeated. 'S all he tell me; 's all I know."

"What's he look like?"

"He ain't much," she said. "'Bout you' age; got brustly white moustache, nice eye-glasses."

"It's Charley Lohr!" Adams exclaimed. "I'll go see what he wants."

"But, Virgil," his wife remonstrated, "do finish your coffee; he might stay all evening. Maybe he's come to call."

Adams laughed. "He isn't much of a caller, I expect. Don't worry: I'll take him up to my room." And turning toward Russell, "Ah—if you'll just excuse me," he said; and went out to his visitor.

When he had gone, Mrs. Adams finished her coffee, and, having glanced intelligently from her guest to her daughter, she rose. "I think perhaps I ought to go and shake hands with Mr. Lohr, myself," she said, adding in explanation to Russell, as she reached the door, "He's an old friend of my husband's and it's a very long time since he's been here."

Alice nodded and smiled to her brightly, but upon the closing of the door, the smile vanished; all her liveliness disappeared; and with this change of expression her complexion itself appeared to change, so that her rouge became obvious, for she was pale beneath it. However, Russell did not see the alteration, for he did not look at her; and it was but a momentary lapse—the vacation of a tired girl, who for ten seconds lets herself look as she feels. Then she shot her vivacity back into place as by some powerful spring.

"Penny for your thoughts!" she cried, and tossed one of the wilted roses at him, across the table. "I'll bid more than a penny; I'll bid tuppence—no, a poor little dead rose—a rose for your thoughts, Mr. Arthur Russell! What are they?"

He shook his head. "I'm afraid I haven't any."

"No, of course not," she said. "Who could have thoughts in weather like this? Will you *ever* forgive us?"

"What for?"

"Making you eat such a heavy dinner—I mean *look* at such a heavy dinner, because you certainly didn't do more than look at it—on such a night! But the crime draws to a close, and you can begin to cheer up!" She laughed gaily, and, rising, moved to the door. "Let's go in the other room; your fearful duty is almost done, and you can run home as soon as you want to. That's what you're dying to do."

"Not at all," he said in a voice so feeble that she laughed aloud.

"Good gracious!" she cried. "I hadn't realized it was *that* bad!"

For this, though he contrived to laugh, he seemed to have no verbal retort whatever; but followed her into the "living-room," where she stopped and turned, facing him.

"Has it really been so frightful?" she asked.

"Why, of course not. Not at all."

"Of course yes, though, you mean!"

"Not at all. It's been most kind of your mother and father and you."

"Do you know," she said, "you've never once looked at me for more than a second at a time the whole evening? And it seemed to me I looked rather nice to-night, too!"

"You always do," he murmured.

"I don't see how you know," she returned; and then stepping closer to him, spoke with gentle solicitude: "Tell me: you're really feeling wretchedly, aren't you? I know you've got a fearful headache, or something. Tell me!"

"Not at all."

"You are ill—I'm sure of it."

"Not at all."

"On your word?"

"I'm really quite all right."

"But if you are——" she began; and then, looking at him with a desperate sweetness, as if this were her last resource to rouse him, "What's the matter, little boy?" she said with lisping tenderness. "Tell auntie!"

It was a mistake, for he seemed to flinch, and to lean backward, however, slightly. She turned away instantly, with a flippant lift and drop of both hands. "Oh, my dear!" she laughed. "I won't eat you!"

And as the discomfited young man watched her, seeming able to lift his eyes, now that her back was turned, she went to the front door and pushed open the screen. "Let's go out on the porch," she said. "Where we belong!"

Then, when he had followed her out, and they were seated, "Isn't this better?" she asked. "Don't you feel more like yourself out here?"

He began a murmur: "Not at——"

But she cut him off sharply: "Please don't say 'Not at all' again!"

"I'm sorry."

"You do seem sorry about something," she said. "What is it? Isn't it time you were telling me what's the matter?"

"Nothing. Indeed nothing's the matter. Of course one *is* rather affected by such weather as this. It may make one a little quieter than usual, of course."

She sighed, and let the tired muscles of her face rest. Under the hard lights, indoors, they had served her until they ached, and it was a luxury to feel that in the darkness no grimacings need call upon them.

"Of course, if you won't tell me——" she said.

"I can only assure you there's nothing to tell."

"I know what an ugly little house it is," she said. "Maybe it was the furniture—or mama's vases that upset you. Or was it mama herself—or papa?"

"Nothing 'upset' me."

At that she uttered a monosyllable of doubting laughter. "I wonder why you say that."

"Because it's so."

"No. It's because you're too kind, or too conscientious, or too embarrassed—anyhow too something—to tell me." She leaned forward, elbows on knees and chin in hands, in the reflective attitude she knew how to make graceful. "I have a feeling that you're not going to tell me," she said, slowly. "Yes—even that you're never going to tell me. I wonder—I wonder——"

"Yes? What do you wonder?"

"I was just thinking—I wonder if they haven't done it, after all."

"I don't understand."

"I wonder," she went on, still slowly, and in a voice of reflection, "I wonder who *has* been talking about me to you, after all? Isn't that it?"

"Not at——" he began, but checked himself and substituted another form of denial. "Nothing is 'it.'"

"Are you sure?"

"Why, yes."

"How curious!" she said.

"Why?"

"Because all evening you've been so utterly different."

"But in this weather——"

"No. That wouldn't make you afraid to look at me all evening!"

"But I did look at you. Often."

"No. Not really a *look*."

"But I'm looking at you now."

"Yes—in the dark!" she said. "No—the weather might make you even quieter than usual, but it wouldn't strike you so nearly dumb. No—and it wouldn't make you seem to be under such a strain—as if you thought only of escape!"

"But I haven't——"

"You shouldn't," she interrupted, gently. "There's nothing you have to escape from, you know. You aren't committed to—to this friendship."

"I'm sorry you think——" he began, but did not complete the fragment.

She took it up. "You're sorry I think you're so different, you mean to say, don't you? Never mind: that's what you did mean to say, but you couldn't finish it because you're not good at deceiving."

"Oh, no," he protested, feebly. "I'm not deceiving. "I'm ——"

"Never mind," she said again. "You're sorry I think you're so different—and all in one day—since last night. Yes, your voice *sounds* sorry, too. It sounds sorrier than it would just because of my thinking something you could change my mind about in a minute—so it means you're sorry you *are* different."

"No—I——"

But disregarding the faint denial, "Never mind," she said. "Do you remember one night when you told me that nothing anybody else could do would ever keep you from coming here? That if you—if you left me—it would be because I drove you away myself?"

"Yes," he said, huskily. "It was true."

"Are you sure?"

"Indeed I am," he answered in a low voice, but with conviction.

"Then——" She paused. "Well—but I haven't driven you away."

"No."

"And yet you've gone," she said, quietly.

"Do I seem so stupid as all that?"

"You know what I mean." She leaned back in her chair again, and her hands, inactive for once, lay motionless in her lap. When she spoke it was in a rueful whisper:

"I wonder if I *have* driven you away?"

"You've done nothing—nothing at all," he said.

"I wonder——" she said once more, but she stopped. In her mind she was going back over their time together since the first meeting—fragments of talk, moments of silence, little things of no importance, little things that might be important; moonshine, sunshine, starlight; and her thoughts zigzagged among the jumbling memories; but, as if she made for herself a picture of all these fragments, throwing them upon the canvas haphazard, she saw them all just touched with the one tainting quality that gave them coherence, the faint, false haze she had put over this friendship by her own pretendings. And, if this terrible dinner, or anything, or everything, had shown that saffron tint in its true colour to the man at her side, last night almost a lover, then she had indeed of herself driven him away, and might well feel that she was lost.

"Do you know?" she said, suddenly, in a clear, loud voice. "I have the strangest feeling. I feel as if I were going to be with you only about five minutes more in all the rest of my life!"

"Why, no," he said. "Of course I'm coming to see you—often. I——"

"No," she interrupted. "I've never had a feeling like this before. It's—it's just *so*; that's all! You're *going*—why, you're never coming here again!" She stood up, abruptly, beginning to tremble all over. "Why, it's *finished*, isn't it?" she said, and her trembling was manifest now in her voice. "Why, it's all *over*, isn't it? Why, yes!"

He had risen as she did. "I'm afraid you're awfully tired and nervous," he said. "I really ought to be going."

"Yes, of *course* you ought," she cried, despairingly. "There's nothing else for you to do. When anything's spoiled, people *can't* do anything but run away from it. So good-bye!"

"At least," he returned, huskily, "we'll only—only say good-night."

Then, as moving to go, he stumbled upon the veranda steps, "Your *hat*!" she cried. "I'd like to keep it for a souvenir, but I'm afraid you need it!"

She ran into the hall and brought his straw hat from the chair where he had left it. "You poor thing!" she said, with quavering laughter. "Don't you know you can't go without your hat?"

Then, as they faced each other for the short moment which both of them knew would be the last of all their veranda moments, Alice's broken laughter grew louder. "What a thing to say!" she cried. "What a romantic parting—talking about *hats*!"

Her laughter continued as he turned away, but other sounds came from within the house, clearly audible with the opening of a door upstairs—a long and wailing cry of lamentation in the voice of Mrs. Adams. Russell paused at the steps, uncertain, but Alice waved to him to go on.

"Oh, don't bother," she said. "We have lots of that in this funny little old house! Good-bye!"

And as he went down the steps, she ran back into the house and closed the door heavily behind her.

Chapter XXIII

HER MOTHER'S wailing could still be heard from overhead, though more faintly; and old Charley Lohr was coming down the stairs alone.

He looked at Alice compassionately. "I was just comin' to suggest maybe you'd excuse yourself from your company," he said. "Your mother was bound not to disturb you, and tried her best to keep you from hearin' how she's takin' on, but I thought probably you better see to her."

"Yes, I'll come. What's the matter?"

"Well," he said, "*I* only stepped over to offer my sympathy and services, as it were. *I* thought of course you folks knew all about it. Fact is, it was in the evening paper—just a little bit of an item on the back page, of course."

"What is it?"

He coughed. "Well, it ain't anything so terrible," he said. "Fact is, your brother Walter's got in a little trouble—well, I suppose you might call it quite a good deal of trouble. Fact is, he's quite considerable short in his accounts down at Lamb and Company."

Alice ran up the stairs and into her father's room, where Mrs. Adams threw herself into her daughter's arms. "Is he gone?" she sobbed. "He didn't hear me, did he? I tried so hard——"

Alice patted the heaving shoulders her arms enclosed. "No, no," she said. "He didn't hear you—it wouldn't have mattered—he doesn't matter anyway."

"Oh, *poor* Walter!" The mother cried. "Oh, the *poor* boy! Poor, poor Walter! Poor, poor, poor, *poor*——"

"Hush, dear, hush!" Alice tried to soothe her, but the lament could not be abated, and from the other side of the room a repetition in a different spirit was as continuous. Adams paced furiously there, pounding his fist into his left palm as he strode. "The dang boy!" he said. "Dang little fool! Dang idiot! Dang fool! Whyn't he *tell* me, the dang little fool?"

"He *did*!" Mrs. Adams sobbed. "He *did* tell you, and you wouldn't *give* it to him."

"He *did*, did he?" Adams shouted at her. "What he begged

me for was money to run away with! He never dreamed of putting back what he took. What the dangnation you talking about—accusing me!"

"He *needed* it," she said. "He needed it to run away with! How could he expect to *live*, after he got away, if he didn't have a little money? Oh, poor, poor, *poor* Walter! Poor, poor, poor——"

She went back to this repetition; and Adams went back to his own, then paused, seeing his old friend standing in the hallway outside the open door.

"Ah—I'll just be goin', I guess, Virgil," Lohr said. "I don't see as there's any use my tryin' to say any more. I'll do anything you want me to, you understand."

"Wait a minute," Adams said, and, groaning, came and went down the stairs with him. "You say you didn't see the old man at all?"

"No, I don't know a thing about what he's going to do," Lohr said, as they reached the lower floor. "Not a thing. But look here, Virgil, I don't see as this calls for you and your wife to take on so hard about—anyhow not as hard as the way you've started."

"No," Adams gulped. "It always seems that way to the other party that's only looking on!"

"Oh, well, I know that, of course," old Charley returned, soothingly. "But look here, Virgil: they *may* not catch the boy; they didn't even seem to be sure what train he made, and if they do get him, why, the ole man might decide not to prosecute if——"

"*Him?*" Adams cried, interrupting. "Him not prosecute? Why, that's what he's been waiting for, all along! He thinks my boy and me both cheated him! Why, he was just letting Walter walk into a trap! Didn't you say they'd been suspecting him for some time back? Didn't you say they'd been watching him and were just about fixing to arrest him?"

"Yes, I know," said Lohr; "but you can't tell, especially if you raise the money and pay it back."

"Every cent!" Adams vociferated. "Every last penny! I can raise it—I *got* to raise it! I'm going to put a loan on my factory to-morrow. Oh, I'll get it for him, you tell him! Every last penny!"

"Well, ole feller, you just try and get quieted down some now." Charley held out his hand in parting. "You and your wife just quiet down some. You *ain't* the healthiest man in the world, you know, and you already been under quite some strain before this happened. You want to take care of yourself for the sake of your wife and that sweet little girl upstairs, you know. Now, good-night," he finished, stepping out upon the veranda. "You send for me if there's anything I can do."

"Do?" Adams echoed. "There ain't anything *anybody* can do!" And then, as his old friend went down the path to the sidewalk, he called after him, "You tell him I'll pay him every last cent! Every last, dang, dirty *penny*!"

He slammed the door and went rapidly up the stairs, talking loudly to himself. "Every dang, last, dirty penny! Thinks *everybody* in this family wants to steal from him, does he? Thinks we're *all* yellow, does he? I'll show him!" And he came into his own room vociferating, "Every last, dang, dirty penny!"

Mrs. Adams had collapsed, and Alice had put her upon his bed, where she lay tossing convulsively and sobbing, "Oh, *poor* Walter!" over and over, but after a time she varied the sorry tune. "Oh, poor Alice!" she moaned, clinging to her daughter's hand. "Oh, poor, *poor* Alice—to have *this* come on the night of your dinner—just when everything seemed to be going so well—at last—oh, poor, poor, *poor*——"

"Hush!" Alice said, sharply. "Don't say 'poor Alice!' I'm all right."

"You *must* be!" her mother cried, clutching her. "You've just *got* to be! *One* of us has got to be all right—surely God wouldn't mind just *one* of us being all right—that wouldn't hurt Him——"

"Hush, hush, mother! Hush!"

But Mrs. Adams only clutched her the more tightly. "He seemed *such* a nice young man, dearie! He may not see this in the paper—Mr. Lohr said it was just a little bit of an item—he *may* not see it, dearie——"

Then her anguish went back to Walter again; and to his needs as a fugitive—she had meant to repair his underwear, but had postponed doing so, and her neglect now appeared to be a detail as lamentable as the calamity itself. She could neither be stilled upon it, nor herself exhaust its urgings to self-reproach, though she finally took up another theme temporarily. Upon an unusually violent outbreak of her husband's, in denunciation of the runaway, she cried out faintly that he was cruel; and further wearied her broken voice with details of Walter's beauty as a baby, and of his bedtime pieties throughout his infancy.

So the hot night wore on. Three had struck before Mrs. Adams was got to bed; and Alice, returning to her own room, could hear her father's bare feet thudding back and forth after that. "Poor papa!" she whispered in helpless imitation of her mother. "Poor papa! Poor mama! Poor Walter! Poor all of us!"

She fell asleep, after a time, while from across the hall the bare feet still thudded over their changeless route; and she woke at seven, hearing Adams pass her door, shod. In her wrapper she ran out into the hallway and found him descending the stairs.

"Papa!"

"Hush," he said, and looked up at her with reddened eyes. "Don't wake your mother."

"I won't," she whispered. "How about you? You haven't slept any at all!"

"Yes, I did. I got some sleep. I'm going over to the works now. I got to throw some figures together to show the bank. Don't worry: I'll get things fixed up. You go back to bed. Good-bye."

"Wait!" she bade him sharply.

"What for?"

"You've got to have some breakfast."

"Don't want 'ny."

"You wait!" she said, imperiously, and disappeared to return almost at once. "I can cook in my bedroom slippers," she explained, "but I don't believe I could in my bare feet!"

Descending softly, she made him wait in the dining-room until she brought him toast and eggs and coffee. "Eat!" she said. "And I'm going to telephone for a taxicab to take you, if you think you've really got to go."

"No, I'm going to walk—I *want* to walk."

She shook her head anxiously. "You don't look able. You've walked all night."

"No, I didn't," he returned. "I tell you I got some sleep. I got all I wanted anyhow."

"But, papa——"

"Here!" he interrupted, looking up at her suddenly and setting down his cup of coffee. "Look here! What about this Mr. Russell? I forgot all about him. What about him?"

Her lip trembled a little, but she controlled it before she spoke. "Well, what about him, papa?" she asked, calmly enough.

"Well, we could hardly——" Adams paused, frowning heavily. "We could hardly expect he wouldn't hear something about all this."

"Yes; of course he'll hear it, papa."

"Well?"

"Well, what?" she asked, gently.

"You don't think he'd be the—the cheap kind it'd make a difference with, of course."

"Oh, no; he isn't cheap. It won't make any difference with him."

Adams suffered a profound sigh to escape him. "Well—I'm glad of that, anyway."

"The difference," she explained—"the difference was made without his hearing anything about Walter. He doesn't know about *that* yet."

"Well, what does he know about?"

"Only," she said, "about me."

"What you mean by that, Alice?" he asked, helplessly.

"Never mind," she said. "It's nothing beside the real trouble we're in—I'll tell you some time. You eat your eggs and toast; you can't keep going on just coffee."

"I can't eat any eggs and toast," he objected, rising. "I can't."

"Then wait till I can bring you something else."

"No," he said, irritably. "I won't do it! I don't want any dang food! And look here"— he spoke sharply to stop her, as she went toward the telephone—"I don't want any dang taxi, either! You look after your mother when she wakes up. I got to be at *work*!"

And though she followed him to the front door, entreating, he could not be stayed or hindered. He went through the quiet morning streets at a rickety, rapid gait, swinging his old straw hat in his hands, and whispering angrily to himself as he went. His grizzled hair, not trimmed for a month, blew back from his damp forehead in the warm breeze; his reddened eyes stared hard at nothing from under blinking lids; and one side of his face twitched startlingly from time to time;—children might have run from him, or mocked him.

When he had come into that fallen quarter his industry had partly revived and wholly made odorous, a negro woman, leaning upon her whitewashed gate, gazed after him and chuckled for the benefit of a gossiping friend in the next tiny yard. "Oh, good Satan! Wha'ssa matter that ole glue man?"

"Who? Him?" the neighbour inquired. "What he do now?"

"Talkin' to his ole se'f!" the first explained, joyously. "Look like gone distracted—ole glue man!"

Adams's legs had grown more uncertain with his hard walk, and he stumbled heavily as he crossed the baked mud of his broad lot, but cared little for that, was almost unaware of it, in fact. Thus his eyes saw as little as his body felt, and so he failed to observe something that would have given him additional light upon an old phrase that already meant quite enough for him.

There are in the wide world people who have never learned its meaning; but most are either young or beautifully unobservant who remain wholly unaware of the inner poignancies the words convey: "a rain of misfortunes." It is a boiling rain, seemingly whimsical in its choice of spots whereon to fall; and, so far as mortal eye can tell, neither the just nor the unjust may hope to avoid it, or need worry themselves by expecting it. It had selected the Adams family for its scaldings; no question.

The glue-works foreman, standing in the doorway of the brick shed, observed his employer's eccentric approach, and doubtfully stroked a whiskered chin. "Well, they ain't no putticular use gettin' so upset over it," he said, as Adams came up. "When a thing happens, why, it happens, and that's all there is to it. When a thing's so, why, it's so. All you can do about it is think if there's anything you *can* do; and that's what you better be doin' with this case."

Adams halted, and seemed to gape at him. "What—case?" he said, with difficulty. "Was it in the morning papers, too?"

"No, it ain't in no morning papers. My land! It don't need to be in no papers; look at the *size* of it!"

"The size of what?"

"Why, great God!" the foreman exclaimed. "He ain't even seen it. Look! Look yonder!"

Adams stared vaguely at the man's outstretched hand and pointing forefinger, then turned and saw a great sign upon the façade of the big factory building across the street. The letters were large enough to be read two blocks away.

"AFTER THE FIFTEENTH OF NEXT MONTH THIS BUILDING WILL BE OCCUPIED BY THE J. A. LAMB LIQUID GLUE CO. INC."

A gray touring-car had just come to rest before the principal entrance of the building, and J. A. Lamb himself descended from it. He glanced over toward the humble rival of his projected great industry, saw his old clerk, and immediately walked across the street and the lot to speak to him.

"Well, Adams," he said, in his husky, cheerful voice, "how's your glue-works?"

Adams uttered an inarticulate sound, and lifted the hand that held his hat as if to make a protestive gesture, but failed to carry it out; and his arm sank limp at his side. The foreman, however, seemed to feel that something ought to be said.

"Our glue-works, hell!" he remarked. "I guess we won't *have* no glue-works over here—not very long, if we got to compete with the sized thing you got over there!"

Lamb chuckled. "I kind of had some such notion," he said. "You see, Virgil, I couldn't exactly let you walk off with it like swallering a pat o' butter, now, could I? It didn't look exactly reasonable to expect me to let go like that, now, did it?"

Adams found a half-choked voice somewhere in his throat. "Do you—would you step into my office a minute, Mr. Lamb?"

"Why, certainly I'm willing to have a little talk with you," the old gentleman said, as he followed his former employee indoors, and he added, "I feel a lot more like it than I did before I got *that* up, over yonder, Virgil!"

Adams threw open the door of the rough room he called his office, having as justification for this title little more than the fact that he had a telephone there and a deal table that served as a desk. "Just step into the office, please," he said.

Lamb glanced at the desk, at the kitchen chair before it, at the telephone, and at the partition walls built of old boards, some covered with ancient paint and some merely weather-beaten, the salvage of a house-wrecker; and he smiled broadly. "So these are your offices, are they?" he asked. "You expect to do quite a business here, I guess, don't you, Virgil?"

Adams turned upon him a stricken and tortured face. "Have you seen Charley Lohr since last night, Mr. Lamb?"

"No; I haven't seen Charley."

"Well, I told him to tell you," Adams began;—"I told him I'd pay you——"

"Pay me what you expect to make out o' glue, you mean, Virgil?"

"No," Adams said, swallowing. "I mean what my boy owes you. That's what I told Charley to tell you. I told him to tell you I'd pay you every last——"

"Well, well!" the old gentleman interrupted, testily. "I don't know anything about that."

"I'm expecting to pay you," Adams went on, swallowing again, painfully. "I was expecting to do it out of a loan I thought I could get on my glue-works."

The old gentleman lifted his frosted eyebrows. "Oh, out o' the *glue*-works? You expected to raise money on the glue-works, did you?"

At that, Adams's agitation increased prodigiously. "How'd you *think* I expected to pay you?" he said. "Did you think I expected to get money on my own old bones?" He slapped himself harshly upon the chest and legs. "Do you think a bank'll lend money on a man's ribs and his broken-down old knee-bones? They won't do it! You got to have some *business* prospects to show 'em, if you haven't got any property nor securities; and what business prospects have I got now, with that sign of yours up over yonder? Why, you don't need to make an *ounce* o' glue; your sign's fixed *me* without your doing another lick! *That's* all you had to do; just put your sign up! You needn't to——"

"Just let me tell you something, Virgil Adams," the old man interrupted, harshly. "I got just one right important thing to tell you before we talk any further business; and that's this: there's some few men in this town made their money in off-colour ways, but there aren't many; and those there are have had to be a darn sight slicker than you know how to be, or ever *will* know how to be! Yes, sir, and they none of them had the little gumption to try to make it out of a man that had the spirit not to let 'em, and the *strength* not to let 'em! I know what *you* thought. 'Here,' you said to yourself, 'here's this ole fool J. A. Lamb; he's kind of worn out and in his second childhood like; I can put it over on him, without his ever——'"

"I did not!" Adams shouted. "A great deal *you* know about my feelings and all what I said to myself! There's one thing I want to tell *you*, and that's what I'm saying to myself *now*, and what my feelings are this *minute*!"

He struck the table a great blow with his thin fist, and shook the damaged knuckles in the air. "I just want to tell you, whatever I did feel, I don't feel *mean* any more; not to-day, I don't. There's a meaner man in this world than *I* am, Mr. Lamb!"

"Oh, so you feel better about yourself to-day, do you, Virgil?"

"You bet I do! You worked till you got me where you want me; and I wouldn't do that to another man, no matter what he did to me! I wouldn't——"

"What you talkin' about! How've I 'got you where I want you?'"

"Ain't it plain enough?" Adams cried. "You even got me where I can't raise the money to pay back what my boy owes you! Do you suppose anybody's fool enough to let me have a cent on this business after one look at what you got over there across the road?"

"No, I don't."

"No, you don't," Adams echoed, hoarsely. "What's more, you knew my house was mortgaged, and my——"

"I did not," Lamb interrupted, angrily. "What do *I* care about your house?"

"What's the use your talking like that?" Adams cried. "You got me where I can't even raise the money to pay what my boy owes the company, so't I can't show any reason to stop the prosecution and keep him out the penitentiary. That's where you worked till you got *me*!"

"What!" Lamb shouted. "You accuse me of——"

"'Accuse you?' What am I telling you? Do you think I got no *eyes*?" And Adams hammered the table again. "Why, you knew the boy was weak——"

"I did not!"

"Listen: you kept him there after you got mad at my leaving the way I did. You kept him there after you suspected him; and you had him watched; you let him go on; just waited to catch him and ruin him!"

"You're crazy!" the old man bellowed. "I didn't know there was anything against the boy till last night. You're *crazy*, I say!"

Adams looked it. With his hair disordered over his haggard forehead and bloodshot eyes; with his bruised hands pounding the table and flying in a hundred wild and absurd gestures, while his feet shuffled constantly to preserve his balance upon staggering legs, he was the picture of a man with a mind gone to rags.

"Maybe I *am* crazy!" he cried, his voice breaking and quavering. "Maybe I am, but I wouldn't stand there and taunt a man with it if I'd done to him what you've done to me! Just look at me: I worked all my life for you, and what I did when I quit never harmed you—it didn't make two cents' worth o' difference in your life and it looked like it'd mean all the difference in the world to my family—and now look what you've *done* to me for it! I tell you, Mr. Lamb, there never was a man looked up to another man the way I looked up to you the whole o' my life, but I don't look up to you any more! You think you got a fine day of it now, riding up in your automobile to look at that sign—and then over here at my poor little works that you've ruined. But listen to me just this one last time!" The cracking voice broke into falsetto, and the gesticulating hands fluttered uncontrollably. "Just you listen!" he panted. "You think I did you a bad turn, and now you got me ruined for it, and you got my works ruined, and my family ruined; and if anybody'd 'a' told me this time last year I'd ever say such a thing to you I'd called him a dang liar, but I *do* say it: I say you've acted toward me like—like a—a doggone mean—man!"

His voice, exhausted, like his body, was just able to do him this final service; then he sank, crumpled, into the chair by the table, his chin down hard upon his chest.

"I tell you, you're crazy!" Lamb said again. "I never in the world——" But he checked himself, staring in sudden perplexity at his accuser. "Look here!" he said. "What's the matter of you? Have you got another of those——?" He put his hand upon Adams's shoulder, which jerked feebly under the touch.

The old man went to the door and called to the foreman.

"Here!" he said. "Run and tell my chauffeur to bring my car over here. Tell him to drive right up over the sidewalk and across the lot. Tell him to hurry!"

So, it happened, the great J. A. Lamb a second time brought his former clerk home, stricken and almost inanimate.

Chapter XXIV

ABOUT five o'clock that afternoon, the old gentleman came back to Adams's house; and when Alice opened the door, he nodded, walked into the "living-room" without speaking; then stood frowning as if he hesitated to decide some perplexing question.

"Well, how is he now?" he asked, finally.

"The doctor was here again a little while ago; he thinks papa's coming through it. He's pretty sure he will."

"Something like the way it was last spring?"

"Yes."

"Not a bit of sense to it!" Lamb said, gruffly. "When he was getting well the other time the doctor told me it wasn't a regular stroke, so to speak—this 'cerebral effusion' thing. Said there wasn't any particular reason for your father to expect he'd ever have another attack, if he'd take a little care of himself. Said he could consider himself well as anybody else long as he did that."

"Yes. But he didn't do it!"

Lamb nodded, sighed aloud, and crossed the room to a chair. "I guess not," he said, as he sat down. "Bustin' his health up over his glue-works, I expect."

"Yes."

"I guess so; I guess so." Then he looked up at her with a glimmer of anxiety in his eyes. "Has he came to yet?"

"Yes. He's talked a little. His mind's clear; he spoke to mama and me—and to Miss Perry." Alice laughed sadly. "We were lucky enough to get her back, but papa didn't seem to think it was lucky. When he recognized her he said, 'Oh, my goodness, 'tisn't *you*, is it!'"

"Well, that's a good sign, if he's getting a little cross. Did he—did he happen to say anything—for instance, about me?"

This question, awkwardly delivered, had the effect of removing the girl's pallor; rosy tints came quickly upon her cheeks. "He—yes, he did," she said. "Naturally, he's troubled about—about——" She stopped.

"About your brother, maybe?"

"Yes, about making up the——"

"Here, now," Lamb said, uncomfortably, as she stopped again. "Listen, young lady; let's don't talk about that just yet. I want to ask you: you understand all about this glue business, I expect, don't you?"

"I'm not sure. I only know——"

"Let me tell you," he interrupted, impatiently. "I'll tell you all about it in two words. The process belonged to me, and your father up and walked off with it; there's no getting around *that* much, anyhow."

"Isn't there?" Alice stared at him. "I think you're mistaken, Mr. Lamb. Didn't papa improve it so that it virtually belonged to him?"

There was a spark in the old blue eyes at this. "What?" he cried. "Is that the way he got around it? Why, in all my life I never heard of such a——" But he left the sentence unfinished; the testiness went out of his husky voice and the anger out of his eyes. "Well, I expect maybe that was the way of it," he said. "Anyhow, it's right for you to stand up for your father; and if you think he had a right to it——"

"But he did!" she cried.

"I expect so," the old man returned, pacifically. "I expect so, probably. Anyhow, it's a question that's neither here nor there, right now. What I was thinking of saying—well, did your father happen to let out that he and I had words this morning?"

"No."

"Well, we did." He sighed and shook his head. "Your father —well, he used some pretty hard expressions toward me, young lady. They weren't *so*, I'm glad to say, but he used 'em to me, and the worst of it was he believed 'em. Well, I been thinking it over, and I thought I'd just have a kind of little talk with you to set matters straight, so to speak."

"Yes, Mr. Lamb."

"For instance," he said, "it's like this. Now, I hope you won't think I mean any indelicacy, but you take your brother's case, since we got to mention it, why, your father had the whole thing worked out in his mind about as wrong as anybody ever got anything. If I'd acted the way your father thought I did about that, why, somebody just ought to take me out and shoot me! Do *you* know what that man thought?"

"I'm not sure."

He frowned at her, and asked, "Well, what do you think about it?"

"I don't know," she said. "I don't believe I think anything at all about anything to-day."

"Well, well," he returned; "I expect not; I expect not. You kind of look to me as if you ought to be in bed yourself, young lady."

"Oh, no."

"I guess you mean 'Oh, yes'; and I won't keep you long, but there's something we got to get fixed up, and I'd rather talk to you than I would to your mother, because you're a smart girl and always friendly; and I want to be sure I'm understood. Now, listen."

"I will," Alice promised, smiling faintly.

"I never even hardly noticed your brother was still working for me," he explained, earnestly. "I never thought anything about it. My sons sort of tried to tease me about the way your father—about his taking up this glue business, so to speak—and one day Albert, Junior, asked me if I felt all right about your brother's staying there after that, and I told him—well, I just asked him to shut up. If the boy wanted to stay there, I didn't consider it my business to send him away on account of any feeling I had toward his father; not as long as he did his work right—and the report showed he did. Well, as it happens, it looks now as if he stayed because he *had* to; he couldn't quit because he'd 'a' been found out if he did. Well, he'd been covering up his shortage for a considerable time—and do you know what your father practically charged me with about that?"

"No, Mr. Lamb."

In his resentment, the old gentleman's ruddy face became ruddier and his husky voice huskier. "Thinks I kept the boy there because I suspected him! Thinks I did it to get even with *him*! Do I look to *you* like a man that'd do such a thing?"

"No," she said, gently. "I don't think you would."

"No!" he exclaimed. "Nor *he* wouldn't think so if he was himself; he's known me too long. But he must been sort of brooding over this whole business—I mean before Walter's trouble—he must been taking it to heart pretty hard for some time back. He thought I didn't think much of him any more

—and I expect he maybe wondered some what I was going to *do*—and there's nothing worse'n that state of mind to make a man suspicious of all kinds of meanness. Well, he practically stood up there and accused me to my face of fixing things so't he couldn't ever raise the money to settle for Walter and ask us not to prosecute. That's the state of mind your father's brooding got him into, young lady—charging me with a trick like that!"

"I'm sorry," she said. "I know you'd never——"

The old man slapped his sturdy knee, angrily. "Why, that dang fool of a Virgil Adams!" he exclaimed. "He wouldn't even give me a chance to talk; and he got me so mad I couldn't hardly talk, anyway! He might 'a' known from the first I wasn't going to let him walk in and beat me out of my own—that is, he might 'a' known I wouldn't let him get ahead of me in a business matter—not with my boys twitting me about it every few minutes! But to talk to me the way he did this morning —well, he was out of his head; that's all! Now, wait just a minute," he interposed, as she seemed about to speak. "In the first place, we aren't going to push this case against your brother. I believe in the law, all right, and business men got to protect themselves; but in a case like this, where restitution's made by the family, why, I expect it's just as well sometimes to use a little influence and let matters drop. Of course your brother'll have to keep out o' this state; that's all."

"But—you said——" she faltered.

"Yes. What'd I say?"

"You said, 'where restitution's made by the family.' That's what seemed to trouble papa so terribly, because—because restitution couldn't——"

"Why, yes, it could. That's what I'm here to talk to you about."

"I don't see——"

"I'm going to *tell* you, ain't I?" he said, gruffly. "Just hold your horses a minute, please." He coughed, rose from his chair, walked up and down the room, then halted before her. "It's like this," he said. "After I brought your father home, this morning, there was one of the things he told me, when he was going for me, over yonder—it kind of stuck in my craw. It was something about all this glue controversy not meaning anything to me in particular, and meaning a whole heap to him and his family. Well, he was wrong about that two ways. The first one was, it did mean a good deal to me to have him go back on me after so many years. I don't need to say any more about it, except just to tell you it meant quite a little more to me than you'd think, maybe. The other way he was wrong is, that how much a thing means to one man and how little it means to another ain't the right way to look at a business matter."

"I suppose it isn't, Mr. Lamb."

"No," he said. "It isn't. It's not the right way to look at anything. Yes, and your father knows it as well as I do, when he's in his right mind; and I expect that's one of the reasons he got so mad at me—but anyhow, I couldn't help thinking about how much all this thing *had* maybe meant to him;—as I say, it kind of stuck in my craw. I want you to tell him something from me, and I want you to go and tell him right off, if he's able and willing to listen. You tell him I got kind of a notion he was pushed into this thing by circumstances, and tell him I've lived long enough to know that circumstances can beat the best of us—you tell him I said 'the *best* of us.' Tell him I haven't got a bit of feeling against him—not any more—and tell him I came here to ask him not to have any against me."

"Yes, Mr. Lamb."

"Tell him I said——" The old man paused abruptly and Alice was surprised, in a dull and tired way, when she saw that his lips had begun to twitch and his eyelids to blink; but he recovered himself almost at once, and continued: "I want him to remember, 'Forgive us our transgressions, as we forgive those that transgress against us'; and if he and I been transgressing against each other, why, tell him I think it's time we *quit* such foolishness!"

He coughed again, smiled heartily upon her, and walked toward the door; then turned back to her with an exclamation: "Well, if I ain't an old fool!"

"What is it?" she asked.

"Why, I forgot what we were just talking about! Your father wants to settle for Walter's deficit. Tell him we'll be glad to accept it; but of course we don't expect him to clean the matter up until he's able to talk business again."

Alice stared at him blankly enough for him to perceive that

further explanations were necessary. "It's like this," he said. "You see, if your father decided to keep his works going over yonder, I don't say but he might give us some little competition for a time, 'specially as he's got the start on us and about ready for the market. Then I was figuring we could use his plant—it's small, but it'd be to our benefit to have the use of it—and he's got a lease on that big lot; it may come in handy for us if we want to expand some. Well, I'd prefer to make a deal with him as quietly as possible—no good in every Tom, Dick and Harry hearing about things like this—but I figured he could sell out to me for a little something more'n enough to cover the mortgage he put on this house, and Walter's deficit, too—*that* don't amount to much in dollars and cents. The way I figure it, I could offer him about ninety-three hundred dollars as a total—or say ninety-three hundred and fifty—and if he feels like accepting, why, I'll send a confidential man up here with the papers soon's your father's able to look 'em over. You tell him, will you, and ask him if he sees his way to accepting that figure?"

"Yes," Alice said; and now her own lips twitched, while her eyes filled so that she saw but a blurred image of the old man, who held out his hand in parting. "I'll tell him. Thank you."

He shook her hand hastily. "Well, let's just keep it kind of quiet," he said, at the door. "No good in every Tom, Dick and Harry knowing all what goes on in town! You telephone me when your papa's ready to go over the papers—and call me up at my house to-night, will you? Let me hear how he's feeling?"

"I will," she said, and through her grateful tears gave him a smile almost radiant. "He'll be better, Mr. Lamb. We all will."

Chapter XXV

ONE MORNING, that autumn, Mrs. Adams came into Alice's room, and found her completing a sober toilet for the street; moreover, the expression revealed in her mirror was harmonious with the business-like severity of her attire. "What makes you look so cross, dearie?" the mother asked. "Couldn't you find anything nicer to wear than that plain old dark dress?"

"I don't believe I'm cross," the girl said, absently. "I believe I'm just thinking. Isn't it about time?"

"Time for what?"

"Time for thinking—for me, I mean?"

Disregarding this, Mrs. Adams looked her over thoughtfully. "I can't see why you don't wear more colour," she said. "At your age it's becoming and proper, too. Anyhow, when you're going on the street, I think you ought to look just as gay and lively as you can manage. You want to show 'em you've got some spunk!"

"How do you mean, mama?"

"I mean about Walter's running away and the mess your father made of his business. It would help to show 'em you're holding up your head just the same."

"Show whom!"

"All these other girls that——"

"Not I!" Alice laughed shortly, shaking her head. "I've quit dressing at them, and if they saw me they wouldn't think what you want 'em to. It's funny; but we don't often make people think what we want 'em to, mama. You do thus and so; and you tell yourself, 'Now, seeing me do thus and so, people will naturally think this and that'; but they don't. They think something else—usually just what you *don't* want 'em to. I suppose about the only good in pretending is the fun we get out of fooling ourselves that we fool somebody."

"Well, but it wouldn't be pretending. You ought to let people see you're still holding your head up because you *are*. You wouldn't want that Mildred Palmer to think you're cast down about—well, you know you wouldn't want *her* not to think you're holding your head up, would you?"

"She wouldn't know whether I am or not, mama." Alice bit her lip, then smiled faintly as she said: "Anyhow, I'm not thinking about my head in that way—not this morning, I'm not."

Mrs. Adams dropped the subject casually. "Are you going down-town?" she inquired.

"Yes."

"What for?"

"Just something I want to see about. I'll tell you when I come back. Anything you want me to do?"

"No; I guess not to-day. I thought you might look for a rug, but I'd rather go with you to select it. We'll have to get a new rug for your father's room, I expect."

"I'm glad you think so, mama. I don't suppose he's ever even noticed it, but that old rug of his—well, really!"

"I didn't mean for him," her mother explained, thoughtfully. "No; he don't mind it, and he'd likely make a fuss if we changed it on his account. No; what I meant—we'll have to put your father in Walter's room. He won't mind, I don't expect—not much."

"No, I suppose not," Alice agreed, rather sadly. "I heard the bell awhile ago. Was it somebody about that?"

"Yes; just before I came upstairs. Mrs. Lohr gave him a note to me, and he was really a very pleasant-looking young man. A *very* pleasant-looking young man," Mrs. Adams repeated with increased animation and a thoughtful glance at her daughter. "He's a Mr. Will Dickson; he has a first-rate position with the gas works, Mrs. Lohr says, and he's fully able to afford a nice room. So if you and I double up in here, then with that young married couple in my room, and this Mr. Dickson in your father's, we'll just about have things settled. I thought maybe I could make one more place at table, too, so that with the other people from outside we'd be serving eleven altogether. You see if I have to pay this cook twelve dollars a week—it can't be helped, I guess—well, one more would certainly help toward a profit. Of course it's a terribly worrying thing to see how we *will* come out. Don't you suppose we could squeeze in one more?"

"I suppose it *could* be managed; yes."

Mrs. Adams brightened. "I'm sure it'll be pleasant having that young married couple in the house—and especially this

Mr. Will Dickson. He seemed very much of a gentleman, and anxious to get settled in good surroundings. I was very favourably impressed with him in every way; and he explained to me about his name; it seems it isn't William, it's just 'Will'; his parents had him christened that way. It's curious." She paused, and then, with an effort to seem casual, which veiled nothing from her daughter: "It's *quite* curious," she said again. "But it's rather attractive and different, don't you think?"

"Poor mama!" Alice laughed compassionately. "Poor mama!"

"He is, though," Mrs. Adams maintained. "He's *very* much of a gentleman, unless I'm no judge of appearances; and it'll really be nice to have him in the house."

"No doubt," Alice said, as she opened her door to depart. "I don't suppose we'll mind having any of 'em as much as we thought we would. Good-bye."

But her mother detained her, catching her by the arm. "Alice, you do hate it, don't you!"

"No," the girl said, quickly. "There wasn't anything else to do."

Mrs. Adams became emotional at once: her face cried tragedy, and her voice misfortune. "There *might* have been something else to do! Oh, Alice, you gave your father bad advice when you upheld him in taking a miserable little ninety-three hundred and fifty from that old wretch! If your father'd just had the gumption to hold out, they'd have had to pay him anything he asked. If he'd just had the gumption and a little manly *courage*——"

"Hush!" Alice whispered, for her mother's voice grew louder. "Hush! He'll hear you, mama."

"Could he hear me too often?" the embittered lady asked. "If he'd listened to me at the right time, would we have to be taking in boarders and sinking *down* in the scale at the end of our lives, instead of going *up*? You were both wrong; we didn't need to be so panicky—that was just what that old man wanted: to scare us and buy us out for nothing! If your father'd just listened to me then, or if for once in his life he'd just been half a *man*——"

Alice put her hand over her mother's mouth. "You mustn't! He *will* hear you!"

But from the other side of Adams's closed door his voice came querulously. "Oh, I *hear* her, all right!"

"You see, mama?" Alice said, and, as Mrs. Adams turned away, weeping, the daughter sighed; then went in to speak to her father.

He was in his old chair by the table, with a pillow behind his head, but the crocheted scarf and Mrs. Adams's wrapper swathed him no more; he wore a dressing-gown his wife had bought for him, and was smoking his pipe. "The old story, is it?" he said, as Alice came in. "The same, same old story! Well, well! Has she gone?"

"Yes, papa?"

"Got your hat on," he said. "Where you going?"

"I'm going down-town on an errand of my own. Is there anything you want, papa?"

"Yes, there is." He smiled at her. "I wish you'd sit down a while and talk to me—unless your errand——"

"No," she said, taking a chair near him. "I was just going down to see about some arrangements I was making for myself. There's no hurry."

"What arrangements for yourself, dearie?"

"I'll tell you afterwards—after I find out something about 'em myself."

"All right," he said, indulgently. "Keep your secrets; keep your secrets." He paused, drew musingly upon his pipe, and shook his head. "Funny—the way your mother looks at things! For the matter o' that, everything's pretty funny, I expect, if you stop to think about it. For instance, let her say all she likes, but we were pushed right spang to the wall, if J. A. Lamb hadn't taken it into his head to make that offer for the works; and there's one of the things I been thinking about lately, Alice: thinking about how funny they work out."

"What did you think about it, papa!"

"Well, I've seen it happen in other people's lives, time and time again; and now it's happened in ours. You think you're going to be pushed right up against the wall; you can't see any way out, or any hope at all; you think you're *gone*—and then something you never counted on turns up; and, while maybe you never do get back to where you used to be, yet somehow you kind of squirm out of being right *spang* against the wall.

You keep on going—maybe you can't go much, but you do go a little. See what I mean?"

"Yes. I understand, dear."

"Yes, I'm afraid you do," he said. "Too bad! You oughtn't to understand it at your age. It seems to me a good deal as if the Lord really meant for the young people to have the good times, and for the old to have the troubles; and when anybody as young as you has trouble there's a big mistake somewhere."

"Oh, no!" she protested.

But he persisted whimsically in this view of divine error: "Yes, it does look a good deal that way. But of course we can't tell; we're never certain about anything—not about anything at all. Sometimes I look at it another way, though. Sometimes it looks to me as if a body's troubles came on him mainly because he hadn't had sense enough to know how not to have any—as if his troubles were kind of like a boy's getting kept in after school by the teacher, to give him discipline, or something or other. But, my, my! We don't learn easy!" He chuckled mournfully. "Not to learn how to live till we're about ready to die, it certainly seems to me dang tough!"

"Then I wouldn't brood on such a notion, papa," she said.

"'Brood?' No!" he returned. "I just kind o' mull it over." He chuckled again, sighed, and then, not looking at her, he said, "That Mr. Russell—your mother tells me he hasn't been here again—not since——"

"No," she said, quietly, as Adams paused. "He never came again."

"Well, but maybe——"

"No," she said. "There isn't any 'maybe.' I told him goodbye that night, papa. It was before he knew about Walter—I told you."

"Well, well," Adams said. "Young people are entitled to their own privacy; I don't want to pry." He emptied his pipe into a chipped saucer on the table beside him, laid the pipe aside, and reverted to a former topic. "Speaking of dying——"

"Well, but we weren't!" Alice protested.

"Yes, about not knowing how to live till you're through living—and *then* maybe not!" he said, chuckling at his own determined pessimism. "I see I'm pretty old because I talk this way—I remember my grandmother saying things a good deal like all what I'm saying now; I used to hear her at it when I was a young fellow—she was a right gloomy old lady, I remember. Well, anyhow, it reminds me: I want to get on my feet again as soon as I can; I got to look around and find something to go into."

Alice shook her head gently. "But, papa, he told you——"

"Never mind throwing that dang doctor up at me!" Adams interrupted, peevishly. "He said I'd be good for *some* kind of light job—if I could find just the right thing. 'Where there wouldn't be either any physical or mental strain,' he said. Well, I got to find something like that. Anyway, I'll feel better if I can just get out *looking* for it."

"But, papa, I'm afraid you won't find it, and you'll be disappointed."

"Well, I want to hunt around and *see*, anyhow."

Alice patted his hand. "You must just be contented, papa. Everything's going to be all right, and you mustn't get to worrying about doing anything. We own this house—it's all clear—and you've taken care of mama and me all our lives; now it's our turn."

"No, sir!" he said, querulously. "I don't like the idea of being the landlady's husband around a boarding-house; it goes against my gizzard. *I* know: makes out the bills for his wife Sunday mornings—works with a screw-driver on somebody's bureau drawer sometimes—'tends the furnace maybe—one the boarders gives him a cigar now and then. That's a *fine* life to look forward to! No, sir; I don't want to finish as a landlady's husband!"

Alice looked grave; for she knew the sketch was but too accurately prophetic in every probability. "But, papa," she said, to console him, "don't you think maybe there isn't such a thing as a 'finish,' after all! You say perhaps we don't learn to live till we die—but maybe that's how it is *after* we die, too—just learning some more, the way we do here, and maybe through trouble again, even after that."

"Oh, it might be," he sighed. "I expect so."

"Well, then," she said, "what's the use of talking about a 'finish?' We do keep looking ahead to things as if they'd finish something, but when we get *to* them, they don't finish anything. They're just part of going on. I'll tell you—I looked ahead all summer to something I was afraid of, and I said to myself, 'Well, if that happens, I'm finished!' But it wasn't so, papa. It did happen, and nothing's finished; I'm going on, just the same—only——" She stopped and blushed.

"Only what?" he asked.

"Well——" She blushed more deeply, then jumped up, and, standing before him, caught both his hands in hers. "Well, don't you think, since we do have to go on, we ought at least to have learned some sense about how to do it?"

He looked up at her adoringly.

"What *I* think," he said, and his voice trembled;—"I think you're the smartest girl in the world! I wouldn't trade you for the whole kit-and-boodle of 'em!"

But as this folly of his threatened to make her tearful, she kissed him hastily, and went forth upon her errand.

Since the night of the tragic-comic dinner she had not seen Russell, nor caught even the remotest chance glimpse of him; and it was curious that she should encounter him as she went upon such an errand as now engaged her. At a corner, not far from that tobacconist's shop she had just left when he overtook her and walked with her for the first time, she met him to-day. He turned the corner, coming toward her, and they were face to face; whereupon that engaging face of Russell's was instantly reddened, but Alice's remained serene.

She stopped short, though; and so did he; then she smiled brightly as she put out her hand.

"Why, Mr. Russell!"

"I'm so—I'm so glad to have this—this chance," he stammered. "I've wanted to tell you—it's just that going into a new undertaking—this business life—one doesn't get to do a great many things he'd like to. I hope you'll let me call again some time, if I can."

"Yes, do!" she said, cordially, and then, with a quick nod, went briskly on.

She breathed more rapidly, but knew that he could not have detected it, and she took some pride in herself for the way she had met this little crisis. But to have met it with such easy courage meant to her something more reassuring than a momentary pride in the serenity she had shown. For she found that what she had resolved in her inmost heart was now really true: she was "through with all that!"

She walked on, but more slowly, for the tobacconist's shop was not far from her now—and, beyond it, that portal of doom, Frincke's Business College. Already Alice could read the begrimed gilt letters of the sign; and although they had spelled destiny never with a more painful imminence than just then, an old habit of dramatizing herself still prevailed with her.

There came into her mind a whimsical comparison of her fate with that of the heroine in a French romance she had read long ago and remembered well, for she had cried over it. The story ended with the heroine's taking the veil after a death blow to love; and the final scene again became vivid to Alice, for a moment. Again, as when she had read and wept, she seemed herself to stand among the great shadows in the cathedral nave; smelled the smoky incense on the enclosed air, and heard the solemn pulses of the organ. She remembered how the novice's father knelt, trembling, beside a pillar of gray stone; how the faithless lover watched and shivered behind the statue of a saint; how stifled sobs and outcries were heard when the novice came to the altar; and how a shaft of light struck through the rose-window, enveloping her in an amber glow.

It was the vision of a moment only, and for no longer than a moment did Alice tell herself that the romance provided a prettier way of taking the veil than she had chosen, and that a faithless lover, shaking with remorse behind a saint's statue, was a greater solace than one left on a street corner protesting that he'd like to call some time—if he could! Her pity for herself vanished more reluctantly; but she shook it off and tried to smile at it, and at her romantic recollections—at all of them. She had something important to think of.

She passed the tobacconist's, and before her was that dark entrance to the wooden stairway leading up to Frincke's Business College—the very doorway she had always looked upon as the end of youth and the end of hope.

How often she had gone by here, hating the dreary obscurity of that stairway; how often she had thought of this obscurity as something lying in wait to obliterate the footsteps of any girl who should ascend into the smoky darkness above! Never had she passed without those ominous imaginings of hers: pretty girls turning into old maids "taking dictation"—old maids of a dozen different types, yet all looking a little like herself.

Well, she was here at last! She looked up and down the street quickly, and then, with a little heave of the shoulders, she went bravely in, under the sign, and began to climb the wooden steps. Half-way up the shadows were heaviest, but after that the place began to seem brighter. There was an open window overhead somewhere, she found, and the steps at the top were gay with sunshine.

IN THE ARENA

Stories of Political Life

To My Father

Contents

"In the First Place"

*T*HE OLD-TIMER, *a lean, retired pantaloon, sitting with loosely slippered feet close to the fire, thus gave of his wisdom to the questioning student:*

"Looking back upon it all, what we most need 'in politics' is more good men. Thousands of good men ARE *in; and they need the others who are not in. More would come if they knew how* MUCH *they are needed. The dilettantes of the clubs who have so easily abused me, for instance, all my life, for being a ward-worker, these and those other reformers who write papers about national corruption when they don't know how their own wards are swung, probably aren't so useful as they might be. The exquisite who says that politics is 'too dirty a business for a gentleman to meddle with' is like the woman who lived in the parlour and complained that the rest of her family kept the other rooms so dirty that she never went into them.*

"There are many thousands of young men belonging to what is for some reason called the 'best class,' who would like to be 'in politics' if they could begin high enough up—as ambassadors, for instance. That is, they would like the country to do something for them, though they wouldn't put it that way. A young man of this sort doesn't know how much he'd miss if his wishes were gratified. For my part, I'd hate not to have begun at the beginning of the game.

"I speak of it as a game," the old gentleman went on, "and in some ways it is. That's where the fun of it comes in. Yet, there are times when it looks to me more like a series of combats, hand-to-hand fights for life, and fierce struggles between men and strange powers. You buy your newspaper and that's your ticket to the amphitheatre. But the distance is hazy and far; there are clouds of dust and you can't see clearly. To make out just what is going on you ought to get down in the arena yourself. Once you're in it, the view you'll have and the fighting that will come your way will more than repay you. Still, I don't think we ought to go in with the idea of being repaid.

"It seems an odd thing to me that so many men feel they haven't any time for politics; can't put in even a little, trying to see how

their cities (let alone their states and the country) are run. When we have a war, look at the millions of volunteers that lay down everything and answer the call of the country. Well, in politics, the country needs ALL *the men who have any patriotism*—NOT *to be seeking office, but to watch and to understand what is going on. It doesn't take a great deal of time; you can attend to your business and do that much, too. When wrong things are going on and all the good men understand them, that is all that is needed. The wrong things stop going on."*

Boss Gorgett

"I GUESS I've been what you might call kind of an assistant boss pretty much all my life; at least, ever since I could vote; and I was something of a ward-heeler even before that. I don't suppose there's any way a man of my disposition could have put in his time to less advantage and greater cost to himself. I've never got a thing by it, all these years, not a job, not a penny—nothing but injury to my business and trouble with my wife. *She* begins going for me, first of every campaign.

Yet I just can't seem to keep out of it. It takes a hold on a man that I never could get away from; and when I reach my second childhood and the boys have turned me out, I reckon I'll potter along trying to look knowing and secretive, like the rest of the has-beens, letting on as if I still had a place inside. Lord, if I'd put in the energy at my business that I've frittered away on small politics! But what's the use thinking about it?"

Plenty of men go to pot horse-racing and stock gambling; and I guess this has just been my way of working off some of my nature in another fashion. There's a good many like me, too; not out for office or contracts, nor anything that you can put your finger on in particular—nothing except the *game*. Of course, it's a pleasure, knowing you've got more influence than some, but I believe the most you ever get out of it is in being able to help your friends, to get a man you like a job, or a good contract, something he wants, when he needs it.

I tell you *then's* when you feel satisfied, and your time don't seem to have been so much thrown away. You go and buy a higher-priced cigar than you can afford, and sit and smoke it with your feet out in the sunshine on your porch railing, and watch your neighbour's children playing in their yard; and they look mighty nice to you; and you feel kind, and as if everybody else was.

But that wasn't the way I felt when I helped to hand over to a reformer the nomination for mayor; then it was just selfish desperation and nothing else. We had to do it. You see, it was this way: the other side had had the city for four terms, and, naturally, they'd earned the name of being rotten by that time.

Big Lafe Gorgett was their best. "Boss Gorgett," of course our papers called him when they went for him, which was all the time; and pretty considerable of a man he was, too. Most people that knew him liked Lafe. I did. But he got a bad name, as they say, by the end of his fourth term as Mayor—and who wouldn't? Of course, the cry went up all round that he and his crowd were making a fat thing out of it, which wasn't so much the case as that Lafe had got to depending on humouring the gamblers and the brewers for campaign funds and so forth. In fact, he had the reputation of running a disorderly town, and the truth is, it *was* too wide open.

But *we* hadn't been much better when we'd had it, before Lafe beat us and got in; and everybody remembered that. The "respectable element" wouldn't come over to us strong enough for anybody we could pick of our own crowd; and so, after trying it on four times, we started in to play it another way, and nominated Farwell Knowles, who was already running on an independent ticket, got out by the reform and purity people. That is: we made him a fusion candidate, hoping to find some way to control him later. We'd never have done it if we hadn't thought it was our only hope. Gorgett was too strong, and he handled the darkeys better than any man I ever knew. He had an organization for it which we couldn't break; and the coloured voters really held the balance of power with us, you know, as they do so many other places near the same size. They were getting pretty well on to it, too, and cost more every election. Our best chance seemed to be in so satisfying the "law-and-order" people that they'd do something to counterbalance this vote—which they never did.

Well, sir, it was a mighty curious campaign. There never really was a day when we could tell where we stood, for certain. As anybody knows, the "better element" can't be depended on. There's too many of 'em forget to vote, and if the weather isn't just right they won't go to the polls. Some of 'em won't go anyway—act as if they looked down on politics; say it's only helping one boodler against another. So your true aristocrat won't vote for either. The real truth is, he don't *care*. Don't care as much about the management of his city, State, and country as about the way his club is run. Or he's ignorant about the whole business, and what between ignorance and indifference the worse and smarter of the two rings gets in again and old Mr. Aristocrat gets soaked some more on his sewer assessments. *Then* he'll holler like a stabbed hand-organ; but he'll keep on talking about politics being too low a business for a gentleman to mix in, just the same!

Somebody said a pessimist is a man who has a choice of two evils, and takes both. There's your man that don't vote.

And the best-dressed wards are the ones that fool us oftenest. We're always thinking they'll do something, and they don't. But we thought, when we took Farwell Knowles, that we had 'em at last. Fact is, they did seem stirred up, too. They called it a "moral victory" when we were forced to nominate Knowles to have any chance of beating Gorgett. That was because it was *their* victory.

Farwell Knowles was a young man, about thirty-two, an editorial writer on the *Herald*, an independent paper. I'd known him all his life, and his wife—too, a mighty sweet-looking lady she was. I'd always thought Farwell was kind of a dreamer, and too excitable; he was always reading papers to literary clubs, and on the speech-making side he wasn't so bad—he liked it; but he hadn't seemed to me to know any more about politics and people than a royal family would. He was always talking about life and writing about corruption, when, all the time, so it struck me, it was only books he was really interested in; and he saw things along book lines. Of course he was a tin god, politically.

He was for "stern virtue" only, and everlastingly lashed compromise and temporizing; called politicians all the elegant hard names there are, in every one of his editorials, especially Lafe Gorgett, whom he'd never seen. He made mighty free with Lafe, referred to him habitually as "Boodler Gorgett," and never let up on him from one year's end to another.

I was against our adopting him, not only for our own sakes —because I knew he'd be a hard man to handle—but for Farwell's too. I'd been a friend of his father's, and I liked his wife —everybody liked his wife. But the boys overruled me, and I had to turn in and give it to him.

Not without a lot of misgivings, you can be sure. I had one little experience with him right at the start that made me uneasy and got me to thinking he was what you might call too literary, or theatrical, or something, and that he was more interested in being things than doing them. I'd been aware, ever since he got back from Harvard, that *I* was one of his literary interests, so to speak. He had a way of talking to me in a quizzical, condescending style, in the belief that he was drawing me out, the way you talk to some old book-peddler in your office when you've got nothing to do for a while; and it was easy to see he regarded me as a "character" and thought he was studying me. Besides, he felt it his duty to study the wickedness of politics in a Parkhurstian fashion, and I was one of the lost.

One day, just after we'd nominated him, he came to me and said he had a friend who wanted to meet me. Asked me couldn't I go with him right away. It was about five in the afternoon; I hadn't anything to do and said, "Certainly," thinking he meant to introduce me to some friend of his who thought I'd talk politics with him. I took that for granted so much that I didn't ask a question, just followed along up street, talking weather. He turned in at old General Buskirk's, and may I be shot if the person he meant wasn't Buskirk's daughter, Bella! He'd brought me to call on a girl young enough to be my daughter. Maybe you won't believe I felt like a fool!

I knew Buskirk, of course (he didn't appear), but I hadn't seen Bella since she was a child. She'd been "highly educated" and had been living abroad a good deal, but I can't say that my visit made me *for* her—not very strong. She was good-looking enough, in her thinnish, solemn way, but it seemed to me she was kind of overdressed and too grand. You could see in a minute that she was intense and dreamy and theatrical with herself and superior, like Farwell; and I guess I thought they thought they'd discovered they were "kindred souls," and that each of them understood (without saying it) that both of them felt that Farwell's lot in life was a hard one because Mrs. Knowles wasn't up to him. Bella gave him little, quiet, deep glances, that seemed to help her play the part of a person who understood everything—especially him, and reverenced greatness—especially his. I remember a fellow who called the sort of game it struck me they were carrying on "those soully flirtations."

Well, sir, I wasn't long puzzling over why he had brought *me* up there. It stuck out all over, though they didn't know it, and would have been mighty astonished to think that I saw. It was in their manner, in her condescending ways with me, in her assumption of serious interest, and in his going through the trick of "drawing me out," and exhibiting me to her. I'll have to admit that these young people viewed me in the light of a "character." That was the part Farwell had me there to play.

I can't say I was too pleased with the notion, and I was kind of sorry for Mrs. Knowles, too. I'd have staked a good deal that my guess was right, for instance: that Farwell had gone first to this girl for her congratulations when he got the nomination, instead of to his wife; and that she felt—or pretended she felt—a soully sympathy with his ambitions; that she wanted to be, or to play the part of, a woman of affairs, and that he talked over everything he knew with her. I imagined they thought they were studying political reform together, and she, in her novel-reading way, wanted to pose to herself as the brilliant lady diplomat, kind of a Madam Roland advising statesmen, or something of that sort. And I was there as part of their political studies, an object-lesson, to bring her "more closely in touch" (as Farwell would say) with the realities he had to contend with. I was one of the "evils of politics," because I knew how to control a few wards, and get out the darkey vote almost as well as Gorgett. Gorgett would have been better, but Farwell couldn't very easily get at him.

I had to sit there for a little while, of course, like a ninny between them; and I wasn't the more comfortable because I thought Knowles looked like a bigger fool than I did. Bella's presence seemed to excite him to a kind of exaltation; he had a dark flush on his face and his eyes were large and shiny.

I got out as soon as I could, naturally, wondering what my wife would say if she knew; and while I was fumbling around among the knickknacks and fancy things in the hall for my hat and coat, I heard Farwell get up and cross the room to a chair nearer Bella, and then she said, in a sort of pungent whisper, that came out to me distinctly:

"My knight!" That's what she called him. "My knight!" That's what she said.

I don't know whether I was more disgusted with myself for hearing, or with old Buskirk who spent his whole time frittering around the club library, and let his daughter go in for the sort of soulliness she was carrying on with Farwell Knowles.

Trouble in our ranks began right away. Our nominee knew too much, and did all the wrong things from the start; he began by antagonizing most of our old wheel-horses; he wouldn't consult with us, and advised with his own kind. In spite of that, we had a good organization working for him, and by a week before election I felt pretty confident that our show was as good as Gorgett's. It looked like it would be close.

Just about then things happened. We had dropped onto one of Lafe's little tricks mighty smartly. We got one of his heelers fixed (of course we usually tried to keep all that kind of work dark from Farwell Knowles), and this heeler showed the whole business up for a consideration. There was a precinct certain to be strong for Knowles, where the balloting was to take place in the office-room of a hook-and-ladder company. In the corner was a small closet with one shelf, high up toward the ceiling. It was in the good old free and easy Hayes and Wheeler times, and when the polls closed at six o'clock it was planned that the election officers should set the ballot-box up on this shelf, lock the closet door, and go out for their suppers, leaving one of each side to watch in the room so that nobody could open the closet-door with a pass-key and tamper with the ballots before they were counted. Now, the ceiling over the shelf in the closet wasn't plastered, and it formed, of course, part of the flooring in the room above. The boards were to be loosened by a Gorgett man upstairs, as soon as the box was locked in; he would take up a piece of planking—enough to get an arm in—and stuff the box with Gorgett ballots till it grunted. Then he would replace the board and slide out. Of course, when they began the count our people would know there was something wrong, but they would be practically up against it, and the precinct would be counted for Gorgett.

They brought the heeler up to me, not at headquarters (I was city chairman) but at a hotel room I'd hired as a convenient place for the more important conferences and to keep out of the way of every Tom-Dick-and-Harry grafter. Bob

Crowder, a ward committee-man, brought him up and stayed in the room, while the fellow—his name was Genz—went over the whole thing.

"What do you think of it?" says Bob, when Genz finished. "Ain't it worth the money? I declare, it's so neat and simple and so almighty smart besides, I'm almost ashamed some of our boys hadn't thought of it for us."

I was just opening my mouth to answer, when there was a signal knock at the door and a young fellow we had as a kind of watcher in the next room (opening into the one I used) put his head in and said Mr. Knowles wanted to see me.

"Ask him to wait a minute," said I, for I didn't want him to know anything about Genz. "I'll be there right away."

Then came Farwell Knowles's voice from the other room, sharp and excited. "I believe I'll not wait," says he. "I'll come in there now!"

And that's what he did, pushing by our watcher before I could hustle Genz into the hall through an outer door, though I tried to. There's no denying it looked a little suspicious.

Farwell came to a dead halt in the middle of the room.

"I know that person!" he said, pointing at Genz, his brow mighty black. "I saw him and Crowder sneaking into the hotel by the back way, half an hour ago, and I knew there was some devilish—"

"Keep your shirt on, Farwell," said I.

He was pretty hot. "I'll be obliged to you," he returned, "if you'll explain what you're doing here in secret with this low hound of Gorgett's. Do you think you can play with me the way you do with your petty committee-men? If you do, I'll *show* you! You're not dealing with a child, and I'm not going to be tricked or sold out of this elec—"

I took him by the shoulders and sat him down hard on a cane-bottomed chair. "That's a dirty thought," said I, "and if you knew enough to be responsible I reckon you'd have to account for it. As it is—why, I don't care whether you apologize or not."

He weakened right away, or, at least, he saw his mistake. "Then won't you give me some explanation," he asked, in a less excitable way, "why are you closeted here with a notorious member of Gorgett's ring?"

"No," said I, "I won't."

"Be careful," said he. "This won't look well in print."

That was just so plumb foolish that I began to laugh at him; and when I got to laughing I couldn't keep up being angry. It *was* ridiculous, his childishness and suspiciousness. Right there was where I made my mistake.

"All right," says I to Bob Crowder, giving way to the impulse. "He's the candidate. Tell him."

"Do you mean it?" asks Bob, surprised.

"Yes. Tell him the whole thing."

So Bob did, helped by Genz, who was more or less sulky, of course; and it wasn't long till I saw how stupid I'd been. Knowles went straight up in the air.

"I knew it was a dirty business, politics," he said, jumping out of his chair, "but I didn't *realize* it before. And I'd like to know," he went on, turning to me, "how you learn to sit there so calmly and listen to such iniquities. How do you dull your conscience so that you can do it? And what course do you propose to follow in the matter of this confession?"

"Me?" I answered. "Why, I'm going to send supper in to our fellows, and the box'll never see that closet. The man upstairs may get a little tired. I reckon the laugh's on Gorgett; it's his scheme and—"

Farwell interrupted me; his face was outrageously red. "*What!* You actually mean you hadn't intended to expose this infamy?"

"Steady," I said. I was getting a little hot, too, and talked more than I ought. "Mr. Genz here has our pledge that he's not given away, or he'd never have—"

"*Mister* Genz!" sneered Farwell. "*Mister* Genz has your pledge, has he? Allow me to tell you that I represent the people, the *honest* people, in this campaign, and that the people and I have made no pledges to *Mister* Genz. You've paid the scoundrel—"

"*Here!*" says Genz.

"The scoundrel!" Farwell repeated, his voice rising and rising, "paid him for his information, and I tell you by that act and your silence on such a matter you make yourself a party to a conspiracy."

"Shut the transom," says I to Crowder.

"*I'm* under no pledge, I say," shouted Farwell, "and I do not compound felonies. You're not conducting my campaign. I'm doing that, and I don't conduct it along such lines. It's precisely the kind of fraud and corruption that I intend to stamp out in this town, and this is where I begin to work."

"How?" said I.

"You'll see—and you'll see soon! The penitentiaries are built for just this—"

"*Sh, sh!*" said I, but he paid no attention.

"They say Gorgett owns the Grand Jury," he went on. "Well, let him! Within a week I'll be mayor of this town—and Gorgett's Grand Jury won't outlast his defeat very long. By his own confession this man Genz is party to a conspiracy with Gorgett, and you and Crowder are witnesses to the confession. I'll see that you have the pleasure of giving your testimony before a Grand Jury of determined men. Do you hear me? And to-morrow afternoon's *Herald* will have the whole infamous story to the last word. I give you my solemn oath upon it!"

All three of us, Crowder, Genz, and I, sprang to our feet. We were considerably worked up, and none of us said anything for a minute or so, just looked at Knowles.

"Yes, you're a little shocked," he said. "It's always shocking to men like you to come in contact with honesty that won't compromise. You needn't talk to me; you can't say anything that would change me to save your lives. I've taken my oath upon it, and you couldn't alter me a hair's breadth if you burned me at a slow fire. Light, light, that's what you need, the light of day and publicity! I'm going to clear this town of fraud, and if Gorgett don't wear the stripes for this my name's not Farwell Knowles! He'll go over the road, handcuffed to a deputy, before three months are gone. Don't tell me I'm injuring *you* and the party by it. Pah! It will give me a thousand more votes. I'm not exactly a child, my friends! On my honour, the whole thing will be printed in to-morrow's paper!"

"For God's sake—" Crowder broke out, but Knowles cut him off.

"I bid you good-afternoon," he said, sharply. We all started toward him, but before we'd got half across the room he was gone, and the door slammed behind him.

Bob dropped into a chair; he was looking considerably pale; I guess I was, too, but Genz was ghastly.

"Let me out of here," he said in a sick voice. "Let me out of here!"

"Sit down!" I told him.

"Just let me out of here," he said again. And before I could stop him, he'd gone, too, in a blind hurry.

Bob and I were left alone, and not talking any.

Not for a while. Then Bob said: "Where do you reckon he's gone?"

"Reckon who's gone?"

"Genz."

"To see Lafe."

"What?"

"Of course he has. What else can he do? He's gone up any way. The best he can do is to try to square himself a little by owning up the whole thing. Gorgett will know it all any way, to-morrow afternoon, when the *Herald* comes out."

"I guess you're right," said Bob. "We're done up along with Gorgett; but I believe that idiot's right, he won't lose votes by playing hob with *us*. What's to be done?"

"Nothing," I answered. "You can't head Farwell off. It's all my fault, Bob."

"Isn't there any way to get hold of him? A crazy man could see that his best friend couldn't *beg* it out of him, and that he wouldn't spare any of us; but don't you know of some bludgeon we could hang up over him?"

"Nothing. It's up to Gorgett."

"Well," said Bob, "Lafe's mighty smart, but it looks like God-help-Gorgett now!"

Well, sir, I couldn't think of anything better to do than to go around and see Gorgett; so, after waiting long enough for Genz to see him and get away, I went. Lafe was always cool and slow; but I own I expected to find him flustered, and was astonished to see right away that he wasn't. He was smoking, as usual, and wearing his hat, as he always did, indoors and out, sitting with his feet upon his desk, and a pleasant look of contemplation on his face.

"Oh," says I, "then Genz hasn't been here?"

"Yes," says he, "he has. I reckon you folks have 'most spoiled Genz's usefulness for me."

"You're taking it mighty easy," I told him.

"Yep. Isn't it all in the game? What's the use of getting excited because you've blocked us on one precinct? We'll leave that closet out of our calculations, that's all."

"Almighty Powers, I don't mean *that*! Didn't Genz tell you—"

"About Mr. Knowles and the *Herald*? Oh, yes," he answered, knocking the ashes off his cigar quietly. "And about the thousand votes he'll gain? Oh, yes. And about incidentally showing you and Crowder up as bribing Genz and promising to protect him—making your methods public? Oh, yes. And about the Grand Jury? Yes, Genz told me. And about me and the penitentiary. Yes, he told me. Mr. Knowles is a rather excitable young man. Don't you think so?"

"Well?"

"Well, what's the trouble?"

"Trouble!" I said. "I'd like to know what you're going to do?"

"What's Knowles going to do?"

"He's sworn to expose the whole deal, as you've just told me you knew; one of the preliminaries to having us all up before the next Grand Jury and sending you and Genz over the road, that's all!"

Gorgett laughed that old, fat laugh of his, tilting farther back, with his hands in his pockets and his eyes twinkling under his last summer's straw hat-brim.

"He can't hardly afford it, can he," he drawled, "he being the representative of the law and order and purity people? They're mighty sensitive, those folks. A little thing turns 'em."

"I don't understand," said I.

"Well, I hardly reckoned you would," he returned. "But I expect if Mr. Knowles wants it warm all round, *I'm* willing. We may be able to do some of the heating up, ourselves."

This surprised me, coming from him, and I felt pretty sore. "You mean, then," I said, "that you think you've got a line on something our boys have been planning—like the way we got onto the closet trick—and you're going to show *us* up because we can't control Knowles; that you hold that over me as a threat unless I shut him up? Then I tell you plainly I know I can't shut him up, and you can go ahead and do us the worst you can."

"Whatever little tricks I may or may not have discovered," he answered, "that isn't what I mean, though I don't know as I'd be above making such a threat if I thought it was my only way to keep out of the penitentiary. I know as well as you do that such a threat would only give Knowles pleasure. He'd take the credit for forcing me to expose you, and he's convinced that everything of that kind he does makes him solider with the people and brings him a step nearer this chair I'm sitting in, which he regards as a step itself to the governorship and Heaven knows what not. He thinks he's detached himself from you and your organization till he stands alone. *That* boy's head was turned even before you fellows nominated him. He's a wonder. I've been noticing him long before he turned up as a candidate, and I believe the great surprise of his life was that John the Baptist didn't precede and herald *him*. Oh, no, going for you wouldn't stop him—not by a thousand miles. It would only do him good."

"Well, what *are* you going to do? Are you going to see him?"

"No, sir!" Lafe spoke sharply.

"Well, well! What?"

"I'm not bothering to run around asking audiences of Farwell Knowleses; you ought to know that!"

"Given it up?"

"Not exactly. I've sent a fellow around to talk to him."

"What use will that be?"

Gorgett brought his feet down off the desk with a bang.

"*Then* he can come to see *me*, if he wants to. D'you think I've been fool enough not to know what sort of man I was going up against? D'you think that, knowing him as I do, I've not been ready for something of this kind? And that's all you'll get out of *me*, this afternoon!"

And it was all I did.

It may have been about one o'clock, that night, or perhaps a little earlier, as I lay tossing about, unable to sleep because I was too much disturbed in my mind—too angry with myself—when there came a loud, startling ring at the front-door bell. I got up at once and threw open a window over the door, calling out to know what was wanted.

"It's I," said a voice I didn't know— a queer, hoarse voice. "Come down."

"Who's 'I'?" I asked.

"Farwell Knowles," said the voice. "Let me in!"

I started, and looked down.

He was standing on the steps where the light of a street-lamp fell on him, and I saw even by the poor glimmer that something was wrong; he was white as a dead man. There was something wild in his attitude; he had no hat, and looked all mixed-up and disarranged.

"Come down—come down!" he begged thickly, beckoning me with his arm.

I got on some clothes, slipped downstairs without wakening my wife, lit the hall light, and took him into the library. He dropped in a chair with a quick breath like a sob, and when I turned from lighting the gas I was shocked by the change in him since afternoon. I never saw such a look before. It was like a rat you've seen running along the gutter side of the curb-stone with a terrier after it.

"What's the matter, Farwell?" I asked.

"Oh, my God!" he whispered.

"What's happened?"

"It's hard to tell you," said he. "Oh, but it's hard to tell."

"Want some whiskey?" I asked, reaching for a decanter that stood handy. He nodded and I gave him good allowance.

"Now," said I, when he'd gulped it down, "let's hear what's turned up."

He looked at me kind of dimly, and I'll be shot if two tears didn't well up in his eyes and run down his cheeks. "I've come to ask you," he said slowly and brokenly, "to ask you—if you won't intercede with Gorgett for me; to ask you if you won't beg him to—to grant me—an interview before to-morrow noon."

"*What!*"

"Will you do it?"

"Certainly. Have you asked for an interview with him yourself?"

He struck the back of his hand across his forehead—struck hard, too.

"Have I tried? I've been following him like a dog since five o'clock this afternoon, beseeching him to give me twenty minutes' talk in private. He *laughed* at me! He isn't a man; he's an iron-hearted devil! Then I went to his house and waited three hours for him. When he came, all he would say was that you were supposed to be running this campaign for me, and I'd better consult with you. Then he turned me out of his house!"

"You seem to have altered a little since this afternoon." I couldn't resist that.

"This afternoon!" he shuddered. "I think that was a thousand years ago!"

"What do you want to see him for?"

"What for? To see if there isn't a little human pity in him for a fellow-being in agony—to end my suspense and know whether or not he means to ruin me and my happiness and my home forever!"

Farwell didn't seem to be regarding me so much in the light of a character as usual; still, one thing puzzled me, and I asked him how he happened to come to me.

"Because I thought if anyone in the world could do anything with Gorgett, you'd be the one," he answered. "Because it seemed to me he'd listen to you, and because I thought—in my wild clutching at the remotest hope—that he meant to make my humiliation more awful by sending me to you to ask you to go back to him for me."

"Well, well," I said, "I guess if you want me to be of any use you'll have to tell me what it's all about."

"I suppose so," he said, and choked, with a kind of despairing sound; "I don't see any way out of it."

"Go ahead," I told him. "I reckon I'm old enough to keep my counsel. Let it go, Farwell."

"Do you know," he began, with a sharp grinding of his teeth, "that dishonourable scoundrel has had me *watched*, ever since there was talk of me for the fusion candidate? He's had me followed, *shadowed*, till he knows more about me than I do myself."

I saw right there that I'd never really measured Gorgett for as tall as he really was. "Have a cigar?" I asked Knowles, and lit one myself. But he shook his head and went on:

"You remember my taking you to call on General Buskirk's daughter?"

"Quite well," said I, puffing pretty hard.

"An angel! A white angel! And this beast, this *boodler* has the mud in his hands to desecrate her white garments!"

"Oh," says I.

The angel's knight began to pace the room as he talked, clinching and unclinching his hands, while the perspiration got his hair all scraggly on his forehead. You see Farwell was doing some suffering and he wasn't used to it.

"When she came home from abroad, a year ago," he said, "it seemed to me that a light came into my life. I've got to tell you the whole thing," he groaned, "but it's hard! Well, my wife is taken up with our little boy and housekeeping—I don't complain of her, mind that—but she really hasn't entered into my ambitions, my inner life. She doesn't often read my editorials, and when she does, she hasn't been serious in her consideration of them and of my purposes. Sometimes she differed openly from me and sometimes greeted my work for truth and light with indifference! I had learned to bear this, and more; to save myself pain I had come to shrink from exposing my real self to her. Then, when this young girl came, for the first time in my life I found real sympathy and knew what I thought I never should know; a heart attuned to my own, a mind that sought my own ideals, a soul of the same aspirations—and a perfect faith in what I was and in what it was my right to attain. She met me with open hands, and lifted me to my best self. What, unhappily, I did not find at home, I found in her—encouragement. I went to her in every mood, always to be greeted by the most exquisite perception, always the same delicate receptiveness. She gave me a sister's love!"

I nodded; I knew he thought so.

"Well, when I went into this campaign, what more natural than that I should seek her ready sympathy at every turn, than that I should consult with her at each crisis, and, when I became the fusion candidate, that I should go to her with the news that I had taken my first great step toward my goal and had achieved thus far in my struggle for the cause of our hearts —reform?"

"You went up to Buskirk's after the convention?" I asked.

"No; the night before." He took his head in his hands and groaned, but without pausing in his march up and down the room. "You remember, it was known by ten o'clock, after the primaries, that I should receive the nomination. As soon as I was sure, I went to her; and I found her in the same state of exaltation and pride that I was experiencing myself. There was *always* the answer in her, I tell you, always the response that such a nature as mine craves. She took both my hands and looked at me just as a proud sister would. 'I *read* your news,' she said. 'It is in your face!' Wasn't that touching? Then we sat in silence for a while, each understanding the other's joy and triumph in the great blow I had struck for the right. I left very soon, and she came with me to the door. We stood for a moment on the step—and—for the first time, the only time in my life—I received a—a sister's caress."

"Oh," said I. I understood how Gorgett had managed to be so calm that afternoon.

"It was the purest kiss ever given!" Farwell groaned again.

"Who was it saw you?" I asked.

He dropped into a chair and I saw the tears of rage and humiliation welling up again in his eyes.

"We might as well have been standing by the footlights in a theatre!" he burst out, brokenly. "Who saw it? Who *didn't* see it? Gorgett's sleuth-hound, the man he sent to me this afternoon, for one; the policeman on the beat that he'd stopped for a chat in front of the house, for another; a maid in the hall behind us, the policeman's sweetheart *she* is, for another! Oh!" he cried, "the desecration! That one caress, one that I'd thought a sacred secret between us forever—and in plain sight of those three hideous vulgarians, all belonging to my enemy, Gorgett! Ah, the horror of it—what *horror*!"

Farwell wrung his hands and sat, gulping as if he were sick, without speaking for several moments.

"What terms did the man he sent offer from Gorgett?" I asked.

"*No* terms! He said to go ahead and print my story about the closet; it was a matter of perfect indifference to him; that he meant to print this about me in their damnable party-organ to-morrow, in any event, and only warned me so that I should have time to prepare Miss Buskirk. Of course he don't care! *I'll* be ruined, that's all. Oh, the hideous injustice of it, the unreason! Don't you see the frightful irony of it? The best thing in my life, the widest and deepest; my friendship with a good woman becomes a joke and a horror! Don't you see that the personal scandal about me absolutely undermines me and nullifies the political scandal of the closet affair? Gorgett will come in again and the Grand Jury would laugh at any attack on him. I'm ruined for good, for good and all, for good and all!"

"Have you told Miss Buskirk?"

He uttered a kind of a shriek. "*No!* I can't! How could I? What do you think I'm made of? And there's her father—and all her relatives, and mine, and my wife—my wife! If she leaves me—"

A fit of nausea seemed to overcome him and he struggled with it, shivering. "My God! Do you think I can *face* it? I've come to you for help in the most wretched hour of my life—all darkness, darkness! Just on the eve of triumph to be stricken down—it's so cruel, so devilish! And to think of the horrible comic-weekly misery of it, caught kissing a girl, by a policeman and his sweetheart, the chambermaid! Ugh! The vulgar ridicule—the hideous laughter!" He raised his hands to me, the most grovelling figure of a man I ever saw.

"Oh, for God's sake, help me, help me. . . ."

Well, sir, it was sickening enough, but after he had gone, and I tumbled into bed again, I thought of Gorgett and laughed myself to sleep with admiration.

When Farwell and I got to Gorgett's office, fairly early the next morning, Lafe was sitting there alone, expecting us, of course, as I knew he would be, but in the same characteristic, lazy attitude I'd found him in, the day before; feet up on the desk, hat-brim tilted 'way forward, cigar in the right-hand corner of his mouth, his hands in his pockets, his double-chin mashing down his limp collar. He didn't even turn to look at us as we came in and closed the door.

"Come in, gentlemen, come in," says he, not moving. "I kind of thought you'd be along, about this time."

"Looking for us, were you?" I asked.

"Yes," said he. "Sit down."

We did; Farwell looking pretty pale and red-eyed, and swallowing a good deal.

There was a long, long silence. We just sat and watched Gorgett. *I* didn't want to say anything; and I believe Farwell couldn't. It lasted so long that it began to look as if the little blue haze at the end of Lafe's cigar was all that was going to happen. But by and by he turned his head ever so little, and looked at Knowles.

"Got your story for the *Herald* set up yet?" he asked.

Farwell swallowed some more and just shook his head.

"Haven't begun to work up the case for the Grand Jury yet?"

"No," answered Farwell, in almost a whisper, his head hanging.

"Why," Lafe said, in a tone of quiet surprise; "you haven't given all that up, have you?"

"Yes."

"Well, ain't that strange?" said Lafe. "What's the trouble?"

Knowles didn't answer. In fact, I felt mighty sorry for him.

All at once, Gorgett's manner changed; he threw away his cigar, the only time I ever saw him do it without lighting another at the end of it. His feet came down to the floor and he wheeled round on Farwell.

"I understand your wife's a mighty nice lady, Mr. Knowles."

Farwell's head sank lower till we couldn't see his face, only his fingers working kind of pitifully.

"I guess you've had rather a bad night?" said Gorgett, inquiringly.

"Oh, my God!" The words came out in a whisper from under Knowles's tilted hat-brim.

"I believe I'd advise you to stick to your wife," Gorgett went on, quietly, "and let politics alone. Somehow I don't believe you're the kind of man for it. I've taken considerable interest in you for some time back, Mr. Knowles, though I don't suppose you've noticed it until lately; and I don't believe you understand the game. You've said some pretty hard things in your paper about me; you've been more or less excitable in your statements; but that's all right. What I don't like altogether, though, is that it seems to me you've been really tooting your own horn all the time—calling everybody dishonest and scoundrels, to shove *yourself* forward. That always ends in sort of a lonely position. I reckon you feel considerably lonely, just now? Well, yesterday, I understand you were talking pretty free about the penitentiary. Now, that ain't just the way to act, according to my notion. It's a bad word. Here we are, he and I"—he pointed to me—"carrying on our little fight according to the rules, enjoying it and blocking each other, gaining a point here and losing one there, everything perfectly good-natured, when *you* turn up and begin to talk about the penitentiary! That ain't quite the thing. You see words like that are liable to stir up the passions. It's dangerous. You were trusted, when they told you the closet story, to regard it as a confidence—though they didn't go through the form of pledging you—because your people had given their word not to betray Genz. But you couldn't see it and there you went, talking about the Grand Jury and stripes and so on, stirring up passions and ugly feelings. And I want to tell you that the man who can afford to do that has to be mighty immaculate himself. The only way to play politics, whatever you're *for*, is to learn the game first. Then you'll know how far you can go and what your own record will stand. There ain't a man alive whose record will stand too much, Mr. Knowles—and when you get to thinking about that and what your own is, it makes you feel more like treating your fellow-sinners a good deal gentler than you would otherwise. Now *I've* got a wife and two little girls, and my old mother's proud of me (though you wouldn't think it) and they'd hate it a good deal to see me sent over the road for playing the game the best I could as I found it."

He paused for a moment, looking sad and almost embarrassed. "It ain't any great pleasure to me," he said, "to think that the people have let it get to be the game that it is. But I reckon it's good for *you*. I reckon the best thing that ever happened to you is having to come here this morning to ask mercy of a man you looked down on."

Farwell shifted a little in his chair, but he didn't speak, and Gorgett went on:

"I suppose you think it's mighty hard that your private character should be used against you in a political question by a man you call a public corruptionist. But I'm in a position where I can't take any chances against an antagonist that won't play the game my way. I had to find your vulnerable point to defend myself, and, in finding it, I find that there's no need to defend myself any longer, because it makes all your weapons ineffective. I believe the trouble with you, Mr. Knowles, is that you've never realized that politicians are human beings. But we are: we breathe and laugh and like to do right, like other folks. And, like most men, you've thought you were different from other men, and you aren't. So, here you are. I believe you said you'd had a hard night?"

Knowles looked up at last, his lips working for a while before he could speak. "I'll resign now—if you'll—if you'll let me off," he said.

Gorgett shook his head. "I've got the election in my hand," he answered, "though you fellows don't know it. You've got nothing to offer me, and you couldn't buy me if you had."

At that, Knowles just sank into himself with a little, faint cry, in a kind of heap. There wasn't anything but anguish and despair *to* him. Big tears were sliding down his cheeks.

I didn't say anything. Gorgett sat looking at him for a good while; and then his fat chin began to tremble a little and I saw his eyes shining in the shadow under his old hat-brim.

He got up and went over to Farwell with slow steps and put his hand gently on his shoulder.

"Go on home to your wife," he said, in a low voice that was the saddest I ever heard. "I don't bear you any ill-will in the world. Nobody's going to give you away."

The Aliens

PIETRO TOBIGLI, that gay young chestnut vender—he of the radiant smiles—gave forth, in his warm tenor, his own interpretation of "Ach du lieber Augustine," whenever Bertha, rosy waitress in the little German restaurant, showed her face at the door. For a month it had been a courtship; and the merchant sang often:

> *"Ahaha, du libra Ogostine,*
> *Ogostine, Ogostine!*
> *Ahaha, du libra Ogostine,*
> *Nees coma ross."*

The acquaintance, begun by the song and Pietro's wonderful laugh, had grown tender. The chestnut vender had a way with him; he looked like the "Neapolitan Fisher Lad" of the chromos, and you could have fancied him of two centuries ago, putting a rose in his hair; even as it was, he had the earrings. But the smile of him it was that won Bertha, when she came to work in the little restaurant. It was a smile that put the world at its ease; it proclaimed the coming of morning over the meadows, and, taking every bystander into an April friendship, ran on suddenly into a laugh that was like silver, and like a strange puppy's claiming you for the lost master.

So it befell that Bertha was fascinated; that, blushing, she laughed back to him, and was nothing offended when, at his first sight of her, he rippled out at once into "Ahaha, du libra Ogostine."

Within two weeks he was closing his business (no intricate matter) every evening, to walk home with her, through the September moonlight. Then extraordinary things happened to the English language.

"I ain'd nefer can like no foreigner!" she often joked back to a question of his. "Nefer, nefer! you t'ink I'm takin' up mit a hant-orkan maan, Mister Toby?"

Whereupon he would carol out the tender taunt, "Ahaha, du libra Ogostine!"

"Yoost a hant-orkan maan!"

"No! *No!* No oragan! I am a greata—greata merchant. Vote a Republican! Polititshian! Tobigli, Chititzen Republican. Naturalasize! March in a parade!"

Never lived native American prouder of his citizenship than this adopted one. Had he not voted at the election? Was he not a member of the great Republican party? He had eagerly joined it, for the reason that he had been a Republican in Italy, and he had drawn with him to the polls his second cousin, Leo Vesschi, and the five other Italians with whom he lived. For this, he had been rewarded by Pixley, his precinct committeeman, who allowed him to carry pink torches in three night processions.

"You keeb oud politigs," said Bertha, earnestly, one evening. "My uncle, Louie Gratz, he iss got a neighbour-lady; her man gone in politigs. After*vorts* he git it! He iss in der bennidenshierry two years. You know why?"

"Democrat!" shouted the chestnut vender triumphantly.

"No, sir! Yoost politigs," replied the unpartisan Bertha. "You keeb oud politigs."

"Ahaha, du libra Ogostine,
Ogostine, Ogostine!
Ahaha, du libra Ogostine,
Nees coma ross."

The song was always a teasing of her and carried all his friendly laughter at her, because of her German ways; but it became softly exultant whenever she betrayed her interest in him.

"Libra Ogostine, she afraid I go penitensh?" he inquired.

"Me!" she jeered with uneasy laughter. "*I* ain'd care! but you —you don' look oud, you git in dod voikhouse!"

He turned upon her, suddenly, a face like a mother's, and touched her hand with a light caress.

"I stay in a workhouse sevena-hunder' year," he said gently, "you come seeta by window some-a-time."

At this Bertha turned away, was silent for a space, leaning on the gate-post in front of her uncle's house, whither they were now come. Finally she answered brokenly: "I ain'd sit by no vinder for yoost a jessnut maan." This was her way of stimulating his ambition.

"Ahaha!" he cried. "You don' know? I'm goin' buy beeg stan'! Candy! Peanut! Banan'! Make some-a-time four dollar a day! 'Tis a greata countra! Bimaby git a store! Ride a buggy! Smoke a cigar! You play piano! Vote a Republican!"

"Toby!"

"Tis true!"

"Toby," she said tearfully; "Toby, you voik hart, und safe your money?"

"You help?" he whispered.

"I help—*you*!" she cried loudly. Then, with a sudden fit of sobbing, she flung open the gate and ran at the top of her speed into the house.

Halcyon the days for Pietro Tobigli, extravagant the jocularity of this betrothed one. And, as his happiness, so did his prosperity increase; the little chestnut furnace became the smallest adjunct of his affairs; for he leaped (almost at one bound) to the proprietorship of a wooden stand, shaped like the crate of an upright piano and backed up against the brick wall of the restaurant—a mercantile house which was closed at night by putting the lid on. All day long Toby's smile arrested pedestrians, and compelled them to buy of him, making his wares sweeter in the mouth. Bertha dwelt in a perpetual serenade: on warm days, when the restaurant doors were open, she could hear him singing, not always "Ogostine," but festal lilts of Italy, liquid and strangely sweet to her; and at such times, when the actual voice was not in her ears, still she blushed with delight to hear in her heart the thrilling echoes of his barcaroles, and found them humming cheerily upon her own lips.

Toby was to save five hundred dollars before they married, a great sum, but they were patient and both worked very hard. The winter would have fallen bitterly upon an outdoor merchant lacking Toby's confident heart, but on the coldest days, when Bertha looked out, she always found him slapping his hands and trudging up and down in the snow in front of the little box; and, as soon as he caught sight of her—"Ahaha, du libra Ogostine, Ogostine, Ogostine!"

She saved her own money with German persistence, and on Christmas day her present to her betrothed, in return for a coral pin, was a pair of rubber boots filled with little cakes.

Elysium was the dwelling-place of Pietro Tobigli, though, apparently, he abode in a horrible slum cellar with Leo Vesschi and the five Latti brothers. In this place our purveyor of sweetmeats was the only light. Thither he had carried his songs and his laugh and his furnace when he came from Italy to join Vesschi; and there he remained, partly out of loyalty to his unprosperous comrades, and partly because his share of the expense was only twenty-five cents a week, and every saving was a saving for Bertha. Every evening, on the homeward walk, the affianced pair passed the hideous stairway that led down to the cellar, and Bertha, neat soul, never failed to shudder at it. She did not know that Pietro lived there, for he feared it might distress her; nor could she ever persuade him to tell her where he lived.

Because of this mystery, upon which he merrily insisted, she affected a fear that he would some day desert her. "You don' tell me where you lif, I t'ink you goin' ran away of me, Toby. I vake opp some day; git a ledder dod you gone back home by 'Talian lady dod's grazy 'bout you!"

"Ahaha! Libra Ogostine, you believe I can make a write weet a pen-a-paper? I don' know that-a *how*. Some-a-time you *see* that gran' palazzo where I leef. Eesa greata-great sooraprise!"

In the gran' palazzo, it was as much as he could do to keep clean his own grim little bunk in the corner. His comrades, sullen, hopeless, came at evening from ten hours' desperate shovelling, and exhibited no ambition for water or brooms, but sat hunched and silent, or morosely muttering and coughing, in the dark room with its sodden earthen floor, stained walls, and one smoky lamp.

To this uncomfortable chamber repaired, one March evening, Mr. Frank Pixley, Republican precinct committee-man, nor was its dinginess an unharmonious setting for that political brilliant. He was a pock-pitted, damp-looking, soiled little fungus of a man, who had attained to his office because, in the dirtiest precinct of the wickedest ward in the city, he had, through the operation of a befitting ingenuity, forced a recognition of his leadership. From such an office, manned by a Pixley, there leads an upward ramification of wires, invisible to all except manipulators, which extends to higher surfaces. Usually the Pixley is a deep-sea puppet, wholly controlled by the dingily gilded wires that run down to him; but there are times when the Pixley gives forth initial impulses of his own, such as may alter the upper surface; for, in a system of this character, every twitch is felt throughout the whole ramification.

"Hello, boys," the committee-man called out with automatic geniality, as he descended the broken steps. "How are ye? All here? That's good; that's the stuff! Good work!"

Only Toby replied with more than an indifferent grunt; but he ran forward, carrying an empty beer keg which he placed as a seat for the guest.

"Aha*ha*, Meesa Peeslay! Make a parade? Torchlight? Banda-play—ta ra, la la la? Firework? Fzzz! Boum! Eh?"

The politician responded to Toby's extravagantly friendly laughter with some mechanical cachinnations which, like an obliging salesman, he turned on and off with no effort. "Not by a dern sight!" he answered. "The campaign ain't begun yet."

"Champagne?" inquired Tobigli politely.

"Campaign, campaign," explained Pixley. "Not much champagne in yours!" he chuckled beneath his breath. "Blame lucky to git Chicago bowl!"

"What is that, that campaign?"

"Why—why, it's the campaign. Workin' up public sentiment; gittin' you boys in line, 'lectioneerin'—fixin' it *right*."

Tobigli shook his head. "Campaign?" he repeated.

"Why—Gee, *you* know! Free beer, cigars, speakin', handshakin', paradin'—"

"Ahaha!" The merchant sprang to his feet with a shout. "Yes! Hoor-r-ra! Vote a Republican! Dam-a Democrat!"

"That's it," replied the committee-man somewhat languidly. "You see, this is a Republican precinct, and it turns the ward—"

"Allaways a Republican!" vociferated Pietro. "That eesa right?"

"Well," said the other, "of course, whichever way you go, you want to follow your precinct committee-man—that's me."

"Yess! Vote a Republican."

Pixley looked about the room, his little red eyes peering out cannily from under his crooked brows at each of the sulky figures in the damp shadows.

"You boys all vote the way Pete says?" he asked.

"Vote same Pietro," answered Vesschi. "Allaways."

"Allaways a Republican," added Pietro sparkingly, with abundant gesture. "'Tis a greata-great countra. Republican here same a Republican at home—eena Etallee. Republican eternall! All good Republican eena thees house! Hoor-r-ra!"

"Well," said Pixley, with a furtiveness half habit, as he rose to go, "of course, you want to keep your eye on your committee-man, and kind of foller along with him, whatever he does. That's me." He placed a dingy bottle on the keg. "I jest dropped in to see how you boys were gittin' along—mighty tidy little place you got here." He changed the stub of his burnt-out cigar to the other side of his mouth, shifting his eyes in the opposite direction, as he continued benevolently: "I thought I'd look in and leave this bottle o' gin fer ye, with my compliments. I'll be around ag'in some evenin', and I reckon before 'lection day comes there may be somep'n doin'—I might have better fer ye than a bottle. Keep your eye on me, boys, an' foller the leader. That's the idea. So long!"

"Vote a Republican!" Pietro shouted after him gaily.

Pixley turned.

"Jest foller yer leader," he rejoined. "That's the way to learn politics, boys."

Now as the rough spring wore on into the happier season, with the days like spiced warm wine, when people on the street are no longer driven by the weather but are won by it to loiter; now, indeed, did commerce at Toby's new stand so mightily thrive that, when summer came, Bertha was troubled as to the safety of Toby's profits.

"You yoost put your money by der builtun-loan 'sociation, Toby," she advised gently. "Dey safe ut fer you."

"T'ree hunder' fifta dolla—*no!*" answered her betrothed. "I keep in de pock'!" He showed her where the bills were pinned into his corduroy waistcoat pocket. "See! Eesa *you*! Onna my heart, libra Ogostine!"

"Toby, uf you ain'd dake ut by der builtun-loan, *blease* put ut in der bink?"

"I keep!" he repeated, shaking his head seriously. "In t'ree-four mont' eesa five-hunder-dolla. Nobody but me eesa tross weet that money."

Nor could Bertha persuade him. It was their happiness he watched over. Who to guard it as he, the dingy, precious parcel of bills? He pictured for himself a swampy forest through which he was laying a pathway to Bertha, and each of the soiled green notes that he pinned in his waistcoat was a strip of firm ground he had made, over which he advanced a few steps nearer her. And Bertha was very happy, even forgetting, for a while, to be afraid of the smallpox, which had thrown out little flags, like auction signs, here and there about the city.

When the full heat of summer came, Pietro laughed at the dog-days; and it was Bertha's to suffer in the hot little restaurant; but she smiled and waved to Pietro, so that he should not know. Also she made him sell iced lemonade and birch beer, which was well for the corduroy waistcoat pocket. Never have you seen a more alluring merchant. One glance toward the stand; you caught that flashing smile, the owner of it a-tiptoe to serve you; and Pietro managed, too, by a light jog to the table on which stood his big, bedewed, earthen jars, that you became aware of the tinkle of ice and a cold, liquid murmur—what mortal could deny the inward call and pass without stopping to buy?

There fell a night in September when Bertha beheld her lover glorious. She had been warned that he was to officiate in the great opening function of the campaign; and she stood on the corner for an hour before the head of the procession appeared. On they came—Pietro's party, three thousand strong; brass bands, fireworks, red fire, tumultuous citizens, political clubs, local potentates in open carriages, policemen, boys, dogs, bicycles—the procession doing all the cheering for itself, the crowds of spectators only feebly responding to this enthusiasm, as is our national custom. At the end of it all marched a plentiful crew of tatterdemalions, a few bleared white men, and the rest negroes. They bore aloft a crazy transparency, exhibiting the legend:

"FRANK PIXLEY'S HARD-MONEY LEAGUE.

WE STAND FOR OUR PRINCIPALS.

WE ARE SOLLID!

NO FOOLING THE PEOPLE GOES!

WE VOTE AS ONE MAN FOR

TAYLOR P. SINGLETON!"

Bertha's eyes had not rested upon Toby where they innocently sought him, in the front ranks, even scanning the carriages, seeking him in all positions which she conceived as highest in honour, and she would have missed him altogether, had not there reached her, out of chaotic clamours, a clear, high, rollicking tenor:

"Ahaha! du libra Ogostine,
Ogostine, Ogostine!
Ahaha! du libra Ogostine,
Nees coma ross!"

Then the eager eyes found their pleasure, for there, in the last line of Pixley's pirates, the very tail of the procession, danced Pietro Tobigli, waving his pink torch at her, proud, happy, triumphant, a true Republican, believing all company equal in the republic, and the rear rank as good as the first.

"Vote a Republican!" he shouted. "Republican—Republican eternall!"

Strangely enough, a like fervid protestation (vociferated in greeting) evoked no reciprocal enthusiasm in the breast of Mr. Pixley, when the committee-man called upon Toby and his friends at their apartment one evening, a fortnight later.

"That's right," he responded languidly. "That's right in gineral, I *should* say. Cert'nly, in *gineral*, I ain't got no quarrel with no man's Republicanism. But this here's kind of a puttickler case, boys. The election's liable to be mighty close."

"Republican win!" laughed Toby. "Meelyun man eena parade!"

Mr. Pixley's small eyes lowered furtively. He glanced once toward the door, stroked his stubby chin, and answered softly: "Don't you be too sure of that, young feller. Them banks is fightin' each other ag'in!"

"Bank? Fight? W'at eesa that?" inquired the merchant, with an entirely blank mind.

"There's one thing it *ain't*," replied the other, in the same confidential tone. "It ain't no two-by-four campaign. All I got to say to you boys is: 'Foller yer leader'—and you'll wear pearl collar-buttons!"

"Vote a Republican," interjected Leo Vesschi gutturally.

The furtiveness of Mr. Pixley increased. "Well—mebbe," he responded, very deliberately. "I reckon I better put you boys next, right now's well's any other time. Ain't nothin' ever gained by not bein' open 'n' above-board; that's my motto, and I ack up to it. You kin ast 'em, jest ast the boys, and you'll hear it from each-an-dall: 'Frank Pixley's *square*!' That's what they'll tell ye. Now see here, this is the way it is. I ain't worryin' much about who goes to the legislature, or who's county-commissioners, nor none o' *that*. *Why* ain't I worryin'? Because it's picayune. It's peanut politics. It ain't where the money is. No, sir, this campaign is on the treasurership. Taylor P. Singleton is runnin' fer treasurer on the Republican ticket, and Gil. Maxim on the Democratic. But that ain't where the fight is." Mr. Pixley spat contemptuously. "Pah! whichever of 'em gits it won't no more'n draw his salary. It's the banks. If Singleton wins out, the Washington National gits the use of the county's money fer the term; if Maxim's elected, Florenheim's bank gits it. Florenheim laid down the cash fer Maxim's nomination, and the Washington National fixed it fer Singleton. And it's big money, don't you git no wrong idea about *that*!"

"Vote a Republican," said Toby politely.

A look of pain appeared upon the brow of the committeeman.

"I reckon I ain't hardly made myself clear," he observed, somewhat plaintively. "Now here, you listen: I reckon it would be kind of resky to trust you boys to scratch the ticket—it's a mixed up business, anyway—"

"Vote a straight!" cried Pietro, nodding his head, cheerfully. "*Yess!* I teach Leo; yess, teach all these"—he waved his hands to indicate the melancholy listeners—"teach them all. Stamp in a circle by that eagle. Vote a Republican!"

"What I was goin' to say," went on the official, exhibiting tokens of impatience and perturbation, "was that if we *should* make any switch this year, I guess you boys would have to switch straight."

"'Tis true!" was the hearty response. "Vote a straight Republican. Republican eternall!"

Pixley wiped his forehead with a dirty handkerchief, and scratched his head. "See here," he said, after a pause, to Toby.

"I've got to go down to Collins's saloon, and I'd like to have you come along. Feel like going?"

"Certumalee," answered Toby with alacrity, reaching for his hat.

But no one could have been more surprised than the chestnut vender when, on reaching the vacant street, his companion glancing cautiously about, beckoned him into the darkness of an alley-way, and, noiselessly upsetting a barrel, indicated it as a seat for both.

"Here," said Pixley, "I reckon this is better. Jest two men by theirselves kin fix up a thing like this a lot quicker, and I seen you didn't want to talk too much before *them*. You make your own deal with 'em afterwards, or none at all, jest as you like! They'll do whatever you say, anyway. I sized you up to run *that* bunch, first time I ever laid eyes on the outfit. Now see here, Pete, you listen to me. I reckon I kin turn a little trick here that'll do you some good. You kin bet I see that the men I pick fer my leaders—like you, Pete—git their rights! Now here: there's you and the other six, that's seven; it'll be three dollars in your pocket if you deliver the goods."

"No! no!" said Pietro in earnest protestation. "We seven a good Republican. We vote a Republican—same las' time, all a time. Eet eesa not a need to pay us to vote a Republican. You save that a money, Meesa Peaslay."

"You don't understand," groaned Pixley, with an inclination to weep over the foreigner's thick-headedness. "There's a chance fer a big deal here for all the boys in the precinck. Gil. Maxim's backers'll pay *big* fer votes enough to swing it. The best of 'em don't know where they're at, I tell you. Now here, you see here"—he took an affectionate grip of Pietro's collar—"I'm goin' to have a talk with Maxim's manager to-morrow, I've had one or two a'ready, and I'll put up the price all round on them people. It's no more'n right, when you count up what we're doin' fer them. Look here, you swing them six in line and march 'em up, and all of ye stamp the rooster instead of the eagle this time, and help me to show Maxim that Frank Pixley's there with the goods, and I'll hand you a five-dollar bill and a full box o' *cig*ars, see?"

Pietro nodded and smiled through the darkness. "Stamp that eagle!" he answered, "eesa all *right*, Meesa Peasley. Don't you have afraid. We all seven a good Republican! Stamp that eagle! Hoor-r-ra! Republican *eternall*!"

Pixley was left sitting on the barrel, looking after the light figure of the young man joyously tripping back to the cellar, and turning to wave a hand in farewell from the street.

"Well, I *am* damned!" the politician remarked, with unwitting veracity. "Did the dern Dago bluff me, does he want more, er did he reely didn't un'erstand fer honest?" Then, as he took up his way, crossing the street at the warning of some red and green smallpox lanterns, "I'll git those seven votes, though, *some*way. I'm out fer a record this time, and I'll *git* 'em!"

Bertha went with her fiancé to select the home that was to be theirs. They found a clean, tidy, furnished room, with a canary bird thrown in, and Toby, in the wild joy of his heart, seized his sweetheart round the waist and tried to force her to dance under the amazed eyes of the landlady.

"You yoost behafed awful!" exclaimed the blushing waitress that evening, with tears of laughter at the remembrance.

She was as happy as her lover, except for two small worries that she had: she feared that her uncle, Louie Gratz, with whom she lived, or one of her few friends, might, when they found she was to marry Toby, allude to him as a "Dago," in which case she had an intuition that he would slap the offender; and she was afraid of the smallpox, which had caused the quarantine of two shanties not far from her uncle's house. The former of her fears she did not mention, but the latter she spoke of frequently, telling Pietro how Gratz was panic-stricken, and talked of moving, and how glad she was that Toby's "gran' palazzo" was in another quarter of the city, as he had led her to believe. Laughing her humours almost away, he told her that the red and green lanterns, threatening murkily down the street, were for only wicked ones, like that Meesa Peaslay, for whom she discovered, Pietro's admiration had diminished. And when she thought of the new home—far across the city from the ugly flags and lanterns—the tiny room with its engraving of the "Rock of Ages" and its canary, she forgot both her troubles entirely; for now, at last, the marvellous fact was assured: the five hundred dollars was pinned into the waistcoat pocket, lying upon Pietro's heart day and night, the precious lump that meant to him Bertha and a home. The good Republican set election-day for the happiest holiday of his life, for that would be his wedding-day.

He left her at her own gate, the evening before that glorious day, and sang his way down the street, feeling that he floated on the airy uplift of his own barcarole beneath sapphire skies, for Bertha had put her arms about him at last.

"Toby," she said, "lieber Toby, I am so all-lofing by you—you are sitch a good maan—I am so—so—I am yoost all-*lofing* by you!" And she cried heartily upon his shoulder. "Toby, uf you ain'd here for me to-morrow by eckseckly dwelf o'glock, uf you are von minutes late, I'm goin' yoost fall down deat! Don' you led nothings happen mit you, Toby."

And she had whispered to him, in love with his old tender mockery of her, to sing "Libra Ogostine" for her before he said good-night.

Mr. Pixley, again seated upon the barrel which he had used for his interview with Toby, beheld the transfigured face of the young man as the chestnut vender passed the mouth of the alley, and the committee-man released from his soul a burdening profanity in the ear of his companion and confidant, a policeman who would be on duty in Pixley's precinct on the morrow, and who had now reported for instructions not necessarily received in a too public rendezvous.

"After I talked to him out here on this very barrel," said Pixley, his anathema concluded, "I raised the bid on him; yessir, you kin skin me fer a dead skunk if I didn't offer him ten dollars and a box of *cig*ars fer the bunch; and him jest settin' there laughin' like a plumb fool and tellin' me I didn't need to worry, they'd all vote Republican fer nothin'! Talked like a parrot: 'Vote a Republican! Republican eternal!' *Republican!* Faugh, he don't know no more why he's a Republican than a yeller dog'd know! I went around to-night, when he was out, thought mebbe I could fix it up with the others. No, *sir*! Couldn't git nothing out of 'em except some more parrot-cackle: 'Vote same Petro. All a good Republican!' It's enough to sicken a man!"

"Do we need this gang bad?" inquired the policeman deferentially.

"I need everybody bad! This is a good-sized job fer me, and I want to do it right. Throwin' the precinck to Maxim is goin' to do me *some* wrong with the Republican crowd, even if they don't git on that it was throwed; and I want to throw it *good*! I couldn't feel like I'd done right if I didn't. I've give my word that they'll git a majority of sixty-eight votes, and that'll be jest twicet as much in my pocket as a plain majority. And I want them seven Dagoes! I've give up on *votin'* 'em; it can't be done. It'd make a saint cuss to try to reason with 'em, and it's no good. They can't be fooled, neither. They know where the polls is, and they know how to vote—blast the Australian ballot system! The most that can be done is to keep 'em away from the polls."

"Can't you git 'em out of town in the morning?"

"D' you reckon I ain't tried that? *No*, sir! That Dago wouldn't take a pass to *heaven*! Everything else is all right. Doc Morgan's niggers stays right here and *votes*. I *know* them boys, and they'll walk up and stamp the rooster all right, all right. Them other niggers, that Hell-Valley gang, ain't that kind; and them and Tooms's crowd's goin' to be took out to Smelter's ice-houses in three express wagons at four o'clock in the morning. It ain't goin' to cost over two dollars a head, whiskey and all. Then, Dan Kelly is fixed, and the Loo boys. Mike, I don't like to brag, and I ain't around throwin' no bokays at myself as a reg'lar thing, but I want to say right here, there ain't another man in this city—no, nor the State neither—that could of worked his precinck better'n I have this. I tell you, I'm within five or six votes of the majority they set for their big money."

"Have you give the Dagoes up altogether?"

"No, by——!" cried the committee-man harshly, bringing his dirty fist down on the other's knee. "Did you ever hear of Frank Pixley weakenin'? Did you ever see the man that said Frank Pixley wasn't game?" He rose to his feet, a ragged and sinister silhouette against the sputtering electric light at the alley mouth. "Didn't you ever hear that Frank Pixley had a barrel of schemes to any other man's bucket o' wind? What's Frank Pixley's repitation lemme ast you that? I git what I go after, don't I? Now look here, you listen to me," he said, lowering his voice and shaking a bent forefinger earnestly in the policeman's face; "I'm goin' to turn the trick. And I *ought* to do it, too. That there Pete, he ain't worth the powder to blow him up—you couldn't learn him no politics if you set up with him night after night fer a year. Didn't I *try*? *Try?* I dern near bust my head open jest thinkin' up ways to make the flathead *see*. And he wouldn't make no effort, jest set there and parrot out 'Vote a Republican!' He's ongrateful, that's what he is. Well, him and them other Dagoes are goin' to stay at home fer two weeks, beginnin' to-night."

"I'll be dogged if I see how," said the policeman, lifting his helmet to scratch his head.

"I'll show you how. I don't claim no credit fer the idea, I ain't around blowin' my own horn too often, but I'd like fer somebody to jest show me any other man in this city could have thought it out! I'd like to be showed jest one, that's all, jest one! Now, you look here; you see that nigger shanty over there, with the smallpox lanterns outside?"

The policeman shivered slightly. "Yes."

"Look here; they're rebuildin' the pest-house, ain't they?"

"Yes."

"Leavin' smallpox patients in their own holes under quarantine guard till they git a place to put 'em, ain't they?"

"Yes."

"You know how many niggers in that shack?"

"Four, ain't they?"

"Yessir, four of 'em. One died to-night, another's goin' to, another ain't tellin' which way he's goin' yit; and the last one, Joe Cribbins, was the first to take it; and he's almost plumb as good as ever ag'in. He's up and around the house, helpin' nurse the sick ones, and fit fer hard labour. Now look here; that nigger does what I *tell* him and he does it quick—see? Well, he knows what I want him to do to-night. So does Charley Gruder, the guard over there. Charley's fixed; I seen to that; and knows he ain't goin' to lose no job fer the nigger's gittin' out of the back winder to go make a little sociable call this evening."

"What!" exclaimed the policeman, startled; "Charley ain't goin' to let that nigger out!"

"Ain't he? Oh, you needn't worry, he ain't goin' *fur*! All he's waiting fer is fer you to give the signal."

"Me!" The man in the helmet drew back.

"Yessir, you! You walk out there and lounge up towards the drug-store and jest look over to Charley and nod twice. Then you stand on the corner and watch and see what you see. When you *see* it, you yell fer Charley and git into the drug store telephone, and call up the health office and git their men up here and into that Dago cellar like hell! The nigger'll be there. They don't know him, and he'll just drop in to try and sell the Dagoes some policy tickets. You understand *me*?"

"Mother Mary in heaven!" The policeman sprang up. "What are you going to do?"

"What am I going to do?" shrilled the other, the light of a monstrous pride in his little eyes. "I'm goin' to quarantine them Dagoes fer fourteen days. They'll learn some politics before I git through with 'em. Maybe they'll know enough United States language to foller their leader next time!"

"By all that's mighty, Pixley," said the policeman, with an admiration that was almost reverence, "you *are* a schemer!"

"Mein Gott!" screeched Bertha's uncle, snapping his teeth fiercely on his pipe-stem, as he flung open the door of the girl's room. "You want to disgraze me mit der whole neighbourhoot, 'lection night? Quid ut! Stob ut! Beoples in der streed stant owidside und litzen to dod grying. You *voult* goin' to marry mit a Dago mens, voult you! Ha, ha! Soife you right! He run away!" The old man laughed unamiably. "Ha, ha! Dago mens foolt dod smard Bertha. Dod's pooty tough. But, bei Gott, you stop dod noise und ect lige a detzent voomans, or you goin' haf droubles mit your uncle Louie Gratz!"

But Bertha, an undistinguishable heap on the floor of the unlit room, only gasped brokenly for breath and wept on.

"Ach, ach, ach, lieber Gott in Himmel!" sobbed Bertha. "Why didn't Toby come for me? Ach, ach! What iss happened mit Toby? Somedings iss happened—I *know* ut!"

"Ya, ya!" jibed Gratz; "somedings iss heppened, I bet you! Brop'ly he's got anoder vife, dod's vot heppened! Brop'ly *leffing* ad you mit anoder voomans! Vot for dit he nefer tolt you vere he lif? So you voultn't ketch him; dod's der reason! You're a pooty vun, *you* are! Runnin' efter a doity Dago mens! Bei Gott! you bedder git oop und back your glo'es, und stob dod gryin'. I'm goin' to mofe owid to-morrow; und you kin go verefer you blease. I ain'd goin' to sday anoder day in sitch a neighbourhoot. Fife more smallpox lanterns yoost oop der streed. I'm goin' mofe glean to der oder ent of der city. Und you can come by me or you can run efter your Dago mens und his voomans! Dod's why he dittn't come to marry you, you grazy—ut's a voomans!"

"No, *no*," screamed Bertha, stopping her ears with her forefingers. "Lies, lies, lies!"

A slatternly negro woman dawdled down the street the following afternoon, and, encountering a friend of like description near the cottage which had been tenanted by Louie Gratz and his niece, paused for conversation.

"Howdy, honey," she began, leaning restfully against the gate-post. "How's you ma?"

"She right spry," returned the friend. "How you'self an' you good husban', Miz Mo'ton?"

Mrs. Morton laughed cheerily. "Oh, he enjoyin' de 'leckshum. He 'uz on de picnic yas'day, to Smeltuh's ice-houses; an' 'count er Mist' Maxim's gitting 'lected, dey gi'n him bottle er whiskey an' two dollahs. He up at de house now, entuhtainin' some ge'lemen frien's wi' de bones, honey."

"Um hum." The other lady sighed reflectively. "I on'y wisht my po' husban' could er live to enjoy de fruits er politics."

"Yas'm," returned Mrs. Morton. "You right. It are a great intrus' in a man's life. Dat what de ornator say in de speech f'm de back er de groce'y wagon, yas'm, a great intrus' in a man's life. Decla'h, I b'lieve Goe'ge think mo' er politics dan he do er me! Well ma'am," she concluded, glancing idly up and down the street and leaning back more comfortably against the gate-post, "I mus' be goin' on my urrant."

"What urrant's dat?" inquired the widow.

"Mighty quare urrant," replied Mrs. Morton. "Mighty quare urrant, honey. You see back yon'eh dat new smallpox flag?"

"Sho."

"Well ma'am, night fo' las', dat Joe Cribbins, dat one-eye nigger what sell de policy tickets, an's done be'n havin' de smallpox, he crope out de back way, when's de gyahd weren't lookin', an', my Lawd, ef dey ain't ketch him down in dat Dago cellar, tryin' sell dem Dagoes policy tickets! Yahah, honey!"

Mrs. Morton threw back her head to laugh. "Ain't dat de beatenest nigger, dat one-eyed Joe?"

"What den, Miz Mo'ton?" pursued the listener.

"Den dey quahumteem dem Dagoes; sot a gyahd dah: you kin see him settin' out dah now. Well ma'am, 'cordin' to dat gyahd, one er dem Dagoes like ter go inter fits all day yas'day. Dat man hatter go in an' quiet him down ev'y few minute'. Seem 't he boun' sen' a message an' cain't git no one to ca'y it fer him. De gyahd, he cain't go; he willin' sen' de message, but cain't git nobody come nigh enough de place fer to tell 'em what it is. 'Sides, it 'leckshum-day, an' mos' folks hangin' 'roun' de polls. Well ma'am, dis aft'noon, I so'nter'n by, an' de gyahd holler out an' ask me do I want make a dollah, an' I say I do. I ain't 'fraid no smallpox, done had it two year' ago. So I say I take de message."

"What is it?"

"Law, honey, it ain't wrote. Dem Dago folks hain't got no writin' ner readin'. Dey mo' er less like de beasts er de fiel'. Dat message by word er mouf. I goin' tell nuffin 'bout de quahumteem. I'm gotter say: 'Toby sen' word to liebuh Augustine dat she needn' worry. He li'l sick, not much, but de doctah ain' 'low him out fer two weeks; an' 'mejutly at de en' er dat time he come an' git her an' den kin go on home wheres de canary bu'd is.' Honey, you evah hyuh o' sich a foolishness? But de gyahd, he say de message gotter be ca'yied dass dataways."

"Lan' name!" ejaculated the widow. "Who dat message to?"

"Hit to a Dutch gal."

"My Lawd!" The widow lifted amazed hands to heaven. "De impidence er dem Dagoes! *Little* mo' an' dey'll be sen'in' messages to you er me!—What her name?"

"Name Bertha Grass," responded Mrs. Morton, "an', nigh as I kin make out, she live in one er dese little w'ite-paint cottages, right 'long yere."

"Yas'm! I knows dat Dutch gal, ole man Grass, de tailor, dass his niece. W'y, dey done move out dis mawn, right f'um dis ve'y house you stan'in in front de gate of. De ole man skeered er de smallpox, an' he mad, too, an' de neighbuhs ask him whuh he gwine, he won't tell; so mad he won't speak to nobody. None on 'em 'round hyuh knows an' dey's considabul cyu'us 'bout it, too. Dey gone off in bofe d'rections—him one way, her 'nother. 'Peak lak dey be'n quollun!"

"Now look at dat!" cried Mrs. Morton dolefully. "Look at dat! Ain't dat de doggonest luck in de wide worl'! De gyahd he say dat Dago willin' pay fifty cents a day fo' me to teck an' bring a message eve'y mawn' tell de quahumteem took off de cellar. Now dat Dutch gal gone an' loss dat money fo' me—movin' 'way whuh nobody cain't fine 'er!"

"Sho!" laughed the widow. "Ef I'se in you place, Miz Mo'ton, an' you's in mine, dat money sho'lly, sho'lly nevah would be los', indeed hit wouldn't. I dass go in t' de do' an' tu'n right 'roun' back ag'in an' go down to dat gyahd an' say de Dutch gal 'ceive de message wid de bes' er 'bligin' politeness an' sent her kine regyahds to de Dago man an' all inquirin' frien's, an' hope de Dago man soon come an' git 'er. To-morrer de same, nex' day de same—"

"Lawd, ef dat ain't de beatenest!" cried Mrs. Morton delightedly. "Well, honey, I thank you long as I live, 'cause I nevah'd a wuk dat out by myself in de livin' worl', an' I sho does needs de money. I'm goin' do exackly dass de way you say. Dat man he ain' goin' know no diffunce till he git out—an' den, honey," she let loose upon the quiet air a sudden, great salvo of laughter, "dass let him fine Lize Mo'ton!"

Bertha went to live in the tiny room with the canary bird and the engraving of the "Rock of Ages." This was putting lime to the canker, but, somehow, she felt that she could go to no other place. She told the landlady that her young man had not done so well in business as they had expected, and had sought work in another city. He would come back, she said.

She woke from troubled dreams each morning to stifle her sobbing in the pillow. "Ach, Toby, coultn't you sented me yoost one word, you *might* sented me yoost one word, yoost one, to tell me what has happened mit you! Ach, Toby, Toby!"

The canary sang happily; she loved it and tended it, and the gay little prisoner tried to reward her by the most marvellous trilling in his power, but her heart was the sorer for every song.

After a time she went back drearily to the kraut-smelling restaurant, to the work she had thought to leave forever, that day when Toby had not come for her. She went out twenty times every morning, and oftener as it wore on towards evening, to look at his closed stand, always with a choking hope in her heart, always to drag leaden feet back into the restaurant. Several times, her breath failing for shame, she approached Italians in the street, or where there was one to be found at a stand of any sort she stopped and made a purchase, and asked for some word of Toby—without result, always. She knew no other way to seek for him.

One day, as she trudged homeward, two coloured women met on the pavement in front of her, exchanged greetings, and continued for a little way together.

"How you enjoyin' you' money, dese fine days, Miz Mo'ton?" inquired one, with a laugh that attested to the richness of the joke between the two.

"Law, honey," answered the other, "dat good luck di'n' las' ve'y long. Dey done shut off my supplies."

"No!"

"Yas'm, dey sho did. Dat man done tuck de smallpox; all on 'em ketched it, ev'y las' one, off'n dat no 'count Joe Cribbins, an' now dat dey got de new pes'-house finish', dey haul 'em off yon'eh, yas'day. Reckon dat ain' make no diffunce in my urrant runnin'. Dat Dago man, he outer he hade two day fo' dey haul 'em away, an' ain' sen' no mo' messages. So dat spile *my* job! Hit dass my luck. Dey's sho' a voodoo on Lize Mo'ton!"

Bertha, catching but fragments of this conversation, had no realization that it bore in any way upon the mystery of Toby; and she stumbled homeward through the twilight with her tired eyes on the ground.

When she opened the door of the tiny room, the landlady's lean black cat ran out surreptitiously. The bird-cage lay on the floor, upside down, and of its jovial little inhabitant the tokens were a few yellow feathers.

Bertha did not know until a month after, when Leo Vesschi found her at the restaurant and told her, that out in the new pest-house, that other songster and prisoner, the gay little chestnut vender, Pietro Tobigli, had called lamentably upon the name of his God and upon "Libra Ogostine," and now lay still forever, with the corduroy waistcoat and its precious burden tightly clenched to his breast. Even in his delirium they had been unable to coax or force him to part from it for a second.

The Need of Money

FAR BACK in his corner on the Democratic side of the House, Uncle Billy Rollinson sat through the dragging routine of the legislative session, wondering what most of it meant. When anybody spoke to him, in passing, he would answer, in his gentle, timid voice, "Howdy-do, sir." Then his cheeks would grow a little red and he would stroke his long, white beard elaborately, to cover his embarrassment. When a vote was taken, his name was called toward the last of the roll, so that he had ample time, after the leader of his side of the House, young Hurlbut, had voted, to clear his throat several times and say "Aye" or "No" in quite a firm voice. But the instant the word had left his lips he found himself terribly frightened, and stroked his beard a great many times, the while he stared seriously up at the ceiling, partly to avoid meeting anybody's eye, and partly in the belief that it concealed his agitation and gave him the air of knowing what he was about. Usually he did not know, any more than he knew how he had happened to be sent to the legislature by his county. But he liked it. He liked the feeling of being a person to be considered; he liked to think that he was making the laws of his State. He liked the handsome desk and the easy leather chair; he liked the row of fat, expensive volumes, the unlimited stationery, and the free penknives which were furnished him. He enjoyed the attentions of the coloured men in the cloak-room, who brushed him ostentatiously and always called him (and the other Representatives) "Senator," to make up to themselves for the airs which the janitors of the "Upper House" assumed. Most of these things surprised him; he had not expected to be treated with such liberality by the State and never realized that he and his colleagues were treating themselves to all these things at the expense of the people, and so, although he bore off as much note-paper as he could carry, now and then, to send to his son, Henry, he was horrified and dumbfounded when the bill was proposed appropriating $135,000 for the expenses of the seventy days' session of the legislature.

He was surprised to find that among his "perquisites" were

passes (good during the session) on all the railroads that entered the State, and others for use on many inter-urban trolley lines. These, he thought, might be gratifying to Henry, who was fond of travel, and had often been unhappy when his father failed to scrape up enough money to send him to a circus in the next county. It was "very accommodating of the railroads," Uncle Billy thought, to maintain this pleasant custom, because the members' travelling expenses were paid by the State just the same; hence the economical could "draw their mileage" at the Treasurer's office, and add it to their salaries. He heard—only vaguely understanding—many joking references to other ways of adding to salaries.

Most of the members of his party had taken rooms at one of the hotels, whither those who had sought cheaper apartments repaired in the evening, when the place became a noisy and crowded club, admission to which was not by card. Most of the rougher man-to-man lobbying was done here; and at times it was Babel.

Through the crowds Uncle Billy wandered shyly, stroking his beard and saying, "Howdy-do, sir," in his gentle voice, getting out of the way of people who hurried, and in great trouble of mind if any one asked him how he intended to vote upon a bill. When this happened he looked at the interrogator in the plaintive way which was his habit, and answered slowly: "I reckon I'll have to think it over." He was not in Hurlbut's councils.

There was much bustle all about him, but he was not part of it. The newspaper reporters remarked the quiet, inoffensive old figure pottering about aimlessly on the outskirts of the crowd, and thought Uncle Billy as lonely as a man might well be, for he seemed less a part of the political arrangement than any member they had ever seen. He would have looked less lonely and more in place trudging alone through the furrows of his home fields in a wintry twilight.

And yet, everybody liked the old man, Hurlbut in particular, if Uncle Billy had known it; for Hurlbut watched the votes very closely and was often struck by the soundness of Representative Rollinson's intelligence in voting.

In return, Uncle Billy liked Hurlbut better than any other man he had ever known—except Henry, of course. On the first day of the session, when the young leader had been pointed out to him, Uncle Billy's humble soul was prostrate with admiration, and when Hurlbut led the first attack on the monopolistic tendencies of the Republican party, Representative Rollinson, chuckling in his beard at the handsome youth's audacity, himself dared so greatly as to clap his hands aloud. Hurlbut, on the floor, was always a storm centre: tall, dramatic, bold, the members put down their newspapers whenever his strong voice was heard demanding recognition, and his "Mr. Speaker!" was like the first rumble of thunder. The tempest nearly always followed, and there were times when it threatened to become more than vocal; when, all order lost, nine-tenths of the men on the other side of the House were on their feet shouting jeers and denunciations, and the orator faced them, out-thundering them all, with his own cohorts, flushed and cheering, gathered round him. Then, indeed, Uncle Billy would have thought him a god, if he had known what a god was.

Sometimes Uncle Billy saw him in the hotel lobby, but he seemed always to be making for the elevator in a hurry, with half-a-dozen people trying to detain him, or descending momentarily from the stairway for a quick, sharp talk with one or two members, their heads close together, after which Hurlbut would dart upward again.

Sometimes the old man sat down at one of the writing tables, in a corner of the lobby, and, annexing a sheet of the hotel note-paper, "wrote home" to Henry. He sat with his head bent far over, the broad brim of his felt hat now and then touching the hand with which he kept the paper from sliding; and he pressed diligently upon his pen, usually breaking it before the letter was finished. He looked so like a man bent upon concealment that the reporters were wont to say: "There's Uncle Billy humped up over his guilty secret again."

The secret usually took this form:

Dear Son Henry:

I would be glad if you was here. There is big doings. Hurlbut give it to them to-day. He don't give the Republicans no rest. he lights into them like sixty you would like to see him. They are plenty nice fellows in the Republicans too but they lay mighty low when Hurlbut gets after them. He was just in the office but went out. He always has a segar in his mouth but not lit. I expect hes quit. I send you enclosed last week's salary all but $11.80 which I had to use as living is pretty high in our capital city of the state. If you would like some of this hotel writing paper better than the kind I sent you of the General Assembly I can send you some the boys say it is free. I think it is all right you sold the calf but Wilkes didn't give you good price. Hurlbut come in while I was writing then. You bet he can always count on Wm. Rollinson's vote.

Well I must draw to a close, Yours truly

Your father.

"Wm. Rollinson" did not know that he was known to his colleagues and the lobby and the Press as "Uncle Billy" until informed thereof by a public print. He stood, one night, on the edge of a laughing group, when a reporter turned to him and said:

"The *Constellation* would like to know Representative Rollinson's opinion of the scandalous story that has just been told."

The old man, who had not in the least understood the story, summoned all his faculties, and, after long deliberation, bent his plaintive eyes upon the youth and replied:

"Well, sir, it's a-stonishing, a-stonishing!"

"Think it's pretty bad, do you?"

Some of the crowd turned to listen, and the old fellow, hopelessly puzzled, stroked his beard with a trembling hand, and then, muttering, "Well, young man, I expect you better excuse me," hurried away and left the place. The next morning he found the following item tacked to the tail of the "Legislative Gossip" column of the *Constellation*:

UNCLE BILLY ROLLINSON HORRIFIED

Yesterday a curious and amusing story was current among the solons at the Nagmore Hotel. It seems that the wife of a country member of the last legislature had been spending the day at the hotel and the wife of a present member from the country complained to her of the greatly increased expenditure appertaining to the cost of living in the Capital City. "Indeed," replied the wife of the former member, "that is curious. But I suppose my husband is much more economical than yours, for he brought home $1.500, that he'd saved out of his salary." As the salary is only $456, and the gentleman in question did not play poker, much hilarity was indulged in, and there were conjectures that the economy referred to concerned his vote upon a certain bill before the last session, anent which the lobby pushing it were far from economical. Uncle Billy Rollinson, the Gentleman from Wixinockee, heard the story, as it passed from mouth to mouth, but he had no laughter to greet it. Uncle Billy, as every one who comes in contact with him knows, is as honest as the day is long, and the story grieved and shocked him. He expressed the utmost horror and consternation, and requested to be excused from speaking further upon a subject so repugnant to his feelings. If there were more men of this stamp in politics, who find corruption revolting instead of amusing, our legislatures would enjoy a better fame.

Uncle Billy had always been agitated by the sight of his name in print. Even in the Wixinockee County *Clarion*, it dumbfounded him and gave him a strange feeling that it must mean somebody else, but this sudden blaze of metropolitan fame made him almost giddy. He folded the paper quickly and placed it under his coat, feeling vaguely that it would not do to be seen reading it. He murmured feeble answers during the day, when some of his colleagues referred to it; but when he reached his own little room that evening, he spread it out under his oil-smelling lamp and read it again. Perhaps he read it twenty times over before the supper bell rang. Perhaps the fact that he was still intent upon it accounted for his not hearing the bell, so that his landlady had to call him.

What he liked was the phrase: "Honest as the day is long." He did not go to the hotel that night. He went back to his room and read the *Constellation*. He liked the *Constellation*. Newspapers were very kind, he thought. Now and then, he would pick up his pile of legislative bills and try to spell through the ponderous sentences, but he always gave it up and went back to the *Constellation*. He wondered if Hurlbut had read it. Hurlbut had. The leader had even told the author of the item that he was glad somebody could appreciate the kind of a man Uncle Billy was, and his value to the body politic.

"Honest as the day is long," Uncle Billy repeated to himself, in the little room, nodding his head gravely. Then he thought for a long while about the member who had, according to the story, gone home with $1,500. He sat up, that evening, until almost ten o'clock. Even after he had gone to bed, he lay awake with his eyes wide open in the darkness, thinking of the colossal sum. If anybody should come to *him* and offer him all that money to vote a certain way upon a bill, he believed he would not take it, for that would be bribery; though Henry would be glad to have the money. Henry always needed money; sometimes the need was imperative—once, indeed, so imperative that the small, unfertile farm had been mortgaged beyond its value, otherwise very serious things must have happened to Henry. Uncle Billy wondered how offers of money to members were refused without hurting the intending donor's feelings. And what a great deal could be done with $1,500, if a member could get it and still be as honest as the day is long!

About the second month of the session the floor of the House began steadily to grow more and more tumultuous. To an unpolitical onlooker, leaning over the gallery rail, it was often an incomprehensible Bedlam, or perhaps one might have been reminded of an ant-heap by the hurry and scurry and life and death haste in a hundred directions at once, quite without any distinguishable purpose. Twenty men might be rampaging up and down the aisles, all shouting, some of them furiously, others with a determination that was deadly, all with arms waving at the Speaker, some of the hands clenched, some of them fluttering documents, while pages ran everywhere in mad haste, stumbling and falling in the aisles. In the midst of this, other members, seated, wrote studiously; others mildly read newspapers; others lounged, half-standing against their desks, unlighted cigars in their mouths, laughing; all the while the patient Speaker tapped with his gavel on a small square of marble. Suddenly perfect calm would come and the voice of the reading clerk drone for half an hour or more, like a single bee in a country garden on Sunday morning.

Of all this Uncle Billy was as much a layman spectator as any tramp who crept into the gallery for a few hours out of the cold. The hurry and seethe of the racing sea touched him not at all, except to bewilderment, while he was carried with it, unknowing, toward the breakers. The shout of those breakers was already in the ears of many, for the crisis of the session was coming. This was the fight that was to be made on Hurlbut's "Railroad Bill," which was, indeed, but in another sense, known as the "Breaker."

Uncle Billy had heard of the "Breaker." He couldn't have helped that. He had heard a dozen say: "Then's when it's going to be warm times, when that 'Breaker' comes up!" or, "Look out for that 'Breaker.' We're going to have big trouble." He knew, too, that Hurlbut was interested in the "Breaker," but upon which side he was for a long time ignorant.

Hurlbut always nodded to the old man, now, as he came down the aisle to his own desk. He had begun that, the day after the *Constellation* item. Uncle Billy never failed to be in his seat early in the morning, waiting for the nod. He answered it with his usual "Howdy-do, sir," then stroked his beard and gazed profoundly at the row of fat volumes in front of him, swallowing painfully once or twice.

This was all that really happened for Uncle Billy during the turmoil and scramble that went on about him all the day long. He had not been forced to discover a way to meet an offer of $1,500, without hurting the putative donor's feelings. No lobbyist had the faintest idea of "approaching" the old man in that way. The members and the hordes of camp-followers and all the lobby had settled into a belief that Representative Rollinson was a sea-green Incorruptible, that of all honest members he was the most honest. He had become typical of honesty: sayings were current—"You might as well try to bribe Uncle Billy Rollinson!" "As honest as old Uncle Billy Rollinson." Hurlbut often used such phrases in private.

The "Breaker" was Hurlbut's own bill; he had planned it and written it, though it came over to the House from the Senate under a Senator's name. It was one of those "anti-monopolistic" measures which Democrats put their whole hearts into, sometimes, and believe in and fight for magnificently; an idea conceived in honesty and for a beneficent purpose, in the belief that a legislature by the wave of a hand can conjure the millennium to appear; and born out of an utter misconception of man and railroads. The bill needs no farther description than this: if it passed and became an enforced law, the dividends of every railroad entering the State would be reduced by two-fifths. There is one thing that will fight harder than a Democrat—that is a railroad.

The "Breaker" had been kept very dark until Hurlbut felt that he was ready; then it was swept through the Senate before the railroad lobby, previously lulled into unsuspicion, could collect itself and block it. This was as Hurlbut had planned: that the fight should be in his own House. It was the bill of his heart and he set his reputation upon it. He needed fifty-one votes to pass it, and he had them, and one to spare; for he took his followers, who formed the majority, into caucus upon it. It was in the caucus Uncle Billy learned that Hurlbut was "for" the bill. He watched the leader with humble, wavering eyes, thinking how strong and clear his voice was, and wondering if he never lit the cigar he always carried in his hand, or if he ever got into trouble, like Henry, being a young man. If he did, Uncle Billy would have liked the chance to help him out.

He had plenty of such chances with Henry; indeed, the opportunity may be said to have been unintermittent, and Uncle Billy was never free from a dim fear of the day when his son would get in so deeply that he could not get him out. Verily, the day seemed near at hand: Henry's letters were growing desperate and the old man walked the floor of his little room at night, more and more hopeless. Once or twice, even as he sat at his desk in the House, his eyes became so watery that he forced himself into long spells of coughing, to account for it, in case any one might be noticing him.

The caucus was uneventful and quiet, for it had all been talked over, and was no more than a matter of form.

The Republicans did not caucus upon the bill (they had reasons), but they were solidly against it. Naturally it follows that the assault of the railroad lobby had to be made upon the virtue of the Democrats *as* Democrats. That is, whether a member upon the majority side cared about the bill for its own sake or not, right or wrong, he felt it his duty as a Democrat to vote for it. If he had a conscience higher than a political conscience, and believed the bill was bad, his duty was to "bolt the caucus"; but all of the Democratic side believed in the righteousness of the bill, except two. One had already been bought and the other was Uncle Billy, who knew nothing about it, except that Hurlbut was "for" it and it seemed to be making a "big stir."

The man who had been bought sat not far from Uncle Billy. He was a furtive, untidy slouch of a man, formerly a Republican; he had a great capacity for "handling the coloured vote" and his name was Pixley. Hurlbut mistrusted him; the young man had that instinct, which good leaders need, for feeling the weak places in his following; and he had the leader's way, too, of ever bracing up the weakness and fortifying it; so he stopped, four or five times a day, at Pixley's desk, urging the necessity of standing fast for the "Breaker," and expressing convictions as to the political future of a Democrat who should fail to vote for it; to which Pixley assented in his husky, tough-ward voice.

All day long now, Hurlbut and his lieutenants, disregarding the routine of bills, went up and down the lines, fending off the lobbyists and such Republicans as were working openly for the bill. They encouraged and threatened and never let themselves be too confident of their seeming strength. Some of those who were known, or guessed, to be of the "weaker brethren" were not left to themselves for half an hour at a time, from their breakfasts until they went to bed. There was always at elbow the "*Hold fast!*" whisper of Hurlbut and his lieutenants. None of them ever thought of speaking to Uncle Billy.

Hurlbut's "work was cut out for him," as they said. What work it is to keep every one of fifty men honest under great temptation for three weeks (which time it took for the hampered and filibustered bill to come up for its passage or defeat), is known to those who have tried to do it. The railroads were outraged and incensed by the measure; they sincerely believed it to be monstrous and thievish. "Let the legislature try to confiscate two-fifths of the lawyers', or the bakers', or the ironmoulders' just earnings," said they, "and see what will happen!"

When such a bill as this comes to the floor for the third time the fight is already over, oratory is futile; and Cicero could not budge a vote. The railroads were forced to fight as best they could; this was the old way that they have learned is most effective in such a case. Votes could not be had to "oblige a friend" on the "Breaker" bill; nor could they be procured by arguments to prove the bill unjust. In brief: the railroad lobby had no need to buy Republican votes (with the exception of the one or two who charged out of habit whenever legislation concerned corporations), for the Republicans were against the bill, but they did mortally need to buy two Democratic votes, and were willing to pay handsomely for them. Nevertheless, Mr. Pixley's price was not exorbitant, considering the situation; nor need he have congratulated himself so heartily as he did (in moments of retirement from public life) upon his prospective

$2,000 (when the goods should be delivered) since his vote was assisting the railroads to save many million dollars a year.

Of course the lobby attacked the bill noisily; there were big guns going all day long; but those in charge knew perfectly well that the noise accomplished nothing in itself. It was used to cover the whispering. Still, Hurlbut held his line firm and the bill passed its second reading with fifty-two votes, Mr. Pixley being directed by his owners to vote for it on that occasion.

As time went on the lobby began to grow desperate; even Pixley had been consulted upon his opinion by Barrett, the young lawyer through whom negotiations in his case had been conducted. Pixley suggested the name of Rollinson and Barrett dismissed this counsel with as much disgust for Pixley's stupidity as he had for the man's person. (One likes a *dog* when he buys him.)

"But why not?" Pixley had whined as he reached the door. "Uncle Billy ain't so much! You listen to me. He wouldn't take it out-an'-out—I don't say as he would. But you needn't work that way. Everybody thinks it's no use to tackle him—but nobody never *tried*! What's he *done* to make you scared of him? *Nothing!* Jest set there and *looked*!"

After he had gone the fellow's words came back to Barrett: "Nobody never tried!" And then, to satisfy his conscience that he was leaving no stone unturned, yet laughing at the uselessness of it, he wrote a letter to a confidant of his, formerly a colleague in the lobby, who lived in the county-seat near which Uncle Billy's mortgaged acres lay. The answer came the night after the second vote on the "Breaker."

Dear Barrett:

I agree with your grafter. I don't believe Rollinson would be hard to approach if it were done with tact—of course you don't want to tackle him the way you would a swine like Pixley. A good many people around here always thought the old man simple-minded. He was given the nomination almost in joke—nobody else wanted it, because they all thought the Republicans had a sure thing of it; but Rollinson slid in on the general Democratic landslide in this district. He's got one son, a worthless pup, Henry, a sort of yokel Don Juan, always half drunk when his father has any money to give him, and just smart enough to keep the old man mesmerized. Lately Henry's been in a mighty serious peck of trouble. Last fall he got married to a girl here in town. Three weeks ago a family named Johnson, the most shiftless in the county, the real low-down white trash sort, living on a truck patch out Rollinson's way, heard that Henry was on a toot in town, spending money freely, and they went after him. A client of mine rents their ground to them and told me all about it. It seems they claim that one of the daughters in the Johnson family was Henry's common-law wife before he married the other girl, and it's more than likely they can prove it. They are hollering for $600, and if Henry doesn't raise it mighty quick they swear they'll get him sent over the road for bigamy. I think the old man would sell his soul to keep his boy out of the penitentiary and he's at his wits' ends; he hasn't anything to raise the money on and he's up against it. He'll do any thing on earth for Henry. Hope this'll be of some service to you, and if there's anything more I can do about it you better call me up on the long distance.

Yours faithfully,
J. P. WATSON.

P. S.—You might mention to our old boss that I don't want anything if services are needed; but a pass for self and family to New York and return would come in handy.

Barrett telegraphed an answer at once: "If it goes you can have annual for yourself and family. Will call you up at two sharp to-morrow."

It was late the following night when the lobbyist concluded his interview with Representative Rollinson, in the latter's little room, half lighted by the oil-smelling lamp.

"I knew you would understand, Mr. Rollinson," said Barrett as he rose to go. His eyes danced and his jaws set with the thought that had been jubilant within him for the last half-hour: "We've got 'em! We've got 'em! We've got 'em!" The railroads had defended their own again.

"Of course," he went on, "we wouldn't have dreamed of coming to you and asking you to vote against this outrageous bill if we thought for a minute that you had any real belief in it or considered it a good bill. But you say, yourself, your only feeling about it was to oblige Mr. Hurlbut, and you admit, too, that you've voted his way on every other bill of the session. Surely, as I've already said so many times, you don't think he'd be so unreasonable as to be angry with you for differing with him on the merits of only one! No, no, Hurlbut's a very sensible fellow about such matters. You don't need to worry about *that*! After all I've said, surely you won't give it another thought, will you?"

Uncle Billy sat in the shadow, bent far over, slowly twisting his thin, corded hands, the fingers tightly interlocked. It was a long time before he spoke, and his interlocutor had to urge him again before he answered, in his gentle, quavering voice.

"No, I reckon not, if you say so."

"Certainly not," said Barrett briskly. "Why of course, we'd never have thought of making you a money offer to vote either for or against your principles. Not much! We don't do business that way! We simply want to do something for you. We've wanted to, all during the session, but the opportunity hadn't offered until I happened to hear your son was in trouble."

Out of the shadow came a long, tremulous sigh. There was a moment's pause; then Uncle Billy's head sank slowly lower and rested on his hands.

"You see," the other continued cheerfully, "we make no conditions, none in the world. We feel friendly to you and want to oblige you, but of course we do think you ought to show a little good-will towards *us*. I believe it's all understood: to-morrow night Mr. Watson will drive out in his buggy to this Johnson place, and he's empowered by us to settle the whole business and obtain a written statement from the family that they have no claim on your son. How he will settle it is neither your affair nor mine; nor whether it costs money or not. But he *will* settle it. We do that out of good-will to you, as long as we feel as friendly to you as we do now, and all we ask is that you show your good-will to us."

It was plain, even to Uncle Billy, that if he voted against Mr. Barrett's friends in the afternoon those friends might not feel so much good-will toward him in the evening as they did now; and Mr. Watson might not go to the trouble of hitching up his buggy to drive out to the Johnsons'.

"You see, it's all out of friendship," said Barrett, his hand on the door knob. "And we can count on yours to-morrow, can't we—absolutely?"

The grey head sank a little lower, and then after a moment the quavering voice answered:

"Yes, sir—I'll be friendly."

Before morning, Hurlbut lost another vote. One of his best men left on a night train for the bedside of his dying wife. This meant that the "Breaker" needed every one of the fifty-one remaining Democratic votes in order to pass. Hurlbut more than distrusted Pixley, yet he felt sure of the other fifty, and if, upon the reading of the bill, Pixley proved false, the bill would not be lost, since there would be a majority of votes in its favour, though not the constitutional majority of fifty-one required for its passage, and it could be brought up again and carried when the absent man returned. Thus, on the chance that Pixley had withstood tampering, Hurlbut made no effort to prevent the bill from coming to the floor in its regular order in the afternoon, feeling that it could not possibly be killed by a majority against it, for he trusted his fifty, now, as strongly as he distrusted Pixley.

And so the roll-call on the "Breaker" began, rather quietly, though there was no man's face in the hall that was not set to show the tensity of high-strung nerves. The great crowd that had gathered and choked the galleries and the floor beyond the bar, and the Senators who had left their own chamber to watch the bill in the House, all began to feel disappointed; for nothing happened until Pixley's name was called.

Pixley voted "No!"

Uncle Billy, sitting far down in his leather chair on the small of his back, heard the outburst of shouting that followed; but he could not see Pixley, for the traitor was instantly surrounded by a ring of men, and all that was visible from where he sat was their backs and upraised, gesticulating hands. Uncle Billy began to tremble violently; he had not calculated on this; but surely such things would not happen to *him*!

The Speaker's gavel clicked through the uproar and the roll-call proceeded.

The clerk reached the name of Rollinson. Uncle Billy swallowed, threw a pale look about him and wrapped his damp hands in the skirts of his shiny old coat, as if to warm them. For a moment he could not answer. People turned to look at him.

"Rollinson!" shouted the clerk again.

"No," said Uncle Billy.

Immediately he saw above him and all about him a blur of men's faces and figures risen to their feet, he heard a hundred voices say breathlessly: "*What!*" and one that said: "My God, that kills the bill!"

Then a horrible and incredible storm burst upon him, and he who had sat all the session shrinking unnoticed in his quiet, back seat, unnerved when a colleague asked the simplest question, found himself the centre and point of attack in the wildest mêlée that legislature ever saw. A dozen men, red, frantic, with upraised arms, came at him, Hurlbut the first of them. But the lobby was there, too; for it was not part of its calculations that the old man should be frightened into changing his vote.

There need have been no fear of that. Uncle Billy was beyond the power of speech. The lobby's agents swarmed on the floor, and, with half-a-dozen hysterically laughing Republicans, met the onset of Hurlbut and his men. It became a riot immediately. Sane men were swept up in it to be as mad as the rest, while the galleries screamed and shouted. All round the old man the fury was greatest; his head sank over his desk and rested on his hands as it had the night before; for he dared not lift it to see the avalanche he had loosed upon himself. He would have liked to stop his ears to shut out the egregious clamour of cursing and yelling that beset him, as his bent head kept the glazed eyes from seeing the impossible vision of the attack that strove to reach him. He remembered awful dreams that were like this; and now, as then, he shuddered in a cold sweat, being as one who would draw the covers over his head to shelter him from horrors in great darkness. As Uncle Billy felt, so might a naked soul feel at the judgment day, tossed alone into the pit with all the myriads of eyes in the universe fastened on its sins.

He was pressed and jostled by his defenders; once a man's shoulders were bent back down over his own and he was crushed against the desk until his ribs ached; voices thundered and wailed at him, threatening, imploring, cursing, cajoling, raving.

Smaller groups were struggling and shouting in every part of the room, the distracted sergeants-at-arms roaring and wrestling with the rest. On the high dais the Speaker, white but imperturbable, having broken his gavel, beat steadily with the handle of an umbrella upon the square of marble on his desk. Fifteen or twenty members, raging dementedly, were beneath him, about the clerk's desk and on the steps leading up to his chair, each howling hoarsely:

"A point of *order*! A point of *or-der*!"

When the semblance of order came at last, the roll was finished, "reconsidered," the "Breaker" was beaten, 50 to 49, was dead; and Uncle Billy Rollinson was creeping down the outer steps of the State-house in the cold February slush and rain.

He was glad to be out of the nightmare, though it seemed still upon him, the horrible clamours, all gonging and blaring at *him*; the red, maddened faces, the clenched fists, the open mouths, all raging at *him*—all the ruck and uproar swam about the dazed old man as he made his slow, unseeing way through the wet streets.

He was too late for dinner at his dingy boarding house, having wandered far, and he found himself in his room without knowing very well how he had come there, indeed, scarcely more than half-conscious that he *was* there. He sat, for a long time, in the dark. After a while he mechanically lit the lamp, sat again to stare at it, then, finding his eyes watering, he turned from it with an incoherent whimper, as if it had been a person from whom he would conceal the fact that he was weeping. He leaned his arm against the window sill and dried his eyes on the shiny sleeve.

An hour later, there came a hard, imperative knock on the door. Uncle Billy raised his head and said gently:

"Come in."

He rose to his feet uncertain, aghast, when he saw who his visitor was. It was Hurlbut.

The young man confronted him darkly, for a moment, in silence. He was dripping with rain; his hat, unremoved, shaded lank black locks over a white face; his nostrils were wide with wrath; the "dry cigar" wagged between gritting teeth.

"Will ye take a chair?" faltered Uncle Billy.

The room rang to the loud answer of the other: "I'd see you in Hell before I'd sit in a chair of yours!"

He raised an arm, straight as a rod, to point at the old man. "Rollinson," he said, "I've come here to tell you what I think of you! I've never done that in my life before, because I never thought any man worth it. I do it because I need the luxury of it

—because I'm sick of myself not to have had gumption enough to see what you were all the time and have you watched!"

Uncle Billy was stung to a moment's life. "Look here," he quavered, "you hadn't ought to talk that way to me. There ain't a cent of money passed my fingers—"

Hurlbut's bitter laugh cut him short. "*No?* Don't you suppose *I know* how it was done? Do you suppose there's a man in the whole Assembly doesn't know how you were sold? I had it by the long distance an hour ago, from your own home. Do you suppose *we* have no friends there, or that it was hard to find out about the whole dirty business? Your son's not going to stand trial for bigamy; that was the price you charged for killing the bill. You and Pixley are the only men whom they could buy with all their millions! Oh, I know a dozen men who could be bought on other issues, but not on *this*! You and Pixley stand alone. Well, you've broken the caucus and you've betrayed the Democratic party. I've come to tell you that the party doesn't want you any more. You are out of it, do you hear? We don't want even to use you!"

The old man had sunk back into his chair, stricken white, his hands fluttering helplessly. "I didn't go to hurt your feelings, Mr. Hurlbut," he said. "I never knowed how it would be, but I don't think you ought to say I done anything dishonest. I just felt kind of friendly to the railroads—"

The leader's laugh cut him off again. "Friendly! Yes, that's what you were! Well, you can go back to your friends; you'll need them!—Mother in Heaven! How you fooled us! We thought you were the straightest man and the staunchest Democrat—"

"I b'en a Democrat all my life, Mr. Hurlbut. I voted fer—"

"Well, you're a Democrat no longer. You're done for, do you understand? And we're done with you!"

"You mean," the old man's voice shook almost beyond control; "you mean you're tryin' to read me out of the party?"

"Trying to!" Hurlbut turned to the door. "You're out! It's done. You can thank God that your 'friends' did their work so well that we can't prove what we know. On my soul, you dog, if we could I believe some of the boys would send you over the road."

An hour after he had gone, Uncle Billy roused himself from his stupor, and the astonished landlady heard his shuffling step on the stair. She followed him softly and curiously to the front door, and watched him. He was bare-headed but had not far to go. The night-flare of the cheap, all-night saloon across the sodden street silhouetted the stooping figure for a moment and then the swinging doors shut the old man from her view. She returned to her parlour and sat waiting for his return until she fell asleep in her chair. She awoke at two o'clock, went to his room, and was aghast to find it still vacant.

"The Lord have mercy on us all!" she cried aloud. "To think that old rascal'd go out on a spree! He'd better of stayed in the country where he belonged."

It was the next morning that the House received a shock which loosed another riot, but one of a kind different from that which greeted Representative Rollinson's vote on the "Breaker." The reading clerk had sung his way through an inconsequent bill; most of the members were buried in newspapers, gossiping, idling, or smoking in the lobbies, when a loud, cracked voice was heard shrilly demanding recognition.

"Mr. Speaker!" Every one turned with a start. There was Uncle Billy, on his feet, violently waving his hands at the Speaker. "Mr. Speaker, Mr. Speaker, Mr. Speaker!" His dress was disordered and muddy; his eyes shone with a fierce, absurd, liquorish light; and with each syllable that he uttered his beard wagged to an unspeakable effect of comedy. He offered the most grotesque spectacle ever seen in that hall—a notable distinction.

For a moment the House sat in paralytic astonishment. Then came an awed whisper from a Republican: "Has the old fool really found his voice?"

"No, he's drunk," said a neighbour. "I guess he can afford it, after his vote yesterday!"

"Mister Speaker! *Mister* Speaker!"

The cracked voice startled the lobbies. The hangers-on, the typewriters, the janitors, the smoking members came pouring into the chamber and stood, transfixed and open-mouthed.

"*Mister Speaker!*"

Then the place rocked with the gust of laughter and ironical cheering that swept over the Assembly. Members climbed upon their chairs and on desks, waving handkerchiefs, sheets of foolscap, and waste-baskets. "Hear 'im! *He-ear* 'im!" rang the derisive cry.

The Speaker yielded in the same spirit and said:

"The Gentleman from Wixinockee."

A semi-quiet followed and the cracked voice rose defiantly:

"That's who I am! I'm the Gentleman from Wixinockee an' I stan' here to defen' the principles of the Democratic party!"

The Democrats responded with violent hootings, supplemented by cheers of approval from the Republicans. The high voice out-shrieked them all: "Once a Democrat, always a Democrat! I voted Dem'cratic tick't forty year, born a Democrat an' die a Democrat. Fellow sizzens, I want to say to you right here an' now that principles of Dem'cratic party saved this country a hun'erd times from Republican mal-'diministration an' degerdation! Lemme tell you this: you kin take my life away but you can't say I don' stan' by Dem'cratic party, mos' glorious party of Douglas an' Tilden, Hen'ricks, Henry Clay, an' George Washin'ton. I say to you they *hain't* no other party an' I'm member of it till death an' Hell an' f'rever after, so help me *God*!"

He smote the desk beside him with the back of his hand, using all his strength, skinning his knuckles so that the blood dripped from them, unnoticed. He waved both arms continually, bending his body almost double and straightening up again, in crucial efforts for emphasis. All the old jingo platitudes that he had learned from campaign speakers throughout his life, the nonsense and brag and blat, the cheap phrases, all the empty balderdash of the platform, rushed to his incoherent lips.

The lord of misrule reigned at the end of each sentence, as the members sprang again upon the chairs and desks, roaring, waving, purple with laughter. The Speaker leaned back exhausted in his chair and let the gavel rest. Spectators, pages, galleries whooped and howled with the members. Finally the climax came.

"I want to say to you just this *here*," shrilled the cracked voice, "an' you can tell the Republican party that I said so, tell 'em straight from *me*, an' I hain't goin' back on it; I reckon they know who I am, too; I'm a man that's honest—I'm as honest as the day is long, I am—as honest as the day is long—"

He was interrupted by a loud voice. "*Yes*," it cried, "*when that day is the twenty-first of December*!"

That let pandemonium loose again, wilder, madder than before. A member threw a pamphlet at Uncle Billy. In a moment the air was thick with a Brobdingnagian snow-storm: pamphlets, huge wads of foolscap, bills, books, newspapers, waste-baskets went flying at the grotesque target from every quarter of the room. Members "rushed" the old man, hooting, cheering; he was tossed about, half thrown down, bruised, but, clamorous over all other clamours, jumping up and down to shriek over the heads of those who hustled him, his hands waving frantically in the air, his long beard wagging absurdly, still desperately vociferating his Democracy and his honesty.

That was only the beginning. He had, indeed, "found his voice"; for he seldom went now to the boarding-house for his meals, but patronized the free-lunch counter and other allurements of the establishment across the way. Every day he rose in the House to speak, never failing to reach the assertion that he was "as honest as the day is long," which was always greeted in the same way.

For a time he was one of the jokes that lightened the tedious business of law-making, and the members looked forward to his "*Mis-ter Speaker*" as schoolboys look forward to recess. But, after a week, the novelty was gone.

The old man became a bore. The Speaker refused to recognize him, and grew weary of the persistent shrilling. The day came when Uncle Billy was forcibly put into his seat by a disgusted sergeant-at-arms. He was half drunk (as he had come to be most of the time), but this humiliation seemed to pierce the alcoholic vapours that surrounded his always feeble intelligence. He put his hands up to his face and cried like a whimpering child. Then he shuffled out and went back to the saloon. He soon acquired the habit of leaving his seat in the House vacant; he was no longer allowed to make speeches there; he made them in the saloon, to the amusement of the loafers and roughs who infested it. They badgered him, but they let him harangue them, and applauded his rhodomontades.

Hurlbut, passing the place one night at the end of the session, heard the quavering, drunken voice, and paused in the darkness to listen.

"I tell you, fellow-countrymen, I've voted Dem'cratic tick't forty year, live a Dem'crat, die a Dem'crat! An' I'm's honest as day is long!"

It was five years after that session, when Hurlbut, now in the national Congress, was called to the district in which Wixinockee lies, to assist his hard-pressed brethren in a campaign. He was driving, one afternoon, to a political meeting in the country, when a recollection came to him and he turned to the committee chairman, who accompanied him, and said:

"Didn't Uncle Billy Rollinson live somewhere near here?"

"Why, yes. You knew him in the legislature, didn't you?"

"A little. Where is he now?"

"Just up ahead here. I'll show you."

They reached the gate of a small, unkempt, weedy graveyard and stopped.

"The inscription on the head-board is more or less amusing," said the chairman, as he got out of the buggy, "considering that he was thought to be pretty crooked, and I seem to remember that he was 'read out of the party,' too. But he wrote the inscription himself, on his death-bed, and his son put it there."

There was a sparse crop of brown grass growing on the grave to which he led his companion. A cracked wooden head-board, already tilting rakishly, marked Henry's devotion. It had been white-washed and the inscription done in black letters, now partly washed away by the rain, but still legible:

HERE LIES
THE MORTAL REMAINS
OF
WILLIAM ROLLINSON
A LIFE-LONG
DEMOCRAT
AND
A
MAN
AS HONEST AS THE DAY IS LONG

The chairman laughed. "Don't that beat thunder? You knew his record in the legislature didn't you?"

"Yes."

"He *was* as crooked as they say he was, wasn't he?"

Hurlbut had grown much older in five years, and he was in Congress. He was climbing the ladder, and, to hold the position he had gained, and to insure his continued climbing, he had made some sacrifices within himself by obliging his friends —sacrifices which he did not name.

"I could hardly say," he answered gently, his down-bent eyes fastened on the sparse, brown grass. "It's not for us to judge too much. I believe, maybe, that if he could hear me now, I'd ask his pardon for some things I said to him once."

Hector

IT ISN'T the party manager, you understand, that gets the fame; it's the candidate. The manager tries to keep his candidate in what the newspapers call a "blaze of publicity"; that is, to keep certain spots of him in the blaze, while sometimes it is the fact that a candidate does not know much of what is really going on; he gets all the red fire and sky-rockets, and, in the general dazzle and nervousness, is unconscious of the forces which are to elect or defeat him. Strange as it is, the more glare and conspicuousness he has, the more he usually wants. But the more a working political manager gets, the less he wants. You see, it's a great advantage to keep out of the high lights.

For my part, not even being known or important enough to be named "Dictator," now and then, in the papers, I've had my fun in the game very quietly. Yet I did come pretty near being a famous man once, a good while ago, for about a week. That was just after Hector J. Ransom made his great speech on the "Patriotism of the Pasture" which set the country to talking about him and, in time, brought him all he desired.

You remember what a big stir that speech made, of course —everybody remembers it. The people in his State went just wild with pride, and all over the country the papers had a sort of catch head-line: "Another Daniel Webster Come to Judgment!" When the reporters in my own town found out that Ransom was a second cousin of mine, I was put into a scare-head for the only time in my life. For a week I was a public character and important to other people besides the boys that do the work at primaries. I was interviewed every few minutes; and a reporter got me up one night at half-past twelve to ask for some anecdotes of Hector's "Boyhood Days and Rise to Fame."

I didn't oblige that young man, but I knew enough. I was always fond of my first cousin, Mary Ransom, Hector's mother; and in the old days I never passed through Greenville, the little town where they lived, without stopping over, a train or two, to visit with her, and I saw plenty of Hector! I never knew a boy that left the other boys to come into the parlour (when there was company) quicker than Hector, and I certainly never saw a boy that "showed off" more. His mother was wrapped up in him; you could see in a minute that she fairly worshipped him; but I don't know, if it hadn't been for Mary, that I'd have praised his recitations and elocution so much, myself.

Mary and I wouldn't any more than get to tell each other how long since we'd heard from Aunt Sue, before Hector would grow uneasy and switch around on the sofa and say: "Ma, I'd rather you wouldn't tell cousin Ben about what happened at the G. A. R. reunion. I don't want to go through all that stuff again."

At that, Mary's eyes would light up and she'd say: "You must, Hector, you must! I want him to hear you do it; he mustn't go away without that!" Then she'd go on to tell me how Hector had recited Lincoln's Gettysburg speech at a meeting of the local post of the G. A. R. and how he was applauded, and that many of the veterans had told him if he kept on he'd be Governor of his State some day, and how proud she was of him and how he was so different from ordinary boys that she was often anxious about him. Then she would urge him to let me have it—and he always would, especially if I said: "Oh, don't *make* the boy do it, Mary!"

He would stand out in the middle of the floor and thrust his chin out, knitting his brow and widening his nostrils, and shout "Of the people, By the people, and For the people" at the top of his lungs in that little parlour. He always had a great talent for mimicry, a talent of which I think he was absolutely unconscious. He would give his speeches in exactly the boy-orator style; that is, he imitated speakers who imitated others who had heard Daniel Webster. Mary and he, however, had no idea that he imitated anybody; they thought it was creative genius.

When he had finished Lincoln, he would say: "Well, I've got another that's a good deal better, but I don't want to go through that to-day; it's too much trouble," with the result that in a few minutes Patrick Henry would take a turn or two in his grave. Hector always placed himself by a table for "Liberty or Death," and barked his knuckles on it for emphasis. Little he cared, so long as he thought he'd got his effect! You could see, in spite of the intensity of his expression, that he was perfectly happy.

When he'd worked us through that, and perhaps "Horatius at the Bridge" and the quarrel scene between Brutus and Cassius and was pretty well emptied, he'd hang about and interrupt in a way that made me restless. Neither Mary nor I could get out two sentences before the boy would cut in with something like: "Don't tell cousin Ben about that day I recited in school; I'm tired of all that guff!"

Then Mary would answer: "It isn't guff, precious. I never was prouder of you in my life." And she'd go on to tell me about another of his triumphs, and how he made up speeches of his own sometimes, and would get up on a box and deliver them to his boy friends, though she didn't say how the boys received them. All the while, Hector would stare at me like a neighbour's cat on your front steps, to see what impression it made on me; and I was conscious that he was sure that I knew he was a wonderful boy. I think he felt that everybody knew it. Hector kind of palled on me.

When he was about sixteen, Mary wrote me that she was in great distress about him because he had decided to go on the stage; that he had written to John McCullough, offering to take the place of leading man in his company to begin with. Mary was sure, she said, that the life of an actor was a hard one; Hector had always been very delicate (I had known him to eat a whole mince pie without apparent distress afterward) and she wanted me to write and urge him to change his mind. She felt sure Mr. McCullough would send for him at once, because Hector had written him that he already knew all the principal Shakespearian rôles, could play Brutus, Cassius, or Mark Antony as desired; and he had added a letter of recommendation from the Mayor of their city, declaring that Hector was a finer elocutionist and tragedian than any actor he had ever seen.

The dear woman's anxiety was needless, for she wrote me, with as much surprise as pleasure, two months later, that for some reason Mr. McCullough had not answered the letter, and that she was very happy; she had persuaded Hector to go to college.

How she kept him there, the first two years, I don't know, for her husband had only left her about four hundred dollars a year. Of course, living in Greenville isn't expensive, but it does cost something, and I honestly believe Mary came near to living on nothing. It was a small college that she'd sent the boy to, but it was a mother's point with her that Hector should be as comfortable as anyone there.

I stopped off at Greenville, one day, toward the end of his second year, but before he'd come home, and I saw how it was. Mary seemed as glad as ever to see me—it was the same old bright greeting that she'd always given me. She saw me from the dining-room window where she was eating her supper, and she came out, running down to the gate to meet me, like a girl; but she looked thin and pale.

I said I'd go right in and have some supper with her, and at that the roses came back quickly to her cheeks. "No," she said, "I wasn't really at supper; only having a bite beforehand; I'm going up-town now to get the things for supper. You smoke a cigar out on the porch till I get back, and—"

I took her by the arm. "Not much, Mary," I said. "I'm going to have the same supper you had for yourself."

So I went straight out to the dining-room; and all I found on the table was some dry bread toasted and a baked apple without cream or sugar. It gave me a pretty good idea of what the general run of her meals must have been.

I had a long talk with her that night, and I wormed it out of her that Hector's college expenses were about twenty-five dollars a month, which left her six to live on. The truth is, she didn't have enough to eat, and you could see how happy it made her. She read me a good many of Hector's letters, her voice often trembling with happiness over his triumphs. The letters were long, I'll say that for Hector, which may have been to his credit as a son, or it may have been because he had such an interesting subject. There was no doubt that he had worked hard; he had taken all the chief prizes for oratory and essay writing and so forth that were open to him; he also allowed it to be seen that he was the chief person in the consideration of his class and the fraternity he had joined. Mary had a sort of humbleness about being the mother of such a son.

But I settled one thing with her that night, though I had to hurt her feelings to do it. I owned a couple of small notes which had just fallen due, and I could spare the money. I put it as a loan to Hector himself; he was to pay me back when he got started, and so it was arranged that he could finish his course without his mother's living on apples and toast.

I went over to his Commencement with Mary and we hadn't been in the town an hour before we saw that Hector was the king of the place. He had *all* the honours; first in his class, first in oratory; first in everything; professors and students all kow-towed and sounded the hew-gag before him. Most of Mary's time was put in crying with happiness. As for Hector himself, he had changed in just one way: he no longer looked at people to see his effect on them; he was too confident of it.

His face had grown to be the most determined I have ever seen. There was no obstinacy in it—he wasn't a bull-dog—only set determination. No one could have failed to read in it an immensely powerful will. In a curious way he seemed "on edge" all the time. His nostrils were always distended, the muscles of his lean jaw were never lax, but continually at tension, thrusting the chin forward with his teeth hard together. His eyebrows were contracted, I think, even in his sleep, and he looked at everything with a sort of quick, fierce appearance of scrutiny, though at that time I imagined that he saw very little. He had a loud, rich voice, his pronunciation was clipped to a deadly distinctness; he was so straight and his head so high in the air that he seemed almost to tilt back. With his tall figure and black hair, he was a boy who would have attracted attention, as they say, in any crowd, so that he might have been taken for a young actor.

His best friend, a kind of Man Friday to him, was another young fellow from Greenville, whose name was Joe Lane. I liked Joe. I'd known him since he was a boy. He was lazy and pleasant-looking, with reddish hair and a drawling, low voice. He had a humorous, sensible expression, though he was dissipated, I'd heard, but very gentle in his manners. I had a talk with him under the trees of the college campus in the moonlight, Commencement night. I can see the boy lying there now, sprawling on the grass with a cigar in his mouth.

"Hector's done well," I said.

"Oh, Lord, yes!" Joe answered. "He always will. He's going 'way up in the world."

"What makes you think so?"

"Because he's so sure of it. It only needs a little luck to make him a great man. In fact, he already is a great man."

"You mean you think he has a great mind?"

"Why, no, sir; but I think he has a purpose so big and so set, that it might be called great, and it will make him great."

"What purpose?"

Joe answered quietly but very slowly, pulling at his cigar after each syllable: "Hec—tor—J. Ran—som!"

"I declare," I put in, "I thought you were his friend!"

"So I am," the young fellow returned. "Friend, admirer, and doer-in ordinary to Hector J. Ransom, that's my quality. I've done errands and odd jobs for him all my life. Most people who meet him do; though it might be hard to say why. I haven't hitched my wagon to a star; nobody'll get to do that, because this star isn't going to take anything to the zenith but itself."

"Going to the zenith, is he?"

"Surely."

"You mean," said I, "that he's going to make a fine lawyer?"

"Oh, no, I think not. He might have been called one in the last generation, but, as I understand it, nowadays a lawyer has to work out business propositions more than oratory."

"And you think Hector has only his oratory?"

"I think that's his vehicle; it's his racing sulky and he'll drive it pretty hard. We're good friends, but if you want me to be frank, I should say that he'd drive on over my dead body if it lay in the road to where he was going." Lane rolled over in the grass with a little chuckle. "Of course," he went on, "I talk about him this way because I know what you've done for him and I'd like to help you to be sure that he's going to be a success. He'll do you credit!"

"What are you going to do, yourself, Joe?" I asked.

"Me?" He sat up, looking surprised. "Why, didn't you know? I didn't get my degree. They threw me out at the eleventh hour for getting too publicly tight—celebrating Hector's winning the works of Lord Byron, the prize in the senior debate! I'll never be a credit to anybody; and as for what I'm going to do—go back to Greenville and loaf in Tim's pool-room, I suppose, and watch Hector's balloon."

However, Hector's balloon seemed uninclined to soar, at the set-off—though Hector didn't. The next summer began a presidential campaign, and Hector, knowing that I was chairman of my county committee, and strangely overestimating my importance, came up to see me: he asked me to use my influence with the National Committee to have him sent to make speeches in one of the doubtful States; he thought he could carry it for us. I explained that I had no wires leading up so far as the National Committee. There were other things I might have explained, but it didn't seem much use. Hector would have thought I wanted to "keep him down."

He thought so anyway, because, after a crestfallen moment, he began to look at me in his fierce eye-to-eye way with what seemed to me a dark suspicion. He came and struck my desk with his clinched fist (he was always strong on that), and exclaimed:

"Then by the eternal gods, if my own flesh and blood won't help me, I'll go to Chicago myself, lay my credentials before the committee, unaided, and wring from them—"

"Hold on, Hector," I said. "Why didn't you say you had credentials? What are they?"

"What are they?" he answered in a rising voice. "You ask me what are my credentials? The credentials of my patriotism, my poverty, and my pride! You ask me for my credentials? The credentials of youth!" (He hit the desk every few words.) "The credentials of enthusiasm! The credentials of strength! You ask for my credentials? The credentials of red blood, of red corpuscles, of young manhood, ripest in the glorious young West! The credentials of vitality! Of virile—"

"Hold on," I said again, but I couldn't stop him. He went on for probably fifteen minutes, pacing the room and gesticulating and thundering at me, though we two were all alone. I felt mighty ridiculous, but, of course, I'd been through much the same thing with one or two candidates and orators before. I thought then that he was practising on me, but I came afterward to see that I was partly wrong. "Oratory" was his only way of expressing himself; he couldn't just *talk*, to save his life. All you could do, when he began, was to sit and take it till he got through, which consumed some valuable time for me that afternoon. I suppose I was profane inside, for having given him that cue with "credentials." Finally I got in a question:

"Why not begin a little more mildly, Hector? Why don't you make some speeches in your own county first?"

"I have consented to make the Fourth of July oration at Greenville," he answered.

Before he could go on, I got up and slapped him on the back. "That's right!" I said. "That's right! Go back and show the home folks what you can do, and I'll come down to hear it!"

And so I did. Mary was, if possible, more flustered and upset than at Hector's Commencement. She and Joe Lane and I had a bench close up to the stand, and on the other side of Mary sat a girl I'd never seen before. Mary introduced me to her in a way that made me risk a guess that Hector liked her more than common. Her name was Laura Rainey, and she'd come to Greenville, a year before, to teach in the high school. She was young, not quite twenty, I reckoned, and as pretty and dainty a girl as ever I saw; thin and delicate-looking, though not in the sense of poor health; and she struck me as being very sweet and thoughtful. Joe Lane told me, with his little chuckle, that she'd had a good deal of trouble in the school on account of all the older boys falling in love with her.

Something in the way he spoke made me watch Joe, and I was sure if he'd been one of her pupils he wouldn't have lightened her worries much in that direction. He had it himself. I saw it, or, I should say, I felt it, in spite of his never seeming to look at her. She looked at him, however, and pretty often, too; and there was a good deal of interest in her eyes, only it was a sad kind, which I understood, I thought, when I found that Joe had been on a long spree and had just sobered up the day before.

Hector sat above us on the platform, with the Mayor and the County Judge, and when the latter introduced him, and the same old white pitcher and glass of water on a pine table, the boy came forward with slow and impressive steps, and, setting his left fist on his hip, allowed his right arm to hang straight by his side till his hand rested on the table, like a statesman of the day standing for a photograph. His brow contained a commanding frown, and he stood for some moments in that position, while, to my astonishment, the crowd cheered itself hoarse.

There was no mistaking the genuine enthusiasm that he evoked. I didn't feel it myself, but I suppose the only explanation is that he had a great deal of what is called "magnetism." What made it I don't know. He was good-looking enough, with his dark eyes and hair, and white, intense face and black clothes; but there was more in the cheering than appreciation of that. I could not doubt that he produced on the crowd, by his quiet attitude, an apparition of greatness. There was some kind of hypnotism in it, I suppose.

The speech was about what I was looking for: bombastic platitudes delivered with such earnestness and velocity that "every point scored" and the cheering came whenever he wanted it.

For instance: he would retire a few steps toward the rear, and, pointing to the sky, adjure it in a solemn voice which made every one lean forward in a dead hush:

"Tell me, ye silent stars, that seem to slumber 'neath the auroral coverlet of day, tell me, down what laurelled pathways among ye walk our dead, the heroes whose blood was our benison, bequeathing to us the heritage of this flower-strewn land; they who have passed to that bourne whence no traveller returns? Answer me: Are not *theirs* the loftiest names inscribed on your marble catalogues of the nations?" He let his voice out startlingly and shouted: "CREEPS there a creature of the earth with spirit so sordid as to doubt it, to doubt *who* heads those gilded rolls! If there be, then *I* say to him, 'Beware!' For the names I see written above me to-day on the immemorial canopy of heaven begin with that of the spotless knight, the unsceptred and uncrowned king, the godlike and immaculate"—(here he turned suddenly, ran to the front of the stage, and, with outstretched fist shaking violently over our heads, thundered at the full power of his lungs): "GEORGE WASHINGTON!"

He did the same for Jefferson, Jackson, Lincoln, Grant, and four or five governors and senators of the State; and at every name the crowd went wild, worked up to it by Hector in the same way. But what surprised me was his daring to conclude his list with a votive offering laid at the feet of Passley Trimmer. Trimmer was the congressional representative of that district and one of the meanest men and smartest politicians in the world. He was always creeping out of tight places and money-scandals by the skin of his teeth; and yet, by building up the finest personal machine in the State, he stuck to his seat in Congress term after term, in spite of the fact that most of the intelligent and honest men in his district despised him. It was a proof of the power Hector held over his audience that, by his tribute to Trimmer, he was able to evoke the noisiest enthusiasm of the afternoon.

Nevertheless, what really tickled me most was the boy's peroration. It gave me a pretty clear insight into his "innard workings." He led up to it in his favourite way: stepping backward a pace or two and sinking his voice to a kind of Edwin Booth quiet; gradually growing a little louder; then suddenly turning on the thunder and running forward.

"You ask *me* for our credentials?" he roared. (Nobody had, this time.) "In the Lexicon of the Peoples, you ask *me* for my country's credentials? The credentials of our pastures, our population and our pride! You ask me for my country's credentials? I reply: 'The credentials of our youth and our enthusiasm! Of red corpuscles! Of red blood! The credentials of the virility and of the magnificent manhood of the Columbian Continent!' You ask for my country's credentials and I answer: 'The credentials of Glory! By right of the eternal and Almighty God!'"

Of course there was a great deal more, but that's enough to show how he had polished it.

I walked back to Mary's with Joe Lane, while Hector followed, making a kind of Royal Progress through the crowds, with his mother and Miss Rainey.

"You see it now, yourself, don't you?" Joe said to me.

"You mean about his doing well?"

"What else? He's just shown what he can do with people. The day will come when you'll have to take him at his own valuation."

I couldn't help laughing. "Well, Joe," I said, "that sounds as if *you*, at least, already took Hector at his own valuation."

"In some things," he answered, "I think I do. Don't you take him for an ass, sir. Sometimes I believe he's guided by a really superior intelligence—"

"Must be a sub-consciousness, then, Joe!"

"Exactly," he said seriously. "He doesn't make a single mistake. He's trained his manner so that, while a very few people laugh at him, he does things that the town would resent in any one else. He doesn't go round with the boys, and they look up to him for it. He isn't pompous, but he's acquired a kind of stateliness of manner that's made Greenville call him 'Mister Ransom' instead of 'Hec.' You probably think that his request to the National Committee only shows he's got all the nerve in the world; but I believe, on my soul, that if it had been granted he could have made good."

"What did he want to run Passley Trimmer into his Pantheon for, to-day?" I asked.

Joe's honest face looked a little dark at this. "It's only another proof of the shrewdness that directs him, though it was, maybe, a little bit sickening. He talks gold and stars and eternal gods, about sweetness and light and pure politics and reform, but he wants Passley Trimmer's machine to take him up. Passley Trimmer and his brother, Link, are a good-sized curse to this district, I expect you know, but Hector's courting them. Link is the dirtiest we've ever had here, and he holds all the rottenest in this county solid for Passley. He's overbearing; ugly, too; shot a nigger in the hip a year ago, and crippled him for life on account of a little back-talk, and got off scot-free. I had a row with him in a saloon last week; I was tight, I suppose, though there's always been bad blood between us, anyway, drunk or sober, and I didn't know much what happened, except that I refused to drink in his company and he cursed me out and I blacked an eye for him before they separated us. Well, sir, next day, here was Hector demanding that I go and apologize to Link. I said I'd as soon apologize to a rattlesnake, and Hector upbraided me in his rhetoric, but with a whole lot of real feeling, too. He was even pathetic about it: put it on the ground that I owed it to morality, by which he meant Hector. I was known to be his most intimate friend; I had done him an irrecoverable injury with the Trimmers, who would extend their retaliation and let *him* have a share of it, as my friend. He ended by declaring that he should withhold the light of his countenance from me until I had repaired the wrong done to his cause, and had apologized to Link!"

"Did you do it?"

The good fellow answered with his little chuckle: "Of course! Don't you see that he gets everybody to do what he wants? It's almost sheer will, and he's a true cloud-compeller."

I wanted to understand something else, and I didn't know how much Mary could tell me; that is, I was sure that she would think that Miss Rainey was in love with Hector. Mary wouldn't be able to see how any girl could help it.

"Joe," I said, "does Hector seem much taken with this Miss Rainey?"

We had come to the gate, and Lane stopped to relight a cigar before he answered. He kept the match at the stub until it burned out, half hiding his face from me with his hands, shielding the flame from a breeze that wasn't blowing.

"Yes," he said finally, "as much as he could be with anybody—at least he wants her to be taken with him."

"Do you think she is?"

He swung the gate open, and stood to let me pass in first. "She could be of great help to him. We've all got to help Hector."

I was going on: "You believe she will—"

"Did you ever hear," he interrupted, "of Jane Welsh Carlyle?"

I thought about that answer of Joe's most of the evening, and it struck me he was right. It was one of those things you couldn't possibly explain to save your life, but you knew it: everybody had *got* to help Hector. Everybody had to get behind him and push. Hector took it for granted in a way that passed the love of woman!

And yet, as we sat at Mary's supper-table, that evening, I don't know that I ever felt less real liking for any of my kin than I felt for Hector, though, perhaps, that was because he seemed to keep rubbing it in on me in indirect ways that I had done him an injury by not helping him with the National Committee, and that I ought to know it, after his triumph of the afternoon. I could see that Mary agreed with him, though in her gentle way.

Young Lane and Miss Rainey stayed for supper, too, and were very quiet. Miss Rainey struck me as a quiet girl generally, and Joe never talked, anyway, when in Hector's company. For that matter, nobody else did; there was mighty little chance. The truth is, Hector had an impediment of speech: he couldn't listen.

Of course he talked only about himself. That followed, because it was all there was in him. Not that it always *seemed* to be about himself. For instance, I remember one of his ways of rubbing it into me, that evening. He had been delivering himself of some opinions on the nature of Genius, fragments (like his "credentials"—I had a sneaking idea) of some undeveloped oration or other. "Look at Napoleon!" he bade us, while Mary was cutting the pie. "Could Barras with all his jealous and malevolent opposition, could Barras with all his craft, all his machinations, with all the machinery of the State, could Barras oppose the upward flight of that mighty spirit? No! Barras, who should have been the faithful friend, the helper, the disciple and believer, Barras, I say, set himself to destroy the youth whose genius he denied, and Barras was himself destroyed! He fell, for he had dared to oppose the path of one of the eternal stars!"

That was a sample, and I don't exaggerate it. I couldn't exaggerate Hector; it's beyond me; he always exaggerated himself beyond anybody else's power to do it. But I loved to hear Joe Lane's chuckle and I got one out of him when I offered him a cigar as we went out on the porch.

"Take one," I said. "It's one of Barras's best."

"Better get in line," was all he added to the chuckle.

A good many visitors dropped in, during the evening, Greenville's greatest come to congratulate Hector on the speech. Everybody in the county was talking about him that night, they said. Hector received these people in his old-fashioned-statesman manner, though I noticed that already he shook hands like a candidate. He would grasp the caller's hand quickly and decidedly, instead of letting the other do the gripping. And I could see that all those who came in, even hard-headed men twice his age, treated him deferentially, with the air of intimate respect that he somehow managed to exact from people. Perhaps I don't do him justice; he was a "mighty myster'us" boy!

I sat and smoked, lounging in one of Mary's comfortable porch-chairs. I managed without trouble to be in the background and I couldn't help putting in most of my time studying Joe Lane and Miss Rainey. Those two were sitting on the side-steps of the porch, a little apart from the rest of us—and a little apart from each other, too. Lord knows how you get such strong impressions, but I was very soon perfectly sure that these two young people were in love with each other and that they both knew it, but that they had given each other up. I was sure, too, that they were both under Hector's spell, and preposterous as it may seem, that they were under his *will*, and that Hector's plans included Miss Rainey for himself.

It was a mighty pretty evening; full of flower-smells and breezes from the woods, which began just across the village street. Joe sat in a sort of doubled-up fashion he had, his thin hands clasped like a strap round his knees. She sat straight and trim, both of them looking out toward where the twilight was fading. As the darkness came on I could barely make them out, a couple of quiet shadows, seemingly as far away from the group about the lamp-lit doorway where Hector sat, as if they were alone on big Jupiter who was setting up to be the whole thing, far out yonder in the lonely sky.

By and by, the moon oozed round from behind the house and leaked through the trees and I could see them plainer, two silhouettes against the foliage of some bright lilac-bushes. Joe hadn't budged, but the back of Miss Rainey's head wasn't toward me as it had been before; it was her profile. She was leaning back a little, against a post, and looking at Joe—just looking at him. Neither of them spoke a word the whole time, and somehow I felt they didn't need to, and that what they had to say to each other had never been spoken and never would be. It was mighty pretty—and sad, too.

I felt so sorry for them, but it made me more or less impatient with Hector, and with Joe—especially with Joe, I think. It seemed to me he needn't have taken his temperament so hopelessly. But what's the use of judging? When a man has a temperament like that, people who haven't can't tell what he's got to contend with.

*

That Fourth of July speech gave Hector his chance. His district managers and the Trimmer faction saw they could use him; and they sent him round stumping the district. Two campaigns later the State Committee was using him, and parts of his speeches were being printed in all the party papers over the State. Locally, I suppose you might say, he had become a famous man; at least he acted like one—not that there was any essential change in him. His style had undergone a large improvement, however; his language was less mixed-up, and he seemed clear-headed enough on "questions of the day," showing himself to be well-informed and of a fine judgment.

In these things I thought I saw the hand of Laura Rainey. The teacher was helping him. The seriousness of his face had increased, he had always entirely lacked humour; yet the spell he managed to cast over his audiences was greater. He never once failed to "get them going," as they say. At twenty-nine he was no longer called "a rising young orator"; no, he was usually introduced as the "Hon. Hector J. Ransom, the Silver-tongued Lochinvar of the West."

Things hadn't changed much at Greenville. Mary had always been so proud of Hector that she hadn't inflated any more on account of his wider successes. She couldn't, because she hadn't any room left for it.

Joe Lane still went on his periodical sprees quite regularly, about one week every three months, and he was the least offensive tippler I ever knew. He came up to the city during one of his lapses, and called at my office. He was dressed with unusual care (he was always a good deal of a dandy), and he did not stagger nor slush his syllables; indeed, the only way I could have told what was the matter with him, at first, was by the solemn preoccupation of his expression. A little black pickaninny followed him, grinning and carrying a big bundle, covered with a new lace window-curtain.

"I am but a bearer of votive flowers," Joe said, bowing. Then turning to the little darky, he waved his hand loftily. "Unveil the offering!"

The pickaninny did so, removing the lace curtain to reveal a shiny new coal-bucket in which was a lump of ice, whereon reposed a pair of white kid gloves and a large wreath of artificial daisies.

"With love," said Joe. "From Hector." And he stalked majestically out.

There was a card on the wreath, which Joe had inscribed: "To announce the betrothal. No regrets."

Sure enough, the next morning I had a letter from Mary, telling me that Hector and Miss Rainey were engaged, that they had been so without announcing it, for several years, and she feared the engagement must last much longer before they could be married. So did I, for all of Hector's glittering had brought him very little money. While he had some law practice, of course it was small, in Greenville, and what he had he neglected. Nor was he a good lawyer. I knew him to be heavily in debt to Lane, whose father had died lately, leaving Joe fairly well off; and I knew also that this debt sat very lightly on Hector. I judged so, because in the matter of the advances I had made for his education, I never heard him refer to them. Probably he forgot all about it, having so many more important things to think of.

Mary was right: it was a very long engagement. It had lasted seven years in all, when Passley Trimmer declared himself a candidate for the nomination for Governor and gave Hector the great chance he had been waiting for. Hector "came out" for Trimmer, and came out strong. He worked for him day and night, and he was one of the best cards in Trimmer's hand.

It was easy enough to understand: Trimmer's nomination would leave his seat in Congress vacant and the Trimmer crowd would throw it to Hector.

You could see that the "young Lochinvar" was really a power, and I think they counted on him almost as much as on the personal machine Trimmer had built up. Most of all, they counted on Hector's speech, nominating Trimmer, to stampede the convention. If it was to be done, Hector was the man to do it. There's no doubt in the world of the extraordinary capacity he had for whirling a crowd along into a kind of insane enthusiasm. He could make his audience enthusiastic about *anything*; he could have brought them to their feet waving and cheering for Ben Butler himself, if he had set out to do it.

I believe that most of us who were against Trimmer were more afraid of Hector's stampeding the convention than of Trimmer's machine and all the money he was spending.

I was working all I knew for another man, Henderson, of my county, and our delegation would go into the convention sixty-three solid for Henderson, first, last, and all the time. On that account I had to play Barras again to the young Napoleon. He came to see me, and made one of his orations, imploring me to swing half of our delegation for Trimmer on the first ballot, and all of it on the second.

"But they count on me!" he declaimed. "They count on me to turn you! Is a man to be denied by his own flesh and blood? Are the ties of relationship nothing? Can't you see that my whole future is put in jeopardy by your refusal? Here is my opportunity at last and you endanger it. My marriage and my fortune depend on it; the cup is at my lips. My long years of toil and preparation, the bitter, bitter waiting—are these things to go for nothing? I tell you that if you refuse me you may blast the most sacred hopes that ever dwelt in a human breast!"

I only smoked on, and so he did "the jury pathetic," and he was sincere in it, too.

"Have you no heart?" he inquired, his voice shaking. "Can you think calmly of my mother? Remember the years she has waited to see this recognition come to her son! Am I to go back to her and tell her that your answer was 'No'? I ask you to think of her, I ask you to put self out of your thoughts, to forget your own interests for once, and to think of my mother, waiting in the old home in the quiet village street where you knew her in her bright girlhood. Remember that she awaits your answer; forget *me* if you will, but remember what it means to *her*, I say, and *then* if there is a stone in your breast, instead of a human heart, speak the word 'No'!"

I spoke it, and, as he had to catch his train, he departed more in anger than in sorrow, leaving me to my conscience, he told me. At the door he turned.

"I warn you," he said, "that this faction of yours shall go down to defeat! Trimmer will win this fight, and I shall take his seat in Congress! That is my first stepping-stone, and I *will* take it! I have worked too hard and waited too long, for such as you to successfully oppose me. I tell you that we shall meet in the convention, and you and your machine will be broken! The rewards, then, to us, the victors!"

"Why, of course," I said, "if you win."

The Trimmer people were strong with the State Executive Committee, and, in spite of us, worked things a good deal their own way. They took the convention away from the State Capital to Greenville, which was, of course, a great advantage for Trimmer. The fact is, that most of the best people in that district didn't like him, but you know how we all are: he *was* one *of* them, and as soon as it seemed he had a chance to beat men from other parts of the State, they began to shout themselves black in the face for their own. When I went down there, the day before the convention, the place was one mass of Trimmer flags, banners, badges, transparencies, buttons, and brass bands.

I went around to see Mary right away, and while she wasn't exactly cold to me—the dear woman never could be that to anybody—she was different; her eyes met mine sadly and her old, sweet voice was a little tremulous, as if she were sorry that I had done something wrong.

I didn't stay long. I started back to the Henderson headquarters in the hotel, but on my way I passed a big store-room on a corner of the Square, which Trimmer had fitted up as his own headquarters. There was quite a crowd of the boys going in and out, looking cheerful, fresh cigars in their mouths, and a drink or two inside, band coming down the street, everything the way an old-timer likes to see it.

Passley Trimmer himself came out as I was going by, and with him were his brother, Link, and two or three other men, among them a weasel-faced little fellow named Hugo Siffles, who kept a drug-store on the next corner. Hugo wasn't anybody; nobody ever paid any attention to him at all; but he was one of those empty-headed village talkers who are always trying to look as if they were behind the scenes, always trying to walk with important people. Everybody knows them. They whisper to the undertaker at funerals; and during campaigns they have something confidential to communicate to United States Senators. They meddle and intrude and waste as much time for you as they can.

When Trimmer saw me, he held out his hand. "Hello, Ben! I hear you're not *for* me!" he said cordially.

"How are you running?" I came back at him, laughing.

"Oh, we're going to beat you," he answered, in the same way.

"Well, you'll see a good run, first, I expect!"

He walked along with me, Link and the others following a little way behind; but Hugo Siffles, of course, walking with us, partly to listen and tell at the drug-store later, and partly to look like state secrets.

"Sorry you couldn't see your way to join us," Trimmer said. "But we'll win out all right, anyway. I shouldn't think that would be much of a disappointment to you, though. It will be a great thing for one of your family."

"Oh, yes," I said, "Hector."

Trimmer took on a little of his benevolent statesman's manner, which they nearly all get in time. "I have the greatest confidence in that young man's future," he said. "He may go to the very top. All he needs is money. I speak to you as a relative: he ought to drop that school-teacher and marry a girl with money. He could, easily enough."

That made me a little ugly. "Oh, no," I said. "He can make plenty in Congress outside of his salary, can't he? I understand some of them do."

Of course Trimmer didn't lose his temper; instead, he laughed out loud, and then put his hand on my shoulder.

"Look here," he said. "I'm his friend and you're his cousin. He's one of my own crowd and I have his best interests at heart. That isn't the girl for him. He tells me that, for a long while, she used to advise him against having too much to do with *me*, until he showed her that winning my influence in his favour was his only chance to rise. Now, if *you* have his best interests at heart, as I have, you'll help persuade him to let her go. Why shouldn't he marry better? She's not so young any longer, and she's pretty much lost her looks. And then, you know people will talk—"

"Talk about what?" I said.

"Well, if he goes to Congress, and, with his prospects, throws himself away on a skinny little old-maid school-teacher in the backwoods, one that he's been making love to for years, they might say almost anything. Why can't he hand her over to Joe Lane? I'm sure—"

"That'll do," I interrupted roughly. "I suppose you've been talking that way to Hector?"

"Why, certainly. I have his best interests at—"

"Good-day, *sir*!" I said, and turned in at the hotel and left him, with Hugo Siffles's little bright pig's eyes peeking at me round Trimmer's shoulder.

Sore enough I was, and cursing Trimmer and Hector in my heart, so that when some one knocked on my door, while I was washing up for supper, I said "Come in!" as if I were telling a dog to get out.

It was Joe Lane and he was pretty drunk. He walked over to the bed and caught himself unsteadily once or twice. I'd never seen him stagger before. He didn't speak until he had sat down on the coverlet; then he shaded his eyes with his hand and stared at me as if he wanted to make sure that it *was* I.

"I've just been down to Hugo Siffles's drug-store," he said, speaking very slowly and carefully, "and Hugo was telling a crowd about a conver—conversation between you and Passley Trimmer. He said Trimmer said Hector Ransom ought to drop Miss Rainey—and 'hand her over to Joe Lane.' Is that true?"

"Yes," I answered. "The beast said that."

"There was more," Joe said heavily. "More that im—implied —might be taken to imply scandal, which I believe Trimmer did not seriously believe—but thought—thought might be used as an argument with Hector to persuade him to jilt her?"

"Yes."

"What was said ex—actly? It is being repeated about town in various forms. I want to know."

Like a fool I told him the whole thing. I didn't think, didn't dream, of course, what was in that poor, drunken, devoted head, and I wanted to blow off my own steam, I was so hot.

He sat very quietly until I had finished; then he took his head in both hands and rocked himself gently to and fro upon the bed, and I saw tears trickling down his cheeks. It was a wretched spectacle in a way, he being drunk and crying like a child, but I don't think I despised him.

"And she so true," he sobbed, "so good, so faithful to him!

She's given him her youth, her whole sweet youth—all of it for him!" He got to his feet and went to the door.

"Hold on, Joe," I said, "where are you going?"

"'Nother drink!" he said, and closed the door behind him.

After supper I went to work with Henderson and three or four others in a little back-room in our headquarters; and we were hard at it when one of the boys held up his hand and said: "Listen!"

The sounds of a big disturbance came in through the open windows: shouting and yelling, and crowds running in the streets below. The town had been so noisy all evening that I thought nothing of it. "It's only some delegation getting in," I said. "Go on with the lists."

But I'd no more than got the words out of my mouth than the noise rolled into the outer rooms of our headquarters like a wave, and there was a violent hammering on the door of our room, some one calling my name in a loud frightened voice. I threw open the door and Hugo Siffles fell in, his pig's eyes starting out of his pale, foolish face.

"Come with me!" he shouted, all in one breath, and laying hold of me by the lapel of my coat, tried to drag me after him. "There's hell to pay! Joe Lane came into Trimmer's headquarters, drunk, twenty minutes ago, and slapped Passley Trimmer's face for what he said to us this afternoon. Link Trimmer came in, a minute later, drunk too, and heard what had happened. He followed Joe to Hodge's saloon and shot him. They've carried him to the drug-store and he's asked to speak to you."

I had the satisfaction of kicking that little cuss through the door ahead of me, though I knew it was myself I ought to have kicked.

It was true that Joe had asked to speak to me, but when I reached the drug-store the doctor wouldn't let me come into the back-room where he lay, so I sat on a stool in the store. They'd turned all the people out, except four or five friends of Joe's; and the glass doors and the windows were solid with flattened faces, some of them coloured by the blue and green lights so that it sickened me, and all staring horribly. After about four years the doctor's assistant came out to get something from a shelf and I jumped at him, getting mighty little satisfaction, you can be sure.

"It seems to be very serious indeed," was all he would say. I knew that for myself, because one of the men in the store had told me that it was in the left side.

Half-an-hour after this—by the clock—the young man came out again and called us in to carry Joe home. It was not more than a hundred yards to the old Lane place, and six of us, walking very slowly, carried him on a cot through the crowd. He was conscious, for he thanked us in a weakish whisper, when we lifted him carefully into his own bed. Then the doctor sent us all out except the assistant, and we went to the front porch and waited, hating the crowd that had lined up against the fence and about the gate. They looked like a lot of buzzards; I couldn't bear the sight of them, so I went back into the little hall and sat down near Joe's door.

After a while the assistant opened the door, holding a glass pitcher in his hand.

"Here," he said, when he saw me, "will you fill this with cold water from the well?"

I took it and hurried out to the kitchen, where four or five people were sitting and glumly whispering around an old coloured woman, Joe's cook, who was crying and rocking herself in a chair. I hushed her up and told her to show me the pump. It was in an orchard behind the house, and was one of those old-fashioned things that sound like a siren whistle with the hiccups.

It took me about five minutes to get the water up, and when I got back to Joe's room, a woman was there with the doctors. It was Miss Rainey. She had her hat off, her sleeves were rolled up and, though her face was the whitest I ever saw, she was cool and steady. It was she who took the water from me at the door.

I heard low voices in the parlour, where a lamp was lit, and I went in there. Mary was sitting on a sofa, with a handkerchief hard against her eyes, and Hector was standing in the middle of the room, saying over and over, "My God!" and shaking. I went to the sofa and sat by Mary with my hand on her shoulder.

"To think of it!" Hector moaned. "To think of its coming at such a time! To think of what it means to me!"

His mother spoke to him from behind her handkerchief: "You mustn't do it; you *can't* Hector—oh, you can't, you *can't*."

For answer he struck himself desperately across the forehead with the palm of his hand.

"What is it," I asked, "that your mother wants you not to do?"

"She wants me to give up Trimmer—to refuse to make the nominating speech for him to-morrow."

"You've *got* to give him up!" cried his mother; and then went on with reiterations as passionate as they were weak and broken in utterance. "You can't make the speech, you can't do it, you *can't*—"

"Then I'm done for!" he said. "Don't you see what a frightful blow this pitiful, drunken folly of poor Joe's has dealt Trimmer's candidacy? Don't you see that they rely on me more than ever, *now*? Are you so blind you don't see that I am the only man who can save Trimmer the nomination? If I go back on him now, he's done for and I'm done for with him! It's my only chance!"

"No, no," she sobbed, "you'll have other chances; you'll have plenty of chances, dear; you're young—"

"My only chance," he went on rapidly, ignoring her, "and if I can carry it through, it will mean everything to me. The tide's running strong against Trimmer to-night, and I am the only man in the world who can turn it the other way. If I go into the convention for him, faithful to him, and, out of the highest sense of justice, explain that, even though Lane has been my closest friend, he was in the wrong and that—"

Mary rose to her feet and went to her son and clung to him. "No, no!" she cried; "no, *no*!"

"I've got to!" he said.

"What is that you must do, Hector?" It was Miss Rainey's voice, and came from just behind me. She was standing in the doorway that led from the hall, and her eyes were glowing with a brilliant, warm light. We all started as she spoke, and I sprang up and turned toward her.

"He's going to get well," she said, understanding me. "They say it is surely so!"

At that Mary ran and threw her arms about her and kissed

her—and I came near it! Hector gave a sort of shout of relief and sank into a chair.

"What is that you must do, Hector?" Miss Rainey said again in her steady voice.

"Stick to Trimmer!" he explained. "Don't you see that I must? He needs me now more than ever, and it's my only chance."

Miss Rainey looked at him over Mary's shoulder. She looked at him a long while before she spoke. "You know why Mr. Lane struck that blow?"

"Oh, I suppose so," he answered uneasily. "At least Siffles—"

"Yes," she said. "You know. What are you going to do?"

"The right thing!" Hector rose and walked toward her. "I put right before all. I shall be loyal and I shall be just. It might have been a terribly hard thing to carry through, but, since dear old Joe will recover, I know I can do it."

The girl's eyes widened suddenly, while the warm glow in them flashed into a fiery and profound scrutiny.

"You are going to make the nominating speech," she said. It was not a question but a declaration, in the tone of one to whom he stood wholly revealed.

"Yes," he answered eagerly. "I knew you would see: it's my chance, my whole career—"

But his mother, turning swiftly, put her hand over his mouth, though it was to Miss Rainey that she cried:

"Oh, don't let him say it—he can't; you mustn't let him!"

The girl drew her gently away and put an arm about her, saying: "Do you think *I* could stop him?"

"But do you wish to stop me?" asked Hector sadly, as he stepped toward her. "Do you set yourself not only in the way of my great chance, but against justice and truth? Don't you see that I must do it?"

"It is your chance—yes. I see the truth, Hector." Her eyes had fallen and she looked at him no more, but, with a little movement away from him, offered her hand to him at arm's length. It was done in a curious way, and he looked perplexed for a second, and then frightened. He dropped her hand, and his lips twitched. "Laura," he said, and could not go on.

"You must go now," she said to all three of us. "The house should be very quiet. I shall be his nurse, and the doctor will stay all night. Isn't it beautiful that Joe is going to get well!"

She went out quickly, before Hector could detain her, back to the room where Lane was.

There's no need my telling you the details of that convention: Henderson was beaten from the start, and Hector's speech was all that happened. If he hadn't made it, there might have been a consolidation on a dark horse, for feeling was high against Trimmer. It isn't an easy thing to go into a convention with a brother locked up in jail on a charge of attempted murder!

I'll never forget Hector's rising to make that speech. There wasn't any cheering, there was a dead, cold hush. This wasn't because his magnetism had deserted him; indeed, I don't think it had ever before been felt so strongly. He was white as white paper, and his face had a look of suffering; altogether I believe I couldn't give a better notion of him than saying that he somehow made me think of Hamlet.

He began in a very low but very penetrating voice, and I don't think anybody in the farthest corner missed a single clear-cut syllable from the first. As I may have indicated, I had never been a warm admirer of his, but with all my prejudice, I think I admired him when he stood up to his task that day. For the effect he intended, his speech was a masterpiece, no less. I saw it before he had finished three sentences. And he delivered it, knowing that even while he did so he was losing the woman he loved; for Hector did love Laura Rainey, next to himself, and she had been part of his life and necessary to him. But though the heavens fell, he stuck to what he had set out to do, and did it masterfully.

Not that what he said could bear the analysis of a cool mind: nothing that Hector ever did or said has been able to do that. But for the purpose, it was perfect. For once he began at the beginning, without rhetoric, and he made it all the more effective by beginning with himself.

"Doubtless there are many among you who think it strange to see me rise to fulfil the charge with which you know me to be intrusted. My oldest and most intimate friend lies wounded on a bed of suffering, stricken down by the hand of another friend whose heart is in the cause for which I have risen. Therefore, you might well question me; you might well say: 'To whom is your loyalty?' Well might I ask myself that same question. And I will give you my answer: 'There are things beyond the personal friendship of man and man, things greater than individual differences and individual tragedies, things as far higher and greater than these as the skies of God are higher than the roof of a child's doll-house. These higher things are the good of the State and the Law of Justice!'"

That brought the first applause; and Trimmer's people, seeing the crowd had taken Hector's point, sprang to their feet and began to cheer. At a tense moment, such as this, cheering is often hypnotic, and good managers know how to make use of it on the floor. The noise grew thunderous, and when it subsided Hector was master of the convention. Then, for the first time, I saw how far he would go—and why. I had laughed at him all my life, but now I believed there was "something in him," as they say. The Lord knows what, but it was there; and as I looked at him and listened it seemed to me that the world was at his feet.

He was infinitely daring, yet he skirted the cause of the quarrel with perfect tact: "The misinterpretation of a few careless and kindly words, said in passing, and repeated, with garbling additions, to a man who was not himself. . . . The brooding of a mind most unhappily beset with alcohol. . . . A blow resented by a too devoted but too violent kinsman. . . ."

Then, with the greatest skill, and rather quietly, he passed to a eulogium of Trimmer's public career, gradually increasing the warmth of his praise but controlling it as perfectly as he controlled the enthusiasm and excitement which followed each of his points. For myself, I only looked away from him once, and caught a glimpse of Henderson looking sick.

Hector finished with a great stroke. He went back to the original theme. "You ask me where my duty lies!" His great voice rose and rang through the hall magnificently: "I reply—'first to my State and her needs'! Is that answer enough? If it be necessary that I should answer for my personal loyalty to one man or another then I ask *you*: 'Shall it go to the friend who, without cause, struck the first blow? Shall it go to that other friend who went out hot-headed and struck back to avenge a brother's wrongs? Is it only between these that I—and many of you—are to choose to-day? Is there not a *third*?' I tell you that I have chosen, and that my loyalty and all my strength are devoted to that other, to that man who has suffered most of all, to him who received a blow and did not avenge it, because in his greatness he knew that his assailant knew not what he did!"

That carried them off their feet. Hector had turned Trimmer's greatest danger into the means of victory. The Trimmer people led one of those extraordinary hysterical processions round the aisles that you see sometimes in a convention (a thing I never get used to), and it was all Trimmer, or rather, it was all Hector. Trimmer was nominated on the first ballot.

There was a recess, and I hurried out, meaning to slip round to Joe Lane's for a moment to find out how he was. I'd seen the doctor in the morning and he said his patient had passed a good night and that Miss Rainey was still there. "I think she's going to stay," he added, and smiled and shook hands with me.

Joe's old darky cook let me in, and, after a moment, came to say I might go into Mr. Lane's room; Mr. Lane wanted to see me.

Joe was lying very flat on his back, but with his face turned toward the door, and beside him sat Laura Rainey, their thin hands clasped together. I stopped on the threshold with the door half opened.

"Come in," said Joe weakly. "Hector made it, I'm sure."

"Yes," I answered, and in earnest. "He's a great man."

Joe's face quivered with a pain that did not come from his hurt. "Oh, it's knowing that, that makes me feel like such a scoundrel," he said. "I suppose you've come to congratulate me."

"Yes," I said, "the doctor says it's a wonderful case, and that you're one of the lucky ones with a charmed life, thank God!"

Joe smiled sadly at Miss Rainey. "He hasn't heard," he said. Then she gave me her left hand, not relinquishing Joe's with her right.

"We were married this morning," she said, "just after the convention began."

The tears came into Joe's eyes as she spoke. "It's a shame, isn't it?" he said to me. "You must see it so. And I the kind of man I am, the town drunkard—"

Then his wife leaned over and kissed his forehead.

"Even so it was right—and so beautiful for me," she said.

Mrs. Protheroe

WHEN ALONZO RAWSON took his seat as the Senator from Stackpole in the upper branch of the General Assembly of the State, an expression of pleasure and of greatness appeared to be permanently imprinted upon his countenance. He felt that if he had not quite arrived at all which he meant to make his own, at least he had emerged upon the arena where he was to win it, and he looked about him for a few other strong spirits with whom to construct a focus of power which should control the senate. The young man had not long to look, for within a week after the beginning of the session these others showed themselves to his view, rising above the general level of mediocrity and timidity, party-leaders and chiefs of faction, men who were on their feet continually, speaking half-a-dozen times a day, freely and loudly. To these, and that house at large, he felt it necessary to introduce himself by a speech which must prove him one of the elect, and he awaited impatiently an opening.

Alonzo had no timidity himself. He was not one of those who first try their voices on motions to adjourn, written in form and handed out to novices by presiding officers and leaders. He was too conscious of his own gifts, and he had been "accustomed to speaking" ever since his days in the Stackpole City Seminary. He was under the impression, also, that his appearance alone would command attention from his colleagues and the gallery. He was tall; his hair was long, with a rich waviness, rippling over both brow and collar, and he had, by years of endeavour, succeeded in moulding his features to present an aspect of stern and thoughtful majesty whenever he "spoke."

The opportunity to show his fellows that new greatness was among them delayed not over-long, and Senator Rawson arose, long and bony in his best clothes, to address the senate with a huge voice in denunciation of the "Sunday Baseball Bill," then upon second reading. The classical references, which, as a born orator, he felt it necessary to introduce, were received with acclamations which the gavel of the Lieutenant-Governor had no power to still.

"What led to the De-cline and Fall of the Roman Empire?" he exclaimed. "I await an answer from the advocates of this *de*-generate measure! I *demand* an answer from them! Let me hear from them on *that* subject! Why don't they speak up? They can't give one. Not because they ain't familiar with history, no sir! That's not the reason! It's because they *daren't*, because their answer would have to go on record *against* 'em! Don't any of you try to raise it against me that I ain't speakin' to the point, for I tell you that when you encourage Sunday Baseball, or any kind of Sabbath-breakin' on Sunday, you're tryin' to start this State on the downward path that beset Rome! *I'll* tell you what ruined it. The Roman Empire started out to be the greatest nation on earth, and they had a good start, too, just like the United States has got to-day. *Then* what happened to 'em? Why, them old ancient fellers got more interested in athletic games and gladiatorial combats and racing and all kinds of out-door sports, and bettin' on 'em, than they were in oratory, or literature, or charitable institutions and good works of all kinds. At first they were moderate and the country was prosperous. But six days in the week wouldn't content 'em, and they went at it all the time, so that at last they gave up the seventh day to their sports, the way this bill wants *us* to do, and from that time on the result was *de*-generacy and *de*-gredation! You better remember *that* lesson, my friends, and don't try to sink this State to the level of Rome!"

When Alonzo Rawson wiped his dampened brow, and dropped into his chair, he was satisfied to the core of his heart with the effect of his maiden effort. There was not one eye in the place that was not fixed upon him and shining with surprise and delight, while the kindly Lieutenant-Governor, his face very red, rapped for order. The young senator across the aisle leaned over and shook Alonzo's hand excitedly.

"That was beautiful, Senator Rawson!" he whispered. "I'm *for* the bill, but I can respect a masterly opponent."

"I thank you, Senator Truslow," Alonzo returned graciously. "I am glad to have your good opinion, Senator."

"You have it, Senator," said Truslow enthusiastically. "I hope you intend to speak often?"

"I do, Senator. I intend to make myself heard," the other answered gravely, "upon all questions of moment."

"You will fill a great place among us, Senator!"

Then Alonzo Rawson wondered if he had not underestimated his neighbour across the aisle; he had formed an opinion of Truslow as one of small account and no power, for he had observed that, although this was Truslow's second term, he had not once demanded recognition nor attempted to take part in a debate. Instead, he seemed to spend most of his time frittering over some desk work, though now and then he walked up and down the aisles talking in a low voice to various senators. How such a man could have been elected at all, Alonzo failed to understand. Also, Truslow was physically inconsequent, in his colleague's estimation—"a little insignificant, dudish kind of a man," he had thought; one whom he would have darkly suspected of cigarettes had he not been dumbfounded to behold Truslow smoking an old black pipe in the lobby. The Senator from Stackpole had looked over the other's clothes with a disapproval that amounted to bitterness. Truslow's attire reminded him of pictures in New York magazines, or the dress of boys newly home from college, he didn't know which, but he did know that it was contemptible. Consequently, after receiving the young man's congratulations, Alonzo was conscious of the keenest surprise at his own feeling that there might be something in him after all.

He decided to look him over again, more carefully to take the measure of one who had shown himself so frankly an admirer. Waiting, therefore, a few moments until he felt sure that Truslow's gaze had ceased to rest upon himself, he turned to bend a surreptitious but piercing scrutiny upon his neighbour. His glance, however, sweeping across Truslow's shoulder toward the face, suddenly encountered another pair of eyes beyond, so intently fixed upon himself that he started. The clash was like two search-lights meeting—and the glorious brown eyes that shot into Alonzo's were not the eyes of Truslow.

Truslow's desk was upon the outer aisle, and along the wall were placed comfortable leather chairs and settees, originally intended for the use of members of the upper house, but nearly always occupied by their wives and daughters, or "lady-lobbyists," or other women spectators. Leaning back with extraordinary grace, in the chair nearest Truslow, sat the handsomest woman Alonzo had ever seen in his life. Her long coat of soft grey fur was unrecognizable to him in connection with any familiar breed of squirrel; her broad flat hat of the same fur was wound with a grey veil, underneath which her heavy brown hair seemed to exhale a mysterious glow, and never, not even in a lithograph, had he seen features so regular or a skin so clear! And to look into her eyes seemed to Alonzo like diving deep into clear water and turning to stare up at the light.

His own eyes fell first. In the breathless awkwardness that beset him they seemed to stumble shamefully down to his desk, like a country-boy getting back to his seat after a thrashing on the teacher's platform. For the lady's gaze, profoundly liquid as it was, had not been friendly.

Alonzo Rawson had neither the habit of petty analysis, nor the inclination toward it; yet there arose within him a wonder at his own emotion, at its strangeness and the violent reaction of it. A moment ago his soul had been steeped in satisfaction over the figure he had cut with his speech and the extreme enthusiasm which had been accorded it—an extraordinarily pleasant feeling: suddenly this was gone, and in its place he found himself almost choking with a dazed sense of having been scathed, and at the same time understood in a way in which he did not understand himself. And yet—he and this most unusual lady had been so mutually conscious of each other in their mysterious interchange that he felt almost acquainted with her. Why, then, should his head be hot with resentment? Nobody had *said* anything to him!

He seized upon the fattest of the expensive books supplied to him by the State, opened it with emphasis and began not to read it, with abysmal abstraction, tinglingly alert to the circumstance that Truslow was holding a low-toned but lively conversation with the unknown. Her laugh came to him, at once musical, quiet, and of a quality which irritated him into saying bitterly to himself that he guessed there was just as much refinement in Stackpole as there was in the Capital City, and just as many old families! The clerk calling his vote upon the "Baseball Bill" at that moment, he roared "No!" in a tone which was profane. It seemed to him that he was avenging himself upon somebody for something and it gave him a great deal of satisfaction.

He returned immediately to his imitation of Archimedes, only relaxing the intensity of his attention to the text (which blurred into jargon before his fixed gaze) when he heard that light laugh again. He pursed his lips, looked up at the ceiling as if slightly puzzled by some profound question beyond the reach of womankind; solved it almost immediately, and, setting his hand to pen and paper, wrote the capital letter "O" several hundred times on note-paper furnished by the State. So oblivious was he, apparently, to everything but the question of statecraft which occupied him, that he did not even look up when the morning's session was adjourned and the lawmakers began to pass noisily out, until Truslow stretched an arm across the aisle and touched him upon the shoulder.

"In a moment, Senator!" answered Alonzo in his deepest chest tones. He made it a very short moment, indeed, for he had a wild, breath-taking suspicion of what was coming.

"I want you to meet Mrs. Protheroe, Senator," said Truslow, rising, as Rawson, after folding his writings with infinite care, placed them in his breast pocket.

"I am pleased to make your acquaintance, ma'am," Alonzo said in a loud, firm voice, as he got to his feet, though the place grew vague about him when the lady stretched a charming, slender, gloved hand to him across Truslow's desk. He gave it several solemn shakes.

"We shouldn't have disturbed you, perhaps?" she asked, smiling radiantly upon him. "You were at some important work, I'm afraid."

He met her eyes again, and their beauty and the thoughtful kindliness of them fairly took his breath. "I am the chairman, ma'am," he replied, swallowing, "of the committee on drains and dikes."

"I knew it was something of great moment," she said gravely, "but I was anxious to tell you that I was interested in your speech."

A few minutes later, without knowing how he had got his hat and coat from the cloak-room, Alonzo Rawson found himself walking slowly through the marble vistas of the State-house to the great outer doors with the lady and Truslow. They were talking inconsequently of the weather, and of various legislators, but Alonzo did not know it. He vaguely formed replies to her questions and he hardly realized what the questions were; he was too stirringly conscious of the rich quiet of her voice and of the caress of the grey fur of her cloak when the back of his hand touched it—rather accidentally—now and then, as they moved on together.

It was a cold, quick air to which they emerged and Alonzo, daring to look at her, found that she had pulled the veil down over her face, the colour of which, in the keen wind, was like that of June roses seen through morning mists. At the curb a long, low, rakish black automobile was in waiting, the driver a mere indistinguishable cylinder of fur.

Truslow, opening the little door of the tonneau, offered his hand to the lady. "Come over to the club, Senator, and lunch with me," he said. "Mrs. Protheroe won't mind dropping us there on her way."

That was an eerie ride for Alonzo, whose feet were falling upon strange places. His pulses jumped and his eyes swam with the tears of unlawful speed, but his big ungloved hand tingled not with the cold so much as with the touch of that divine grey fur upon his little finger.

"You intend to make many speeches, Mr. Truslow tells me," he heard the rich voice saying.

"Yes ma'am," he summoned himself to answer. "I expect I will. Yes ma'am." He paused, and then repeated, "Yes ma'am."

She looked at him for a moment. "But you will do some work, too, won't you?" she asked slowly.

Her intention in this passed by Alonzo at the time. "Yes ma'am," he answered. "The committee work interests me greatly, especially drains and dikes."

"I have heard," she said, as if searching his opinion, "that almost as much is accomplished in the committee-rooms as on the floor? There—and in the lobby and in the hotels and clubs?"

"I don't have much to do with that!" he returned quickly. "I guess none of them lobbyists will get much out of me! I even sent back all their railroad tickets. They needn't come near me!"

After a pause which she may have filled with unexpressed admiration, she ventured, almost timidly: "Do you remember that it was said that Napoleon once attributed the secret of his power over other men to one quality?"

"I am an admirer of Napoleon," returned the Senator from Stackpole. "I admire all great men."

"He said that he held men by his reserve."

"It can be done," observed Alonzo, and stopped, feeling that it was more reserved to add nothing to the sentence.

"But I suppose that such a policy," she smiled upon him inquiringly, "wouldn't have helped him much with women?"

"No," he agreed immediately. "My opinion is that a man ought to tell a *good* woman everything. What is more sacred than—"

The car, turning a corner much too quickly, performed a gymnastic squirm about an unexpected street-car and the speech ended in a gasp, as Alonzo, not of his own volition, half rose and pressed his cheek closely against hers. Instantaneous as it was, his heart leaped violently, but not with fear. Could all the things of his life that had seemed beautiful have been compressed into one instant, it would not have brought him even the suggestion of the wild shock of joy of that one, wherein he knew the glamorous perfume of Mrs. Protheroe's brown hair and felt her cold cheek firm against his, with only the grey veil between.

"I'm afraid this driver of mine will kill me some day," she said, laughing and composedly straightening her hat. "Do you care for big machines?"

"Yes ma'am," he answered huskily. "I haven't been in many."

"Then I'll take you again," said Mrs. Protheroe. "If you like I'll come down to the State-house and take you out for a run in the country."

"When?" said the lost young man, staring at her with his mouth open. "When?"

"Saturday afternoon if you like. I'll be there at two."

They were in front of the club and Truslow had already jumped out. Mrs. Protheroe gave him her hand and they exchanged a glance significant of something more than a friendly good-bye. Indeed, one might have hazarded that there was something almost businesslike about it. The confused Senator from Stackpole, climbing out reluctantly, observed it not, nor could he have understood even if he had seen, that delicate signal which passed between his two companions.

When he was upon the ground Mrs. Protheroe extended her hand without speaking, but her lips formed the word,

"Saturday." Then she was carried away quickly, while Alonzo, his heart hammering, stood looking after her, born into a strange world, the touch of the grey fur upon his little finger, the odour of her hair faintly about him, one side of his face red, the other pale.

"To-day is Wednesday," he said, half aloud.

"Come on, Senator." Truslow took his arm and turned him toward the club doors.

The other looked upon his new friend vaguely. "Why, I forgot to thank her for the ride," he said.

"You'll have other chances, Senator," Truslow assured him. "Mrs. Protheroe has a hobby for studying politics and she expects to come down often. She has plenty of time—she's a widow, you know."

"I hope you didn't think," exclaimed Alonzo indignantly, "that I thought she was a married woman!"

After lunch they walked back to the State-house together, Truslow regarding his thoughtful companion with sidelong whimsicalness. Mrs. Protheroe's question, suggestive of a difference between work and speechmaking, had recurred to Alonzo, and he had determined to make himself felt, off the floor as well as upon it. He set to this with a fine energy, that afternoon, in his committee-room, and the Senator from Stackpole knew his subject. On drains and dikes he had no equal. He spoke convincingly to his colleagues of the committee upon every bill that was before them, and he compelled their humblest respect. He went earnestly at it, indeed, and sat very late that night, in his room at a nearby boarding house, studying bills, trying to keep his mind upon them and not to think of his strange morning and of Saturday. Finally his neighbour in the next room, Senator Ezra Trumbull, long abed, was awakened by his praying and groaned slightly. Trumbull meant to speak to Rawson about his prayers, for Trumbull was an early one to bed and they woke him every night. The partition was flimsy and Alonzo addressed his Maker in the loud voice of those accustomed to talking across wide out-of-door spaces. Trumbull considered it especially unnecessary in the city; though, as a citizen of a county which loved but little his neighbour's district, he felt that in Stackpole there was good reason for a person to shout his prayers at the top of his voice and even then have small chance to carry through the distance. Still, it was a delicate matter to mention and he put it off from day to day.

Thursday passed slowly for Alonzo Rawson, nor was his voice lifted in debate. There was little but routine; and the main interest of the chamber was in the lobbying that was being done upon the "Sunday Baseball Bill" which had passed to its third reading and would come up for final disposition within a fortnight. This was the measure which Alonzo had set his heart upon defeating. It was a simple enough bill: it provided, in substance, that baseball might be played on Sunday by professionals in the State capital, which was proud of its league team. Naturally, it was denounced by clergymen, and deputations of ministers and committees from women's religious societies were constantly arriving at the State-house to protest against its passage. The Senator from Stackpole reassured all of these with whom he talked, and was one of their staunchest allies and supporters. He was active in leading the wavering among his colleagues, or even the inimical, out to meet and face the deputations. It was in this occupation that he was engaged, on Friday afternoon, when he received a shock.

A committee of women from a church society was waiting in the corridor, and he had rounded-up a reluctant half-dozen senators and led them forth to be interrogated as to their intentions regarding the bill. The committee and the lawmakers soon distributed themselves into little argumentative clumps, and Alonzo found himself in the centre of these, with one of the ladies who had unfortunately—but, in her enthusiasm, without misgivings—begun a reproachful appeal to an advocate of the bill whose name was Goldstein.

"Senator Goldstein," she exclaimed, "I could not believe it when I heard that you were in favour of this measure! I have heard my husband speak in the highest terms of your old father. May I ask you what *he* thinks of it? If you voted for the desecration of Sunday by a low baseball game, could you dare go home and face that good old man?"

"Yes, madam," said Goldstein mildly; "we are *both* Jews."

A low laugh rippled out from near-by, and Alonzo, turning almost violently, beheld his lady of the furs. She was leaning back against a broad pilaster, her hands sweeping the same big coat behind her, her face turned toward him, but her eyes, sparklingly delighted, resting upon Goldstein. Under the broad fur hat she made a picture as enraging, to Alonzo Rawson, as it was bewitching. She appeared not to see him, to be quite unconscious of him—and he believed it. Truslow and five or six members of both houses were about her, and they all seemed to be bending eagerly toward her. Alonzo was furious with her.

Her laugh lingered upon the air for a moment, then her glance swept round the other way, omitting the Senator from Stackpole, who, immediately putting into practice a reserve which would have astonished Napoleon, swung about and quitted the deputation without a word of farewell or explanation. He turned into the cloak-room and paced the floor for three minutes with a malevolence which awed the coloured attendants into not brushing his coat; but, when he returned to the corridor, cautious inquiries addressed to the tobacconist elicited the information that the handsome lady with Senator Truslow had departed.

Truslow himself had not gone. He was lounging in his seat when Alonzo returned and was genially talkative. The latter refrained from replying in kind, not altogether out of reserve, but more because of a dim suspicion (which rose within him, the third time Truslow called him "Senator" in one sentence) that his first opinion of the young man as a light-minded person might have been correct.

There was no session the following afternoon, but Alonzo watched the street from the windows of his committee-room, which overlooked the splendid breadth of stone steps leading down from the great doors to the pavement. There were some big bookcases in the room, whose glass doors served as mirrors in which he more and more sternly regarded the soft image of an entirely new grey satin tie, while the conviction grew within him that (arguing from her behaviour of the previous day) she would not come, and that the Stackpole girls were nobler by far at heart than many who might wear a king's-ransom's-worth of jewels round their throats at the opera-house in a large city. This sentiment was heartily confirmed by the clock when it marked half-past two. He faced the bookcase doors and struck his breast, his open hand falling across the grey tie with tragic violence; after which, turning for the last time to the windows, he uttered a loud exclamation and, laying hands upon an ulster and a grey felt hat, each as new as the satin tie, ran hurriedly from the room. The black automobile was waiting.

"I thought it possible you might see me from a window," said Mrs. Protheroe as he opened the little door.

"I was just coming out," he returned, gasping for breath. "I thought—from yesterday—you'd probably forgotten."

"Why 'from yesterday'?" she asked.

"I thought—I thought—" He faltered to a stop as the full glorious sense of her presence overcame him. She wore the same veil.

"You thought I did not see you yesterday in the corridor?"

"I thought you might have acted more—more—"

"More cordially?"

"Well," he said, looking down at his hands, "more like you knew we'd been introduced."

At that she sat silent, looking away from him, and he, daring a quick glance at her, found that he might let his eyes remain upon her face. That was a dangerous place for eyes to rest, yet Alonzo Rawson was anxious for the risk. The car flew along the even asphalt on its way to the country like a wild goose on a long slant of wind, and, with his foolish fury melted inexplicably into honey, Alonzo looked at her—and looked at her—till he would have given an arm for another quick corner and a street-car to send his cheek against that veiled, cold cheek of hers again. It was not until they reached the alternate vacant lots and bleak Queen Anne cottages of the city's ragged edge that she broke the silence.

"You were talking to some one else," she said almost inaudibly.

"Yes ma'am, Goldstein, but—"

"Oh, no!" She turned toward him, lifting her hand. "You were quite the lion among ladies."

"I don't know what you mean, Mrs. Protheroe," he said, truthfully.

"What were you talking to all those women about?"

"It was about the 'Sunday Baseball Bill.'"

"Ah! The bill you attacked in your speech, last Wednesday?"

"Yes ma'am."

"I hear you haven't made any speeches since then," she said indifferently.

"No ma'am," he answered gently. "I kind of got the idea that I'd better lay low for a while, at first, and get in some quiet hard work."

"I understand. You are a man of intensely reserved nature."

"With men," said Alonzo, "I am. With ladies I am not so much so. I think a good woman ought to be told—"

"But you are interested," she interrupted, "in defeating that bill?"

"Yes ma'am," he returned. "It is an iniquitous measure."

"Why?"

"Mrs. Protheroe!" he exclaimed, taken aback. "I thought all the ladies were against it. My own mother wrote to me from Stackpole that she'd rather see me in my grave than votin' for such a bill, and I'd rather see myself there!"

"But are you sure that you understand it?"

"I only know it desecrates the Sabbath. That's enough for me!"

She leaned toward him and his breath came quickly.

"No. You're wrong," she said, and rested the tips of her fingers upon his sleeve.

"I don't understand why—why you say that," he faltered. "It sounds kind of—surprising to me—"

"Listen," she said. "Perhaps Mr. Truslow told you that I am studying such things. I do not want to be an idle woman; I want to be of use to the world, even if it must be only in small ways."

"I think that is a noble ambition!" he exclaimed. "I think all good women ought—"

"Wait," she interrupted gently. "Now, that bill is a worthy one, though it astonishes you to hear me say so. Perhaps you don't understand the conditions. Sunday is the labouring-man's only day of recreation—and what recreation is he offered?"

"He ought to go to church," said Alonzo promptly.

"But the fact is that he doesn't—not often—not at *all* in the afternoon. Wouldn't it be well to give him some wholesome way of employing his Sunday afternoons? This bill provides for just that, and it keeps him away from drinking too, for it forbids the sale of liquor on the grounds."

"Yes, I know," said Alonzo plaintively. "But it ain't *right*! I was raised to respect the Sabbath and—"

"Ah, that's what you should do! You think *I* could believe in anything that wouldn't make it better and more sacred?"

"Oh, no, ma'am!" he cried reproachfully. "It's only that I don't see—"

"I am telling you." She lifted her veil and let him have the full dazzle of her beauty. "Do you know that many thousands of labouring people spend their Sundays drinking and carousing about the low country road-houses because the game is played at such places on Sunday? They go there because they never get a chance to see it played in the city. And don't you understand that there would be no Sunday liquor trade, no working-men poisoning themselves every seventh day in the low groggeries, as hundreds of them do now, if they had something to see that would interest them?—something as wholesome and fine as this sport would be, under the conditions of this bill; something to keep them in the open air, something to bring a little gaiety into their dull lives!" Her voice had grown louder and it shook a little, with a rising emotion, though its sweetness was only the more poignant. "Oh, my dear Senator," she cried, "don't you *see* how wrong you are? Don't you want to *help* these poor people?"

Her fingers, which had tightened upon his sleeve, relaxed and she leaned back, pulling the veil down over her face as if wishing to conceal from him that her lips trembled slightly; then resting her arm upon the leather cushions, she turned her head away from him, staring fixedly into the gaunt beech woods lining the country road along which they were now coursing. For a time she heard nothing from him, and the only sound was the monotonous chug of the machine.

"I suppose you think it rather shocking to hear a woman talking practically of such commonplace things," she said at last, in a cold voice, just loud enough to be heard.

"No ma'am," he said huskily.

"Then what *do* you think?" she cried, turning toward him again with a quick imperious gesture.

"I think I'd better go back to Stackpole," he answered very slowly, "and resign my job. I don't see as I've got any business in the Legislature."

"I don't understand you."

He shook his head mournfully. "It's a simple enough matter. I've studied out a good many bills and talked 'em over and I've picked up some influence and —"

"I know you have," she interrupted eagerly. "Mr. Truslow says that the members of your drains-and-dikes committee follow your vote on every bill."

"Yes ma'am," said Alonzo Rawson meekly, "but I expect they oughtn't to. I've had a lesson this afternoon."

"You mean to say—"

"I mean that I didn't know what I was doing about that baseball bill. I was just pig-headedly goin' ahead against it, not knowing nothing about the conditions, and it took a lady to show me what they were. I would have done a wrong thing if you hadn't stopped me."

"You mean," she cried, her splendid eyes widening with excitement and delight; "you mean that you—that you—"

"I mean that I will vote for the bill!" He struck his clenched fist upon his knee. "I come to the Legislature to do *right*!"

"You will, ah, you *will* do right in this!" Mrs. Protheroe thrust up her veil again and her face was flushed and radiant with triumph. "And you'll work, and you'll make a speech for the bill?"

At this the righteous exaltation began rather abruptly to simmer down in the soul of Alonzo Rawson. He saw the consequences of too violently reversing, and knew how difficult they might be to face.

"Well, not—not exactly," he said weakly. "I expect our best plan would be for me to lay kind of low and not say any more about the bill at all. Of course, I'll quit workin' against it; and on the roll-call I'll edge up close to the clerk and say 'Aye' so that only him'll hear me. That's done every day—and I—well, I don't just exactly like to come out too publicly for it, after my speech and all I've done against it."

She looked at him sharply for a short second, and then offered him her hand and said: "Let's shake hands *now*, on the vote. Think what a triumph it is for me to know that I helped to show you the right."

"Yes ma'am," he answered confusedly, too much occupied with shaking her hand to know what he said. She spoke one word in an undertone to the driver and the machine took the very shortest way back to the city.

After this excursion, several days passed, before Mrs. Protheroe came to the State-house again. Rawson was bending over the desk of Senator Josephus Battle, the white-bearded leader of the opposition to the "Sunday Baseball Bill," and was explaining to him the intricacies of a certain drainage measure, when Battle, whose attention had wandered, plucked his sleeve and whispered:

"If you want to see a mighty pretty woman that's doin' no good here, look behind you, over there in the chair by the big fireplace at the back of the room."

Alonzo looked.

It was she whose counterpart had been in his dream's eye every moment of the dragging days which had been vacant of her living presence. A number of his colleagues were hanging over her almost idiotically; her face was gay and her voice came to his ears, as he turned, with the accent of her cadenced laughter running through her talk like a chime of tiny bells flitting through a strain of music.

"This is the third time she's been here," said Battle, rubbing his beard the wrong way. "She's lobbyin' for that infernal Sabbath-Desecration bill, but we'll beat her, my son."

"Have you made her acquaintance, Senator?" asked Alonzo stiffly.

"No, sir, and I don't want to. But I knew her father—the slickest old beat and the smoothest talker that ever waltzed up the pike. She married rich; her husband left her a lot of real estate around here, but she spends most of her time away. Whatever struck her to come down and lobby for that bill I don't know—yet—but I will! Truslow's helping her to help himself; he's got stock in the company that runs the baseball team, but what she's up to—well, I'll bet there's a nigger in the woodpile *some*where!"

"I expect there's a lot of talk like that!" said Alonzo, red with anger, and taking up his papers abruptly.

"Yes, *sir*!" said Battle emphatically, utterly misunderstanding the other's tone and manner. "Don't you worry, my son. We'll kill that venomous bill right here in this chamber! We'll kill it so dead that it won't make one flop after the axe hits it.

You and me and some others'll tend to *that*! Let her work that pretty face and those eyes of hers all she wants to! I'm keepin' a little lookout, too—and I'll—"

He broke off, for the angry and perturbed Alonzo had left him and gone to his own desk. Battle, slightly surprised, rubbed his beard the wrong way and sauntered out to the lobby to muse over a cigar. Alonzo, loathing Battle with a great loathing, formed bitter phrases concerning that vicious-minded old gentleman, while for a moment he affected to be setting his desk in order. Then he walked slowly up the aisle, conscious of a roaring in his ears (though not aware how red they were) as he approached the semi-circle about her.

He paused within three feet of her in a sudden panic of timidity, and then, to his consternation, she looked him squarely in the face, over the shoulders of two of the group, and the only sign of recognition that she exhibited was a slight frown of unmistakable repulsion, which appeared between her handsome eyebrows.

It was very swift; only Alonzo saw it; the others had no eyes for anything but her, and were not aware of his presence behind them, for she did not even pause in what she was saying.

Alonzo walked slowly away with the wormwood in his heart. He had not grown up among the young people of Stackpole without similar experiences, but it had been his youthful boast that no girl had ever "stopped speaking" to him without reason, or "cut a dance" with him and afterward found opportunity to repeat the indignity.

"What have I *done* to *her*?" was perhaps the hottest cry of his bruised soul, for the mystery was as great as the sting of it.

It was no balm upon that sting to see her pass him at the top of the outer steps, half an hour later, on the arm of that one of his colleagues who had been called the "best-dressed man in the Legislature." She swept by him without a sign, laughing that same laugh at some sally of her escort, and they got into the black automobile together and were whirled away and out of sight by the impassive bundle of furs who manipulated the wheel.

For the rest of that afternoon and the whole of that night no man, woman, or child heard the voice of Alonzo Rawson, for he spoke to none. He came not to the evening meal, nor was he seen by any who had his acquaintance. He entered his room at about midnight, and Trumbull was awakened by his neighbour's overturning a chair. No match was struck, however, and Trumbull was relieved to think that the Senator from Stackpole intended going directly to bed without troubling to light the gas, and that his prayers would soon be over. Such was not the case, for no other sound came from the room, nor were Alonzo's prayers uttered that night, though the unhappy statesman in the next apartment could not get to sleep for several hours on account of his nervous expectancy of them.

After this, as the day approached upon which hung the fate of the bill which Mr. Josephus Battle was fighting, Mrs. Protheroe came to the Senate Chamber nearly every morning and afternoon. Not once did she appear to be conscious of Alonzo Rawson's presence, nor once did he allow his eyes to delay upon her, though it cannot be truthfully said that he did not always know when she came, when she left, and with whom she stood or sat or talked. He evaded all mention or discussion of the bill or of Mrs. Protheroe; avoided Truslow (who, strangely enough, was avoiding *him*) and, spending upon drains and dikes all the energy that he could manage to concentrate, burned the midnight oil and rubbed salt into his wounds to such marked effect that by the evening of the Governor's Reception—upon the morning following which the mooted bill was to come up—he offered an impression so haggard and worn that an actor might have studied him for a make-up as a young statesman going into a decline.

Nevertheless, he dressed with great care and bitterness, and placed the fragrant blossom of a geranium—taken from a plant belonging to his landlady—in the lapel of his long coat before he set out.

And yet, when he came down the Governor's broad stairs, and wandered through the big rooms, with the glare of lights above him and the shouting of the guests ringing in his ears, a sense of emptiness beset him; the crowded place seemed vacant and without meaning. Even the noise sounded hollow and remote—and why had he bothered about the geranium? He hated her and would never look at her again—but why was she not there?

By-and-by, he found himself standing against a wall, where

he had been pushed by the press of people. He was wondering drearily what he was to do with a clean plate and a napkin which a courteous negro had handed him, half-an-hour earlier, when he felt a quick jerk at his sleeve. It was Truslow, who had worked his way along the wall and who now, standing on tiptoe, spoke rapidly but cautiously, close to his ear.

"Senator, be quick," he said sharply, at the same time alert to see that they were unobserved. "Mrs. Protheroe wants to speak to you at once. You'll find her near the big palms under the stairway in the hall."

He was gone—he had wormed his way half across the room —before the other, in his simple amazement could answer. When Alonzo at last found a word, it was only a monosyllable, which, with his accompanying action, left a matron of years, who was at that moment being pressed fondly to his side, in a state of mind almost as dumbfounded as his own. "*Here!*" was all he said as he pressed the plate and napkin into her hand and departed forcibly for the hall, leaving a spectacular wreckage of trains behind him.

The upward flight of the stairway left a space underneath, upon which, as it was screened (save for a narrow entrance) by a thicket of palms, the crowd had not encroached. Here were placed a divan and a couple of chairs; there was shade from the glare of gas, and the light was dim and cool. Mrs. Protheroe had risen from the divan when Alonzo entered this grotto, and stood waiting for him.

He stopped in the green entrance-way with a quick exclamation.

She did not seem the same woman who had put such slights upon him, this tall, white vision of silk, with the summery scarf falling from her shoulders. His great wrath melted at the sight of her; the pain of his racked pride, which had been so hot in his breast, gave way to a species of fear. She seemed not a human being, but a white spirit of beauty and goodness who stood before him, extending two fine arms to him in long, white gloves.

She left him to his trance for a moment, then seized both his hands in hers and cried to him in her rapturous, low voice: "Ah, Senator, you have come! I *knew* you understood!"

"Yes ma'am," he whispered chokily.

She drew him to one of the chairs and sank gracefully down upon the divan near him.

"Mr. Truslow was so afraid you wouldn't," she went on rapidly, "but I was sure. You see I didn't want anybody to suspect that I had any influence with you. I didn't want them to know, even, that I'd talked to you. It all came to me after the first day that we met. You see I've believed in you, in your power and in your reserve, from the first. I want all that you do to seem to come from yourself and not from me or any one else. Oh, I *believe* in great, strong men who stand upon their own feet and conquer the world for themselves! That's *your* way, Senator Rawson. So, you see, as they think I'm lobbying for the bill, I wanted them to believe that your speech for it to-morrow comes from your own great, strong mind and heart and your sense of right, and not from any suggestion of mine."

"My speech!" he stammered.

"Oh, I know," she cried; "I know you think I don't believe much in speeches, and I don't ordinarily, but a few, simple, straightforward and vigorous words from you, to-morrow, may carry the bill through. You've made such *progress*, you've been so *reserved*, that you'll carry great weight—and there are three votes of the drains-and-dikes that are against us now, but will follow yours absolutely. Do you think I would have 'cut' *you* if it hadn't been *best*?"

"But I—"

"Oh, I know you didn't actually promise me to speak, that day. But I knew you would when the time came! I knew that a man of power goes over *all* obstacles, once his sense of *right* is aroused! I *knew*—I never doubted it, that once *you* felt a thing to be right you would strike for it, with all your great strength —at all costs—at all—"

"I can't—I—I—can't!" he whispered nervously. "Don't you see—don't you see—I—"

She leaned toward him, lifting her face close to his. She was so near him that the faint odour of her hair came to him again, and once more the unfortunate Senator from Stackpole risked a meeting of his eyes with hers, and saw the light shining far down in their depths.

At this moment the shadow of a portly man who was stroking his beard the wrong way projected itself upon them from the narrow, green entrance to the grotto. Neither of them perceived it.

Senator Josephus Battle passed on, but when Alonzo Rawson emerged, a few moments later, he was pledged to utter a few simple, straightforward and vigorous words in favour of the bill. And—let the shame fall upon the head of the scribe who tells it—he had kissed Mrs. Protheroe!

The fight upon the "Sunday Baseball Bill," the next morning, was the warmest of that part of the session, though for a while the reporters were disappointed. They were waiting for Senator Battle, who was famous among them for the vituperative vigour of his attacks and for the kind of personalities which made valuable copy. And yet, until the debate was almost over, he contented himself with going quietly up and down the aisles, whispering to the occupants of the desks, and writing and sending a multitude of notes to his colleagues. Meanwhile, the orators upon both sides harangued their fellows, the lobby, the unpolitical audience, and the patient presiding officer to no effect, so far as votes went. The general impression was that it would be close.

Alonzo Rawson sat, bent over his desk, his eyes fixed with gentle steadiness upon Mrs. Protheroe, who occupied the chair wherein he had first seen her. A senator of the opposition was finishing his denunciation, when she turned and nodded almost imperceptibly to the young man.

He gave her one last look of pathetic tenderness and rose.

"The Senator from Stackpole!"

"I want," Alonzo began, in his big voice: "I want to say a few simple, straightforward but vigorous words about this bill. You may remember I spoke against it on its second reading—"

"You did *that*!" shouted Senator Battle suddenly.

"I want to say now," the Senator from Stackpole continued, "that at that time I hadn't studied the subject sufficiently. I didn't know the conditions of the case, nor the facts, but since then a great light has broke in upon me—"

"I should say it had! I saw it break!" was Senator Battle's second violent interruption.

When order was restored, Alonzo, who had become very pale, summoned his voice again. "I think we'd ought to take into consideration that Sunday is the working-man's only day of recreation and not drive him into low groggeries, but give him a chance in the open air to indulge his love of wholesome sport—"

"Such as the ancient Romans enjoyed!" interposed Battle vindictively.

"No, sir!" Alonzo wheeled upon him, stung to the quick. "Such a sport as free-born Americans and *only* free-born Americans can play in this wide world—the American game of base-ball, in which no other nation of the *Earth* is our equal!"

This was a point scored and the cheering lasted two minutes. Then the orator resumed:

"I say: 'Give the working-man a chance!' Is his life a happy one? You know it ain't! Give him his one day. *Don't* spoil it for him with your laws—he's only got one! I'm not goin' to take up any more of your time, but if there's anybody here who thinks my well-considered opinion worth following I say: '*Vote for this bill.*' It is right and virtuous and ennobling, and it ought to be passed! I say: '*Vote for it.*'"

The reporters decided that the Senator from Stackpole had "wakened things up." The gavel rapped a long time before the chamber quieted down, and when it did, Josephus Battle was on his feet and had obtained the recognition of the chair.

"I wish to say, right here," he began, with a rasping leisureliness, "that I hope no member of this honoured body will take my remarks as personal or unparliamentary—*but*"—he raised a big forefinger and shook it with menace at the presiding officer, at the same time suddenly lifting his voice to an unprintable shriek—"I say to *you*, sir, that the song of the siren has been *heard* in the land, and the call of Delilah has been answered! When the Senator from Stackpole rose in this chamber, less than three weeks ago, and denounced this iniquitous measure, I heard him with pleasure—we *all* heard him with pleasure—*and* respect! In spite of his youth and the poor quality of his expression, *we* listened to him. *We* knew he was sincere! What has caused the change in him? What *has*, I ask? I shall not tell you, upon this floor, but I've taken mighty good care to let most of you know, during the morning, either by word of mouth or by *note* of hand! Especially those of you of the drains-and-dikes and others who might follow this young Samson, whose locks have been shore! *I've* told you all about that, and more—*I've* told you the *inside* history of some *facts* about the bill that I will not make public, because I am too confident of our strength to defeat this devilish measure, and prefer to let our vote speak our opinion of it! Let me not detain you longer. *I* thank you!"

Long before he had finished, the Senator from Stackpole was being held down in his chair by Truslow and several senators whose seats were adjacent; and the vote was taken amid an uproar of shouting and confusion. When the clerk managed to proclaim the result over all other noises, the bill was shown to be defeated and "killed," by a majority of five votes.

A few minutes later, Alonzo Rawson, his neck-wear disordered and his face white with rage, stumbled out of the great doors upon the trail of Battle, who had quietly hurried away to his hotel for lunch as soon as he had voted.

The black automobile was vanishing round a corner. Truslow stood upon the edge of the pavement staring after it ruefully:

"Where is Mrs. Protheroe?" gasped the Senator from Stackpole.

"She's gone," said the other.

"Gone where?"

"Gone back to Paris. She sails day after to-morrow. She just had time enough to catch her train for New York after waiting to hear how the vote went. She told me to tell you goodbye, and that she was sorry. Don't stare at me Rawson! I guess we're in the same boat!—Where are you going?" he finished abruptly.

Alonzo swung by him and started across the street. "To find Battle!" the hoarse answer came back.

The conquering Josephus was leaning meditatively upon the counter of the cigar-stand of his hotel when Alonzo found him. He took one look at the latter's face and backed to the wall, tightening his grasp upon the heavy-headed ebony cane it was his habit to carry, a habit upon which he now congratulated himself.

But his precautions were needless. Alonzo stopped out of reaching distance.

"You tell me," he said in a breaking voice; "you tell me what you meant about Delilah and sirens and Samsons and inside facts! You tell me!"

"You wild ass of the prairies," said Battle, "I saw you last night behind them pa'ms! But don't you think I told it—or ever will! I just passed the word around that she'd argued you into her way of thinkin', same as she had a good many others. And as for the rest of it, I found out where the nigger in the woodpile was, and I handed that out, too. Don't you take it hard, my son, but I told you her husband left her a good deal of land around here. She owns the ground that they use for the baseball park, and her lease would be worth considerable more if they could have got the right to play on Sundays!"

Senator Trumbull sat up straight, in bed, that night, and, for the first time during his martyrdom, listened with no impatience to the prayer which fell upon his ears.

"O Lord Almighty," through the flimsy partition came the voice of Alonzo Rawson, quaveringly, but with growing strength: "Aid Thou me to see my way more clear! I find it hard to tell right from wrong, and I find myself beset with tangled wires. O God, I feel that I am ignorant, and fall into many devices. These are strange paths wherein Thou hast set my feet, but I feel that through Thy help, and through great anguish, I am learning!"

Great Men's Sons

MME. BERNHARDT and M. Coquelin were playing "L'Aiglon." Toward the end of the second act people began to slide down in their seats, shift their elbows, or casually rub their eyes; by the close of the third, most of the taller gentlemen were sitting on the small of their backs with their knees as high as decorum permitted, and many were openly coughing; but when the fourth came to an end, active resistance ceased, hopelessness prevailed, the attitudes were those of the stricken field, and the over-crowded house was like a college chapel during an interminable compulsory lecture. Here and there—but most rarely—one saw an eager woman with bright eyes, head bent forward and body spellbound, still enchantedly following the course of the play. Between the acts the orchestra pattered ragtime and inanities from the new comic operas, while the audience in general took some heart. When the play was over, we were all enthusiastic; though our admiration, however vehement in the words employed to express it, was somewhat subdued as to the accompanying manner, which consisted, mainly, of sighs and resigned murmurs. In the lobby a thin old man with a grizzled chin-beard dropped his hand lightly on my shoulder, and greeted me in a tone of plaintive inquiry:

"Well, son?"

Turning, I recognized a patron of my early youth, in whose woodshed I had smoked my first cigar, an old friend whom I had not seen for years; and to find him there, with his long, dust-coloured coat, his black string tie and rusty hat, brushed on every side by opera cloaks and feathers, was a rich surprise, warming the cockles of my heart. His name is Tom Martin; he lives in a small country town, where he commands the trade in Dry Goods and Men's Clothing; his speech is pitched in a high key, is very slow, sometimes whines faintly; and he always calls me "Son."

"What in the world!" I exclaimed, as we shook hands.

"Well," he drawled, "I dunno why I shouldn't be as meetropolitan as anybody. I come over on the afternoon accommodation for the show. Let's you and me make a night of it. What say, son?"

"What did you think of the play?" I asked, as we turned up the street toward the club.

"I think they done it about as well as they could."

"That all?"

"Well," he rejoined with solemnity, "there was a heap *of* it, wasn't there!"

We talked of other things, then, until such time as we found ourselves seated by a small table at the club, old Tom somewhat uneasily regarding a twisted cigar he was smoking and plainly confounded by the "carbonated" syphon, for which, indeed, he had no use in the world. We had been joined by little Fiderson, the youngest member of the club, whose whole nervous person jerkily sparkled "L'Aiglon" enthusiasm.

"Such an evening!" he cried, in his little spiky voice. "Mr. Martin, it does one good to realize that our country towns are sending representatives to us when we have such things; that they wish to get in touch with what is greatest in Art. They should do it often. To think that a journey of only seventy miles brings into your life the magnificence of Rostand's point of view made living fire by the genius of a Bernhardt and a Coquelin!"

"Yes," said Mr. Martin, with a curious helplessness, after an ensuing pause, which I refused to break, "yes, sir, they seemed to be doing it about as well as they could."

Fiderson gasped slightly. "It was magnificent! Those two great artists! But over all the play—the play! Romance newborn; poesy marching with victorious banners; a great spirit breathing! Like 'Cyrano'—the birth-mark of immortality on this work!"

There was another pause, after which old Tom turned slowly to me, and said: "Homer Tibbs's opened up a cigar-stand at the deepo. Carries a line of candy, magazines, and fruit, too. "Home's a hustler."

Fiderson passed his hand through his hair.

"That death scene!" he exclaimed at me, giving Martin up as a log accidentally rolled in from the woods. "I thought that after 'Wagram' I could feel nothing more; emotion was exhausted; but then came that magnificent death! It was tragedy made ecstatic; pathos made into music; the grandeur of a gentle spirit, conquered physically but morally unconquerable! Goethe's 'More Light' outshone!"

Old Tom's eyes followed the smoke of his perplexing cigar along its heavy strata in the still air of the room, as he inquired if I remembered Orlando T. Bickner's boy, Mel. I had never heard of him, and said so.

"No, I expect not," rejoined Martin. "Prob'ly you wouldn't; Bickner was governor along in *my* early days, and I reckon he ain't hardly more than jest a name to you two. But *we* kind of thought he was the biggest man this country had ever seen, or was goin' to see, and he *was* a big man. He made one president, and could have been it himself, instead, if he'd be'n willing to do a kind of underhand trick, but I expect without it he was about as big a man as anybody'd care to be; governor, senator, secretary of state—and just owned his party! And, my law!—the whole earth bowin' down to him; torchlight processions and sky-rockets when he come home in the night; bands and cannon if his train got in, daytime; home-folks so proud of him they couldn't see; everybody's hat off; and all the most important men in the country following at his heels—a country, too, that'd put up consider'ble of a comparison with everything Napoleon had when he'd licked 'em all, over there.

"Of course he had enemies, and, of course, year by year, they got to be more of 'em, and they finally downed him for good; and like other public men so fixed, he didn't live long after that. He had a son, Melville, mighty likable young fellow, studyin' law when his paw died. I was livin' in their town then, and I knowed Mel Bickner pretty well; he was consider'ble of a man.

"I don't know as I ever heard him speak of that's bein' the reason, but I expect it may've be'n partly in the hope of carryin' out some of his paw's notions, Mel tried hard to git into politics; but the old man's local enemies jumped on every move he made, and his friends wouldn't help any; you can't tell why, except that it generally *is* thataway. Folks always like to laugh at a great man's son and say *he* can't amount to anything. Of course that comes partly from fellows like that ornery little cuss we saw to-night, thinkin' they're a good deal because somebody else done something, and the somebody else happened to be their paw; and the women run after 'em, and they git low-down like he was, and so on."

"Mr. Martin," interrupted Fiderson, with indignation, "will you kindly inform me in what way 'L'Aiglon' was 'low-down'?"

"Well, sir, didn't that huntin'-lodge appointment kind of put you in mind of a camp-meetin' scandal?" returned old Tom quietly. "It did me."

"But—"

"Well, sir, I can't say as I understood the French of it, but I read the book in English before I come up, and it seemed to me he was pretty much of a low-down boy; yet I wanted to see how they'd make him out; hearin' it was thought, the country over, to be such a great *play*; though to tell the truth all I could tell about *that* was that every line seemed to end in 'awze'; and 't they all talked in rhyme, and it did strike me as kind of enervatin' to be expected to believe that people could keep it up that long; and that it wasn't only the boy that never quit on the subject of himself and his folks, but pretty near any of 'em, if he'd git the chanst, did the same thing, so't almost I sort of wondered if Rostand wasn't that kind."

"Go on with Melville Bickner," said I.

"What do you expect," retorted Mr. Martin with a vindictive gleam in his eye, "when you give a man one of these here spiral staircase cigars? Old Peter himself couldn't keep straight along one subject if he tackled a cigar like this. Well, sir, I always thought Mel had a mighty mean time of it. He had to take care of his mother and two sisters, his little brother and an aunt that lived with them; and there was mighty little to do it on; big men don't usually leave much but debts, and in this country, of course, a man can't eat and spend long on his paw's reputation, like that little Dook of Reishtod—"

"I beg to tell you, Mr. Martin—" Fiderson began hotly.

Martin waved his bony hand soothingly.

"Oh, I know; they was money in his mother's family, and they give him his vit'als and clothes, and plenty, too. *His* paw didn't leave much either—though he'd stole more than Boss Tweed. I suppose—and, just lookin' at things from the point of what they'd *earned*, his maw's folks had stole a good deal, too; or else you can say they were a kind of public charity; old Metternich, by what I can learn, bein' the only one in the whole possetucky of 'em that really *did* anything to deserve his salary—" Mr. Martin broke off suddenly, observing that I was about to speak, and continued:

"Mel didn't git much law practice, jest about enough to keep the house goin' and pay taxes. He kept workin' for the party jest the same and jest as cheerfully as if it didn't turn him down hard every time he tried to git anything for himself. They lived some ways out from town; and he sold the horses to keep the little brother in school, one winter, and used to walk in to his office and out again, twice a day, over the worst roads in the State, rain or shine, snow, sleet, or wind, without any overcoat; and he got kind of a skimpy, froze-up look to him that lasted clean through summer. He worked like a mule, that boy did, jest barely makin' ends meet. He had to quit runnin' with the girls and goin' to parties and everything like that; and I expect it may have been some hard to do; for if they ever *was* a boy loved to dance and be gay, and up to anything in the line of fun and junketin' round, it was Mel Bickner. He had a laugh I can hear yet—made you feel friendly to everybody you saw; feel like stoppin' the next man you met and shakin' hands and havin' a joke with him.

"Mel was engaged to Jane Grandis when Governor Bickner died. He had to go and tell her to take somebody else—it was the only thing to do. He couldn't give Jane anything but his poverty, and she wasn't used to it. They say she offered to come to him anyway, but he wouldn't hear of it, and no more would he let her wait for him; told her she mustn't grow into an old maid, lonely, and still waitin' for the lightning to strike him—that is, his luck to come; and actually advised her to take 'Gene Callender, who'd be'n pressin' pretty close to Mel for her before the engagement. The boy didn't talk to her this way with tears in his eyes and mourning and groaning. No, sir! It was done *cheerful*; and so much so that Jane never *was* quite sure after*werds* whether Mel wasn't kind of glad to git rid of her or not. Fact is, they say she quit speakin' to him. Mel *knowed*; a state of puzzlement or even a good *mad's* a mighty sight better than bein' all harrowed up and grief-stricken. And he never give her—nor any one else—a chanst to be sorry for him. His maw was the only one heard him walk the floor nights, and after he found out she could hear him he walked in his socks.

"Yes, sir! Meet that boy on the street, or go up in his office, you'd think that he was the gayest feller in town. I tell you there wasn't anything pathetic about Mel Bickner! He didn't believe in it. And at home he had a funny story every evening of the world, about something 'd happened during the day; and 'd whistle to the guitar, or git his maw into a game of cards with his aunt and the girls. La! that boy didn't believe in no house of mourning. He'd be up at four in the morning, hoein' up their old garden; raised garden-truck for their table, sparrow-grass and sweet corn—yes, and roses, too; always had the house full of roses in June-time; never *was* a house sweeter-smellin' to go into.

"Mel was what I call a useful citizen. As I said, I knowed him well. I don't recollect I ever heard him speak of himself, nor yet of his father but once—for *that*, I reckon, he jest couldn't; and for himself; I don't believe it ever occurred to him.

"And he was a *smart* boy. Now, you take it, all in all, a boy can't be as smart as Mel was, and work as hard as he did, and not *git* somewhere—in this State, anyway! And so, about the fifth year, things took a sudden change for him; his father's enemies and his own friends, both, had to jest about own they was beat. The crowd that had been running the conventions and keepin' their own men in all the offices, had got to be pretty unpopular, and they had the sense to see that they'd have to branch out and connect up with some mighty good men, jest to keep the party in power. Well, sir, Mel had got to be about the most popular and respected man in the county. Then one day I met him on the street; he was on his way to buy an overcoat, and he was lookin' skimpier and more froze-up and genialer than ever. It was March, and up to jest that time things had be'n hardest of all for Mel. I walked around to the store with him, and he was mighty happy; goin' to send his mother north in the summer, and the girls were goin' to have a party, and Bob, his little brother, could go to the best school in the country in the fall. Things had come his way at last, and that very morning the crowd had called him in and told him they were goin' to run him for county clerk.

"Well, sir, the next evening I heard Mel was sick. Seein' him only the day before on the street, out and well, I didn't think anything of it—thought prob'ly a cold or something like that;

but in the morning I heard the doctor said he was likely to die. Of course I couldn't hardly believe it; thing like that never *does* seem possible, but they all said it was true, and there wasn't anybody on the street that day that didn't look blue or talked about anything else. Nobody seemed to know what was the matter with him exactly, and I reckon the doctor did jest the wrong thing for it. Near as I can make out, it was what they call appendicitis nowadays, and had come on him in the night.

"Along in the afternoon I went out there to see if there was anything I could do. You know what a house in that condition is like. Old Fes Bainbridge, who was some sort of a relation, and me sat on the stairs together outside Mel's room. We could hear his voice, clear and strong and hearty as ever. He was out of pain; and he had to die with the full flush of health and strength on him, and he knowed it. Not *wantin'* to go, through the waste and wear of a long sickness, but with all the ties of life clinchin' him here, and success jest comin.' We heard him speak of us, amongst others, old Fes and me; wanted 'em to be sure not fergit to tell me to remember to vote fer Fillmore if the ground-hog saw his shadow election year, which was an old joke I always had with him. He was awful worried about his mother, though he tried not to show it, and when the minister wanted to pray fer him, we heard him say, 'No, sir, you pray fer my mamma!' That was the only thing that was different from his usual way of speakin'; he called his mother 'mamma,' and he wouldn't let 'em pray fer him neither; not once; all the time he could spare for their prayin' was put in fer her.

"He called in old Fes to tell him all about his life insurance. He'd carried a heavy load of it, and it was all paid up; and the sweat it must have took to do it you'd hardly like to think about. He give directions about everything as careful and painstaking as any day of his life. He asked to speak to Fes alone a minute, and later I helped Fes do what he told him. 'Cousin Fes,' he says, 'it's bad weather, but I expect mother'll want all the flowers taken out to the cemetery and you better let her have her way. But there wouldn't be any good of their stayin' there; snowed on, like as not. I wish you'd wait till after she's come away, and git a wagon and take 'em in to the hospital. You can fix up the anchors and so forth so they won't look like funeral flowers.'

"About an hour later his mother broke out with a scream, sobbin' and cryin', and he tried to quiet her by tellin' over one of their old-time family funny stories; it made her worse, so he quit. 'Oh, Mel,' she says, 'you'll be with your father—'

"I don't know as Mel had much of a belief in a hereafter; certainly he wasn't a great church-goer. 'Well,' he says, mighty slow, but hearty and smiling, too, 'if I see father, I—guess—I'll—be—pretty—well—fixed!' Then he jest lay still, tryin' to quiet her and pettin' her head. And so—that's the way he went."

Fiderson made one of his impatient little gestures, but Mr. Martin drowned his first words with a loud fit of coughing.

"Well, sir," he observed, "I read that 'Leglong' book down home; and I heard two or three countries, and especially ourn, had gone middling crazy over it; it seemed kind of funny that *we* should, too, so I thought I better come up and see it for myself, how it *was*, on the stage, where you could *look* at it; and—I expect they done it as well as they could. But when that little boy, that'd always had his board and clothes and education free, saw that he'd jest about talked himself to death, and called for the press notices about his christening to be read to him to soothe his last spasms—why, I wasn't overly put in mind of Melville Bickner."

Mr. Martin's train left for Plattsville at two in the morning. Little Fiderson and I escorted him to the station. As the old fellow waved us good-bye from within the gates, Fiderson turned and said:

"Just the type of sodden-headed old pioneer that you couldn't hope to make understand a beautiful thing like 'L'Aiglon' in a thousand years. I thought it better not to try, didn't you?"

CHRONOLOGY

NOTE ON THE TEXTS

NOTES

Chronology

1869 Newton Booth Tarkington born July 29, the second child of John S. Tarkington and Elizabeth Booth. (His father, a thirty-seven-year-old lawyer, had been the Indiana governor's private secretary and had held political office in the state's House of Representatives. He helped organize and served as captain in the 132nd Indiana Volunteers during the Civil War. Father's family roots are Southern; Tarkington's grandfather, a Methodist minister, had moved to Indiana from Tennessee. Tarkington's thirty-five-year-old mother, a shopkeeper's daughter, was raised in Terre Haute and educated at a Catholic school, though she is Presbyterian. Her New England forebears include Thomas Hooker, who founded the colony of Connecticut. Her brother, the successful entrepreneur and politician Newton Booth, for whom Tarkington is named, will serve as governor of California and as its U.S. senator. The Tarkingtons were married in 1857; their daughter Mary Booth, known as Hautie, was born in 1858.) Family lives at 520 Meridian Street in a well-to-do neighborhood of Indianapolis.

1870 Father elected judge of the Fifth Circuit Court, a post he occupies for two years before returning to private practice.

1872 Mother takes Tarkington and his sister for a summer visit with Newton Booth in California, where they are guests at the governor's mansion in Sacramento.

1873 Financial panic wipes out much of the family's wealth and forces them to sell their home and move to a rented two-family house on New York Street.

1875 Finances improving, the family moves to a larger and more accommodating rented house on North Delaware Street.

1876–80 In summer 1876, Newton Booth, now a U.S. senator, visits Indianapolis to campaign for Republican candidates; he provides funds for a large brick house to be built for the Tarkingtons at 1100 North Pennsylvania Street. Family moves into completed house the following year, establishing a home that will be Tarkington's Indianapolis residence for the next forty-six years. Tarkington is befriended by the poet James Whitcomb Riley on Riley's visits to court his sister. Attends Public School Number Two, and performs well until fourth grade, when, disliking his teacher, he begins doing poorly and feigns illness; parents send him to live for a time with grandmother in Terre Haute, and after he returns he repeats part of fourth grade. Writes stories as a youngster. Reads Shakespeare, Dickens, Scott, and other literary writers as well as popular boys' stories.

1881–87 Begins keeping diary. In summer of 1881, visits Marshall, Indiana, later the basis for Plattville, the locale for his first novel, *The Gentleman from Indiana*. Composes fourteen-act play about the career of the outlaw Jesse James. Writes poetry and enjoys drawing, which his parents encourage; makes whimsical addition to proposed cover design for James Whitcomb Riley's *The Boss Girl*, which is retained in the published book cover. Travels to New Orleans with his uncle Newton. Attends Shortridge High School. During junior year, because he is afraid to admit to his parents that he played hooky from school, neglects attendance for nine weeks until his mother discovers his truancy. Parents do not send him back to school but arrange for private lessons in singing and drawing for the duration of the academic term, then enroll him for the 1887 fall term at Phillips Exeter Academy in New Hampshire, his mother hoping he will attend Princeton (Tarkington himself expects to go to Harvard). He arrives a month after classes have begun, living as other students do in a boardinghouse. Takes to the school's social environment and applies himself to his studies.

1888–89 During spring recess in 1888, visits a classmate's family in New York City, where he attends a performance of *The Taming of the Shrew*. On trips to Boston and New York City he visits the Museum of Fine Arts and the Metropolitan Museum, respectively. Graduates from Exeter after the 1889 spring term but stays on to work on the class yearbook. Father is now working in banking but debts prevent the family from sending Tarkington to college in the fall. He lives at home in Indianapolis, taking business and art classes.

1890–91 Vacationing in summer in northern Indiana, meets Geneve Reynolds of Lafayette, Indiana, home of Purdue University, and, charmed by her literary conversation and seeking to court her, he persuades his parents to send him to Purdue for the time being rather than Princeton. Matriculates at Purdue in fall 1891. Writes column for a Lafayette newspaper and plays a starring role in *Tom Cobb* by Gilbert and Sullivan. Due to lack of money, writes mother and asks her to "give up the idea of Princeton" so that he can "go to work." Admitted to Princeton for fall 1891 term as a special student (a status conferred because he lacks knowledge of Latin and Greek, and he will not be able to earn a degree). Joins Ivy Club and is soon a popular and gregarious figure on campus; though casual about his studies, he passes his courses easily. Accepted into Glee Club and becomes a soloist.

1892 Serves as president of the Dramatic Association (soon to be called the Triangle Club), which performs the musical comedy *The Honorable Julius Caesar*, for which he has written the book. Writes for and edits student publications. Death of Newton Booth, whose modest bequest to Tarkington will provide him some financial stability while he is attempting to establish himself after college as a writer. During winter break, tours with Glee Club through several midwestern cities, performing one of his own songs, "It's All Over Now."

1893 After finishing at Princeton, summers in Jamestown, Rhode Island, and visits Bar Harbor, Maine, the setting of his farcical comedy "The Ruse," which is performed by the Indianapolis Dramatic Club in December with Tarkington in the starring role. In autumn, begins novel *The Gentleman from Indiana* but sets it aside after a few months.

1894–95 Publishes stories and poems in local publications in Indiana. Writes prolifically for several years while living in family home but his stories and drawings are rejected by New York publishers; acquires reputation for smoking, sleeping during the day, and nocturnal walks. Writes historical drama "The Prodigals," set in Trenton, New Jersey, in 1790, and plays the starring role when it is performed by the Indianapolis Dramatic Club. "In the Borderland," short prose piece with his accompanying drawing, sells to *Life* magazine for $20 ($13 for the drawing, $7 for the text). In fall 1895, travels to New York City after the agent Elizabeth Marbury, to whom Tarkington's sister has given "The Prodigals," requests he revise the play for potential Broadway staging. Lives in Manhattan for several months, unsuccessfully revising "The Prodigals" and other plays and writing stories. At Thanksgiving, encounters William Dean Howells at The Lantern, a literary club, but finds himself unable to speak to him; prompted to sing, feels embarrassed by his nervous performance. Sees Sarah Bernhardt act.

1896 Works on a novel about the theater. Returns to Indianapolis in the spring. Writes play set during the French Revolution, the basis for the one-act comedy "Mlle de Marmontel," which is performed by the Indianapolis Dramatic Club in November with Tarkington in the cast. Contributes pseudonymous poems, prose pieces, and drawings to the short-lived little magazine *John-a-Dreams*, based in Greenwich Village. His work elicits admiring letter to the magazine from Helen Pitkin, whom by coincidence Tarkington had met in New Orleans when he was fifteen, and they begin a spirited correspondence.

1897–98 Writes novella *Monsieur Beaucaire*, set in eighteenth-century England, but cannot get it published. Death in December 1897 of John Cleve Green, a Princeton friend to whom he will dedicate *The Gentleman from Indiana*. Resumes working on *The Gentleman from Indiana*, which he had abandoned nearly five years earlier. Late in 1898, his sister, without his knowledge, attempts to sell *Monsieur Beaucaire* to the publisher S. S. McClure while in New York and, though unsuccessful, interests him in *The Gentleman from Indiana*, now nearly complete.

1899 Manuscript of *The Gentleman from Indiana* is read by the novelist Hamlin Garland, who writes Tarkington: "You are a novelist." McClure accepts the manuscript and requests that Tarkington come to New York as soon as possible to cut it down for serial publication. Leaves Indianapolis at the end of January and is greeted enthusiastically at McClure's offices, where he meets not only the publisher but also Garland and the journalist Ida Tarbell. During a stay at McClure's house on Long Island, makes cuts to *The Gentleman from Indiana*. Turns down McClure's offer of an editorial position at his firm and an invitation to join him on a European trip the following summer. Attends dinner hosted by F. N. Doubleday, a member of McClure's company, and meets Rudyard Kipling. Serialization of *The Gentleman from Indiana* in *McClure's Magazine* begins in May; *Monsieur Beaucaire* is serialized there starting in December. Book version of *The Gentleman from Indiana* is published in October and sells well, the first of many popular successes (in the next fifty years, more than five million copies of his books will be sold). In November, guides William Dean Howells around Indianapolis before Howells gives a lecture and attends dinner for the eminent author and editor organized by Tarkington's sister; other guests include former president Benjamin Harrison, a family friend. Howells tells Tarkington he has read and liked *The Gentleman from Indiana*.

1900–01 Writes twelve weekly book columns for the *Indianapolis Press* from January through May. Visits Louisiana and becomes engaged to Helen Pitkin, but the engagement is broken after her grandmother objects and makes Tarkington promise not to write her for several months. *Monsieur Beaucaire* is brought out in book form by McClure, Phillips & Co. in May 1900, but McClure discourages Tarkington from publishing *Cherry*, a historical romance set in eighteenth-century New Jersey. Evelyn Sutherland, a drama critic and playwright from Boston, offers to assist with a stage adaptation of *Monsieur Beaucaire*, which Tarkington starts work on, ceding one-third of the stage rights to her. The actor Richard Mansfield agrees to perform the play with his company but demands, over Sutherland's objections (and threats of litigation), that the play be further revised during rehearsals, which Tarkington assents to. Finishes play about a United States senator, *The Man on Horseback*, which is not produced until 1912. *Monsieur Beaucaire* begins pre-Broadway tryouts in Philadelphia on October 7, 1900. Returns to Indiana and begins work on historical novel *The Two Vanrevels. Cherry* is serialized in *Harper's* in January and February 1901. Meets Louisa Fletcher (b. 1878), a banker's daughter and Smith College graduate, and soon begins courting her.

1902 Enters Republican primary for a seat in the Indiana House of Representatives and wins handily, without campaigning. In April, finishes *The Two Vanrevels*, which is published in October. Holds party for Woodrow Wilson, whom he had known at Princeton. Makes a curtain call during performance of *Monsieur Beaucaire*, now on tour after its relatively brief Broadway run. Travels east, visiting New York City and Lancaster, Pennsylvania. Marries Louisa Fletcher in a ceremony at her family home in Indianapolis on June 18; they embark on a honeymoon that includes stops in New York City, Quebec, and Mackinac Island, Michigan. Reluctantly campaigns for House of Representatives seat, which he wins in November. Visits New York City and attends a birthday dinner in honor of Mark Twain.

1903 Enters Indiana House of Representatives and has eye-opening introduction to the rough-and-tumble of politics. Struggling with public speaking, delivers only one speech as a representative, which lasts six minutes. Opposes bill supported by Indiana's governor that would allow the governor, in an act of political retaliation, to replace the board of the state reformatory; when a compromise bill passes that denies the governor such powers, Tarkington is praised by the *Indianapolis News* for grasping "the question in its true light" and having "the courage and independence to stand up for what he believed to be right." After legislature adjourns in March, vacations with Louisa at French Lick in southern Indiana and, drawing from his political experiences, writes the short stories "Boss Gorgett" and "The Aliens," the first of the six political stories that will be collected in *In the Arena*. Contracts typhoid fever and, severely ill for several weeks, loses eighty pounds; on doctor's orders he leaves Indiana to convalesce in Kennebunkport, Maine, for the summer. Is so taken with the place that eventually and for all of his later life he will be a part-time resident, dividing his time between there and Indianapolis. Continues recuperation during an eleven-month European trip, arriving in England with his wife and parents at the beginning of the fall. After a brief stay in London, arrives in Paris and is immediately smitten with the city. Travels through Italy and spends a month on Capri before settling in Rome for the winter. *Cherry* is published by Harper and Bros. in October.

1904 Visits Germany and Belgium, where he rides for the first time in an automobile, as well as the Netherlands, before returning to Paris. Arrives back in the United States in August, living with Louisa in a Manhattan apartment. Writes stories, essays, and a dramatic adaptation of *The Gentleman from Indiana* for the producer George Tyler. In December, receives invitation to the White House from Theodore Roosevelt, who, Tarkington learns during their luncheon, has read and admired his political stories in magazines.

1905 *In the Arena* is published by McClure Phillips & Co. on January 30. Stage version of *The Gentleman from Indiana* opens in Indianapolis in February but, unsuccessful in tryout runs in Chicago and Boston, is not staged in New York. Publishes widely in magazines. Attends annual dinner of the Periodical Publishers Association in Lakewood, New Jersey, where he and the playwright Harry Leon Wilson lay the groundwork for their lengthy collaboration on works for the stage. Writes novel *The Conquest of Canaan*, set in contemporary Indiana, which begins serialization before he is finished; book version, with brisk sales, is published by Harper in the fall. After a short visit to Indianapolis, travels to Capri with Louisa, Wilson and his wife Rose O'Neill (the creator of the Kewpie doll), as well as his future collaborator Julian Street and his wife; rents the villa of the American artist Elihu Vedder. Finds himself unable to write while on Capri. With Louisa now pregnant, the Tarkingtons settle by year's end in Rome in advance of the delivery, living in a penthouse apartment at the Palace Hotel.

1906 Daughter Laurel born on February 11. Rejects proposal from D. Appleton and Company to buy the rights to his work for $20,000. Relocates family to Paris in April and takes automobile tour of surrounding countryside to the southeast; leaves Paris residence in May to settle nearby at a villa in Champigny-sur-Marne, with a hilltop view of the city. Travels to London and Normandy and along the Loire. Resumes working after long fallow period, writing for *Harper's* the novella *His Own People*, about a young American in Rome. Displeased himself with its aesthetic merits, is informed that *Harper's* will not publish it because of moral objections to a drunken kiss described in the narrative. Contracts with *The Saturday Evening Post* to publish it instead, the first of many fictional works accepted by the editor, George Lorimer, and his successors; book version is accepted by F. N. Doubleday, now the founder and head of his own company. With Harry Leon Wilson, writes play *The Man from Home*. At the end of December, leaves Champigny-sur-Marne villa for a Left Bank apartment at 20, rue de Tournon, in Paris, for which he has signed a three-year lease.

1907 In spring, starts novel *The Guest of Quesnay*, which he completes in four months. Travels in summer with Wilson to New York, where they meet George Tyler, whose production of *The Man from Home* is scheduled for tryouts in Louisville and Chicago in the fall. At the home of a friend from his Princeton days, meets Susanah Robinson (née Kiefer, b. 1870; she has divorced her first husband). Serialization of *The Guest of Quesnay* in *Everybody's Magazine* begins in November.

1908 *The Man from Home* premieres on Broadway and is an enormous success. Abandons fiction for playwriting for the time being, and during the next two years, though he continues to be based in Paris, makes regular trips to New York and Indiana. Writes two plays with Wilson: *Cameo Kirby* and *Foreign Exchange.*

1909 After a visit to Indianapolis, learns that his mother has died of a heart attack on April 17; returns to Indiana for the funeral. Writes four plays with Wilson, including *Your Humble Servant* and *Getting a Polish.* Expands the previously published story "Beasley and the Hunchback" (1905) into the book-length *Beasley's Christmas Party*, published by Harper in October. Tiring of traveling between Paris and New York because of his plays, has furniture and other personal effects shipped home and decides not to renew his Paris lease.

1910 Father remarries. *Getting a Polish*, revised as a farce, is staged in Kennebunkport and then in New York. Drinks heavily, and domestic tensions between the Tarkingtons strain their marriage to the breaking point.

1911 Writes little. Separates from Louisa in July. Goes to Europe with his sister's husband and his nephew John, a Princeton undergraduate, visiting Paris, Switzerland, northern Italy, and Germany. During the trip, writes frequent, mostly unanswered letters to Louisa. Arrives in New York in August, and discovers that Louisa has filed for divorce, seeking custody of Laurel and claiming mental cruelty, which is reported in the Indianapolis newspapers. Divorce is granted in November, with Louisa retracting her charges of cruelty; she is given custody of Laurel for eleven months of the year, with Tarkington allowed visitation rights and one month of custody during the summer. Sees the English novelist Arnold Bennett, whom he had met in London, in New York and Indianapolis. Returning to the writing of fiction, begins story "Mary Smith."

1912 Suffers heart attack that requires lengthy convalescence. On January 16, vows successfully to give up drinking. Begins working on novel *The Flirt*, finishing in the summer; it is accepted by *The Saturday Evening Post* for a two-month serialization beginning in December. Courts Susanah Robinson, visiting her several times in Dayton, Ohio, where they are married on November 6.

1913 Book version of *The Flirt* published by Doubleday, Page & Co. on March 8. Susanah, after reading the English author Horace Vachell's novel *The Hill*, gives it to Tarkington and, when he claims that its depiction of boys is unrealistic, she asks him to write something more lifelike. He responds with the story "Penrod and the Pageant" (later retitled "A Boy and His Dog"), the début of Penrod Schofield, boy protagonist of a series of many stories that begin appearing in magazines in June. Dressed in a bathrobe and writing in longhand (he never learns to use a typewriter), works according to an intensive schedule that occupies nearly all his waking hours.

1914 From January through March writes *The Turmoil*, novel set in Indiana that is critical of American business values. *Penrod*, comprising thirty-one stories, is published on March 26 by Doubleday, Page. Serialization of *The Turmoil* in *Harper's* begins in August. Novella about the theater, *Harlequin and Columbine*, serialized in *Metropolitan Magazine*, September–November. Works on the comic novel *Seventeen*.

1915 *Seventeen* begins serialization in *Metropolitan*. *The Turmoil*, published in February by Harper, garners critical praise, including from William Dean Howells, and sells well. Writes Woodrow Wilson and advocates for a massive preparedness campaign for the American military in support of the Allies in World War I; in the months leading up to America's entry into the war he will regularly publish essays in support of Allies and against claims made by pro-German Americans. After a hiatus from playwriting of several years, drafts comedy about an Italian immigrant organ-grinder, *Mister Antonio*. While summering in Maine, accepts lunch invitation from Howells, beginning a friendship that lasts until Howells's death five years later. With Julian Street, works on comic play *The Ohio Lady*, early version of *The Country Cousin*.

1916 In remarks published in the *Cleveland Leader*, makes distinction between his approaches to plays and fiction: "When I am writing a play, I think of what the public wants. When I see that the public doesn't want anything in one of my plays, I try to cut it out and write something that it does want. But I do not make these concessions when I am writing fiction." *Seventeen* is published in book form by Harper in March. First of several film adaptations of *The Flirt* are released, as is film of *Seventeen*. Buys eighteen acres of land in Maine on a hill near Kennebunkport. *Mister Antonio*, starring Otis Skinner, premieres on Broadway in September. Second Penrod book, *Penrod and Sam*, is published in October by Doubleday, Page.

1917 Begins writing novel *The Magnificent Ambersons*, a return to the social and regional themes he had treated in *The Turmoil*. Increasingly concerned with the war in Europe, publishes acerbic satire "Laughing in German," directed largely at the government's toleration of German harassment of American ships; whips up support for a demonstration protesting the German use of Belgian forced labor and serves as Indianapolis chairman of the American Rights Committee. After the U.S. enters the war, writes pro-war pamphlets and the story "Captain Schlotterwerz," which results in a rejection from *Collier's*, his first in over a decade, because it is too propagandistic (*The Saturday Evening Post* accepts it). Encourages toleration of Americans of German extraction. Builds colonial frame house, called Seawood, on Kennebunkport land and will live there for much of the year for the rest of his life. Adaptation of *Seventeen*, starring Ruth Gordon, is staged in Indianapolis; production will run for eight months on Broadway the following year. Revises *The Ohio Lady* for Broadway staging as *The Country Cousin*, produced by George Tyler, which is attended on opening night by Theodore Roosevelt.

1918 Writes *Ramsay Milholland*, novel that culminates in its young protagonist enlisting in the army, for serialization beginning in November and book publication the following year. Continues pamphleteering for the war effort, claiming to have "long since dropped all work of my own." In June, in pamphlet of the League to Enforce Peace, disputes points raised against the League of Nations by Indiana's former U.S. senator Alfred Beveridge. Begins publishing in *Collier's* the stories that will be collected in

Gentle Julia. Edward E. Rose's stage adaptation of *Penrod* is staged on Broadway. *The Magnificent Ambersons* is published in October by Doubleday, Page, which also issues an edition of his collected works under his supervision and the biographical-critical study *Booth Tarkington* by Robert Cortes Holliday. Writes the comic play *Clarence* for actor Alfred Lunt, who has taken over the starring role for the touring production of *The Country Cousin*; also intends to feature the young actor Helen Hayes, who has been cast in the Broadway adaptation of *Penrod*.

1919 For *The Magnificent Ambersons*, is awarded the first of his two Pulitzer Prizes. Begins lifelong friendship with Kenneth Roberts, a journalist and later a novelist who is his neighbor in Maine. With Wilson, writes plays *Up from Nowhere*, which flops on Broadway and closes in two weeks, and *The Gibson Upright*, a farce attacking communism that is performed only in Indianapolis. But *Clarence*, starring Lunt and Hayes, opens in September to popular and critical success and a long theatrical run. Writes silent film scenarios for movies about boy protagonist Edgar Pomeroy.

1920 In summer, writes novel *Alice Adams*. *Poldekin*, anticommunist play, opens on Broadway in September and, harshly reviewed, closes the following month.

1921 *Alice Adams*, published by Doubleday, Page in May after being serialized in *Pictorial Review*, is hailed by critics and sells well. Tarkington tops list of booksellers' poll in *Publishers Weekly* ranking most significant living American authors. Writes play *The Wren*, set in Maine, as a vehicle for Helen Hayes; reviewed unfavorably, it closes after a three-week Broadway run in October. Completes comedy *The Intimate Strangers* and is asked by its producers, including Florenz Ziegfeld, to direct it; Ziegfeld's wife Billie Burke plays a starring role. Visits the Harding White House with a group of journalists early in November and while in Washington is recognized at a tryout matinee of *The Intimate Strangers* by Woodrow Wilson, infirm and, as Tarkington writes to his father, "unutterably shattered."

1922 Awarded the Pulitzer Prize for *Alice Adams*, and is lauded in polls conducted by *Literary Digest* and *The New York Times* as the greatest living American author and as one of ten great Americans, respectively. Book version of *Gentle Julia*, whose stories were published in magazines in

1918–1919, is brought out by Doubleday, Page in April. After a successful three months on Broadway and a tour, *The Intimate Strangers* closes. Asked by Ziegfeld and Billie Burke to write a new comedy, answers with *Rose Briar*, written in Maine in the summer and opening on Broadway Christmas night to positive reviews. The secretary of the New York Society for the Suppression of Vice, advocating a censorship process for book manuscripts, cites him as one writer whose material is never salacious. Interviewed by *The New York Times* about censorship and his views on sexually candid literature, he claims at the outset, "the fact is I don't write about such things, simply because I don't think about such things," then voices respect for Zola but criticizes the French writer's imitators as well as those of Wells and Shaw, laments the "breaking down in taste" among the reading public, and, while mostly opposing censorship, says that a man like Will H. Hays (later head of the so-called Hays Office to monitor the content of motion pictures) could be trusted with such power. Undergoes treatment for cataracts. Begins working on novel *The Midlander*. Visited after Christmas by distraught daughter Laurel, who has quarreled with her mother (now remarried and living in Boston) over her recently born stepsister and has been sent away.

1923 Father dies in January. Laurel continues to show mental distress; she contracts pneumonia and dies on April 13. *The Fascinating Stranger and Other Stories* is published in April. *Tweedles*, revised version of an unperformed comedy written with Wilson several years before, opens on Broadway to good reviews, unlike his play *Magnolia*, which is panned and closes after a few weeks. Moves out of family home; for the portion of every year he spends in Indianapolis, will now live in a large house he has bought at 4270 North Meridian Street, away from the city center. Movie *Boy of Mine*, with scenario written by Tarkington, is released in December by First National Pictures. Limited edition of *The Midlander* is published by Doubleday, Page in December, with a trade edition following in January.

1924 Stops writing for the theater for several years, though his plays, including several one-acts, continue to be brought out in book form. Writes short stories that will be collected in *Women*. Dislikes film adaptation of *Monsieur Beaucaire* starring Rudolph Valentino ("I don't know what Mr. Valentino was doing, but it certainly wasn't my intention").

1925 Takes six months off from writing to visit North Africa and to make what will be his final trip to Europe, traveling by car from Algiers to Tunis before crossing the Mediterranean for Sicily, which he also tours by car; visits several Italian cities, spends five weeks in Paris (where he sees F. Scott Fitzgerald and meets Hemingway), and sails back to the United States in early June. Works on novel *The Plutocrat*, which draws from his recent travels, as does the novel that follows, *Claire Ambler*. *Women* is published in November. Is sued for $500,000 by a Texas woman claiming he has stolen her scenario for the film *Boy of Mine*, but the case is thrown out of court.

1926 *Hello, Lola!*, musical of *Seventeen* with book and lyrics by Dorothy Donnelly and music by William B. Kernell, has its New York premiere on January 15. Vision becomes increasingly impaired.

1927 *The Plutocrat* is published in January. Collects *The Magnificent Ambersons*, *The Turmoil*, and *The Midlander* (under the title *National Avenue*) in one volume, *Growth*.

1928 Gives extensive editorial advice to Kenneth Roberts on the plot, structure, and prose of the novel *Arundel*, as he will for several of Roberts's books. Autobiographical essay collection *The World Does Move* is published by Doubleday, Doran in November. His vision deteriorating, he begins dictating his writing to his secretary, Betty Trotter. In November, goes to Baltimore in preparation for eye surgery conducted by William Wilmer, a noted ophthalmologist at Johns Hopkins.

1929 Undergoes eye surgery in February, the first of five such procedures performed over the next two years. Works on final play, *Colonel Satan*, a drama about Aaron Burr, after he is asked to take on the subject by the actor George Arliss (who will later decline to play the role in George Tyler's Broadway production). Novel *Young Mrs. Greeley* is serialized in *Ladies' Home Journal* from March to May and is published by Doubleday, Doran, which also brings out new Penrod collection, *Penrod Jashber*, in September. Play *How's Your Health?*, written with Wilson most likely in 1923, runs for forty-seven performances on Broadway.

1930 Works on novel *Mirthful Haven*, published in book form in September, the title's locale a stand-in for Kennebunkport. Begins to be represented by Carl Brandt, who will be his agent for the rest of his life. Writes dialogue for *The Millionaire*, movie starring George Arliss. Vision fails completely in August, and he is rushed from Maine to Baltimore for an operation on his right eye, which is followed by two additional operations in the latter half of the year.

1931 Completes recovery after the last of his eye surgeries and, after five months of blindness, is able to see better than he has in years, though his physical energy is diminished for the rest of his life. *Colonel Satan* opens on Broadway but fails to win over the critics and closes after seventeen performances. Having built up a modest art collection, begins to devote more attention to the acquisition of art and takes advantage of a fall in prices to buy many Old Master paintings. Collects three Penrod books in *Penrod: His Complete Story.*

1932 Novel *Mary's Neck* is brought out by Doubleday, Doran in February; a historical novel set in Restoration England and inspired by two portraits he owns, *Wanton Mally*, is published in November after being serialized in *Ladies' Home Journal.* Writes novella *Pretty Twenty*, which is serialized but never collected in book form.

1933 Receives gold medal from National Institute of Arts and Letters. Writes a juvenile radio serial based in part on *Gentle Julia* that is broadcast three times a week on WJZ in New York City. In June, the first of his many stories about seven-year-old protagonist "Little Orvie" is published in *The Saturday Evening Post.* Novel *Presenting Lily Mars* is published in August. In November, radio play "The Help Each Other Club," about unemployed young people during the Depression written for the United Charities Campaign and the Boy Scouts, is broadcast on CBS and NBC; Tarkington, who prospers during the Depression through his still-popular fiction, tends to avoid public political engagement but opposes the New Deal policies of Franklin D. Roosevelt, reflecting a core conservatism that elicits negative views of his work from writers and critics during the 1930s.

1934–35 Completes novella *This Boy Joe* but *American Magazine*, which commissioned it, rejects it; the version published in the *Chicago Tribune* in the summer of 1935 contains significant and unauthorized cuts. Novella *Rennie Peddigoe* is serialized in *Women's Home Companion*, December

1934–April 1935. RKO film adaptation of *Alice Adams* starring Katharine Hepburn, for which she will receive an Oscar nomination, is released in August 1935. Little Orvie stories are collected in book form. Novel *The Lorenzo Bunch* is serialized in *McCall's*, July–November 1935, though its editors ask for changes, only some of which Tarkington agrees to; final chapter is published only in book version, which comes out early the following year.

1936–39 First of numerous stories featuring the art dealer Mr. Rumbin is published in *The Saturday Evening Post* in January 1936. Many are collected in *Rumbin Galleries*, brought out in October 1937 by Doubleday, Doran. Sues Warner Brothers on copyright grounds because its *Penrod and His Twin Brother* has not used any of Tarkington's material other than the boy's name. Stage adaptations of *Seventeen* and *Aromatic Aaron Burr*, rewritten version of *Colonel Satan*, are performed in Kennebunkport in the summer of 1938, followed the next summer by *Karabash*, a rewrite of his anti-communist play *Podelkin*, along with his one-act *The Ghost Story* and *Tweedles*. Novella *Uncertain Mrs. Collicut* appears in *Pictorial Review*, December 1938. In July 1939 profile in *The New York Times*, expresses his long-held view that technological and social changes—most especially the rise of the automobile—have diminished the richness and vigor of American life: "When the old livery stable was cleaned up and took on the odor of gasoline . . . then something went out from American life," adding, "I wonder if the people as a whole are either as happy or as cultured as their parents were. They are surely not as hardy." *Some Old Portraits: A Book About Art and Human Beings*, discussing works from his own collection, is published in November 1939 by Doubleday, Doran. Begins writing novel "Today and Forever," published in 1941 as *The Heritage of Hatcher Ide* (title changed because the same title had been given to a forthcoming Pearl S. Buck book; Tarkington's novel was serialized as "The Man of the Family").

1940 Having long rejected honorary degrees because of his reluctance to make public appearances, accepts a degree from Purdue University because the ceremony is held at his Indianapolis home. Publicly supports presidential campaign of Wendell Willkie, a personal acquaintance; his letter to Indiana U.S. senator Frederick Van Nuys urging passage of Lend-Lease Bill over the objections of many of the senator's constituents is published in *Life* magazine. Writes *Lady Hamilton and Her Nelson*, propagandistic radio play urging national readiness for war. Joins board of the John Herron Art Institute (later the Indianapolis Museum of Art) and chairs its Fine Arts Committee.

1941 Reminiscences of childhood and early adulthood, "As I Seem to Me," are serialized in *The Saturday Evening Post.* Settles out of court with Warner Brothers on Penrod lawsuit, receiving a small amount in damages and a promise that any future use of the Penrod character is subject to his approval. *The Fighting Littles*, novel based in part on stories published as far back as 1937 (one of which had been rejected by *The Saturday Evening Post* as "anti–New Deal propaganda"), appears in the fall.

1942 Writes for government agencies and publishes editorials in support of the war effort in magazines, as he will do for the duration of World War II. Joins Coast Guard Auxiliary and uses his personal motorboat to patrol the Maine coast near Kennebunkport. *The Saturday Evening Post* requests a serial about a man whose successful career in business is due to his wife but rejects his submission, which is then serialized as "The Hardest Wife to Be" in *Ladies' Home Journal* (June–September) and published as the novel *Kate Fennigan* the following year.

1943 Asked by *The Saturday Evening Post* to write something to accompany a Norman Rockwell illustration extolling freedom of speech, submits story about a fanciful meeting between Hitler and Mussolini before either man rose to power. Eight of his plays are performed in the Pasadena Playhouse's annual summer festival in Pasadena, California.

1944 As Fine Arts Committee chairman, dismissively rejects the Herron Art Institute's proposed purchase of a Cubist painting by Picasso. Enthusiastically reviews Willkie's *One World* and writes letter to Indiana Republicans urging them to eschew isolationism in a postwar world and confront global problems, noting, "When the next war comes all of the military powers concerned will almost certainly be in possession of an implement able to wipe out such a city as New York within ten minutes so effectively that no living being could get anywhere near the place during the next three or four months." Works on novel *The Image of*

Josephine, drawing from his experience as a trustee at the Herron.

1945 Just after an abridged version of *The Image of Josephine* appears in *American Magazine* as "Lovely Hellion," book version is published in February. Awarded William Dean Howells medal from American Academy of Arts and Letters. Works on unfinished novel *The Show Piece*. Novella *Walterson* is serialized in *Good Housekeeping*, October–November.

1946 Makes final public appearance when he attends a performance of a stage adaptation of *Alice Adams* undertaken by his secretary, Betty Trotter. Falls ill later in March, and begins to lose strength precipitously; is unable to make his yearly move to Kennebunkport. Dies on May 19 at home. Buried at Crown Hill Cemetery in Indianapolis.

Note on the Texts

This volume contains Booth Tarkington's novels *The Magnificent Ambersons* (1918) and *Alice Adams* (1921), along with the collection *In the Arena: Stories of Political Life* (1906).

One of the most popular authors of his time, Tarkington wrote prolifically and, except for periods when he was traveling abroad, maintained a demanding daily schedule of writing throughout his career. Tarkington usually did not revise his works after they were published; the texts of his novels were not reset for collected editions brought out during his lifetime, such as the Autograph Edition (1918–28) and the Seawood Edition (1922–28). Therefore the texts of the works printed here are taken from their first American editions. Tarkington did make some changes to the three previously published novels that were brought together as the *Growth* trilogy in 1927, including *The Magnificent Ambersons.* On the whole he made these revisions, which were significant though not extensive, to loosely connect the three novels and make them seem more unified. (A lengthy variant passage in the *Growth* version of *The Magnificent Ambersons* is given in this volume's Notes.)

The Magnificent Ambersons was written in 1917, during a time when Tarkington was devoting most of his other efforts as a writer to supporting the war effort. Serialized in *Metropolitan* from December 1917 to September 1918, the novel was published in October 1918 by Doubleday, Page & Company in New York and by Hodder & Stoughton in London (as with the other books collected here, the novel was not revised for the English publication). Translations into Swedish and German followed in 1919. The novel garnered Tarkington the first of his two Pulitzer Prizes. This volume prints the text of the 1918 Doubleday, Page edition of *The Magnificent Ambersons.*

Alice Adams was completed over a relatively short span of time in the summer of 1920, while Tarkington was living at his Kennebunkport, Maine, home. The novel was published in installments in *Pictorial Review*, February–May 1921, and was brought out in book form by Doubleday, Page & Company in May. An error in the first printing, "I can't see you why don't" (508.13), was corrected to "I can't see why you don't" in later printings and is also corrected here. Hodder & Stoughton's English edition was published in October. In 1922 Tarkington was awarded his second Pulitzer Prize, for *Alice Adams.* The 1921 Doubleday, Page edition contains the text printed here.

Tarkington wrote the stories collected in *In the Arena* not long after the end of his brief career as a politician in 1903 (see Chronology). "Boss Gorgett" and "The Aliens" were composed first, while Tarkington was vacationing with his first wife that spring in French Lick, Indiana. Four of the six stories appeared in magazines before *In the Arena* was published in book form by McClure, Phillips & Company in late January 1905: "Boss Gorgett" in *Everybody's Magazine*, December 1903; "The Aliens" in *McClure's*, February 1904; "The Need of Money" in *McClure's*, November 1904; and "Hector" in *Everybody's Magazine*, December 1904.

"In the First Place," the volume's preface, drew inspiration from Tarkington's meeting with Theodore Roosevelt at the White House shortly before Christmas 1904. Roosevelt had invited the author for a visit because he had read and admired Tarkington's political stories in magazines. He wrote to Roosevelt that the preface "was almost directly your suggestion. When, in last December, I had the honor of lunching with you, you spoke of the danger that my purpose in these stories might be misunderstood, and that exhibiting too much of the uglier side [of politics] might have no good effect. So I prefixed the Preface, hoping that if you happened to see it you would believe that the professor was at least trying to do his best."

In April 1905, a few months after its American publication, *In the Arena* was published by John Murray in London. The text printed here is taken from the 1905 McClure, Phillips & Company edition of *In the Arena.*

This volume presents the texts of the original printings chosen for inclusion here, but it does not attempt to reproduce nontextual features of their typographic design. The texts are presented without change, except for the correction of typographical errors. Spelling, punctuation, and capitalization are often expressive features and are not altered, even when inconsistent or irregular. The following is a list of typographical errors corrected, cited by page and line number: 8.18, Diavola."; 24.33, papier-maché; 38.11, I I was; 40.3, they were; 49.17, girls'; 50.3, sympathetically, Well,; 89.11, Dr; 94.2, though; 96.22, me,; 104.19, says, lately."; 120.2, Class.; 138.17, Better——."; 172.27, toknow; 178.30, "Goodnight."; 186.16, bend; 238.17, that he; 306.9, door; 312.10, In; 328.27, slap you-on-the-back; 329.30, made; 335.32, matter.; 365.6, room.'; 382.26, o 'me; 387.18, were!'; 446.21, chiamo; 466.1, 'shouldn't.'"; 467.8, here.; 473.19, worry,; 478.12, minute."; 485.4, Mrs; 508.13, you why; 530.12, and is; 536.34, sharp,; 570.24, ironmoulders',; 571.30, "I agree; 573.36, your's; 606.12, do?; 618.16, State-house; 625.5, have."; 630.37, sencere!.

Notes

In the notes below, the reference numbers denote page and line of this volume (the line count includes headings). These notes, as well as the Chronology and Note on the Texts, were prepared in-house at Library of America and were reviewed and approved by this volume's editor. No note is made for material included in standard desk-reference books. Quotations from Shakespeare are keyed to *The Riverside Shakespeare*, ed. G. Blakemore Evans (Boston: Houghton Mifflin, 1974). Biblical quotations are keyed to the King James Version. For further biographical information than is included in the Chronology, see *America Moved: Booth Tarkington's Memoirs of Time and Place, 1869–1928*, ed. Jeremy Beer (Eugene, OR: Front Porch Republic Books, 2015); Dorothy Ritter Russo and Thelma L. Sullivan, *A Bibliography of Booth Tarkington, 1869–1946* (Indianapolis: Indiana Historical Society, 1949); and James Woodress, *Booth Tarkington: Gentleman from Indiana* (Philadelphia: J. B. Lippincott, 1955).

THE MAGNIFICENT AMBERSONS

3.5 Magnificent Lorenzo] The Florentine ruler and arts patron Lorenzo de' Medici (1449–1492), known as "the Magnificent."

4.4 "congress gaiters"] Ankle-high boots designed for comfort, with elastic inserts in the sides for flexibility.

4.26–27 Kaiserliche boar-tusk moustache] A pointed and curled mustache in the style of the German emperor Wilhelm II (1859–1941; ruled 1888–1918).

4.28 Dundreary whiskers] Style of oversized bushy whiskers popular in the mid-nineteenth century, named for Lord Dundreary, a character in *Our American Cousin* (1858), play by the English playwright Tom Taylor (1817–1880).

8.13–14 "You'll Remember Me," . . . Marble Halls,"] Arias from the light opera *The Bohemian Girl* (1843), music by the Irish composer Michael W. Balfe (1808–1870), libretto by the English theater manager Alfred Bunn (1796–1860).

8.14 "Silver Threads Among the Gold,"] Popular ballad (1873), with lyrics by the American poet Eben Rexford (1848–1916) and music by the American songwriter Hart Pease Danks (1834–1903).

8.14–15 "Kathleen Mavourneen,"] Song (1839) with music by the English-born American composer Frederick W. Nicholls Crouch (1808–1896); the

"Mrs. Crawford" credited with its words has been identified variously as several women with that married name.

8.15 "The Soldier's Farewell."] Of the several nineteenth-century songs with this title or subtitle, most likely a composition by the German composer Johanna Kinkel (1810–1858).

8.17 "Olivette" and "The Mascotte"] Comic operas (1879, 1880) by the French composer Edmond Audran (1840–1901).

8.17–18 "The Chimes of Normandy"] Comic opera (1877) by the French composer Robert Planquets (1848–1903), originally staged in Paris as *Les Cloches de Corneville.*

8.18 "Giroflé-Girofla" and "Fra Diavolo."] Comic operas (1874, 1830) by, respectively, the French composers Charles Lecocq (1832–1918) and Daniel Auber (1782–1871).

8.19–20 "Pinafore" and "The Pirates of Penzance" and of "Patience."] Operettas (1878, 1879, 1881), three of the many stage collaborations of the English poet and librettist W. S. Gilbert (1836–1911) and the English composer Arthur Sullivan (1842–1900).

8.20–23 This last was needed . . . furniture.] *Patience* satirizes the Aesthetic Movement, which made the appreciation and creation of beauty a supreme value and championed "art for art's sake" in all spheres of creative expression, especially painting, poetry, interior design, and furniture. Its furnishings incorporated forms derived from nature (flowers, peacock feathers) and were often influenced by the decorative arts of Japan and China.

8.23 what-nots] Lightweight furniture with shelves, so called because they were meant to display a variety of small ornamental items.

9.4 Tosti's new songs] Beginning in the 1880s, the songs of the Italian-born English composer Paolo Tosti (1846–1916) were enormously popular in England and abroad.

9.11 Edwin Booth] American classical and Shakespearean actor (1833–1893), one of the most renowned actors of his era.

9.13 "The Black Crook" . . . shocking girls dressed as fairies.] Lavish musical melodrama (1866) with music selected and composed by Thomas Baker, with book by Charles M. Barras (1826–1873); it featured a large contingent of scantily clad female dancers.

13.8 "Hazel Kirke"] Long-running domestic comedy (1880) by the American playwright Steele MacKaye (1842–1894).

16.13–23 the Fauntleroy period had set in . . . "Lean on *me*, grandfather,"] In *Little Lord Fauntleroy* (1886), best-selling novel by the English-American writer Frances Hodgson Burnett (1849–1924), the American boy Cedric Errol discovers he is heir to a British title and goes to live with his grandfather on an English estate. The book's success made the protagonist's black velvet suit, lace collar, and long curly hairstyle a popular style for young boys. When the seven-year-old Cedric first encounters his cantankerous grandfather, who suffers from gout, the boy helps him take a short walk after asking the old man to lean on him.

23.16–17 "Turn down your pants, you would-be dude! Raining in dear ole Lunnon!] The accusation is that George is affecting a foppish urban fashion, rolling up his trouser legs as if he were in London (so they would not get wet from the rain). This was a familiar joke in the newspapers of the 1890s.

24.17 Lillian Russell] Renowned beauty (1861–1922) whose stage vehicles included *The Grand Duchess* (1890) and, with the burlesque team Weber and Fields, *Fiddle-dee-dee* (1900) and *Whoop-dee-doo* (1903).

24.22 "Sappho,"] *Sapho*, novel (1884) and play (1885) by the French writer Alphonse Daudet (1840–1897).

24.22–23 "Mr. Barnes of New York,"] Popular novel (1887) by the American novelist and playwright Archibald Clavering Gunter (1847–1907).

24.25 "The Little Minister,"] Novel (1891) and play (1897) by the British writer J. M. Barrie (1860–1937).

24.29 Della Fox in "Wang"] the American comic actor and singer Della Fox (1870–1913) played the role of Prince Mataya in the comic opera *Wang* (1891), music by Woolson Morse (1858–1897), book and lyrics by J. Cheever Goodwin (1850–1912).

24.30–31 John L. Sullivan] American heavyweight boxer (1858–1918), the last of the bare-knuckles prizefighting champions.

24.32 "A Reading From Homer."] Painting (1885) by the Dutch-born British artist Lawrence Alma-Tadema (1836–1912).

32.26 "The Fencing Master"] Operetta (1892) by the American composer Reginald DeKoven (1859–1920).

34.4 "Oh, Promise Me"] Song (1889) with music by Reginald DeKoven and lyrics by the English writer Clement Scott (1841–1902).

35.20 Edward the Seventh beard.] Closely trimmed beard in imitation of the style worn by the British king Edward VII (1841–1910; ruled 1901–1910).

36.7 "*La Paloma*."] "The Dove," popular song (1859) by the Spanish composer Sebastian de Yradier (1809–1865).

41.19 cutter] Sleigh with a single seatboard meant to carry two people and to be drawn by a single horse.

43.26 Pitt, at twenty-one, prime minister of England] The twenty-one-year-old William Pitt the Younger (1759–1806) became a member of Parliament (not the prime minister) in January 1781. He would become the youngest prime minister in British history in 1783, at age twenty-four.

54.10 surry] A Surrey sleigh, which had front and rear seating compartments that could transport two passengers each.

55.29 a real Brummell] Byword for a man who is consistently fashionably dressed, after the English dandy Beau Brummell (1778–1840).

58.36–38 more rejoicing in heaven over one sinner repented than over all the saints who consistently remain holy] A paraphrase of Luke 15:7.

64.7–9 She breathes, she stirs; she seems to feel a thrill of life along her keel!"] Cf. "The Building of the Ship" (1849), poem by Henry Wadsworth Longfellow (1807–1882), lines 349–50: "She starts,—she moves,—she seems to feel / The thrill of life along her keel."

64.13–14 "The Danube River."] Popular song (1864) by the English poet, novelist, and dramatist Charles Hamilton Aide (1829–1906).

66.33–34 "O moon of my delight that knows no wane"] Cf. rubái 74 in *The Rubáiyát of Omar Khayyám*, freely translated (1859) from the eleventh-century Persian by Edward FitzGerald (1809–1883): "Ah, Moon of my Delight who know'st no wane."

78.6 Modjeska] Helena Modjeska (1840–1909), Polish actor renowned for her Shakespearean performances.

79.17–18 "Henry Esmond" and "The Virginians."] Novels (1852, 1857–59) by the English novelist William Makepeace Thackeray (1811–1863).

82.39 "Thrift, Horatio!"] From Shakespeare, *Hamlet*, I.ii.180.

98.7–13 "As I walk along the Boy de Balong . . . bank at Monte Carlo!"] Chorus from "The Man Who Broke the Bank at Monte Carlo" (1892), popular song by the English theatrical agent and songwriter Fred Gilbert (1850–1903). "Boy de Balong" is the Bois de Boulogne, the large park at the edge of the sixteenth arrondissement of Paris.

118.3 Mister Bones] A stock minstrel-show character, who banters with and answers questions from a Mr. Interlocutor.

135.38 duck skirt] Skirt made from cotton or linen duck cloth.

142.24 an old air from "Fra Diavolo."] See note 8.18; the comic opera contains the song "On Yonder Rock Reclining" mentioned just below.

181.5–6 the romantic ballad of Lord Bateman.] Traditional ballad with origins in Scotland and England.

199.20–29 "'Tis not alone my inky cloak . . . trappings and the suits of Woe."] Hamlet's lines in *Hamlet*, I.ii.77–78, 85–86. The phrase "times, so out of joint" (199.25) make reference to I.v.188–89: "The time is out of joint—O cursed spite, / That ever I was born to set it right!"

210.16 *marche funèbre*] The third movement of Frédéric Chopin's Piano Sonata no. 2 in B-flat Minor, op. 35.

210.21 "Robin Adair" . . . "Bedelia"] "Robin Adair," traditional Scottish tune with words written in the mid-eighteenth century by Lady Caroline Keppel (c. 1734–1769) during her romance with the Irish surgeon Robin Adair; "Bedelia" (1903), song by the American songwriting duo William Jerome (1865–1932) and Jean Schwartz (1878–1956).

211.17 But the great change was in the citizenry itself.] For the version of *The Magnificent Ambersons* that was included in the *Growth* trilogy (1927), Tarkington added the following passage:

> But another had prophesied more passionately—not as Eugene did, upon evidence and reason—but out of the new inspirational faith in Bigness that was growing to its climax in the land. The inner necessity for Giantism, the craving for it in the American heart, now manifested itself in works, and the city almost reached to the border of that "Ornaby Addition" Isabel had once thought part of the insanity of her friend's son, Dan Oliphant. This dreamer, the great prophet of his time, was now thought not so mad; and there were new names that began to be lustrous "downtown"; one among them, Sheridan, being held of significance. Also, there were Kohns and Hensels and Komiskeys.
>
> For there was a change in the citizenry itself. [. . .]

257.14 Almanach de Gotha, or Burke] Guides to European and British aristocracy, respectively.

272.34–35 "Oh, love for a year . . . alway—"] From "Sweethearts" (1875), song by Gilbert and Sullivan that is based on their operetta of the same name first staged the previous year.

ALICE ADAMS

306.14 Georgette with Malines flounces."] Dress made of a sheer lightweight fabric with lace flounces named for the Belgian city of Malines (the French name for Mechelen).

322.37 tin Lizzie,"] Nickname for the Ford Model T; flivver: a small, old, inexpensive car, a jalopy.

359.31 "La Paloma,"] See note 36.7.

365.8–10 "O, swear not . . . Lest thy love prove——"] *Romeo and Juliet*, II.ii.109–11.

378.13 Nast] Thomas Nast (1840–1902), American political cartoonist and illustrator.

394.20–22 horrible old Juggernaut . . . throwing them under the wheels] An annual festival held in Puri in eastern India is devoted to the Hindu god Jagannath (Juggernaut in its Anglicized form), an avatar of Krishna. Nineteenth-century Protestant missionaries published widely read accounts of processions in which chariots bearing wooden carvings of Jagannath and other deities crushed people under their wheels as they were pulled through the streets of the city.

421.25 The way of the transgressor——"] From Proverbs 13:15: "Good understanding giveth favor; but the way of the transgressor is hard."

446.21 "*Mi chiamano Mimi,*"] Aria ("They call me Mimi") from *La Bohème* (1895), opera by Giacomo Puccini (1858–1924).

IN THE ARENA

526.10 Parkhurstian fashion] Charles H. Parkhurst (1842–1933), a Presbyterian minister, was president of the Society for the Prevention of Crime, 1891–1909, and author of *Our Fight with Tammany* (1895), which recounted his struggles with the city's Democratic Party political machine.

527.19 Madam Roland] The French revolutionary and salonnière born Jeanne-Marie Phillipon (1754–1793).

528.20 good old free and easy Hayes and Wheeler times] The Republican president Rutherford B. Hayes (1822–1893) and his vice president William A. Wheeler (1819–1887), whose victory in the disputed 1876 presidential election was marred by fraud and corruption on the part of election officials.

534.19 that John the Baptist didn't precede and herald *him.*] I.e., he thinks he's as good as Jesus, whom John the Baptist prophesied to be "mightier than I, whose shoes I am not worthy to bear" (Matthew 3:11).

543.4 "Ach du lieber Augustine,"] "Ach Du Lieber Augustin" ("Oh, dear Augustin"), Austrian folk song about the Great Plague of Vienna in 1679 and attributed to the seventeenth-century Austrian minstrel Marx Augustin. The song is based on an anecdote of the plague in which a drunken Augustin passes out and, mistakenly thought to be dead, is thrown into a corpse-pit but awakes before being buried alive.

543.15 chromos] Chromolithographs.

551.32 that eagle. Vote a Republican!"] Referring to the Republican Party being represented by an eagle on ballots; the Democratic Party's emblem was a rooster.

560.23 engraving of the "Rock of Ages."] Print made after a painting (1867) by the German-born American artist and clergyman Johannes Adam Simon Oertel (1823–1909) showing a woman clinging to a cross in the midst of a raging sea. This work's popular title (not Oertel's) was taken from the hymn "Rock of Ages," whose words, written in 1776 by Anglican cleric Augustus Montague Toplady (1740–1778), were adapted and set to music in the nineteenth century.

568.19 sea-green Incorruptible] Epithet applied to the French revolutionary François Maximilien Isidore de Robespierre (1759–1794).

579.17–19 Dem'cratic party, mos' glorious party of Douglas . . . Washin'ton.] Stephen A. Douglas (1813–1861) was a Democratic U.S. congressman from Illinois, 1843–47, a senator, 1847–61, and a candidate for president in 1860. New York governor Samuel Tilden (1814–1886) and Indiana governor Thomas Hendricks (1819–1885; later U.S. vice president in 1885) were the Democratic presidential and vice presidential candidates in the 1876 election. The politician and statesman Henry Clay (1777–1852) was a member and co-founder of both the National Republican and Whig Parties; George Washington did not belong to a political party.

583.24 "Another Daniel Webster] The American politician, statesman, and attorney Daniel Webster (1782–1852) was a renowned orator.

584.11 G. A. R. reunion] Grand Army of the Republic.

585.3–4 "Horatius at the Bridge"] Widely popular ballad (1842) by the English historian, essayist, and poet Thomas Babington Macaulay, 1st Baron Macaulay (1800–1859).

585.4–5 quarrel scene between Brutus and Cassius] In Shakespeare's *Julius Caesar*, IV.iii.

591.24–25 that bourne whence no traveller returns?] Cf. *Hamlet*, III.i.78–79.

592.16 Edwin Booth] See note 9.11.

595.14–21 Barras . . . dared to oppose the path of one of the eternal stars!"] Paul François Jean Nicolas, vicomte de Barras (1755–1829), was a member of the five-man Directory that ruled France during the French Revolution, which was abolished after the bloodless coup d'état of November 9 (18 Brumaire), 1799, which made Napoleon first consul.

597.20 Lochinvar] Romantic hero in the long narrative poem *Marmion* (1808), Canto V, by Sir Walter Scott (1771–1832); he abducts his beloved on the evening of her betrothal to another man.

608.40–609.2 that man who has suffered most of all . . . did!"] Jesus; "knew not what he did" refers to his words while being crucified as given in Luke 23:34: "Father, forgive them; for they know not what they do."

630.30–31–631.2 the call of Delilah . . . locks have been shore!] See Judges 16, where Delilah, in exchange for payment from the leaders of the Philistines, discovers from the Israelite judge and warrior Samson that shaving his head will diminish his great strength. One night, while Samson is sleeping on her lap, Delilah orders her servant to cut off his hair, which enables the Philistines to capture and blind him. Samson later takes revenge when, after God grants his wish for a final act of superhuman strength, he pulls down the pillars of a temple, killing himself and the people inside.

633.2 MME. BERNHARDT and M. Coquelin] The renowned French actors Sarah Bernhardt (1844–1923) and Constant-Benoît Coquelin (1841–1909).

633.3 "L'Aiglon."] Historical drama (1900) set in 1830–32 by the French playwright Edmond Rostand (1868–1918) whose title character ("the eaglet") is Napoléon François Joseph Charles Bonaparte (1811–1832), the son of Napoléon and his second wife, Marie-Louise, duchess of Parma (1791–1847). Living in Austria for most of his life, François Bonaparte (Napoléon II) was known as Franz and by his title the duke of Reichstadt (the "Dook of Reishtod" mentioned at 636.31).

634.30 'Cyrano'] Rostand's *Cyrano de Bergerac* (1897).

634.37–39 "That death scene!" . . . after 'Wagram'] Wagram, the site in Austria of a battle Napoleon won in 1809, provides the setting for the fifth act of Rostand's play; François Napoléon dies in the final act while a description of his christening in Paris during his father's reign is read aloud.

635.3 Goethe's 'More Light'] The last words of the German writer Johann Wolfgang von Goethe (1749–1832) are said to have been "More light! More light!"

636.5 that huntin'-lodge appointment] In act 4 of *L'Aiglon* the play's hero asks the young woman Thérèse to meet him for a tryst (which never takes place) at his hunting lodge.

636.15 they all talked in rhyme] Rostand's play was written in rhyming alexandrines.

636.17–18 never quit on the subject of himself and his folks] In the political, not personal, sense: the play's hero has to decide, given significant Bonapartist support, whether to return to France to install himself as emperor in continuation of his father's line.

636.36–37 he'd stole more than Boss Tweed.] William Marcy Tweed (1823–1878), New York City Democratic politician and leader of the party's Tammany Hall political machine. With others, Boss Tweed swindled millions of dollars from the city treasury and was convicted on charges related to his corrupt activities in 1873.

636.40 old Metternich] The diplomat Klemens Wenzel von Metternich (1773–1859), chancellor, 1821–48, and foreign minister of Austria, 1809–48; a prominent character in Rostand's play.

639.19–20 Fillmore . . . election year] U.S. politician Millard Fillmore (1800–1874), who became president as a Whig on the death of Zachary Taylor in 1850, lost his only presidential campaign as a Know Nothing candidate in 1856; he also served in the U.S. House of Representatives, 1833–35, 1837–43.

640.21 the press notices about his christening] See note 634.37–39.

This book is set in 10 point ITC Galliard, a face designed for digital composition by Matthew Carter and based on the sixteenth-century face Granjon. The paper is acid-free lightweight opaque that will not turn yellow or brittle with age. The binding is sewn, which allows the book to open easily and lie flat. The binding board is covered in Brillianta, a woven rayon cloth made by Van Heek–Scholco Textielfabrieken, Holland. Composition by Dedicated Book Services. Printing and binding by LSC Communications. Designed by Bruce Campbell.

THE LIBRARY OF AMERICA SERIES

Library of America fosters appreciation of America's literary heritage by publishing, and keeping permanently in print, authoritative editions of America's best and most significant writing. An independent nonprofit organization, it was founded in 1979 with seed funding from the National Endowment for the Humanities and the Ford Foundation.

1. Herman Melville: Typee, Omoo, Mardi
2. Nathaniel Hawthorne: Tales & Sketches
3. Walt Whitman: Poetry & Prose
4. Harriet Beecher Stowe: Three Novels
5. Mark Twain: Mississippi Writings
6. Jack London: Novels & Stories
7. Jack London: Novels & Social Writings
8. William Dean Howells: Novels 1875–1886
9. Herman Melville: Redburn, White-Jacket, Moby-Dick
10. Nathaniel Hawthorne: Collected Novels

11 & 12. Francis Parkman: France and England in North America

13. Henry James: Novels 1871–1880
14. Henry Adams: Novels, Mont Saint Michel, The Education
15. Ralph Waldo Emerson: Essays & Lectures
16. Washington Irving: History, Tales & Sketches
17. Thomas Jefferson: Writings
18. Stephen Crane: Prose & Poetry
19. Edgar Allan Poe: Poetry & Tales
20. Edgar Allan Poe: Essays & Reviews
21. Mark Twain: The Innocents Abroad, Roughing It

22 & 23. Henry James: Literary Criticism

24. Herman Melville: Pierre, Israel Potter, The Confidence-Man, Tales & Billy Budd
25. William Faulkner: Novels 1930–1935

26 & 27. James Fenimore Cooper: The Leatherstocking Tales

28. Henry David Thoreau: A Week, Walden, The Maine Woods, Cape Cod
29. Henry James: Novels 1881–1886
30. Edith Wharton: Novels

31 & 32. Henry Adams: History of the U.S. during the Administrations of Jefferson & Madison

33. Frank Norris: Novels & Essays
34. W.E.B. Du Bois: Writings
35. Willa Cather: Early Novels & Stories
36. Theodore Dreiser: Sister Carrie, Jennie Gerhardt, Twelve Men
37. Benjamin Franklin: Writings (2 vols.)
38. William James: Writings 1902–1910
39. Flannery O'Connor: Collected Works

40, 41, & 42. Eugene O'Neill: Complete Plays

43. Henry James: Novels 1886–1890
44. William Dean Howells: Novels 1886–1888

45 & 46. Abraham Lincoln: Speeches & Writings

47. Edith Wharton: Novellas & Other Writings
48. William Faulkner: Novels 1936–1940
49. Willa Cather: Later Novels
50. Ulysses S. Grant: Memoirs & Selected Letters
51. William Tecumseh Sherman: Memoirs
52. Washington Irving: Bracebridge Hall, Tales of a Traveller, The Alhambra
53. Francis Parkman: The Oregon Trail, The Conspiracy of Pontiac
54. James Fenimore Cooper: Sea Tales

55 & 56. Richard Wright: Works

57. Willa Cather: Stories, Poems, & Other Writings
58. William James: Writings 1878–1899
59. Sinclair Lewis: Main Street & Babbitt

60 & 61. Mark Twain: Collected Tales, Sketches, Speeches, & Essays

62 & 63. The Debate on the Constitution

64 & 65. Henry James: Collected Travel Writings

66 & 67. American Poetry: The Nineteenth Century

68. Frederick Douglass: Autobiographies
69. Sarah Orne Jewett: Novels & Stories
70. Ralph Waldo Emerson: Collected Poems & Translations
71. Mark Twain: Historical Romances
72. John Steinbeck: Novels & Stories 1932–1937
73. William Faulkner: Novels 1942–1954

74 & 75. Zora Neale Hurston: Novels, Stories, & Other Writings

76. Thomas Paine: Collected Writings

77 & 78. Reporting World War II: American Journalism

79 & 80. Raymond Chandler: Novels, Stories, & Other Writings

81. Robert Frost: Collected Poems, Prose, & Plays
82 & 83. Henry James: Complete Stories 1892–1910
84. William Bartram: Travels & Other Writings
85. John Dos Passos: U.S.A.
86. John Steinbeck: The Grapes of Wrath & Other Writings 1936–1941
87, 88, & 89. Vladimir Nabokov: Novels & Other Writings
90. James Thurber: Writings & Drawings
91. George Washington: Writings
92. John Muir: Nature Writings
93. Nathanael West: Novels & Other Writings
94 & 95. Crime Novels: American Noir of the 1930s, 40s, & 50s
96. Wallace Stevens: Collected Poetry & Prose
97. James Baldwin: Early Novels & Stories
98. James Baldwin: Collected Essays
99 & 100. Gertrude Stein: Writings
101 & 102. Eudora Welty: Novels, Stories, & Other Writings
103. Charles Brockden Brown: Three Gothic Novels
104 & 105. Reporting Vietnam: American Journalism
106 & 107. Henry James: Complete Stories 1874–1891
108. American Sermons
109. James Madison: Writings
110. Dashiell Hammett: Complete Novels
111. Henry James: Complete Stories 1864–1874
112. William Faulkner: Novels 1957–1962
113. John James Audubon: Writings & Drawings
114. Slave Narratives
115 & 116. American Poetry: The Twentieth Century
117. F. Scott Fitzgerald: Novels & Stories 1920–1922
118. Henry Wadsworth Longfellow: Poems & Other Writings
119 & 120. Tennessee Williams: Collected Plays
121 & 122. Edith Wharton: Collected Stories
123. The American Revolution: Writings from the War of Independence
124. Henry David Thoreau: Collected Essays & Poems
125. Dashiell Hammett: Crime Stories & Other Writings
126 & 127. Dawn Powell: Novels
128. Carson McCullers: Complete Novels
129. Alexander Hamilton: Writings
130. Mark Twain: The Gilded Age & Later Novels
131. Charles W. Chesnutt: Stories, Novels, & Essays
132. John Steinbeck: Novels 1942–1952
133. Sinclair Lewis: Arrowsmith, Elmer Gantry, Dodsworth
134 & 135. Paul Bowles: Novels, Stories, & Other Writings
136. Kate Chopin: Complete Novels & Stories
137 & 138. Reporting Civil Rights: American Journalism
139. Henry James: Novels 1896–1899
140. Theodore Dreiser: An American Tragedy
141. Saul Bellow: Novels 1944–1953
142. John Dos Passos: Novels 1920–1925
143. John Dos Passos: Travel Books & Other Writings
144. Ezra Pound: Poems & Translations
145. James Weldon Johnson: Writings
146. Washington Irving: Three Western Narratives
147. Alexis de Tocqueville: Democracy in America
148. James T. Farrell: Studs Lonigan Trilogy
149, 150, & 151. Isaac Bashevis Singer: Collected Stories
152. Kaufman & Co.: Broadway Comedies
153. Theodore Roosevelt: Rough Riders, An Autobiography
154. Theodore Roosevelt: Letters & Speeches
155. H. P. Lovecraft: Tales
156. Louisa May Alcott: Little Women, Little Men, Jo's Boys
157. Philip Roth: Novels & Stories 1959–1962
158. Philip Roth: Novels 1967–1972
159. James Agee: Let Us Now Praise Famous Men, A Death in the Family, Shorter Fiction
160. James Agee: Film Writing & Selected Journalism
161. Richard Henry Dana Jr.: Two Years Before the Mast & Other Voyages
162. Henry James: Novels 1901–1902
163. Arthur Miller: Plays 1944–1961
164. William Faulkner: Novels 1926–1929
165. Philip Roth: Novels 1973–1977

166 & 167. American Speeches: Political Oratory
168. Hart Crane: Complete Poems & Selected Letters
169. Saul Bellow: Novels 1956–1964
170. John Steinbeck: Travels with Charley & Later Novels
171. Capt. John Smith: Writings with Other Narratives
172. Thornton Wilder: Collected Plays & Writings on Theater
173. Philip K. Dick: Four Novels of the 1960s
174. Jack Kerouac: Road Novels 1957–1960
175. Philip Roth: Zuckerman Bound
176 & 177. Edmund Wilson: Literary Essays & Reviews
178. American Poetry: The 17th & 18th Centuries
179. William Maxwell: Early Novels & Stories
180. Elizabeth Bishop: Poems, Prose, & Letters
181. A. J. Liebling: World War II Writings
182. American Earth: Environmental Writing Since Thoreau
183. Philip K. Dick: Five Novels of the 1960s & 70s
184. William Maxwell: Later Novels & Stories
185. Philip Roth: Novels & Other Narratives 1986–1991
186. Katherine Anne Porter: Collected Stories & Other Writings
187. John Ashbery: Collected Poems 1956–1987
188 & 189. John Cheever: Complete Novels & Collected Stories
190. Lafcadio Hearn: American Writings
191. A. J. Liebling: The Sweet Science & Other Writings
192. The Lincoln Anthology
193. Philip K. Dick: VALIS & Later Novels
194. Thornton Wilder: The Bridge of San Luis Rey & Other Novels 1926–1948
195. Raymond Carver: Collected Stories
196 & 197. American Fantastic Tales
198. John Marshall: Writings
199. The Mark Twain Anthology
200. Mark Twain: A Tramp Abroad, Following the Equator, Other Travels
201 & 202. Ralph Waldo Emerson: Selected Journals
203. The American Stage: Writing on Theater
204. Shirley Jackson: Novels & Stories
205. Philip Roth: Novels 1993–1995
206 & 207. H. L. Mencken: Prejudices
208. John Kenneth Galbraith: The Affluent Society & Other Writings 1952–1967
209. Saul Bellow: Novels 1970–1982
210 & 211. Lynd Ward: Six Novels in Woodcuts
212. The Civil War: The First Year
213 & 214. John Adams: Revolutionary Writings
215. Henry James: Novels 1903–1911
216. Kurt Vonnegut: Novels & Stories 1963–1973
217 & 218. Harlem Renaissance Novels
219. Ambrose Bierce: The Devil's Dictionary, Tales, & Memoirs
220. Philip Roth: The American Trilogy 1997–2000
221. The Civil War: The Second Year
222. Barbara W. Tuchman: The Guns of August, The Proud Tower
223. Arthur Miller: Plays 1964–1982
224. Thornton Wilder: The Eighth Day, Theophilus North, Autobiographical Writings
225. David Goodis: Five Noir Novels of the 1940s & 50s
226. Kurt Vonnegut: Novels & Stories 1950–1962
227 & 228. American Science Fiction: Nine Novels of the 1950s
229 & 230. Laura Ingalls Wilder: The Little House Books
231. Jack Kerouac: Collected Poems
232. The War of 1812
233. American Antislavery Writings
234. The Civil War: The Third Year
235. Sherwood Anderson: Collected Stories
236. Philip Roth: Novels 2001–2007
237. Philip Roth: Nemeses
238. Aldo Leopold: A Sand County Almanac & Other Writings
239. May Swenson: Collected Poems
240 & 241. W. S. Merwin: Collected Poems
242 & 243. John Updike: Collected Stories
244. Ring Lardner: Stories & Other Writings
245. Jonathan Edwards: Writings from the Great Awakening
246. Susan Sontag: Essays of the 1960s & 70s

247. William Wells Brown: Clotel & Other Writings
248 & 249. Bernard Malamud: Novels & Stories of the 1940s, 50s, & 60s
250. The Civil War: The Final Year
251. Shakespeare in America
252. Kurt Vonnegut: Novels 1976–1985
253 & 254. American Musicals 1927–1969
255. Elmore Leonard: Four Novels of the 1970s
256. Louisa May Alcott: Work, Eight Cousins, Rose in Bloom, Stories & Other Writings
257. H. L. Mencken: The Days Trilogy
258. Virgil Thomson: Music Chronicles 1940–1954
259. Art in America 1945–1970
260. Saul Bellow: Novels 1984–2000
261. Arthur Miller: Plays 1987–2004
262. Jack Kerouac: Visions of Cody, Visions of Gerard, Big Sur
263. Reinhold Niebuhr: Major Works on Religion & Politics
264. Ross Macdonald: Four Novels of the 1950s
265 & 266. The American Revolution: Writings from the Pamphlet Debate
267. Elmore Leonard: Four Novels of the 1980s
268 & 269. Women Crime Writers: Suspense Novels of the 1940s & 50s
270. Frederick Law Olmsted: Writings on Landscape, Culture, & Society
271. Edith Wharton: Four Novels of the 1920s
272. James Baldwin: Later Novels
273. Kurt Vonnegut: Novels 1987–1997
274. Henry James: Autobiographies
275. Abigail Adams: Letters
276. John Adams: Writings from the New Nation 1784–1826
277. Virgil Thomson: The State of Music & Other Writings
278. War No More: American Antiwar & Peace Writing
279. Ross Macdonald: Three Novels of the Early 1960s
280. Elmore Leonard: Four Later Novels
281. Ursula K. Le Guin: The Complete Orsinia
282. John O'Hara: Stories
283. The Unknown Kerouac: Rare, Unpublished & Newly Translated Writings
284. Albert Murray: Collected Essays & Memoirs
285 & 286. Loren Eiseley: Collected Essays on Evolution, Nature, & the Cosmos
287. Carson McCullers: Stories, Plays & Other Writings
288. Jane Bowles: Collected Writings
289. World War I and America: Told by the Americans Who Lived It
290 & 291. Mary McCarthy: The Complete Fiction
292. Susan Sontag: Later Essays
293 & 294. John Quincy Adams: Diaries
295. Ross Macdonald: Four Later Novels
296 & 297. Ursula K. Le Guin: The Hainish Novels & Stories
298 & 299. Peter Taylor: The Complete Stories
300. Philip Roth: Why Write? Collected Nonfiction 1960–2013
301. John Ashbery: Collected Poems 1991–2000
302. Wendell Berry: Port William Novels & Stories: The Civil War to World War II
303. Reconstruction: Voices from America's First Great Struggle for Racial Equality
304. Albert Murray: Collected Novels & Poems
305 & 306. Norman Mailer: The Sixties
307. Rachel Carson: Silent Spring & Other Writings on the Environment
308. Elmore Leonard: Westerns
309 & 310. Madeleine L'Engle: The Kairos Novels
311. John Updike: Novels 1959–1965
312. James Fenimore Cooper: Two Novels of the American Revolution
313. John O'Hara: Four Novels of the 1930s
314. Ann Petry: The Street, The Narrows
315. Ursula K. Le Guin: Always Coming Home
316 & 317. Wendell Berry: Collected Essays
318. Cornelius Ryan: The Longest Day, A Bridge Too Far